CRESCENT CITY

HOUSE
of
FLAME
and
SHADOW

Books by Sarah J. Maas

The Throne of Glass series

The Assassin's Blade
Throne of Glass
Crown of Midnight
Heir of Fire
Queen of Shadows
Empire of Storms
Tower of Dawn
Kingdom of Ash

•

The Throne of Glass Colouring Book

The Court of Thorns and Roses series

A Court of Thorns and Roses
A Court of Mist and Fury
A Court of Wings and Ruin
A Court of Frost and Starlight
A Court of Silver Flames

•

A Court of Thorns and Roses Colouring Book

The Crescent City series

House of Earth and Blood
House of Sky and Breath
House of Flame and Shadow

CRESCENT CITY

HOUSE
of
FLAME
and
SHADOW

SARAH J. MAAS

BLOOMSBURY PUBLISHING
LONDON · OXFORD · NEW YORK · NEW DELHI · SYDNEY

BLOOMSBURY PUBLISHING
Bloomsbury Publishing Plc
50 Bedford Square, London WC1B 3DP, UK
29 Earlsfort Terrace, Dublin 2, Ireland

BLOOMSBURY, BLOOMSBURY PUBLISHING, and the Diana logo
are trademarks of Bloomsbury Publishing Plc

First published in the United States in 2024 by Bloomsbury Publishing
First published in Great Britain in 2024 by Bloomsbury Publishing Plc

A catalogue record for this book is available from the British Library

ISBN: HB: 978-1-4088-8444-7; TPB: 978-1-5266-2823-7; eBook: 978-1-4088-8445-4;
ePDF: 978-1-5266-5035-1; Waterstones: 978-1-5266-6824-0;
Digitally signed edition: 978-1-5266-6823-3

2 4 6 8 10 9 7 5 3 1

Typeset by Westchester Publishing Services

Printed and bound in Great Britain by CPI (UK) Ltd, Croydon, CRO 4YY

For Sloane,
who lights up entire universes with her smile

LUNATHION

CRESCENT CITY

THE ANGELS' GATE

CENTRAL BUSINESS DISTRICT

THE MEAT MARKET

THE MERCHANTS' GATE

WESTERN ROAD

ISTROS RIVER

THE FOUR HOUSES OF
MIDGARD

*As decreed in 33 V.E. by the Imperial Senate
in the Eternal City*

HOUSE OF EARTH AND BLOOD

Shifters, humans, witches, ordinary animals, and many others
to whom Cthona calls, as well as some chosen by Luna

HOUSE OF SKY AND BREATH

Malakim (angels), Fae, elementals, sprites,* and those who
are blessed by Solas, along with some favored by Luna

HOUSE OF MANY WATERS

River-spirits, mer, water beasts, nymphs, kelpies, nøkks,
and others watched over by Ogenas

HOUSE OF FLAME AND SHADOW

Daemonaki, Reapers, wraiths, vampyrs, draki, dragons,
necromancers, and many wicked and unnamed things
that even Urd herself cannot see

**Sprites were kicked out of their House as a result of their participation in the
Fall, and are now considered Lowers, though many of them refuse to accept this.*

PROLOGUE

The Hind knelt before her undying masters and contemplated how it would feel to tear out their throats.

Around her own throat, a silver torque lay cool and heavy. It never warmed against her skin. As if the taken lives it symbolized wanted her to endure death's icy grip as well.

A silver dart on a dreadwolf uniform: the trophy for a rebel wiped off the face of Midgard. Lidia had acquired so many that her imperial grays couldn't hold them all. So many that they'd been melted down into that torque.

Did anyone in this chamber see the necklace for what it truly was?

A collar. With a golden leash leading right to the monsters before her.

And did those monsters ever suspect that their faithful pet sat at their feet and pondered the taste and texture of their blood on her tongue? On her teeth?

But here she would kneel, until given leave to rise. As this world would kneel until the six enthroned Asteri drained it dry and left its carcass to rot in the emptiness of space.

The staff of the Eternal Palace had cleaned the blood from the shining crystal floor beneath her knees. No coppery tang lingered in the sterile air, no errant drops marred the columns flanking the chamber. As if the events of two days ago had never occurred.

But Lidia Cervos could not let herself dwell on those events. Not while surrounded by her enemies. Not with Pollux kneeling beside her, one of his shining wings resting atop her calf. From another, it might have been a gesture of comfort, of solidarity.

From Pollux, from the Hammer, it meant nothing but possession.

Lidia willed her eyes dead and cold. Willed her heart to be the same, and focused on the two Fae Kings pleading their cases.

"My late son acted of his own accord," declared Morven, King of the Avallen Fae, his bone-white face grave. The tall, dark-haired male wore all black, but no heavy air of mourning lay upon him. "Had I known of Cormac's treason, I would have handed him over myself."

Lidia flicked her gaze to the panel of parasites seated on their crystal thrones.

Rigelus, veiled as usual in the body of a Fae teenage boy, propped his delicate chin on a fist. "I find it difficult to believe that you had no knowledge of your son's activities, considering how tightly you held his reins."

Shadows whispered over Morven's broad shoulders, trailing off his scaled armor. "He was a defiant boy. I thought I'd beaten it out of him long ago."

"You thought wrong," sneered Hesperus, the Evening Star, who'd taken on the shape of a blond nymph. Her long, slim fingers tapped the glimmering arm of her throne. "We can only assume that his treachery stemmed from some decay within your royal house. One that must now be scourged."

For the first time in the decades the Hind had known him, King Morven held his tongue. He'd had no choice but to answer the Asteri's summons yesterday, but he clearly did not appreciate the reminder that his autonomy was a mere illusion, even on the misty isle of Avallen.

Some small part of her relished it—seeing the male who'd strutted through Summits and meetings and balls now weighing his every word. Knowing it might be his last.

Morven growled, "I had no knowledge of my son's activities or of his craven heart. I swear it upon Luna's golden bow." His voice rang clear as he added with impressive fury, "I condemn all that Cormac was and stood for. He shall not be honored with a grave nor a burial. There will be no ship to sail his body into the Summerlands. I will ensure that his name is wiped from all records of my house."

For a heartbeat, Lidia allowed herself a shred of pity for the Ophion agent she'd known. For the Fae Prince of Avallen who'd given everything to destroy the beings before her.

As she had given everything. Would still give everything.

Polaris, the North Star—wearing the body of a white-winged, dark-skinned female angel—drawled, "There will be no ship to sail Cormac's body to the Summerlands because the boy immolated himself. And tried to take us with him." Polaris let out a soft, hateful laugh that raked talons down Lidia's skin. "As if a paltry flame might do such a thing."

Morven said nothing. He'd offered what he could, short of getting on his knees to plead. It might very well come to that, but for now, the Fae King of Avallen held his head high.

Legend claimed that even the Asteri could not pierce the mists that shrouded Avallen, but Lidia had never heard of it being tested. Perhaps that was also why Morven had come—to keep the Asteri from having a reason to explore whether the legend was true.

If they were somehow repelled by whatever ancient power lay around Avallen, that would be a secret worth abasing oneself to keep.

Rigelus crossed an ankle over his knee. Lidia had seen the Bright Hand order entire families executed with the same casual air. "And you, Einar? What have you to say for your son?"

"Traitorous shit," spat Pollux from where he knelt beside Lidia. His wing still rested on her leg like he owned it. Owned her.

The Autumn King ignored the Hammer. Ignored everyone except Rigelus as he flatly replied, "Ruhn has been wild since birth. I did what I could to contain him. I have little doubt that he was lured into this business through his sister's machinations."

Lidia kept her fingers loose, even as they ached to curl into fists. Steadied her heart into a sluggish, ordinary beat that no Vanir ears would detect as unusual.

"So you would seek to spare one child by damning the other?" Rigelus asked, lips curling into a mild smile. "What sort of father are you, Einar?"

"Neither Bryce Quinlan nor Ruhn Danaan has the right to call themselves my children any longer."

Rigelus angled his head, his short, dark hair shimmering in the glow of the crystal room. "I thought she had claimed the name Bryce Danaan. Have you revoked her royal status?"

A muscle ticked in the Autumn King's cheek. "I have yet to decide a fitting punishment for her."

Pollux's wings rustled, but the angel kept his head down as he snarled to the Autumn King, "When I get my hands on your cunt of a daughter, you'll be glad to have disavowed her. What she did to the Harpy, I shall do to her tenfold."

"You'd have to find her first," the Autumn King said coolly. Lidia supposed Einar Danaan was one of the few Fae on Midgard who could openly taunt an angel as powerful as the Malleus. The Fae King's amber eyes, so like his daughter's, lifted to the Asteri. "Have your mystics discovered her whereabouts yet?"

"Do you not wish to know where your son is?" asked Octartis, the Southern Star, with a coy smile.

"I know where Ruhn is," the Autumn King countered, unmoved. "He deserves to be there." He half turned toward where Lidia knelt, and surveyed her coldly. "I hope you wring every last answer from him."

Lidia held his stare, her face like stone, like ice—like death.

The Autumn King's gaze flicked over the silver torque at her throat, a faint, approving curve gracing his mouth. But he asked Rigelus, with an authority that she could only admire, "Where is Bryce?"

Rigelus sighed, bored and annoyed—a lethal combination. "She has chosen to vacate Midgard."

"A mistake we shall soon rectify," Polaris added.

Rigelus shot the lesser Asteri a warning look.

The Autumn King said, his voice a shade faint, "Bryce is no longer in this world?"

Morven glanced warily at the other Fae King. As far as anyone knew, there was only one place that could be accessed from Midgard—there was an entire wall circling the Northern Rift in Nena to prevent its denizens from crossing into this world. If Bryce was no longer on Midgard, she had to be in Hel.

It had never occurred to Lidia that the wall around the Rift would also keep Midgardians from getting *out*.

Well, most Midgardians.

Rigelus said tightly, "That knowledge is not to be shared with anyone." The edge sharpening his words implied the rest: *under pain of death.*

Lidia had been present when the other Asteri had demanded to know how it had happened: how Bryce Quinlan had opened a gate to another world in their own palace and slipped through the Bright Hand's fingers. Their disbelief and rage had been a small comfort in the wake of all that had happened, all that was still churning through Lidia.

A silvery bell rang from behind the Asteri's thrones in a polite reminder that another meeting had been scheduled shortly.

"This discussion is not yet finished," Rigelus warned the two Fae Kings. He pointed with a skinny finger to the double doors open to the hall beyond. "Speak of what you have heard today, and you will find that there is no place on this planet where you will be safe from our wrath."

The Fae Kings bowed and left without another word.

The weight of the Asteri's gazes landed upon Lidia, singeing her very soul. She withstood it, as she had withstood all the other horrors in her life.

"Rise, Lidia," Rigelus said with something that bordered on affection. Then, to Pollux, "Rise, my Hammer." Lidia shoved down the bile that burned like acid and got to her feet, Pollux with her. His white wing brushed against her cheek, the softness of his feathers at odds with the rot of his soul.

The bell tinkled again, but Rigelus lifted a hand to the attendant waiting in the shadows of the nearby pillars. The next meeting could wait another moment.

"How go the interrogations?" Rigelus slouched on his throne as if he had asked about the weather.

"We are in the opening movements," Lidia said, her mouth somehow distant from her body. "Athalar and Danaan will require time to break."

"And the Helhound?" asked Hesperus, the nymph's dark eyes gleaming with malice.

"I am still assessing him." Lidia kept her chin high and tucked her hands behind her back. "But trust that I shall get what we need from all of them, Your Graces."

"As you always do," Rigelus said, gaze dipping to her silver collar. "We give you leave to do your finest work, Hind."

Lidia bowed at the waist with imperial precision. Pollux did the same, wings folding elegantly. The portrait of a perfect soldier—the one he'd been bred to become.

It wasn't until they'd entered the long corridor beyond the throne room that the Hammer spoke. "Do you think that little bitch really went to Hel?" Pollux jerked his head behind them, toward the dull, silent crystal Gate at the opposite end of the hall.

The busts lining the walkway—all the Asteri in their various forms throughout the centuries—had been replaced. The windows that had been shattered by Athalar's lightning had been repaired.

As in the throne room, not one hint of what had occurred remained here. And beyond the crystal walls of this palace, no whisper had surfaced in the news.

The only proof: the two Asterian Guards now flanking either side of the Gate. Their white-and-gold regalia shone in the streaming sunlight, the tips of the spears gripped in their gloved hands like fallen stars. With their golden helmets' visors down, she could make out nothing of the faces beneath. It didn't matter, she supposed. There was no individuality, no life in them. The elite, highborn angels had been bred for obedience and service. Just as they'd been bred to bear those glowing white wings. As the angel beside her had.

Lidia maintained her unhurried pace toward the elevators. "I won't waste time trying to find out. But Bryce Quinlan will no doubt return one day, regardless of where she wound up."

Beyond the windows, the seven hills of the Eternal City rippled under the sunlight, most of them crusted with buildings crowned by terra-cotta roofs. A barren mountain—more of a hill, really—lay among several nearly identical peaks just north of the city border, the metallic gleam atop it like a beacon.

Was it an intentional taunt to Athalar that the mountain, Mount Hermon—where he and the Archangel Shahar had staged the doomed first and final battle of their rebellion—today housed scores of the Asteri's new hybrid mech-suits? Down in the dungeons, Athalar would have no way of seeing them, but knowing Rigelus, the positioning of the new machines was definitely symbolic.

Lidia had read the report yesterday morning about what the Asteri had cooked up these last few weeks, despite Ophion's attempts to stop it. Despite *her* attempts to stop it. But the written details had been nothing compared to the suits' appearance at sunset. The city had been abuzz as the military transports had crested the hill and deposited them, one by one, with news crews rushing out to report on the cutting-edge tech.

Her stomach had churned to see the suits—and did so again now as she gazed at their steel husks glinting in the sun.

Further proof of Ophion's failure. They'd destroyed the mech-suit on Ydra, obliterated the lab days ago—yet it had all been too late. In secret, Rigelus had crafted this metal army and stationed it atop Mount Hermon's barren peak. An improvement on the hybrids, these did not even require pilots to operate them, though they still had the capacity to hold a single Vanir soldier, if need be. As if the hybrids had been a well-calculated distraction for Ophion while Rigelus had secretly perfected *these*. Magic and tech now blended with lethal efficiency, with minimal cost to military life. But those suits spelled death for any remaining rebels, and damned the rest of the rebellion.

She should have caught Rigelus's sleight of hand—but she hadn't. And now that horror would be unleashed on the world.

The elevator opened, and Lidia and Pollux entered in silence. Lidia hit the button for the lowest sublevel—well, second lowest. The elevators did not descend to the catacombs, which could only be accessed by a winding crystal staircase. There, one thousand mystics slumbered.

Each of whom were now focused on a single task: *Find Bryce Quinlan.*

It begged the question: If everyone knew that the Northern Rift and other Gates only opened to Hel, why did the Asteri bother to expend such resources in hunting for her? Bryce had landed in Hel—surely there was no need to order the mystics to find her.

Unless Bryce Quinlan had wound up somewhere *other* than Hel. A different world, perhaps. And if that was the case . . .

How long would it take? How many worlds existed beyond Midgard? And what were the odds of Bryce surviving on any of them—or ever getting back to Midgard?

The elevators opened into the dank dimness of the dungeons. Pollux prowled down the stone walkway, wings tightly furled. Like he didn't want one speck of dirt from this place marring their pristine white feathers. "Is that why you're keeping them alive? As bait for that bitch?"

"Yes." Lidia followed the screams past the guttering firstlight sconces along the wall. "Quinlan and Athalar are mates. She will return to this world because of that bond. And when she does, she will go straight to him."

"And the brother?"

"Ruhn and Bryce are Starborn," Lidia said, heaving open the iron door to the large interrogation chamber beyond. Metal grated against stone, its shriek eerily similar to the sounds of torment all around them. "She will want to free him—as her brother and her ally."

She stalked down the exposed steps into the heart of the chamber, where three males hung from gorsian shackles in the center of the room. Blood pooled beneath them, dribbling into the grate below their bare feet.

She shut down every part of her that felt, that breathed.

Athalar and Baxian dangled unconscious from the ceiling, their torsos patchworks of scars and burns. And their backs . . .

A constant drip sounded in the otherwise silent chamber, like a leaking faucet. The blood still oozed from the stumps where their wings had been. The gorsian shackles had slowed their healing to near-human levels—keeping them from dying entirely, but ensuring that they suffered through every moment of pain.

Lidia couldn't look at the third figure hanging between them. Couldn't get a breath down near him.

Leather whispered over stone, and Lidia dove deep within herself as Pollux's whip cracked. It snapped against Athalar's raw, bloody back, and the Umbra Mortis jolted, swaying on his chains.

"Wake up," the Hammer sneered. "It's a beautiful day."

Athalar's swollen eyes cracked open. Hate blazed in their dark depths.

The halo inked anew upon his brow seemed darker than the shadows of the dungeon. His battered mouth parted in a feral smile, revealing bloodstained teeth. "Morning, sunshine."

A soft, broken rasp of a laugh sounded to Athalar's right. And though she knew it was folly, Lidia looked.

Ruhn Danaan, Crown Prince of the Valbaran Fae, was staring at her.

His lip was swollen from where Pollux had torn out his piercing. His eyebrow was crusted with blood from where that hoop had been ripped out, too. Across his tattooed torso, along the arms above his head, blood and dirt and bruises mingled.

The prince's striking blue eyes were sharp with loathing.

For her.

Pollux slashed his whip into Athalar's back again, not bothering with questions. No, this was the warm-up. Interrogation would come later.

Baxian still hung unconscious. Pollux had beaten him into a bloody pulp last night after severing his and Athalar's wings with a blunt-toothed saw. The Helhound didn't so much as stir.

Night, Lidia tried, casting her voice into the moldy air between herself and the Fae Prince. They'd never spoken mind-to-mind outside of their dreaming, but she'd been trying since he'd arrived here. Again and again, she'd cast her mind toward his. Only silence answered.

Just as it had from the moment Ruhn had learned who she was. What she was.

She knew he could communicate, even with the gorsian stones halting his magic and slowing his healing. Knew he'd done so with his sister before Bryce had escaped.

Night.

Ruhn's lip pulled back in a silent snarl, blood snaking down his chin.

Pollux's phone rang, a shrill, strange sound in this ancient shrine to pain. His ministrations halted, a terrible silence in their wake. "Mordoc," the Hammer said, whip still in one hand. He pivoted from Athalar's swinging, brutalized body. "Report."

Lidia didn't bother to protest the fact that her captain was reporting to the Hammer. Pollux had taken the Harpy's death personally—he'd commandeered Mordoc and the dreadwolves to find any hint of where Bryce Quinlan might have gone.

That he still believed Bryce was responsible for the Harpy's death was only because Athalar and Ruhn hadn't revealed that it was Lidia who'd murdered the Harpy. They knew who she was, and only the fact that she was vital to the rebellion kept them from spilling her secrets.

For a moment, with Pollux turned away, Lidia let her mask drop. Let Ruhn see her true face. The one that had kissed his soul and shared her own with him, their very beings melding.

Ruhn, she pleaded into his mind. *Ruhn.*

But the Fae Prince did not answer. The hate in his eyes did not lessen. So Lidia donned her Hind's mask once again.

And as Pollux pocketed his phone and angled his whip anew, the Hind ordered the Hammer in the low, lifeless voice that had been her shield for so long now, "Get the barbed wire instead."

PART I

THE DROP

1

Bryce Quinlan sat in a chamber so far beneath the mountain above that daylight must have been a myth to the creatures who dwelled there.

For a place that apparently *wasn't* Hel, her surroundings sure appeared like it: black stone, subterranean palace, even-more-subterranean interrogation cell . . . The darkness seemed inherent to the three people standing across from her: a petite female in gray silk, and two winged males clad in black scalelike armor, one of them—the beautiful, powerful male in the center of the trio—literally rippling with shadows and stars.

Rhysand, he'd called himself. The one who looked so much like Ruhn.

It couldn't be coincidence. Bryce had leapt through the Gate intending to reach Hel, to finally take up Aidas's and Apollion's repeated offers to send their armies to Midgard and stop this cycle of galactic conquest. But she'd wound up here instead.

Bryce glanced to the warrior beside Ruhn's almost-twin. The male who'd found her. Who'd carried the black dagger that had reacted to the Starsword.

His hazel eyes held nothing but cold, predatory alertness.

"Someone has to start talking," the short female said—the one who'd seemed so shocked to hear Bryce speak in the Old

Language, to see the sword. Flickering braziers of something that resembled firstlight gilded the silken strands of her chin-length bob, casting the shadow of her slender jaw in stark relief. Her eyes, a remarkable shade of silver, slid over Bryce but remained unimpressed. "You said your name is Bryce Quinlan. That you come from another world—Midgard."

Rhysand murmured to the winged male beside him. Translating, perhaps.

The female went on, "If you are to be believed, how is it that you came here? *Why* did you come here?"

Bryce surveyed the otherwise empty cell. No table glittering with torture instruments, no breaks in the solid stone beyond the door and the grate in the center of the floor, a few feet away. A grate from which she could have sworn a hissing sound emanated.

"What world is this?" Bryce rasped, the words gravelly. After Ruhn's body double had introduced himself in that lovely, cozy foyer, he'd grabbed her hand. The strength of his grip, the brush of his calluses against her skin had been the only solid things as wind and darkness had roared around them, the world dropping away—and then there was only solid rock and dim lighting. She'd been brought to a palace carved beneath a mountain, and then down the narrow stairs to this dungeon. Where he'd pointed to the lone chair in the center of the room in silent command.

So she'd sat, waiting for the handcuffs or shackles or whatever restraints they used in this world, but none had come.

The short female countered, "Why do you speak the Old Language?"

Bryce jerked her chin at the female. "Why do you?"

The female's red-painted lips curved upward. It wasn't a reassuring sight. "Why are you covered in blood that is not your own?"

Score: one for the female.

Bryce knew her blood-soaked clothes, now stiff and dark, and her blood-crusted hands did her no favors. It was the Harpy's blood, and a bit of Lidia's. All coating Bryce as a part of a careful game to keep her alive, to keep their secrets safe, while Hunt and Ruhn had—

Her breath began sawing in and out. She'd left them. Her mate and her brother. She'd left them in Rigelus's hands.

The walls and ceiling pushed in, squeezing the air from her lungs.

Rhysand lifted a broad hand wreathed in stars. "We won't harm you." Bryce found the rest of the sentence lurking within the dense shadows around him: *if you don't try to harm us.*

She closed her eyes, fighting past the jagged breathing, the crushing weight of the stone above and around her.

Less than an hour ago, she'd been sprinting away from Rigelus's power, dodging exploding marble busts and shattering windows, and Hunt's lightning had speared through her chest, into the Gate, opening a portal. She'd leapt toward Hel—

And now . . . now she was here. Her hands shook. She balled them into fists and squeezed.

Bryce took a slow, shuddering breath. Another. Then opened her eyes and asked again, her voice solid and clear, "What world is this?"

Her three interrogators said nothing.

So Bryce fixed her eyes on the female, the smallest but by no means the least deadly of the group. "You said the Old Language hasn't been spoken here in fifteen thousand years. Why?"

That they were Fae and knew the language at all suggested some link between here and Midgard, a link that was slowly dawning on her with terrible clarity.

"How did you come to be in possession of the lost sword Gwydion?" was the female's cool reply.

"What . . . You mean the Starsword?" Another link between their worlds.

All of them just stared at her again. An impenetrable wall of people accustomed to getting answers in whatever way necessary.

Bryce had no weapons, nothing beyond the magic in her veins, the Archesian amulet around her neck, and the Horn tattooed into her back. But to wield it, she needed power, needed to be fueled up like some stupid fucking battery—

So talking was her best weapon. Good thing she'd spent years as a master of spinning bullshit, according to Hunt.

"It's a family heirloom," Bryce said. "It's been in my world since it was brought there by my ancestors . . . fifteen thousand years ago." She let the last few words land with a pointed glance at the female. Let her do the math, as Bryce had.

But the beautiful male—Rhysand—said in a voice like midnight, "How did you find this world?"

This was not a male to be fucked with. None of these people were, but this one . . . Authority rippled off him. As if he was the entire axis of this place. A king of some sort, then.

"I didn't." Bryce met his star-flecked stare. Some primal part of her quailed at the raw power within his gaze. "I told you: I meant to go to Hel. I landed here instead."

"How?"

The things far below the grate hissed louder, as if sensing his wrath. Demanding blood.

Bryce swallowed. If they learned about the Horn, her power, the Gates . . . what was to stop them from using her as Rigelus had wanted to? Or from viewing her as a threat to be removed?

Master of spinning bullshit. She could do this.

"There are Gates within my world that open into other worlds. For fifteen thousand years, they've mostly opened into Hel. Well, the Northern Rift opens directly into Hel, but . . ." Let them think her rambling. An idiot. The party girl most of Midgard had labeled her, that Micah had believed her to be, until she was vacuuming up his fucking ashes. "This Gate sent me here with a one-way ticket."

Did they have tickets in this world? Transportation?

She clarified into their silence, "A companion of mine gambled that he could send me to Hel using his power. But I think . . ." She sorted through all that Rigelus had told her in those last moments. That the star on her chest somehow acted as a beacon to the original world of the Starborn people.

Grasping at straws, she nodded to the warrior's dagger. "There's a prophecy in my world about my sword and a missing knife. That when they're reunited, so will the Fae of Midgard be."

Master of spinning bullshit, indeed.

"So maybe I'm here for that. Maybe the sword sensed that dagger and . . . brought me to it."

Silence. Then the silent, hazel-eyed warrior laughed quietly.

How had he understood without Rhysand translating? Unless he could simply read her body language, her tone, her scent—

The warrior spoke with a low voice that skittered down her spine. Rhysand glanced at him with raised brows, then translated for Bryce with equal menace, "You're lying."

Bryce blinked, the portrait of innocence and outrage. "About what?"

"You tell us." Darkness gathered in the shadow of Rhysand's wings. Not a good sign.

She was in another world, with strangers who were clearly powerful and wouldn't hesitate to kill her. Every word from her lips was vital to her safety and survival.

"I just watched my mate and my brother get captured by a group of intergalactic parasites," she snarled. "I have no interest in doing anything except finding a way to help them."

Rhysand looked to the warrior, who nodded, not taking his gaze off Bryce for so much as a blink.

"Well," Rhysand said to Bryce, crossing his muscled arms. "*That's* true, at least."

Yet the petite female remained unmoved. In fact, her features had tightened at Bryce's outburst. "Explain."

They were Fae. There was nothing to suggest that they were better than the pieces of shit Bryce had known for most of her life. And somehow, despite appearing to be stuck a few centuries behind her own world, they seemed even more powerful than the Midgardian Fae, which could only lead to *more* arrogance and entitlement.

She needed to get to Hel. Or at the very least back to Midgard. And if she said too much . . .

The female noted her hesitation and said, "Just look in her mind already, Rhys."

Bryce went rigid. Oh gods. He could pry into her head, see anything he wanted—

Rhysand glanced at the female. She held his stare with a ferocity that belied her small stature. If Rhysand was in charge, his underlings certainly weren't expected to be silent cronies.

Bryce eyed the lone door. No way to reach it in time, even on the off chance they'd left it unlocked. Running wouldn't save her. Would the Archesian amulet provide any protection? It hadn't prevented Ruhn's mind-speaking, but—

I do not pry where I am not willingly invited.

Bryce lurched back in the chair, nearly knocking it over at the smooth male voice in her mind. Rhysand's voice.

But she answered, thanking Luna for keeping her own voice cool and collected, *Code of mind-speaking ethics?*

She felt him pause—as if almost amused. *You've encountered this method of communication before.*

Yes. It was all she'd say about Ruhn.

May I look in your memories? To see for myself?

No. You may not.

Rhysand blinked slowly. Then he said aloud, "Then we'll have to rely on your words."

The petite female gaped at him. *"But—"*

Rhysand snapped his fingers and three chairs appeared behind them. He sank gracefully onto one, crossing an ankle over a knee. The epitome of Fae beauty and arrogance. He glanced up at his companions. "Azriel." He motioned lazily to the male. Then to the female. "Amren."

Then he motioned to Bryce and said neutrally, "Bryce . . . Quinlan."

Bryce nodded slowly.

Rhysand examined his trimmed, clean nails. "So your sword . . . it's been in your world for fifteen thousand years?"

"Brought by my ancestor." She debated the next bit, then added,

"Queen Theia. Or Prince Pelias, depending on what propaganda's being spun."

Amren stiffened slightly. Rhysand slid his eyes to her, clocking the movement.

Bryce dared to push, "You . . . know of them?"

Amren surveyed Bryce from her blood-splattered neon-pink shoes to her high ponytail. The blood smeared on Bryce's face, now stiff and sticky. "No one has spoken those names here in a very, very long time."

In fifteen thousand years, Bryce was willing to bet.

"But you have heard of them?" Bryce's heart thundered.

"They once . . . dwelled here," Amren said carefully.

It was the last scrap of confirmation Bryce needed about what this planet was. Something settled deep in her, a loose thread at last pulling taut. "So this is it, then. This is where we—the Midgard Fae—originated. My ancestors left this world and went to Midgard . . . and we forgot where we came from."

Silence again. Azriel spoke in their own language, and Rhysand translated. Perhaps Rhysand had been translating for Azriel mind-to-mind these last few minutes.

"He says we have no such stories about our people migrating to another world."

Yet Amren let out a small, choked sound.

Rhysand turned slowly, a bit incredulous. "Do we?" he asked smoothly.

Amren picked at an invisible speck on her silk blouse. "It's murky. I went in before . . ." She shook her head. "But when I came out, there were rumors. That a great number of people had vanished, as if they had never been. Some said to another world, others said they'd moved on to distant lands, still others said they'd been chosen by the Cauldron and spirited away somewhere."

"They must have gone to Midgard," Bryce said. "Led by Theia and Pelias—"

Amren held up a hand. "We can hear your myths later, girl.

What I want to know"—her eyes sharpened, and it was all Bryce could do to weather the scrutiny—"is why *you* came here, when you meant to go elsewhere."

"I'd like to know that, too," Bryce said, perhaps a bit more boldly than could be deemed wise. "Believe me, I'd like nothing more than to get out of your hair immediately."

"To go to . . . Hel," Rhysand said neutrally. "To find this Prince Aidas."

These people weren't her friends or allies. This might be the home world of the Fae, but who the fuck knew what they wanted or aspired to? Rhysand and Azriel *looked* pretty, but Urd knew the Fae of Midgard had used their beauty for millennia to get what they wanted.

Rhysand didn't need to read her mind—no, he seemed to read all that on her own face. He uncrossed his legs, bracing both feet on the stone floor. "Allow me to lay out the situation for you, Bryce Quinlan."

She made herself meet his star-flecked stare. She'd taken on the Asteri and Archangels and Fae Kings and walked away. She'd take him on, too.

The corner of Rhysand's mouth curled upward. "We will not torture it from you, nor will I pry it from your mind. If you choose not to talk, it is indeed your choice. Precisely as it will be *my* choice to keep you down here until you decide otherwise."

Bryce couldn't stop herself from coolly surveying the room, her attention lingering on the grate and the hissing that drifted up from it. "I'll be sure to recommend it to my friends as a vacation spot."

Stars winked out in Rhysand's eyes. "Can we expect any others to arrive here from your world?"

She gave the truest answer she could. "No. As far as I know, they've been looking for this place for fifteen thousand years, but I'm the only one who's ever made it back."

"Who is *they*?"

"The Asteri. I told you—intergalactic parasites."

"What does that mean?"

"They are . . ." Bryce paused. Who was to say these people

wouldn't hand her right over to Rigelus? Bow to him? Theia had come from this world and fought the Asteri, but Pelias had bought what they were selling and gleefully knelt at their immortal feet.

Her pause said enough. Amren snorted. "Don't waste your breath, Rhysand."

Rhysand angled his head, a predator studying prey. Bryce withstood it, chin high. Her mother would have been proud of her.

He snapped his fingers again, and the blood, the dirt on her, disappeared. A stickiness still coated her skin, but it was clean. She blinked down at herself, then up at him.

A cruel half smile graced his mouth. "To incentivize you."

Amren and Azriel remained stone-faced. Waiting.

She'd be stupid to believe Rhysand's *incentive* meant anything good about him. But she could play this game.

So Bryce said, "The Asteri are ancient. Like tens of thousands of years old." She winced at the memory of that room beneath their palace, the records of conquests going back millennia, complete with their own unique dating system.

Her captors didn't reply, didn't so much as blink. Fine—insane old age wasn't totally nuts to them.

"They arrived in my world fifteen thousand years ago. No one knows from where."

"What do you mean by *arrived*?" Rhysand asked.

"Honestly? I have no idea how they first got to Midgard. The history they spun was that they were . . . liberators. Enlighteners. According to them, they found Midgard little more than a backwater planet occupied by non-magical humans and animals. The Asteri chose it as the place to begin creating a perfect empire, and creatures and races from other worlds soon flocked to it through a giant rip between worlds called the Northern Rift. Which now only opens to Hel, but it used to open to . . . anywhere."

Amren pushed, "A rip. How does that happen?"

"Beats me," Bryce said. "No one's ever figured out how it's even possible—why it's at that spot in Midgard, and not others."

Rhysand asked, "What happened after these beings arrived in your world?"

Bryce sucked her teeth before saying, "In the *official* version of this story, another world, Hel, tried to invade Midgard. To destroy the fledgling empire—and everyone living in it. But the Asteri unified all these new people under one banner and pushed Hel back to its own realm. In the process, the Northern Rift was fixed with its destination permanently on Hel. After that, it remained mostly closed. A massive wall was erected around it to keep any Hel-born stragglers from getting through the cracks, and the Asteri built a glorious empire meant to last for eternity. Or so we're all ordered to believe."

The faces in front of her remained impassive. Rhysand asked quietly, "And what is the unofficial story?"

Bryce swallowed, the room in the archives flashing through her memory. "The Asteri are ancient, immortal beings who feed on the power of others—they harvest the magic of a people, a world, and then eat it. We call it firstlight. It fuels our entire world, but mostly them. We're required to hand it over upon reaching immortality— well, as close to immortality as we can get. We seize our full, mature power through a ritual called the Drop, and in the process, some of our power is siphoned off and given over to the firstlight stores for the Asteri. It's like a tax on our magic."

She wasn't even going to touch upon what happened after death. How the power that lingered in their souls was eventually harvested as well, forced by the Under-King into the Dead Gate and turned into secondlight to fuel the Asteri even more. Whatever reached them after the Under-King ate his fill.

Amren angled her head, sleek bob shifting with the movement. "A tax on your magic, taken by ancient beings for their own nourishment and power." Azriel's gaze shifted to her, Rhysand presumably still translating mind-to-mind. But Amren murmured to herself, as if the words triggered something, "A tithe."

Rhysand's brows rose. But he waved a broad, elegant hand at Bryce to continue. "What else?"

She swallowed again. "Midgard is only the latest in a long line of worlds invaded by the Asteri. They have an entire archive of different planets they've either conquered or tried to conquer. I saw it right before I came here. And, as far as I know, there were only three planets that were able to kick them out—to fight back and defeat them. Hel, a planet called Iphraxia, and . . . a world occupied by the Fae. The original, Starborn Fae." She nodded to the dagger at Azriel's side, which had flared with dark light in the presence of the Starsword. "You know my sword by a different name, but you recognize what it is."

Only Amren nodded.

"I think it's because it came from this world," Bryce said. "It seems connected to that dagger somehow. It was forged here, became part of your history, then vanished . . . right? You haven't seen it in fifteen thousand years, or spoken this language in nearly as long—which lines up perfectly with the timeline of the Starborn Fae arriving in Midgard."

The Starborn—Theia, their queen, and Pelias, the traitor-prince who'd usurped her. Theia had brought two daughters with her into Midgard: Helena, who'd been forced to wed Pelias, and another, whose name had been lost to history. Much of the truth about Theia had been lost as well, either through time or the Asteri's propaganda. Aidas, Prince of the Chasm, had loved her—that much Bryce knew. Theia had fought alongside Hel against the Asteri to free Midgard. Had been killed by Pelias in the end, her name nearly wiped from all memory. Bryce bore Theia's light—Aidas had confirmed it. But beyond that, even the Asteri Archives had provided no information about the long-dead queen.

"So you believe," Amren said slowly, silver eyes flickering, "that *our* world is this third planet that resisted these . . . Asteri."

It was Bryce's turn to nod. She motioned to the cell, the realm above it. "From what I learned, long before the Asteri came to my world, they were *here*. They conquered and meddled with and ruled this world. But eventually the Fae managed to overthrow them—to defeat them." She loosed a tight breath, scanning each of their faces. "How?" The question was hoarse, desperate. "How did you do it?"

But Rhysand glanced warily to Amren. She had to be some sort of court historian or scholar if he kept consulting her about the past. He said to her, "Our history doesn't include an event like that."

Bryce cut in, "Well, the Asteri remember your world. They're still holding a grudge. Rigelus, their leader, told me it's his personal mission to find this place and punish you all for kicking them to the curb. You're basically public enemy number one."

"It is in our history, Rhysand," Amren said gravely. "But the Asteri were not known by that name. Here, they were called the Daglan."

Bryce could have sworn Rhysand's golden face paled slightly. Azriel shifted in his chair, wings rustling. Rhysand said firmly, "The Daglan were all killed."

Amren shuddered. The gesture seemed to spark more alarm in Rhysand's expression. "Apparently not," she said.

Bryce pushed Amren, "Do you have any record about how they were defeated?" A kernel of hope glowed in her chest.

"Nothing beyond old songs of bloody battles and tremendous losses."

"But the story . . . it rings true to you?" Bryce asked. "Immortal, vicious overseers once ruled this world, and you guys banded together and overthrew them?"

Their silence was confirmation enough.

Yet Rhysand shook his head, as if still not quite believing it. "And you think . . ." He met Bryce's stare, his eyes once again full of that predatory focus. Gods, he was terrifying. "You believe the Daglan—these *Asteri*—want to come back here for revenge. After at least fifteen thousand years." Doubt dripped from every word.

"That's, like, five minutes for Rigelus," Bryce countered. "He's got infinite time—and resources."

"What kind of resources?" Cold, sharp words—a leader assessing the threat to his people.

How to begin describing guns or brimstone missiles or mech-suits or Omega-boats or even the Asteri's power? How to convey the ruthless, swift horror of a bullet? And maybe it was reckless, but . . . She extended her hand to Rhysand. "I'll show you."

Amren and Azriel cut him sharp looks. Like this might be a trap.

"Hold on," Rhysand said, and vanished into nothing.

Bryce started. "You—you can teleport?"

"We call it winnowing," Amren drawled. Bryce could have sworn Azriel was smirking. But Amren asked, "Can you do it?"

"No," Bryce lied. If Azriel sensed her lie, he didn't call her out this time. "There are only two Fae who can."

It was Amren's turn to start. "Two—on your entire planet?"

"I'm guessing you have more?"

Azriel, without Rhysand to translate, watched in silence. Bryce could have sworn shadows wreathed him, like Ruhn's, yet . . . wilder. The way Cormac's had been.

Amren's chin dipped. "Only the most powerful, but yes. Many can."

As if on cue, Rhysand appeared again, a small silver orb in one hand.

"The Veritas orb?" Amren said, and Azriel lifted an eyebrow.

But Rhysand ignored them and extended his other hand, in which lay a small silver bean.

Bryce took it, peering at the orb he laid on the floor. "What are these?"

Rhysand nodded to the orb. "Hold it, think of what you want to show us, and the memories shall be captured within for us to view."

Easy enough. Like a camera for her mind. She gingerly approached the orb and picked it up. The metal was smooth and cold. Lighter than it should have been. Hollow inside.

"Here goes," she said, and closed her eyes. Pictured the weapons, the wars, the battlefields she'd seen on television, the mech-suits, the guns she'd learned to fire, the lessons with Randall, the power Rigelus had blasted down the hall after her—

She shut it off at that point. Before she leapt into the Gate, before she left Hunt and Ruhn behind. She didn't want to relive that. To show what she could do. To reveal the Horn or her ability to teleport.

Bryce opened her eyes. The ball remained quiet and dim. She put it back on the floor and rolled it toward Rhysand.

He floated it on a phantom wind to his hand, then touched its top. And all that had been in her mind played out.

It was worse, seeing it as a sort of memory-montage: the violence, the brutality of how easily the Asteri and their minions killed, how indiscriminately.

But whatever she felt was nothing compared to the surprise and dread on her captors' faces.

"Guns," Bryce said, pointing to the rifle Randall fired in her displayed memory, landing a perfect bulls-eye shot in a target half a mile off. "Brimstone missiles." She pointed to the blooming golden light of destruction as the buildings of Lunathion ruptured around her. "Omega-boats." The *SPQM Faustus* hunted through the dark depths of the seas. "Asteri." Rigelus's white-hot power blasted apart stone and glass and the world itself.

Rhysand mastered himself, a cool mask sliding into place. "You live in such a world."

It wasn't entirely a question. But Bryce nodded. "Yes."

"And they want to bring all of that . . . here."

"Yes."

Rhysand stared ahead. Thinking it through. Azriel just kept his eyes on the space where the orb had displayed the utter destruction of her world. Dreading—and yet calculating. She'd seen that look before on Hunt's face. A warrior's mind at work.

Amren turned to Rhys, meeting his stare. Bryce knew that look, too. A silent conversation passing between them. As Bryce and Ruhn had often spoken.

Her heart wrenched to see it, to remember. It steadied her, though. Sharpened her focus.

The Asteri had been here—under a different name, but they'd been here. The ancestors of these Fae had defeated them. And Urd had sent her here—here, not Hel. Here, where she'd instantly encountered a dagger that made the Starsword sing. Like it had been the lodestone that had drawn her to this world, to that riverbank. Could it really be the knife from the prophecy?

She'd believed that destroying the Asteri would be as simple as obliterating that firstlight core, yet Urd had sent her here. To the original world of the Midgardian Fae. She had no choice but to trust Urd's judgment. And pray that Ruhn, that Hunt, that everyone she loved in Midgard could hold on until she found a way to get home.

And if she couldn't . . .

Bryce examined the silver bean that lay smooth and gleaming in her hand. Amren said without looking at her, "You swallow it, and it will translate our mother tongue for you. Allow you to speak it, too."

"Fancy," Bryce murmured.

She had to find a way home. If that meant navigating this world first . . . language skills would be useful, considering the extent of bullshit still to be spun. And, sure, she didn't trust these people for one moment, but considering all the questions they kept lobbing her way, she highly doubted they were going to poison her. Or go to such lengths to do so, when a slit throat would be way easier.

Not a comforting thought, but Bryce nonetheless popped the silver bean into her mouth, worked up enough saliva, and swallowed. Its metal was cool against her tongue, her throat, and she could have sworn she felt its slickness sliding into her stomach.

Lightning cleaved her brain. She was being ripped in two. Her body couldn't hold all the searing light—

Then blackness slammed in. Quiet and restful and eternal.

No—that was the room around her. She was on the floor, curled over her knees, and . . . glowing. Brightly enough to illuminate Rhysand's and Amren's shocked faces.

Azriel was already poised over her, that deadly dagger drawn and gleaming with a strange black light.

He noted the darkness leaking from the blade and blinked. It was the most shock Bryce had seen him display.

"Put it away, you fool," Amren said. "It sings for her, and by bringing it close—"

The blade vanished from Azriel's hand, whisked away by a shadow. Silence, taut and rippling, spread through the room.

Bryce stood slowly—as Randall and her mom had taught her to move in front of Vanir and other predators.

And as she rose, she found it in her brain: the knowledge of a language that she had not known before. It sat on her tongue, ready to be spoken, as instinctual as her own. It shimmered along her skin, stinging down her spine, her shoulder blades—wait.

Oh no. No, no, no.

Bryce didn't dare reach for the tattoo of the Horn, to call attention to the letters that formed the words *Through love, all is possible.* She could feel them reacting to whatever had been in that spell that set her glowing and could only pray it wasn't visible.

Her prayers were in vain.

Amren turned to Rhysand and said in that new, strange language—*their* language: "The glowing letters inked on her back . . . they're the same as those in the *Book of Breathings.*"

They must have seen the words through her T-shirt when she'd been on the floor. With every breath, the tingling lessened, like the glow was fading. But the damage was already done.

They once again assessed her. Three apex killers, contemplating a threat.

Then Azriel said in a soft, lethal voice, "Explain or you die."

2

Tharion's blood dripped into the porcelain sink of the hushed, humid bathroom, the roar of the crowd a distant rumble through the cracked green tiles. He breathed in through his nose. Out through his mouth. Pain rippled along his aching ribs.

Stay upright.

His hands clenched the chipped edges of the sink. He inhaled again, focusing on the words, willing his knees not to buckle. *Keep standing, damn you.* He'd taken a beating tonight.

The minotaur he'd faced in the Viper Queen's ring had been twice his weight and at least four feet taller than him. He had a hole in his shoulder leaking blood down the sink drain thanks to the horns he hadn't been fast enough to avoid. And several broken ribs thanks to blows from fists the size of his head.

Tharion loosed another breath, wincing, and reached for the small medkit on the lip of the sink. His fingers shook, fumbling with the vial of potion that would blunt the edge of the pain and accelerate the healing his Vanir body was already doing.

He chucked the cork into the trash can beside the sink, atop the wads of bloodied cotton bandages and wipes he'd used to clean his face. It had somehow been more important than addressing the pain—the hole in his shoulder—that he should be able to see his face, the male beneath.

The reflection wasn't kind. Purple smudges beneath his eyes matched the bruises along his jaw, the cuts on his lip, his swollen nose. All things that would fade and heal swiftly enough, but the hollowness in his eyes . . . It was his face, and yet a stranger's.

Tharion didn't meet his own gaze in the mirror as he tipped back the vial and chugged it. Silky, tasteless liquid coated his mouth, his throat. He'd once done shots with the same abandon. In the span of a few weeks, everything had gone to shit. His whole fucking life had gone to shit.

He'd given up everything he was and had been and ever would be.

He'd chosen this, being chained to the Viper Queen. He'd been desperate, but the burden of his decision weighed on him. He hadn't been allowed to leave the warren of warehouses in the two days since arriving—hadn't really wanted to, anyway. Even the need to return to the water was taken care of for him: a special tub had been prepared below this level with water pumped in directly from the Istros.

So he hadn't been in the river, or felt the wind and the sun, or heard the chatter and rhythmic beats of normal life in days. Hadn't so much as found an exterior window.

The door groaned open, and a familiar female scent announced the identity of the new arrival. As if at this hour, in this bathroom, it could be anyone else.

The Viper Queen had a crew of fighters. But the two of them . . . she treated them like prized racehorses. They fought during the prime-time slots. This bathroom was for their private use, along with the suite upstairs.

The Viper Queen owned them. And she wanted everyone to know it.

"I warmed them up for you," Tharion rasped over a shoulder at Ariadne. The dark-haired dragon, clad in a black bodysuit that accentuated her luscious curves, turned toward him.

Tharion and Ariadne were required to look sexy and stylish,

even as the Viper Queen bade them to bloody themselves for the crowd's amusement.

Ariadne halted at a sink a few feet away, surveying the angles of her face in the mirror as she washed her hands.

"Still as pretty as ever," Tharion managed to tease.

That earned him a sidelong assessment. "You look like shit."

"Nice to see you, too," he drawled, the healing potion tingling through him.

Her nostrils flared delicately. It wasn't wise to taunt a dragon. But he'd been on a hot streak of making stupid decisions lately, so why stop now?

"You have a hole in your shoulder," she said without taking her gaze from his.

Tharion peered at the ghastly wound, even as his skin knitted closed, the sensation like spiders crawling over the area. "Builds character."

Ariadne snorted, returning to her reflection. "You know, you throw around your attraction to females quite a bit. I'm starting to think it's a shield."

He stiffened. "Against what?"

"Don't know, don't really care."

"Ouch."

Ariadne continued examining herself in the mirror. Was she hunting for herself—the person she'd been before coming here—as well? Or maybe the person she'd been before the Astronomer had trapped her inside a ring and worn her on his finger for decades?

Tharion had done what the Viper Queen had asked regarding Ari: he'd woven a web of lies to his Aux contacts about the dragon being commandeered for security purposes. So the Viper Queen didn't technically own Ari as a slave—Ari remained a slave owned by someone else. She just . . . lived here now.

"Your adoring public awaits," Tharion said, grabbing another cotton wipe and holding it under the running water before beginning to clean the blood from his bare chest. He could have jumped in one of the showers to his left, but it would have stung like Hel on his still-mending wounds. He twisted, straining for the particularly nasty slice along his left shoulder blade. It remained out of reach, even for his long fingers.

"Here," Ariadne said, taking the wipe from his hand.

"Thanks, Ar—Ariadne." He'd almost called her Ari, but it didn't seem wise to antagonize her when she'd offered to help him.

Tharion braced his hands on the sink. Ariadne dabbed along the wound, wiping up blood, and he clenched the porcelain hard enough for it to groan beneath his fingers. He gritted his teeth against the stinging, and into the silence, the dragon said, "You can call me Ari."

"I thought you hated that nickname."

"Everyone seems inclined to use it, so it might as well be my choice for you to do so."

"Was that your thinking when you abandoned my friends right before a deathstalker attacked them?" He couldn't keep the bite from his voice, antagonizing her be damned. "Everyone expected the worst of you, so why not just be the worst?"

She snorted. "Your friends . . . you mean the witch and the redhead?"

"Yes. Real honorable of you to ditch them."

"They seemed capable of looking after themselves."

"They are. But you bailed all the same."

"If you're so invested in their safety, perhaps you should have been there." Ari tossed the wipe in the trash and grabbed another one. "Who taught you to fight, anyway?"

He let the argument drop—it'd get them nowhere. He couldn't even have said why he'd felt inclined to bring it up now, of all times. "Here I was, thinking you didn't care to know anything about me."

"Call it curiosity. You don't seem . . . serious enough to be the River Queen's Captain of Intelligence."

"Such a flatterer."

But embers sparked in her eyes, so Tharion shrugged. "I learned how to fight the usual way: I enrolled in the Blue Court Military

Academy after school, and have spent the years since honing those skills. Nothing cool. You?"

"Survival."

He opened his mouth to respond, but the dragon turned on a booted heel. "Ari—" he called before she could reach the door. "We didn't, you know."

She turned, eyebrows rising. "Didn't what?"

"Expect the worst of you."

Her face twisted—rage and sorrow and a drop of shame. Or maybe he was imagining that last bit. She didn't answer before stalking out.

The dripping of his blood again filled the bathroom.

Tharion waited until the potion patched most of the holes in his skin, and didn't bother tugging the upper half of the black bodysuit on before following the dragon back to the heat and smells and light of the fighting ring.

Ari was just getting started. With impressive calm, she squared off against three male lion shifters, the enormous cats circling her with deadly precision. She turned with them, not letting the lions get behind her, her skin beginning to glow with molten scales, her black eyes flickering red.

Across the pit, the one-way window that peered over the ring reflected the glaring spotlights. But Tharion knew who stood on the other side of it, amid the plush finery of her private quarters. Who watched the dragon fight, assessing the intensity of the crowd's roar.

"Traitor," someone hissed to his left.

Tharion found two young mer males glaring at him from the risers above. Both clutched beers and had the glazed look of guys who'd already downed a few.

Tharion gave them a bland nod and faced the ring again.

"Fucking loser," the other male spat.

Tharion kept his eyes on Ari. Steam rippled from the dragon's mouth. One of the lions lunged, swiping with fingers that ended in curved claws, but she ducked away. The concrete floor singed where her feet had been. Preliminary blast marks.

"Some fucking captain," the first male taunted.

Tharion ground his teeth. This wasn't the first time in the past few days that one of his people had recognized him and told him precisely how they felt. Everyone knew Tharion had defected from the Blue Court. Everyone knew he'd defected and come *here* to serve the Meat Market's depraved ruler. The River Queen and her daughter had made sure of it.

Captain Whatever, Ithan Holstrom had once called him. It seemed he truly embodied it now.

You gave that up, he reminded himself. He could never again so much as set foot in the Istros. The moment he did, his former queen would kill him. Or order her sobeks to rip him to shreds. Something twisted in his gut.

He was aware that his parents lived only because he'd gotten messages from them expressing their outrage and disappointment. *We already lost one child,* his mother had written. *Now we lose another. Defecting, Tharion? What in Ogenas's depths were you thinking?*

He didn't write back. Didn't apologize for being so reckless and selfish that he hadn't thought of their safety before committing this act of insanity. He'd not only sworn himself to the Viper Queen, he'd bound himself to her, too. After all the shit that had gone down in Pangera . . . no place else was safe for him, anyway. Only here, where the Viper Queen was allowed to rule.

He watched Ari pace in the ring. *You gave that up,* he told himself again firmly. *For this.*

"You're a disgrace," the other mer male went on.

Something liquid and foamy splashed on Tharion's head, his bare shoulders. The fucker had thrown his beer.

Tharion snarled up at them, and the males had the good sense to back up a step, like they might have finally remembered what Tharion was capable of when provoked. But before he could beat the living shit out of them, one of the Viper Queen's personal guards—one of those glassy-eyed Fae defectors—said, "Fishboy. Boss wants you. Now."

Tharion stiffened, but he had no choice. The tugging sensation in his gut would only worsen the longer he resisted. Best to get this over with now.

So he left the assholes behind. Left Ari with the lions, who'd be deep-fried in about twenty minutes, or whenever the dragon had put on enough of a show to please the audience and did what she could have accomplished without so much as stepping into the ring.

He had no doubt there'd be some vendor waiting in the wings to scoop up the cooked carcasses and sell them in a food stall nearby. It wasn't called the Meat Market for nothing.

The walk upstairs, to the room behind that one-way window, was long and quiet. He willed his mind to be that way, too. To stop caring.

It was easier said than done, when everything kept circling: the failed attack on the lab, Cormac's death . . . They'd all been so fucking dumb, thinking they could take on the Asteri. And now here he was.

Honestly, he'd been headed this way for a while before that. Starting with the debacle with the River Queen's daughter. Then Lesia's death a year ago. This last month had been a culmination of that shit. Of what a pathetic, weak failure he'd always been beneath the surface.

Tharion knocked once on the wooden door, then entered.

The Viper Queen stood at the window overlooking the pit, where Ari had switched to taunting the lions. They were now frantic to escape. Everywhere the cats lunged to flee the ring, a wall of flame blocked their exit.

"She's a natural performer," the Viper Queen observed without turning. The ruler of the Meat Market wore a white silk romper cut to her slim figure, feet bare. A cigarette dangled from her manicured hand. "You could learn from her."

Tharion leaned against the wooden doorframe. "Is that an order or a suggestion?"

The Viper Queen pivoted, shiny dark hair swaying with her. Her lips were painted their usual dark purple, offsetting the snake shifter's pale skin. "Do you know the lengths I went to in procuring that minotaur for you tonight?"

Tharion kept his mouth shut. How many times had he stood like this in front of the River Queen, silent while she ripped into him? He'd lost count long ago.

The Viper Queen's teeth flashed, delicate fangs stark against the purple of her lips. "Five minutes, Tharion?" Her voice dropped to a deadly purr. "A great deal of effort on my part, and all I get out of it, all my crowd gets, is a five-minute fight?"

Tharion gestured to his shoulder. "I'd think goring me and then hurling me across the ring was spectacle enough."

"I'd have liked to see that several more times. Not witness you flying into a rage and snapping the bull's neck."

She crooked a finger. That tugging in his gut increased. As if they possessed a mind of their own, his feet and legs moved. They carried him to the window, to her side.

He hated it—not the summoning, but the fact that he'd stopped any attempt at defying it.

"To make up for you blowing your load," the Viper Queen drawled, "I told Ari to drag out her fight." She inclined her head to the ring. Ari's face had gone empty and cold as she made the lions scream under her flames.

Tharion's gut churned. No wonder Ari hadn't stayed long to talk to him. But she'd helped him anyway. He had no idea how to unpack that.

"Try a little harder next time," the Viper Queen hissed in his ear, lips brushing his skin. She sniffed. "The mer punks really drenched you."

Tharion stepped away. "Is there a reason you called me up here?" He wanted a shower, and the relief that only sleep could offer him.

Her lips curled upward. She tugged back the pristine sleeve of her romper, exposing her moon-pale wrist. "Considering how little heart you put into your performance, I thought you might need a pick-me-up."

Tharion clenched his teeth. He wasn't a slave—though he'd

been stupid and desperate enough to offer himself as such to her. But instead she'd offered him something nearly as bad: the venom only she could produce.

And now, after that initial taste of it . . . His mouth filled with saliva. The scent of her skin, the blood and venom beneath it—he was helpless before her, a hungry fucking animal.

"Maybe if I offered you some before your fights," she mused, forearm extended to him like a personal feast, "you would find a bit more . . . stamina."

With every scrap of will left in him, Tharion lifted his eyes to hers. Let her see how much he hated this, hated her, hated himself.

She smiled. She knew. Had known when he'd defected to her, to this life. He'd told himself that this was a place of refuge, but it was getting harder to hide from what it really was.

A long-overdue punishment.

The Viper Queen slid one of her gold-painted nails down her wrist. Opened a vein churning with that milky, opalescent venom that made him see the gods themselves.

"Go ahead," she urged, and Tharion wanted to scream, to weep, to run, as he grabbed her arm to his mouth and sucked in a mouthful of the venom.

It was beautiful. It was horrific. And it punched through him. Stars flickered in the air. Time slowed to a syrupy, languid scroll. Exhaustion and pain faded to nothing.

He'd heard the whispers long before he'd come here: her venom was the best high an immortal could ever attain. Having tasted it, he didn't disagree. Didn't blame those Fae defectors who served as her bodyguards in exchange for hits of this.

He'd once pitied them, scorned them.

Now he was one of them.

The Viper Queen's hand trailed up his chest to his neck, tracing over the spot where his gills usually appeared. She scraped her painted nails over it—a mark of pure ownership. Not only of his body, but of who he was, who he'd once been.

Her fingers tightened on his throat. An invitation, this time.

The Viper Queen's lips brushed against his ear again as she whispered, "Let's see what kind of stamina you have now, Tharion."

"We can't just leave Tharion in here."

"Trust me, Holstrom, Captain Whatever can look after himself."

Ithan frowned deeply at Tristan Flynn from across the rickety table. Declan Emmet and his boyfriend, Marc, were chatting up a vendor at one of the Meat Market's many stalls. The owl-headed Vanir was the third person they'd spoken to tonight, hoping to get news of their imprisoned friends—the twelfth lowlife they'd contacted in the past two days.

And Ithan was getting sick enough of their fruitless talking that he taunted Flynn, "Is this what Fae do? Leave their friends to suffer?"

"Fuck you, wolf," Flynn said, but didn't take his eyes off where Declan and Marc worked their charm. Even the usually unflappable Flynn now had bags beneath his eyes. He'd rarely smiled in the past few days. Seemed to be sleeping as little as Ithan was.

Yet despite all that, Ithan went for the throat. "So Ruhn's life means more—"

"Ruhn is in a fucking *dungeon* being tortured by the Asteri," Flynn snarled. "Tharion is here because he defected. He made that choice."

"Technically, Ruhn also made a choice to go to the Eternal City—"

Flynn dragged his hands through his brown hair. "If you're going to complain, then get the fuck out of here."

"I'm not complaining. I'm just saying that we've got a friend in a bad situation literally *right there* and we're not even trying to help him." Ithan pointed to the second level of the cavernous warehouse, the nondescript door that led into the Viper Queen's private quarters.

"Again, Ketos defected. Not much we can do."

"He was desperate—"

"We're all fucking desperate," Flynn murmured, eyeing a passing draki male carrying a sack of what smelled like elk meat. He sighed. "Seriously, Holstrom—go back to the house. Get some rest." Again, Ithan noted the Fae lord's exhausted face. "And," Flynn added, "take that one with you." Flynn nodded to the female sitting ramrod straight at a nearby table, alert and tense. The three fire sprites lay draped around her shoulders, dozing.

Right. The other source of Ithan's frustration these days: playing babysitter for Sigrid Fendyr.

It would have been smarter to leave her back at the Fae males' house—his house now, he supposed—but she'd refused. Had insisted on accompanying them.

Sigrid insisted on seeing and knowing *everything*. If he'd thought she'd crawl out of her mystic's tank and cower, he'd thought wrong. She'd been a pain in his ass for two days now, wanting the complete history of the Fendyrs, their enemies, Ithan's enemies . . . anything and everything that had happened while she'd been the Astronomer's captive.

She hadn't offered up much of her own past—not even a crumb about her father, whose history she hadn't known until Ithan had filled her in, how the male had long ago been Prime Apparent until his sister, Sabine, had challenged him and won. Ithan had thought she'd killed him, but she'd apparently sent Sigrid's father off into exile instead, where Sigrid had been born. Anything other than that was a complete mystery. Part of Ithan didn't want to know what circumstances had been so dire as to make a Fendyr sell his heir—sell an *Alpha*—to the Astronomer.

That heir was only sitting quietly right now because she'd taken two steps into the Meat Market and sneered, *Who'd want to shop at a disgusting place like this?* Promptly making Declan and Marc's work infinitely harder by earning the ire of any vendor within earshot.

The whisper network here put them all within earshot.

So Flynn had ordered her to sit alone. Well, alone apart from her fiery little cabal. Wherever Sigrid went, the sprites went with her.

Ithan had no idea if that bond was from the years in the

tank, or from a shared trauma, or just because they were females living in a very male house, but the four of them together were a headache.

"It's too dangerous for her to be out in the open," Flynn went on. "Anyone can report a sighting."

"No one knows who she is. To them, she's a random wolf."

"Yeah, and all it takes is one mention to Amelie or Sabine that a female wolf is in your company, and they'll know. I'm shocked they haven't run right over here already."

"Sabine's ruthless, but she's not dumb. She wouldn't start shit on the Viper Queen's turf."

"No, she'll wait until we cross into the CBD and then ambush us." The angels had long ignored anything that went on at street level in their district, too preoccupied with the comings and goings in their lofty towers.

Ithan glared at the male. Normally, he got along fine with Flynn. Liked him, even. But since Ruhn and Hunt and Bryce had disappeared . . .

Disappeared wasn't the right word, at least for Ruhn and Hunt. They'd been taken prisoner, but Bryce . . . no one knew what had happened to her. Hence their presence here, seeking any intel they could get their hands on after Declan's computer searches had been fruitless.

Any information on Bryce, on Ruhn, on Athalar . . . they were desperate for it. For a direction. A spark to light the way. Something that was better than sitting on their asses, not knowing.

Ithan glanced at the chair beneath him. *He* was currently sitting on his ass. Not knowing anything.

Before he could let self-loathing sink its teeth into him, he rose and stalked over to where Sigrid sat monitoring the patrons of the Meat Market. She lifted brown eyes full of irritation and disdain to him. "This is a bad place."

No shit, he refrained from saying. "It has it uses," he hedged.

He'd gone straight to the Fae males' house when he'd hauled Sigrid out of the Astronomer's tank. They'd stayed there while Flynn and Declan pretended that all was normal in their world. While they continued working for the Aux, Prince Ruhn's absence dismissed as a much-needed vacation.

Ithan had been waiting for soldiers to show up. Or assassins, sent by the Asteri or Sabine or the Astronomer.

Yet there had been no questions. No interrogations. No arrests. The Autumn King hadn't even grilled Flynn and Dec, though he no doubt knew something had happened to his son. And that where Ruhn went, his two best friends went with him.

The public had no idea what had happened in the Eternal City. Granted, Ithan and the Fae warriors didn't know much either, but they knew that their friends had gone into the Asteri stronghold and hadn't come out again. The Asteri, the other powers at play . . . they knew that Ithan and the others had also been involved, even if they hadn't been present. And yet they hadn't made a move to punish them.

It wasn't a comforting thought.

Sigrid angled her head with lupine curiosity. "Do you come here often?"

With anyone else, he might have made a joke about pickup lines, but Sigrid didn't know or care about humor. He couldn't blame her, after what she'd been through. So Ithan said, "When my work for the Aux or my pack demands it. But rarely, thank the gods."

Her mouth tightened. "The Astronomer frequented this place." That day Ithan had gone back to the Astronomer's place to free her, he remembered, the ancient male had been over here buying some part for her tank.

"Any idea who he patronizes?" It was more of a casual question than anything.

Sigrid peered around. If she'd been in wolf form, he had no doubt her ears would have been flicking, picking up every sound. She replied without taking her focus off the teeming market, "A satyr, I heard him say once. Who sells salts and other things."

Ithan glanced to the balcony level—to the shut green door where the satyr lived. He knew who she was talking about, thanks to all those past visits on behalf of the Aux. The lowlife peddled in all kinds of contraband.

Sigrid marked his shift in attention, tracing his line of sight. "That's his place?"

Ithan gave a slow nod.

Sigrid shot to her feet, eyes gleaming with predatory intent.

"Where are you going?" Ithan demanded, stepping into her path.

The sprites jolted from their nap, clinging to Sigrid's long brown hair to keep from being thrown off her shoulders.

"Are we done?" Malana asked, yawning.

"We're terribly bored," Sasa agreed, stretching her plump body along Sigrid's neck. Rithi, the third sister, hummed in agreement.

Ignoring the sprites, Sigrid's teeth flashed as she faced Ithan. "I want to see why this satyr thinks it appropriate to supply people like the Astrono—"

"We're not here to cause trouble," Ithan said, and didn't move an inch from her path. But she stomped around him, pure Fendyr. A force of nature—one he'd just begun to see unleashed.

Despite that noble bloodline, Ithan grabbed her arm. "Do *not* go up there," he snarled softly, fingers digging into her bony arm.

She looked down at his hand, then up at his face. Her nose crinkled with anger. "Or what?"

The steel of an Alpha rang in her voice. Ithan's very bones cried out to submit, to bow away, to step aside.

But he fought it, pushed against it—met it with his own dominance. The Fendyrs might have been Alphas for generations, but the Holstroms weren't pushovers. They were Alphas, too—leaders and warriors in their own right.

Like Hel would he let this female push him around, Fendyr or no.

Flynn's chair scraped the ground, but Ithan didn't take his eyes from Sigrid as the Fae male stalked over and hissed, "What the fuck is wrong with you two? Go snarl at each other somewhere it won't be noticed by everyone in the gods-damned Meat Market."

Ithan bared his teeth at Sigrid. She bared hers right back.

He said to Flynn, still not breaking Sigrid's stare, "She wants to go confront the salt dealer about his association with the Astronomer. The satyr who got in all that trouble last year."

Flynn sighed at the wooden ceiling. "Now's not the time to go on a self-righteous warpath, sweetheart."

Sigrid looked away from Ithan at last, though the wolf part of him knew she wasn't conceding in their battle of wills. No, it was because she'd found another opponent to face. "Don't speak to me like I'm some common female," Sigrid raged at Flynn, who held up his hands. She whipped her head back to Ithan, "It's within my rights—"

"You have no rights," a male voice said. Marc. The leopard shifter had stalked up behind them with preternatural grace. Though he was in jeans and a long-sleeved T-shirt, the male still had an air of sleek professionalism. "Since you technically don't even exist. You're a ghost, for all intents and purposes."

Sigrid slowly turned, lip curling. "Did I ask for your opinion, *cat*?"

Normally, Ithan would have been glad to engage in some intershifter rivalry. But Marc was a good male—her disdain was utterly misplaced. Declan sauntered up beside his boyfriend and slung an arm around his broad shoulders. "I think it's past someone's bedtime."

Sigrid growled. But the sprites drifted from her shoulders to float in front of her face as Sasa said carefully, "Siggy, we *are* here to . . . do other things. Perhaps we could come back another time."

Ithan almost laughed at the nickname. Someone as intense as the female before him had no business being called *Siggy*.

"The next time they let us out of the house," Sigrid said, bristling. "In days or weeks."

"I'll remind you," Declan drawled, "that you're currently Sabine's primary enemy."

"Let her come find me," Sigrid said without an ounce of fear. "I've a score to settle."

"Luna spare me," Flynn muttered. Ithan could have sworn he caught the sprites nodding their agreement as they resettled themselves on Sigrid's shoulders. The Fae lord turned to Declan and Marc. "Anything?"

The couple shook their heads. "No. It really does seem like the Asteri put a lock on the information. Nothing's getting in or out." Silence fell, heavy and tense.

It was Sigrid who said, "So what now?"

Only two days out of the tank and she was already assuming the mantle of leader, whether she knew it or not. A true Alpha, expecting to be answered . . . and obeyed.

"We keep trying to find out what's going on," Declan said with a one-shouldered shrug.

Flynn blew out an exasperated breath and plopped onto his chair again. "We're no closer than we were two days ago: Ruhn and Athalar are being held as traitors. That's all we know." That was all Marc's inside source at the Eternal City had been able to glean. Nothing else.

Declan sank into a seat and rubbed his eyes with his thumb and index finger. "Honestly? We're lucky we aren't in those dungeons, too."

"We have to break them out," Flynn said, crossing his muscled arms. Rithi, on his left shoulder, made an identical gesture.

"Urd knows what shape they're in," Declan said bleakly. "We'd need medwitches on hand, probably."

"You've got healing magic," Flynn countered.

"Yeah," Dec said, shaking his head, "but the kind of injuries they'd have . . . I'd need to be working alongside a team of trained professionals."

The thought of what those injuries might be to require such a team of medwitches made them all fall silent again. A heavy, miserable sort of quiet.

"And," Declan challenged, head lifting, "where would we even go once we rescued them? There's no one on Midgard who could hide or harbor us."

"What about that mer ship?" Flynn mused. "The one that picked them up at Ydra. It outran the Omega-boats. Seems pretty damned good at hiding from the Asteri, too."

"Flynn," Marc warned with a glance at the teeming market. All those listening ears.

Ithan kept his voice low. "Tharion could get us onto that ship."

He expected Flynn to roll his eyes at the mention of helping Ketos, but the male glanced to the second level. "He can't set foot beyond this market."

None of them had seen or heard from the mer male since he'd left for Pangera. But they'd learned of his whereabouts thanks to a neon-green piece of paper taped to a lamppost, advertising an upcoming match in the Viper Queen's fighting pit with Tharion as the main event. It was clear enough what had happened: the male had defected from the Blue Court and run straight here.

Ithan countered, "Then we ask Tharion how to get a message to them."

Declan shook his head. "And what then? We all live under the ocean forever?"

Ithan shifted on his feet. The wolf in him would go insane. No ability to run freely, to respond to the moon calling his name—

"*She* lived in a tank for the gods know how long," Flynn said, gaze darting to Sigrid. "I think we can manage a cushy, city-sized submarine."

Sigrid flinched—a crack in her usually cocky exterior.

"Careful," Ithan warned Flynn.

The sprites murmured their comfort to Sigrid, their flames now a deep raspberry. But Sigrid silently rose from her seat and walked toward a nearby vendor selling opals. The sweatshirt and pants Ithan had given her hung off her lean frame, swishing with each step.

"You need to remind her to shower," Dec said a shade quietly, eyes shining with concern.

She hadn't known what shampoo was. Or soap. Or conditioner. Hadn't even known what a shower was, and had refused to step into the stream until Ithan had done so himself, fully clothed, to demonstrate that it was safe. That it wasn't some version of a tank.

She'd never slept in a proper bed before, either. Or at least not one that she remembered.

"Okay," Declan said, drawing attention back to the matter at hand. "We're clearly not learning anything by asking around, but let's think about it . . . Ruhn has to be alive. The Asteri wouldn't kill him right away—he's too big of a political presence."

"Yeah, so let's go rescue him," Flynn pushed. "Him and Athalar."

"What about Bryce?" Declan asked so softly it was barely a whisper.

"She's gone," Flynn said tightly. "Went wherever."

Ithan didn't like that tone—not one bit. "What, you think Bryce bailed?" he demanded. "You think she'd willingly leave Ruhn and Hunt to the Asteri? Come on."

Flynn leaned back in his chair. "You got a better guess about where she might be?"

Ithan restrained the urge to punch the Fae lord in the throat. Flynn was angry and hurting and scared, Ithan reminded himself. "Bryce doesn't give up on the people she loves. If she went somewhere, it's gotta be important."

"Doesn't matter where she went," Flynn said. "All I know is we have to get Ruhn out before it's too late."

Ithan glanced at the second level again, that sunball captain part of his mind calculating, thinking it through . . .

Dec gripped Flynn's shoulder, squeezing tight. "Look, the mer ship isn't a bad idea, but we need to think long-term. Need to consider our families, too."

"My parents and sister can go to Hel for all I care," Flynn said.

"Well, I want my family to be safe," Declan snapped. "*If* we're going to rescue Ruhn and Athalar, we need to make sure no one else gets caught in the cross fire."

Dec looked to Ithan, and Ithan shrugged. He had no one left to warn. Would anyone even miss him if he were gone? His duty was to protect the wolf at the stall across the way. Out of some stupid hope that she might . . . He had no idea. Challenge and defeat Sabine? Correct the dangerous path Sabine was leading the wolves down? Fill the void that Danika had left?

Sigrid was a loose cannon. An Alpha, yes, but she had no training.

Her impulses were all over the place, too unpredictable. With time, she might learn the necessary skills, but time wasn't their ally these days.

So Ithan said, "You want to save Ruhn and Athalar? That mer ship is the only way we can cross the ocean unnoticed. Maybe the mer on it will have some idea how to break them out. They might even help us if we're lucky." He pointed to the second level. "Tharion's our way in."

"Seems convenient," Flynn said at last, "given that you were insisting we needed to spring him loose from here."

"Two birds, one stone."

"Tharion can't leave," Marc mused, "but nothing's stopping him from talking to us. Maybe he can provide contact information."

"Only one way to find out," Ithan said.

Flynn sighed, which Ithan took as acceptance. "Someone's gotta tell her to go home." He jabbed a thumb over his shoulder toward Sigrid.

"And be her escort," Dec added.

"Not it," Flynn and Ithan said at the same moment.

Declan whipped his head to Marc and said, "Not it," before the leopard could grasp what was going on.

Marc rubbed his temples. "Remind me how it is that the three of you are considered some of the most feared warriors in this city?"

Dec just kissed his cheek.

Marc sighed. "If I have to bring *Siggy* home, then Holstrom has to be the one to tell her."

Ithan opened his mouth, but . . . fine. With a mocking smile to the males, he walked over to retrieve the Alpha. And spare the opal dealer from her endless questions.

How do you know *it bestows luck or love or joy? What do the colors have to do with anything? What proof do you have that these work?*

He couldn't tell if it was curiosity, pent up from years in that tank, or sheer Alphaness, needing to question everyone and everything. Needing order in the world.

Ithan put a hand on Sigrid's elbow to alert her of his presence, but again she flinched. Ithan backed away a step, hands up as the opal dealer watched warily. "Sorry."

She didn't like being touched. She'd only let him touch her to wash her hair that first night, when she'd had no idea how to do it.

Ithan motioned her to walk back toward the males, and she fell into step beside him, a healthy distance away. Most wolves needed touch—craved it. Had the instinct been robbed from her by those years in the tank?

It made it hard to be annoyed with her when he thought about it like that.

"How do you get used to it?" Sigrid asked over the hiss of cooking meat and bartering shoppers. Behind her, the sprites were still hovering by the array of opals, exclaiming over the stones. How the three sprites had adapted so quickly to this strange, open world was beyond him. They'd been trapped by the Astronomer, too, locked in his rings.

Ithan asked, "Used to what?"

Sigrid peered at her hands, her thin body beneath the sweats. Passing shoppers noted her—him—and gave them a wide berth. "Feeling like you're stranded in a rotting corpse."

He blinked. "I, ah . . ." He couldn't imagine himself in her shoes, suddenly a body of flesh and blood and bone after the weightless years in the isolation tank. "You just need time."

Her eyes lowered. It didn't seem to be the answer she was looking for.

"Sigrid," he said again. "You're . . . you're doing great."

"Why do you keep calling me that?" she asked.

"That's the name Sasa chose for you," Ithan said, offering a friendly smile.

"Why do I need a name? I've lived this long without one."

"An Alpha should have one. A *person* should have one. The Astronomer let you take the Drop—you'll be alive for centuries."

When pressed, she'd revealed that she'd somehow made the Drop in the isolation tank. She couldn't tell him when or how, but he'd been relieved to hear she had that protection.

"I don't want to talk about the Drop." Her voice was flat, dead.

"Neither do I." He would have liked some answers about what she'd experienced, but not now. Not when they'd reached the three waiting males. The sprites, finally emerging from the depths of the opal stall, raced over, three plumes of flame streaming across the bone-dry warehouse.

"So, do we go knock?" Flynn asked, pointing to the metal, vault-like door at the top of the stairs. The entrance to the Viper Queen's private lair.

Marc caught Ithan's eye. Had he explained to Sigrid that Marc would escort her home?

Ithan cringed. No, he hadn't.

Marc glared. *Coward,* the leopard's look seemed to say. But he tensed, going still. "Stay quiet."

The others obeyed, the two Fae males reaching for the guns at their sides. The Meat Market bustled on unawares, selling and trading and feeding, and yet . . .

Marc's tawny eyes scanned the warehouse, the skylights. He sniffed.

Ithan did the same. As shifters, their senses were sharper than those of the Fae.

From the doorway behind them, the blend of smells from the open night leaked in, the reek of the sewers beyond . . .

And the scent of converging wolves.

3

I don't know what language the tattoo is in," Bryce insisted. "My friend got it inked on me when I was blackout—"

"Do not *lie*," Rhysand warned with soft menace. He'd kill her. Whatever the language was, it was apparently so bad that it might as well say *Stick knife here.*

Amren stalked around Bryce, peering at the tattoo no doubt still glowing from beneath the material of her white shirt. "I can feel something in the letters . . ." Bryce tensed. "Get Nesta."

Azriel murmured, "Cassian won't be happy."

"Cassian will deal. Nesta will be able to sense this better than I can." Bryce turned, placing Amren and Azriel back in her line of sight right as the former insisted, "Get her, Rhysand."

Bryce's knees bent into a defensive crouch. How much would this hurt? Would she stand any chance of—

Rhysand vanished again.

Before Bryce had finished rising to her feet, he returned, a familiar female with golden-brown hair in tow. As she had earlier in the foyer, the female wore dark leathers akin to those on Azriel and Rhysand, and stood with an unruffled, cool sort of calm. A warrior.

Her blue-gray eyes slid over Bryce.

Bryce slowly, almost numbly sank back into her chair. Whatever was in those eyes—

The female said quietly to the others, voice flat, almost bored, "I told you earlier: There's something Made on her. Beyond that sword she carried."

"Made?" Bryce, caution be damned, asked the newcomer—Nesta, she could only assume—at the same time Amren pointed to Bryce's back and asked, "Is it that tattoo?"

Nesta just said, "Yes."

All of them stared at Bryce once more, expressions unreadable. Which one would strike first? Four against one—she wasn't getting out of here alive.

Amren said quietly to Rhysand, "What do you want to do with her, Rhys?"

Bryce clenched her jaw. Even if she stood zero chance of winning, like Hel would she take her death lying down. She'd fight in whatever way she could—

Nesta jerked her chin at Bryce, haughty and aloof. "You can fight us, but you'll lose."

Fuck that. Bryce held the female's stare, finding a will of pure steel gleaming in it. "You try to touch that tattoo and you'll find out why the Asteri want me dead so badly."

She regretted the retort instantly. Azriel's hand drifted toward the dagger at his side. But Nesta stepped closer, unimpressed and unintimidated.

"What is it?" Nesta asked Bryce, motioning to her back. "How is a bit of writing on your skin . . . Made?"

"I can't answer the question until you tell me what the fuck *Made* means."

"Don't tell her anything," Amren warned Nesta. She pointed to the doorway. "You did your job and told us what we needed. We'll see you later."

Nesta's brows rose at the dismissal. But she looked at Bryce and smiled sharply. "It's in your best interests to cooperate with them, you know."

"So they've told me," Bryce said, fingers curling into fists at the sides of her chair. She tucked them under her thighs to keep from doing anything stupid.

Nesta's eyes gleamed with amusement, marking the movement.

"Our . . . visitor needs rest," Rhysand said, and gracefully stalked to the door. Order given, Amren and Azriel strode after him, Nesta following only after staring at Bryce for another heartbeat. A taunting, daring look.

Yet as Azriel reached the threshold, Bryce blurted to the winged warrior, "The sword—where is it?"

Azriel paused, glancing over a shoulder. "Somewhere safe."

Bryce held Azriel's gaze, meeting his ice with her own—with that expression she knew Ruhn always thought looked so much like their father's. The face she'd let the world see so very rarely. "The sword is mine. I want it back."

Azriel's mouth kicked up at the corners. "Then give us a good reason to return it to you."

Time dripped by. Trays of simple food appeared at fairly regular intervals: bread, beef stew—or what she assumed was beef stew—hard cheese. Foods similar to ones back home.

Even the herbs were familiar—had the Fae of this world introduced them to Midgard? Or were plants like thyme and rosemary somehow universal? Strewn across space?

Or maybe the Asteri had brought those herbs from their own home world and planted them on all their conquered planets.

She knew it was a stupid thing to contemplate. That she had way bigger things to consider than an intergalactic garden. But she quickly lost interest in eating, and thinking about everything else was . . . too much.

No one else came to see her. Bryce entertained herself by tossing peas from her stew into the grate in the center of the floor, counting the long seconds until she heard a faint *plink*, and then the hiss and roar of whatever lurked down there.

She didn't want to know. Her imagination conjured plenty of options, all with sharp teeth and ravenous appetites.

She tried the door only once. It wasn't locked, but a wall of black night filled the doorway, obscuring the hall beyond from sight. Blocking anyone from going in or out. She'd flared her starlight, but even it had muted in the face of that darkness.

Maybe it was some kind of fucked-up test. To see if she could get through their strongest powers and wards. To feel her out as an opponent. Maybe to see what the Horn—whatever was *Made* about it—could do. But she didn't need to throw her starlight against that darkness to know it wasn't budging. Its might thundered in her very bones.

Bryce scoured her memory for any alternative escape tactic, reviewing everything Randall had taught her, but none of it was applicable to getting through that impenetrable power.

So Bryce sat. And ate. And threw peas at the monsters below.

Even if she got out of here, she couldn't get off-planet. Not without someone to power her up, activating the Horn in the process. And from Apollion's hints, Hunt's power was far more compatible with hers than most. Granted, Hypaxia had powered her up against the deathstalker, but there was no guarantee the witch-queen's magic would have been enough to open a gate.

And did she *need* a gate to get home? Micah had used the Horn in her back to open all seven Gates in Crescent City, blocks away. When she'd landed here, there had been no gate-like structure nearby. Just a grassy front lawn, the river, and the house she could barely make out through the dense mists.

Only the dagger—and Azriel wielding it—had been there. Like *that* was where she'd needed to be.

"When knife and sword are reunited, so shall our people be," Bryce murmured into the quiet.

To what end, though? The Fae were horrible. The ones here weren't much different from the ones she knew, as far as she could tell. And the Fae on Midgard had proved their moral rot again this spring, locking vulnerable people out of their villas during the demon attack. Proved it with their laws and rules keeping females oppressed, little more than chattel. Bryce had twisted their rules against them at the Autumn Equinox to marry Hunt, but according to those same rules, she now technically *belonged* to him. She was a princess, for Urd's sake, and yet she was still the property of the untitled male she'd married.

Maybe the Fae weren't worth uniting.

But it still left her with the problem of getting off this planet—one of the few worlds to have ever succeeded in ousting the Asteri. Daglan. Whatever they were called.

Bryce leaned against a wall of the cell, knees to her chest, and tried to sort through it all, laying out the pieces before her.

Hours stretched on. Nothing came to her.

Bryce rubbed at her face. She'd stumbled into the home world of the Fae. The world from which the Starborn Fae—Theia and Pelias and Helena—had come. From which the Starsword had come, and where its knife had been waiting. If Urd had some intention in sending her here . . . she sure as fuck had no idea what it was.

Or how she'd get out of this mess.

"We shouldn't have brought her with us," Flynn murmured as they hurried through the stalls of the Meat Market, aiming for an alternate exit on the quieter side of the warehouse. "I fucking *told* you, Holstrom—"

"I ordered him to bring me," Sigrid cut in, keeping pace beside Ithan, the sprites dimmed to a pale yellow as they hunched on her shoulders. Something in Ithan twinged at that—an Alpha, defending him. Taking the responsibility, even if it implied that he *could* be ordered. The Alphas he'd lived under for the past few years had used their power and dominance for themselves. Danika had used her position to support those under her, in her own brash way, but Danika was gone. He'd thought he'd never encounter another like her, but maybe—

"Sabine would have found us anyway," Ithan said, "whether we were here or at the house. It was only a matter of time."

They entered a long service corridor with a dented metal door at its other end, a half-assed *EXIT* painted on it in white lettering.

Definitely not up to code. Though he doubted a city health and safety inspector had ever set foot in this warren of misery.

"Do we split up?" Dec asked. "Try to shake them that way?"

"No," Marc said, claws glinting at his fingertips. "Their sense of smell's too good. They'll be able to tell which of us she's with."

As if in answer, howls rent the warehouse proper. Ithan's entire body locked up. He knew the tenor of those howls. *Prey on the run.* He gritted his teeth to keep from answering, to clamp his responding howl inside his body.

Beside him, Sigrid was a live wire. Like the howls had triggered a response in her, too.

"So we make a run for it," Flynn said. "Where do we rendezvous if we get separated?"

The question hung in the air. Where the fuck was safe in this city, on this planet? Considering their connections to imprisoned traitors, the list of options was short as fuck. Where would Bryce have gone? She would have found someone bigger and badder . . . or smarter, at least. She would have gone to the gallery, maybe, to its protective wards, but Jesiba Roga's sanctum was gone. Griffin Antiquities had never been repaired or reopened. Which left—

"We make it to the Comitium," Ithan said. "Isaiah Tiberian will shelter us."

Dec lifted a brow. "You know Tiberian?"

"No, but Athalar's his friend. And I've heard he's a good male."

"For an angel," Flynn muttered.

Sigrid demanded, "We're going to the angels?" Disdain and distrust spiked each word.

The howls in the warehouse closed in: *We stalk the darkness together.*

"I don't see another option," Dec admitted. "It's a gamble, though. Tiberian might go right to Celestina."

"The Governor's cool," Flynn said.

"I don't trust any Archangel," Marc said. "They're bred and raised into unchecked power. They go to those secretive academies, ripped away from any family. It's not conducive to raising well-balanced people. *Good* people."

At the exit, they paused, listening carefully to the sounds beyond. They couldn't smell anything through the metal door, but the howls behind them drew closer. Whoever was in the warehouse would reach this hall in a matter of moments.

Another howl—this one familiar. "Amelie," Ithan breathed. If they turned back, they'd face a fight with the second-most powerful wolf pack in Lunathion. Yet to go through that door into the unforgiving city, no certain allies to shelter them—

Sigrid did them all a favor and shoved the door open.

And there, standing in the alley beyond, stood Sabine Fendyr.

Sabine let out a joyless laugh. Her eyes met Ithan's, filled with nothing but hate, and then she faced Sigrid, Ithan's dismissal clear. He was nothing and no one to her. Not even a wolf to acknowledge.

Ithan bared his teeth. Flynn, Dec, and Marc clicked off the safeties on their guns.

But Sabine just said to Sigrid through a mouth full of fangs, "You look exactly like him."

4

Pain and dark and quiet. That was the entirety of Hunt Athalar's world.

No, that wasn't true.

Those things were the entirety of the world beyond his tortured body, his sawed-off wings, the aching hunger writhing in his stomach and thirst burning his throat, the slave brand stamped on his wrist. The halo inked anew upon his brow by Rigelus himself, its oppressive power somehow heavier and oilier than the first. All that he had achieved, regained . . . wiped away. His very existence belonged to the Asteri once more.

But inside him, beyond that sea of pain and despair, Bryce was the entirety of his world.

His mate. His wife. His princess.

Prince Hunt Athalar Danaan. He would have hated the last name were it not for the fact that it was a marker of her ownership over his soul, his heart.

There was Bryce, and nothing else. Not even Pollux's barbed-wire whips could rip her face from his mind. Not even that blunt-toothed saw had severed it from him, even as it had hewn through his wings.

Bryce, who had gotten away. Gone to Hel to seek aid. He'd stay here, let Pollux rip him to shreds, cut through his wings again and again, if it meant that the Asteri's attention stayed away from her. If it bought her time to rally the force needed to take on these fuckers.

He'd die before he told them where she was. His only consolation was that Ruhn would do the same.

Baxian, bloody and swaying on the other side of Ruhn, didn't know where Bryce had gone, but he knew plenty about what Bryce had been up to lately. Yet the Helhound hadn't given Pollux an inch. Hunt would have expected nothing less of a male Urd had chosen to be Danika Fendyr's mate.

It was quiet now—the only sound the clank of their chains. Blood and piss and shit coated the floor beneath them, the smell almost as unbearable as the pain.

Pollux was creative, Hunt would give him that. Where others might have gone for stabbing in the gut and twisting, the Hammer had learned the exact points on the feet to whip and burn to cause maximum agony while keeping his victims conscious.

Or maybe it was the Hind who'd learned those tricks. She stood behind her lover and watched with dead eyes as the Hammer slowly—so slowly—took them apart.

That was the other secret he and Danaan would keep. The Hind—what and who she was.

Oblivion beckoned, a sweet release Hunt had come to crave as much as Bryce's body entwined with his. He pretended, sometimes, that when he fell into the blackness, he was falling into her arms, into her sweet, tight heat.

Bryce. Bryce. Bryce.

Her name was a prayer, an order.

He had little hope of leaving this place alive. His only job was to make sure he held out long enough for Bryce to do what she had to do. After his series of colossal fuckups over the centuries . . . it was the least he could offer up.

He should have seen it coming—part of him *had* seen it coming a few weeks ago, when he'd tried to convince Bryce not to go down this road. He should have fought harder. Should have told her this outcome was inevitable, especially if he was involved.

He'd *known* not to trust Celestina with her whole *new Governor, new rules* bullshit. He'd let her win him over, and the Archangel had fucking betrayed them. All that talk about being a friend of Shahar's—he'd eaten it up. Let the memory of his long-dead lover cloud his instincts, as Celestina had surely gambled it would.

What was this but another Fallen rebellion? On a smaller scale, yes, but the stakes had been so much higher this time. Then, he'd lost an army, lost his lover—had known she was dying as time had stretched and slowed around him. Had known she was dead when time had resumed its normal speed once more, and the whole world had changed.

Yet the ties that now bound him to others—not only Bryce, but to the two males in this dungeon with him—had become unbearable. Their pain was his pain. Perhaps worse than what he endured before.

Shahar had been given the easy end. To die at Sandriel's hand, to die on the battlefield, swift and final . . . It had been easier.

A few feet away, Baxian groaned softly.

Hunt's arms had gone numb, shoulders popping out of their sockets from trying to support the weight of their bodies. He mustered his energy, his focus, enough to say to Baxian, "How . . . how you doing?"

Baxian let out a wet cough. "Great."

Next to Hunt, Ruhn grunted. It might have been a laugh. Their only options were screaming and sobbing, or laughing at this giant fucking disaster.

Indeed, Ruhn said, "Wanna . . . hear a . . . joke?" The prince didn't wait for a reply before he continued, "Two angels . . . and a Fae Prince . . . walk into . . . a dungeon . . ."

Ruhn didn't finish, and didn't need to. A broken, rasping laugh came out of Hunt. Then Baxian. Then Ruhn.

Though every heave shrieked through his arms, his back, his broken body, Hunt couldn't stop laughing. The sound bordered on hysteria. Soon tears were leaking down his cheeks, and he knew from the scent that the others were laughing and crying as well, like it was the funniest fucking thing in the world.

The door to the chamber banged open, echoing off the stones like a thunderclap.

"Shut the fuck up," Pollux barked, stalking down the stairs, wings blazing in the dimness.

Hunt laughed louder. Footsteps trailed behind the Hammer—a dark-haired, brown-skinned male followed him in: the Hawk. The final member of Sandriel's triarii. "What the Hel is wrong with them?" he sneered at Pollux.

"They're stupid shits, that's what," Pollux said, strutting to the rack of torture devices and grabbing an iron poker. He thrust it into the embers of the fire, the light gilding his white wings into a mockery of a heavenly aura.

The Hawk prowled closer, peering at the three of them with a close scrutiny that echoed his namesake. Like Baxian, the Hawk hailed from two peoples: angels, who had granted him his white wings, and hawk shifters, who'd granted him his ability to transform into a bird of prey.

Those were about all the similarities between the two males. For starters, Baxian had a soul. The Hawk . . .

The Hawk's gaze lingered on Hunt. Nothing of life, of joy, lay in those eyes.

"Athalar."

Hunt nodded to the male in greeting. "Asshole."

Ruhn snickered. The Hawk pivoted to the rack, where he pulled out a long, curving knife. The kind that was designed to yank out organs on the withdraw. Hunt remembered that one—from last time.

Ruhn laughed again, as if almost drunk. "Creative."

"We'll see how you laugh in a moment, princeling," the Hawk said, earning a grin from Pollux as the Hammer waited for the poker to heat. "I heard your cousin Cormac pleaded for mercy before the end."

"Fuck you," Ruhn snarled.

The hawk shifter weighed the knife in his hands. "His father has disowned him. Or whatever's left of his body." A wink at Ruhn. "Your father has done the same."

Hunt didn't miss the shock that rippled over Ruhn's face. At his father's betrayal? Or at his cousin's demise? Did such things even matter down here?

Baxian rasped to the Hawk, "You're a fucking liar. Always were . . . always will be."

The Hawk smiled up at Baxian. "How about we start with your tongue today, traitor?"

To Baxian's credit, he stuck out his tongue toward the Hawk in invitation.

Hunt smirked. Yeah—they were all in this together. To the bitter end.

The Hawk cut his stare toward Hunt. "You'll be next, Athalar."

"Come and get it," Hunt gasped. Ruhn extended his tongue as well.

The Hawk simmered with rage at their defiance, white wings glowing with unearthly power. But slowly, a smile lit his face— horrific in its calculation, its gradual delight as Pollux turned, the poker white-hot and rippling with heat.

"Who's first?" the Hammer crooned. The angel stood poised, silhouetted against the blazing fire behind him.

Hunt opened his mouth, his last bit of bravado before the shit-show began, but in the shadows behind Pollux, beyond the fire-place, something dark moved. Something darker than shadow.

Not Ruhn's shadows. The prince didn't seem to be able to access those when constrained by the gorsian shackles. Only the prince's mind-speaking abilities remained.

This shadow was different—darker, older. Watching them.

Watching Hunt.

Hallucinations: Bad, because it meant he had some infection that even his immortal body couldn't fight off. Good, because it meant he might quietly slip away into death's embrace. Bad, because it meant the Asteri might turn their attention fully to Bryce. Good, because the pain would be gone. Bad, because he still held out some stupid, fool's hope deep in his heart of seeing her again. Good, because Bryce wouldn't come looking for him if he was dead.

Across the room, the thing in the shadows moved. Just slightly. Like it had crooked a finger at him.

Death. That was the thing in the shadows.

And now it beckoned.

Night.

Borne on a raft of oblivion, Ruhn drifted across a sea of pain.

The last thing he remembered was the sound and sight of his small intestine splattering on the ground, pain as sharp as—well, as sharp as the curved knife the Hawk had plunged into his gut.

He wondered when the shifter would disembowel them with his talons in his hawk form, as he was fond of doing. Ruhn could imagine it easily: the Hawk perching on his torso and clawing out his organs, pecking at them with that razor-sharp beak. He'd heal, and then the Hawk would begin again. Over and over—

Ruhn had been a fool to think nothing that happened down here could be worse than the years of torture at his father's hands. The burns, the gorsian shackles his father had put him in to keep him from fighting back, keep him from healing—then, at least, he'd developed his own ways of surviving, of recovering. But now there was only pain, then oblivion, then pain again.

Had he died? Or been a whisper away from death, as Vanir could be if the blow wasn't truly fatal? His Fae body would regenerate the organs, even slowed by the gorsian shackles.

Night.

The female voice echoed across the starlit sea. Like a lighthouse shining in the distance.

Night.

Here, there was no escape from her voice. If he roused himself, the pain would wash over the raft and he'd drown in it. So he had no choice but to listen, to drift toward that beacon.

Gods, what did he do to you?

Anger and grief filled the question as it came from all around him, from inside him.

Ruhn managed to say, *Nothing you haven't done a thousand times yourself.*

Then she stood there with him, on his raft. Lidia. Fire streamed off her body, but he could see her perfect face. The most beautiful female he'd ever seen. A flawless mask over a rotted heart.

His enemy. His lover. The soul he'd thought was—

She knelt and extended a hand toward him. *I'm so sorry.*

Ruhn shifted beyond her reach. As much movement as he could manage, even here. Something like agony flashed in her eyes, but she didn't try to touch him again.

He must have been killed today. Or come close to it, if she was here. If he had no defenses left and she'd broken through that mental wall for the first time since he'd learned who she was.

What had they done to Cormac to render him irrevocably dead?

He couldn't stop the memory from flooding him, of sitting beside Cormac in that bar before they went to the Eternal City, of that one moment he thought he'd glimpsed the person his cousin might have been. The friend Cormac might have become, if he hadn't been systematically stripped of kindness by King Morven.

It shouldn't have been a shock to Ruhn, that the two kings had disowned their sons. Though one king had fire in his veins and the other shadows, Einar and Morven were more alike than anyone realized.

Ruhn had always held some scrap of hope that his father saw the Asteri for what they truly were, and that if it ever came down to it, his father would make the right choice. That the orrery in his study, the years spent looking for patterns in light and space . . . that it had meant something larger. That it wasn't simply the idle studying of a bored royal who needed to feel more important in the grand scheme of things than he actually was.

That hope was dead. His father was a spineless fucking coward.

Ruhn, Lidia said, and he hated the sound of his name on her lips. He hated *her.* He turned on his side, putting his back to her.

I understand why you're angry, why you must hate me, she began hoarsely. *Ruhn, the . . . the things I've done . . . I need you to understand why I did them. Why I'll keep doing them.*

Save your sob story for someone who gives a shit.

Ruhn, please.

The raft groaned, and he knew she was reaching for him again. But he couldn't bear that touch, the pleading in her voice, the emotion that no one else in the world but him had ever heard from the Hind.

So Ruhn said, *Fuck your excuses.* And rolled off that mental raft to let the sea of pain drown him.

5

Ithan's heart stalled as Sabine smiled savagely, advancing toward the warehouse's side door. The alley behind her was empty—no witnesses. Exactly what Ithan and all those who served under Sabine had been trained to ensure.

Sigrid backed up a step, right into Declan. The sprites clung to her neck, yellow flames trembling.

"I knew my brother let me find him and your sister too easily," Sabine snarled, eyes fixed wholly on Sigrid, as if the two Fae warriors with guns pointed at her head were nothing. "I *knew* he lied about how many pups he had."

Sigrid halted her retreat. Ithan didn't dare take his eyes off Sabine to read her face.

"All that effort—for *you?*" Sabine surveyed her curving claws. "I promise to make this quick, at least. It's more than I can say for your sister. Poor pup."

"Leave her alone," Ithan snarled, balancing on the balls of his feet, readying to leap for Sabine. To make this final, disastrous stand.

Sabine laughed humorlessly, acknowledging his existence at last. "Some guard, Holstrom."

"You have two fucking seconds, Sabine, to get lost," Declan said.

Sabine's smile crinkled her nose—sheer lupine fury. "You'll need more than bullets to down me, Faeling." Ithan had told Flynn that Sabine wasn't dumb enough to start shit on the Viper Queen's turf, but at the sight of the Prime Apparent's hateful expression, he wondered if her rage and fear had overridden any scrap of common sense.

He unsheathed his claws. "How about these?" He snarled again. "You're dead fucking meat when we tell the authorities about this."

Sabine's smile became icy cold. "Who will you tell? Celestina won't care. And the Autumn King wants a clean slate for the Valbaran Fae. He'll have nothing to do with this."

A low, thunderous growl rattled from behind Ithan.

The hair on his arms rose. It was a growl of pure challenge. One he'd heard from Danika. From Connor. The challenge of a wolf who wouldn't back down.

Sabine glanced to Sigrid in surprise.

"I went into the tank for my sister," Sigrid rasped, agony and rage contorting her face. "To keep her fed. To keep her safe. And you killed her." Her voice rose, full of command that had the wolf in him sitting up, readying to strike at her signal. "I'll rip out your throat, you soulless thief. I'm going to piss on your rotting *corpse*—"

Sabine leapt.

Declan fired his gun at the same time Flynn unleashed a second, blasting shot.

Sigrid dropped to her knees, claws scratching at her face as she shielded her ears against the noise. Flynn advanced, gun at the ready, firing again at the downed wolf leaking blood onto the grimy alley pavement.

Dec's shot had been for Sabine's knee—to incapacitate her. But Flynn had blasted Sabine's face clean off.

"Hurry," Flynn said, grabbing Sigrid's arm. The trembling sprites leapt onto his shoulders. "We have to get to the river—we'll grab one of the boats."

Yet Ithan could only stare at Sabine's body, the blood and gore splattered around the alley. She would no doubt heal from this wound, but not soon enough to stop them from leaving.

Every muscle in his body locked up. As if screaming, *Help her!*

Protect and save your Alpha! Even if something in his gut whispered, *Rip her to pieces.*

The others began running for the alley, but Ithan didn't move.

"Stop," he said. They didn't hear him. *"Stop!"* His shout echoed over stone and corpse and blood—and they halted within steps of the alley exit.

"What?" Marc said, his cat's eyes gleaming in the dimness.

"The other wolves . . . they went quiet." The howls that had been closing in behind them had stopped entirely.

"Glad someone finally noticed," drawled a female voice from the end of the alley.

The Viper Queen lounged against a filthy wall, cigarette smoldering between her fingers, her white jumpsuit glowing like the moon in the flickering firstlight from the lampposts. Her eyes dropped to Sabine's body. Her purple-painted lips curved upward as her gaze lifted to Ithan's.

"Bad dog," she purred.

"This is a most unorthodox request, Lidia."

Lidia kept her chin high, hands tucked behind her back as she walked with clipped precision along the crystal hallway. The perfect imperial soldier. "Yes, but I believe Irithys might be . . . motivating for Athalar."

Rigelus kept pace beside her, graceful despite his long, gangly legs. The teenage Fae body masked the immortal monster beneath.

As they began to descend a winding staircase, lit only by first-lights guttering in tiny alcoves, Rigelus sniffed, "She is mostly cooperative, but she might balk at the order."

Now a step behind him, Lidia fixed her gaze on his scrawny neck. It would be so easy, were he any other being, to wrap her hands around it and twist. She could almost feel the echo of his crunching bones reverberating against her palms.

"Irithys will do what she's told," Lidia said as they descended into the gloom.

Rigelus said nothing more as they wound around and around,

into the earth beneath the Eternal Palace. Even deeper than the dungeons where Ruhn and the others were kept. Most believed this place little more than myth.

Rigelus at last halted before a metal door. Lead—six inches thick.

Lidia had been here only once over her time with the Asteri. Accompanied by Rigelus then as well, along with her father.

A private tour of the palace, given by the Bright Hand himself to one of his most loyal subjects—and one of his wealthiest. And Lidia, young and still brimming with hate and disdain for the world, had been all too willing to join them.

She became that person again as Rigelus laid a hand on the door. The lead glowed, and then the door swung open.

The oppressive heat and humidity of this place hadn't changed since that first visit. As Lidia stepped inside after Rigelus, it once again pushed with damp fingers on her face, her neck.

The hall stretched ahead, the one thousand sunken tubs in the stone floor shining with pale light that illuminated the bodies floating within. Masks and tubes and machines hummed and hissed; salt crusted the stones between the tanks, some sections piled thick with it. And before the machines, already bowing at the waist to Rigelus . . .

A withered humanoid form, veiled and dressed in gray robes, the material gauzy enough to reveal the bony body beneath, stood at the massive desk at the entrance of the room. The Mistress of the Mystics. If she had a name, Lidia had never heard it uttered.

Above her veiled head, a hologram of images spun, stars and planets whizzing by. Every constellation and galaxy the mystics now searched for Bryce Quinlan. How many corners of the universe remained?

That wasn't Lidia's concern—not today. Not as Rigelus said, "I have need of Irithys."

The mistress lifted her head, but her body remained stooped with age, so thin the knobs of her spine jutted from beneath her gauzy robe. "The queen has been sullen, Your Brilliance. I fear she will not be amenable to your requests."

Rigelus only gestured to the hall, bored. "We shall try, nonetheless."

The mistress bowed again and hobbled past the sunken tubs and machinery, the trail of her robes white with salt.

Rigelus strode past the mystics without so much as a downward glance. They were mere cogs in a machine to help facilitate his needs. But Lidia couldn't help assessing the watery faces as she passed. All slumbering, whether they wanted to or not.

Where had they come from, the dreamers locked down here? What Hel had they or their families endured to make it worth it? And what skills did they possess to warrant this alleged honor of honors, to serve the Asteri themselves?

Rigelus neared the dimly glowing center of the hall. There, in a crystal bubble the size of a cantaloupe, a female made of pure flame slumbered.

Her long hair lay draped around her in golden waves and curls of fire, her lean, graceful limbs nude. The Sprite Queen was perhaps no bigger than Lidia's hand, yet even in repose, she had a presence. Like she was the small sun around which this place orbited.

It was close to the truth, Lidia supposed.

The mistress hobbled to the warded and bespelled orb and rapped on it with her knobbly knuckles. "Get up. Your master's here to see you."

Irithys opened eyes like glowing coals. Even crafted of flame, she seemed to simmer with hate. Especially as her gaze landed on Rigelus.

The Bright Hand inclined his head mockingly. "Your Majesty."

Slowly, with dancer-like grace, Irithys sat up. Her eyes slid from Rigelus to her mistress to Lidia. Nothing but calculation and resentment shone on her face—an uncommonly plain face, considering the usual beauty of her kind.

Rigelus gestured to Lidia, the golden rings on his long fingers sparkling in Irithys's light. "My Hind has a request of you."

My Hind. Lidia ignored the possession in the words. The way they raked down her very soul.

She stepped closer to the bubble, hands once again clasped behind her back. "I have three prisoners in the dungeon who will find your sort of fire particularly motivating. I require you to come to the dungeons, to help me convince them to talk."

The Mistress of the Mystics whipped her head to Lidia. "You can't mean for her to *leave* here—"

Not sparing the crone a look, Lidia said, "Surely, as mistress of this place, you can find it in yourself to protect your wards for a few hours."

Beneath the thin veil, she could have sworn the mistress's eyes sparked with hostility. "Irithys is here *because* of the need for her specific kind of protection. Because of her light, a beacon against the darkness of Hel—"

Lidia only leveled a bored look at Rigelus.

He smirked, always amused by the cruelty of others, and said to the mistress, "Should Hel come knocking, send word and I will assist you personally." A huge honor—and an indication of how badly he needed Athalar broken. Ruhn and Baxian, she wasn't entirely sure about, but Athalar . . .

The mistress bowed her head. Leaving Irithys now staring at Lidia.

Lidia lifted her chin. "Will you be amenable to assisting me?"

Irithys glanced down at herself, as if she could see the small band of tattoos around her throat. A halo of sorts—inked on the Sprite Queen by an imperial hag to keep her power in check.

The queen's gesture was a silent question.

Rigelus said, "The ink remains. You can wield enough of your powers to prove useful."

Lidia kept quiet. Let Irithys study her.

She'd been kept down here more than a century. Had not seen daylight or left that crystal bubble in all that time. There was a good chance that behind the glimmering eyes, the queen had gone mad.

But Lidia didn't need her sanity. She could do the thinking for the two of them.

Irithys's chin dipped slightly.

Rigelus turned to Lidia. "You have a week with her."

Lidia held the sprite's blazing stare, let her see the cold fire within her own soul. "Breaking Athalar won't take that long."

Bryce left what she assumed was dinner—roast chicken, more bread, and some herbed potatoes—uneaten on the tray. No one had come by in the hours that had passed, so she assumed they'd either check in with her tomorrow, or perhaps wait until she was banging on that wall of night and howling for someone to come talk to her.

Neither of which seemed like an appealing option.

That left two choices, really. See if she could break through the magical barrier, then make her way out of this mountain and into a strange new world with no idea where she was going, or . . .

She glanced down. Or she could see what lay at the bottom of the grate, if there was some opening beyond the beasts that might take her out of this place . . . and into a strange new world with no idea where she was going.

Hours, and that was the best she could come up with.

"Pathetic," she muttered, zipping the Archesian amulet along its chain. "Fucking pathetic."

What was happening to Hunt? To Ruhn? Were they even—

She wouldn't let herself think about it.

Her captors had taken her phone before bringing her here, so she had no idea what time it was. Or at least what time it was on Midgard. She didn't even want to wade into the tangle of how time might pass faster or slower on this world. And how long had actually passed since that run down the hallway in the Eternal Palace—

Bryce stood from her crouched position against the wall. Stalked to the grate in the center of the room. A chorus of hissing rose from it as she approached.

"Yeah, yeah, I hear you," she murmured, kneeling and prying the grate out of the floor, her fingers straining painfully with the effort. But inch by inch, it pulled away, scraping too loudly against the stone floor.

She waited a moment, listening for the sounds of her approaching captors. When no one came to investigate the noise, Bryce peered into the yawning dark pit she'd opened.

She lowered her head a little toward the hole. The hissing stopped.

Bryce willed starlight to her hand and held it up. Nothing but emptiness waited below. Bryce fisted her palm, balling the starlight into an orb, and dropped it down—

A writhing sea of black, scaled bodies silvered by her light appeared.

Bryce scrambled back.

Sobeks—or their dark twins. Tharion had faced them when they'd escaped the Bone Quarter, concentrating his water magic into lethal spears that pierced their thick hides, but . . ."Fuck," she breathed.

She glanced over a shoulder to the door. To the shield that echoed there with a sense of Rhysand. Power the likes of which she'd never encountered—at least, other than from the Asteri.

If he had as much power as an Asteri . . . It was all a hunch, really, but if he could be manipulated into helping her, somehow coming back to Midgard with her and kicking ass—

She might very well replace six conquerors for another. And something had to change, the cycle had to stop *now*, but not if it began anew with another overlord. And if Rhysand did indeed have that much power, she doubted these interrogations would continue so peaceably for much longer. Especially now that they knew she had something of importance tattooed on her back. Whatever *Made* meant, it held considerable weight with them. She had little doubt their patience would soon wear thin.

And whether it'd manifest in Rhysand going against his oh-so-polite insistence on her consent to be mentally probed or in Azriel carving her up with that black knife . . . she didn't want to be around to find out.

Bryce peered at the hole, the beasts below.

That kernel of magic that had altered the language in her

brain and set the Horn glowing had left something in her chest. Just enough fuel.

She'd have a nanosecond to teleport—winnow, as they called it here—down to the beasts. To that sliver of rock she'd noted jutting above them, little wider than her foot. Then she'd have to see if there was any way out. Some tunnel through which they moved beneath this place.

Unless it was only a pit, a veritable cage where they sat in darkness and waited for meat—dead or alive—to be thrown to them.

It would be a true leap of faith.

Her hands shook, but she balled them into fists. She'd outrun an Asteri. Granted, that was with Hunt's lightning, but . . .

Every minute here counted. Every minute left Hunt and Ruhn in Rigelus's hands. If they were even still alive.

"Hunt. Ruhn. Mom. Dad. Fury. June. Syrinx." She whispered their names, fighting the tightness in her throat.

She had to get out of here. Before these people decided the risk she posed was too great, and dealt with her the smart way. Or before they decided they liked the sound of Midgard, of Rigelus, and knew she'd be a wonderful peace offering—

"Get the fuck up," she grunted. "Get the fuck up and do something."

Hunt would tell her she was out of her mind. Ruhn would tell her to try to spin some more bullshit, try to win her captors over. But Danika . . .

Danika would have jumped.

Danika *had* jumped—down into the depths of the Drop with Bryce. Knowing there'd be no return trip for her.

Danika, whose death Rigelus had engineered, manipulating Micah into killing her.

A white haze blurred Bryce's vision. Primal wrath pumped through her, the sort only the Fae could descend into. It sharpened her vision. Tautened her muscles. The star on her chest flared with soft light.

"Fuck this," she growled.

And teleported into the pit.

Tharion supposed he was still high, still hallucinating, when Ithan Holstrom, Declan Emmet, Tristan Flynn, Marc Rosarin, and an unfamiliar female wolf—carrying three *very* familiar sprites—walked into the suite. They were escorted by the Viper Queen and six of her drugged-out Fae bodyguards.

Lying on the couch in front of the TV, so chill it was as if his very bones had melted into the cushions, Tharion could barely lift his head as the group filed in. He gave them a lazy, blissed-out smile. "Hi, friends."

Declan blew out a breath. "Burning fucking Solas, Tharion."

Tharion's face heated. He had a good idea how he looked. But he couldn't convince his body to move. His head was too heavy, limbs too limp. He closed his eyes, sinking back into that sweet heaviness.

"What the fuck is happening here?" Flynn growled. "Did you do that to him?"

Tharion only realized that Ari had entered the living space when she hissed at Flynn, "*Me?* You think I go around drugging helpless people?"

"You go around abandoning them," Flynn countered. "Or was that reserved for Bryce and Hypaxia?"

"Go back to your partying, pretty boy," Ari spat.

"I'll leave you all to catch up," the Viper Queen crooned, and stalked out, shutting the door behind her with a soft click.

Tharion managed to open his eyes. "Why are you guys here?" Ogenas, his mouth felt so far away.

Declan paced a few steps. "Bryce, Athalar, and Ruhn didn't make it out of the Eternal Palace."

Was it the news or the venom that made his entire world spin? "Dead?" The word was like ash on his tongue.

"No," Declan said. "As far as we know. Bryce disappeared, and Ruhn and Hunt are now being held in the Asteri's dungeons."

Tharion just stared at the Fae warrior—Declan's form blurring at the edges—and let the news sink in.

"Dude, your pupils are huge," Flynn said. No wonder his vision was so foggy. "What are you on?"

"You don't want to know."

"Her venom," Ari snapped. "That's what he's on."

"You look terrible," Declan said, stepping closer to peer down at Tharion. "Your shoulder—"

"Minotaur," Tharion grunted. "It's healing. And I don't want to talk about it. Where did Bryce go?"

"We don't know," Declan said.

"Fuck." Tharion said the word on a long exhale. It echoed in every bone and blood vessel. Before he could ask more, he noticed Ari sizing up the group, her gaze landing on the female wolf beside Holstrom. "I know you."

The female wolf's chin lifted. "Likewise, dragon."

Tharion must have made a confused face, because Holstrom said, "This is Sigrid . . . Fendyr."

Yeah, he was hallucinating. There was only *one* Fendyr other than the Prime: Sabine. And he was pretty sure she didn't have any secret daughters.

"We'll get to the particulars later," Declan said, and slumped into the nearest chair. His boyfriend stood beside him, a hand on his shoulder. "We have to sort through this clusterfuck."

Flynn swore. "What is there to sort through? We killed Sabine."

Tharion jolted—or tried to. His body wouldn't move.

"*You* killed Sabine," Declan said. "I shot her in the leg."

"She's not dead-dead," Flynn said.

"She doesn't have a *face*," Dec countered. "That's pretty—"

"What happened to the other wolves?" Holstrom asked none of them in particular.

Oh, wait—he was asking Tharion and Ari. Ari gave Holstrom a blank look. "What wolves?"

"We were being chased by the Black Rose Pack," Ithan explained, "and then . . . we weren't. Where did the Viper Queen take them?"

"Start looking in the river," Tharion mumbled.

"She wouldn't have killed them," Marc said. "It'd be a head-ache, even for her. Her goons must have knocked them out and moved them elsewhere."

"What about Sabine?" Holstrom asked.

Gods, Tharion's head was throbbing. This had to be some weird dream.

"The Viper Queen will twist this to her own advantage some-how," Marc said. "She'll either present herself as Sabine's rescuer or hand us over."

Tharion lifted his brows at Marc.

Marc caught the look and explained, "I've had a few clients get into trouble with the Viper Queen over the years. I learned a thing or two about her tactics."

Tharion nodded, as if this was perfectly fucking normal, and closed his eyes again.

"Pathetic," Ari hissed—probably at him. But then she asked the others, "So you're all the Viper Queen's captives?"

"Not sure," Declan said. "She caught us in the act of, uh . . . downing Sabine. When she told us to follow, it seemed like an order."

"But she said nothing else?" Ari asked. Tharion cracked an eye, fighting to stay present.

"Just that we can crash here tonight," Flynn said, plopping on the couch beside Tharion and grabbing the remote. He flipped to some sports highlights.

"We should make a run for Tiberian or for the river," Declan said.

"You're not getting out if the Viper Queen doesn't want you to," Tharion rasped.

"So we're trapped?" Sigrid's voice hitched with something like panic.

"No," Holstrom said. "But we need to think through our steps carefully. It's a question of strategy."

"Lead on, oh great sunball captain," Flynn intoned with mock solemnity.

Ithan rolled his eyes, and the gesture was so normal, so friendly, that something in Tharion's chest tightened. He'd thrown all this away, any shot at a normal life. And now his friends were here . . . seeing him like this.

Tharion closed his eyes once more, this time because he couldn't stand the sight of his friends. Couldn't stand the worry and pity in Holstrom's eyes as the wolf took in his sorry state.

Captain Whatever. More like Captain Worthless.

The beasts were much larger, much fouler-smelling up close. Bryce's magic sputtered as they turned her way. She teetered on the rock ledge before steadying herself.

One leap upward, and they'd devour her. Her star illuminated only the closest ones, all hissing mouths, writhing bodies, slashing tails—

She rallied her power, but . . . nothing. Just glittering stardust in her veins. Only enough to keep that star glowing on her chest. No teleporting, then. Could these creatures see enough to be blinded? They dwelled in the darkness. Could they have evolved past the need for sight?

The thoughts raced and crashed through her. The grate was thirty feet up—no way to go back now. And the floor of the pit was covered with these things, all smelling her, assessing her.

But not . . . advancing. Like something about her gave them pause.

Made. Maybe it also meant something to these creatures.

Bryce tugged the neckline of her T-shirt down, revealing the star in all its glory. The beasts shrank back, hissing, tossing massive, scaled heads. Their teeth glinted in the starlight.

A tunnel stretched on either side of the pit. She could only make out the cavernous mouths, but it seemed like this pit sat in the middle of a passage. To where, though? This was the stupidest thing she'd ever done. In a life full of stupid ideas and mistakes, that was saying something, but . . .

Bryce turned toward one of the tunnels, trying to better see what lay beyond. The star in her chest dimmed. Like her magic was rapidly fading. She whirled toward the other tunnel, trying to see what she could before the magic vanished—

The star flared brightly again.

"Huh," she murmured. Bryce turned back the other way. The star faded. To the opposite side: it brightened.

Rigelus had said the star reacted to people—those loyal to her, her chosen knights or whatever. He'd also said that Theia herself had borne this star on her chest. And in this world, this home planet of Theia and the Starborn . . .

Bryce had no choice but to trust that star.

"That way, then," she said, her voice echoing in the chamber. But she still had to get over the gulf of those beasts between her and the next rocky outcropping in the tunnel wall.

She'd never before wished for wings, but fuck if they wouldn't have been handy right then. If Hunt had been here with her—

Her throat closed up. The beasts hissed, tails lashing. As if they could sense her shift in attention.

Bryce focused on her breathing, as she'd learned to do in the wake of losing Danika, as she'd learned to do in the face of all those Vanir and Fae who'd sneered at her. The star kept glowing, pointing the way. The creatures settled, as if her emotions were theirs.

She willed herself to calm. To feel no fear. The creatures settled further. Some laid their heads down.

She glanced at the star in her chest. Still glowing brightly. *They are your champions, too,* it seemed to say. The star hadn't been wrong about Hunt. Or Cormac.

So Bryce stuck one foot over the ledge. The beasts didn't move. She let her foot drop a little lower, dangling bait—

Nothing.

Her heartbeat ratcheted up, and a massive head rose, pivoting her way—

Through love, all is possible. She called up the memory of Danika's love and let it course through her, steady her as she lowered herself onto the ground.

Into the beasts' nest.

They lay before her like obedient dogs. She didn't question it. Didn't think of anything but the star on her chest and the tunnel it pointed toward and the desire to see the faces of those she loved once more.

Bryce took a step, her neon-pink sneaker outrageously bright amid the dark scales so terrifyingly close. Then another step. The creatures watched, but they didn't move a single talon.

Ruhn had called her a queen before she left. And for the first time in her life, as she walked through that sea of death . . . she might have lifted her chin a bit higher. Might have felt a mantle settle on her shoulders, a train of starlight in her wake.

Might have felt something like a crown settle upon her head. Guiding her into the dark.

Tharion finally worked up enough concentration and energy to get to his feet and amble toward his room. Holstrom cornered him a second later.

"What the Hel happened?" the wolf asked, halting Tharion on the threshold.

"The River Queen was gunning for me." Gods, his voice sounded dead, even to his ears. "It was either death or imprisonment at her hands or . . . this."

"You should have come to me."

"For what?" Tharion's laugh was as dead as his voice. "You're a defector, too. We're packless wolves." Tharion nodded to the wolf now sitting on the couch beside Flynn. "Speaking of which . . . Sigrid *Fendyr*?"

"Long story. She's Sabine's niece." Ithan's mouth tightened. "She was the female mystic in the Astronomer's place. I pulled her out two days ago."

Tharion's head spun. "So what are you doing here?"

"Before Sabine showed up to kill Sigrid, we were just getting to the part where I convinced everyone to come free you from this shithole so we could get onto the *Depth Charger* and save Ruhn and Athalar."

"That's . . . a lot of words." Tharion's heart was swimming with them.

Or maybe that was the venom. His stomach was churning, and he really needed a toilet or a bed or a single moment of peace.

"You can't stay here," Ithan said, but his voice seemed distant as Tharion walked to his bed and collapsed face-first onto the mattress. "We're gonna find a way to get you out."

"Too late, wolf," Tharion said, words muffled against the pillows. They slurred further as sleep grabbed him with sharp talons and tugged him down. "There's no saving me."

Ithan found Sigrid pacing before the window overlooking the now-dim fighting pit. It was late enough that even its lights had been shut off.

"You should sleep—the couch is yours."

Dec, Flynn, and Marc had all claimed spots on the floor—though from their breathing patterns, Ithan knew they were awake. After the night they'd had, how could any of them sleep?

Sigrid wrapped her arms around her thin body. "We're trapped here."

"No," Ithan insisted. "I won't let that happen."

"I can't be trapped again." Her voice broke. "I *can't*."

"You're getting out of here," Ithan said. "No matter what."

"Then why not go for the door right now?" she demanded, waving a hand toward the exterior door to the suite.

"Because there are six drugged-up Fae assassins on the other side, waiting to kill us if we do."

Her face blanched and she rubbed at her chest. "*Trapping us.* I need to get out."

"You will."

She closed her eyes, breathing shallowly, losing herself in panic.

Ithan glanced across the room. The three sprites—now curled up beside Flynn and dozing as violet balls of flame—hadn't seemed too panicked. Quiet, but . . . focused. Like they were accustomed to facing fear. It made his guts twist to think about it.

"Sabine will come for me again," Sigrid said. "Won't she?"

"She'll try, but we'll be long out of the city by the time she recovers."

Her eyes narrowed. "Why didn't we leave immediately? When you took me out of the tank?"

Ithan stiffened. "Because I didn't know where else to go."

"A house with those *buffoons* was the best—"

"Those buffoons are my friends, and some of the best fighters I know," Ithan warned, temper flaring. "Those buffoons risked their lives for you tonight—*saved* you tonight."

Her teeth bared. "If Sabine will recover, then let me get to her body and rip it to—"

"Believe me, the thought crossed my mind. But . . ."

He didn't finish the thought.

"But what?"

He shook his head, not letting himself go there, even mentally. "It's late," he said. "You should sleep."

"I won't be able to."

"Then try," he said, perhaps a bit more sharply than necessary.

Sigrid glared at him, then glanced toward the door to Tharion's bedroom. "Was *that* the mer you wanted to get to help us?"

"Yes."

She snorted. "I don't think he'll be much help to anyone. Not even himself."

"You should sleep," he said again. He'd had enough of this.

"Is this a thing you do frequently?" she asked suddenly. "Liberate people enslaved to others?"

"Only recently," he said wearily.

He didn't wait for her to reply before he walked to Tharion's room, threw himself on the ground beside the heavily sleeping male, and closed his eyes.

6

About twenty feet into the tunnel, the beasts tapered off. They remained still, watchful, until Bryce had passed the last of them. Until she found bars blocking the way, save for a small door on the left side of the barrier. The door swung open at the touch of her hand. She had to stoop to get through, but it had clearly been designed to keep the beasts from getting out.

She made sure to shut the door behind her.

The metal groaned, and then hissing, like a swarm of angry wasps, filled the tunnel.

The beasts were writhing again, snapping jaws and heaving bodies scraping against each other, as if shutting the door had knocked them from their stupor. Bryce stumbled back in time to see one particularly massive beast lunge for the bars.

The iron shook with the impact—but held.

Bryce panted, surveying the sinuous death once again in motion. But the beasts were far too large to squeeze through the bars.

She let out a shaky breath and surveyed the tunnel ahead. The star flared brighter, as if urging her onward.

"All right," she said, patting her chest. "All right."

* * *

Bryce walked for hours. Or what she assumed was hours, judging by how sore her legs became, how her feet ached, even with the cushioning of her sneakers.

The tunnel could lead nowhere. It could last for a hundred miles.

She should have grabbed some supplies—stuffed some of the food from her tray into her pockets and bra. Filled up on water.

She saw no deviations, no alternate tunnels or crossroads. Just one long, endless stretch into the dark.

Her mouth dried out, and though she knew she shouldn't, Bryce stopped. Sitting down against the age-worn wall, she swallowed the dryness in her mouth. She had no choice but to keep going.

She closed her eyes for a heartbeat. Only one—

Bryce's eyes flew open.

She'd fallen asleep. Somehow, she'd *fallen asleep*, so fucking exhausted from the last gods knew how many hours that she hadn't even realized it, and—

The star on her chest was still glowing beneath her T-shirt. She remained in the tunnel.

But it was no longer empty.

Nesta stood over her, a sword strapped down her back. The female's blue-gray eyes seemed to gleam with power in the starlight.

Bryce didn't dare move.

Nesta tossed her a leather-wrapped canteen. "Do yourself a favor and drink before you pass out again."

Bryce sipped from the canteen of what seemed to be—thankfully—water, and watched the other female over the rim of the bottle. Nesta sat against the opposite wall of the tunnel, monitoring Bryce with a feline curiosity.

They'd been silent in the minutes since Bryce had awoken. Nesta had barely moved, other than to take a seat.

At last, Bryce capped the canteen and tossed it back to Nesta.

The female caught it with ease. "How'd you learn that I left the cell?" No need to reveal that she could teleport.

Nesta gave her a bored look—as if Bryce should have already known the answer. "We have people who can talk to shadows. They told us you went through the grate."

Interesting—and creepy. But Bryce asked, "So you're here to drag me back to the cell?"

Nesta shoved the canteen into her pack and rose, the movement sure and graceful. The sword strapped down her back . . . it wasn't the Starsword, though Bryce could have sworn there was something similar about the blade. A kind of presence, a tug toward it.

The female inclined her head to the tunnel behind them—the way back. "I was sent to escort you."

"Semantics." Bryce got to her feet. Her versus this female . . . decent odds, but the sword presented a problem. As did whatever sort of presence thrummed from Nesta, apparently able to detect the Horn in Bryce's back. Battling an opponent whose skills and powers were unknown, if not wholly alien, was probably unwise. "Look. I'm not here to start trouble—"

"Then don't. Walk back with me."

Bryce eyed the tunnel behind them. "How'd you even get past the beasts?"

A slight smile. "It pays to know people with wings."

Bryce grunted, despite the ache in her chest. "So someone flew you to the gate—"

"And will fly us out." A corner of her mouth kicked up. "Or haul you, if you decide to do this the hard way."

Bryce scanned the path behind Nesta. Only deep shadows lingered. No sign of anyone with wings waiting to snatch her. "You might be bluffing."

She could have sworn silver fire danced in Nesta's eyes. "Do you want to find out?"

Bryce held her stare. Clearly, they didn't want her dead, if they'd sent someone to retrieve her, not hunt her down. But if she returned to that cell, how long would they keep her there? Even hours could make a difference for Hunt and Ruhn—

"I'm always up for a day of discovery," Bryce said.

Then she erupted with light.

Nesta cursed, but Bryce didn't wait to see if the light had blinded her before bolting down the passage. Without any weapons, a running head start was her best chance of making it.

A force like a stone wall hit her from behind. The world tilted, her breath rushing from her as she collided with the stone ground, bones barking in pain. Shadows had wrapped around her, pinning her, and she thrashed, kicking and swatting at them.

She flared her light, a blast of incandescence that sent the shadows splintering in every direction.

She might not have enough magic left in her veins to teleport, but she could buy herself some time with this, at least. She scrambled to her feet, the shadows leaping upon her again, a pack of wolves set on devouring her.

She let them swarm her for just a moment before her magic exploded outward, a bomb of light in every direction. It sent those shadows flying into the ceiling, the walls. Where shadow met stone, debris tumbled from the ceiling. The mountain shook.

Bryce ran. Deeper into the tunnel, into the dark, her star flaring as she raced away from the crumbling rock all around—

The world shook and roared again, sending her sprawling amid a cloud of dust.

And then there was silence, interrupted only by the skittering rocks from the wall of stones now blocking the way back. But a cave-in wouldn't stop Vanir or Fae for long. Bryce lunged upward—

Metal bit into her throat. Icy, deathly cold.

"Do not," Nesta said quietly, panting, "move."

Bryce glared up at the female but didn't shove the blade from her throat. Her very bones roared at her not to touch the sword more than necessary. "Neat trick with the shadows."

Nesta just stared imperiously at her. "Get up."

"Put down your sword and I will."

Their gazes clashed, but the sword moved a fraction. Bryce got to her feet, wiping dust and debris from her clothes. "What now?"

Her knees buckled with exhaustion. Her magic was spent, her veins utterly devoid of starlight.

Nesta glanced to the cave-in. Whatever shadow magic she possessed seemed to have little ability to move it. The warrior nodded to the tunnel ahead. "I suppose you're getting your way."

"I didn't mean to cause that—"

"It doesn't matter. There's only one way out now. If there's a way out at all."

Bryce sighed, frowning at the star on her chest, still gleaming into the dark through her T-shirt. Illuminating all the dirt now smeared on the white cotton. "I didn't intend to drag anyone else into this with me."

"Then you should have stayed in the Hewn City."

Bryce tucked away that kernel of knowledge—the place she'd been kept was called the Hewn City. "Look, this star . . ." She tapped her chest. "It's pointing me this way. I have no idea why, but I have to follow it."

Nesta gestured with her blade to the dark path ahead. Bryce could have sworn the sword sang through the air. "So lead on."

"You won't stop me?"

Nesta sheathed the sword down her back with enviable grace. "We're trapped down here. We might as well see what lies ahead."

It was a better reaction than Bryce could have hoped for. Especially from the Fae.

With a shrug, Bryce walked into the dark, one eye on the female at her side. And prayed Urd knew where she was leading them.

7

Lidia carried the crystal bubble containing the Queen of the Fire Sprites through the dim halls, Irithys's flame splashing gold upon the marble floors and walls.

She said nothing to the sprite—not with all the cameras mounted throughout the Asteri's palace. Irithys didn't seem to care. She rested on the bottom of the orb with her legs folded serenely. After several long minutes, though, the sprite said, "The dungeons aren't this way."

"And you're so familiar with the layout of this place?"

"I have a keen memory," the queen said flatly, her long hair floating above her head in a twirl of yellow flame. "I need only see something once to remember it. I recall the entire walk down here to the mystics in perfect detail."

A helpful gift. But Lidia said, "We're not going to the dungeons."

From the corner of her eye, she noted Irithys peering at her. "But you told Rigelus—"

"It has been a long while since you left your bubble . . . and used your powers." Whatever embers were left with the halo's constraints. "I think it wise that we warm you up a bit before the main event."

"What do you mean?" the queen demanded, flame shifting to a wary orange, but Lidia said nothing as she unlocked an unmarked iron door on a quiet lower level. Lidia offered up silent thanks to Luna that her hands didn't shake as she reached for the handle, the gold-and-ruby ring on her finger shimmering in Irithys's light.

Between one breath and the next, Lidia buried that part of her that begged to distant gods, the part that doubted. She became still and flat, expression as undisturbed as the surface of a forgotten forest pool.

The door creaked open to reveal a table, a chair in front of it, and on the other side of the table, chained with gorsian shackles, an imperial hag.

The hag lifted baleful, yellow-tinged eyes to Lidia as the Hind shut the door behind her. Those eyes lowered to the bubble, the Sprite Queen glowing orange inside it.

Lidia slid into the chair across from the prisoner, setting the sprite's crystal on the table between them as if it were no more than a handbag. "Thank you for meeting me, Hilde."

"I had no choice in the matter," the hag rasped, her thinning white hair glimmering like strands of wispy moonlight. A wretched, twisted creature, but one of hidden beauty. "Ever since your *dogs* arrested me on trumped-up charges—"

"You were found in possession of a comm-crystal known to be used by Ophion rebels."

"I never saw that crystal in all my life," Hilde snapped, shards of brown teeth glinting. "Someone framed me."

"Yes, yes," Lidia said, waving a hand. Irithys watched every movement, still that alert shade of orange. "You can plead your case before Rigelus."

The imperial hag had the good sense to look nervous. "Then why are you here?"

Lidia smirked at Irithys. "To warm you up."

The Sprite Queen caught her meaning, and simmered into a deep, threatening red.

But the hag let out a hacking laugh. She still wore her imperial uniform, the crest of the Republic frayed over her sagging breasts. "I've got nothing to tell you, *Lidia*."

Lidia crossed one leg over the other. "We'll see."

Hilde hissed, "You think yourself so mighty, so untouchable."

"Is this the part where you tell me you'll have your revenge?"

"I knew your mother, girl," the hag snapped.

Lidia had enough training and self-control to keep her face blank, tone utterly bored. "My mother was a witch-queen. Plenty of people knew her."

"Ah, but I *knew* her—flew in her unit in our fighting days."

Lidia angled her head. "Before or after you sold your soul to Flame and Shadow?"

"I swore allegiance to Flame and Shadow *because* of your mother. Because she was weak and spineless and had no taste for punishment."

"I suppose my mother and I differ on that front, then."

Hilde swept her rheumy gaze over Lidia. "Better than that disgrace of a sister who now calls herself queen."

"Hypaxia is half Flame and Shadow—she should have your allegiance on both fronts."

Lidia knew Irithys monitored each word. If she could remember things after seeing them only once, did it also apply to what she heard?

"Your mother was a fool to give you away," Hilde grumbled.

Lidia arched a brow. "Is that a compliment?"

"Take it as you will." The hag flashed her rotting teeth in a nightmare of a smile. "You're a born killer—like any true witch. That girl on the throne is as softhearted as your mother. She'll bring down the entire Valbaran witch-dynasty."

"Alas, my father was a smart negotiator," Lidia said, making a good show of admiring the ruby ring on her finger, the stone as red as Irithys's flame. "But enough about me." She gestured to the hag, then to the sprite. "Irithys, Queen of the Sprites. Hilde, Grand Hag of the Imperial Coven."

"I know who you are," Irithys said, her voice quiet with leashed rage. She now floated in the center of the orb, her body bloodred. "You put this collar on me."

Hilde again smiled, wide enough to reveal her blackened gums. A lesser person would have cowered at that smile. "I had the honor of doing it to the little bitch who bore the crown before you, too."

Hilde didn't mean Irithys's mother, who had never been queen at all. No, when the last Sprite Queen had died, the line had passed to a different branch of the family, with Irithys first to inherit.

A damned inheritance—she'd gained the title and a prison sentence in the same breath. Irithys had barely had her crown for a day before Rigelus had her brought into the dungeons.

Lidia said blandly, "Yes, Hilde. We all know how skilled you are. Athalar himself can thank you for his first halo. But let's talk about why you chose to betray us."

"*I did no such thing.*" Even with the gorsian shackles, a crackling sort of energy leaked from the hag.

Lidia sighed at the ceiling. "I do have appointments today, Hilde. Shall we speed this up?"

She gave no warning before tapping the top of Irithys's crystal. It melted away to nothing, leaving only air between the hag and the Sprite Queen.

Irithys didn't move. Didn't try to run or erupt. She just stood there like a living, burning ruby. As if being free of the crystal after all these years—

Lidia shut down the thought, her voice as dead as her eyes as she said, "Let's see how motivational you can be, Your Majesty."

Hilde glared daggers, but didn't cower or tremble.

Yet Irithys turned to Lidia, hair swirling above her. "No."

Lidia arched a brow. "No?"

Across the table, Hilde was still bristling—but listening carefully.

Irithys said boldly, unafraid, "No."

"It wasn't a request." Lidia nodded to the hag. "Burn her hand."

Hilde snatched her gnarled hands off the table. As if that could save her.

Irithys's chin lifted. "I may be your captive, but I do not have to obey you."

"Hilde is a traitor to the Republic—"

"These are *lies*," Hilde interrupted.

"Your pity is wasted on her," Lidia went on.

"It is not pity," Irithys said, ruby flame darkening to a color like rich wine. "It is honor. There is none in attacking a person who cannot fight back, enemy or no."

Lidia's upper lip curled back from her teeth. "Burn. Her."

Irithys glowed a violet blue, like hottest flame. *"No."*

Hilde let out a caw of laughter.

Lidia said with a calm that usually made enemies start begging, "I will ask you one more time—"

"And I will tell you a thousand more times: no. On my honor, no."

"You have no honor down here. It means nothing in this place."

"Honor is all I have," Irithys said, the heat of her indigo flames strong enough to warm Lidia's chilled hands. "Honor, and my name. I will not sully or yield them. No matter what my enemy has done. Or what you threaten me with, Hind."

Lidia held the sprite's blazing stare and found only unbreaking, unrelenting will there.

So Lidia inclined her head mockingly at the queen. And with a wave of her hand, she activated the magic Rigelus had gifted her for the week. Like a ball of ice melting in reverse, the crystal orb formed around Irithys again.

"Then I have no need of you," Lidia said, and picked up the crystal, stalking for the door.

Irithys said nothing, but her flame burned a bright, royal blue.

Lidia had just opened the metal door again when Hilde called from the table, "And what of me?"

Lidia threw the imperial hag a cool look. "I suggest you beg Rigelus for mercy." She didn't let the hag reply before slamming the door behind her.

Mercy. Lidia had held none in her heart two days ago, when she'd walked past Hilde in the upper corridors and slipped her own comm-crystal into the hag's pocket. With Ruhn in the dungeons, no one was accessing the other end of the line, anyway. The crystal was, for all intents and purposes, dead. But in Hilde's possession, when Mordoc had sniffed it out on Lidia's suspicion . . . the crystal once again became invaluable.

She could think of no one, other than the Asteri themselves, that Irithys might hate more than the hag who had inked the tattoo on her burning throat. No one that Irithys might enjoy hurting more than Hilde.

And yet the Sprite Queen had refused.

The mistress was nowhere to be found when Lidia returned to the heat and humidity of the mystics' hall, nor when Lidia set Irithys back on her stand in the center of it.

"What of the other prisoners?" Irithys demanded as Lidia stepped back.

Lidia paused, sliding her hands into her pockets. "Why should I waste my time trying to convince you to assist me with them?"

Indeed, time was running thin. She had places to be, and quickly.

"You went to an awful lot of trouble to get me out today. For nothing."

Lidia shrugged, then began prowling for the exit. "I know when I'm losing a battle." She tossed over a shoulder, "Enjoy your name and honor. I hope they're good company in that crystal ball."

Bryce and Nesta walked in fraught, heavy silence for ages.

Bryce's feet had begun aching again, the soreness continuing all the way up her legs. Normally, she would have resorted to talking to distract herself from the discomfort, but Bryce knew better than to ask prying questions about this world, about Nesta's people.

It would be too suspicious. If she sought to tell them as little as possible about herself and Midgard, then they probably wished to do the same regarding their home.

Without warning, Nesta stopped, holding up a fist.

Bryce halted beside her, glancing sidelong to find Nesta's blue-gray eyes making a slow sweep over the tunnel ahead. Icy calm had settled on her face.

Bryce murmured, "What is it?"

Nesta's eyes again flicked over the terrain.

As Bryce stepped forward, her star illuminated what had given the warrior pause: the tunnel widened into a large chamber, its ceiling so high even Bryce's starlight didn't reach it. And in the center of it . . . the path dropped away on either side, leaving only a sliver of a rocky bridge over what seemed to be an endless chasm.

Bryce knew it wasn't endless only because far, far below, water roared. A large subterranean river, if the sound was this loud even up here. Bits of spray floated from the darkness, the damp air laced with a thick, metallic scent—iron. There must have been deposits of it down here.

Nesta said with equal quiet, "That bridge is the perfect place for an ambush."

"From *who*?" Bryce hissed.

"I haven't lived long enough to know every horror in this world, but I can tell you that dark places tend to breed dark things. Especially ones as old and forgotten as this."

"Great. So how do we get across without attracting said dark things?"

"I don't know—this tunnel is foreign to me."

Bryce turned to her in surprise. "You've never been down this way?"

Nesta cut her a look. "No. No one has."

Bryce snorted, surveying the chasm and bridge ahead. No movement, no sound other than the rushing water far below. "Who'd you piss off to get sent to retrieve me, anyway?"

She could have sworn Nesta's lips curved into a smile. "On a good day, too many people to count. But today . . . I volunteered."

Bryce arched a brow. "Why?"

That silvery flame flashed in Nesta's eyes. A shiver slithered along Bryce's spine. Fae and yet . . . not.

"Call it intuition," Nesta said, and stepped onto the bridge.

They'd made it halfway across the narrow bridge—Bryce doing everything she could not to think about the lack of railings, the seemingly endless drop to that thundering river—when they heard it. A new noise, barely audible above the rapids' roar.

Talons skittering over stone.

From above *and* below.

"Hurry." Nesta drew that plain-yet-remarkable sword. At the touch of her hand, silver flames skittered down the blade and—

The breath whooshed out of Bryce. The sword pulsed, as if all the air around it had vanished. It was like the Starsword, somehow. A sword, but more. Just as Nesta was Fae but more.

"What is your sword—"

"Hurry," Nesta repeated, stalking across the rest of the bridge.

Bryce mastered herself enough to obey, moving as fast as she dared given the plunge gaping on either side.

Leathery wings fluttered. Those talons scraped along the stone mere feet ahead—

Bryce damned caution to Hel and jogged toward the tunnel mouth beyond, where Nesta was waving at her to hurry the fuck up, sword gleaming faintly in her other hand.

Then Bryce's star illuminated the rock framing the tunnel's mouth.

She ran.

A teeming mass of *things* crusted the entrance, smaller than the beasts beneath the dungeon, but almost worse. Cruder, more leathery. Like some sort of primordial bat-lizard hybrid. Black tongues tasted the air between flesh-shredding, clear teeth. Like the kristallos, bred and raised for eons in darkness—

A few of the creatures leapt, swooping into the void below, off on the hunt—

The tunnel, the bridge, rumbled.

Bryce staggered, the drop looming sickeningly closer, and a white wave of panic blinded every sense—

Training and Fae grace caught her, and Bryce could have wept with relief that she hadn't tumbled into that void. Especially as something massive and slimy lurched from below, the size of two city buses.

An enormous worm, gleaming with water and mud.

A mouth full of rows of teeth opened wide and *snapped*—

Bryce fell back on her ass as the worm caught three of the flying lizards between those teeth. Swallowed them all in one bite.

Her starlight flared, casting the whole cavern in light and shadow.

The creatures on the walls screeched—either at the worm or the light—flapping off their perches and right into the creature's opening jaws. Another snapping bite, river water and metallic-reeking mud spraying with the movement, and more vanished down the worm's throat.

Bryce could only stare.

One twist of its behemoth body and it'd be upon her. One bite and she'd be swallowed. Her starlight could do nothing against it. It had no eyes. It likely operated on smell, and there she was, a trembling treat offered up on that bridge—

A strong, slim hand grabbed Bryce under the shoulder and dragged her back.

Sensations pelted her: rock scraping beneath her as she was dragged, light and shadows and shrieking flying things, her back stinging as debris sliced her skin, the wet slap of the worm's massive body as it surged from the depths again, snatching at the beasts—

She couldn't stop shaking as Nesta dropped her a safe distance into the tunnel. The worm took a few more bites at the air, the cavern shuddering with each of its powerful thrusts upward. The iron smell grew stronger—blood. It misted the air alongside the river water.

Every snap of the worm's jaws boomed through the rock, through Bryce's bones.

She could only watch in mute horror as more creatures disappeared between those teeth. As the tang of more blood filled the air. Until the worm at last began sinking down, down, down. Back toward the river and wherever its lair lay below.

Nesta's breathing was as harsh as Bryce's, and when Bryce finally peered at the warrior, she found Nesta's gaze already on her. Displeasure and something like disappointment filled Nesta's pretty face as she said, "You froze out there."

Hot anger washed away Bryce's lingering shudders, the stinging from her scraped skin, and she shoved to her feet. "What the fuck was that thing?"

Nesta glanced to the shadows behind Bryce, as if someone stood there. But she said, "A Middengard Wyrm."

"Middengard?" Bryce started at the word. "Like—*Midgard*? Did they come from my world originally?"

Horrific as the creature was, to have another being from her world here was . . . oddly comforting. And maybe finding a scrap of comfort in that fact proved how fucking desperate she was.

"I don't know," Nesta said.

"Are they common around here?" If they were, no wonder the Fae had bailed on this world.

"No," Nesta said, a muscle ticking in her jaw. "As far as I know, they're rare. But I've seen my sister's paintings of the one she defeated. I thought her renderings exaggerated, but it was as monstrous as she depicted it." She shook her head, shock honing into something cold and sharp once more. "I didn't know more than one existed." Her eyes swept over Bryce in a warrior's wary assessment. "What manner of power is it that you possess? What sort of light is this?"

Bryce slowly shook her head. "Light. Just . . . light." Strange, terrible light from another world, she'd once been told.

From this world.

Nesta's eyes glimmered. "What court did your ancestors hail from?"

"I don't know. The Fae ancestor whose powers I bear, Theia— she was Starborn. Like me."

"That term means nothing here." Nesta pulled Bryce to her

feet with ease. "But Amren told me what you said of Theia, the queen who went to your world from ours."

Bryce brushed the dust and rock off her back, her ass. Her ego. "My ancestor, yes."

"Theia was High Queen of these lands. Before she left," Nesta said.

"She was?" A powerful ruler here as well as in Midgard. Her ancestor had been *High* Queen. Bryce carried not only Theia's starlight—she carried her royal ties to this world. Which could land her in some major hot water with these people, if they felt threatened by Bryce's lineage—if they believed she might have some sort of claim to their throne.

Nesta's eyes drifted to the star on Bryce's chest, then to the shadows behind her. But she let the subject drop, turning toward the tunnel ahead. "If we encounter something that wants to eat us again," the warrior said, "don't stare at it like a startled deer. Either run, or fight."

Randall would like this female. The thought pained her. But she snapped back, "I've been doing that my entire life. I don't need a lesson from you about it."

"Then don't make me risk my neck dragging you out of danger next time," Nesta said coolly.

"I didn't ask you to save me," Bryce growled.

But Nesta began walking into the tunnel once more—not waiting for Bryce or her star to light the way. "You've gotten us into enough of a mess as it is," the warrior said without looking back. "Keep close."

8

The shadows were watching him again.

Baxian and Ruhn had passed out, and Hunt had thought he'd lost consciousness, too, but . . . here he was. Watching a shadow watch him back. It stood beside the rack of devices Pollux and the Hawk had used on him.

Lidia hadn't appeared today. He didn't know whether that was a good sign. Didn't dare ask Ruhn for his take on it. Hunt supposed that, out of all of them, he himself should be the one to know whether it was a good sign. He'd lived through this shit for years.

But he should have known a lot of other things, too.

Hunt had lost feeling in his hands, his shoulders. The itching from his slowly regenerating wings continued, though. Like streams of ants tickling down his spine. No writhing could help it.

He should have known not to tangle with Archangels, with the Asteri. He should have warned Bryce more strongly—should have tried harder to get her to back down from this insane path.

Isaiah had tried to convince him all those centuries ago. Hunt hadn't listened . . . and he'd lived with the consequences. He should have learned.

His blood cooled as it ran along his body. Dripped to the floor.

But he hadn't learned a fucking thing, apparently. One didn't take on the Asteri and their hierarchies and win. *He should have known.*

The shadow smiled at him.

So Hunt smiled back. And then the shadow spoke.

"You would do well in Hel."

Too drugged with agony, Hunt didn't even quiver at the familiar male voice. One he'd already heard in another dream, another life.

"Apollion," he grunted. Not Death at all, then.

He tried not to let disappointment sink in his gut.

"What a sorry state you're in," the Prince of the Pit purred. He remained hidden in the shifting shadows. The demon prince inhaled, as if tasting the air. "What delicious pain you feel."

"I'd be happy to share."

A terrifyingly soft laugh. "Your good humor, it seems, remains intact. Even with the halo inked anew upon your brow."

Hunt smiled savagely. "I had the honor of having it done by Rigelus's hand this time."

"Interesting that he would do it himself, rather than employ an imperial hag. Do you detect a difference?"

Hunt's chin dipped. "This one . . . stings. The hag's halo felt like cold iron. This burns like acid." He'd just finished voicing the last word when a thought slammed into him. "Bryce. Is she . . . is she with you?" If they'd hurt her, if Apollion gave one suggestion that—

"No." The shadow seemed to blink. "Why?"

Horror leached through Hunt, colder than ice. "Bryce didn't make it to Hel?" Where was she, then? Had she made it anywhere, or was she tumbling through time and space, forever trapped—

He must have made some pitiful noise because Apollion said, "One moment before the hysterics, Athalar," and vanished.

Hunt couldn't breathe. Maybe it was the weight of his body crushing his lungs, but . . . Bryce hadn't made it. She hadn't fucking made it to Hel, and he was stuck here, and—

Apollion appeared again, a second shadow at his side. Taller and thinner, with eyes like blue opals.

"*Where is Bryce?*" hissed the Prince of the Chasm.

"She went to find you." Hunt's voice broke. Beside him, Ruhn groaned, stirring. "She went to fucking find *you*, Aidas." The Princes of Hel looked at each other, some wordless conversation passing between them. Hunt pushed, "You two told her to find you. Fed us all that bullshit about armies and wanting to help and getting her ready—"

"Is it possible," Aidas said to his brother, ignoring Hunt entirely, "after everything . . . ?"

"Don't fall into romanticism," Apollion cautioned.

"The star might have guided her," Aidas countered.

"Please," Hunt cut in, not caring if he was begging. *"Tell me where she is."* Baxian grunted, rising to consciousness.

Aidas said quietly, "I have a suspicion, but I can't tell you, Athalar, lest Rigelus wring it from you. Though he has likely already arrived at the same conclusion."

"Fuck you," Hunt spat.

But Apollion said to his brother, "We must leave."

"Then what was the point of all this watching me from the shadows?" Hunt demanded.

"To ensure that we can continue to rely on you when the time comes."

"To do what?" Hunt ground out.

"What you were born to do—to accomplish the task for which your father brought you into existence," Apollion said before fading into nothing, leaving Aidas standing alone before the prisoners.

Shock reared up in Hunt, dampened by the weight of an old, unbidden hurt. "I have no father."

Aidas's expression was sad as he stepped out of the shadows. "You spent too long asking the wrong questions."

"What the fuck does *that* mean?"

Aidas shook his head. "The black crown once again circling your brow is not a new torment from the Asteri. It has existed for millennia."

"Tell me the fucking truth for *once*—"

"Stay alive, Athalar." The Prince of the Chasm followed his brother, vanishing into darkness and embers.

* * *

Tharion woke with a pounding headache that echoed through every inch of his body.

From the smell in his room, Holstrom had slept there, likely on the floor, but the space was empty. Squinting against his headache, Tharion padded into the main living space to find Holstrom on the couch, Flynn beside him, and Declan and Marc nursing coffees at the small table by the window overlooking the fighting pit. Ariadne sat in a chair, reading a book, her demeanor completely at odds with the female who'd roasted those lions last night.

No sign of the Fendyr heir. Or the sprites. Maybe he'd hallucinated that part.

"Morning," he grumbled, shutting one eye against the brightness of the room.

None of them answered.

Fine. He'd deal with them in a moment. After coffee. He padded to the wet bar across the room, the glare of the muted television sending a spike of pain through his left eye, and turned on the coffee machine by muscle memory. Tharion shoved a cup under the nozzle and hit a button that vaguely resembled the main one.

"You really do look like shit," Flynn drawled as Tharion inhaled the aroma of the coffee. "Ari, of course, looks gorgeous as always."

The dragon kept her attention on her book, ignoring the Fae lord. She didn't move a muscle, as if she wanted them to forget she was there. Like such a thing was even possible.

But Flynn focused on Tharion again. "Why didn't you come to us for help?"

Tharion sipped his coffee, wincing at the heat that burned his mouth. "It's too early for this conversation."

"Bullshit," Holstrom said. "We would have helped you. Why come here?"

Tharion couldn't keep the snap from his voice. "Because the River Queen would have wiped you guys off the map. I didn't want that on my conscience."

"And this is better?" Ithan demanded.

Flynn added, "Now you're stuck here, taking whatever she

dishes out, not to mention the shit she's offering you on the side. How could you be so fucking dumb?"

Tharion cut him a look. "You're one to talk about doing dumb shit, Flynn."

Flynn's eyes flickered—a rare glimmer of the powerful Fae lord lurking beneath the casual facade. "Even I would never sell my soul to the Viper Queen, Ketos."

Holstrom added, "There's gotta be some way to get you out of this. You defected from the Blue Court. Who's to say you can't defect from—"

"Look," Tharion said, grinding his teeth, "I know you've got some savior complex, Holstrom—"

"Fuck you. You're my friend. You don't get to ignore the danger you're drowning in."

Tharion couldn't decide whether to glare at the wolf or hug him. He drank from his boiling-hot coffee again. Welcomed its sear down his throat.

Ithan said hoarsely, "We're all that's left. It's only us now."

Declan said quietly from the table, "It's all fucked up. Ruhn, Athalar, Bryce . . ." Marc laid a comforting hand on his shoulder.

"I know," Tharion said. "And Cormac's dead."

"What?" Flynn spat his coffee back into his mug.

Tharion filled them in on what had gone down in the lab, and fuck—he really could have used some of that venom right now. By the time he'd finished explaining his arrangement with the Viper Queen, they were all silent again.

Until Flynn said, "Okay. Next steps: We need to get to the *Depth Charger*, and then to Pangera. To the Eternal City." He nodded to Tharion. "Before we got ambushed by Sabine, we had just decided to seek you out—to bail you out of this shit, and to see if you could get us in with the mer on the ship."

"There's no way in Hel the Vipe lets him go," Ari said, breaking her silence.

The males blinked at her, as if they'd indeed forgotten that a dragon sat in their midst. Marc's mouth tightened as he realized how much she'd heard.

But Flynn asked her, brow arching, "And you're an authority on the Vipe now?"

"I'm an authority on assholes," Ari countered smoothly, giving Flynn a look as if to indicate that he was included on that list. "And by asking her to free him, you'll make her cling tighter."

"She's right," Tharion said. "I can try to think of a way to contact Commander Sendes—"

"No," Ithan said. "We *all* go."

"I'm touched," Tharion said, setting his coffee down on the counter behind him. "Really. But it's not as easy as saying *I defect* and walking out."

Ithan bristled, but Sigrid appeared in the bathroom doorway, steam rippling out. She must have showered. "What would it take?"

Tharion eyed the female. Definitely an Alpha, with that solid stance, those bright eyes. The lack of fear in them. "The Vipe's all about business."

"You're rich," Ari said to Flynn.

"It's not about money for her," Marc said. "She's got more than she knows what to do with. It'd take a trade."

Tharion frowned toward the hallway—the door that led to the Viper Queen's private chambers. "Who's with her right now?"

"Some female," Ari answered, rising to her feet and padding toward the hall. She reached the door to her room and said over a shoulder, "Pretty blond in an imperial uniform." The dragon didn't say anything else as she shut her bedroom door. Then locked it.

"We need to get out of here," Declan said, voice low. "Immediately."

"What's wrong?" Flynn asked. Declan was already reaching for his handgun, Marc easing to his feet beside him with feline grace.

Tharion peered down the hall in time to see the door swing open. The Viper Queen, clad in a blue silk tracksuit and white high-top sneakers, sauntered toward them, hooped gold earrings swaying beneath her black bob. "Just a moment," she said to whoever was in the room behind her. "Your kind of poison's downstairs. Takes a minute to get."

Tharion stiffened as the snake shifter entered the room, surveying his friends.

"You missed a spot of Sabine's blood on your hands," she drawled to Flynn.

They all glared at her. But it was the Fendyr heir who shot to her feet and snapped, "You're no better than the Astronomer, keeping these people here, drugging and—"

The Viper Queen cut her off. "Lower the hackles, little Fendyr." She surveyed Sigrid from her wet hair to her baggy sweats. "Staying here's free, but a wardrobe upgrade will cost you."

"Let them go," Sigrid commanded, voice like thunder. "The dragon and the mer—let them go."

Tharion didn't let the Alpha's ferocity get his hopes up. Not as the Viper Queen laughed. "Why would I do that? They bring in good business." She cut Tharion a mocking smirk as she stalked for the door, headed to get whatever drugs her client down the hall wanted. "When they're not blowing their load after a few minutes."

Tharion bristled, crossing his arms. But as soon as the Viper Queen had shut the door, vanishing outside, clipped footsteps sounded from down the hall.

Dec and Flynn drew their guns. Holstrom had his claws out. Tharion unsheathed his own, his entire body tensing.

"Put those away," said a cool female voice. Terror stole any last traces of Tharion's brain fog.

"Oh fuck," Flynn breathed.

"You open that door," the Hind said mildly, "and Prince Ruhn dies."

9

Bryce and Nesta pushed through the tunnel for hours, tense silence filling the space between them again. Worse than before.

It was typical, Bryce realized, of her interactions with the Fae she knew from her own world. She didn't know why it somehow . . . disappointed her to realize it.

They paused once, Nesta wordlessly tossing her a water canteen along with a roll of dark bread.

"You brought provisions," Bryce said around a mouthful of the faintly sweet, moist roll. "Seems weird, considering you intended to bring me right back to the cell."

Nesta only swigged from her canteen. "I had a feeling I might be running around after you for a while."

"Long enough to need to stop to eat?" Their gazes met, Nesta's silvered in Bryce's starlight.

"We don't know these caves. I prepared for anything."

"Not the Wyrm, apparently."

"You're alive, aren't you?"

Bryce couldn't help her snort. "Fair enough."

There was no more talk after that.

It was possible they could walk right into a dead end and have wasted miles and hours down here. But the tunnel seemed . . . intentional. And Bryce wasn't about to pose a question about the potential fruitlessness of their trek if it would make Nesta try to drag her back to the cave-in to wait to be dug out.

She was getting her way—for better or worse.

Bryce was deep enough in her thoughts that she didn't notice the fork in the tunnel until she'd nearly passed the tunnel that veered to the right. She drew up short, the halt of Nesta's footsteps behind her telling her the warrior had done the same.

Bryce tugged the neck of her T-shirt down to reveal more of her starlight, illuminating the two options gaping before them.

To the left, the tunnel continued, old, rough rock walls curving into the gloom.

To the right . . . Around the natural archway, an array of stars and planets had been carved, crowned at its apex by a large setting or rising sun. Bryce's star glowed brighter as she faced it, guiding her there.

She could dimly make out more scenes of violence and bloodshed covering the walls inside the tunnel.

"I'm going to take a guess and say let's go right." Bryce sighed, covering her star again with her shirt.

"Very well," Nesta said, and strode for the archway.

Bryce lunged before Nesta could clear it, grabbing the warrior by the back of her collar. With a twirl and a flash, Nesta was on her, sword at Bryce's throat. Its metal was impossibly cold.

Bryce held up her hands, trying not to breathe too loudly, to bring her skin into any more contact with that horrific blade than necessary. "No—look." She nodded as minutely as she could to the carvings in the tunnel just beyond the archway.

Nesta didn't remove the blade, which seemed to throb against Bryce's skin, like the sword was alive and aware. But Nesta's gaze shifted to where Bryce had indicated.

"What is it?"

"Those carvings," Bryce breathed. "Back home, my job is to look at ancient art, to study it and sell it, and . . . never mind, that's not really relevant. I just mean I've seen a *lot* of ancient Fae artwork, and that stuff on the walls—it's spelling out a warning. So if you want to get impaled by a bunch of rusty spears, keep walking." ·

Nesta blinked, head angling, more feline than Fae. But the sword lowered.

Bryce tried not to gasp in relief as that icy metal left her skin, her soul. She never wanted to endure anything like it again.

Nesta either didn't know or didn't care about the sword's impact on Bryce as she surveyed the carvings. The one closest to them.

A female, clearly Fae nobility from the ornate robes and fancy jewelry, stared out from the wall. As if she were addressing an audience, welcoming the newcomers to the tunnel. She was young and beautiful, yet stood with a presence that seemed regal. Long hair flowed around her like a silent river, framing her delicate, heart-shaped face.

Bryce shook off the last of her dread and translated the inscription. "Her name was Silene."

Nesta peered at the writing beneath the image. "That's all it says?"

Bryce shrugged. "Old-school Fae. Lots of fancy titles and lineage. You know how they liked to preen."

Nesta's lips quirked upward. Bryce motioned at the embossed panels that continued onward.

"The warning is in the story she's telling here," Bryce said.

A field of corpses had been carved into the wall, a battlefield stretching ahead. Crucifixes loomed over the battlefield, bodies hanging from them. Great, dark beasts of scales and talons—the ones from the pit beneath her cell, she realized with a shudder—feasted on screaming victims. Blood eagles were splayed out on stone altars.

"Mother above," Nesta murmured.

"Those holes along the corpses there—the ones that look like wounds . . . I'd bet anything there are mechanisms in them to send weapons at passersby," Bryce said. "As some fucked-up 'artistic' way of making the viewer experience the pain and terror of these Fae victims."

Bryce could have sworn something like surprise and embarrassment—that perhaps the warrior herself hadn't spotted the threat—crossed Nesta's face.

"How do you propose we get through, then?" A weighted question. A test.

Like Hel would Bryce *freeze* again. She held out a hand. "Pass me something heavy. I'll see if I can trigger the mechanism to fire."

Nesta sighed, as if annoyed again. Bryce turned to her, about to snap something about having a better idea, when Nesta lifted an arm. Silver flame wreathed her fingers. Bryce backed away a step.

It was fire but not fire. It was like ice turned into flame. It echoed in Nesta's eyes as she laid her hand on the stone wall. Silver fire rippled over the carvings.

Mechanisms clicked—and misfired. Rusty metal bolts shot from the walls. Or tried to. They barely cleared the wall before they melted into dust.

Nesta's power shivered down the walls, disappearing into the dark. Faint clicking and hissing faded away into the gloom; the sound of the traps turned to ashes.

Nesta met Bryce's stare. The fire wreathing her hand winked out, but the silver flame still flickered in her eyes. "You have my gratitude" was all Nesta said before striding ahead.

Later, Bryce and Nesta again dined on hard cheese and more of that dark bread, their resting place a small alcove in the tunnel wall. Bryce's starlight still provided the only glow, muted through her T-shirt. It was cold enough that she looked with envy at Nesta's dark cape, wrapped tightly around the warrior.

She distracted herself by peering at the carvings etched into the walls: Fae kneeling before impossibly tall, robed humanoids, glowing bits of starlight in their upraised hands. Magic. An offering to the crowned creatures before them. One of the beings was reaching a hand toward the nearest Fae, her fingers stretching toward that offered light.

Bryce's stomach twisted as she noted that behind the supplicating Fae, chained humans lay prostrate on the earth, their crudely carved faces a sharp contrast to the otherworldly, pristine beauty of the Fae. Another bit of fucked-up artistry: Humans were little more than rock and dirt compared to the Fae and their godlike masters. Not even worth the effort of carving them. Present only for the Fae to lord their power over them, to crush the humans beneath their heels.

From far away, Rigelus's voice sounded in Bryce's memory. The Asteri had once given the humans to the Vanir to have someone to rule over, to keep them from thinking about how they were hardly better off, all of them slaves to the Asteri. It continued on Midgard today, this false sense of superiority and ownership. And it seemed it existed in this world as well.

Nesta finished her cheese, gnawing it right down to the rind, and said without looking at Bryce, "Your star always glows like that?"

"No," Bryce said, swallowing down the bread. "But down here, it seems to."

"Why?"

"That's what I wanted to find out: What it's leading me toward in this tunnel. *Why* it's leading me there."

"Why you stumbled into our world." Rhysand or the others must have filled Nesta in on everything before siccing her on Bryce.

Bryce motioned to the tunnel and its ancient carvings. "What is this place, anyway?"

"I told you earlier: We don't know. Until you crept past the beasts, even Rhys didn't know this tunnel existed. He certainly didn't know there were carvings down here."

"And Rhysand is . . . your king?"

Nesta snorted. "He'd like to be. But no. He's the High Lord of the Night Court."

Bryce arched a brow. "So he serves a king?"

"We have no kings in these lands. Only seven courts, each ruled by a High Lord. Sometimes a High Lady beside them."

A rock skittered in the distance. Bryce twisted toward it, but—nothing. Only darkness.

She found Nesta watching her carefully. Nesta asked, "Why not let me get impaled earlier? You could have let me walk right into a trap and run."

"I have no reason to want you dead."

"Yet you ran from the cell."

"I know how interrogations tend to end."

"No one was going to torture you."

"Not yet, you mean."

Nesta didn't reply. At the sound of another scuff in the darkness, Bryce whipped her head to it and found Nesta watching her once more.

"What is that?" Bryce asked quietly.

Nesta's eyes gleamed like a cat's in the dimness. "Just the shadows."

10

Tharion knew this wouldn't end well. Not with Flynn and Dec pointing guns at the Hind, Marc's claws gleaming and poised to shred flesh. Not with Holstrom crouched, teeth bared, angled in front of Sigrid. The Fendyr heir glanced between them all with predatory assessment, understanding a threat at hand but not what it was.

Well, fuck. That left him as the voice of reason.

So Tharion did what he did best: dragged up the smile of the person he'd once been and sauntered over to Tristan Flynn.

He laid a claw-tipped finger on the barrel of the Fae lord's gun, pushing it down. "Take a breath," Tharion crooned. "We're all on neutral territory. Even Lidia wouldn't be so stupid as to harm you here." He winked at the Hind, though his insides trembled. "Would you?"

The Hind's face held no emotion, but her chin dipped.

Sigrid stepped forward. "Who are you?"

The Hind's golden eyes swept over the female wolf. Her nostrils flared delicately. "I think," she murmured quietly, "the better question is who are *you*?"

"None of your business," Ithan cut in.

The Hind gave him a look that said she had her suspicions but it wasn't her priority—yet. She said to the Fendyr heir, "A moment of privacy, if you will."

Holstrom growled. "Whatever you have to say, you can say it in front of her."

Declan said quietly, "Holstrom, maybe she can . . . go join the dragon for a minute."

Ithan turned outraged eyes on Declan but then seemed to relent. If this was about Ruhn, if the only way for the Hind to talk was to get Sigrid out of earshot . . .

Tharion chimed in, "Ari locked her door, so I'm pretty sure that means *alone time*." He nodded to the door beside Ari's. "But go ahead and take my room."

Sigrid scoffed. "I'm not some pup to be ordered about—"

"Please," Declan said with a helpless gesture. Marc again laid a gentle hand on his shoulder.

There was a moment, then, when Ithan and Sigrid looked at each other—when Tharion could have sworn some sort of battle of wills passed between them.

Sigrid bristled, then spat, "Fine," and stalked off toward Tharion's bedroom.

The sprites zoomed after her, but the Hind halted them. "You three—wait."

Sasa, Malana, and Rithi turned, wide eyes on the Hind. But she didn't speak again until Sigrid had slammed the door to Tharion's room. Perhaps a bit petulantly.

Tharion didn't miss Ithan's sigh.

The Hind glanced at her watch, likely calculating how much time remained until the Viper Queen returned, then said to Flynn and Dec, "I went looking for you two, but no one was at your . . . house." Her tone dripped with enough disdain that it was clear what she thought of their house off Archer Street. "But I knew that Ketos had defected and come to the Meat Market for refuge—so I guessed you might be hiding here as well."

"Guessed?" Declan demanded. "Or someone sold us out?"

"Don't flatter yourself," the Hind said, crossing her arms. "You're extremely predictable."

"Well, you're fucking wrong," Flynn said, still not holstering his gun. "We're not here to hide."

Declan coughed, as if to say, *This is what you choose to lie about?* Marc hid a smile.

"I don't care why you're here," the Hind said. "We don't have much time. Ruhn's life depends on you listening to me."

"What the fuck have you done to Ruhn?" Flynn cut in.

Tharion could have sworn something like pain flashed across the Hind's face. "Ruhn lives. As do Athalar and Argos."

"Bryce?" Ithan asked hoarsely.

"I don't know. She . . ." The Hind shook her head.

But Declan asked, "Baxian got involved? The Helhound?"

Before she could finish, Flynn demanded, "Why are you *here*?" His voice broke. "To arrest us? To rub our failure in our faces?"

The Hind pivoted to the Fae lord, and—yes, that was pain shining in her eyes. "I'm here to help you rescue Ruhn."

Even Tharion blinked.

"This is a trap," Declan said.

"It's no trap." The Hind surveyed them bleakly. "Athalar, Baxian, and Ruhn are being held in the dungeons beneath the Asteri's palace. The Hammer and the Hawk torture them daily. They . . ." A muscle ticked in her slim jaw. "Your friends haven't talked. But I'm not sure how much longer the Asteri will be entertained by their suffering."

"I'm sorry," Declan spat, "but aren't *you* their lead interrogator?"

The Hind turned her unnaturally perfect face toward the Fae warrior. "The world knows me as such, yes. I don't have time to tell you everything. But I require your help, Declan Emmet. I'm one of a few people on Midgard who can get into those dungeons unchallenged. And I'm the only one who can get them out. But I need *you* to help hack the cameras in the palace. I know you've done so once before."

"Yeah," Dec muttered. "But even with the cameras hacked, our plans haven't exactly turned out great lately. Ask Cormac how well our last big adventure went."

The words pelted Tharion like stones. The memory of the Fae

Prince immolating himself slammed into him. A flash, and Cormac was dead—

"It only failed because Rigelus knew they were coming," the Hind said, not unkindly. "Celestina sold them out."

Shock rippled through the room. But Marc murmured to Declan, "I told you: Archangels are creeps."

Flynn threw up his hands. "Am I the only one who feels like they're on a bad acid trip?"

Tharion scrubbed at his face. "I'm still on one, I think." Flynn snorted, but Tharion mastered himself, clearing his throat before saying to the Hind, "Allow me to clarify a few things: You are the Asteri's most skilled interrogator and spy-breaker. You and your dreadwolves tormented us nonstop not so long ago, in this very city. You are, not to put too fine a point on it, pretty much the soul of evil. Yet you're asking us to help you free our friends. And you expect us not to be suspicious?"

She surveyed them all for a long moment, and Tharion had the good sense to sit down before she said evenly, "I'm Agent Daybright."

"Bullshit," Flynn spat, angling his gun at her again.

Daybright, who was high up in the Asteri's innermost circles. Daybright, who knew of their plans before the Asteri ever acted. Daybright, the most vital link in the rebels' information chain . . .

"She smells like Ruhn," Ithan murmured. They all blinked at him. The wolf sniffed again. "Just barely. Smell her—it's there."

To Tharion's shock, a bit of color stained the Hind's cheeks. "He and I . . ."

"Don't for one fucking second believe this," Flynn snapped. "She probably rolled around in his blood in the dungeons."

Her teeth flashed in a snarl, the first hint of a crack in that cool exterior. "I would never hurt him. Everything I've done recently, everything I'm doing now, has been to keep Ruhn alive. Do you know how hard it is to keep Pollux at bay? To convince him to go slow? Do you have *any idea what that's like?*" She screamed the last part at Flynn, who backed away a step. The Hind heaved a breath, shaking. "I need to get him out. If you don't help me, then his death is on you. And I will *destroy you*, Tristan Flynn."

Flynn slowly shook his head, confusion and disbelief stark on his face.

The Hind turned to Tharion, and he withstood her blazing look. "I made sure the *Depth Charger* was there to pick you up after Agent Silverbow sacrificed himself, trying to bring the Asteri down with him; I filled Commander Sendes in about Ruhn and Athalar and Baxian being captured, and Bryce going missing. I'm the one who's kept Rigelus off your scent, kept the Asteri from killing anyone who has ever meant anything to Ruhn, Bryce, or Athalar."

"Or you're the one," Tharion said, "who got the information out of the real Agent Daybright and are here to entrap us, too."

"Believe what you want," the Hind said, and true exhaustion slumped her shoulders. For a heartbeat, Tharion pitied her. "But in three days, I am going to free them. And I will fail if I don't have your help."

"Even if we believe you," Declan said, "we have families who the Asteri would kill without a thought. People we love."

"Then use this time to get them into hiding. But the more people who know, the more likely we will be discovered."

"You can't be fucking serious," Flynn said to Declan. "You're trusting this monster?"

Declan met the Hind's eyes, and Tharion knew he was weighing whatever he found there. "It makes sense, Flynn. Everything Ruhn told us about Daybright . . . it adds up."

"Does Ruhn know what you are?" Flynn spat.

Lidia ignored him, and instead looked to Tharion. "I need you, too, Ketos."

Tharion shrugged with a nonchalance he didn't feel. "Unfortunately, I can't leave the building."

"Find a way out. I need you to be my ally and advocate on the *Depth Charger* after we have completed the rescue."

Holstrom said, "The Viper Queen's apparently your drug dealer—why don't you ask her to let Tharion go?"

Lidia held his stare with a dominance that belied her deer-shifter heritage. "Why don't you, Ithan Holstrom?"

There was something in her voice that Tharion didn't quite understand—a challenge, perhaps. A gauntlet thrown.

"Does Ruhn know?" Flynn demanded again.

"Yes," the Hind said. "He, Athalar, and Bryce know. Baxian doesn't."

Flynn's throat bobbed. "You lied to Ruhn."

"We lied to each other," she said, some sort of emotion flickering in her golden eyes. "Our identities weren't supposed to be revealed. We both . . . went too far."

"Why bother to save them?" Declan asked. "Ruhn and Hunt have no value to Ophion, other than being good fighters. And Argos isn't connected with Ophion at all."

"Hunt Athalar is valuable to Bryce Quinlan, and to activating her power. Baxian Argos is a powerful warrior and skilled spy. He is therefore valuable to all of us."

"And Ruhn?" Ithan asked, brows high.

"Ruhn is valuable to me," the Hind said without an ounce of doubt. "At sunrise in two days' time, a skiff will be waiting for you at Ionia's harbor, at the very end of the north dock. Get on it, and the captain will take you a few miles offshore. Throw this into the water and wait." She chucked a small white stone to Tharion.

He'd seen one like it before—that day in the sea off Ydra. She'd thrown one into the water then, and the *Depth Charger* had appeared.

She must have noted his shock, because she said, "I summoned the ship that day after what happened at Ydra. Drop that stone into the ocean, and the *Depth Charger* will come again and carry you to Pangera."

Silence filled the room.

Lidia looked to the sprites crouching at Flynn's neck and said, "I have questions for you three."

"Us?" Sasa squawked, ducking behind Flynn's left ear. Her flame illuminated it, casting his skin a glowing red.

Lidia said, "About your queen."

"Irithys?" Malana said, flaring a deep violet. "Where—"

"I know where she is," Lidia said calmly, though Tharion noted with surprise that her hands were shaking. "But I want to know what *you* know about her. Her temperament."

"Where have the Asteri been keeping her?" Sasa demanded, turning white-hot with anger.

Lidia tipped her chin upward. "Answer my questions, and I'll tell you."

"We only know of her through rumor," Rithi said, poking her head out from behind Flynn's right ear. "She is noble, and brave—"

"Is she trustworthy?" Lidia asked.

Rithi ducked behind Flynn's ear again, but Sasa snapped, "She is our queen. She is honor itself."

Lidia looked coolly at the sprite. "I know plenty of rulers who don't embody that virtue one bit." Tharion could only stare at the Hind—Agent Daybright. Their . . . ally. "What else?"

"That is all we know," Malana said, "all we have heard. Now tell us: Where *is* she?"

Lidia's mouth curved upward. "Would you rush to free her?"

"Don't patronize them," Flynn snapped with rare gravitas. The sprites huddled closer to him.

To Tharion's shock, Lidia inclined her head. "Apologies. Your courage and loyalty are commendable. I wish I had a thousand like you at my disposal."

"To Hel with your compliments," Sasa snarled, her flame blazing bright. "You promised—"

"The Asteri have her in their palace."

"Beyond that!" Sasa cried, flaring white-hot again.

"You should have bargained better if you wanted to know more."

Tharion tensed. This female might be an ally, but fuck, she was slippery.

In the furious silence, the Hind walked to the door. She halted before opening it, and didn't turn around as she said to them all, "I know you don't trust me. I don't blame you. That you don't tells me I've done my job very well. But . . ."

She looked over a shoulder, and Tharion saw her throat bob.

"Ruhn and Athalar are in danger. As we speak, Rigelus is debating which one of them will die. It all boils down to how it might impact Quinlan. But once he decides, there will be nothing I can do to stop it. So I am . . ." Her voice caught. "I am begging you. Before it's too late. Help me pull this off. Find a way out of this situation with the Viper Queen"—a nod to Tharion, then a nod to Declan—"be ready at a moment's notice from me to hack into the cameras at the Eternal Palace"—and finally a look toward the rest of them—"and for Luna's sake, be on that dock in two days' time."

With that, she left. For a long moment, none of them could speak.

"Well, Flynn," Declan finally rasped, "looks like you got your wish."

11

Rushing water roared through the cavern, its spray coating Bryce's face with drops so cold they were kisses of ice.

The strange carvings had continued all the way here, showing great Fae battles and lovemaking and childbirth. Showing a masked queen, a crown upon her head, bearing instruments in her hand and standing before an adoring crowd. Behind her, a great mountaintop palace rose toward the sky, winged horses soaring among the clouds. No doubt some religious iconography of her divine right to rule. Beyond the mountaintop palace, a lush archipelago spread into the distance, rendered with remarkable detail and skill.

Scenes of a blessed land, a thriving civilization. One relief had been so similar to the frieze of the Fae male forging the sword at the Crescent City Ballet that Bryce had nearly gasped. The last carving before the river had been one of transition: a Fae King and Queen seated on thrones, a mountain—different from the one with the palace atop it—behind them with three stars rising above it. A different kingdom, then. *Some ancient High Lord and Lady,* Nesta had suggested before approaching the river.

She hadn't commented on the lower half of the carving, which depicted a Helscape beneath their thrones, some kind of underworld. Humanoid figures writhed in pain amid what looked like icicles and snapping, scaly beasts—either past enemies conquered or an indication of what failure to bow to the rulers would bring upon the defiant.

The suffering stretched throughout, lingering even underneath that archipelago and its mountaintop palace. Even here, in paradise, death and evil remained. A common motif in Midgardian art, too, usually with the caption: *Et in Avallen ego.*

Even in Avallen, there am I.

A whispered promise from Death. Another version of *memento mori.* A reminder that death was always, always waiting. Even in the blessed Fae isle of Avallen.

Maybe all the ancient art that glorified the idea of *memento mori* had been brought to Midgard by these people.

Maybe she was thinking too much about shit that really didn't matter at the moment. Especially with an impassable river before her.

Bryce and Nesta peered down at the cascade rushing past, the night-dark waters flowing deeper into the caverns. The scent of iron was stronger here, likely because they now stood closer to the river than they had before. It didn't matter. All that mattered was the fact that the tunnel continued on the other side, and the gap was large enough that jumping wasn't an option.

"Now would be a good time for your friends with wings to find us," Bryce muttered. Her star shone ahead, faint but still pointing the way to the path across the river.

Nesta glanced over a shoulder. "You winnowed out of the cell." So the shadows *had* told Nesta and the others everything. "You can't do so again?"

"I, ah . . . It drained me." She hated to reveal any sort of weakness, but didn't see a way around it. "I'm still recovering."

"Surely your magic should have replenished by now. You were able to use some against me before the cave-in. And the star on your chest still glows. Some magic must remain in you."

"I was always able to get it to glow," Bryce confessed, "long before I ever had true power." For a heartbeat, Bryce debated telling Nesta how she'd attained her depth of power, how she could get even *more* if someone fueled her up. Just to let the warrior know she wasn't some loser who froze in the face of an enemy, giant Wyrm or no.

But that would reveal more about her abilities than was wise.

"You can't, uh . . . winnow?" Bryce asked Nesta.

"I've never tried," Nesta admitted. "My powers are unusual amongst the High Fae."

"High Fae? As opposed to . . . normal Fae?"

Nesta shrugged. "They use the *High* part to make themselves sound more important than they are."

Bryce's mouth twitched upward. "Sounds like the Fae in my world." She angled her head. "But you're High Fae. You . . . talk about them like you're not."

"I'm new to the Fae realms," Nesta said, her focus again on the river. "I was born human and turned High Fae against my will." She sighed. "It's a long story. But I've only lived in the faerie lands for a handful of years now. Much of this is still strange to me."

"I know the feeling," Bryce said. "My mother is human, my father Fae. I've lived between two worlds my entire life."

Nesta nodded shallowly. "None of that helps us get across the river."

Bryce surveyed her companion. If Nesta was originally human and had been turned Fae—however the fuck *that* was possible— maybe her sympathies still lay with humankind. Maybe she'd understand how it was to be powerless and frightened in a world designed to oppress and kill her—

Or maybe she'd been sent to win Bryce's sympathy and trust, working for a so-called High Lord. Everything she'd said in these tunnels could have been a lie. And she was powerful enough that she'd been called in to look at the Horn on Bryce's back—she was no defenseless lamb.

"Up for a swim?" Bryce asked the warrior, kneeling to dip a hand into the river. She hissed at its ice-cold bite.

Great. Just . . . great.

She frowned at the dark, rushing water, illuminated by the light from her star. Smooth white pebbles glimmered brightly far beneath the surface. *Really* brightly.

Bryce glanced at her star. It was glowing more strongly now. She stood, wiping her wet, chilled hand on the thigh of her leggings. The star dimmed.

"What is it?" Nesta took a step closer, a hand rising toward the sword at her back.

Bryce knelt again, plunging her hand back into the frigid river. Her star glowed brighter as she angled its light over the water. She twisted on her knees, toward the gloom downriver. The starlight flared in answer. It faded to a dull light when she pivoted back toward the tunnel ahead.

"You've gotta be kidding me," Bryce muttered, rising to her feet again.

"What?" Nesta asked, scanning the river, the darkness around them.

Bryce didn't reply. The star had led her this far. If it wanted her in the river . . .

Bryce glanced over a shoulder to Nesta. "See you at the bottom." And with a wink, Bryce jumped into the roaring water.

The cold knocked the breath from Bryce.

The thrashing river was illuminated by her star, the water a clear, striking blue in the small bubble of her light. It glazed the high cavern ceiling, and it was all Bryce could do to keep her head above the rapids, from being smashed against the boulders spiking up throughout the twisting length of the river.

Behind her, Nesta had jumped in—as Bryce had rounded a bend a moment ago, she'd heard Nesta's snapped *"Reckless idiot!"* before the roar of the river swallowed all sounds once more.

The star had to be leading her somewhere. To something.

Bryce was hurled around another bend in the caverns, and as she struggled to keep her head clear of the water, her star seemed to extend a beam into the darkness.

The ray of silvery light landed upon a small pool bulging out of the opposite side of the river. A break in the rapids. Right in front of a small bank . . . and another looming tunnel entrance beyond.

Bryce began swimming for the pool, her body screaming with the effort of pushing perpendicular to the current, racing to reach that sliver of calm water before she was swept past. Stroke after stroke, kick after kick, she aimed for that narrow shore.

She turned to warn Nesta to make for the shore, too, but found that the female was a few feet behind her, swimming like mad for the bank. So Bryce continued swimming, arms straining as the river pulled her forward mercilessly. If she and Nesta didn't reach the little pool soon, they'd miss it entirely—

The tug of the water relented. Bryce's strokes became easier, her pace faster.

And then she was in the pool, the water still and light compared to the raging beast behind her. She clawed at the rocky shore, hauling herself onto it.

Rocks scraped against each other beside her, and then Nesta's heavy, wet breathing sounded. "What . . ." Nesta panted. "The . . ." Another breath. *"Fuck."*

Bryce inhaled all that beautiful, wonderful air, even as intense cold began to shake through her very bones. "The star said to go this way," she managed to say.

"Some warning would have been good," Nesta growled.

Bryce rose onto her elbows, gasping down breath after breath. "Why? You would have tried to talk me out of it."

"Because," Nesta bit out, wiping the water from her eyes as she got to her knees, "we could have come down here without having to get wet. I'm not to let you out of my sight—not even for a moment, so I had no choice but to go after you. But since you jumped in so damned fast . . . Now we're freezing."

"How could we have reached here without getting wet?" Bryce asked, shuddering with cold, teeth already clacking against each other.

Nesta rolled her eyes and said to the shadows, "You might as well come out now."

Bryce whirled on her knees, reaching for a weapon that wasn't there as Azriel landed from above them.

His wings were spread so wide they nearly touched either side of the cavern, and the black dagger hung at his hip, its dark hilt gleaming faintly in the light of her star. And peeking above a broad shoulder, its matching dark hilt like shadow given form, was the Starsword.

"What the fuck do you mean Bryce isn't in Hel?" Ruhn managed to say around what was left of his tongue, every breath like shards of glass slicing down his throat.

Hunt gave no answer, and Ruhn supposed he hadn't really expected one, anyway.

Baxian grunted, "Where?" It was about all the angel could get out, Ruhn realized.

"Dunno," Hunt said, voice gravelly from screaming.

The Hawk had yanked the lever that sent them all plunging, laughing when they'd yelped as their injuries collided with cold stone. As reeking puddles of their own blood and waste splashed onto them. But at least they were on the floor.

Still chained at the wrists and ankles, Ruhn had only been able to lie there, shuddering, tears leaking from his eyes at the relief in his shoulders, his arms, his lungs.

The Hawk had slid a tray of food toward them before he left— but kept it far enough away that they'd have to crawl through their piss and shit to get to it before the rats converged.

Baxian was currently trying to reach the tray, legs pushing against the stones, the half-grown stumps of his wings stained red. He stretched a filthy hand toward the broth and water, and groaned deeply. Blood leaked from a wound in his ribs.

Ruhn wasn't sure he could eat, though his body screamed for food. He took breath after sawing breath.

The Oracle had told him that the royal bloodline ended with him. Had she seen that he'd wind up here—and never walk out alive? Cold worse than the dungeons' damp chill crept through him.

He had come to peace with the possibility of this fate for himself a long time ago. Granted, not this particular demise, but an untimely end in some vague sense. But now that Bryce was a true royal, the prophecy shed light on her fate, too. If she hadn't made it to Hel . . . perhaps she hadn't made it anywhere. Thus ending the royal bloodline with both of their deaths.

He couldn't share his suspicions with Athalar. Couldn't offer up that bit of despair that would break the Umbra Mortis worse than any of Pollux's tools. It would be Ruhn's secret to keep. His own wretched truth, left to fester in his heart.

The smell of stale bread filled his nostrils, rising above the stench as the tray slid in front of him. Splashing through a puddle of—Ruhn didn't want to know what the liquid was. Though his nose offered up a few unpleasant suggestions.

"Gotta eat," Hunt said, hands shaking as he brought a cup of broth to his mouth.

"Don't want us dead, then," Baxian said, slowly lifting a piece of bread.

"Not yet." Athalar sipped slowly. Like he didn't trust his body not to chuck it all up. "Eat, Danaan."

It was a command, and Ruhn found himself reaching his weak, trembling fingers toward the broth. It took all his focus, all his strength, to raise it to his lips. He could barely taste it. Right— his tongue was still regrowing. He sipped again.

"I don't know where Bryce is," Hunt said, voice raw. He picked up a piece of bread with his good hand. The burned fingers on his other hand were twisted at different angles. Some were missing nails.

Fuck, how had their lives come to this?

Athalar took the last bite of bread and lay back—right in the reeking piles and puddles. He closed his eyes. The halo gleamed darkly on the angel's brow. Ruhn knew Athalar's relaxed posture belied his thoughts. Knew the angel was probably frantic with worry and dread.

Guilt was likely eating Athalar alive. Guilt that wasn't his to bear—they'd all made choices that had landed them here. But the words were too heavy, too painful for Ruhn to voice.

Baxian finished and lay down as well, instantly asleep. The Hammer and the Hawk had come down especially hard on the Helhound.

It was personal with them—Baxian had been one of their own. A brother-in-arms, a partner in cruelty. Now they'd take him apart piece by piece.

Ruhn lifted his cup again—a silicone one that couldn't be broken to use as a weapon—and peered into the water within. Watched it ripple with his breath.

"We need to get out of here," Ruhn said, and nothing had ever sounded more stupid. Of course they needed to get out of here. For so many fucking reasons.

But Athalar cracked open an eye. Met his stare. Pain and rage and determination shone there, unbroken despite the halo and slave brand on his wrist. "Then talk to your . . . person." *Girlfriend,* the angel didn't say.

Ruhn ground his teeth, and his ravaged mouth gave a burst of pain. He'd rather die here than beg the Hind for help. "Another way."

"I was in these dungeons . . . for seven years," Hunt said. "No way out. Especially not with Pollux so invested in ripping us apart."

Ruhn glanced again at the halo. He knew the angel didn't only mean a way out of the dungeons. The Asteri owned them now.

Baxian stirred from his slumber to wearily rasp, "I never appreciated it, Athalar. What you went through."

"I'm surprised I didn't get a badge of honor when I left here." The light words were at odds with the utter emptiness of Hunt's stare. Ruhn couldn't stand to see it there, in the eyes of the Umbra Mortis.

Baxian chuckled brokenly, playing along. "Maybe Pollux will give you one this time."

If Ruhn got free, Pollux would be the first asshole he ended. He didn't dwell on why. Didn't dwell on the rage that coursed through him whenever he saw the white-winged angel.

He'd been so stupid. Naïve and reckless and *stupid* to let himself get in so deep with Day—with Lidia—and forget the Oracle's warning. Delude himself into thinking that it probably meant he wouldn't have kids. He'd been so fucking pathetic and lonely that he'd needed to think the best, even though it was clear he'd always had a one-way ticket to disaster.

The only thing left to do was put an end to it.

So Ruhn said, "You were alone then, Athalar."

Hunt met Ruhn's stare, as if to say, *Oh yeah?* Ruhn just nodded. Friends, brothers, whatever—he had Athalar's back.

Something glimmered in Athalar's eyes. Gratitude, maybe. Or hope. Much better than what had been there moments ago. It sharpened Ruhn's focus. Cleared the pain-fogged bits of his brain. This might be a one-way ticket for him, but it didn't have to be for Hunt. And Bryce . . .

Ruhn looked away before Hunt could read the fear that filled his eyes, his heart.

Thankfully, Baxian added, "And you weren't . . . the Umbra Mortis back then, either. You've changed, Athalar."

Hunt let out a grating laugh, full of challenge and defiance. Thank the gods for that. "What are you thinking, Danaan?"

12

You've been here this whole time?" Bryce eyed the shadow-wreathed warrior as they left the river behind, walking through the lower tunnel passage. They followed the light of Bryce's star, once again pointing ahead, faintly illuminating the carvings all around them. Her teeth chattered with cold, but moving helped warm her frozen body—just a fraction.

Azriel, striding a few feet behind Bryce as Nesta led the way through the tunnel, said, "Yes."

Nesta snorted. "That's about all you'll get out of him."

Bryce peered over a shoulder at the male, trying to calm her shivers. "Those were your shadows against my light earlier?"

"Yes," Azriel said again.

Nesta chuckled. "And he's probably been put out about it ever since."

"Seeing you go into that freezing river helped," Azriel said mildly, and Bryce could have sworn she caught a hint of a smile gracing his beautiful face.

But she asked, "Why keep hidden at all?"

"To observe," Nesta answered for him, stride unfaltering. "To see what you'd do. Where you'd lead me. As soon as we realized there was a tunnel, we got supplies together and followed you." Hence her pack of food.

They passed by more carvings—all disarmed well ahead of their approach by Nesta's silver flame. These were more peaceful: They showed small children playing. Time passing with trees blooming, then barren, then blooming again. Pretty, perfect scenes at odds with the conversation at hand.

Bryce gestured to the passageway and the carvings. "Your guess remains as good as mine. I'm just following the light."

"Right into the river," Nesta grumbled. Azriel snickered behind her.

Bryce glanced at him again, at the wings and armor. At his ears—she realized now that they weren't arched, but round like a human's. There had been carvings earlier of warriors that looked like him—armies of them. "Do you have Vanir in this world?"

His eyes narrowed. "What's that?"

Bryce slowed her pace, allowing herself to fall into step beside him. Though perhaps he allowed it as well. "In Midgard—my world—it's a term for all magical, non-human beings. Fae, angels, shifters, mer, sprites . . ." Azriel's brows rose with each word. "Basically, they're the top of the food chain."

"In this world," Nesta said from ahead, rubbing her wet, cold arms to get some semblance of warmth into them, "we have the humans and the Fae. But amongst the Fae, there are High Fae, like . . . me. Amren. And what some call lesser faeries: any other magical creatures. And then there are people like Azriel, who is just . . . Illyrian."

"So Rhysand is Illyrian, too?" Bryce pried. "He's got the wings."

"Half," Nesta corrected. "Half High Fae, half Illyrian." Azriel cleared his throat as if to warn her to stop talking so much, and Nesta added sharply, "And with the combined arrogance of both."

Azriel *really* cleared his throat then, and Bryce couldn't help her smile, despite her clacking teeth.

Her gaze flicked to the Starsword strapped to Azriel's back, then to his side, to the knife hanging there. Her ears hollowed out for a moment, a dull thump sounding once, and her hand spasmed, seemingly tugged toward those blades.

Azriel's wings twitched at the same moment, and he rolled his shoulders, like he was shaking off some phantom touch. A peek at Nesta revealed her studying the male, as if such a display was unusual.

Bryce put aside her questions, rubbing her frozen hands together for warmth. *Eyes on the prize,* she reminded herself as they continued on. *Master of spinning bullshit.*

Carrying both the dagger and the Starsword was clearly bothering Azriel.

As they pushed into the gloom, clothes slowly drying, bodies slowly thawing, Bryce counted his wings twitching or shoulders rolling no less than six times.

Not to mention the occasional hollow thump in her own ears if she drew too near to him.

They crossed a stream, wide enough to be a river, but shallow and rocky all the way across. Her blazing star, thankfully, pointed to the tunnel on the other side. No swimming necessary this time. As they crossed, the star illuminated slimy white creatures slithering out of their path. Bryce reined in the urge to cringe down at them. Or at the iron-rich water scent that stuffed itself up her nose. She said, if only to distract herself from the gross fauna of the stream, "Did the Fae make these tunnels?"

A few steps ahead, Nesta said nothing. But Azriel, trailing behind, mused after a moment, "I don't think so. From the consistent size of them, I'd guess that a Middengard Wyrm originally made these passages. Maybe it even used these waterways to get around."

"Does it matter?" Nesta said without looking back.

"Possibly," Azriel murmured. "We should be on alert. It might still use them to access the tunnel system."

Alarm flared through Bryce. "What makes you say that?"

Azriel nodded to a pile of white things that she'd mistaken for more of the writhing, newt-like creatures. "Bones. Of those things from the bridge chamber, probably."

Bryce stumbled on a slippery rock, going down into the frigid water, palms and knees smarting—

A strong hand was instantly at her back, but too late to avoid the stinging cuts that now peppered her hands and legs. "Careful," Azriel warned, setting her on a sturdier rock.

Bryce's stomach hollowed out with her ears this time, and the dagger was right there, the sword so close—

Azriel let out a grunt, going rigid. Like he could feel it, too, the weapons' demand to be together or apart or whatever it was, the strange power of them in proximity to each other—

"Watch your footing" was all the male said before stepping back. Far enough away that the sword and the dagger halted their strange tugging at Bryce. Her stomach eased, her hearing with it.

Reaching the bank, she shook off the stinging in her palms, the scent of her blood stronger than that of the river, and wiped the blood from her torn knees. She'd liked these leggings, damn it. Mud came away with the blood, and she clicked her tongue as she wiped her hand along the rock wall, trying to smear it away.

She realized too late that she'd smudged the blood and dirt over a carving of two serene, lute-playing Fae females. With an apologetic look to them and their long-dead carver, Bryce continued on. And on. And on.

"Your hands aren't healing," Azriel said from behind Bryce the next day. Or whenever it was now, considering that they'd all slept for a few hours with nothing in the darkness to indicate the passing of time. Bryce had dozed lightly, fitfully, aware of every drip of moisture and scrape of rock in the tunnel, the breathing from the warriors beside her.

She knew they'd been monitoring *her* every breath.

After a quick meal, they'd been on their way. And apparently, Azriel hadn't missed the scent of her hands still leaking blood.

Nesta halted ahead, as if concerned by Azriel's words, and when the female backtracked, hand outstretched, Bryce showed her scraped-up palms.

"Something in the water?" Nesta murmured to Azriel.

"Her knees healed," Azriel murmured back.

Bryce didn't want to know how he knew that. She peered at her raw, scraped hands, the smeared blood and lingering mud on them. "Maybe my magic's weird down here. It'd explain why the star is doing its . . . GPS thing."

Her tongue stumbled over the *GPS* pronunciation in their language, but if they had no idea what the Hel she was talking about, they didn't let on.

Instead, Azriel asked, "How fast do you usually heal?" He reached for her hand, her starlight washing over the golden skin of his own hands . . . and the scars there. Covering every inch.

She'd seen them during their first encounter on that misty riverbank, but had forgotten until now. She'd never seen such extensive burn scars.

The sword and dagger, so close now, began their thrumming and tugging. Her hearing hollowed out, her gut with it.

Azriel's wings twitched once again.

But Bryce said of her bleeding hands, blocking out the blades' call, "I'm half-human, so I'm used to slower healing, but since making the Drop, I've been healing at relatively normal Vanir speeds."

Nesta must have been filled in on the Drop as well, because she didn't question what it was. She only said, "Maybe it has something to do with your magic needing so long to replenish, too."

"Again," Azriel reminded them, "her knees have healed."

Bryce glanced at the thick scarring over his fingers. What— who—had done such a brutal thing to him? And though she knew it was dumb to open up, to show any vulnerability, she said quietly, "The male who fathered me . . . he used to burn my brother to punish him. The scars never healed for him, either." Ruhn had just tattooed over them. A fact she'd only learned right before she'd come here, and knowing about the pain he'd suffered—

Azriel dropped her hand. But he said nothing as he stepped back, far enough away that the sword and dagger stopped chattering to Bryce. If they continued plaguing him, he made no sign. He only motioned them to keep moving before prowling off into the gloom, taking the lead this time. Bryce watched him for a moment before following, heart heavy in her chest for some reason she couldn't place.

Nesta continued down the tunnel, this time staying a little closer to Bryce. The female said a shade quietly, "I'm sorry about your brother's suffering."

The words steadied Bryce, focused her. "I'll make sure my sire pays for it one day."

"Good" was all Nesta said. "Good."

"Tell me about the Daglan." Bryce's voice echoed too loudly in the otherwise silent cave from where she sat against the tunnel wall, a carving of three dancing Fae females above her. The scent of her blood filled the cave, the wounds on her hands still open and bleeding. Not enough to be alarming, but a small, steady ooze every now and then.

Azriel and Nesta, sitting beside each other with the ease of familiarity, both frowned. Nesta said, "I don't know anything about them." She considered, then added, "I slew one of their contemporaries, though. About seven months ago."

Bryce's brows rose. "So not an Asteri—Daglan, I mean?"

Azriel shifted. Nesta glanced sidelong at him, marking the movement, but said to Bryce, "I don't think so. The creature—Lanthys—was a breed unto himself. He was . . . horrible."

Bryce angled her head. "How did you kill him?"

Nesta said nothing.

Bryce's gaze lifted to the sword hilt peeking above the warrior's shoulder. "With that?"

Nesta just said, "Its name is Ataraxia."

"That's an Old Language word." Nesta nodded. Bryce murmured, "Inner Peace—that's your sword's name?"

"Lanthys laughed when he heard it, too."

"I'm not laughing," Bryce said, meeting the female's stare.

She found nothing but open curiosity on Nesta's face. Nesta said, "The scar your light comes from . . . it's shaped like an eight-pointed star. Why?"

Bryce peered at where the light was muffled by her T-shirt. "It's the symbol of the Starborn, I think."

"And the magic marked you in this way?"

"Yes. When I . . . revealed who I was, what I am, to the world, I drew the star out of my chest. It left that scar in its wake." She glanced to Azriel. "Like a burn."

His face was an unreadable mask. But Nesta asked, "So you have a star *within* you? An actual star?"

Bryce shrugged with one shoulder. "Yeah? I mean, not literally. It's not like a giant ball of gas spinning in space. But it's starlight."

Nesta didn't seem particularly impressed. "And you said these Asteri of yours . . . they also have stars within them?"

Bryce winced. "Yes."

"So what's the difference between you and them?" Nesta asked.

"Aside from the fact that I'm not an intergalactic colonialist creep?"

She could have sworn Nesta's mouth kicked up at a corner. That Azriel chuckled, the sound soft as shadow. "Right," Nesta said.

"I, uh . . . I don't know." Bryce considered. "I never really thought about it. But . . ." Those final moments running from Rigelus flashed in her memory, the bursts of his power rupturing marble and glass, searing past her cheek—

"My light is just that," Bryce said. "Light. The Asteri claim their powers are from holy stars inside themselves, but they can physically manipulate things with that light. Kill and destroy. Is starlight that can shatter rock actually light? Everything they've told us is basically a lie, so it's possible they don't have stars inside them at all—that it's merely bright magic that *looks* like a star, and they called it a holy star to wow everyone."

Azriel said, wings rustling, "Does it matter what their power is called, then?"

"No," Nesta admitted. "I was only curious."

Bryce chewed on her lip. What *was* the Asteri's power? Or hers? Hers was light, but perhaps theirs was actually the brute force of a star—a sun. So hot and strong it could destroy all in its path. It wasn't a comforting thought, so Bryce asked Nesta, in need of a new subject, "What kind of sword is that, anyway?" Its simple, ordinary hilt jutted above Nesta's shoulder.

"One that can kill the unkillable," Nesta answered.

"So is the Starsword," Bryce said quietly, then nodded to Azriel's side. "Can your dagger kill the unkillable, too?"

"It's called Truth-Teller," he said in that soft voice, like shadows given sound. "And no, it cannot."

Bryce arched a brow. "So does it . . . tell the truth?"

A hint of a smile, more chilling than the frigid air around them. "It gets people to do so."

Bryce might have shuddered had she not caught Nesta rolling her eyes. It gave her enough courage to dare ask the winged warrior, "Where did the dagger come from?"

Azriel's hazel eyes held nothing but cool wariness. "Why do you want to know?"

"Because the Starsword"—she motioned to the blade he had down his back—"sings to it. I know you're feeling it, too." *Let it be out in the open.* "It's driving you nuts, right?" Bryce pushed. "And it gets worse when I'm near."

Azriel's face again revealed nothing.

"It is," Nesta answered for him. "I've never seen him so fidgety."

Azriel glowered at his friend. But he admitted, "They seem to want to be near each other."

Bryce nodded. "When I landed on that lawn, they instantly reacted when they were close together."

"Like calls to like," Nesta mused. "Plenty of magical things react to one another."

"This was unique. It felt like . . . like an answer. My sword blazed with light. That dagger shone with darkness. Both of them are crafted of the same black metal. Iridium, right?" She jerked her chin to Azriel, to the dagger at his side. "Ore from a fallen meteorite?"

Azriel's silence was confirmation enough.

"I told you guys back in that dungeon," Bryce went on. "There's literally a prophecy in my world about my sword and a dagger reuniting our people. *When knife and sword are reunited, so shall our people be.*"

Nesta frowned deeply. "And you truly think this is that particular dagger?"

"It checks too many boxes not to be." Bryce lifted a still-bloody hand, and she didn't miss the way they both tensed. But she furled her fingers and said, "I can feel them. It gets stronger the closer I get to them."

"Then don't get too close," Nesta warned, and Bryce lowered her hand.

Bryce surveyed the carved walls, pivoting. "These reliefs tell a narrative, too, you know."

Nesta peered up at the images: the three dancing Fae in the foreground, the stars overhead, the scattered islands. The mountain island with the castle atop its highest peak. And again, always the reminder of that suffering underworld beneath it. *Memento mori. Et in Avallen ego.* "What sort of narrative?"

Bryce shrugged. "If I had a few weeks, I could walk the whole length and analyze it."

"But you don't know our history," Nesta said. "It'd have no context for you."

"I don't need context. Art has a universal language."

"Like the one tattooed on your back?" Nesta said.

All right. Their turn to ask questions. "Your friend—Amren. She said it was the same as the language in some book?"

Azriel asked, stone-faced, "What do you call it in your world—that language?"

Bryce shook her head. "I don't know. I told the truth earlier. My friend and I got . . . We had a lot to drink one night." And smoked a fuck-ton of mirthroot, but they didn't need to know that, or need an explanation about the drugs of Midgard. "I barely remember it. She said it meant *Through love, all is possible.*"

Nesta clicked her tongue, but not with disdain. Something like understanding.

Bryce went on, "She claimed she picked the alphabet out of a book in the tattoo shop, but . . . I don't think that was the case." She needed to steer this away from the Horn. Quickly. Especially since Nesta had been the one they'd called to inspect her tattoo.

Azriel asked, "How did your friend know the language?"

"I still don't know. I've been trying to figure out what she knew for months now."

"Why not just ask her?" Nesta countered.

"Because she's dead." The words came out flatter than Bryce had intended. But something cracked in her to say them, even if she'd lived with that reality every day for more than two years now. "The Asteri had her assassinated, then had it framed as a demonic murder. She was getting close to discovering some major truth about the Asteri and our world, so they had her killed."

"What truth?" This from Azriel.

"I've been trying to uncover that, too," Bryce said.

"Was the language of your tattoo part of it?" Azriel pressed.

"I don't know—I only got as far as learning that she'd uncovered what the Asteri truly are, what they do to the worlds they conquer. If I ever get home . . ." Her heart became unbearably heavy. "If I ever get home, maybe I'll learn the rest."

Silence fell. Then Nesta nodded to the three dancing Fae figures above Bryce. "So what does that mean, then? If you don't need the context."

Bryce examined the relief. Took in the dancing, the stars, the idyllic islands in the background. And she said softly, "It means that there was once joy in this world."

Silence. Then Nesta said, "That's it?"

Bryce kept her eyes on the dancers, the stars, the lush lands. Ignored the darkness beneath. Focused on the good—always the good. "Isn't that all that matters?"

13

It took five hours for the Viper Queen to deign to meet Ithan.

Five hours, plus the fact that Ithan had opened the door to the hallway where two Fae assassins stood posted and threatened to start ripping apart the warehouse.

Then and only then was he escorted here, to her office.

He'd left Flynn, Dec, Marc, and Tharion quietly debating not only how the fuck they'd get out of the Meat Market, but also whether to trust the Hind. The sprites, shocked by her mention of their lost queen, had retreated into Tharion's bedroom with Sigrid. The dragon hadn't yet emerged from her own.

But Ithan had had enough of debating, of asking questions. He'd never been good with that shit. Maybe it was the athlete in him, but he just wanted to *do* something.

It didn't matter if they could trust the Hind or not. If she could get them to Pangera, closer to their friends . . . he'd take that. But he had to get one friend out first.

Ithan sat in an ancient green chair in a truly derelict office, watching the Viper Queen type key by key into a computer that could have doubled as a cement block.

A statue of Luna sat atop that computer, arrow pointed at the Viper Queen's face. A few more deliberate *click-clacks* of her long nails on the keyboard, and then her green eyes slid to Ithan.

"So what was all the yelping about?"

Ithan crossed his arms. On the desk itself sat a statuette of Cthona, carved from black stone. In one arm the goddess cradled an infant to her bare breast. In the other, she extended an orb—Midgard—out into the room. Cthona, birther of worlds. He touched it idly, gathering his courage.

"I want to discuss what you're going to do about Sabine," he said.

The Viper Queen leaned back in her seat, sleek bob swaying. "As far as I know, when Amelie Ravenscroft woke up from having her throat cut by my guards, she tracked down the Prime Apparent, dragged her carcass home, and has been feeding Sabine a steady diet of firstlight to regenerate her. She's already back on her feet."

Ithan's blood curdled. "So Sabine recovered quickly."

The Viper Queen cocked her head. "Were you hoping otherwise?"

He didn't answer. Instead, he asked, "And you're going to hand Sigrid and me over to her?"

The Viper Queen opened a drawer, pulled out a silver tin of cigarettes, and lifted one to her mouth. "Depends on how nicely you ask me not to, Holstrom." The cigarette rose and fell with the words. She lifted a lighter and ignited the tip, taking a long drag.

"What'll it take?"

Smoke rippled from her mouth as the Viper Queen sized him up. Her tongue darted over her purple lower lip. Tasting—scenting. The way snakes smelled.

"Let's introduce ourselves first. We've never met, have we?"

"Hi. Nice to meet you."

"So testy. I thought you'd be a big old softy."

He flashed his teeth. "I don't know why you'd assume that."

She took another long drag of her cigarette. "Did you not go against Sabine's orders and lead a small group of wolves into Asphodel Meadows to save humans? To save the most vulnerable of the House of Earth and Blood?"

He growled. "I was doing a nice thing. There wasn't much more to it than that."

The Viper Queen exhaled a plume of smoke, more dragon than the one upstairs. "That remains to be seen."

Ithan challenged, "You sent your people to help that day, too."

"I was doing a nice thing," the Viper Queen echoed mildly. "There wasn't much more to it than that."

"Maybe you'll feel inclined to do the nice thing today, too."

"Buying or selling, Holstrom?"

Ithan leashed the wolf inside howling at him to start shredding things. "Look, I don't play games."

"Pity." She examined her manicured nails. "Sabine doesn't, either. All you wolves are so *boring*."

Ithan opened his mouth, then shut it. Considered what she'd said, what she'd done. "You don't like Sabine."

Her lips curved slowly. "Does anyone?"

He clenched his hands into fists. "If you don't like her, why let her go?"

"I'd ask the same of you, pup. You had her down—why not finish the kill?" Ithan couldn't help the way his body tensed. "Of course," the Viper Queen went on, "the Fendyr heir—Sigrid, is it?—should be the one to do it. Don't you wolves call it . . . challenging?"

"Only in open combat, when witnessed by pack-members of the Den. If Sigrid had killed Sabine last night, it would have been an assassination."

"Semantics."

A chill skittered down his spine. "You want Sabine truly dead." She said nothing. "Is this your cost, then? You want me to kill—"

"Oh, no. I wouldn't *dare* tangle in politics like that."

"Just drugs and misery, right?"

Again, that slow smile. "What would your dear brother say if he knew you were here with the likes of me?"

Ithan wouldn't give her the satisfaction of a reaction. "Tell me what it'll take to get all of us out of here."

"A fight." She extinguished her cigarette. "Just one fight. From you. A private event," the Viper Queen purred. "Only for me."

"Why?" Ithan demanded.

"I place a high value on amusement. Especially my own." She smiled again. "One fight for safe passage—and Ketos's freedom. You win, and it's all yours. Nothing more required beyond that."

Fuck, he should have brought Marc with him—he'd have thought this through, would have spotted any pitfalls a mile off.

But Ithan knew if he walked out, if he went to get someone else, the option would be off the table. It came down to him, and him alone.

"I fight, and you'll let us all go. Immediately."

Her chin dipped. "I'll even provide a car to take you wherever you want to go."

One fight. He'd fought plenty in his life. "I'm not taking your venom," Ithan said.

"Who said I was offering?" Her lips curled.

"You'll let Tharion free of that, too," Ithan added. "No more enthralling bullshit."

"I'm offended, Holstrom. It's a sacred bond amongst my kind."

"Nothing is sacred to you."

The Viper Queen lifted a finger and turned the statuette of Luna toward him, the arrow now pointing his way. "Oh?"

"The trappings mean nothing if you don't follow it up with actions."

Another little smile. "So self-righteous."

Ithan held her stare, letting her see the wolf within, whatever bones of it remained.

There had to be a catch. But time was running out—and he didn't see an alternative to getting out of this mess.

"Fine," Ithan said. "One fight."

"It's a deal," the Viper Queen crooned. She rose and stalked to the door, body moving with sinuous grace. "The fight's at ten tomorrow night. Your friends can come watch, if they want." She opened the door, an order to leave. Ithan obeyed, and she pulled out yet another cigarette tin—this one gold—and flicked it open. He was passing over the threshold when she said, "I'll give you a worthy opponent, don't worry."

The Viper Queen smirked. And then added before she slammed the door shut in his face, "Make your brother proud."

Lidia Cervos brushed out her hair, seated at her vanity in her ornate room in the Asteri's palace. A monstrosity of gold silk, ivory velvet, and polished oak overlooking the seven hills of the city. The perfect room for the pampered, loyal pet of the Asteri.

No one had thought twice or even questioned her when she'd gone to Lunathion earlier to deliver a message to Celestina and make a pit stop at the Meat Market to pick up some "party favors." Even Mordoc hadn't cared.

But her allies believed she was their enemies' faithful pet, too.

So here she was. Alone. Praying that Declan Emmet and his friends would meet her. Praying that she'd correctly judged the Sprite Queen, many levels below.

The door to the bathroom opened, steam rippling out, and Pollux emerged, wholly naked and gleaming from the shower.

"You're not dressed?" he asked, frowning at her dove-gray silk dressing robe. The frown deepened as his eyes drifted over her hair, still down and unstyled. "We're leaving in fifteen minutes."

Here it was—the beginning of an intricate dance.

"My cycle is starting," she said, putting a hand to her lower abdomen. "Make excuses for me."

Pollux slicked back his blond hair and stalked over to her, his heavy cock swinging with each step. His white wings dripped a trail of water over the cream carpet. "Rigelus personally asked us to be there. Take a tonic."

"I did," she said, letting a bit of her temper show. It wasn't a lie. She *had* taken a potion—one of her emergency contraceptives, lest her usual plan fail. It had jump-started her cycle two weeks ahead of schedule.

Right on cue, Pollux sniffed, scenting her blood. "You're early."

He knew, because he didn't like to fuck her when she was bleeding. She'd come to cherish her cycle. Pollux usually tormented someone else that week.

She met his stare, if only because his cock was in her face and she had little interest in looking at it for another second of her existence. The tonic did its job in that moment, and nausea churned in her gut—along with a slice of pain.

She didn't have to fake her wince. "Tell Rigelus I apologize."

Pollux observed her without an ounce of mercy. To the contrary—his cock thickened. A cat enjoying the suffering of its dinner.

But she ignored it, going back to the mirror. A broad, powerful hand stroked down her hair, brushing it aside. Then lips found her neck, his tongue flicking beneath her ear. "I hope you'll feel better soon."

Lidia made herself lift a hand to his hair. Run her fingers through the damp strands and let out a low sound. It might have been pain or lust. To the Malleus, it was all the same. He pulled back, a hand pumping his cock as he headed into the dressing room, wings glowing white behind him.

She was in their bed—a great mass of down pillows and silken sheets—when Pollux left fifteen minutes later, wearing a tux with devastating effect. Such a beautiful exterior, this monster.

"Lidia," the Hammer purred, possession in his rich voice, and then he was gone.

She lay in bed, fighting past the twisting in her gut, the nausea that wasn't solely from her cycle. Only after ten minutes had gone by did she rise from the mattress.

She hurried into the bathroom, still humid from Pollux's shower—usually so hot she wondered if he was trying to scald the evil from himself—and pulled out the bag of feminine hygiene products that she knew he'd never open. As if touching a tampon might make his cock shrivel up and drop off.

Inside the bag lay a burner phone. A different one arrived in a box of tampons every month. She ran the shower again, blocking out any identifying noises that could be picked up from the palace's cameras on the walls outside or by anyone on the other end of the line. Then she dialed.

An operator answered. "Fincher Tiles and Flooring."

She shifted her voice into a lilting, sweet croon. "I'm looking for custom ash-wood floors, seven-by-seven pieces?"

"One moment, please."

Another ring. Then another female said, "This is Custom Ash-Wood Floors, Seven by Seven."

Lidia let out a small breath. She had only called once before, long ago. They'd sent her burner phone after burner phone, in case of an emergency. Each month she'd destroyed them, unused.

Well, this was an emergency.

"This is Daybright," she said in her normal voice.

The female on the line sucked in a breath. "Solas."

Lidia continued quickly, "I need all agents mobilized and ready to move in three days."

The female on the line cleared her throat. "I . . . Agent Daybright, I don't think there's anyone to mobilize."

Lidia blinked slowly. "Explain."

"We've taken too many hits, lost too many people. And after the death of Agent Silverbow, a good number abandoned the cause."

"How many are left?"

"A couple hundred, perhaps."

Lidia closed her eyes. "And none can be spared right now to—"

"Command's put an end to all missions. They're going into hiding."

"Patch me through to Command, then."

"I . . . I'm not authorized to do that."

Lidia opened her eyes. "Tell Command I'll speak to them and only them. This information is something that might buy them a shot at survival."

The dispatcher paused, considering. "If it's not—"

"It is. Tell them it's about something they've wanted to do for a very long time."

Another pause. Thinking through all she knew, probably. "One moment."

It was the work of a few minutes to get the human male on the phone. For Lidia to use the passcodes to identify herself and verify her identity, as well as his. To explain the plan she'd slowly been forming. For Ophion to survive another day, yes . . . but even more so, for their unwitting help in making sure Ruhn survived.

Two days. Lidia left him with a time, a start location, and an order to be ready. There'd be no missing the signal. She could only hope Ophion would show up as the commander had promised.

Lidia ended the call, and crushed the phone in her fist until only shards of plastic and glass remained. Then she opened the bathroom window, pretending to air out the steam as the tiny pieces blew into the starry night.

Bryce faced another river, this one waist-deep and frigid. But at least the star kept pointing ahead this time, no swimming required. They splashed through the water in silence, Bryce's still-bleeding hands stinging at the river's kiss, and she shivered as they emerged on the other side.

"So that eight-pointed star," Nesta said into the quiet as they began walking again, shoes squishing, "it's a symbol of the Starborn people in your world. It means nothing else?"

"Why all the questions about it?" Bryce asked through chattering teeth. Azriel walked a few steps behind, silent as death, but she knew he was listening to every word.

Nesta went silent, and Bryce thought she might not answer, but then she said, "I had a tattoo on my back—recently. A magical one, now gone. But it was of an eight-pointed star."

"And?"

"And the magic, the power of the bargain that caused the tattoo to appear . . . it chose the design. The star meant nothing to me. I thought maybe it was related to my training, but its shape was identical to the scar on your chest."

"So we're obviously destined to be best friends," Bryce teased. Nesta didn't smile or laugh. Bryce asked, "Is that . . . is that why you volunteered to come to get me?"

"I've been in the Fae realms long enough to know that there are forces that sometimes guide us, push us along. I've learned to let them. And to listen." Nesta smirked. "It's why I didn't kill you for following your starlight into the river. You were doing the same thing."

Bryce's chest tightened. The female had a story to tell, and one Bryce would, in any other circumstance, like to hear. But before she could even consider asking, something massive and white appeared ahead. A skeleton of enormous bones.

"The Wyrm?" Bryce asked, even as she realized it wasn't. This thing was different, with a body like a sobek's. Each tooth was as large as Bryce's hand.

"No," Azriel said from behind them, the rushing river muffling his soft words. "And I don't think the Wyrm ate it, if its skeleton is intact like this."

"Do you know what it is?" Bryce asked.

"No," Azriel said again. "And part of me is glad not to."

"You think there are more down here?" Nesta asked Azriel, scanning the dark.

"I hope not," Azriel answered. Bryce shuddered and took the opportunity to continue onward, leading the way, leaving those ancient, terrifying bones far behind.

The river was still a thunderous roar when the carvings changed. Normally, they were full of life and action and movement. But this one was simple, clearly meant to be the sole focus. Something of great importance to whoever had carved it.

An archway had been etched, stars glimmering around it. And in that archway stood a male figure, the image created with impressive depth. His hand was upraised in greeting.

And Bryce might have looked closer, had the Middengard Wyrm not exploded from the river behind them.

14

The Middengard Wyrm had arrived at last. Precisely according to Bryce's plan.

She'd been dripping blood for it all this way, leaving a trail, constantly scraping off her scabs to reopen her wounds—ones she'd intentionally inflicted on herself by "falling" into the stream. If the Wyrm relied on scent to hunt, then she'd left a veritable neon sign leading right to them. She hadn't known when or how it would attack, but she'd been waiting.

And she was ready.

Bryce fell back as not only shadows, but blue light flared from Azriel—right alongside the ripple of silver flame from Nesta. Back-to-back, they faced the massive creature with razor-sharp focus. Ataraxia gleamed in Nesta's hand. Truth-Teller pulsed with darkness in Azriel's.

Now or never. Her legs tensed, readying to sprint.

Nesta's eyes slid to Bryce's for a heartbeat. As if understanding at last: Bryce's "unhealing" hand. The blood she'd wiped on the walls. Her musing about the linked river system in these caves, sussing out what they knew regarding the terrain and the Wyrm. To unleash this thing—on *them*.

"I'm sorry," Bryce said to her. And ran.

She meant them no harm—she hadn't lied about that. They could undoubtedly face the Wyrm and live. Nesta had said her sister had done exactly that.

But Bryce needed to learn whatever Urd had sent her to discover. If it was intel that could help or harm her world . . . she didn't want these people knowing. Using it against her. Offering it up to the Asteri. Or wielding it against Midgard for their own gain. Whatever lay ahead was for her alone.

Bryce raced down the tunnel, her path lit by flashes of silver flame and blue magic. Nesta's and Azriel's powers, flaring like lightning against the nightmare of the Wyrm.

The faces of the tunnel carvings watched Bryce's flight with cold, damning eyes. Her breath sawed in her throat. She had no idea how far she had to run, but if she could get a little farther—

A shout bounced off the rocks behind her. Not one of pursuit, but of pain. Azriel. She glanced over a shoulder just as his blue light went out.

Then a female shout resounded through the cavern, and Nesta's silver flame vanished, too, leaving Bryce's starlight to illuminate the way. Leaving only darkness and silence behind her.

She had to keep going. They were seasoned warriors. They were fine.

But that silence, interrupted by Bryce's breathing, her rushing steps . . .

She was the master of spinning bullshit. She'd kept them distracted, kept them from thinking her a manipulative little shit, but . . .

Bryce slowed to a stop. The darkness behind her loomed.

She found herself face-to-face with a scene depicting a great battlefield before the high walls of a city, Fae and winged horrors and snarling beasts all at war, entrenched in pain and suffering. One of the Fae stood in the foreground, spearing a fellow Fae warrior in the mouth.

Fae against Fae. It shouldn't have bothered her. Shouldn't have grabbed her as it did: the warrior-female's merciless expression as she embedded her spear in the agonized face of the female soldier before her. It shouldn't have unsettled something in Bryce to see it.

She'd long ago understood that this kind of thing wasn't beyond the Fae. She took comfort in knowing she wasn't like them, would never be that way.

Yet what she'd just done . . .

She wasn't a monster. Was she?

Maybe she'd regret it. She knew Hunt would have yelled at her for setting a trap only to go help the people she'd ensnared.

But Bryce began running again, hurtling through the cave. Back toward Nesta and Azriel.

And prayed there was something left for her to save.

Bryce realized now, as she retraced her steps, that what she'd earlier thought to be the roaring of the river was in fact the thunderous movement of the Wyrm's massive body. Azriel and Nesta must have made the same mistake.

In the dark, her starlight silvered the walls, casting the world into stark relief.

Her starlight hadn't felt so . . . empty before. While it had been guiding them, it had been comforting, had brought some color and spark to this realm of eternal night. Now, bobbing with every sprinting step, it seemed harsh. Devoid of color.

Like even the light was disgusted by her.

Nesta and Azriel weren't in the tunnel by the carving of the archway. From the shaking of the ground and the snapping of jaws ahead, they'd driven the Wyrm back to the river.

Bryce checked herself in time to slow to a walk before reaching the bank, reminding herself of Randall's training.

Observe, assess, decide.

So she crept up the last few feet toward the rushing water, a hand over her star to dim it, and—

They weren't there. No sign of the Wyrm or its meal. Her stomach dropped. They'd seemed supremely badass and capable. Surely that Wyrm couldn't have . . .

It had.

Nesta lay sprawled on a large rock in the river not ten feet away. No sign of the Wyrm or Azriel. Perhaps it had eaten him already. And would soon return for the other part of its meal.

Oh gods, she'd done this, she'd fucked up beyond forgiveness—

Bryce raced to Nesta's prone form, splashing through the icy water, slipping over stones, the river foaming around her waist in a strong current as she reached to turn the female over—

Nesta's eyes were open. And blazing with fury.

A hand wrapped around Bryce's throat. A blade poked into her back. And Azriel's voice was whisper-soft as he snarled, "Give me one reason not to bury this knife in your spine."

Bryce bared her teeth. "Because I came back to help?"

Nesta snorted, getting to her feet. Utterly unharmed.

"The Wyrm?" Bryce managed to ask, trying not to think about the knife angled to slide into her body. Or about the tug and thrum of the Starsword and the dagger, so near to her now.

"It's hunting us," Nesta seethed, eyeing the river, the tunnel.

"Then fucking *run*," Bryce panted. "The tunnel's open—"

"We're not leaving that thing alive in the world," Azriel said with quiet venom. Nesta unsheathed Ataraxia, the blade glowing faintly. Her demeanor was calm, as if this was all in a day's work.

Solas burn her. Randall would kill her for being so stupid. "You lured me here."

Nesta nodded to Azriel, who withdrew his blade but kept a hand on Bryce's shoulder, either to prevent her from moving or to hold her steady in the river's current. "You saved me from the traps in the walls. It only made sense that you'd have a guilty conscience to go with that soft heart."

Scratch that: her *mother* would kill her for being so stupid.

"I—" Bryce began, but Nesta said, "Save it."

The sharp tone was enough to make Bryce peer into the river's darkness, the tunnel on either side. Even the call of the Starsword and Truth-Teller became secondary as she asked, "How did it disappear?"

"Deep pits in the riverbed," Azriel murmured. "It got one whiff of Nesta's power and dove into one. But from the shaking of the stone . . . it's staying close. Watching us."

"Then why the fuck are we standing in the river?"

Nesta smirked at her. "Bait."

Make your brother proud.

The Viper Queen might as well have shot Ithan in the fucking gut. Like she knew precisely how ashamed Connor would have been of how far he'd fallen.

"What's she going to do about Sabine?" Tharion asked Ithan as he entered the suite once more. Right—he'd told them that was what he wanted to learn from her.

"Nothing," Ithan said.

Sigrid sat on the couch beside Declan, watching his fingers fly over his phone.

"Where's Marc?" Ithan asked.

"Pulled the lawyer privileges card," Flynn answered for Dec. "Fed the guards some crap about legal stuff. He got a message from the Viper Queen a minute after you left, saying he was free to go."

So that was what the Viper Queen had been typing on her computer.

"Go where?"

"To his firm," Dec said, still focusing on his phone. "He's going to look into whether there's a legal way to get us all out of this shitshow."

"I might have a solution for that," Ithan said. They all looked at him.

Tharion asked quietly, "What did she offer you, pup?"

"Nothing I can't handle."

Tharion stood from the table by the fighting ring window. "Did you—"

"One fight—from me. Tomorrow night."

Sigrid's eyes widened. "What sort of fight?"

Ithan pointed to the window behind Tharion. "One of her fancy ones. Down there."

"Did she say *who*?" He'd never seen Ketos's face so serious. "You should have made her specify. She's going to screw you over—screw us all over somehow." Tharion's voice sharpened. "What the Hel were you thinking?"

"I was thinking," Ithan shot back, "that *you* made a stupid choice, and I was trying to get you out of it. Get us all out of this mess."

Tharion blinked at him, eyes dark. Cold. "I didn't ask you to get me out of it. You think I can just walk out of here? I *can't*."

"The Viper Queen said you could—"

"And what then?" The mer got to his feet. "I'll be right back at the mercy of the River Queen. The Viper Queen knows that—she knows I don't have any choice but to stay here, with her." Tharion shook his head in disgust. "You dumb fucking idiot." With that, the mer stalked out of the room.

Silence reigned for a moment. Then Declan said, "You should have talked to us first."

"Yeah, well, I didn't," Ithan snapped. Then sighed. "The Hind gave us two days. Marc's a genius and all that, but legal shit takes time. We don't have that."

"The mer is right," Sigrid said darkly. "You shouldn't trust someone like her. Anyone who traffics in lives has no honor."

"I know," Ithan said. And for a moment, he could see it in Sigrid's eyes—the rigid, yet fair Alpha she might be. With the emotional scars to understand the importance and value of each life.

Maybe he should have encouraged her to kill Sabine last night. Ithan sighed again.

Flynn walked to the wet bar. "Better drink up, Holstrom."

"I never drink before a game," Ithan said. "Even the day before."

"Trust me," Flynn said, pressing a glass of whiskey into Ithan's hand, "with the Vipe hand-selecting your opponent, you'll want something to take the edge off."

"You left your blood all over the place to lead it along," Nesta said. "It's after you—not us. So *you're* going to draw it back here."

Bryce glanced between Nesta and Azriel. They were completely serious.

Bryce pointed to the boulder Nesta had been lying upon moments ago. "So, what, I'm supposed to sit on this rock and wait for the Wyrm to show up and eat me?"

"That last bit is up to you," Nesta said, turning toward the other end of the river. "But from what I just saw, you're a fast runner. You'll get away in time. Probably."

Asshole.

Azriel murmured, "Quiet," and Bryce, without much of an alternative, obeyed.

It didn't matter how brightly her starlight shone. The Wyrm was blind. And it was only a matter of time until it came sniffing again—

It was a matter of seconds, actually.

One moment, there was only the rushing river. The next, a wall of water exploded in front of Azriel, the behemoth body of the Wyrm dwarfing even the warrior's powerful form.

Bryce had never seen such a horrible creature, even during the attack on Crescent City this spring. Rays of blue light flared from Azriel, spearing for the creature—

They pierced its dark, wet skin and vanished.

It was all Bryce saw before she leapt off the rock, splashing through the water, aiming for the tunnel archway.

Nesta shot past her, Ataraxia in hand, silver fire wreathing the other. But the Wyrm vanished—as fast as it had appeared, it went back into the sinkhole.

"Where is it?" Nesta shouted to Azriel, who pivoted, scanning the river, the tunnel—

Behind them, closer to Bryce, the Wyrm erupted from the water again from another sinkhole. Silver fire blasted past her. The Wyrm screeched as the raw power slammed into its side, setting the caverns shaking, debris and rock splashing into the river.

Then the fire vanished, sucked into its skin. The Wyrm again plunged beneath the water, into the sinkhole.

Azriel and Nesta returned to their back-to-back position, and Bryce gathered her wits enough to say, "What happened?"

"It . . . it ate my power," Nesta murmured.

"That's not possible," Azriel said, eyes fixed on the river.

"It *did*," Nesta snapped. "I felt it."

"Shit," Azriel said.

"We need to run," Bryce said.

"No," Nesta said, silver fire in her eyes again. "That thing doesn't get out of this fight alive."

As if in answer and challenge, the Wyrm leapt from the water, a massive, powerful surge, jaws opening wide toward Nesta and Azriel and Bryce—

A flap of Azriel's wings and the three of them were airborne, faster than even the Wyrm could attack. It narrowly missed Azriel's booted feet as it dove again, vanishing once more.

"We need it restrained," Nesta said to Azriel. "So I can get close with Ataraxia."

"If your power didn't kill it, there's no saying Ataraxia will, either," Azriel panted, landing them on the bank. "It breaks through my tethers like they're spiderwebs."

"Then we get something else to do the fighting for us," Nesta said, and Azriel whirled to her, as if in alarm.

But Bryce said, "Fine." And reached a hand out to Azriel. "Give me the Starsword." She'd led them into this mess—she could try to get them out of it. The Starsword had killed Reapers. Maybe it would kill this thing, too.

"Don't you dare," Azriel began—but not to Bryce. Dread paled his golden skin. "Nesta—"

Something metallic gleamed like sunshine in Nesta's hand. A mask.

"*Nesta*," Azriel warned, panic sharpening his voice, but too late. She closed her eyes and shoved it onto her face. A strange, cold breeze swept through the tunnel.

Bryce had endured that wind before, in the Bone Quarter. A wind of death, of decay, of quiet. The hair on her arms rose. And her blood chilled to ice as Nesta opened her eyes to reveal only silver flame shining there.

Whatever that mask was, whatever power it had . . . death lay within it.

"Take it off," Azriel snarled, but Nesta extended a hand into the darkness of the tunnel.

Mortal, an ancient, bone-dry voice whispered in Bryce's head. *You are mortal, and you shall die. Memento mori. Memento mori, memento—*

Bone clicked in the darkness. The earth shook.

Azriel grabbed Bryce, tugging her back against him as he retreated toward the wall, as if it'd offer any shelter from whatever approached. The Starsword and Truth-Teller hummed and pulled at Bryce's spine, and her hands itched, like she could feel the weapons in her palms—

She didn't see what it was that Nesta drew from the dark before the Wyrm found them.

As it had before, it leapt from the river, thrashing into the narrow tunnel, blocking the way back. Azriel's shield glowed blue around them. Jaws open wide to reveal rows of flesh-shredding teeth, the Wyrm shot right for them.

But something massive and white slammed into the Wyrm instead. A creature of pure bone, larger than the Wyrm.

The skeleton they'd encountered down the tunnel. Reanimated.

Its jaws snapped for the Wyrm, long arms ending in claws finding purchase on either side of the Wyrm's unholy mouth.

The Wyrm shrieked, but the creature held firm, biting down on the Wyrm's head and shaking, shaking, *shaking*—

Azriel dragged Bryce back, sword and dagger calling to her to draw them, use them. But he kept pulling her away, deeper into the tunnel as the undead thing and the Wyrm grappled with each other. The ceiling shook, debris shattering on the floor. Azriel arched a wing, shielding them both from its slicing rain.

But there was nothing in that world to shield them from the being standing a few feet away.

Hair drifting on a phantom breeze, Nesta glowed with silver fire. Still wearing her mask. A finger pointed toward the fight. Commanding that creature of bone and death to attack the Wyrm. Again. Again.

"What is she—" Bryce began, but Azriel clamped a hand over her mouth, hauling her farther down the tunnel.

So Bryce could only watch in awe and utter terror as Nesta's fingers closed into a fist.

The beast's jaws encircled the Wyrm's entire front end and smashed it down into the earth, pinning it. The ground rocked with the impact, and even Azriel stumbled, his hand flying from Bryce's mouth.

The Wyrm thrashed, but the undead creature held it firm. Held it down as Nesta drew Ataraxia once more and approached.

"We need to help her," Bryce panted to Azriel.

"I promise you, she's fine," Azriel countered, urging them further into the tunnel. Out of the impact zone, Bryce realized.

The Wyrm must have sensed the sword's approach, because it bucked against the bones and claws pinning it to the rock.

It managed to nudge the undead creature back, but only for a heartbeat.

Nesta raised her free hand again, and the undead creature slammed the Wyrm back into the ground. The Wyrm thrashed, desperate now.

With a dancer's grace, Nesta scaled the undead beast's tail, running along the knobs of its spine like rocks in a stream. Getting to higher ground, to a better angle.

The Wyrm shrieked, but Nesta had reached the undead beast's white skull. And then she was jumping, sword arcing above her, then down, down—

Straight into the head of the Wyrm.

A shudder of silver fire rushed down the Wyrm. That cold, dry wind shivered through the caves again, death in its wake.

The Wyrm slumped to the ground.

The silence was worse than the sound.

Azriel was instantly gone, wings tucking in tight as he rushed toward Nesta and the undead beast that still held the Wyrm in its grip.

"Take it off," Azriel ordered her.

The female turned her head toward him with a smooth motion that Bryce had only seen from possessed dolls in horror movies.

"Take it off," Azriel snarled.

Still staring at him, Nesta yanked Ataraxia from the Wyrm's body and slid down its side, landing with that preternatural ease on the rock.

Every muscle in Bryce's body went taught, that voice whispering over and over to her, *Mortal. You shall die. You shall die. You shall die.*

She hated how she shook at Nesta's stalking approach. How both the human and Vanir parts of her trembled at this thing, whatever it was, contained within the mask.

Azriel didn't yield a single step. Nesta came to a stop before him. Nothing human or Fae looked out through the eyeholes of the mask.

"Take it off," he said, voice pure ice. "Let the creature rest again."

A blink, and the undead creature collapsed once more into a pile of bones.

"Cassian's waiting for you, Nesta," Azriel said—tone gentling. "Take off the Mask." Nesta stayed silent, Ataraxia ready in her hand. One swipe, and Azriel would be dead. "He's waiting for you at the House of Wind," Azriel went on. "At home."

Another blink from Nesta. The silver fire banked a little.

Like whoever Cassian was, and whatever the House of Wind was . . . they might be the only things capable of fighting the siren song of the Mask.

"Gwyn and Emerie are waiting," Azriel pushed. "And Feyre and Elain." The silver flame flared at that. Then Azriel said, "Nyx is waiting, too."

The silver flame went out entirely.

The Mask fell from Nesta's face, clattering on the stone.

Nesta swayed, but Azriel was there, catching her, bringing her to his chest, scarred hands stroking her hair. "Thank the Mother," he breathed. "Thank the Mother."

Bryce began to turn away, sensing that she was witnessing something deeply personal.

But Nesta pulled back from Azriel. Steadied her feet before facing Bryce, Ataraxia still in one hand. She flicked the fingers of her other hand and the Mask instantly vanished, off to wherever she'd summoned it from.

Bryce had so many words in her head that none of them came out.

Nesta just sheathed Ataraxia down her spine again and said to Bryce, "Keep walking."

15

It took Bryce hours to stop shaking. To chase that cold, deadly wind from her skin. To stop hearing the whispering of her death, the death of all things.

She'd never encountered anything like that mask. Nesta had seemed at its mercy, brought back to herself only by Azriel's list of whoever those people were—clearly people Nesta cared about.

Through love, all is possible. Even getting free of death-masks.

Nesta didn't speak, staying close beside Azriel. Or maybe he was the one staying close to her. The male didn't seem to want her farther away than he could grab.

Eventually, Bryce could stand it no longer. "I'm sorry," she said.

At their silence, she twisted to look back at them. They wore twin expressions of ice.

"I'm . . . I'm really fucking sorry," Bryce said, heart thundering.

"You're proving," Nesta said tightly, "to be more trouble than you're worth."

"Then why not just kill me?" Bryce snapped.

"Because whatever you think you'll find at the end of these tunnels," Azriel said with lethal quiet, "whatever warrants the effort of trying to kill us . . . that has to be something worth seeing."

"You could leave me here and go ahead yourselves." She probably shouldn't have suggested that. Too late now.

"That star on your chest suggests otherwise," Nesta said, and left Azriel's side at last to head into the dark. "We've put this much effort into seeing what you'll do. Might as well see it through."

"Effort?" But even as she spoke, Bryce understood. "You knew I'd go through the grate."

"Rhysand guessed, yes—and you made him smug as hell when you winnowed. Granted, he was surprised that you could winnow at all, but . . . the bastard sent us after you." Nesta spoke without turning around, striding with that unfaltering confidence into the gloom. "He had us make sure there was only one path forward. Make sure *you* believed there was only one path forward, too. So you'd show your hand—show us what you truly wanted here."

"You caused the cave-in."

Nesta shrugged. "Azriel caused it. But yes."

"Why—why do any of this? Why do you *care*?"

Nesta was quiet for a beat. Azriel didn't say a word, a wall of silent menace at her back. Then Nesta said, "Because I've seen that star on your chest before."

"Yeah, you said that," Bryce said. "Your tattoo—"

"Not my tattoo."

"Then where?" Bryce breathed. If she could get answers—

But Nesta strode ahead again into the darkness. "No place good."

After another fitful rest, Azriel and Nesta were both still clearly pissed at Bryce. Rightly so, but wasn't she allowed to be pissed, too? They'd manipulated her every step of the way, watching her like some animal in a zoo, making her think she'd caused that cave-in when they'd engineered it themselves . . .

She shot Azriel a sidelong glare as they walked through the tunnel. He gave her a cool look in return.

Behind him, the carvings continued, showing Fae frolicking over hills and thriving in ancient-looking walled cities. A scene of growth and change. But Azriel's eyes slid ahead—and he nodded at where Nesta had stopped.

"We have a problem," Nesta murmured as they stepped up to her side.

A chasm stretched before them, Bryce's starlight glowing in a single ray straight across it. Bryce swallowed.

Yeah, they really fucking did.

Ruhn managed to keep his food down, and that was about all he could say for himself as he lay on the filthy, reeking floor and slept.

Maybe it was because he hadn't managed to truly sleep in days. Maybe it was because Athalar had asked him to do it, and he knew, deep down, that he needed to grow the fuck up. But here he was. On a familiar-looking mental bridge. Staring at a burning female figure.

Ruhn? Lidia's voice caught. *What happened?*

"I need to pass along intel." Each word was cold and clipped.

The flame around Lidia banked until it was nothing but her flowing golden hair, and it killed him. She was so fucking beautiful. It wouldn't have mattered to him, *hadn't* mattered to him during those weeks they'd gotten to know each other, but . . .

She kept ten feet away. He hadn't bothered with his stars and night. He didn't care.

"Bryce . . . was trying to go to Hel to ask for help. She didn't make it there."

Lidia's face was impassive. "How can you possibly know this?"

"The Prince of the Pit paid Hunt a visit. He confirmed that Bryce isn't with him—or his brothers."

To her credit, Lidia didn't balk at the mention of Apollion— she didn't even question why Hunt was in contact with him. "Where did she go?"

"We don't know. The plan was for her to head there to raise their armies and bring them back, but if she's not there, we're shit out of luck."

"Was there . . . was there a chance that Hel might have actually allied with you?" Disbelief laced every word.

"Yeah. There still is."

"Why tell me any of this?"

He clenched his jaw. "We weren't sure if you or Command had any suspicions about where Bryce went, or if you were hoping she'd carry out some sort of miracle when she got back here. But we figured you should know that doesn't seem like an option."

Lidia swore. She looked at her hands, as if she could see whatever plans Ophion might have had crumbling away. "We weren't counting on any assistance from your sister or Hel, but I'll pass along the warning nonetheless." Her eyes churned with worry. "Is she . . ."

Trust Day to get right to the heart of the matter.

"I don't know." His flat tone conveyed everything.

She angled her head, and he knew her well enough to know she was considering all he'd told her. The Oracle's warning.

But Lidia said, "She's not dead." Nothing but pure confidence filled her words.

"Oh yeah?" He couldn't keep his snide tone in check. "What makes you so sure?"

She took his nastiness in stride. "Rigelus has his mystics hunting for her. He wants her found."

"He doesn't know what I know."

"No—he knows *more* than you. He wouldn't waste the effort if he believed Bryce was dead. Or in Hel. He knows she's somewhere else."

Ruhn ignored the kernel of hope in his chest. "So what does it mean, then?"

"It means he thinks Bryce's location might make some difference." She crossed her arms. "It means wherever he suspects she might be . . . it has him worried."

"I don't see how it *could* make any difference."

"Then you underestimate your sister."

"Fuck you," he snapped.

"Rigelus isn't underestimating Bryce for one moment," she went on, tone sharpening. "One thousand mystics, Ruhn—all looking for her. Do you know how many tasks he usually has them doing? But they are all focused on finding her. That tells me he's very, very scared."

Ruhn swallowed hard. "What would happen if his mystics found her location?"

Lidia shook her head, flames twining through the strands. "I don't know. But he must have some plan in mind."

Ruhn asked, "Why can't they find her? I thought his mystics could find anything."

"The universe is vast. Even a thousand mystics need some time to comb every galaxy and star system."

"How much time?"

Her eyes simmered. "Not as much as Bryce likely needs—if she is indeed trying to do the impossible."

"Which is what?"

"Find help."

It was about as much as Ruhn could take. He turned back toward his end of the bridge. "Ruhn."

He halted, shuddering at the way she spoke his name, the memory of how it had felt to hear it the first time, after the equinox ball, when she'd learned who he was.

But that was the problem, wasn't it? She knew who he was . . . and he knew who *she* was. Knew that while she might be Agent Daybright, she'd been the Hind for decades before she'd decided to turn rebel. Had committed plenty of despicable acts for Sandriel and the Asteri long before she'd killed the Harpy to save his life. Did changing sides erase the stain?

She said quietly, "I'm doing what I can to help you."

Ruhn looked over a shoulder. She'd wrapped her arms around her middle. "I don't give a fuck what you're doing. I'm only here because other people's lives might depend on it."

Hurt flashed in her eyes, and it was kindling to his temper. How dare she look that way, look like *she* was hurt, when it was *his* fucking heart—

"You're dead to me," Ruhn hissed, and vanished.

16

Too narrow for me to fly," Azriel said, assessing the seemingly endless chasm between them and the rest of the tunnel. No bridge this time. Only a narrow, endless drop. Far too slim for Azriel to spread his wings. Far too wide for any of them to jump.

"Is this another manipulation?" Bryce asked Nesta coolly.

Nesta snorted. "The rock doesn't lie. He can't even spread his wings halfway."

To get this far and turn back with no answers, nothing to help her get home . . . The star still blazed ahead. Pointing to the tunnel across the chasm.

"No one's got any rope?" Bryce asked pathetically. She was met with incredulous silence. Bryce nodded to Azriel. "Those shadows of yours could take form—they caused that cave-in. Can't you, like, make a bridge or something? Or your blue light . . . you seemed to think it could have restrained the Wyrm. Make a rope with that."

His brows rose. "Neither of those things is remotely possible. The shadows are made of magic, just very condensed. These"—he motioned to the blue stones in his armor—"concentrate my power and allow me to craft it into things that resemble weapons. But they're still only magic—power."

Bryce's mouth twisted to the side. "So it's like a laser?" With the language now imprinted on her brain, her tongue stumbled over *laser* like it was truly the foreign word it was for them. She spoke it like she did in Midgard, but with the accent of this world layered over it, warping the word slightly.

"I don't know what that is," Azriel said, at the same time Nesta declared, "This still doesn't solve the issue of getting over there."

But Bryce frowned deeply at Azriel. "Do you ever use that power to, uh, charge people up?"

"Charge?"

"Fuel. Um. Give your power to someone else to help *their* power."

"Are you implying that I could do such a thing to you?"

"I'm pretty sure the concept of a battery won't have much meaning here, but yeah. My magic can be amplified by someone else's power." The other untranslatable word—*battery*—lay heavy on her tongue.

But Nesta looked her over. "For what purpose?"

"So I can teleport." Another word that didn't translate. "Winnow." She pointed to the other side of the divide. "I could winnow us over there."

Azriel said, "Give me a reason to believe you won't winnow out of here and leave us."

"I can't. You'll have to trust me."

"After what you just pulled?"

"Remember that I'll be trusting you not to blast a hole through my heart." She tapped the star. "Aim right there."

"I told you already: we don't want to kill you."

"Then aim carefully."

Azriel and Nesta exchanged a glance.

Bryce added, "Look, I'd offer you something in return if I could. But you literally took everything of value from me." She pointed to the sword at Azriel's back.

Nesta angled her head. Then reached into her pocket. "What about this?"

Her phone.

Her *phone*. With Nesta's movement, the lock screen came on, blaring bright in the gloom, with Hunt's face right there. His beautiful, wonderful face, so full of joy—

Azriel and Nesta were blinking at the bright light, the photo, and then the phone was gone, stashed in Nesta's pocket again.

"There's a portrait hidden inside its encasing," Nesta added. "Of you and three females."

The photo of Bryce, Danika, June, and Fury. She'd forgotten she'd put it in there before heading to Pangera. But there, in Nesta's pocket, shielded by those fancy-ass waterproofing spells she'd purchased, was her only link back to Midgard. To the people who mattered. And if she was stuck in this fucking world . . . that might very well be all she had left of her own.

"Were you waiting to dangle that in front of me?" Bryce asked.

A shrug from Nesta. "I guessed you might find it valuable."

"Who's to say I'm not playing you? Making you think it means something to me so I can leave you down here anyway?"

"Same reason you came running back to see if we were alive," Azriel said coolly.

Fine. She'd exposed herself with that one. So she said to Azriel, "Hit the star."

"How much power?"

Gods, this was potentially a really bad idea. Experimenting with power she didn't know or understand—

"A little. Just make sure you don't deep-fry me."

After the shit with the Wyrm, he'd probably like nothing more than to do exactly that. But Azriel's lips tugged upward. "I'll try my best."

Bryce braced herself, sucking in a deep breath—

Azriel struck before she could exhale. Searing, sharp power, a bolt of blue right into her star. Bryce bent over, coughing, breathing around the burn, the alien strangeness of the power.

"Are you all right?" Nesta asked with something like concern.

Was it his power? Or something about this world? Even Hunt's hadn't felt like this—so undiluted, like one-hundred-proof liquor.

Bryce closed her eyes and counted to ten, breathing hard. Letting it ease into her blood. Her bones. It tingled along her limbs.

Slowly, she straightened, opening her eyes. From the way the others' faces were illuminated, she knew her gaze had turned incandescent.

They tensed, reaching for their weapons, bracing for her to flee or attack. But Bryce extended her hands—now glowing white—to them.

Nesta took one first. Then Azriel's hand, battered and deeply scarred, slid around hers. Light leaked from where their skin met. She could have sworn his shadows hovered, watching like curious snakes.

Bryce pictured the tunnel mouth. She wanted to go there—

A blink, and it was done.

The raw power in her faded with the jump. Enough that the incandescence vanished and her skin returned to its normal state. Until only her star remained glowing once more.

But she found Azriel and Nesta observing her with different expressions than before. Wariness, yet something like respect, too.

"Let's go," Azriel said, and released her hand. Because the sword and dagger weren't merely tugging now. They were singing, and all she had to do was reach out for them—

But before she could give in to temptation, Azriel stalked into the dark.

Staying a few feet behind him still wasn't enough to block out the blades' song. But Bryce tried to ignore it, well aware of Nesta's watchful gaze. Tried to pretend that everything was totally fine.

Even if she knew that it wasn't. Not even close. And she had a feeling that whatever waited at the end of these tunnels would be way worse.

"The Cauldron," Nesta said hours later, pointing to yet another carving on the wall. It indeed showed a giant cauldron, perched atop what seemed to be a barren mountain peak with three stars above it.

Azriel halted, angling his head. "That's Ramiel." At Bryce's questioning look, he explained, "A mountain sacred to the Illyrians."

Bryce nodded to the carving. "What's the big deal about a cauldron?"

"*The* Cauldron," Azriel amended. Bryce shook her head, not understanding. "You don't have stories of it in your world? The Fae didn't bring that tradition with them?"

Bryce surveyed the giant cauldron. "No. We have five gods, but no cauldron. What does it do?"

"All life came and comes from it," Azriel said with something like reverence. "The Mother poured it into this world, and from it, life blossomed."

Nesta said quietly, "But it is also real—not a myth." Her swallow was audible. "I was turned High Fae when an enemy shoved me into it. It's raw power, but also . . . sentient."

"Like that mask you put on earlier."

Azriel folded his wings tightly, clearly wary of discussing such a powerful instrument with a potential enemy. But Nesta asked, "You detected a sentience in the Mask?"

Bryce nodded. "It didn't, like, talk to me or anything. I could just . . . sense it."

"What did it feel like?" Nesta asked quietly.

"Like death," Bryce breathed. "Like death incarnate."

Nesta's eyes grew distant, grave. "That's what the Mask can do. Give its wearer power over Death itself."

Bryce's blood chilled. "And this is a . . . normal type of weapon here?"

"No," Azriel said from ahead, shoulders tense. "It is not."

Nesta explained, "The Mask is one of three objects of catastrophic power, Made by the Cauldron itself. The Dread Trove, we call it."

"And the Mask is . . . yours?"

"I was also Made by the Cauldron," Nesta said, "which allows me to wield it." She spoke with no pride or boasting. Merely cold resignation and responsibility.

"Made," Bryce mused. "You said that my tattoo was Made."

"It is a mystery to us," Nesta said. "You'd need to have had the ink Made by the Cauldron, in this world, for it to be so."

The Horn had come from here. Had been brought by Theia

and Pelias into Midgard. Perhaps it, too, had been forged by the Cauldron.

Bryce tucked away the knowledge, the questions it raised. "We don't have anything like the Cauldron on Midgard. Solas is our sun god, Cthona his mate and the earth goddess. Luna is his sister, the moon; Ogenas, Cthona's jealous sister in the seas. And Urd guides all—she's the weaver of fate, of destiny." Bryce added after a moment, "I think she's the reason I'm here."

"Urd," Nesta murmured. "The Fae say the Cauldron holds our fates. Maybe it became this Urd."

"I don't know," Bryce said. "I always wondered what happened to the gods of the original worlds, when their people crossed into Midgard. Did they follow them? Did I bring Urd or Luna or any of them with me?" She gestured to the caves. "Are they here, or am I alone, stranded in your world with no gods to call my own?"

They began walking again, the questions hanging there unanswered.

Bryce asked, because some small part of her had to know after what she'd seen of the Mask, "When you die, where do your souls go?" Did they even believe in the concept of a soul? Maybe she should have led with that.

But Azriel said softly, "They return to the Mother, where they rest in joy within her heart until she finds another purpose for us. Another life or world to live in." He glanced sidelong at her. "What about your world?"

Bryce's gut twisted. "It's . . . complicated."

With nothing else to do as they walked, she explained it: the Bone Quarter and other Quiet Realms, the Under-King and the Sailings. The black boats tipping or making it to shore. The Death Marks that could purchase passage. And then she explained the secondlight, the meat grinder of souls that churned their lingering energy into more food for the Asteri.

Her companions were silent when she finished. Not with contemplation, but with horror.

"So that is what awaits you?" Nesta asked at last. "To become . . . food?"

"Not me," Bryce said quietly. "I, ah . . . I don't know what's coming for me."

"Why?" Azriel asked.

"That friend I mentioned—the one who learned the truth about the Asteri? When she died, I worried that she might not be given the honor of making it to shore during her Sailing. I . . . couldn't let her bear that final disrespect. I didn't know then about the second-light. So I bargained with the Under-King: my soul, my place in the Bone Quarter in exchange for hers." Again, that horrified quiet. "So when I die, I won't rest there. I don't know where I'll go."

"It has to be a relief," Nesta said, "to at least know you won't go to the Bone Quarter. To be harvested." She shuddered.

"Yeah," Bryce agreed. "But what's the alternative?"

"Do you still have a soul?" Nesta asked.

"Honestly? I don't know," Bryce admitted. "It feels like I do. But what will live on when I die?" She blew out a breath. "And if I were to die in this world . . . what would happen to my soul? Would it find its way back to Midgard, or linger here?" The words sounded even more depressing out loud.

Something glaringly bright blinded her—her phone. Hunt's face smiled up at her.

"Here," Nesta said. Bryce wordlessly took the phone, blinking back her tears at the sight of Hunt. "You kept your word and winnowed us. So take it."

Bryce knew it was for more than that, but she nodded her thanks all the same.

She flashed the screen at Nesta and Azriel. "That's Hunt," she said hoarsely. "My mate."

Azriel peered at the picture. "He has wings."

Bryce nodded, throat unbearably tight. "He's an angel—a malakh." But talking about him made the burning in her eyes worse, so she slid the phone into her pocket.

As they walked on, Nesta said, "When we stop again . . . can you show me how that contraption works?"

"The phone?" The word couldn't be translated into their language, and it sounded outright silly in their accent.

But Nesta nodded, her eyes fixed on the tunnel ahead. "Trying to figure out what it does has been driving us all crazy."

Tharion cornered the dragon in the pit's bathroom. He could barely stand on his left leg thanks to a gash he'd taken in his thigh from the claws of the jaguar shifter he'd faced as the lunchtime entertainment. No prime time for him tonight, though—not with Ithan in the pit.

"Do not fucking kill Holstrom," he warned Ariadne.

She tilted her head back, eyes flashing as they met his. "Oh? Who said I'm facing him?"

Tharion and the others had spent most of the last twenty-four hours debating who the Viper Queen would select to face Ithan. And now, with less than an hour left until the fight and no opponent announced . . . "Who else would the Vipe unleash on him? You're the only one here who's stronger. The only one worth a fight."

"So flattering."

"Don't kill him," Tharion snarled.

She batted her eyelashes. "Or what?"

Tharion clenched his teeth. "He's a good male, and a valuable one to a lot of people, and if you kill him, you'll be playing into the Vipe's hands. Make the fight fast, and make it as painless as you can."

Ari let out a cool laugh that belied the blazing heat in her eyes. "You don't give me orders."

"No, I don't," Tharion said. "But I'm giving you advice. You kill Ithan, you hurt him beyond repair, and you will have more enemies than you know what to do with. Starting with Tristan Flynn—who might seem like an irreverent idiot, but is fully capable of ripping you apart with his bare hands—and ending with me."

Ariadne let out a snort and tried to stride around him. Tharion gripped her by the arm, the claws at the tips of his fingers digging into her soft flesh. "I mean it."

"And what about me?" she sneered.

"What about you?"

"Are you warning Ithan Holstrom not to harm me?"

He blinked. "You're a *dragon*."

Another one of those humorless laughs. "I have a job to do. I swore oaths, too."

"Always looking out for number one."

She tried to pry her arm free, but he dug his fingers in further. She hissed, "I'm not a part of your little cabal, and I don't want to be. I don't give a shit about you, or whatever you're trying to pull against the Asteri. It's clearly going to get you all killed."

"Then what *do* you want, Ari? A life of *this*?"

Her skin heated, searing his palm, and he had no choice but to release her. She stalked toward the hall door that led to the eerily quiet pit. As the Viper Queen had promised, only she would watch.

Ariadne opened the door, but tossed over a shoulder, "Do you like your wolf cooked with barbecue sauce or gravy?"

"So a phone," Nesta said, overpronouncing the word as they crossed yet another small stream, hopping from stone to stone, "can take these *photographs* that capture a moment in time, but not the people in it?"

"Phones have cameras," Bryce answered, "and the camera is the thing that . . . yeah. It's like an instant drawing of the moment." Gods, so many words and terms from her own language to explain. She forged ahead. "But with all the details rendered perfectly. And don't ask me more than that, because I seriously have no idea how it actually works."

Nesta chuckled as she landed gracefully on the opposite bank. Azriel strode ahead into the dark, the carvings around him lit by Bryce's star: more war, more death, more suffering . . . this time on a larger scale, entire cities burning, people screaming in pain, devastation and grief on a whole new level. No paradise to counter the suffering. Just death.

Nesta paused on the stream bank to wait for Bryce to finish crossing. "And it also holds music. Like a Symphonia?"

"I don't know what that is, but yes, it holds music. I've got a few thousand songs on here."

"*Thousand?*" Nesta whirled as Bryce jumped from the last stone onto the bank, pebbles skittering from beneath her sneakers. "In that tiny thing? You recorded it all?"

"No—there's a whole industry of people whose job it is to record it, and again, I don't know how it works." Finding her footing, Bryce followed Azriel, now a hulking shadow silhouetted against the larger dark.

Nesta fell into step beside her. "And it's a way of talking mind-to-mind with other people."

"Sort of. It can connect to other people's phones, and your voices are linked in real time . . ."

"And let me guess: you don't know exactly how it works."

Bryce snorted. "Pathetic, but true. We take our tech and don't ask what the Hel makes it operate. I couldn't even tell you how the flash-light in the phone works." To demonstrate, she hit the button and the cave illuminated, the battle scenes and suffering on the walls around them even more stark. Azriel hissed from up ahead, whirling their way with his eyes shielded, and Bryce quickly turned it off.

Nesta smirked. "I'm surprised it can't cook you food and change your clothes, too."

"Give it a few years, and maybe it will."

"But you have magic to do these things?"

Bryce shrugged. "Yeah. Magic and tech kind of overlap in my world. But for those of us without much in the way of the former, tech really helps fill the gap."

"And that weaponry you showed us," Azriel said quietly, pausing his steps to let them catch up. "Those . . . guns."

"That's tech," Bryce said, "not magic. But some Vanir have found ways to combine magic and machine to deadly effect."

Their silence was heavy.

"We're here," Azriel said, motioning to the darkness ahead. The reason, it turned out, that he had halted.

A massive metal wall now blocked their way, thirty feet high and thirty feet wide at least, with a colossal eight-pointed star in its center.

The carvings continued straight up to it: battle and suffering, two females running on either side of the passage, as if running for this very wall . . . Indeed, around the star, an archway had been etched. Like this was the destination all along.

Bryce glanced back at Nesta. "Is this where you saw my star?"

Nesta slowly shook her head, eyeing the wall, the embossed star, the cave that surrounded them. "I don't know where this place is. What it is."

"Only one way to find out," Bryce said with a bravado she didn't feel, and approached the wall. Azriel, a live wire beside her, approached as well, a hand already on Truth-Teller.

The lowest spike of the star extended down, right in front of Bryce. So she laid a hand on the metal and pushed. It didn't budge.

Nesta stalked to Bryce's side, tapping a hand on the metal. A dull thud reverberated against the cave walls. "Did you really think it'd move?"

Bryce grimaced. "It was worth a shot."

Nesta opened her mouth to say something—to make fun of Bryce, probably—but was silenced by groaning metal. She staggered back a step. Azriel threw an arm in front of her, blue light wreathing his scarred hand.

Leaving Bryce alone before the door.

But she couldn't have moved if she'd wanted. Couldn't take her eyes away from the shifting wall.

The spikes of the star began to expand and contract, as if it were breathing. Metal clicked behind it, like gears shifting. Locks opening.

And in the lowest spike of the star, a triangle of a door slid open.

17

Only dry, ancient darkness waited beyond the star door. No sound or hint of life. Just more darkness. Older, somehow, than the tunnel behind them. Heavier. More watchful.

Like it was alive. And hungry.

Bryce stepped into it anyway.

"What is this place?" Bryce breathed, daring another step into the tunnel that lay on the door's other side. Azriel and Nesta quickly fell into step behind her.

A shriek of metal sliced through the air, and Bryce whirled—

Too late. Even Azriel, now mid-stride, hadn't been fast enough to stop the door from sliding shut. Its thud echoed through her feet, up her legs. Dust swirled.

They'd been sealed in.

Bryce's star flared . . . and went out.

A chill rippled up her arms, some primal instinct screaming at her to *run* without knowing why—

Light flared at Azriel's hand—faelight, he'd told her earlier. Two orbs of it drifted ahead, illuminating a short passageway. At its other end lay a vast, circular chamber, its floor carved with symbols and drawings akin to those on the walls of the tunnel.

Nesta whispered, voice breathy with fear, "*This* is the place I last saw the star on your chest." She drew Ataraxia, and the blade gleamed in the dimness. "We call it the Prison."

It was like game day, Ithan told himself. The same restlessness coursing through his body, the same razor-sharp focus settling into place.

Except there would be no ref. No rules. No one to call a time-out.

He stood at the edge of the empty ring in the center of the fighting pit, surrounded by his friends and Sigrid. The sprites, unable to stomach the violence, had opted to stay away.

There was no sign of the dragon.

He hadn't dared research how bad third-degree burns were. If he'd be in any shape to go help free Athalar and Ruhn. And the Helhound, apparently—what was that about?

Focus. Survive the fight, win, and they could be out of here tonight. He was good at winning. Or he had been, once upon a time.

"She'll try to distract you," Flynn said from beside him, staring at the empty ring. "But get around her flames, and I think you can take her."

"I thought you had the hots for the dragon," Declan muttered. "No pun intended."

"Not when she's about to toast my friend."

Ithan tried and failed to smile.

"Ari won't go easy on you," Tharion finally chimed in. He'd returned to the suite an hour ago, but he'd gone into his bedroom and shut the door. At least he'd come down for the fight.

"So he's supposed to—what, Ketos?" Flynn asked. "Stand there and be burned to a crisp?"

"I bet the Viper Queen would find that *highly* amusing," Declan said grimly.

Ithan, despite himself, finally smiled at that.

Tharion's face remained grave, though, as he said to Ithan,

"Odds are, Ari's going to hurt you. Badly. But she's arrogant—use it against her."

Ithan felt Sigrid's gaze on him, but he nodded at the mer. "Promise to wield that water magic of yours to douse the flames and I'll be fine."

Tharion was in no mood to joke, though. "Holstrom, I . . . Look, I said some shit earlier that I—" He shook his head. "If you can get me out of here, I'll make it count. It means a lot that you'd even try. That you care."

"We're a pack," Ithan said to Tharion, Flynn, and Dec. "It's what we do for each other." None of them contradicted it. His heart strained.

Tharion's eyes glimmered with emotion. "Thanks."

The double doors on the other side of the space creaked open to reveal the Viper Queen in a metallic gold jumpsuit and matching high-tops.

"She'll probably have Ari jump down from the rafters in a ball of flame," Tharion murmured as the snake shifter moved across the chamber with sinuous, unhurried grace. Ithan looked up, but the shadowed top of the ring remained empty as far as his wolf-sharp eyes could see.

The Viper Queen halted a few feet away and frowned at Ithan. "That's what you chose to wear?" He examined his T-shirt and jeans. The same ones he'd been wearing since arriving in this Hel-hole. But she nodded to Tharion. "You should have spruced him up a bit."

Tharion said nothing, his face like stone.

The Viper Queen turned, jumpsuit glimmering like molten gold, and strutted toward the nearest riser. She plunked herself down and waved an elegant hand to Ithan. "Begin."

Ithan glanced to the empty ring. "Where's the dragon?"

The Viper Queen pulled out her phone and typed into it, the screen casting her already pale face in an unearthly pallor. "Ariadne? Oh, she's no longer in my employ."

"*What?*" Tharion and Flynn blurted at the same time.

The Viper Queen didn't look up from her phone, thumbs flying.

The light bounced off her long nails, also painted a metallic gold. "An offer too good to refuse came in an hour ago."

"She's not your slave," Tharion snapped, face more livid than Ithan had ever seen. "You don't fucking own her."

"No," the Viper Queen agreed, typing away, "but the arrangement was . . . advantageous to us both. She agreed." She at last lifted her head. Nothing remotely kind lay within her green eyes as she surveyed Tharion. "If you ask me, I think she said yes in order to avoid having to toast Holstrom to a crisp. I wonder who might have made her feel bad about that?"

They all turned to the mer, who gaped at the Viper Queen.

"Of course," the Vipe went on, typing again on her phone, "I didn't inform her new employer that the dragon's a softhearted worm. But given her new surroundings, I think she'll harden up quickly." The *swish* of a message being sent punctuated her words.

Tharion looked like he was going to be sick. Ithan didn't blame him.

But Ithan willed himself to focus, his breathing to steady. She wanted him off-balance. Wanted him reeling. He squared his shoulders. "So who am I fighting, then?"

The Viper Queen slid her phone into her pocket and smiled, revealing those too-white teeth.

"The Fendyr heir, of course."

"We should get Rhys."

"We'd have to hike up through the mountain, climb down past the wards, then hope we're not too far to reach him mind-to-mind."

Bryce listened to Azriel and Nesta quietly argue, content to let them debate while she took in the chamber.

"This place is lethal," Azriel insisted gravely. "The wards in there are sticky as tar."

"Yes," Nesta admitted, "but we've come all this way, so let's see why we've been dragged here."

"Why *she's* been dragged here—by that star." They both turned toward her at last, expressions taut.

Bryce composed her own face into the portrait of innocence as she asked, "What *is* the Prison?"

Nesta's lips pursed for a heartbeat before she said, "A misty island off the coast of our lands." She glanced at Azriel and mused, "Do you think we somehow walked beneath the ocean?"

Azriel slowly shook his head, his dark hair shining in the faelights bobbing overhead. "There's no way we walked that far. The door must have been a portal of some sort, moving us from the mainland out here."

Nesta's brows lifted. "How is that possible?"

"There are caves and doors throughout the land," Azriel said, "that open into distant places. Maybe that was one of them." His gaze flicked to Bryce, noting how closely she was listening to all that, and said, "Let's go in."

He took Bryce's hand in his broad, callused one, pulling her toward the chamber beyond.

His face was a mask of cold determination in the light of the golden orbs floating over them, his hazel eyes darting around to monitor the gloom.

This close to him, hand in hand, she could feel the sword and dagger again thrumming and pulsing. They throbbed against her eardrums—

The hilt of the Starsword shifted in her direction—she could have reached out and touched it with her other hand. One movement, and its hilt would be in her grip.

Azriel shot her a warning look.

Bryce kept her face bland, bored. Had his glance been to warn her to be careful for her own safety, or for her not to make one wrong move?

Maybe both.

Too soon, too quickly, they neared the entrance to the large, round chamber at the end of the short passage. The faelight danced over carvings etched and embossed onto the stone floor, as ornate and detailed as those in the tunnels leading here. The entire floor of the chamber was covered with them.

But between her and that room hung a sense of foreboding, of heaviness, of *keep the fuck out.*

Even the sword and dagger seemed to go quiet. Her star remained extinguished. Like their task was done. They'd arrived at the place they'd been compelled to bring her.

Bryce sucked in a breath. "I'm going in. Keep a step back," she warned Azriel.

"And miss the fun?" Azriel muttered. Nesta chuckled behind them.

"I mean it," Bryce said, trying to tug her hand from his. "You stay here."

His fingers tightened on hers, not letting go. "What do you sense?"

"Wards," Bryce replied, again scanning the arena-sized cavern ahead. And there, right in the center of the space . . .

Another eight-pointed star.

It must have been the one Nesta had seen before. As if in answer, the star on Bryce's chest flared, then dimmed.

Nesta stepped up beside them, pointing. "The Harp sat atop that star."

"Harp?" Bryce asked, not missing the glare that Azriel directed at Nesta. But Nesta's eyes remained on the star as she said, more to herself than to them, "It was held there by those wards."

Azriel scanned the chamber, still not letting go of Bryce's hand as he said to Nesta, "We don't know what else might be kept at bay in here."

"I didn't sense anything except the Harp last time," Nesta replied, but she still assessed the chamber with a warrior's focus.

"We also didn't sense that there was a second entrance into this place," Azriel countered. "We can assume nothing right now."

Bryce fingered the Archesian amulet around her neck. It had protected her at the gallery . . . had allowed her to walk through Jesiba's grade A wards . . .

There had to be an answer here, somewhere. About something. Anything.

Bryce's fingers tightened around the amulet. Then she looked over Azriel's shoulder, and her eyes widened. "Watch out!"

He dropped her hand instantly, whirling to the unseen, unsensed opponent.

The nonexistent opponent.

Bryce moved with Fae swiftness, and by the time Azriel realized there was nothing there, she'd already crossed the ward line.

Cold fury tightened his features, but Nesta was smirking with something like approval.

"You're on your own now," Azriel said, blue stones glimmering at his hands with a cold fury that matched his expression.

Bryce's brows lifted, walking backward a few steps. "You really can't get through?"

He crouched to trace a scarred hand along the stone floor, anger fading in the face of his curiosity. "No." He peered up at Bryce, mouth twisting to the side. "I don't know whether to be impressed or worried." He rose and jerked his chin at Nesta. "You going in?"

Nesta crossed her arms and remained at his side. "Let's see what happens first."

Bryce scowled. "Thanks."

Nesta didn't smile. She only urged, "Be quick. Look around, but don't linger."

Bryce tried, "I'd feel better if I had my sword."

Azriel said nothing, face impassive. Fine. Sighing, Bryce surveyed the carvings on the floor. Whorls and faces and—

The hair on her arms rose.

"These are Midgard's constellations." Bryce pointed to a cluster. "That's the Great Ladle. And that . . . that's Orion. The hunter."

Hunt. Her Hunt.

Her companions, the tunnels, the world faded away as she traced the stars, plotting their path. The Archesian amulet warmed against her skin, as if working to clear the wards around her.

"The Archer," she breathed. "The Scorpion and the Fish . . . This is a map of *my* cosmos." Her boot knocked against a raised half-orb, a screaming face carved into it. "Siph." The outermost planet. She went to the next, a similar mound with a grave male face. "Orestes."

"Orestes?" Azriel asked sharply, drawing her attention back to where he and Nesta still stood at the tunnel archway. "The warrior?"

She blinked. "Yes."

"Interesting," Nesta said, head angling. "Perhaps the name came from the same source."

Bryce indicated the next mound, the face of a bearded old man. "Oden." The next, closer to the center of the room, was a young, laughing male. "Lakos." Another mound rose on the other side of the star, massive and helmeted. "Thurr," she said. Then she pointed to a mound with a female head. "Farya." And beyond Farya, a large, raised mound with snaking tendrils. "Sol," she whispered, indicating the sun-shaped thing.

She scanned the room again and turned to the eight-pointed star. Directly between Lakos and Thurr. "Midgard." The name seemed to echo in the chamber. "Someone went to an awful lot of trouble to make this floor. Someone who'd been to my world and then came back here." Bryce glanced over a shoulder to Nesta, the warrior's face unreadable. "You said there was a harp on the eight-pointed star?" A shallow nod. "What kind of harp? Was it special in any way?"

"It can move its player between physical places," Nesta said, a shade too quickly.

"What else?" Bryce asked, and her chest glowed again.

Azriel lifted a hand toward Nesta, as if he'd cover her mouth to shut her up, but she said, "The Harp is Made. It can stop time itself."

"It stops *time*?" Bryce's knees wobbled.

She could think of only one group of people in her own world who'd be able to create stuff like that. Who, if they had indeed Made such objects, had a really good reason for wanting to get back into this world. To claim them.

"Was there ever," Bryce ventured, a sudden hunch taking form in her mind, "a Made object called the Horn?"

"I don't know," Nesta said. "Why?"

Bryce gazed at the eight-pointed star, the very heart of this chamber, of this map of the cosmos. "Someone put your Harp there for a reason."

"To keep it hidden," Azriel said.

"No," Bryce said quietly, facing the star fully, her free hand drifting to touch the matching scar on her chest.

It had led her all the way here. To this exact spot, where the Harp had been.

"It was left for someone like me."

"What do you mean?" Nesta demanded, voice bouncing off the rock.

But Bryce went on, the words tumbling out of her faster than she could sort them, "I think . . . I think all those carvings in the tunnels might be to remind us of what happened." She pointed to where they stood, the passage behind them. "The carvings tell a story. And they're an invitation to come *here*."

"Why?" Azriel asked with that lethal softness.

Bryce stared at the eight-pointed star for a moment before she said, "To find the truth."

"Bryce," Nesta cautioned, as if reading her thoughts.

Bryce didn't so much as look back as she stepped onto the star.

18

Hunt coughed, seeing stars with every heave as he sprayed blood.

"Fuck, Athalar," Baxian grunted from where he hung on the other side of Danaan, though he wasn't much better.

They'd had all of a few hours on the floor before Pollux had returned and hauled them back up. Hunt hadn't been able to stop screaming as his shoulders dislocated again.

But Pollux had been called away somewhere, and apparently there was no one else in the palace suitably fucked up to torture them, so they'd been left here.

Bryce. Her name came and went with his wet, rasping breaths. He'd wanted so many things with her. A normal, happy life. Children.

Gods, how many times had he thought about her beautiful face as it would look when she held their little winged children? They'd have their mother's hair and temper, and his gray wings, and occasionally, he'd catch a glimpse of his own mother's smile on their cherubic faces.

The last time he'd been in these dungeons, he'd had no visions of the future to cling to. Shahar had been dead, most of the Fallen with her, and all his dreams with them. But maybe this was worse. To have come *so* close to those dreams, to be able to see them so vividly, to know Bryce was out there . . . and he was not.

Hunt shoved aside the thoughts, the pain that ached worse than his shoulders, his breaking body, and grunted, "Danaan. You're up."

The Hammer's early departure today had left an opening. Everything else, what Apollion and Aidas had implied, that shit about his father and the black crown—the halo—on him . . . it was all secondary.

All his failures on Mount Hermon, the Fallen who'd died, losing Shahar, being enslaved . . . Secondary.

All the repeated failures these past few months, leading them toward disaster, toward this . . . Secondary.

If this was their one shot, he'd put it all behind him. He had been alone the last time. Seven years down here, alone. Only the screams of his fellow tortured Fallen in other chambers to keep him company, to remind him hourly of his failures. Then the two years in Ramuel's dungeons. Nine years alone.

He wouldn't let the two friends beside him endure it.

"Do it now, Danaan," Hunt urged Ruhn.

"Give me . . . a moment," Ruhn panted.

Fuck, the prince had to be in bad shape to have even asked that. Proud bastard.

"Take a few," Hunt said, gentle but firm, even as guilt twisted his gut. To his credit, Ruhn took only a minute, then the creaking of his chains began again.

"Keep it quiet," Baxian warned as Ruhn swayed his body back and forth, swinging his weight. Aiming for the rack of weapons and devices just beyond the reach of his feet.

"Too . . . far," Ruhn said, legs straining toward the rack. Trying to grab the iron poker that, if the prince's abs held out, he could curl upward and position with his feet, nestling it inside the chain links—and twist it until they hopefully snapped free.

It was a long shot—but any shot was worth a try.

"Here," Hunt said, and lifted himself up on his screaming shoulders, feet out. Blocking out the agony, breathing through it, Hunt kicked as Ruhn collided with him. The prince muffled a cry of pain, but arced farther this time, closer to the rack.

"You got this," Baxian murmured.

Ruhn swung back, and Hunt kicked him again, eyes watering at what the movement did to every part of his body.

The rack was still too far. Another few inches and Ruhn's feet could grab the handle of the iron poker, but those inches were insurmountable.

"Stop," Hunt ordered, breathing hard. "We need a new plan."

"I can reach it," Ruhn growled.

"You can't. Not a chance."

Ruhn's swinging came to a gradual halt. And in silence, they hung there, chains clanking. Then Ruhn said, "How strong is your bite, Athalar?"

Hunt stilled. "What the fuck do you mean?"

"If I . . . swing into you . . . ," Ruhn said, gasping. "Can you bite off my hand?"

Shock fired through Hunt like a bullet. From the other side of Ruhn, Baxian protested, *"What?"*

"I'd have more range," Ruhn said, voice eerily calm.

"I'm not biting off your fucking hand," Hunt managed to say.

"It's the only way I'll reach it. It'll grow back."

"This is insane," Baxian said.

Ruhn nodded to Hunt. "We need you to be the Umbra Mortis. He's a badass—he wouldn't hesitate."

"A badass," Hunt said, "not a cannibal."

"Desperate times," Ruhn said, meeting Hunt's stare.

Determination and focus filled the prince's face. Not one trace of doubt or fear.

Pollux probably wouldn't return until morning. It might work.

And the guilt already weighing on Hunt, on his shredded soul . . . What difference would this make, in the end? One more burden for his heart to bear. It was the least he could offer, after all he'd done. After he'd led them into this unmitigated disaster.

Hunt's chin dipped.

"Athalar," Baxian cut in roughly. *"Athalar."*

Hunt dragged his eyes to the Helhound, expecting disgust and dismay. But he found only intense focus as Baxian said, "I'll do it."

Hunt shook his head. Though Baxian could probably reach if Ruhn stretched toward him—

"I'll do it," Baxian insisted. "I've got sharper teeth." It was a lie. Perhaps his teeth were sharper in his Helhound form, but—

"I don't care who fucking does it," Ruhn snarled. "Just do it before I change my mind."

Hunt scanned Baxian's face again. Found only calm—and sorrow. Baxian said softly, "Let me shoulder this burden. You can get the next one."

The Helhound had been Hunt's enemy at Sandriel's fortress for so many years. Where had that male gone? Had he ever existed, or had it been a mask all along? Why had Baxian even fallen in with Sandriel in the first place?

Maybe it didn't matter now. Hunt nodded to Baxian in acceptance and thanks. "You were a worthy mate to Danika," he said.

Pain and love flooded Baxian's eyes. Perhaps the words had touched on a wound, a doubt that had long plagued him.

Hunt's heart strained. He knew the feeling.

But Baxian jerked his chin at Ruhn, holding the prince's stare with the unflinching determination he'd been known for as one of Sandriel's triarii.

Here was the male Hunt had tangled with back then—to devastating results. Including that snaking scar down Baxian's neck, courtesy of Hunt's lightning.

"Get ready," Baxian said quietly to Ruhn. "You can't scream."

With the excuse of her cycle, Lidia found a shred of privacy to think through her plan, to fret over whether it would work, to pace her room and debate whether she'd put her trust in the right people.

Trust was a foreign concept to her—even before she'd turned into Agent Daybright. Her father had certainly never instilled such a thing in her. And after her mother had sent her away at age three, right into the arms of that monstrous man . . . Trust didn't exist in her world.

But right now, she had no choice but to rely on it.

Lidia had just changed her tampon and washed her hands when Pollux strutted into the bathroom.

"Good news," he announced, flashing a dazzling smile. He seemed lighter on his feet than he had since Quinlan had escaped.

She leaned against the bathroom door, inspecting her immaculate uniform. "Oh?"

"I'm surprised you didn't hear it from Rigelus first." Pollux stripped off his bloodied shirt.

Ruhn's blood clung to him, its scent screaming through the room. Ruhn's *blood*—

Muscles rippling under his golden skin, Pollux stalked to the shower, where untold gallons of blood had washed away from his body. A wild sort of excitement seemed to pulse from him as he cranked on the water.

"Rigelus and the others were able to fix the Harpy."

At first, nothing happened as Bryce stood atop the eight-pointed star.

"Well—" Nesta began.

Light flared from the star at Bryce's feet, from her chest, merging and blending, and then a hologram of a dark-haired young female—High Fae—appeared. As if she were addressing an audience.

Bryce knew that heart-shaped face. The long hair.

"Silene," Bryce murmured.

"From the carving?" Nesta asked, and as Bryce glanced to her, the warrior stepped through the wards as if they were nothing. Like she could have done so all along. Azriel didn't try to stop her, but remained standing inside the tunnel mouth. "At the beginning of the tunnels," Nesta said, "there was that carving of a young female . . . you said her name was Silene."

"The carving's an exact likeness," Bryce said, nodding. "But who is she?"

Azriel said softly, voice tinged with pain, "She looks like Rhysand's sister."

Nesta peered back at him with something like curiosity and sympathy. Bryce might have asked what the connection meant, but the hologram spoke.

"My story begins before I was born." The female's voice was heavy—weary. Tired and sad. "During a time I know of only from my mother's stories, my father's memories." She lifted a finger to the space between her brows. "Both of them showed me once, mind-to-mind. So I shall show you."

"Careful," Azriel warned, but too late. Silene's face faded, and mist swirled where she'd stood. It glowed, casting light upon Nesta's shocked face as she came to a stop beside Bryce.

Bryce swapped a look with the female. "First sign of trouble," Nesta said under her breath, "and we run."

Bryce nodded. She could agree to that much. Then Silene's voice spoke from the fog. And any promise of running faded from Bryce's mind.

We were slaves to the Daglan. For five thousand years, our people—the High Fae—knelt before them. They were cruel, powerful, cunning. Any attempt at rebellion was quashed before forces could be rallied. Generations of my ancestors tried. All failed.

The fog cleared at last.

And in its wake spread a field of corpses under a gray sky, the twin to the one carved miles behind in the tunnels: crucifixes, beasts, blood eagles—

The Daglan ruled over the High Fae. And we, in turn, ruled the humans, along with the lands the Daglan allowed us to govern. Yet it was an illusion of power. We knew who our true masters were. We were forced to make the Tithe to them once a year. To offer up kernels of our power in tribute. To fuel their own power—and to limit our own.

Bryce's breath caught in her throat as an image of a Fae female kneeling at the foot of a throne appeared, a seed of light in her upheld hands. Smooth, delicate fingers closed around the Fae female's droplet of power. It flickered, illumining pale skin.

The hand that had claimed the power lifted, and Bryce stilled as the memory zoomed out to reveal the hand's bearer: a black-haired, white-skinned Asteri.

There was no mistaking the cold, otherworldly eyes. She lounged in golden robes, a crown of stars upon her head. Her red lips pulled back in a cold smile as her hand closed tightly around the seed of power.

It faded into nothing, absorbed into the Asteri's body.

The Daglan became arrogant as the millennia passed, sure of their unending dominion over our world. But their overconfidence eventually blinded them to the enemies amassing at their backs, a force like none that had been gathered before.

Bryce's breath remained caught in her throat, Nesta still as death at her side, as the scene shifted to show a golden-haired High Fae female standing a step behind the Asteri's throne. Her chin was lifted, her face as cold as her mistress's.

My mother served at that monster's side for a century, a slave to her every sick whim.

Bryce knew who it was before Silene spoke again. Knew whose truth she'd been led here, across the stars, to learn at last.

Theia.

19

Lidia froze at Pollux's words as he stepped into the steaming spray of the shower. "What do you mean they've fixed the Harpy?"

The Hammer said over the noise of the water, tipping back his head to soak his golden hair, "They've been working on her as a pet project of sorts—Rigelus just told me. Apparently, it's looking good."

"*What* is looking good?" Lidia asked, using all her training to keep her heartbeat calm.

"That she'll wake up. Rigelus needs one more thing." Pollux opened the shower door and reached out a hand for her. An order more than an invitation.

With fingers that felt far away, Lidia unbuttoned her uniform. "What about my cycle?" she asked, as coyly as she could stomach.

"Water will wash the blood away," Pollux said, and she hated the weight of his eyes on her as she stripped. Stepping in, she winced at the burning heat of the water. Pollux only tugged her to his naked body, his erection already pressing into her.

"When will the Harpy wake up?" Lidia asked as Pollux's mouth found her throat and he bit deeply enough for her to wince again.

If the Harpy returned and spoke of what she'd seen, of who had really killed her . . .

None of Lidia's plans, however well laid, would matter.

Pollux's hand slid to her ass, cupping and squeezing. He nipped her ear, wholly unaware of the dread creeping through her as he said against her wet skin, "Soon." Another squeeze, harder this time. "Another day or two and we'll have her back."

The Viper Queen's announcement might as well have been a brimstone missile dropped into the room.

Tharion looked between Ithan, Sigrid, and the snake shifter. The Fendyr heir was staring at the female, face pale with shock.

The Viper Queen drawled to her, "What was it you said to me? That I was no better than the Astronomer?" She waved a manicured hand toward the ring, gold nails glinting. "Well, here's a shot to free yourself. I believe that's more than he ever offered you."

"I'm not fighting Sigrid," Ithan snarled, bristling.

"Then you and your friends will stay here," the Viper Queen said, leaning back on her hands. "And whatever urgent rescue mission you want to stage for your other friends will fail."

This bitch knew everything.

"Let me fight Holstrom," Tharion snapped.

"No," the Viper Queen said with sweet venom. "Holstrom and the girl go into the ring, or the deal's off."

"You fucking—" Flynn started.

"I'll do it," Sigrid said, fingers curling into fists at her sides.

They all turned to the Fendyr heir. Ithan's face twisted, a portrait of anguish.

Tharion noted that pain, and wished he'd never been born. His choices had led them here. His fuckups.

"Good," the Viper Queen said to Sigrid, who bared her teeth at the snake. But the ruler of the Meat Market gave the wolf a serpent's smile. "Looks like it might be your last night on Midgard. Maybe you should have gotten that wardrobe upgrade after all."

* * *

Bryce stared at the hard-faced, beautiful female who could have rivaled the Hind for sheer badassery and beauty. Theia.

Silene's next words only confirmed how alike the ancient Fae Queen and the Hind were:

But my mother, Theia, used the time she served the Daglan to learn all she could about their instruments of conquest. The Dread Trove, we called it in secret. The Mask, the Harp, the Crown, and the Horn.

From the corner of her vision, Bryce spied Nesta glancing her way at the last word.

The Horn had been sister to the Mask, and the Harp Nesta had mentioned. It had come from *here*, and worse, was part of some deadly arsenal of the Asteri—

And Theia.

The carving in the tunnel of the crowned, masked queen—Theia—flashed in Bryce's memory. She'd been holding two instruments: a horn and a harp.

The Daglan, Silene went on, *always quarreled over who should control the Trove, so more often than not, the Trove went unused. It was their downfall.*

Was this it, then? Why she'd been sent to this world? To learn about this Trove—that it might possibly be the thing to destroy the Asteri? But Bryce could only watch as the vision showed Theia's hands snatching the objects from black pedestals. Spiriting them away from the subterranean mountain holds where they were kept, using cave archways to move swiftly across the lands.

Caves like this one. Capable of moving people great distances in a matter of hours. Or an instant.

Snow drifted across the image, and then Theia was standing atop a mountain, a black monolith rising behind her.

"Ramiel," Azriel whispered from behind them, from beyond the wards.

Theia embraced a handsome, broad-shouldered man amid the swirling snow.

My mother and father, Fionn, had kept their love a secret through the years, knowing the Daglan would find it amusing to tear them apart if they learned of the affair. But they were able to meet in secret—and to plan their uprising.

"Fionn . . . ," Azriel murmured, awe lacing his voice, "was your ancestor."

Nesta turned from the vision, frowning toward Azriel. "You might as well come in," she muttered, and pointed. Silver flame rippled in a straight line, spearing for Azriel. He didn't flinch away, only tucking in his wings tightly as streams of smoke filtered up from the floor.

A path through the wards. The spells shimmered against the flames, as if trying to close in on the road she'd made, but Nesta's power held them at bay.

Azriel inclined his head to Nesta as he stepped through that slender passage lined with silver flames, not one ounce of fear on his beautiful face. Only when Azriel had passed through did Nesta release her power, the wards slamming back into place in a shimmering rush, like a wave washing over the shore.

Bryce pointed to the hologram—to the golden-haired Fae male. "Who is he?" she asked quietly. There had never been any mention of Fionn in the histories of Midgard, the lore.

"The first and last High King of these lands," Azriel breathed.

Before Bryce could contemplate this further, Silene went on, *But my mother and father knew they needed the most valuable of all the Daglan's weapons.*

Bryce tensed. This *had* to be the thing that had given them the edge—

The snows around Ramiel parted, revealing a massive bowl of iron at the foot of the monolith. Even through the vision, its presence leaked into the world, a heavy, ominous thing.

"The Cauldron," Nesta said, dread lacing her voice.

Not a useful weapon, then. Bryce braced herself as Silene continued.

The Cauldron was of our world, our heritage. But upon arriving here, the Daglan captured it and used their powers to warp it. To turn it from what it had been into something deadlier. No longer just a tool of creation, but of destruction. And the horrors it produced . . . those, too, my parents would turn to their advantage.

Another shift of memory, and Fionn pulled a long blade from the Cauldron, dripping water. A black blade, whose dark metal absorbed any trace of light around it. Bryce's knees weakened.

The Starsword.

Two other figures stood there, veiled in the thick snow, but Bryce hardly got a chance to wonder about them before Silene's narration began anew.

They fought the Daglan and won, she went on. *Using the Daglan's own weapons, they destroyed them. Yet my parents did not think to learn the Daglan's other secrets—they were too weary, too eager to leave the past behind.*

"Wait," Bryce cut in. "How did they use those weapons?" Nesta and Azriel cast wary looks her way. "How the fuck did they use them? And what other secrets—"

But Silene kept speaking, history unspooling from her lips.

My father became High King, and my mother his queen, yet this island on which you stand, this place . . . my mother claimed it for herself. The very island where she had once served as a slave became her domain, her sanctuary. The Daglan female who'd ruled it before her had chosen it for its natural defensive location, the mists that kept it veiled from the others. So, too, did my mother. But more than that, she told me many times that she and her heirs were the only ones worthy of tending this island.

Nesta murmured to Azriel, "The Prison was once a royal territory?"

Bryce didn't care—and Azriel didn't reply. Silene had glossed over how Theia and Fionn had used the Trove and Cauldron against the Asteri, and why the Hel had she come to this planet if not to learn about that?

Yet once again, Silene's memory plowed forward.

And with the Daglan gone, as the centuries passed, as the Tithe was no longer demanded of us or the land, our powers strengthened. The land strengthened. It returned to what it had been before the Daglan's arrival millennia before. We returned to what we'd been before that time, too, creatures whose very magic was tied to this land. Thus the land's powers became my mother's. Dusk, twilight—that's what the island was in its long-buried heart, what her power bloomed into, the lands rising with it. It was, as she said, as if the island had a soul that now blossomed under her care, nurtured by the court she built here.

Islands, like those they'd seen in the carvings, rose up from the sea, lush and fertile.

Bryce couldn't take her gaze off the wondrous sight, even as Silene continued. *After centuries with an empty womb, my mother bore both my sister and me within a span of five years. My father was fading by then—he was centuries older than my mother. But Fionn did not consider my mother a worthy successor. The crown should go to the eldest child, he said—to my sister, Helena. It was time, he thought, for a new generation to lead.*

It did not sit well with my mother, or with many of those in her court—especially her general, Pelias. He agreed with my mother that Helena was too young to inherit our father's throne. But my mother was still in her prime. Still ripe with power, and it was clear that she'd been blessed by the gods themselves, since she had been gifted children at long last.

So it was just as it had been before: those behind the throne worked to upend it.

The image shifted to some sort of marsh—a bog. Fionn rode a horse between the islands of grass, bow at the ready as he ducked beneath trees in bloom.

My parents often went hunting in the vast slice of land the Daglan had kept for their private game park, where they had crafted terrible monsters to serve as worthy prey. It was there that he met his death.

A dark-haired, pale creature that could have been the relative of the nøkk in Jesiba's gallery dragged a bound and gagged Fionn into the inky depths of the bog, the once-proud king screaming as he went under.

Horror rooted Bryce to the spot.

Theia and Pelias stood at the water's edge, faces impassive.

Petals began falling from the trees. Leaves with them. Birds took flight. As if sudden winter gripped the bog. As if the land had died with its king.

Then the Starsword was thrust from the center of the pool,

sparkling in the gray light. A heartbeat later, a scaled hand lifted a dagger—Truth-Teller. Debris or a gift from the creature, Bryce could only guess as they sparkled in the grayish light, dripping water. It didn't matter—in the face of such treachery and brutality, who fucking cared?

My father had never shown himself to be giving—long had he kept Gwydion and never once offered it to my mother. The dagger that had belonged to his dear friend, slain during the war, hung at his side, unused. But not for long.

Theia extended her hands toward the water, the offered blades. And on phantom wings, sword and dagger soared for her. Summoned to her hands.

Starlight flared from Theia as she snatched the sword and knife out of the air, the blades glowing with their own starlight.

My mother returned that day with only Pelias and my father's blades. As she had helped Make them, they answered to the call in her blood. To her very power.

Bryce knew that call. Had been hearing it since she arrived in this world. A chill rippled down her spine.

And then she took the Trove for herself.

Theia sat, enthroned, the Harp and Horn beside her, the Mask in her lap, and the Crown atop her head.

Unchecked, limitless power sat upon that throne. Bryce could barely get a breath down.

The Theia who Aidas had spoken so highly of . . . she was a murdering *tyrant*?

As if in answer, Silene said, *Our people bowed—what other option did they have in the face of such power? And for a short span, she ruled. I cannot say whether the years were kind to my people—but there was no war. At least there was that.*

"Yeah," Bryce seethed, more to Silene than the others, "at least you guys had that."

My sister and I grew older. My mother educated us herself, always reminding us that though the Daglan had been vanquished, evil lived on. Evil lurked beneath our very feet, always waiting to devour us. I believe she told us this in order to keep us honest and true, certainly more than she had ever been. Yet as we aged and grew into our power, it became clear that only one throne could be inherited. I loved Helena more than anything. Should she have wanted the throne, it was hers. But she had as little interest in it as I did.

It was not enough for my mother. Possessing all she had ever wanted was not enough.

"Classic stage mom," Bryce muttered.

My mother remembered the talk of the Daglan—their mention of other worlds. Places they had conquered. And with two daughters and one throne . . . only entire worlds would do for us. For her legacy.

Bryce shook her head again. She knew where this was going.

Remembering the teachings of her former mistress, my mother knew she might wield the Horn and Harp to open a door. To bring the Fae to new heights, new wealth and prestige.

Bryce rolled her eyes. Same corrupt, delusional Fae rulers, different millennium.

Yet when she announced her vision to her court, many of them refused. They had just overthrown their conquerors—now they would turn conqueror, too? They demanded that she shut the door and leave this madness behind her.

But she would not be deterred. There were enough Fae throughout her lands, along with some of the fire-wielders from the south, who supported the idea, merchants who salivated at the thought of untapped riches in other worlds. And so she gathered a force.

It was Pelias who told her where to cast her intention. Using old, notated star maps from their former masters, he'd selected a world for them.

Bryce's gut churned. The Asteri must have kept archives and records on this world, too. Exactly like the room Bryce had found in the palace, full of notes on conquered planets. *Dusk,* they'd labeled the room—as if out of all the worlds mentioned within, *this* world remained their focus. This place.

Pelias told her it was a world the Daglan had long coveted but had not had the chance to conquer. An empty world, but one of plenty.

She had no way of knowing that he had spent our era of peace learning ancient summoning magic and searching the cosmos for whatever remained of the Daglan on other worlds. What he wanted from them, I can only guess—perhaps he knew that to wrest the Trove from Theia and seize power for himself, he needed someone more powerful than he was.

"You idiot," Bryce spat at the image of Pelias and Theia hovering over a table full of star charts. "Both of you: fucking idiots."

And after all that searching, someone finally answered. A Daglan who had been using his army of mystics to scour galaxies for our world. The Daglan promised him every reward, if only he could nudge my mother toward this moment, to use the Dread Trove to open a portal to the world he indicated.

A step beside her, Nesta clicked her tongue in disgust.

My mother did not question Pelias, her conspirator and ally, when he told her to will the Horn and Harp to open a doorway to this world. She did not question how and why he knew that this island, our misty home, was the best place to do it. She simply gathered our people, all those willing to conquer and colonize—and opened the doorway.

In a chamber—*this* chamber, if the eight-pointed star on the floor was any indication, though the celestial carvings had not yet been added—beside red-haired Fae who looked alarmingly like Bryce's father, Helena and Silene appeared, grown and beautiful, and yet still young—gangly. Teenagers.

In the center of the chamber, a gate opened into a land of green and sunshine. And standing there among the greenery, waiting for them . . .

"Oh fuck." Bryce's mouth dried out. "Rigelus."

The teenage Fae boy, appearing no older than Helena and Silene, smiled at Theia. Raised a hand in greeting.

My mother did not recognize the enemy when they wore a friendly face, beckoning her and the others through the portal. Had she any hesitations upon finding that the empty world she'd been promised was indeed populated, they were calmed when the strangers claimed to be Fae as well, long separated from our world by the Daglan, whom they too claimed to have overthrown. And they had waited all this time to reunite our people.

With a few words from the Daglan, my mother's doubts melted away, and our exodus into Midgard began.

Long lines of Fae passed through the chamber, through the portal, and into Midgard.

Nausea twisted through Bryce. "She opened the front door to the Asteri. Brought the Trove right to them."

"Fool," Nesta growled at the image. "Power-hungry fool."

But if Theia had opened the door to this realm, if she had the Horn and Harp, why hadn't the Asteri immediately pounced on both? They'd wanted this world, wanted the Trove, and Theia had practically hand-delivered both to them. The Asteri were too smart, too wicked, to have forgotten either fact. So there must have been some plan in place—

By the grace of the Mother, she was paranoid enough about any new allies or companions that she hid the Horn and Harp. She created a pocket of nothingness, she told me, and stashed them there. Only she could access that pocket of nothingness—only she could retrieve the Horn and Harp from its depths. But she remained unaware that Pelias had already told the Daglan of their presence. She had no idea that she was allowed to live, if only for a time, so they might figure out where she'd concealed them. So Pelias, under their command, might squeeze their location out of her.

Just as she had no idea that the gate she had left open into our home world . . . the Daglan had been waiting a long, long time for that, too. But they were patient. Content to let more and more of Theia's forces come into the new world—thus leaving her own undefended. Content to wait to gain her trust, so she might hand over the Horn and Harp.

It was a trap, to be played out over months or years. To get the instruments of power from Theia, to march back into our home world and claim it again . . . It was a long, elegant trap, to be sprung at the perfect moment.

And, distracted by the beauty of our new world, we did not consider that it all might be too *easy. Too simple.*

Midgard was a land of plenty. Of green and light and beauty. Much like our own lands—with one enormous exception. The memory spanned to a view from a cliff of a distant plain full of creatures. Some winged, some not. *We were not the only beings to come to this world hoping to claim it. We would learn too late that the other peoples had been lured by the Daglan under similarly friendly guises. And that they, too, had come armed and ready to fight for these lands. But before conflict could erupt between us all, we found that Midgard was already occupied.*

Theia and Pelias, with Helena and Silene trailing, warriors ten deep behind them, stood atop the cliff, surveying the verdant land and the enormous walled city on the horizon.

Bryce's breath caught. She'd spent years working in the company of the lost books of Parthos, knowing that a great human civilization had once flourished within its walls, but here, before her, was proof of the grandeur, the human skill that had existed on Midgard. And had been entirely wiped away.

She braced herself, knowing what came next, hating it.

We found cities in Midgard carved by human hands. This world had been mostly populated by humans, and only a handful of unusual creatures that had kept mostly to themselves. It was a blank slate, as far as worlds went. Little native magic to fight the Daglan's power.

"Fuck you," Bryce breathed. Nesta grunted her agreement. "Blank slate, my ass." Bryce balled her hands into fists, a familiar, long-simmering rage building under her skin.

Yet the humans were not pleased at our arrival. A legion of armored humans lined the exterior of a walled city, built of pale stone. Bryce didn't want to watch—but couldn't tear her eyes away from the sight.

My mother had dealt with human uprisings before. She knew what to do.

Humans lay slaughtered, the sand beneath them bloody. Bryce trembled, jaw clenched so tightly it hurt. So many dead—both soldiers and civilians. Adults and . . . Gods, she couldn't stand the sight of the smallest bodies.

Azriel swore, low and dirty. Nesta was breathing jaggedly.

Yet Silene spoke on, voice unwavering, as if the memory of the merciless bloodshed didn't faze her one bit.

City to city, we moved. Taking the land as we wished. Taking human slaves to build for us.

But some humans resisted, their city-states uniting as we Fae had once united against our masters.

Bryce didn't let her heart lift at the bronze-armored legions in lines and phalanxes ranged against the glimmering armor of the Fae. She knew how this particular tale ended.

Knew it would be wiped from official history.

But had Aidas known what Theia—what Helena and Silene and the Fae—had done? He must have—he'd loved Theia, after all. And yet he still had the fucking *nerve* to talk about her as if she wasn't a murdering piece of shit. To talk about Bryce having her light as if it was something good.

That star in her chest . . . it was the light of a butcher. Her ancestor.

Was this what she had been sent here to learn? That she wasn't some brave savior's scion, but a descendent of a morally corrupt bloodline?

It didn't matter if that was what the star had wanted her to learn or not—she knew it now, and there'd never be any unlearning it.

There would never be any atoning for what her ancestors had done.

The thoughts sliced her heart like shards of glass, and Bryce might have walked out right then and there, might have told Silene's memory to fuck off with her history lesson—but if this unbearable history could offer some hint about how to save Midgard's future . . .

Bryce kept listening.

20

Standing at the edge of the ring, Ithan found he couldn't move.

He was doing this. This ultimate disgrace, this betrayal of all that he was as a person, as a wolf—

Across the ring, Sigrid was so small. So thin and frail and *new* to this world. This reality. Had he freed her from the tank for this? Only to wind up here?

"Begin," the Viper Queen intoned.

Flynn, Dec, and Tharion stood at the sidelines, barely containing their rage.

Tharion had been right. He'd been so fucking stupid to tangle with the Viper Queen like this, to think it'd be as easy as bloodying himself, maybe getting a few burns—

And now Ariadne had been traded away because of it, too. He barely knew the dragon, yet that was also his burden to carry.

"I said *begin*," the Viper Queen snapped.

Ithan met Sigrid's light brown gaze.

Alpha. Fendyr. Prime. That's what he was taking on. All that he'd bowed to, stood for—

Ithan didn't let himself think. Didn't broadcast his moves. He launched himself at her before he could back away from this precipice.

He swung a punch for Sigrid's face and she lunged aside with surprising speed. An Alpha's speed.

Ithan struck again, and she ducked once more, all instinct.

Sigrid leapt—a swipe of claw-tipped hands.

Shock blasted through Ithan at the sight of those claws, so readily drawn. He stood rooted to the floor—a second too long.

She slashed across his ribs, sharp pain blasting like acid through him—

He bounced away to the sound of Flynn cursing. Ithan pushed a hand to his side. Warm blood leaked over his fingers.

Something sharpened in him. Steadied him. They were doing this: wolf to wolf. Alpha to . . . whatever he was. A wolf without a pack.

Ithan lunged again, reaching low—

His fist collided with Sigrid's soft belly, but she didn't go down. She twisted, elbow slamming directly into his nose. It wasn't an elegant maneuver, but it was a smart one. Bone crunched, blood spurted, and then claws were raking at his face—

He staggered back again. She'd gone for his fucking *eyes*. Ithan tackled her, throwing her to the floor.

"Holstrom!" Tharion shouted, and he couldn't tell if it was a warning or a reprimand, but there was no time to think about it as Sigrid's claws punched through his shoulder. Ithan reared back, roaring, wrenching her claws free.

She brought her legs up and *kicked*. Ithan grabbed her ankles, but too slow. Her feet connected with his gut, and then he was soaring back, back—

He hit the other side of the ring with a thud that echoed through his very bones.

Mired in shame, Tharion watched the bloodbath unfold before him.

He deserved to be here, in this place, with the Viper Queen. He didn't deserve to be freed, to be fought for.

Ariadne. Her name clanged through him. Sold—or traded,

whatever the fuck that meant. Because of him. Because of what he'd said to her, apparently.

Everything he touched turned to shit.

"This isn't going to end well," Flynn murmured. "Even if Ithan wins . . ." Whatever state Sigrid would be in, they wouldn't be able to leave tonight.

Yet even through his shame, Tharion had to admit that she was fighting better than he'd expected. Sloppy and untrained, yes, but she was giving as good as she got. Holding her own.

She and Ithan rolled on the floor, claws out, blood spraying—

Ithan took a hit to the jaw, lacerating his skin. Sigrid seemed inclined to rip him to shreds.

"Solas," Flynn muttered, rubbing his jaw in sympathy.

Tharion dug his nails into his palms, drawing blood.

He couldn't watch this. Couldn't let this happen. Not for his sake—not even for his freedom.

Sigrid slashed again, and Ithan rolled to the side, narrowly missing her wrath. But Sigrid was on him in an instant, and Holstrom's roar of pain as her claws connected with his thigh had Flynn lunging for the ring.

Tharion grabbed the Fae lord, fingers grappling into hard muscle. "Easy," he murmured. "He's fine."

Total fucking lie. Neither Ithan nor Sigrid were fine. Not even close.

Flynn struggled, thrashing out of Tharion's grip and whirling on the Viper Queen. "This ends *now.*"

"It ends," the ruler of the Meat Market drawled from the stands, "when I give the order."

Tharion stilled. "It ends at a knockout."

"It ends with one of them on their way to the Bone Quarter," the Viper Queen said, taking out her phone and snapping a photo of the bloodied wolves squaring off in the ring.

A fight to the death. Tharion choked out, "Holstrom won't—"

"We'll see," the Viper Queen said, and a grunt from Ithan had Tharion spinning back to the fight. From the rage flickering in

Ithan's eyes as he dodged another onslaught of blows from Sigrid, the wolf had heard everything.

"Please," Tharion said to the Vipe. "Let me swap in for the Fendyr heir—"

"Enough, fish," the Viper Queen said, pocketing her phone in her gold jumpsuit.

Tharion might have begged, had Ithan not panted from the ring, "It's done, Tharion." Holstrom was already back on his feet, circling Sigrid, leaking blood everywhere. He'd barely touched her.

He wouldn't touch her, Tharion knew. To harm this female who'd faced such misery . . . Holstrom would never do it.

Tharion couldn't get a breath down, his anger a violent sea churning through his body, drowning him. He'd fucking kill the Viper Queen for putting his friends through this. Even if he only needed to look in the mirror to find the person at fault for this mess.

Sigrid slashed her claws again, and Ithan ducked low with athletic grace.

Sigrid launched an offensive then, powerful and steady in a way that told Tharion it was pure instinct. Swipe, punch, duck—

She wasn't just an heir to the Fendyr line. She *was* the Fendyr line, at its most potent.

It was clearly all Ithan could do to keep ahead of each blow. Blood coated his mouth, his teeth. His brown eyes shone bright and furious. Not at the wolf attacking him, but at the female who'd led them to this.

"Fuck, fuck, fuck," Flynn chanted, pulling at his hair.

Ithan's back hit the ropes, and there was nowhere to go, absolutely nowhere at all, as Sigrid slammed her fist toward his face.

Tharion's stomach flipped. This was all for *him*, and he was the biggest fucking loser on the planet—

Ithan had been waiting, though. He ducked—and punched his claws into the Fendyr heir's gut.

Sigrid screamed, staggering back, collapsing to her knees.

Ithan halted, panting hard. His face was empty as he walked

toward the female clutching her bleeding stomach. It had been a hard blow—but not a fatal one. Claws glinted at his fingertips.

Tharion couldn't breathe as Ithan raised his hand to make the final blow.

Silene's voice remained as steady, unmoved, as it had been throughout. A bored immortal, blandly reciting a history of others' suffering.

We were still waging our war on the humans when the door between worlds opened again. More Fae appeared—from another world this time.

Tall, beautiful beings entered. Even Bryce's rage and despair stalled.

Fae from another world—but they looked so similar to the ones from this place. How was it possible? Another ancient conquest of the Asteri? Another place they'd colonized and tampered with, and eventually lost?

They were Fae like us, but not. The ears, the grace, the strength were identical, but they were shape-shifters, all of them. Each capable of turning into an animal. And each, even in their humanoid body, equipped with elongated canine teeth.

It was a puzzle—enough of one that my mother paused her warmongering. There were two types of Fae. From two seemingly unconnected and distant worlds. These new Fae bore elemental magic, strong enough to make Pelias wary of them. They were more aggressive than the Fae we knew—wilder. And they answered directly to Rigelus.

It seemed, in fact, like they'd known Rigelus a long while.

My mother soon began to suspect that our host was not as benevolent as he claimed. But by the time she learned just how wrong she had been about him, it was too late.

"No shit," Nesta growled, disgust coating her voice, and Bryce could only manage a nod.

My mother would trust only us. Pelias, she might have once included, but he had taken to the pleasures of this new world too eagerly, championed by Rigelus himself.

A glimpse through a curtain of Pelias dumping a human woman's body into a river beside a white-stoned villa. Bruised and naked and dead.

Bryce nearly fell to her knees as the brutalized woman's corpse drifted and sank beneath the clear river, Pelias already long gone.

"They've got some nerve," Nesta grated out. "They were murdering children in those human cities."

"It's still going on today," Bryce said hoarsely. "Humans tossed in dumpsters after the Vanir have tormented and killed them. It goes on every single day in Midgard, and it started with *that* fucker." She pointed a shaking finger at the memory. "With him, and Theia, and all those monsters."

She might have truly erupted then, but Silene continued her story.

My mother eventually trusted only Helena and myself to seek the truth. She knew we could be of great use to her, because we bore the shadows as well as starlight.

Helena and Silene crept through the dimness of a mighty crystal palace. Down a winding crystal staircase. "That's the Asteri's palace," Bryce whispered to Azriel and Nesta. "In the Eternal City."

We spent a month hidden in the enemy's stronghold, no more than shadows ourselves. By the time we returned to our mother, we'd learned the truth: Rigelus and his companions were not Fae at all, but parasites who conquered world after world, feeding off the magic and lives of their citizens. The Daglan, now under their true name: the Asteri.

It was then that my mother told us, showed us, what had happened so long ago. All that she had done since. But she did not waste time apologizing for the past. If we had indeed walked into an enemy's trap, she said, then we must defeat them.

Bryce placed a hand over the star-shaped scar on her chest, fingers curling into the fabric of her shirt. Could she carve it out of herself, the connection to these two-faced hypocrites, and walk away from it forever?

My mother had kept the star map that the Daglan had long ago annotated. And a world on it had caught her attention—a world, like ours, that had overthrown the Daglan.

In an elaborate bedroom, standing before a desk with her two daughters, Theia waved a hand. As if she'd pulled them from that pocket of nothingness, the Harp and Horn appeared on the desk, glimmering alongside the Starsword and the knife.

Theia nodded once, slowly, as if making a decision, and then played the Horn and Harp. A portal between worlds swirled. It solidified, an archway to nowhere. A handsome, golden-haired male stood before it, with eyes like blue opals.

Bryce inhaled sharply.

Prince Aidas only asked my mother one thing when she opened the gate to his world: "Have you come to ask for Hel's help, then?"

Hunt cringed as Baxian vomited blood and flesh and bone. All of it splattered on the floor below them, and the smell—

Ruhn was gasping, shaking, but the prince hadn't asked the Helhound to stop.

"A little more," Baxian said, panting hard. Hunt's own stomach churned at the blood sliding down the male's chin. "Two more bites and it'll be off."

Ruhn whimpered but nodded grimly. They swung into each other, legs locking tight, and Baxian gave no warning before he bit down again. There was no time to waste.

Hunt shut out the sounds. The smells. Bryce and his future and those beautiful kids—that was the image he held in his mind instead. Escape—survival—was the goal. Bryce was the goal.

Even if he had no idea how he'd face her again after failing to protect them from this fate. After agreeing to let his friends do this. He had no idea how he'd look her in the eye.

Ruhn let out a muffled shout, and Baxian retched again, mouth still around Ruhn's wrist. Balking.

They'd come too fucking far to stop now. So Hunt said, voice hardening into that cold, flat tone of the Umbra Mortis, just as Ruhn had said they needed, "Again, Baxian."

"Please," Ruhn moaned, and it wasn't a request to stop, but to hurry. To get it over with.

"Again," the Umbra Mortis ordered Baxian.

Baxian, who'd shouldered this unspeakable task for Hunt so he didn't have to endure it—

The Helhound heaved forward, teeth clamping down, and *crunched*.

Ruhn screamed, swinging away wildly.

Hunt didn't know where to look first. At Baxian, spewing blood and flesh onto the stones beneath him. At the hand and part of a wrist still attached to the chain, or at Ruhn surging for the rack, sobbing through his teeth at all the weight now on one arm, feet straining—

Hunt acted, lifting his feet and *pushing*. Ruhn's toes nudged the top of the iron.

"More," Hunt barked. He'd become the Umbra Mortis, become that fucking monster again if it gave his friends a shot at survival—

Ruhn swung toward Hunt, blood everywhere, and Hunt steeled himself, then gave him another kick. The prince's toes connected with the iron poker. Held. And as he swung back—the poker came with him.

Ruhn came to a halt, dangling from that one arm. How the fuck would Ruhn curl upward with *one* arm, not two? Hunt began swinging for him. If he could use his legs and help Ruhn twist—

"What acrobatics," drawled a familiar male voice from the doorway. "And what determination."

Cold horror cracked through Hunt as Rigelus approached, flanked by Pollux and the Hawk.

Ithan panted as he stood over Sigrid, claws raised. The Fendyr heir's face was white with pain, her hand still clutching her bloodied side.

"Kill her, Holstrom," the Viper Queen purred from the sidelines, rising to her feet in a ripple of gold. "And it's done."

The Viper Queen had wanted him to be presented with this choice—this true *amusement*: deciding between saving his friends, saving Athalar and Ruhn and possibly Bryce . . . and Sigrid. The future of the Fendyr line. An alternative to Sabine.

On the ground, Sigrid lifted her head to look at him. Blood dribbled from her nose.

He'd done that to her. He'd never felt so dirty, so worthless as when he'd punched his claws through her stomach.

But Sigrid said with a mouth full of bloody teeth, "I never thanked you."

The entire world stilled. The Viper Queen faded into nothing. "For what?" Ithan panted.

"For getting me out." Her eyes were so trusting, so sad—

Make your brother proud.

If Connor were here . . .

Ithan lowered his claws. Slowly, he turned to the Viper Queen, whose face was tight with displeasure. "Fuck you, and fuck this bargain. If you don't let—"

Sigrid struck.

A cheap, cruel lunge for his throat, designed to rip it out. Ithan barely blocked the blow, her claws sinking into his forearm with a blinding flash of pain.

"Fendyr through and through," the Viper Queen said approvingly. It wasn't a compliment. Ithan wrenched his arm away, flesh tearing with it, and he could hardly breathe around the pain—

Sigrid slashed for his throat again. Then again. She hurled him against the ropes with strength only a Fendyr Alpha could wield. And as he rebounded, shooting right for her, he saw it. The death in her eyes.

She'd kill him. He might have pulled her from the tank, but she was, first and last, an Alpha.

And Alphas did not lose. Not to lesser wolves.

Make your brother proud.

They were the only words in his head as Ithan hurtled through the air. As he met Sigrid's eyes. The primal, intrinsic dominance there that took no prisoners. Had no mercy. Could never have mercy.

Make your brother proud.

Ithan aimed his clawed fist for her shoulder, a blow that would send her to her knees.

But Sigrid was fast—too fast. And did not yet understand how swiftly she could move.

Neither did Ithan.

One moment, his claws were heading for her shoulder. The next, she'd managed to bob to the right, planning to sidestep the blow—

Ithan saw it in slow motion. As if watching someone else—another wolf, caught in this ring.

One moment, Sigrid was dodging him, so swift he didn't have time to pull the punch. The next, she was still, eyes wide with shock and pain.

His claws hadn't gone through her shoulder.

They'd punched straight through her throat.

21

Aidas was a Prince of Hel, Silene went on.

Bryce's breath caught in her throat.

Using rare summoning salts that facilitated communication between worlds, his spies in Midgard had kept him well informed since the Asteri had failed to conquer his planet. Aidas had been assigned to hunt for the Asteri ever since. So their evil might never triumph again. On his world, or any other.

Hel was somehow the force for *good* in all this. How had Aidas been able to see past Theia's atrocities? And more than that, to love her? It made no sense. Unless Aidas was just like Theia, a murdering hypocrite—

Long hours did my mother and Aidas speak through the portal, neither daring to cross into the other's world. For many days afterward, in secret, they planned.

It soon became clear that we needed more troops. Any Fae that were loyal to us . . . and humans. The very enemies my mother had slaughtered and enslaved, she now needed. Their final stronghold lay at Parthos, where all the scholars and thinkers of their day had holed up in the great library. And so it was to Parthos we next went, winnowing under cover of darkness.

"Unbelievable," Nesta seethed.

The white-stoned city rose like a dream from a vast, black-soiled river delta.

Parthos was more beautiful than any city currently on Midgard, adorned with elegant spires and columns, massive obelisks in the market squares, sparkling fountains and complex networks of aqueducts, and humans milling about in relative peace and ease, not fear.

At the edge of the city, overlooking the marshes to the north, sat a massive, columned building—no, a complex of several buildings.

The library of Parthos.

It hadn't only been a place to hold books, Bryce knew. The compound had housed several academies for various fields of study—the arts, sciences, mathematics, philosophy—as well as the vast collection of books, a treasure trove of thousands of years' worth of learning.

Bryce's heart ached to see it—what had once been. What had been lost.

Crowded into an amphitheater in the center of the complex stood a mix of humans and Fae arguing—pointing and shouting.

The meetings did not go well, Silene said. *But my mother stood firm. Explained what she had learned. What the humans had long known, though they had been ignorant of the details.*

The arguing parties slowly sat on the stone benches, quietly listening to Theia.

And when she had finished, the humans revealed their own discovery— one that showed us our doom.

As a lone human woman stood from the crowd, Bryce reminded herself to keep breathing, to steady herself—

The Asteri had infected the water we consumed with a parasite. They'd poisoned the lakes and streams and oceans. The parasites burrowed their way into our bodies, warping our magic.

Holy gods.

The Asteri created a coming-of-age ritual for all magical creatures who had entered Midgard, and their descendants. A blast of magic would be released and then contained—and then fed to the Asteri. It was a greater, more concentrated dose than the seeds of power they'd sucked off us for years in the Tithe. They spun it into a near-religious experience, explained it away as a method to harness energy for fuel, and had been feeding off it ever since.

"The Drop," Bryce whispered, dismay rocking through her. She knew Nesta and Azriel were staring at her, but she couldn't look away from the memory.

Should anyone with power opt out of the ritual, the parasites would suck immortals dry until they withered away to nothing—like humans. It would be dismissed as old age. Lies were planted about the dangers of performing the ritual in any place other than one of the Asteri's harvesting sites, where the power could be contained and filtered to them, and to their cities and their technology.

Bryce was going to be sick.

The Asteri's hold on the people of her world wasn't merely based in military and magical might. These parasites ensured that they fucking *owned* each person, their very power. Their tyranny had wormed itself into the blood of every being on Midgard.

The humans had learned this—the Asteri had been careless in spilling knowledge around them, because without magic, the humans were unaffected. And they'd watched in smug silence while we, their gleeful oppressors, had unwittingly become oppressed. With one sip of water from this world, we belonged to the Asteri. There was no undoing it.

The despair nearly broke us then and there.

At last, Bryce could truly relate. She'd gone somewhere far away from her body. Listened as if from a distance as the last acts of this damned history played out.

But we convinced the humans to trust us. And my mother began reaching out to some of those Fae who had followed us into Midgard—those she hoped she could trust.

In the end, my mother had ten thousand Fae willing to march, most hailing from our dusk-bound lands. And when my mother fully opened the doorway to Hel, Aidas and his brothers brought fifty thousand soldiers with them.

I do not have the words for the war's brutality. For the lives lost, the torment and fear. But my mother did not break.

The Asteri mounted their counteroffensive swiftly, and wisely put Pelias in charge of their forces. Pelias knew my mother and her tactics well.

And though Hel's armies fought valiantly, our people with them, it was not enough.

I was never privy to the story of how my mother and Prince Aidas became lovers. I know only that even in the midst of war, I had never seen my mother so at peace. She told me once, when I marveled at our luck that the portal had opened to Aidas that day, that it was because they were mates—their souls had found each other across galaxies, linking them that fateful day, as if the mating bond between them was indeed some physical thing. That was how deeply they loved each other. And when this war was over, she promised me, we would go to Hel with Aidas. Not to rule, but to live. When this was over, she promised, she would spend the rest of her existence atoning.

She did not get to fulfill that promise.

"Too bad," Nesta said pitilessly.

But Bryce had moved beyond words. Beyond anything other than pure despair and dread.

Word came from the enemy right before they attacked in the dead of night: Surrender, and we would be spared. Fight, and we would be slaughtered.

Our camp had been erected high in the mountains, where we thought the winter snows would protect us from advancing enemies. Instead, we were cold and hungry, with barely any time to ready our forces. Aidas had returned to Hel to recruit more soldiers, so we were spending a rare night with our mother alone.

Hel did not have the chance to come to our aid. My mother did not even bother to try to open a portal to their world. Our forces on Midgard were already depleted—the new recruits wouldn't be amassed for days. We begged her to open the portal anyway, to at least get the princes' help, but my mother believed it would do little good. That what was coming that night was inevitable.

"Fool," Nesta said again, and Bryce nodded numbly.

But my mother didn't ask us to fight.

A bloodied Theia pressed the Horn into Helena's hands, and urged Silene to take the Harp and the dagger. She kept the Starsword for herself.

The place where we had first entered this world was nearby. We'd been camping here in part so that my mother could eventually open a portal again and recruit more Fae to fight. She still did not understand much about voyaging between worlds—she wasn't sure, if she opened a portal in another spot, if it would open to a different place in our world. So she'd gambled on our entry point in Midgard opening precisely into our court once more. From there, she'd planned to take the tunnels that leapt across the lands and build Fae armies. Even knowing they'd opposed her before, knowing they'd probably refuse her or kill her, she had no other options.

But there was no time for that now.

"Play the Horn and Harp," *our mother ordered, pulling them out of that pocket of nothingness,* "and get out of this world." *It would be swift, a momentary opening, too fast for Rigelus to pounce on. We'd open it and be gone before he would even catch wind of what we'd done—and then we would seal the door between worlds forever.*

Theia pressed a kiss to each of their brows.

She warned that Pelias was coming. For both of us. Rigelus had made him Prince of the Fae, and Pelias would use us to legitimize his reign. He meant to father children on us.

Even with all they had done, the crimes they'd committed against humans, Bryce's chest still tightened in panic for the sisters.

Pulling her daughters close, Theia flared with starlight. And in the small space between their bodies, Bryce could just make out Theia plucking a low string on the Harp. In answer, a star—akin to the one Bryce could pull from her own chest—emerged from Theia's body. It split into three shimmering balls of light, one drifting into Silene's chest and another to Helena's before the final one, as if it were the mother from which the other two stars had been born, returned to Theia's body.

For a moment, all three of them glowed. Even Truth-Teller,

in Silene's hand, seemed to ripple, a dark countermelody to how Gwydion flashed in Theia's hand, its light a heartbeat.

She gave us what protection her magic could offer, transferring it from her body into our own using the Harp. Another secret she had learned from her long-ago masters: that the Harp could not only move its bearer through the world, but move things from one place to another—even move magic from her soul to ours.

Gwydion in hand, Theia left the tent. With Fae grace and surety, she leapt onto the back of a magnificent winged horse and was airborne in seconds, soaring into the battle-filled night.

Bryce drew in a sharp breath. Silene hadn't shown the creatures in the earlier memories, or in the initial crossing into Midgard, but there they were. The pegasuses in the tunnels' carvings hadn't been religious iconography, then. And they'd lived long enough in Midgard to grace early art, like the frieze at the Crescent City Ballet. They must have all died out, becoming nothing more than myth and a line of sparkly toys.

Another beautiful thing that Theia and her daughters had destroyed.

Helena's eyes filled with panic as she turned to Silene in the memory.

To escape, it was worth the risk of going back to our home world, even if the Fae there might kill us for our connections to the Asteri, our foolishness in trusting them.

Helena grabbed Silene's hand and hauled her toward the far edge of the camp. Toward the snow-crusted peak ahead—a natural archway of stone. A gateway.

But no matter how fast we ran, it was not fast enough.

Far below, Fae were rushing up the mountain. Not the advancing enemy, but members of their court racing for them, realizing what Helena and Silene were doing. Still glowing with their mother's magic, both princesses stood atop the slope like silver beacons in the night. The Fae masses sprinted for them, bearing small children in their arms, bundled against the cold.

Bryce couldn't endure it, this last atrocity. But she made herself watch. For the memory of those children.

We would not stop. Not even for our people.

Hatred coursed through Bryce at Silene's words, the rage so violent it threatened to consume her as surely as any flame.

Helena lifted the Horn to her lips as Silene plucked a string on the Harp. A shuddering, shining light rippled in the archway, and then a stone room appeared beyond it, dim and empty.

That was when the wolves found us. The shape-shifting Fae, closing in from the other side of the mountain, barreled through the snow. *The Asteri had sent their fiercest warriors to capture us.*

In the back of her mind, Bryce marveled at it: that the wolves, the shifters . . . they had once been *Fae.* So similar to Bryce's sort of Fae, yet so different—

I lifted the Harp again, Silene said, voice finally hitching with emotion, *but my sister did not sound the Horn. And when I turned . . .*

Silene paused, finding Helena standing yards away. Facing the enemy advancing from the snow, the skies. Their frantic, desperate people surging up the side of the mountain, pleas for their children on their lips.

Helena eyed the fleeing people, the wolves closing in. She leaned over to Silene, plucked the shortest string, and shoved her sister, still holding the Harp, backward.

She used the Harp to send me the last of the distance to the archway.

Silene landed in the snow, hundreds of feet now between her and her sister. Wolves advanced on Helena below.

Helena didn't look back as she charged down the mountain, away from the pass. Buying me time. But I took one moment to look. At her, at the wolves giving chase. And at our mother—farther down the mountain, now locked in combat with Pelias, her winged horse dead beside her.

Power blasted from Pelias, power such as I had never seen from him.

The power struck her mother—struck true.

Even their fleeing people halted, looking behind them at the figure lying prone in the gore. At Pelias, stooping to pick up the Starsword.

With an easy, almost graceful flip of his hand, he plunged the sword through Theia's head.

There was a choice for me, then. To stay and avenge my mother, fight alongside my sister . . . or to survive. To shut the door behind me.

Silene jumped through the portal toward the chamber beyond, plucking the Harp as she went.

And as I tumbled between worlds . . . the Horn sounded.

Silene fell and fell and fell, down and sideways. The Horn's keening was cut off abruptly, and then she lay awkwardly on a stone floor, surrounded by darkness.

She was home.

Sobbing, Silene scrambled to her feet, snow spraying from her clothes. Not one shred of pity stirred in Bryce's heart at Silene's tears.

Not as screaming echoed through the walls. Through the stone. Silene's people had reached the pass, and now banged on the rock, begging to be let through.

Silene covered her ears, sinking again to the floor. She clutched the Harp to her chest.

Mother above, open up! a male roared. *We have children here! Take the children!*

Bryce shook her head in mute horror as the screams and pleading faded. Then stopped entirely. As if sucked into the very stones of this place. Right along with the melting snow around Silene.

"You fucking coward," Bryce breathed at last. Her voice broke on the last word. *This* was her heritage.

Heavy quiet fell in the chamber, interrupted only by Silene's broken rasping as she knelt, cradling the Harp.

At that moment, Silene said, *I had only one thought in my mind. That this knowledge would die with me. This world would continue as if the Fae who had gone into Midgard had never been. They would become a story whispered around campfires about people who had vanished. It was the only thing I could think to do to protect this world. To atone.*

Too little, too late. And of course, Silene would have benefitted from hiding her past—if she didn't tell anyone who she was or what she and her family had done, she couldn't be punished for it. How convenient. How *noble.*

Silene studied the spot where she knelt on the eight-pointed star in the center of the room. The only adornment.

She slowly set the Harp atop the star. Snow still melting in her hair, she got to her feet and wiped her tears, then rallied her magic, the sheer concentrated power of her light. It sliced through the stone like a knife through warm butter—a laser.

Light that wasn't just light—light, as the Asteri could wield their power.

Silene carved planets and stars and gods. A map of the cosmos. Of the world she had abandoned. When she finished, she lay beside the Harp, curled around the dagger sheathed at her waist.

Silene traced her fingers over the stone, like she could somehow reach across the stars to her sister. A seed of starlight began to form at her fingertip—

The vision went dark. Then Silene's face appeared again—older, worn. Her clear blue eyes looked out with a steady gaze. *My strength wanes,* she said. *I hope that my life has been spent wisely. Atoning for my mother's crimes and foolishness and love—and trying to make it right. I carved these tunnels, the path here, so some record might exist of what we were, what we did. But first I had to erase all of it from recent memory.*

Her face faded away, and more images began. A faster montage.

Silene, walking away from the Harp and through the empty, beautiful halls of a palace carved into the mountain—*this* mountain.

Our home had been left empty since we'd vanished. As if the other Fae thought it cursed. So I made it truly cursed. Damned it all.

She wandered through rooms that must once have been familiar to her, pausing as if lost in memory. Then she waved a hand, and entire hallways were walled off with natural rock. Another wave, and ornate throne rooms were swallowed by the mountain, until only the lowermost passages, the dungeons and this chamber far beneath, remained.

Despite my efforts to hide what this place had once been, a terrible, ancient power hung in the air. It was as my mother had warned us when we were children: evil always lingered, just below us, waiting to snatch us into its jaws.

So I went to find another monster to conceal it.

Beneath another mountain, far to the south, I found a being of blood and rage and nightmares. Once a pet of the Asteri, it had long been in hiding, feeding off the unwitting. With the dagger and my power, I laid a trap for it. And when it came sniffing, I dragged it back here. Locked it in one of the cells. Warded the door.

One after another, I hunted monsters—the remaining pets of the Daglan—until many of the lowest rooms were filled with them. Until my once-beautiful home became a prison. Until even the land was so disgusted by the evil I'd gathered here that the islands shriveled and the earth became barren. The winged horses who hadn't gone with my mother to Midgard, who had once flown in the skies, playing in the surf . . . they were nearly gone. Not a single living soul remained, except for the monstrosities in the mountain.

No pity or compassion stirred in Bryce. She didn't buy Silene's "for the common good" bullshit. It had all been to cover her own ass, to make sure the Fae in this world never learned how close she and her mother and sister had come to damning them. How Silene and Helena *had* damned the Fae of Midgard, locking them out along with their children. Another few seconds of keeping the portal open and she could have saved dozens of lives. But she hadn't.

So boo-fucking-hoo and to Hel with her atonement.

I left, wandering the lands for a time, seeing how they had moved on without Theia's rule. They'd splintered into several territories, and though they were not at war, they were no longer the unified kingdom I had known.

I will spare you the details of how I came to wed a High Lord's son. Of the years before and after he became the High Lord of Night, and I his lady. He wanted me to be High Lady, as the other lords' mates were, but I refused. I had seen what power had done to my mother, and I wanted none of it.

Yet when my first son was born, when the babe screamed and the sound was full of night, I brought him to the Prison and keyed the wards into his blood. No one knew that the infant who sometimes glowed with starlight had inherited it from me. That it was the light of the evening star. The dusk star.

And this island that had become barren and empty . . . this, too, was his. I told him, when he was old enough, what I had left here for him. So that someone might be able to access this record, to know the risks of using the Trove and the threat of the Asteri, always waiting to return here. I made sure he knew that the buried weapon he'd need against the Asteri was down here. I only asked that he not tell his father, my mate. To my knowledge, he never has. And one day, he has promised to tell his son, and his son after him. A secret shame, a secret history, a secret weapon—all hidden within our bloodline. Our burden to carry forward, carved and recounted here so that if the original history becomes warped or parts of it lost to time . . . here it is, etched in stone.

Nesta murmured to Azriel, "Does Rhys . . . does he know?"

"No," Azriel replied without an ounce of doubt. "Somewhere along the line . . . all this was forgotten, and never passed on."

Bryce couldn't bring herself to care. She knew the truth now, and all that mattered was getting home to Midgard to share it with others. With Hunt.

But to the rest of the world, Silene said, *I ensured that my mother and her lands became a whisper. Then a legend. People wondered if Theia had ever existed. The old generation died off. I clung to life, even after my mate had passed. As an elder, I spun lies for my people and called them truth.*

"No one knows what became of Theia and General Pelias," I told countless generations. *"They betrayed King Fionn, and Gwydion was forever lost, his dagger with it." I lied with every breath.*

"Theia and Fionn had two daughters. Unimportant and unimpressive." That was the hardest, perhaps. Not that my own name was gone. But that I had to erase Helena's, too.

Bryce glowered. Erasing her sister's name was worse than butchering human families?

My son had sons, and I lived long enough to see my grandsons have sons of their own. And then I returned here. To the place that had once been full of light and music, and now housed only terrors.

To leave this account for one whose blood will summon it, child of my child, heir of my heir. To you—I leave my story, your story. To you, in this very stone, I leave the inheritance and the burden that my own mother passed to me.

The image blurred, and there she was again. That old, weary face.

I hope the Mother will forgive me, Silene said, and the hologram dissolved.

"Well, I fucking don't," Bryce spat, and flipped off the place where Silene had stood.

22

Hunt could only watch in despair as the Bright Hand of the Asteri swept into the chamber, followed by Pollux and the Hawk. The Hawk noted the hand still dangling from the chains and laughed.

"Just like a rat," the Hawk taunted, "gnawing off a limb when caught in a trap."

"Get fucked," Baxian spat, Ruhn's blood coating his face, his neck, his chest.

"Language," Rigelus chided, but didn't interfere as Pollux snatched the iron poker from where Ruhn still clutched it between his feet. Ruhn, to his credit, tried to hold on to it, legs curling upward to tuck it close. But weakened and bleeding . . . there was nothing he could do. Pollux ripped it away, beating Ruhn's back once with it—prompting a pained grunt from the prince—then used the poker to prod Ruhn's severed hand from the shackle above.

It landed on the filthy ground with a sickening thump.

Smiling, the Hawk picked it up like it was a shiny new toy.

Observing the three of them, Rigelus said mildly, "If I'd known you were so bored down here, I would have sent Pollux back sooner. Here I was, thinking you'd had enough of pain."

Pollux stalked to the lever, wings glowingly white. With a smirk, the Hammer pulled it and sent all three of them dropping heavily to the ground.

The agony that blasted through Hunt drowned out Ruhn's scream as the prince landed on his severed wrist.

Hunt gave himself one breath, one moment on that filthy floor to sink down into the icy black of the Umbra Mortis. To fight past the pain, the guilt, to focus. To lift his head.

Rigelus stared down at them impassively. "I'm hoping that I will soon have further insight into where Miss Quinlan might have gone," he crooned. "But perhaps you might feel inclined now to talk?"

Ruhn spat, "Fuck off."

Behind Rigelus's back, the Hawk folded the fingers of Ruhn's severed hand until only the middle one remained upright.

Hunt snarled softly. The snarl of the Umbra Mortis.

Yet Rigelus stepped closer to Hunt, immaculate white jacket almost obscenely clean in this place. The golden rings on his fingers glimmered. "It brings me no joy to see you with the halo and slave brand again, Athalar."

"Halo," Hunt asked as solidly as he could, "or black crown?"

Rigelus blinked—the only sign of his surprise—but the term clearly landed with the Bright Hand.

"Been talking to shadows, have you?" Rigelus hissed.

"Umbra Mortis and all that," Hunt said. "Makes sense for the Shadow of Death."

Baxian chuckled.

Rigelus narrowed his eyes at the Helhound, then turned back to Hunt. "What lengths would the Umbra Mortis go to in order to keep these two pathetic specimens alive, I wonder?"

"What the fuck do you want?" Hunt growled. Pollux flashed him a warning look.

"A small task," Rigelus said. "A favor. Unrelated to Miss Quinlan entirely."

"Don't fucking listen to him," Baxian muttered, then cried out as a whip cracked, courtesy of the Hawk.

"I'd be willing to offer a . . . reprieve," Rigelus said to Hunt, ignoring the Helhound entirely. "If you do something for me."

That was what this had been about, then. His mystics would find Bryce—he didn't need the three of them for that. But the torture, the punishment . . . Hunt willed his foggy head to clear, to listen to every word. To cling to that Umbra Mortis he'd once been, what he'd been so happy to leave behind.

"Your lightning is a gift, Athalar," Rigelus continued. "A rare one. Use it once, on my behalf, and perhaps we can find you three more comfortable . . . arrangements."

Ruhn spat, "To do *what*?"

"A side project of mine."

Hunt snapped, "I'm not agreeing to shit."

Rigelus smiled sadly. "I assumed that would be the case. Though I'm still disappointed to hear it." He pulled a sliver of pale rock from his pocket—a crystal. Uncut and about the length of his palm. "It'll be harder to extract it from you without your consent, but not impossible."

Hunt's stomach flipped. "Extract what?"

Rigelus stalked closer, crystal in hand. The Asteri halted steps from Hunt, fingers unfurling so he could examine the hunk of quartz in his palm. "A fine natural conduit," the Bright Hand said thoughtfully. "And an excellent receptacle for power." Then he lifted his gaze up to Hunt. "I'll give you a choice: offer me a sliver of your lightning, and you and your friends will be spared the worst of your suffering."

"No." The word rose from deep in Hunt's gut.

Rigelus's expression remained mild. "Then choose which one of your friends shall die."

"Go to Hel." The Umbra Mortis slipped away, too far to reach.

Rigelus sighed, bored and weary. "Choose, Athalar: Shall it be the Helhound or the Fae Prince?"

He couldn't. Wouldn't.

Pollux was grinning like a fiend, a long knife already in his hand. Whichever of Hunt's friends was chosen, the Hammer would draw out their deaths excruciatingly.

"Well?" Rigelus asked.

He'd do it—the Bright Hand would do this, make him choose between his friends, or just kill both of them.

And Hunt had never hated himself more, but he reached inward, toward his lightning, suppressed and suffocated by the gorsian shackles, but still there, under the surface.

It was all Rigelus needed. He pressed the quartz against Hunt's forearm, and the stone cut into his skin. Searing, acid-sharp lightning surged out of Hunt, ripped from his soul, twisted through the confines of the gorsian shackles, extracted inch by inch into the crystal. Hunt screamed, and he had a moment of brutal clarity: this was what his enemies felt when he flayed them alive, what Sandriel had felt when he'd destroyed her, and oh *gods*, it burned—

And then it stopped.

Like a switch being flipped, only darkness filled him. His lightning sank back into him, but in Rigelus's hands, the crystal now glowed, full of the lightning he'd wrenched from Hunt's body. Like a firstlight battery—like the scrap of power extracted during the Drop.

"I think this will do for now," Rigelus crooned, sliding the stone back into his pocket. It illuminated the dark material of his pants, and Hunt's throat constricted, bile rising.

The Bright Hand turned away, and said to the Hammer and the Hawk without looking back, "I think two out of three will still be a good incentive for Miss Quinlan to return, don't you? Executioner's choice."

"You bastard," Hunt breathed. "I did what you asked."

Rigelus strode for the stairs that led out of the chamber. "Had you agreed to give me your lightning from the start, both of your companions would have been spared. But since you made me go to all that effort . . . I think you need to learn the consequences of your defiance, however short-lived it was."

Baxian seethed, "He'll never stop defying you—and neither will we, asshole."

It meant more than it should have that the Helhound spoke up for him. And also made it worse.

Last time he'd been here, he'd been alone. He'd had only the screams of soldiers to endure. His guilt had devoured him, but it was different than this. Than having to be here with two brothers and bear their suffering along with his own.

Being alone would have been better. So much better.

Rigelus knew it, too. It was why he'd waited this long to come down here, giving Hunt time to comprehend the bind he was in.

The Bright Hand ascended the steps with feline grace. "We shall see what Athalar is willing to give up when it really comes down to it. Where even the Umbra Mortis draws the line."

Lidia's time had run out. If she was to act, it had to be now. There was no margin for error. She needed the prisoners ready—in whatever way she could manage.

But she'd gotten no farther than two steps into the dungeon when the breath whooshed from her body at the sight of the stump where Ruhn's hand should have been.

The prince hung, unconscious, from his chains. Athalar and Baxian were out, too. All three were caked in blood.

Pollux and the Hawk were panting, smiling like fiends. "You missed the fun, Lidia," the Hawk said, and held up—

Held up—

That broad, tattooed hand—Ruhn's hand—had touched her. On that mental plane, soul to soul, those hands had caressed her, gentle and loving.

"Well done," she managed, though she screamed inside. Clawed at the walls of her being and shrieked with fury. "Which one of you claimed the prize?"

"Baxian, actually," the Hammer said, chuckling. "Chewed it off like the dog he is in an attempt to get free."

Lidia made herself turn. Look at the Helhound like she was impressed. Some small part of her was. But the pain Ruhn had endured . . .

She put a hand to her stomach, and her wince wasn't entirely feigned.

"Lidia?" the Hawk asked, white wings rustling.

"Her cycle," Pollux answered for her, disdain coating his voice.

"I'm fine," she snapped, to make the show complete. The Hawk and Pollux swapped looks, as if to say, *Females.* She pulled a velvet case from an interior pocket of her uniform jacket. When she flicked it open, firstlight glowed from the two syringes strapped within.

"What's that?" The Hawk stalked a step closer, peering at the needles.

Lidia made herself smirk at him, then at Pollux. "It seems a shame to me that Athalar and the Helhound's wings are no longer able to be . . . targeted. I thought we'd bring them back into play."

A shot of a medwitch healing potion, laced with firstlight, would regrow their wings within a day or two, even under the repressive power of the gorsian shackles. If she'd known about Ruhn's hand, she would have brought three, but now there would be no way to casually explain the need for it, not without drawing too much attention.

And she needed Athalar and Baxian able to fly.

Pollux smiled. "Clever, Lidia." He jerked his chin toward the unconscious angels. "Do it."

She didn't need the Hammer's permission, but she didn't protest. "Wait until they're fully regrown," she warned Pollux and the Hawk. "Let them savor the hope of having their wings again before you find some interesting way to remove them anew."

Athalar and Baxian were too deeply unconscious to even feel the prick of the needle at the center of their spines. Firstlight glowed along their backs, stretching like shining roots toward the stumps of their wings. The wounds in between healed over slowly, but she'd bade the medwitch who'd crafted the potion to weave a spell in it to target the wings specifically. If she'd healed them both completely, it would have been too suspicious.

Slowly, before her eyes, the stumps on their backs began to rebuild, flesh and sinew and bone creeping together, multiplying.

Lidia turned from the gruesome sight. She could only pray they'd be healed in time.

"I'll take it from here," she said to Pollux and the Hawk, striding to the rack.

"I thought you were here to heal them." The Hawk glanced between her and the angels.

"Only the wings," Lidia said. "Why not play with other parts while they mend?"

The Hammer smiled. "Can I watch?"

"No."

Ruhn stirred, groaning softly, and it was all she could do to keep from pulling one of the long blades from the rack and plunging it through Pollux's gut.

"You know how I like to watch," Pollux purred, and the Hawk chuckled. What an utter waste of life. He'd stood by while the Hammer committed his bloody atrocities. Had delighted in watching during those years with Sandriel, too.

The Malleus's eyes gleamed with naked lust. "Why don't you put on a show for us?"

"Get out," she said, unamused. Pollux might pretend he had control, but he knew who the Asteri favored. Her orders were not to be ignored. "I don't need distractions."

The Hawk snickered, but obeyed, stalking out. A true minion, through and through.

The Hammer, however, walked over to her. With a lover's gentleness, he put a hand on the side of her neck. And then squeezed tight enough to bruise as he said against her mouth, "I'll fuck that disrespect out of you, Lidia. Bloody cunt or not."

Then he was striding up the steps, wings glowing with his wrath. He slammed the door behind him.

Lidia waited, listening. When she was convinced they were both gone, she pulled the lever that sent the prisoners crashing to the floor and rushed to where Ruhn lay sprawled.

"Get up." She kept her voice hard, cold. But the prince opened his beautiful blue eyes.

She scanned his face. *Ruhn.* No one answered. As if pain had carved him up and hollowed him out. *Ruhn, listen to me.*

You're dead to me, he'd said. It seemed he'd killed the connection between them, too. But Lidia still cast her thoughts toward his mind.

Ruhn, I don't have much time. I managed to make contact with people who can help get you out of here, but the Harpy is somehow about to be resurrected, and once she is, the truth will come out. If my plan's to go off without a hitch, if you are to survive, you need to listen—

Ruhn only closed his eyes and didn't open them again.

Silence, heavy and unbearable, filled the chamber beneath the Prison. Bryce stared at the eight-pointed star, revulsion coursing through her in an oily slide.

"They were horrible," she rasped. "Self-serving, reckless monsters."

"Silene and Helena did shut the portal," Nesta countered carefully.

Bryce's gaze snapped to the female. "Only after they opened it again—to *escape*. It was open because they wanted to run. And they left all those people behind. They could have held it open a little longer, could have saved them. But Silene chose herself. She's a fucking *disgrace*."

"Surely their fate at Pelias's hands," Azriel said, "would explain some of their motivation in acting quickly."

Bryce pointed to the place where Silene had stood. "That fucking *bitch* locked out children to save herself and then tried to justify it."

It was no different than what the Valbaran Fae had done this spring in Crescent City—locking the innocents out of their villas while they cowered inside, protected by their wards.

"What did you . . . ," Nesta began, a shade gently. "What was it that you expected to find here?"

"I don't know." Bryce let out a bitter laugh. "I thought maybe . . . maybe they'd have some answer about how to kill the Asteri. But she glossed over *that* part. I thought that in the thousands of years since then, maybe the Fae of Midgard had evolved into the reprehensible shitheads they are. Not that they were reprehensible all along."

She scrubbed at her face, eyes stinging. "I thought having Theia's light was . . . good. Like she was somehow better than Pelias. But she wasn't." And Aidas had *loved* her? "I thought it'd somehow give me an edge in this shitshow. But it fucking doesn't. It just means I'm the heir to a legacy of selfish, scheming assholes."

And worse, that parasite in Midgard's waters . . . what could even be done against that? Bryce sucked in a shuddering breath.

A gentle hand rested on her shoulder. Nesta.

"We need to tell Rhys," Azriel said hoarsely. Like he was still reeling from all he'd heard. "Immediately."

Bryce's gaze snapped to his face. The concern and determination there. Everything he'd seen . . . it was a threat to this world, to the people in it.

Azriel asked her with terrifying calm, "What happened to the Horn?"

Bryce held his stare, seething, beyond trying to spin any bullshit.

But Nesta said, "She *is* the Horn, Azriel. It's inked into her flesh." She lowered her hand from Bryce's shoulder and peered at her. "Isn't that right? It's the only thing that would have made your tattoo react that way earlier."

Azriel's hazel eyes flickered with predatory intent. He'd carve it out of her fucking back.

If she ran for the exit tunnel . . . They'd said something about a climb out of here, then a hike down a mountain.

But this court was an island. She wouldn't be able to get away from them.

Azriel began circling her with an unhurried, calculating precision. Bryce turned with him, keeping him in sight, but doing so exposed her back to Nesta, who she suspected might be the apex predator in the room.

"That's how you got to this world," Nesta went on, backing up a step—no doubt to provide space to draw Ataraxia. "Why you, and no one else, can come. Why you said no one would be able to follow you here. Because only you have the Horn. Only you can move between worlds."

"You got me," Bryce said, throwing up her hands in mock surrender and taking a step out of Nesta's range. "I'm a big, bad, world-jumping monster. Like my ancestors."

"You're a liability," Nesta said flatly, eyes taking on that silvery sheen—that otherworldly fire.

"I told you guys a hundred times already: I didn't even want to come here—"

"It doesn't matter," Nesta said. "You *did* come here, to the place where the Daglan are still apparently dead set on returning."

"The Asteri would need the Horn to open a portal. They might find me, but they can't get in."

"But you want to go home," Nesta said, "and for that you'll have to open a door to Midgard. What if Rigelus is right there? Waiting to come through?"

Bryce turned to keep facing Azriel, but—

Only shadows surrounded her.

Nesta had distracted her, enough that her focus had slipped and Azriel had vanished. They'd worked in silent, perfect tandem.

Not to attack, she realized, as a shadow darker than the ones around it raced for the tunnel across the chamber. But to go get reinforcements.

"No!" Bryce threw out a hand, and light ruptured from her fingers. It slammed into Azriel's shadows, fracturing the darkness and revealing the warrior beneath. But not enough to stop his sprint—

She needed more power.

The eight-pointed star at her feet glimmered. As if her magic had nudged something within it. Like embers flaring in stirred ashes. What if her star hadn't been guiding her to the knowledge, but to something . . . different? Something tangible?

Like calls to like.

To you, in this very stone, Silene had said, *I leave the inheritance and the burden that my own mother passed to me.*

This place, this Prison and the court it had once been, was

Bryce's inheritance. Hers to command, as Silene had commanded it.

And that memory, of Silene lying next to the Harp in the center of this room, reaching for one of the carvings with a kernel of light forming at her finger . . .

In this very stone . . .

Silene had warped her former palace and home into this Prison. She must have imbued some magic in the rock to do it. Must have given over some part of her power to not only change the terrain, but to house the monsters in their cells.

Theia had shown her how to do it. In those last moments with her daughters, Theia had used the Harp to transfer magic from herself into Silene and Helena, to protect them. It had appeared as a star. Had Silene replicated that here?

Was it possible that the Harp, in that moment that Silene reached for it, power at the ready, had been able to transfer her magic to this place?

. . . I leave the inheritance and the burden that my own mother passed to me.

And precisely as Theia had gifted her own power to Silene . . . perhaps Silene had in turn left that same power here, to be claimed by a future scion.

One by one, rapid as shooting stars, the thoughts raced through Bryce. More on instinct than anything else, she dropped to her knees and slammed her hand atop the eight-pointed star. Bryce reached with her mind, through layers of rock and earth—and there it was. Slumbering beneath her.

Not firstlight, not as she knew it on Midgard—but raw Fae power from a time before the Drop. The power ascended toward her through the stone, like a glimmering arrow fired into the dark—

Azriel flapped his wings and was instantly airborne, swooping for the tunnel exit.

Like a small sun emerging from the stone itself, a ball of light burst from the floor. A star, twin to the one in Bryce's chest. Her starlight at last awoke again, as if reaching with shining fingers for that star hovering inches away.

With trembling hands, Bryce guided the star to the one gleaming on her chest. Into her body.

White light erupted everywhere.

Power, uncut and ancient, scorched through her veins. The hair on her head rose. Debris floated upward. She was everywhere and nowhere. She was the evening star and the last rays of color before the dark.

Azriel had nearly reached the tunnel. Another flap of his wings and he'd be swallowed by its dark mouth.

But at a mere thought from Bryce, stalactites and stalagmites formed, closing in on him. The room became a wolf, its jaws snapping for the winged warrior—

The rock had moved for her, as it had for Silene.

"Stop him," she said in a voice that was more like her father's than anything she'd ever heard come out of her mouth.

Azriel swept for the tunnel archway—and slammed into a wall of stone. The exit had sealed.

Slowly, he turned, wings rustling. Blood trickled out of his nose from his face-first collision with the rock now in his path. He spread his wings, bracing for a fight.

The mountain shook, the chamber with it. Debris fell from the ceiling. Walls began shifting, rock groaning against rock. As if the place this had once been was fighting to emerge from the stone.

But Nesta raced at Bryce, Ataraxia drawn, silver flame wreathing the blade.

Bryce lifted a hand, and spike after spike of rock ruptured from the ground, blocking Nesta's advance. The chamber shuddered again—

"*Stop*," Azriel roared, something like panic in his voice. "The cells—"

From far away, she could sense it: the *things* lurking within the mountain, her mountain. Twisted, wretched creatures. Some had been here since Silene had trapped them. Had been contemplating their escape and revenge all this time. She'd let them out if she restored the mountain to its former glory.

And in that moment, the mountain—the island—spoke to her.

Alone. It was so alone—it had been waiting all this time. Cold and adrift in this thrashing gray sea. If she could reach out, if she could open her heart to it . . . it might sing again. Awaken. There was a beating, vibrant heart locked away, far beneath them. If she freed it, the land would rise from its slumber, and such wonders would spring again from its earth—

The mountain shook again. Nesta and Azriel had halted ten feet away, Ataraxia a blazing light, Truth-Teller enveloped by shadows. The Starsword remained sheathed at Azriel's back—but she could have sworn it twitched. As if urging Azriel to draw it.

Nesta warned Bryce, her eyes on the shaking earth, "If you open those cells—"

"I don't want to fight you," Bryce said, voice oddly hollow, like the surge of magic she'd taken from Silene's store had emptied out her soul. "I'm not your enemy."

"Then let us bring you back to our High Lord," Nesta snapped. Ataraxia flashed in answer.

"To do what? Lock me up? Cut the Horn out of my skin?"

"If that's what's necessary," Nesta said coldly, knees bending, readying to strike. "If that's what it takes to keep our world safe."

Bryce bared her teeth in a feral grin. More spikes of rock shot up from the ground, angling toward Nesta and Azriel. "Then come and take it."

With a flap of his wings, Azriel burst toward her, fast as a striking panther—

Bryce stomped her foot. Those spikes of stone stretched higher, blocking his way. Blue light flared from him, smashing through the stones.

Bryce stomped her foot again, summoning more lethal spears of rock—but there were none left. Only a vast, gaping void.

Bryce had only a second to realize there literally *was* a void below her feet, before the ground beneath them collapsed entirely.

23

If the prisoners had done something as drastic as biting off Ruhn's hand, they had to be dangerously close to breaking. Which left Lidia with too little time, and too few options.

The one before her now seemed the wisest and swiftest. She could only trust that Declan Emmet had gotten the coded message she'd sent through her secure labyrinth of channels and was turning the cameras away at this very moment.

The Mistress of the Mystics had scuttled off as soon as Lidia had stalked through the doors to the dank hall—surely to grouse to Rigelus about Lidia's unexpected arrival. She'd ordered Lidia to wait at the front desk.

Lidia had lingered long enough to ensure the mistress had indeed left, then promptly ignored her order.

"Irithys," Lidia said to the sprite lying on the bottom of the crystal ball. Curled on her side, the queen remained asleep. Or pretended to be. "I need your help."

The Sprite Queen cracked open an eye. "To torture more people?"

"To torture *me*."

Irithys opened both eyes this time. Slowly sat up. "What?"

Lidia brought her face close to the crystal and said quietly, "There is an angel in the dungeon. Hunt Athalar."

Irithys sucked in a breath—she knew him. How could she not, as one of the Fallen in her own way? Though Irithys hadn't fought in the failed rebellion, she'd been born into the consequences: heir to a damned people, a queen enslaved upon the moment of her crowning. She'd know every key player in the saga—know every decision that had led to the punishment that rippled across generations of sprites.

"He has begun the fight anew. And this spring, a sprite befriended him; she died to save his mate. Her name was Lehabah. She claimed to be a descendent of Queen Ranthia Drahl." Just as Lidia had seen the footage of Athalar slaying Sandriel, so, too, had she witnessed the final stand of the fire sprite who had saved Bryce Quinlan. Rigelus had considered it imperative that Lidia know everything about the threat to the Asteri's power.

Irithys's eyes widened at the mention of their long-dead queen's line. The bloodline believed gone. The queen whose decision to rebel alongside Athalar and his Archangel had led to this enslaved fate for all sprites, for Irithys herself. But she said evenly, "So?"

Lidia said, "I need you to help me free Hunt Athalar and two of his companions."

Irithys stood, flame a mistrusting yellow. "Is this another *warm-up*?"

Lidia didn't have time for lies, for games. "The warm-up with Hilde was a test. Not to see what you could do, but who you are."

The queen's head angled. The yellow hue remained.

Lidia said, "To see if you were as honorable as I had hoped. As trustworthy."

"For what?" The sprite spat the words, sparks of pure red flying from her.

"To help me with a diversion—one that might save more lives than the three in the dungeon."

Irithys sniffed. "You are Rigelus's pet." She waved with a burning hand to the mystics slumbering in their tanks. "No better than them, obeying him in all things. They would lie if he commanded them to. Would drown themselves, if he so much as breathed the word."

"I can explain later. Right now I only have"—she choked on the word—"trust to offer."

"What of the cameras?" Irithys glanced to the ever-watchful eyes mounted throughout the space.

"I have people in my employ who have ensured that they are looking elsewhere right now," Lidia said, praying that it was true.

And with an appeal to Luna, she tapped the crystal ball, dissolving it. She still had the access Rigelus had granted in her blood to open the ball—she could still make this happen.

She'd intended to use the Sprite Queen to attempt to melt the gorsian shackles off Ruhn, Baxian, and Athalar, but things had changed. She needed Irithys for something far bigger.

Irithys stood in the open air, arms crossed, now a familiar, wary orange shade. "And this?" She gestured to the ink on her neck.

Lidia said quietly, as calmly as she could, "I made a bargain with Hilde for her freedom. She need only do one favor for me when the time comes, and she'll walk free."

Irithys angled her head again. "And the part about me torturing you . . . ?"

"Will come after that. To make it believable."

"Make *what* believable?"

Lidia checked her watch. Not much time. "I need to know if you're in or out."

To her credit, the Sprite Queen didn't waste time. Lidia held her stare, and let the queen see all that lay beneath it. Surprise lit Irithys's face . . . but she nodded slowly, turning a determined hue of ruby.

"Get the hag," the queen said.

It was a matter of a few minutes to get Hilde brought down. The guards didn't question the Hind, and her luck had held—the mistress was still off complaining to Rigelus.

Hilde glared at Lidia as she stood before the sprite, the queen free of her crystal and burning a bright bloodred. "And I walk free as soon as I do this favor for you?"

"No one shall stop you."

Hilde weighed Lidia's expression. "What is it, then?"

Lidia nodded toward Irithys. "Undo what you did years ago. Remove the tattoo from her neck."

Hilde showed no shock, not even a glimmer. Instead, she again glanced between Lidia and the sprite, who remained silent and watchful. "Won't your master punish you for that?"

Lidia said, "All I do is in service of Rigelus's will, even if he cannot always see it." A pretty lie.

But Hilde nodded slowly, her wispy silver hair gleaming with the red of Irithys's flame. "I shall seek shelter in my House until you have officially cleared my name, then."

Lidia produced a key to the hag's gorsian shackles. Irithys simmered beside her, now a tense violet, as the lock clicked.

The hag's shackles fell free.

Before they could hit the floor, Hilde whirled toward Lidia, mouth opening in a scream of fury—

Lidia drew her gun faster than the eye could follow and pressed it against the side of the hag's head. "I don't think so."

"You're a traitorous pile of filth. Rigelus will reward me handsomely when I tell him about this."

Lidia pushed the barrel of the gun into the hag's temple. "Free the queen now, or this bullet goes into your brain. And the shackles go back on."

The injury would be permanent with gorsian shackles slowing the healing. Death would find her almost instantaneously.

Hilde spat, a wad of greenish-brown phlegm splattering at Lidia's feet. "Who's to say you won't kill me afterward?"

"I swear on Luna's golden bow that I shall not kill you."

There were few stronger vows, short of the blood oath of the Fae. It seemed to do the trick for the hag, who bared her rotted teeth but said, "Fine."

A wave of a gnarled hand and some chanted, guttural words, and the ink melted down Irithys's fiery neck. Like black rain, it sluiced down her flaming blue body, dripping to the stones below.

And in its wake, as it cleared, the sprite began to blaze a blinding white.

Lidia lowered the gun from the hag's head. "As promised."

Hilde sneered, "What now? I leave, knowing you have some scheme afoot?"

Lidia slid her gaze to Irithys. "Your move, sprite."

Irithys smiled, and crooked a small, white-hot finger.

Hilde burst into flames. The hag didn't even have time to scream before she was ash on the floor. Amid the acrid smoke curling through the room, Irithys glowed like a newborn star.

"And now, Hind?" the Sprite Queen asked, bright as Solas himself.

Lidia held out her forearm. "Now you make it look like an accident."

"What?"

"Burn me." She nodded to Hilde's ashes. "Not like that, but . . . enough. So it looks convincing when I tell the others you overpowered me and Hilde when I fetched you for more help torturing the prisoners, and then you got away."

Irithys's white flame again turned yellow. "Got away to do *what*, though?"

"Create a diversion."

"It will hurt."

Lidia held the sprite's stare. "Good. In order to be real, it needs to hurt."

She laid out her plan for the queen as quickly as she could, telling her how to navigate the path of disabled cameras to get out of the palace, where to hide, and when and where to strike. And if somehow, against all odds, she succeeded . . . she laid out what would be required of Irithys after that. As insane and unlikely as it was.

All of it relied on the queen. When Lidia had finished, Irithys was shaking her head—not with refusal, but with shock.

"Can I trust you?" Lidia asked the sprite.

Irithys began to glow white again—white-hot. "You don't have any other choice now, do you?"

Lidia extended her arm once more. "Make it hurt, Your Majesty."

Darkness and debris and dust. Coughs and groans.

From the sounds behind her, Bryce knew Nesta and Azriel were alive. What state they were in . . . Well, she didn't particularly care at the moment.

The power she'd siphoned from this place, from Silene herself, thrummed through her body, familiar and yet foreign. It was part of her now—not like a temporary charge from Hunt, but rather something that had *stuck* to her own power, bound itself there.

Like called to like. As if her star had known this magic existed and drawn her toward it, as if they were sister powers—

And they were. Bryce bore Theia's light through Helena's line. And this light . . . it was Theia's light through Silene. Two sisters, united at last. But Silene's light, now mixed with Bryce's . . .

It was light, but it wasn't quite the same as the power she'd possessed before. She couldn't figure it out, didn't have the time to explore its nuances, as she got to her feet and beheld the faint shimmer filling the chamber they'd fallen into. The one that had been hidden a level below the star.

A sarcophagus made of clear quartz lay in the center of the space. And inside it, preserved in eternal youth and beauty, lay a dark-haired female.

Bryce's mind sped through possibilities. This place had once been an Asteri palace before Theia had claimed it. And in the tunnel carvings, made by Silene to depict her mother's teachings . . .

Evil always waited below them.

What if Silene had never realized what, exactly, Theia had meant? That it wasn't just a metaphor?

That here, literally right under them, slumbering in that forgotten coffin . . .

Here lay the evil beneath.

24

Bryce's breath came fast and shallow as she surveyed the crystal coffin in the center of the otherwise empty chamber.

There were no doors into the room. As far as she could discern, the only entrance was through the ceiling that had just collapsed beneath them.

In the crystal sarcophagus, the female lay preserved with unnerving detail.

No, not preserved. Her slim chest rose and fell. Sleeping.

The hair on the back of Bryce's neck rose.

One of the inmates she'd been warned not to release from the Prison. Some ancient, strange being held down here, in a cell beneath their feet, so dangerous she'd been encased in crystal—

That crystal coffin revealed the features of the sleeping female: humanoid, pale-skinned, and slender. Her silky golden gown accentuated every delicate curve of her body.

Bryce had never seen skin that pale. It glowed like a full moon. Her dark hair . . . it was *too* dark, somehow. It didn't reflect the light at all. It shouldn't have existed in nature.

And—was she wearing lipstick? No one had lips that vibrantly red. *Blow Job Red*, Danika had once quipped about a similar shade Bryce had worn.

"What have you done?" Azriel rasped, and Bryce twisted to

find him on his feet, wings tucked in, Nesta leaning against him as if wounded, Ataraxia dangling from her grip. The male now held the Starsword at the ready, Truth-Teller gripped in his other hand.

He must have had some sort of Starborn blood in him, then—a distant ancestor, maybe. Or maybe his possession of the knife somehow allowed him to also bear the Starsword.

As if in answer to Azriel's question, the female in the coffin opened her eyes. They were a crushing blue—and they *glowed*.

Bryce tried to scramble away, but she remained frozen in place as the female's gaze slid toward hers. As those red lips curved upward in a small smile that held no joy. As the female lifted a long, slender hand to the lid of the crystal sarcophagus and said, "Release me, slave."

Even muffled by the crystal, the voice was cold, merciless.

"Have you lost your senses?" Nesta seethed at Bryce, hobbling a step closer.

"I didn't mean to open a cell—" Bryce started.

"This isn't one of the cells," Azriel snarled. "We didn't even know this chamber existed."

The female in the coffin ignored their arguing. "How long have I slumbered?" Again, she pushed against the crystal of her sarcophagus.

Or had it been a cage?

Azriel growled at Bryce, "Did you know she was down here?"

Bryce didn't take her eyes off the coffin and the monster within it. "No."

The female in the coffin banged on the lid, its dull thump echoing off the dark stone walls. "Slave, do as you are told."

"Get fucked," Bryce snapped toward the coffin.

"You dare defy me?" Through the quartz, Bryce could only watch as the encased female's nostrils flared. Sniffing. "Ah. You are a mongrel. Both slave and the slave of our slaves. No wonder your manners are coarse."

Nesta rasped, hefting Ataraxia higher, "What *are* you?"

The female's long nails scraped along the lid of the coffin. She didn't look at them as she tested the lid for weaknesses. "I am your god. I am your master. Do you not know me?"

"We don't have any fucking master," Bryce snarled.

The female's nails gouged deep lines into the crystal, but the lid held. She searched beyond Bryce, her gaze falling upon Azriel. Her lips curled. "A foot soldier. Excellent. Kill this insolent female and free me." She pointed to Bryce.

Azriel didn't move. The caged female hissed, "Kneel, soldier. Make the Tithe so I may regain my strength and leave this cage."

Bryce knew then. Knew what evil had been kept in this coffin all this time.

Beside Azriel, Nesta steadied her stance. Like she'd figured it out, too. The motion drew the creature's gaze—and her eyes flared in pure rage. She glanced between Nesta and Bryce, and her white teeth flashed as she asked the latter, "Was it Theia who stole the Horn for you? Who put it in your flesh?" Her gaze slid back to Nesta. "And you—you are linked to the other parts of the Trove. Did she give them to you?"

"I don't know what you're talking about," Nesta said flatly.

The creature snickered, and drawled to Nesta, "I can smell them on you, girl. Do you not think a blacksmith knows their own creation?"

Bryce's mouth dried out.

The female in the sarcophagus was an Asteri.

Tharion had no words as they walked down the halls of the Meat Market to the car supposedly waiting for them in a side alley. None of them did.

Ithan hadn't spoken since he'd torn out Sigrid's throat.

It had been an accident. Tharion had seen Ithan aiming that blow for Sigrid's shoulder, but the female had dodged so quickly— and chosen the wrong fucking direction, by stupid chance—that the blow had become fatal.

Silence had fallen as Ithan stared at the fist and claws he'd punched clean through Sigrid's throat. His hand was the only thing keeping her body upright as her eyes went vacant—

"*Remove your fist,*" the Viper Queen had commanded.

Ithan's face had gone dead, and the wolf snatched his claws and hand out of Sigrid's throat.

It was the final indignity. The removal of his hand and claws severed what remained of her thin neck.

And as he yanked his bloody fist back, as her body collapsed to the ring floor . . . Sigrid's head rolled away.

Ithan had just stared at what he'd done. And Tharion hadn't been able to find the words to say that they'd all *seen* what Holstrom had intended, all knew he hadn't meant to kill her.

The Viper Queen's assassins stood at the alley door, holding it open. As promised, a black sedan had been parked there.

Tharion took one step—only one—out into the night before the sweet, beckoning scent of the Istros hit him. Every muscle and instinct in his body came alive, begging him to go to the water, to submerge himself in its wildness and magic, to shed legs in favor of fins, to let the river ripple through his gills, into his very blood—

Tharion shut down the demand, the longing. Kept moving toward the sedan, one foot after another.

Still silent, they filed into the car, Flynn taking the wheel, Dec sliding into the passenger seat. Tharion sat in the back beside the male who'd taken on this unholy burden for him.

"You, ah . . . ," Flynn began as he started the car and peered over his shoulder to reverse out of the alley. "You all right, Holstrom?"

Ithan said nothing.

Declan announced quietly, looking down at his phone, "Marc's handling our family stuff. Making sure everyone's safe."

Small fucking consolation.

Three bright lights slammed into the windshield, and they all jumped. But—the sprites. They'd forgotten the sprites.

Flynn rolled down his window and Rithi, Sasa, and Malana sped in. Sasa breathed, *"Go, go, go,"* and Flynn didn't waste time questioning as they reversed out of the alley at full speed. In a smooth shift, he pulled onto a main street and switched into drive—and then they were zooming off through the labyrinth of streets Tharion had thought he'd never see again.

"What's happening?" Declan asked the sprites, who had nestled into the drink holders up front.

"We burned it," Sasa said, a deep orange.

"Burned *what*?" Flynn demanded.

Tharion could only gape as Malana pointed through the rear window, to where flames were now licking the night sky above the Meat Market.

"She'll kill you." Tharion's voice was hoarse. Like he'd been screaming. Maybe he had been. He didn't know.

"She'll have to find us to do that," said Rithi grimly, then turned to Ithan. "She engineered that perfectly. She used you."

"I played right into her hands." Ithan's voice was soft, broken.

No one spoke. No one seemed inclined to. So Tharion figured he might as well ask, "How so?"

Ithan shook his head and looked out the window, face blank, still blood-splattered. He said nothing more.

They drove on through the city, somehow unchanged despite what had just occurred. Drove all the way to the Rose Gate and the Eastern Road beyond it. To the coast, and the ship that would be waiting for them.

And all the consequences that would follow.

Bryce backed away as Azriel advanced a step toward the crystal coffin, Truth-Teller now glowing with black light in his left hand.

Bryce had seen the gold-clad creature who now slumbered in the coffin before, she realized: when Silene had related her mother's story. This female before them . . . she was the Asteri who'd ruled here. Theia's mistress.

The Asteri's blue eyes lowered to the dagger. "You dare draw a weapon before me? Against those who crafted you, soldier, from night and pain?"

"You are no creator of mine," Azriel said coldly. The Starsword gleamed in his other hand. If they bothered him, if they called to him, he didn't let on. Neither hand so much as twitched.

The Asteri's eyes flared with recognition at the long blade. "Did Fionn send you, then? To slay me in my sleep? Or was it that traitor Enalius? I see that you bear his dagger—as his emissary? Or his assassin?"

The words must have meant something to Azriel. The warrior let out a small noise of shock.

"Fionn indeed sent us to finish you off," Nesta lied with impressive menace. "But it looks like now we'll have the pleasure of killing you awake."

The Asteri smiled again. "You'll have to open this sarcophagus to get me."

Bryce smiled back at her, all teeth. "Fionn sent them. But Theia sent *me*."

Blue fire simmered in the creature's eyes. "That traitorous bitch will be dealt with after I handle you."

Azriel started to move along the coffin. Assessing the best way to attack the Asteri, no doubt. "Unfortunately for you," Bryce taunted, "Theia's been dead for fifteen thousand years. So have the rest of your buddies. Your people are little more than a half-forgotten myth in this world."

For a heartbeat, it was the creature's turn to blink. As if a memory had cleared, she said, more to herself than them, "Theia was so charming that day. Told me I looked tired, and to replenish myself in the crystal here, above the well. But she sealed me within instead. To let me starve to death over the eons." Teeth, white as snow, flashed. "And in my dreams, she danced upon the stones above me. Danced upon my grave while I starved beneath her feet."

"Give me the Starsword," Bryce murmured to Azriel. The blade had killed Reapers. Maybe it could kill an Asteri. Maybe that was what she'd come here to learn.

"No," Azriel snarled. "You brought this terror upon us."

"I had no idea she was here—"

"Release me, slaves," the Asteri cut in. "I grow impatient."

Why hadn't Theia warned her daughters that this thing was down here? Why be so irresponsible, so reckless—

Et in Avallen ego. Even here, on this island that had been a paradise during Theia's reign, this evil had existed. And Theia *had* warned her children about it—that evil was always lurking beneath them, waiting to grab them. Literally.

The taint of the Asteri who had ruled here, Silene had claimed, had lingered about this place—a terrible, ancient power. Enough so that it had needed to be concealed by the Prison's wickedness. Silene just hadn't figured out that it remained because an Asteri was still present.

And here, against all odds, was a living link to the past, to answers Bryce needed. If Urd had guided her this far . . .

Bryce said calmly, "I have questions for you. If you don't answer them, I'm happy to leave you down here until the end of eternity."

"Oh, this planet will be long dead before eternity has ended. Its star will expand, and expand, and eventually devour everything in its path. Including this world."

"Thanks for the astronomy lesson."

A slow smile. "I shall answer your questions . . . if you release me from this tomb."

Bryce held her stare.

"Don't you fucking dare," Azriel murmured.

But time pressed down on her. With every minute, Hunt suffered. She was sure of it.

The very stones and wards of this place answered to her will . . .

Azriel lunged for Bryce, but she'd already pointed to the crystal coffin. *"Get up, then."*

A click, loud as thunder, and the lid unlocked.

25

Opening the coffin had been as easy as commanding the stones of the mountain to move.

"What have you done?" Nesta said, silver fire flaring in her eyes, down Ataraxia's blade.

The Asteri laid a hand on the unlocked coffin lid and began to push.

Like Hel would she face this thing unarmed. Bryce extended a hand toward Azriel, casting her will with it.

The Starsword flew from his hand and into hers.

Azriel started, shadows flashing at his shoulders, readying to strike, but Bryce said, "Theia showed me that trick in Silene's little memory montage." It was the feeling she'd been sensing, of the blade calling to her. Being willing to leap into her hand.

Azriel bared his teeth, but drew another sword that had been sheathed in a concealed panel at his back and hefted Truth-Teller in his other hand as Nesta lifted Ataraxia—

Bryce twisted to the coffin in time to see the Asteri slowly climb out, like a hatching spider.

Bryce's chest provided the only light, making the monster's pale skin even whiter, deepening the red of her lips to a near-purple hue. Her long black hair draped down her slim form, pooling on the stone beneath her like liquid night.

But she remained on the floor, hunched over herself. Like she didn't have the strength to stand.

"You go left," Azriel murmured to Nesta, power blazing around them.

"No," Bryce said, not looking back as she approached the Asteri on the floor and sat down, setting the Starsword on the cold stone beside her.

To her shock, Azriel and Nesta didn't attack. But they remained only a step away, weapons at the ready.

"Your companions think you mad for releasing me," the Asteri said, picking at an invisible speck on her golden silk gown as she settled herself into a proper seated position.

"They don't realize that you haven't fed in thousands of years, and I can kick your ass."

"We realized it," Nesta muttered.

"Let's start with the basics, leech," Bryce said to the Asteri. "Where did—"

"You may call me Vesperus." The creature's eyes glowed with irritation.

"Are you related to Hesperus?" Bryce arched a brow at the name, so similar to one of Midgard's Asteri. "The Evening Star?"

"*I* am the Evening Star," Vesperus seethed.

Bryce rolled her eyes. "Fine, we'll call you the Evening Star, too. Happy?"

"Is it not fitting?" A wave of long fingers capped in sharp nails. "I drank from the land's magic, and the land's magic drank from me."

"Where did you come from, before you arrived here?"

Vesperus folded her hands in her lap. "A planet that was once green, as this one is."

"And that wasn't good enough?"

"We grew too populous. Wars broke out between the various beings on our world. Some of us saw the changes in the land beginning—rivers run dry, clouds so thick the sun could not pierce them—and left. Our brightest minds found ways to bend the fabric of worlds. To travel between them. Wayfarers, we called them. World-walkers."

"So you trashed your planet, then went to feed off others?"

"We had to find sustenance."

Bryce's fingers curled against the rock floor, but her voice remained steady. "If you knew how to open portals between worlds, why did you need to rely on the Dread Trove?"

"Once we left our home world, our powers began to dim. Too late, we realized that we had been dependent on our land's inherent magic. The magic in other worlds was not potent enough. Yet we could not find the way back home. Those of us who ventured here found ways to amplify that power, thanks to the gifts of the land. We pooled our power, and imbued those gifts into the Cauldron so that it would work our will. We Made the Trove from it. And then bound the very essence of the Cauldron to the soul of this world."

Solas. "So destroy the Cauldron . . ."

"And you destroy this world. One cannot exist without the other."

Behind them, Nesta sucked in a sharp breath. But Bryce said, "You gave this world a kill switch."

"We gave many worlds . . . kill switches. To protect our interests." She said it with such calm, such surety.

"Do you know Rigelus?"

"You speak his name very casually for a worm."

"We're closely acquainted."

A slight pursing of the lips. "I knew him in passing. I'm assuming you wish to slay him—and have come to ask me how to do it."

Bryce said nothing.

Vesperus leveled a cold look at her. "I will not help you in that regard. I will not betray the secrets of my people."

"Was this sort of compassion the reason Theia didn't kill you?"

Vesperus glowered. "Theia knew that for my kind, this sort of punishment would be far worse than death. To be confined, yet live. To neither breathe, nor eat, nor drink—but to be left in half slumber, starving." That gleam in her eyes—it wasn't solely rage. It was madness. "It would have been a mercy to kill me. Theia did not understand the word. I raised her from childhood not to. She would come down here every now and then and stare at me—I slept, but I could sense her there. Gloating over me. Convinced of her triumph."

A chill skittered down Bryce's spine. "She kept you down here as a trophy."

Vesperus's chin dipped in a nod. "I believe she drew pleasure from my suffering."

"I don't blame her," Bryce snapped, even as a sick feeling filled her stomach. Theia might have helped Midgard in the end, but she was no better than the monster who'd raised her.

"I have questions for you, too, mongrel."

"By all means," Bryce said, waving her hand.

"If we lost the war to Theia, if my people are now a mere myth, how is it that you know Rigelus intimately? Do the Asteri still dwell here?"

"No," Bryce said. "I came from another world. One where the Asteri remain in control."

"How long have the Asteri ruled?"

"Fifteen thousand years."

"Rigelus must be very pleased with himself."

"Oh, he is."

But the Asteri looked from Bryce to Azriel and Nesta behind her, brows lifting. "Is life so unbearable under our rule that you must always defy us?"

Yes. No. For Bryce, life had been fine. Shitty in spots, but fine. But for so many others . . .

"Does it matter," Vesperus pushed on, addressing Bryce once more, "that we take a little of your power? What would you even do with it?"

"It matters that we're lied to," Bryce said. "That our power is not yours for the taking. That your supremacy is unchecked and unearned."

"There is a natural order to the universe, girl. The strong rule the weak, and the weak benefit from it. Everything in nature preys and is preyed upon. You Fae somehow consider this an affront only when it is applied to you."

"I'm not going to debate the ethics of conquest with you. Rigelus and the others have no right to my world, but they've poisoned the water in Midgard—it's full of some sort of parasite that leaches our magic and requires us to offer it up to the Asteri. How do I undo it?"

Vesperus's eyes glowed with delight. "We'd hoped for something of this nature, rather than the Tithe, which required the *consent*"—she spat the word as if it tasted foul—"of our subjects, but we never figured out how . . . The water supply, you say?" A soft laugh. "Rigelus always was clever."

"How the *fuck* do I undo it?"

"You seem to think me inclined to help you, when I would receive nothing in return."

"I know what you want, and you're not getting it."

"And if I were to say that I have no wish to rule, only to live?"

"You'd still be a leech, who'd need to feed on these people. You don't deserve to go free."

"They have a place in this land for creatures like me. The unwanted. It is called the Middle. I have dreamt of it, seen it in my long slumber."

"That's not my decision to make."

"Use the Crown that Made scum over there possesses." Vesperus nodded to Nesta. "You could forge a path to enact your vision by clearing the minds of those before you."

She had no idea what Vesperus meant, but Bryce countered coolly, "You guys had a long fucking time to figure out every way to justify your actions, huh?"

"We are superior beings. We do not need to justify anything."

"You'd fit right in on Midgard."

"If Rigelus has held on to his power for so long, then your world is firmly in his grasp. He will not abandon it. He will have learned from the mistakes my companions and I made on this world and on others."

Bryce's hand curled into a fist. The force of holding her power at bay sang through her.

Vesperus's gaze darted to Bryce's glowing fist. "Is it time for us to battle, then?"

Power thrummed from the Asteri, a steady beat against Bryce's skin.

Even depriving Vesperus of her magic sustenance for this long hadn't killed her. What would taking out that massive core of first-light under the Asteri's palace in the Eternal City do, other than remove their source of nutrition? It wouldn't be enough.

So Bryce let some of her power shimmer to the surface. She could have sworn her starlight was . . . heavier. Different, somehow, with the addition of what she'd claimed from Silene.

"I know you can die," Bryce said, and felt the power glowing in her eyes. "The Fae killed you losers once, and on my world, Apollion ate one of you."

"Ate?" Vesperus's amusement banked.

Bryce smiled slowly. "They call him the Star-Eater. He ate Sirius. I have him on standby, waiting to come eat you, too."

"You lie."

"I wish I could show you the empty throne Rigelus still keeps for Sirius. It's sort of sweet."

"What manner of creature is this Apollion?"

"We call them demons, but you probably know them by some other name. Your kind tried to invade their world, Hel. It didn't go well for you."

"Then Hel and this Apollion shall pay for such sacrilege," Vesperus hissed.

"Somehow, I don't think you'll be the one to make him."

Vesperus's fingers tapped her gold-clad knee. Her eyes guttered to midnight blue, promising death. She braced her hands on the ground and began to push upward—to stand.

"Don't move," Bryce warned, hand closing around the Starsword's hilt. Azriel and Nesta pointed their blades at the Asteri.

But Vesperus completed the motion. Stood to her full height. Bryce had no choice but to shoot to her feet as well. Vesperus swayed, but remained upright.

The Asteri advanced a tentative, testing step. Bryce held her ground.

Vesperus took another step, steadier now, and smiled past Bryce. At Azriel, at Truth-Teller. "You don't know how to use it, do you?"

Azriel pointed the dagger toward the advancing Asteri. "Pretty sure this end's the one that'll go through your gut."

Vesperus chuckled, her dark hair swaying with each inching step closer. "Typical of your kind. You want to play with our weapons, but have no concept of their true abilities. Your mind couldn't hold all the possibilities at once."

Azriel snarled softly, wings flaring, "Try me."

Vesperus took one more step, now barely a foot from Bryce. "I can smell it—how much of what we created here went unused. Ignorant fools."

Bryce let her magic flow. A thought, and her hair drifted around her head, borne aloft once more by the currents of her power, still amplified by what she'd seized from this mountain. She angled the Starsword before her, light rippling along the blade.

Vesperus backed up a half step, hissing at the gleaming weapon. "We hid pockets of our power throughout the lands, in case the vermin should cause . . . problems. It seems our wisdom did not fail us."

"There are no such places," Azriel countered coldly.

"Are there not?" Vesperus grinned broadly, showing all of her too-white teeth. "Have *you* looked beneath every sacred mountain? At their very roots? The magic draws all sorts of creatures. I can sense them even now, slithering about, gnawing on the magic. *My* magic. They're as much vermin as the rest of you."

Bryce carefully didn't glance at Nesta, who was creeping around the crystal coffin. Nesta had claimed earlier that the Middengard Wyrm had eaten her power—was that the sort of creature Vesperus meant?

And perhaps more importantly: Was Nesta still weakened? Or had her power returned?

Bryce clutched the Starsword tighter. Its power thudded into her palms like a heartbeat. "But why store your power *here*? It's an island—not exactly an easy pit stop."

"There are certain places, girl, that are better suited to hold power than others. Places where the veil between worlds is thin, and magic naturally abounds. Our light thrives in such environments, sustained by the regenerative magic of the land." She gestured around them. "This island is a thin place—the mists around it declare it so."

Bryce continued, buying Nesta more time to get closer to Vesperus, "We don't have anything like that on Midgard."

But didn't they? The Bone Quarter, surrounded by impenetrable mists, held all that secondlight.

"Every world has at least one thin place," Vesperus drawled. "And there are always certain people more suited to exploit it—to claim its powers, to travel through them to other worlds."

The Northern Rift was wreathed in mist, too, Bryce realized. A tear between worlds—a thin place. And the riverbank where she'd landed in this world . . . it had been misty there, as well.

"Theia had the gift," Vesperus said, "but did not understand how to claim the light. I made sure never to reveal how during her training—how she might light up entire worlds, if she wished, if she seized the power to amplify her own. But you, Light-Stealer . . . She must have passed the gift down to you. And it seems you have learned what she did not."

Vesperus peered at her bare feet, the rock beneath. "Theia never learned how to access the power I cached beneath my palace. She had no choice but to leave it there, buried in the veins of this mountain. Her loss—and my gain."

Oh gods. There was a fucking firstlight core here, far beneath their feet—

Vesperus smiled. "You really should have killed me when you had the chance."

Light shot up the Asteri's legs, into her body. A blinding flash, and then—

Vesperus's red mouth opened in joy and triumph, but no sound came out. Only black blood.

Bryce blinked at the crunch. The wet spray. The glint of silver that appeared between Vesperus's shining breasts.

The firstlight flowing up the Asteri's body shivered—and vanished.

Nesta had plunged Ataraxia right through Vesperus's chest.

26

Ithan didn't deserve to exist. To breathe.

And yet here he was, sitting in the back of a car as they approached the docks at Ionia. Here he was, praying the Hind hadn't sold them out and that the ship would be waiting to bring them to Pangera.

Kin-slayer. Murderer. The thoughts echoed through his very bones.

Ithan had killed the one person who might have led the Valbaran wolves to a different future, an alternative to Sabine.

It didn't matter that it had been accidental. He'd ripped out her throat. And decapitated her in the process of removing his fist.

To save his friends, he'd done this unspeakable, unforgivable thing. He was no better than the Hind.

Ithan caught a glimpse of his reflection in the car window, and hastily turned away.

Ataraxia had slain the Middengard Wyrm—but there was no indication the blade could also kill an Asteri. That anything, in any world, could do that except for Apollion.

"Get out of range—" Bryce warned Nesta, but the warrior snarled

at Bryce, "She was keeping you talking until she got an opportunity to kill you with that cache of light, you fool."

Black blood dribbled from Vesperus's lips. "You are indeed a fool, girl."

The power slipped from Bryce's grip as Vesperus placed a hand at Ataraxia's tip and shoved. The sword punched back through her chest. The movement was hard enough that Nesta stumbled, shock whitening her face.

Slowly, Vesperus turned. Smiled at Nesta. Then down at the gaping hole between her breasts, already healing. All that firstlight was grade A healing magic. Taken in such a big dose—

"Ataraxia didn't work," Nesta breathed, shock still stark on her face. "The Trove—"

"Do *not* summon the Trove," Azriel ordered. "Don't bring it near her."

Nesta shook her head. "But—"

"Not even for our lives," Azriel snarled.

"Oh, I'll get the Trove soon enough," Vesperus said, and peered at the hole above her coffin, the ruined chamber beyond.

For a heartbeat, Bryce wasn't in the tomb, but back in Griffin Antiquities. A heartbeat, and she was in the library below the gallery, Micah held at bay, Lehabah begging her to go—

She'd found a way then. She'd killed a fucking Archangel.

There were two blades practically screaming for her to use them. Bryce again reached out a hand, her will, toward Azriel. And as surely as the Starsword had done, Truth-Teller flew from his grip. He tried to grab it, but even his swift lunge wasn't fast enough to stop it. To stop Bryce as the knife soared for her fingers.

The dagger's hilt landed in her palm, cool and heavy.

Her body began to hum. Like having one blade in each hand— the Starsword and Truth-Teller—electrified her.

Bryce stepped toward Vesperus. Vesperus swayed back slightly. Just as Bryce had suspected.

Behind her, Nesta and Azriel unleashed twin bolts of magic, one silver, one blue—arcing toward Vesperus from two directions. Splitting Vesperus's attention for a heartbeat—

The heartbeat Bryce had used to kill Micah.

The heartbeat that she used now to spring at the Asteri, sword in one hand, dagger in the other.

Bone collided with metal, and Vesperus screeched in rage as Bryce plunged Truth-Teller and the Starsword into her chest.

Bryce threw her power into the Starsword, light ripping through the black blade, willing it to tear this fucking monster apart—

She willed it into Truth-Teller, and shadows flowed—

And where the two blades met, where Bryce's light merged at their nexus, power met power.

Her ears hollowed out. Magic like lightning surged through her, from her. The chamber rippled, a muffled *boom* echoing through Bryce.

Her blood roared, a beast howling at the moon. She was vaguely aware of a glow, of radiating light that flowed through the Starsword, the dagger—

Vesperus thrashed, falling beyond Bryce's grip, sinking to her knees.

The Asteri hunched over, hands grappling on the hilts of the blades. She hissed as her skin touched the black metal. "I shall *kill* you for this."

But the words were slow . . . dragged out.

No, that was *time* slowing, rippling, as it had with Micah, as if the blades were killing the Asteri, a great world power—

A whip of blue magic shot through the world, a ribbon of cobalt piercing the starlight and darkness. She could see every loop and coil as it wrapped around Vesperus's neck.

Time resumed—sped up to its normal rate. "Stop!" Bryce shouted, but too late.

Vesperus lifted a hand to her neck as Azriel's blue light dissolved into her skin. She let out a strangled laugh as blood leaked from her mouth. "Still so ignorant. Your power is and will always be mine."

Blue magic appeared at her fingertips, absorbed from the Illyrian's attack. She wrapped it around one hand like a glove and grasped the Starsword's handle.

As if it provided the barrier she needed, allowing her to touch the blade, Vesperus yanked the Starsword free and let it clatter to the stones, coated with gore.

It . . . it hadn't worked. The sword and dagger united hadn't killed her.

Hand glowing blue, Vesperus studied the dagger still in her chest and then smiled at Bryce as she wrapped her fingers, still wreathed in lightning, around the hilt. "I'm going to carve you up with this, girl."

Nesta rotated Ataraxia in her hand and swung upward. Azriel shouted at her, "Throw your power in the blade!"

"*No!*" Bryce screamed. The Starsword and Truth-Teller had clearly been weakening the Asteri. If she could figure out how to amplify their power, she'd know how to kill them all—

Vesperus had just yanked Truth-Teller from her chest in a smooth slide when Ataraxia severed flesh and bone, dark blood—or whatever ichor flowed in an Asteri's veins—spraying.

Vesperus's dark head tumbled to the stones.

Silver fire wreathed Ataraxia as Nesta plunged the blade into the Asteri's fallen head. Again. And again. Ichor and light leaked from the broken body, and between one stab and the next, Nesta's arm slowed, slowed, slowed—

That was time slowing again. Bryce could see every spark of silver flame coiling about the blade, see it reflected in Nesta's eyes.

The sword descended into Vesperus's head one last time. Inch by inch, shattering bone and spraying gore—

Time snapped back into movement, but Vesperus did not.

Vesperus, the only Asteri left on this world, lay dead.

There was a small boat waiting for them. That much had gone right.

Tharion couldn't stand to look at Ithan. At any of his friends, even the sprites, who'd done so much for him.

The captain was waving to them, a silent order to hurry up while they still had the cover of darkness. Dawn was beginning to turn the sky gray.

They ditched the car at the end of the dock and walked quickly toward the small boat. Once they were on the *Depth Charger*, they'd be untraceable, even if the Viper Queen tracked the car here.

Tharion slid a hand into his pocket and fingered the white stone that would summon the ship. Dec, Flynn, and the sprites jumped into the boat, Dec quietly talking to the captain, but Holstrom had paused at the edge of the dock.

Silently, Tharion came up beside him.

The water was clear, even twenty feet above the bottom. Where he might have once jumped in, luxuriated in the crisp ocean water . . .

He didn't dare send a ripple through the waters of the world announcing his presence. Coward.

Flynn called to them, "Get on, assholes!"

Tharion glanced to Ithan, but the wolf was staring at the eastern horizon. The rising sun.

"Ready?" Tharion asked.

"I have to go back," Holstrom rasped.

"What?" Tharion faced him fully. "What do you mean?"

The wolf slowly turned to look at him, his eyes bleak. Tharion felt the weight of his guilt at what he'd done to this male, in having Holstrom fight for him.

"To Crescent City," Ithan said, face like stone. "I have to go back."

"Why?"

"Holstrom! Ketos!" Dec hollered as the boat's engine churned.

Ithan just said quietly, "To make it right."

A shudder of muscle and a ripple of light, and the human form became a massive wolf.

"Ithan—" Tharion started.

The wolf turned and sprinted down the dock, back toward the arid countryside, golden in the rising light.

Flynn bellowed, "Holstrom, what the *fuck*!"

But the wolf had already reached the shore. Then the main building of the marina. Then the alley beside it . . . and then he vanished.

Silence fell, interrupted only by the grumble and splash of the engine. Tharion turned back toward the boat, toward the two friends onboard, the sprites gleaming like three small stars between them.

"What the fuck happened?" Flynn demanded.

Tharion shook his head, at a loss for words, and stepped onto the boat.

His fault—all of it. He lifted his face to the sky as the boat peeled toward the open ocean, and wondered if he'd ever see Valbara again.

If he even deserved to.

27

Bryce couldn't move for a moment. Vesperus was dead.

Nesta slashed her hand and the creature's body burned with that strange silver fire.

As the Asteri was reduced to ashes, Bryce grabbed the sword and dagger from the ground, both blades dripping with Vesperus's blood.

She whirled on Nesta, on Azriel. "You shouldn't have killed her. If we could have gotten her under control, the amount of information that we could have pried from her—"

"Do you have any idea what you almost did here?" Nesta raged, covered in Vesperus's dark ichor. She still gripped Ataraxia in one hand, as if not yet decided whether she was done killing. "What you unleashed?"

"Trust me, I know better than you guys what the Asteri can do."

"Then you have even less of an excuse for your actions," Nesta snapped. Her sword rose.

Azriel extended a scarred hand to Bryce, panting hard. "Open the passage out of here. You're coming back with us. Right now."

To that cell under a different mountain. Where she had no doubt she'd be subjected to the interrogation Vesperus should have received.

Bryce snorted. "Like Hel I am." Debris began floating around her. "You killed the one person here who might have given me the answer I needed."

"You're looking for ways to kill the Daglan. Well, *I* just killed that monster," Nesta said. "Isn't that answer enough?"

"No," Bryce said. "You've only left me with more questions."

She let her power flow outward from the star in her chest. From the Horn in her back.

"Don't you *dare*," Azriel warned with lethal softness.

But Bryce shoved out a slice of her power. Sharp and targeted, as Silene had used to carve the stones. As Azriel had focused his own power on her star earlier.

Light cut through stone and sizzled, a line literally drawn at Azriel's feet.

Whatever had changed in her power with the addition of Silene's magic . . . Fuck yeah. This would be useful.

"I won't tell them about you," Bryce said coolly, even as part of her marveled at the laser she'd created out of pure magic. The other part of her cringed from it—from the power that was eerily similar to what Rigelus had used against her before she jumped through the Gate in the Eternal Palace. "I swear it on my mate's life. Even if Rigelus . . ." She shook her head. "I won't breathe a word to them about this place."

Azriel dared to put one foot over the line she'd blasted into the floor. "They'll pry it from you. People like me, like them . . . we always get the information we need." His gaze darkened with the promise of unending pain.

"I won't let it come to that," Bryce said, and sent her power searing through her star again—right into the crystal sarcophagus.

Crystal like the Gate that had opened the way to this world.

The sarcophagus glowed . . . and then darkened into a pit.

"Please," Azriel said, his gaze now on her hands. On the Starsword—and on Truth-Teller. Something like panic filled his hazel eyes.

Shaking her head, Bryce backed toward the hole she'd made in the world. In the universe. She could only pray it would lead her to Midgard.

She met Nesta's stare. Raging silver fire flickered there.

"You're as much of a monster as they are," Nesta accused.

Bryce knew. She'd always known. "Love will do that to you."

Silver flames roared for her in a tidal wave, but Bryce was already leaping, sheathing the blades as she moved. Cold like nothing she'd known tore past her head, her spine—

And then the light from Nesta's silver flame winked out as the gate shut above Bryce, nothing but darkness surrounding her as she plunged deeper and deeper into the pit.

Toward home.

PART II
THE SEARCH

28

Hours after Pollux and the Hawk had left with Rigelus, Hunt was no closer to knowing who they would select to die. His bet was on Baxian, but there was a good chance Pollux would realize that killing Ruhn would devastate Bryce. If Bryce ever got back home to learn of it.

He'd been surprised and disturbed to stir from unconsciousness to find a familiar, growing weight at his back. A glance to Baxian had shown him the source: their wings were somehow regrowing at rapid speed, despite the gorsian shackles. Someone had to have given them something to orchestrate the healing—though it couldn't mean anything good.

He wondered if their captors had realized that the relentless itching would be a torment as awful as the whips and brands. Gritting his teeth against it, Hunt writhed, arching his spine, as if it'd help ease the merciless sensation. He'd give anything, anything, for one scratch—

"Orion." Aidas's voice sounded in his head, in the chamber. A cat with eyes like blue opals crouched on the floor, amid the blood and waste. The same form Rigelus had used to deceive Hunt months ago.

"Aidas . . . or Rigelus?" Hunt groaned.

Aidas was smart enough to get it—Hunt needed proof. The

demon prince said, "Miss Quinlan first met me on a park bench outside of the Oracle's Temple when she was thirteen. I asked her what blinds an Oracle."

The real thing, then. Not some trick of the Asteri.

"Bryce," Hunt moaned.

"I'm looking for her," Aidas said. Hunt could have sworn the cat looked sad.

"What does Rigelus want from my lightning?"

Aidas's tail swished. "So that's why he's working so hard to break you."

"He threatened to kill one of them if I didn't give some to him." A nod to Ruhn and Baxian.

Aidas bristled. "You mustn't do so, Athalar."

"Too late. He harvested it into a crystal like firstlight. And the fucker's going to kill one of them anyway."

Aidas's blue eyes filled with worry, but the prince said nothing. So Hunt said again, "What does he want from my lightning?"

"If I were to guess . . . The same thing Sofie Renast's lightning was hunted for: to resurrect the dead."

Hunt's head swam. "My lightning can't do that. We didn't even know Sofie's lightning could do that."

Aidas blinked. "Well, apparently, Rigelus thinks both sources of lightning can."

"How did you find that out? *We* didn't discover that, and we were trying to dig up information about Sofie for weeks." Hunt fought the fog in his head. No, he knew this wasn't possible.

"I don't just sit around waiting for you to contact me," Aidas said. "My spies hear whispers around Midgard . . . and when some concern me, I go to investigate."

"So the River Queen was on the hunt for Sofie to . . . engage in some necromancy? Why not go to the Bone Quarter?"

"I don't know what the River Queen wanted."

Hunt scoured his memory for what had happened to Sofie's corpse after they'd found it in the morgue aboard the *Depth Charger*. What had Cormac done with it? Was it still on the ship? And if so, did the Ocean Queen know what she had in her possession?

The questions swarmed, but one rose to the forefront. "Why didn't Rigelus just hunt down Sofie's body? Why bother going after me?"

"You presented yourself to him rather conveniently, Athalar. Not to mention that you're alive, and much easier to command than a corpse."

"There are some Archangels who might disagree with you."

Aidas's mouth twitched upward, but he said, "It will likely take time for Rigelus to figure out a way to wield the lightning he extracted from you. Though I admit I am . . . disturbed to learn of his new experimentation. It does not bode well for any of us, if Rigelus is tangling with the dead."

"Why now?" Hunt asked. "I've been enslaved to them for centuries, for Urd's sake."

"Perhaps they've at last learned what your father bred you to be."

Even the miserable itching in his back was forgotten at those words. "What the *fuck* does that mean?"

But Aidas only shook his head. "A tale for another time, Athalar."

"A tale for *now*, Aidas. These cryptic mentions of my father, the *black crown*, secrets about my powers—"

"Mean nothing, if you do not get out of these dungeons."

"Then stop fucking popping out of the shadows and find a key."

"I cannot. My body isn't real here."

"It was real enough in Quinlan's apartment."

"That was a portal, a summoning. This is like . . . a phone call."

"Then send one of your buddies through the Northern Rift to help us—"

"The distance from Nena is too great. They wouldn't arrive in time to make a difference. You will get answers, Athalar, I promise. If you survive. But if the Asteri can use your lightning to raise the dead, in ways swifter and less limited than traditional necromancy, then the armies they might create—"

"You're not making me feel any better about giving some over." Another bit of guilt to burden his soul. He didn't know how he wasn't already broken beneath the sheer weight of it.

"Try not to give him more, then." But Aidas threw him a

pitying look. "I am sorry that one of your companions will die tomorrow."

"Fuck," Hunt said hoarsely. "Any idea who they've picked?"

Aidas angled his head, more feline than princely. Like he could hear things Hunt couldn't. "The one whose death will mean the most to both you and Bryce." Hunt closed his eyes. "The Fae Prince."

This was all Hunt's fault. He'd learned nothing since the Fallen. And he'd been fine with taking on the punishment himself, but for others to do it, for Ruhn to—

"I'm sorry," the Prince of the Chasm said again, and sounded like he meant it.

But Hunt said hoarsely, "If you find her . . . if you see her again . . . tell her . . ."

Not to come back. Not to dare enter this world of pain and suffering and misery. That he was so damn sorry for not stopping all of this.

"I know," Aidas said, not needing Hunt to finish before he vanished into darkness.

29

Bryce had dropped down between worlds. And yet when she landed, she collided sideways with a wall.

Apparently, magical interstellar travel didn't care about physics.

Her head throbbed; her mouth was painfully dry. The rough fibers of a carpet scraped her cheek, muffling the sounds of an enclosed space. It was dry, vaguely musty. Familiar-smelling.

"Isn't this interesting," drawled a male voice in her own language. It was the most wonderful sound she'd ever heard.

Though she'd have wished, perhaps, for the words to have come from someone other than the Autumn King.

He loomed over her, his hands wreathed in flame. Above him, a golden orrery clicked and whirred. She'd landed in her father's private study.

The Autumn King's lips curled in that familiar cruel smile. "And where have *you* been, Bryce Quinlan?"

Bryce opened her mouth, power rallying—

And sputtering out.

"For an old bastard, you move fast," she groaned, straining against the gorsian shackles on her wrists. No chains attached to them, at least—just the cuffs of the shackles. But it was enough. Bryce couldn't so much as summon a flicker of starlight.

Her father knew it. He strolled to his giant wooden desk like he had all the time in the world.

In those initial seconds when she'd landed here, in the worst fucking place in the whole fucking world, he'd not only disabled her power with those shackles—he'd also disarmed her. The Starsword and Truth-Teller now lay behind him on his desk. Along with her phone.

Bryce lifted her chin, though she remained sitting on the ground. "Are Ruhn and Hunt alive?"

Something like distaste flashed in the Autumn King's eyes. As if such mortal bonds should be the least of her concerns. "You show your hand, Bryce Quinlan."

"I thought my name was *Bryce Danaan* now," she seethed.

"To the detriment of the line, yes," the Autumn King said, his eyes sparking. "Where have you been?"

"There was a sample sale at the mall," Bryce said flatly. *"Are Ruhn and Hunt still alive?"*

The Autumn King's head angled, gaze sweeping over her filthy T-shirt, her torn leggings. "I was informed that you were no longer on this planet. Where did you go?"

Bryce declined to answer.

Her father smiled slightly. "I can connect the dots. You arrive from off-world, bearing a knife that matches the Starsword. The dagger from the prophecy, no?" His eyes gleamed with greed. "Not seen since the First Wars. If I were to guess, you managed to reach a place I have long desired to go." He glanced up at the orrery.

"You might want to reconsider before packing your bags," Bryce said. "They don't take kindly to assholes."

"Your journey hasn't impacted that smart mouth of yours, I see."

She smiled with saccharine sweetness. "You're still an absolute bastard, *I see.*"

The Autumn King pursed his lips. "I'd be careful if I were you." He pushed off his desk and stalked toward her. "No one knows you're here."

"Taking your daughter hostage: excellent parenting."

"You are my guest here until I see fit to release you."

"Which will be when?" She batted her eyelashes with exaggerated innocence.

"When I have the reassurances I seek."

Bryce made a show of tapping her chin in contemplation. "How about this: You let me go, and I don't fucking kill you for delaying me?"

A soft, taunting laugh. How had her mother ever loved this cold-blooded reptile?

"I've already sealed off the wards around this villa, and sent away my servants and sentries."

"You mean to tell me we're going to do all our own cooking?"

The intensity on his face didn't falter. "No one shall even know that you are back in this world until I see fit."

"And then you'll tell the Asteri?" Her heart skipped a beat. She couldn't let that happen.

Her father smiled again. "That depends entirely on you."

Ithan ran himself into the ground all the way back to the eastern gate of Crescent City, hundreds of miles from the dock in Ionia where he'd left Tharion and the others.

Make your brother proud.

He hadn't been able to get on that boat. Ketos might be able to walk away from the consequences of his actions, but Ithan couldn't.

Gilded by the setting sun, Crescent City bustled on as usual, unaware of what he'd done. How everything had changed.

He took the coward's path through the city, cutting through FiRo rather than going right to the Istros through Moonwood. If he saw another wolf right now . . .

He didn't want to know what he'd do. What he'd say.

He was no one in the hustle of rush hour, but he kept to the alleys and side streets. He didn't spare a glance for the Heart Gate as he sprinted past it, nor did he let himself look eastward toward Bryce and Danika's old apartment when he passed that, too.

He only looked ahead, toward the approaching river. Toward the Black Dock at the end of the street.

Despite the chaotic throngs of evening commuters in the rest of the city, the Black Dock was silent and empty, wreathed in mist. Down the quay, a few mourners wept on benches, but no one stood on the dock itself.

Ithan couldn't bring himself to look deeper into the mists, toward the Bone Quarter. He prayed Connor wasn't looking his way from across the river.

Ithan shifted into his humanoid form before walking a block westward along the quay. Ithan knew where the entrance was—everyone did.

No one ever went there, of course. No one dared.

The great black door sat in the middle of a matching black marble building—a facade. The building had been styled after an elaborate mausoleum. The door was the focus, the main reason for its existence: to lead one not into the building, but below it.

No one stood guard at the door. Ithan supposed nobody was needed. Anyone who wanted to rob this place would deserve all that they'd face inside.

Crude, ancient markings covered the black door. Like scratches carved by inhuman fingernails. At its center, an etching of a horned, humanoid skull engulfed in flames stared out at him.

Ithan knocked on its hateful face once. Twice. The metal thudded dully.

The door yawned open, silent as a grave. Only darkness waited beyond, and a long, straight staircase into the gloom.

It might as well have been Hel on Midgard.

Ithan felt nothing, was nothing, as he strode in. As the door shut behind him, sealing him in solid, unending night.

Locking him inside the House of Flame and Shadow.

30

If the Autumn King was indeed cooking their meals, then Bryce had to admit that he wasn't a bad chef. Roast chicken, green beans, and some thickly sliced bread waited on the marble table in the vast dining room.

Apparently, she'd arrived around three in the afternoon on a Friday. That was all she'd been able to get out of him while he'd led her from his office to a bedroom on the second floor. Not what the date was, or even the month. Or year.

Nausea coursed through her. Hunt had been kept in the Asteri dungeons for *years* the last time . . . Was he still there? Was he even alive? Was Ruhn? Her family?

There was nothing in her bedroom, an elegant—if bland—blend of marble and overstuffed furniture in varying shades of gray and white, to aid in answering these questions. Her father wanted her cut off from the world, and so it was: No TV. No phone—not even a landline. A glamour shimmered on the floor-to-ceiling windows overlooking an interior lavender garden, blocking prying eyes from seeing in. A peek toward the sky showed an iridescent bubble over the whole place—wards. Like the ones the Fae had established to lock down their territory during the attack this spring.

But it was the screams of pleading Fae parents as Silene locked them out of their home world, leaving their children to the Asteri's cruelty, that echoed through Bryce's head.

And now, sitting across the massive dining table from her father hours later, having showered and changed into a pair of jeans, a T-shirt, and a skintight navy blue athletic jacket that he'd given her—she really fucking hoped they weren't left over from a booty call—Bryce asked, "So is this the plan? Lock me up here until I get so bored that I tell you everything? Or is it to deprive me of information so that I'll tell you anything in exchange for a snippet of news about Hunt?"

Her father sliced into his chicken with a precision that told her exactly how he dealt with his enemies. But he sighed through his nose. "Your hosts in the other world must have had a high tolerance for irreverent nonsense, if you're still alive."

"Most people call it charm."

He sipped from his wine. "How long were you there?"

"Tell me about Ruhn and Hunt."

He sipped again. "That wasn't even a good attempt to surprise me into answering."

"You know, only a real piece of shit would withhold that information."

He set down his wine. "Here is how this shall work. For every question of mine that you answer, *you* shall receive an answer to one of your questions. If I sense that you are lying, you shall not get a reply from me."

"You know, I just played this game with someone even more horrible than you—shocking, I know—and it didn't end well for her. So I suggest we skip the Q and A and you tell me what I want to know."

He only stared. He'd sit here all fucking night.

Bryce tapped her foot on the marble floor, weighing it out. "Fine."

"Did you truly go to the home world of the Fae?"

"Yes."

A muscle ticked in his jaw. "Athalar and Ruhn are still alive."

Bryce tried not to sag with relief. "How long—"

He held up a finger. "My turn."

Fucker.

"What was their world like?"

"I don't know—I only saw a holding cell and some tunnels and caverns. But . . . it seemed free. Of the Asteri, at least." And then, because she knew it would upset him, she said, "The Fae there are stronger than we are. The Asteri take a chunk of our power through the Drop—it feeds them, sustains them. In that other world, the Fae retain their full, pure power."

She could have sworn his face had paled, even under the flattering golden glow of the twin iron chandeliers dangling above. It made her more smug than she'd expected.

"How long was I gone?" she asked.

"Five days."

The timelines between their worlds were similar, then. "And—"

"What did you learn while you were there?"

How to reply? To give him the truth . . . "I'm still processing."

"That's not an acceptable answer."

"I learned," she snapped, "that most of the Fae, no matter what world they're on, are a bunch of selfish assholes."

His eyebrows lifted. "Oh?"

She crossed her arms. "Let's just say that I know a female who could wipe your sorry ass from existence and not break a sweat."

And yet Nesta hadn't done that to Bryce. She'd thought it luck, but was it possible the female had pulled her punches? Nesta hadn't been anything like Silene or Theia.

It didn't matter now, but the thought lingered.

"That still doesn't answer my question. You must have gone to that world for a reason—what did you learn?"

"One, I wound up there by accident. Two, *technically*, I did answer your question, so be more specific next time."

Something dark and lethal passed over her father's face. "How—"

Bryce held up a finger, mocking him. "What happened after I left?"

Her father's whiskey-colored eyes simmered with flame at the sight of that finger, the command and insistence of the right to speak it conveyed. The sight must have been especially galling from a female.

But he seemed to tamp down his anger and said with a smugness of his own, like he was savoring the bad news as much as she had while giving hers, "The Asteri threw Athalar and your brother into their dungeons, and managed to contain the knowledge of what occurred at their palace. They only informed those of us who needed to know." He drained his wine. "Did you bring these Fae back into Midgard with you?"

"Did you *see* them arrive here with me?" No need to tell him that she didn't part on good terms. Azriel might very well have killed her if she'd stayed a moment longer.

Bryce braced her forearms on the table, gorsian shackles thudding against the cool marble. "So you've known Ruhn is in the Asteri's dungeons for five days and have done nothing to help him?"

"Ruhn deserves all that is coming his way. He chose his fate."

Her fingers curled into fists, nails digging into her flesh. "He's your son, for fuck's sake."

"I can have others."

"Not if I kill you first." A familiar white haze crept over her vision.

Her father smiled, as if noting the primal fury of the Fae—but purely human rage. "You're so like your mother." He smirked. "No questions about *her* fate?"

"I know you wouldn't be able to keep from telling me if something had happened to her. You'd take too much pleasure in it. Why have the Asteri kept Hunt and Ruhn alive?"

"I believe it is my turn."

"*I* believe it's *my* turn. *No questions about* her *fate?* counts as a question, asshole."

Her father's eyes flickered, as if amused despite himself—and impressed. "Very well."

"Why have they kept Ruhn and Hunt alive?"

"To use them against you, I assume, though I cannot say for sure." He poured himself more wine, the fading sunlight streaming through the windows making the liquid glow like fresh blood. "Tell me about the knife—it is the one from our prophecies, the sibling to the Starsword?"

"The one and only. They call it Truth-Teller." He opened his mouth again, but she tapped her fingers on the table. Better get the lay of the land, assess where any allies might be—if they survived. "What's the status of Ophion?"

"No attacks since the one on the lab. Their numbers are nearly depleted. Ophion is, for all intents and purposes, dead."

Bryce reined in her wince.

The Autumn King drank from his wine again. At this rate, he'd get through the whole bottle before the sun had fully set. "How did you attain Truth-Teller?"

"I stole it." She smiled slightly at his frown of distaste. "What of my other friends—are they all alive?"

"If you counted that traitor Cormac amongst your friends, then no. But the rest of them, as far as I have heard, are alive and well." Bryce reeled. Cormac was— "Did you steal the dagger to fulfill the prophecy?"

She shrugged with what nonchalance she could muster and set down her fork. "I'm tired of this game."

Cormac was dead. Had he died that day at the lab, or had it been afterward—perhaps in the Asteri's dungeons, under their questioning? Or had they simply sent the male home to his shitty father and let the King of Avallen rip him to shreds for dishonoring his household?

The Autumn King smiled like he'd won. "Then you are dismissed. I shall see you tomorrow."

She pushed past her twisting grief to say, "Fuck you."

He merely inclined his head and resumed eating in silence.

Ithan strode down the steps of the House of Flame and Shadow in darkness so pure that even his wolf eyes couldn't pierce it.

He'd never heard anything about what waited at the bottom of the stairs. But he figured he was out of options.

He lost track of how long he walked downward, the air tight and dry. Like a tomb.

The scuff of his sneakers against the steps echoed off the black walls. His eyes strained with the effort of trying to see, to no avail. If the steps ended in a plunge, he'd have no idea. No warning.

It was true, in the end, that he had no warning. But not for a drop. Metal clanked, and his skull with it, as Ithan slammed into a wall. He rebounded, swearing—

Light, golden and soft, cracked through the stairwell.

It wasn't a wall. It was a door, and beyond it, silhouetted by the light, was a slim female figure. Even before he could make out her face, he knew the voice. Arch, cultured, bored.

"Well, that's one way of knocking," drawled Jesiba Roga.

31

Jesiba Roga led Ithan through a subterranean hall of black stone, lit only by crackling fires in hearths shaped like roaring, fanged mouths. In front of those fireplaces lounged draki of varying hues, vampyrs drinking goblets of blood, and daemonaki in business suits typing away on laptops.

A weirdly . . . normal place. Like a private club.

He supposed it *was* a private club, of sorts. The headquarters of any House were open to all its members, at any time. Some chose to dwell within them, mostly the workers who ran the House's daily operations. But some just came to hang out, to meet, to rest.

Ithan, to his embarrassment, had never been to Lunathion's House of Earth and Blood headquarters. Hadn't been to its main headquarters, either, up in Hilene. Bryce had as a kid, he remembered, but he couldn't recall the details.

Ithan followed Jesiba down the long hall, past people who barely looked his way, and then through a set of double doors of black wood carved with the horned skull sigil of the House.

He didn't know what he'd expected. A council chamber, some fancy office . . .

Not the sleek, onyx bar, lit with deep blue lighting, like the heart of a flame. A jazz quartet played on a small stage beneath an archway in the rear of the space, the many high tables—all adorned with glass votives of that blue light—oriented toward the music. But Roga headed right for the obsidian glass bar, the gilded stools before it.

A golden-scaled draki female in a gauzy black dress worked the bar, and nodded toward Roga. The sorceress nodded back shallowly as she took a seat and patted the stool beside her, ordering Ithan, "Sit."

Ithan threw the sorceress a glare at the blatant reference to his canine nature, but he obeyed.

A moment later, the bartender slid two dark glasses toward them, both rippling with smoke. Jesiba knocked hers back in one go, smoke curling from her mouth as she said, "I thought the porters had smoked too much mirthroot when they told me that Ithan Holstrom was walking down the entry steps."

Ithan peered into his dark glass, at the amber liquid that looked and smelled like whiskey, though he'd never seen whiskey with smoke rising from it.

"It's called a smokeshow," Roga drawled. "Whiskey, grated ginger, and a little draki magic to make it look fancy."

Ithan took her word for it and swallowed the whole thing in one mouthful. It burned all the way down—burned through the nothingness in him.

"Well," Roga said, "based on how eagerly you drank that and the fact that you're here at all, I can assume things are . . . not going well for you."

"I need a necromancer."

"And I need a new assistant, but you'd be surprised how few competent ones are out there."

Ithan didn't hide his glower. "I'm serious."

Roga signaled the bartender for another round. "As am I. Ever since Quinlan left me to go work at the Fae Archives, I've been up to my neck in paperwork."

Ithan was pretty sure that wasn't how it had gone down with Bryce and Jesiba, but he said, "Look, I didn't come here to talk to you—"

"Yes, but you're lucky as Hel that the porters called me to deal with you, and not someone else. One of the vamps might have taken a taste by now."

She nodded to the nearest high table behind them, where two gorgeous blonds in skintight black dresses perched, no drinks before them. They were surveying the people in the room, as if looking over a menu.

Ithan cleared his throat. "I need a necromancer," he said again. "Immediately."

Jesiba sighed, and nodded her thanks to the bartender as she slid over another smokeshow. "Your brother's been dead for too long."

"Not for my brother," Ithan said. "For someone else."

Jesiba drank slowly this time. Smoke fluttered from her lips as she swallowed. "Whatever it is, pup, I'd suggest making peace with it."

"There's *no making peace with it*," Ithan snarled. He could have sworn the glasses rattled, that the jazz quartet faltered, that the two vamps turned his way. A glance from Jesiba, and the room resumed its rhythms.

"Who did you kill?" Jesiba asked, voice so low it was barely audible.

Ithan's throat constricted. He couldn't breathe—

"Holstrom." Her eyes glowed like the flames in the sconces behind the bar.

There was no fixing this, no undoing it. He was a traitor and a murderer and—

"Who do you need to raise?" Roga's question was cold as ice.

Ithan made himself meet her gaze, made himself face what he'd done.

"A lost Fendyr heir."

"I'm assuming the food last night was reheated leftovers, if that shitty little yogurt you left outside my door this morning counts as breakfast," Bryce said to the Autumn King as she plopped into a red leather armchair and watched his orrery tick away.

Her father, sitting across the oversized desk, ignored her.

"How long are you going to keep me here?"

"Are we playing the question game again? I thought you'd tired of it last night." He didn't look up from what he was writing, his sheet of red hair slipping over a broad shoulder.

She clenched her teeth. "Just trying to calculate how much borrowed time I have left."

His golden pen—a fountain pen, for fuck's sake—slashed across the paper. "I shall procure more groceries, if my breakfast provisions are inadequate."

Bryce crossed her legs, the leather chair creaking as she leaned back. "Look at you: cooking your own meals and grocery shopping. Why, you could almost pass as a functional adult and not some pampered brat."

The fabric of his gray T-shirt pulled over his chest as his shoulders tensed.

Bryce pointed to the orrery. "The Astronomer said you had some Avallen craftsmen make that for you. Fancy." The Autumn King's eyes narrowed at the mention of the Astronomer, but he didn't look up from his paper. Bryce plowed on, "He said the orrery is to contemplate fundamental questions about ourselves, like who we are and where we came from. I have a hard time believing you're in here all day, thinking about anything that profound."

His pen stalled on the paper. "The Fae bloodlines have been weakening for generations now. It is my life's work to investigate why. This orrery was built in pursuit of answering that question."

She blew on her nails. "Especially after little old me became a certified Starborn Princess, huh?"

His fingers tightened on his pen, hard enough that she was surprised the gold plating didn't dent. "The question of our failing bloodlines plagued me long before you were born."

"Why? Who cares?"

He lifted his head at last, his eyes cold and dead. "I care if our people are weakening. If we become lesser than the angels, the shifters, the witches."

"So it's about your ego, then."

"It's about our survival. The Fae stand in a favorable position with the Asteri. If our power wanes, they will lose interest in maintaining that. Others will creep in to take what we have, predators around a carcass. And the Asteri won't lift a finger to stop them."

"And this is why you and Morven schemed to throw me and Cormac together?"

"*King* Morven has noticed the fading as well. But he has the luxury of hiding behind Avallen's mists."

Bryce drummed her fingers on the smooth rolled arm of her chair. "Is it true that the Asteri can't pierce the mists around Avallen?"

"Morven is almost certain they can't. Though I don't know if Rigelus has ever tried to breach the barriers." He glanced toward the tall windows to his left, toward the dome of the glamour shimmering above the olive trees and lavender beds. As much of a barrier as he could ever hope to hide behind.

Bryce weighed her options, and ultimately dared to go for it as she asked, "Does the term *thin place* mean anything to you?"

He angled his head, and damn if it didn't freak her the fuck out to see how similar the motion was to her own habits. "No. What is it?"

"Just something I heard once."

"You lie. You learned of it in the home world of the Fae."

Maybe she shouldn't have asked. Maybe it was too dangerous to have revealed this to him. Not for her, but for the world she'd left. Bryce halted her fingers' drumming, laying her hand flat on the cool, smooth leather arm. "I only heard the phrase, not the definition."

He surveyed her, sensing that lie as well, but something like admiration brightened his eyes. "Defiant to a fault."

Still seated, she sketched a half bow.

The Autumn King went on, idly twirling the pen between his fingers, "I always knew your mother was hiding something about you. She went to such lengths to conceal you from me."

"Maybe because you're a sociopath?"

His fingers tightened around the pen once more. "Ember loved me, once upon a time. Only something enormous would have severed that love."

Bryce propped her chin on a fist, all innocent curiosity. "Like when you hit her? Something enormous like that?"

Fire licked along his shoulders, in his long hair. But his voice remained flat. "Let us not retread old ground. I have told you my feelings on the matter."

"Yeah, you're *so* sorry about it. Sorry enough that now you've done exactly what she was so scared of all along: locked me up in your villa."

He motioned to the windows. "Has it occurred to you that here, hidden from the world and any spying eyes, you are safe? That should anyone on Midgard have learned of your return, word would soon have reached the Eternal Palace and you would be dead?"

Bryce put a hand on her chest. "I totally love how you're building yourself up as my savior—really, A for effort on that front—but let's cut the bullshit. I'm locked up here because you want something from me. What is it?"

He didn't answer, and instead twisted to adjust one of the settings on some sort of prism-like device. Whatever he'd done sent the sunlight piercing through the orrery's assortment of planets.

A prism—the total opposite of what she'd done with her powers when she'd fought Nesta and Azriel. Where she'd condensed light, the prism fractured it.

She glanced at her hands, so pale against the bloodred of the leather chair. She'd been riding on adrenaline and despair and bravado. How had she managed to make her light into a laser in those last moments in the Fae world? It had been intuitive in the moment, but now . . . Maybe it was better not to know. Not to think about how her light seemed to be edging closer to the properties of an Asteri's destructive power.

"Ruhn told me that you hole up in here all day looking for patterns," Bryce said, nodding to the orrery, the prism device, the assortment of golden tools on the desk. "What sort of patterns?" She and Ruhn had enjoyed a good laugh over that—the thought of the mighty Autumn King as little more than a conspiracy theorist.

What does he think he's going to find? Ruhn had asked, snickering. *That the universe is playing a giant game of tic-tac-toe?*

Bryce's heart twanged with the memory.

The Autumn King jotted down another note, pen scraping too loudly in the heavy quiet. "Why should I trust a loud-mouthed child with no discretion to keep my secrets?"

"It's a secret, huh? So this is some controversial shit?"

Disdain warped his handsome face. "I once asked your brother to provide me with a seed of his starlight."

"Gross. Don't call it that."

His nostrils flared. "What little *seed* he was able to produce allowed me to use this in a way I found . . . beneficial." He patted the gold-plated device that held the prism.

"I didn't realize making rainbows on the wall was so important to you."

He ignored her. "This device refracts the light, pulling it apart so I might study every facet of it." He pointed to a sister device positioned directly across from it. "That device gathers it back into one beam again. I am attempting to add *more* to the light in the process of re-forming it. If the light might be pulled apart and strengthened in its most basic form, there's a chance that it will coalesce into a more powerful version of itself."

She refrained from mentioning the blue stones Azriel had wielded—how they'd condensed and directed his power. Instead, she drawled, "And this is a good use of your time because . . . ?"

His silence was biting.

"Let me do the math." She began ticking items off on her fingers. "The Asteri are made of light. They feed on firstlight. You are studying light, its properties, beyond what science can already tell us . . ."

A muscle ticked in his jaw.

"Am I getting warm?" Bryce asked. "But if you have such questions about the Asteri, why not ask them yourself?" She hummed in contemplation. "Maybe you want to use this against them?"

He arched a brow. "Your imagination does run rampant."

"Oh, totally. But you took zero interest in me as a kid. And now suddenly, once I revealed my magic light, you want me to be part of your fucked-up little family."

"My only interest in you lies in the bloodline you stand to pass on."

"Too bad Hunt complicates that."

"More than you know."

She paused, but didn't fall for the trap of asking about it. She continued to lead him down the path of her rambling, resuming her counting on her fingers.

"So your daughter has light powers, you're interested in *patterns* in light . . . you want the information hidden from the Asteri . . ." She chuckled, lowering her hand at last. "Oh, don't even try to deny it," she said when he opened his mouth. "If you wanted to help them, you'd have turned me over to them already."

The Autumn King smiled. It was a thing of nightmarish beauty. "You truly are my child. More so than Ruhn ever was."

"That's not a compliment." But she went on, content to needle him with her guesses. "You want to know if I can kill them, don't you? The Asteri. If the Starborn light is different from their light, and *how* it is different. That's where the orrery comes in: contemplating where we come from . . . what sort of light we have, how it can be weaponized."

His nostrils flared again. "And did you learn such things on your journey?"

Bryce tapped her gorsian-shackled wrist. "Remove these and I can show you what I learned."

He smirked, and picked up the prism device again. "I'll wait."

She hadn't thought for a second that would work—but it seemed he knew it, too. That this was a game, a dance between them.

Bryce nodded to where he'd left the Starsword and Truth-Teller on the desk the day before. According to Ruhn, the Autumn King had rarely dared to touch the sword. It seemed like that was true, if he hadn't moved the blades since her crash landing. "Let's talk about how we can add another notch to my Magical Starborn Princess belt: I united the sword and knife. Prophecy fulfilled."

"You don't know anything about that prophecy," the Autumn King said, and returned to his work.

She asked sweetly, "So my interpretation is wrong? *When knife and sword are reunited, so shall our people be.* Well, I went to our old world. Met some people. Reminded them we exist. Came back here. Thus, two people reunited."

He shook his head in pure disgust. "You know as little about those blades as you do your own true nature."

She made a show of yawning. "Well, I do know that only the Chosen One can handle the blades. Wait—does that mean you can't? Since last I checked . . . only Ruhn and I got the Chosen One membership cards."

"Ruhn doesn't possess the raw power to handle such a thing correctly."

"But I do?" she asked innocently. "Is *that* why I'm here? We're going to cooperate in some kind of training montage so I can take down the Asteri for you?"

"Who says I want to get rid of the Asteri?"

"You've been really careful not to mention one way or another how you feel about them. One moment, you're protecting me from them, the next you're trying to keep the Fae in their good graces. Which is it?"

"Can it not be both?"

"Sure. But if you get rid of the Asteri, it'd give you even more power than whatever scheme you had planned that involved my marrying Cormac."

He adjusted a dial on his device, the light shifting a millimeter to the right. "Does it matter who is in power, so long as the Fae survive?"

"Um, yeah. One option is a parasitic blight upon this world. Let's not go with that choice."

He set the device down again. "Explain this . . . parasite. You mentioned something about the Asteri taking some of our power through the Drop."

Bryce debated it. He held her stare, seeing that debate rage in her.

Who would he tell, though? At this point, the more people who knew, even the assholes, the better it was. That way the secret couldn't die with her.

And after all the shit she'd learned and been through . . . maybe it'd help to lay out all the pieces at once.

So Bryce told him. Everything she'd learned about the Asteri, their history, their feeding patterns, the firstlight and secondlight. Gods, it was worse saying it aloud.

She finished, slumping back in the armchair. "So we're basically a giant buffet for the Asteri."

He'd been still and watchful while she'd related the information, but now he said quietly, "Perhaps the Asteri have been taking too much, for too long, from our people. That is why the bloodlines have weakened, generation after generation." He spoke more to himself than to her, but his eyes snapped to Bryce's as he said, "So all the water on Midgard is contaminated."

"I don't think a filter's gonna help you, if that's what you're planning."

He cut her a glare. "Yet the Fae in the other world do not have this affliction?"

"No. The Asteri hadn't developed this nasty little method of theft when they occupied their world." She rubbed her temples. "Maybe that sword and dagger can cleanse the parasite, though." She hummed again, as if thinking it over. "Maybe you should let me impale you with them and we can see what happens."

"You will never understand how they work," he said flatly.

"So you do?" She let her skepticism show in her voice. "How?"

"You're not the only one with access to ancient texts. Jesiba Roga's collection is but a fraction of mine—and a fraction of what lies in Avallen. I have studied the lore long enough to draw some conclusions."

"Good for you. You're a genius."

Fire crackled at his fingertips—the same flame he'd used to burn Ruhn as a kid. She shut down the thought as he warned, "I wouldn't be so impertinent if I were you. Your survival depends entirely upon my goodwill."

Oily, churning nausea coursed through her gut. Whatever game or dance they'd been engaging in . . . he could have this round. "Gods, you're the worst."

He picked up a nearby notebook and cracked open its green cover. It was full of scribbling. His research records and thoughts. A stack of paper lay underneath it, also covered with his writing. Leafing through the notebook, his voice was bland as he said, "I tire of you. Take your leave."

32

Hunt knew what was coming when the Hawk left the door to the dungeons open. Knew it would be bad when they were all dumped to the filthy ground again, Ruhn moaning at what it did to his arm.

All this, to break Hunt to Rigelus's will. A slow sapping of Hunt's resolve, to suffer and see these males suffer beside him, to wear him down to this point, so he'd beg them to stop, would offer up anything to make it cease, to save them—

"Get the fuck up," the Hawk ordered from the doorway as Mordoc and several of his dreadwolves stalked into the chamber. They didn't wait for Hunt to obey the Hawk's command before they reached for him, the silver darts in their imperial uniforms glinting.

Hunt bared his teeth. A few of them stepped back at the expression on his face. At the presence of the Umbra Mortis, still unbroken.

Even Mordoc, with all those silver darts crusting his collar, paused, considering.

Hunt's legs shook, his body roared in pain, but he stood. His barely formed wings twitched, trying to spread in angelic wrath. This might all be his fault, but he'd go down swinging.

"Rigelus requests an audience," the Hawk drawled, tapping an invisible watch on his slender wrist. "Best not to keep His Holiness waiting."

Hunt had no idea how Ruhn or Baxian managed to stand beside him. But groaning, hissing, they did. A sidelong glance to Baxian showed him the Helhound's wings—fully formed, but still as weak as Hunt's own—were tucked in protectively.

Hunt had little hope either of them would keep their wings today. But losing them again would be better than losing Ruhn. Would Bryce ever forgive him if he let Ruhn die? Would he ever forgive himself?

He already knew the answer.

Mordoc aimed a gun at Hunt's head, and the other dread-wolves followed suit with Baxian and Ruhn as their chains were unanchored from the wall.

Hunt caught Ruhn's agonized, exhausted stare. How the fuck would they even make it up the small flight of stairs to where the Hawk stood?

Nice knowing you, Athalar.

The prince's voice was muffled. Like even the energy to talk mind-to-mind was too much. Or maybe that was all the gorsian stone on them.

But somehow . . . Ruhn seemed to know his fate. He didn't appear inclined to fight it.

"One foot at a time, friends," Baxian murmured as they reached the bottom of the stairs. Hunt hated the hand he had to brace on the cold stone wall to help him get up the steps. Hated his jagged breathing, the screaming in his body, the effort required to lift each foot.

But he did as Baxian said. One foot at a time.

And then the Hawk was in front of them, still sneering. Mordoc and the dreadwolves kept their guns trained as the motherfucker bowed mockingly. "This way, friends."

Mordoc snickered, the fucker.

Hunt staggered into the hall, head spinning. The cup of thin broth and dry bread had been a pathetic excuse for a meal. Quinlan would have had some smart remark about it. He could almost hear her saying to the Hawk, *Where's my pizza, bird-boy?*

Hunt laughed to himself, earning a quizzical look over the shoulder from the Hawk.

Ruhn stumbled, nearly eating stone. The dreadwolves swept in, hauling him up before he could collapse. The prince's feet scraped and pushed feebly at the floor, trying to stand, but his body failed him.

Hunt could do nothing but watch as two dreadwolves dragged Ruhn along like a fucking duffel bag.

Maybe it would be a mercy for Ruhn to die. The thought was abhorrent, but—

"Please let us take the elevator," Baxian muttered from behind him, and Hunt chuckled again. He might have been on the verge of hysteria.

"Shut the fuck up," Mordoc snarled, and Baxian grunted, no doubt from a blow the dreadwolf had landed on his battered body.

Thank the gods, they were indeed herded down the hall toward the elevator bay. As if on cue, the gold-plated doors parted to reveal the Hind in her pristine uniform.

"Good morning, boys," she purred, face cold as death as she held the door open with a slender hand. Her other arm was in a sling, heavily bandaged.

"Lidia," the Hawk drawled, and nodded to her injured arm. "How are the burns healing up?"

Limping into the elevator beside Lidia, Hunt eyed the Hind's sling. Had she finished playing rebel and gone back to her true self? Maybe she'd been using fire to persuade a prisoner to talk and gotten a little too enthusiastic. Ruhn's face remained wholly blank. He was back on his feet again, slowly approaching the elevator.

"Fine." Lidia leaned against the button panel, fire in her golden eyes. She sniffed at Baxian, then said to the Hawk, "You couldn't wash them first?"

"Rigelus said immediately," the Hawk said, shoving Ruhn in.

The prince hit the glass wall at the rear of the elevator and slumped to the floor with a groan. The Hawk reached to push in Baxian, but the Helhound bared his teeth, and even the Hawk didn't try anything as the Helhound took up a place beside Hunt, limping only slightly.

How much had changed since those years with Sandriel. And how little.

"Room for two," Lidia snapped at her dreadwolves, and a pair of stone-faced soldiers slipped in. Each had at least a dozen silver darts along the collars of their gray uniforms. Lidia ordered Mordoc, "Be waiting outside the bay upstairs."

Mordoc nodded, golden eyes bright with anticipated blood-shed, and snarled something to the dreadwolf unit that had them marching swiftly for the stairs. With feral delight dancing over his face, Mordoc trailed them out.

Lidia waited until the dreadwolves and their captain had left the landing before removing her hand from the door. The elevator sealed shut, and the car began to slide upward.

They emerged from the underground levels, rising into the crystal palace above.

Blinding light pierced Hunt's eyes—daylight. His eyes, accustomed to the dark, couldn't focus—he couldn't make out anything of the world around him. He lifted a wing to block out the light, body barking in pain with the movement. Ruhn and Baxian hissed, recoiling from the light as well.

The Hawk snickered. "Just a taste of what Rigelus will do to you." The two dreadwolves chuckled with him.

Hunt squinted as he lowered his wing and met the shithead's eyes. "Fuck you." Like Hel would these assholes make him beg and grovel—either for his own life or Ruhn's.

Lidia said mildly, "I couldn't have said it better myself, Athalar." Hunt looked, but not fast enough.

The Hawk certainly didn't look fast enough.

And Hunt knew he'd treasure this moment forever: the moment when Lidia Cervos pulled out her gun and fired it right between the Hawk's eyes.

33

All Ruhn knew was blinding light, and the blast of gunshots.

Three bodies hit the floor. The Hawk, followed by two dread-wolves. And before them, lowering her gun to her side . . . Lidia.

"What the *fuck*!" Baxian shouted.

He didn't know—Ruhn had never told him. Even in his rage and loathing, he'd never dared risk sharing the knowledge of Daybright's identity with another person who could betray her.

Using her good hand, Lidia hit a button on the elevator. "We have one minute and thirty-five seconds to get to the car." She yanked a ring of keys from her pocket and knelt in front of Athalar. Fumbling a bit with her bandaged hand, she freed first his ankles, then his wrists from the gorsian shackles. Then Baxian's.

Ruhn blinked and she was in front of him, eyes bright and clear. "Hang on," she whispered. Her slender fingers brushed his skin, and gorsian stone fell away. His magic swelled, a tide of starlight rising within him.

It stopped at the end of his arm. He was missing his fucking *hand*—

He swayed. Lidia caught him, hauling him upright with ease. But he didn't miss the grunt of pain from whatever it did to her arm, now free of its sling.

Her scent hit him, wrapping around him, holding him awake as surely as she wrapped her arm around his middle to help keep him standing.

"How long, Lidia?" Baxian asked. "How long since you've turned?" His face was slack with shock.

"There'll be time enough to trade rebel background stories," she said shortly, watching the changing floor numbers. "When the doors open, go left, then take the first door, then down two flights, take the door after that, then jump into the car. It's large enough to fit all of you—and the wings." She glanced over a shoulder, gaze sweeping over Hunt, then Baxian. "Are they healed enough to fly? Did the firstlight injection work?"

She was the one to thank for the angels' healing—in anticipation of this escape?

"Weak, but functional," Baxian panted. "But you're insane if you believe we can get out—"

"Shut up," she snapped, her good arm tightening around Ruhn's side before she angled him toward the door. "We only have one minute now."

The elevator dinged, and Ruhn knew he should be bracing himself as Hunt and Baxian were, but he couldn't move his body, his agonized, weak body, even when the doors opened—

Lidia moved him instead. She charged into the hall, half dragging him, and cut left, Athalar and Baxian behind her.

Sparks flickered in Ruhn's vision, blackness creeping in at the edges. It was all he could do to keep his feet under him, keep them moving, as Lidia raced them down the corridor to that door she'd indicated, then the stairs—

Ruhn stumbled on the first step, and she was there, heaving him over her slender back, lifting him. Fucking *carrying* him, despite that injured arm. He might have been mortified had each movement not set every nerve in his arm screaming.

Down, then through the glass door into the above-ground parking garage. An imperial open-air jeep with an unmanned gunner mounted in the back waited at the curb.

"Baxian: gunner," Lidia ordered as she dumped Ruhn into the front passenger seat, pain threatening to tear his fragile consciousness from him.

The Helhound needed no further explanation before crawling up to the machine gun. Athalar threw himself across the back row, wings barely able to squeeze in with him. And then Lidia slung herself into the driver's seat. A stomp of her feet on the pedals as she slammed the stick shift into place, and the car rocketed off.

The many-tiered garage was crammed full of military vehicles. Someone was going to see them, someone was going to come—

On a downward turn, Ruhn collided with the side paneling, and the impact reverberated painfully through his body as Lidia let the car drift, drift—then punched it forward, flying down a ramp. Hunt let out a broken laugh, apparently impressed. Athalar cut it short, though.

Ruhn saw why a second later. The guard station. Six guards had been stationed around it: two angels, four wolves. They'd heard the racing car.

They hardly had time to notice Baxian at the gunner. They didn't even manage to raise their rifles or summon a spark of magic before the Helhound unleashed a hundred rounds of bullets. With the angle of the down-ramp, they stood right in his line of fire.

Blood sprayed in a mist as Lidia sailed through them—the car bumping over their bodies with sickening thuds. She shattered the barrier.

They burst into the sunlight, but there was no relief. They were now in the middle of the city, with enemies all around. Ruhn couldn't get a breath down.

A voice crackled over the radio—Declan Emmet's voice. "Daybright, you read?"

Hot tears began to streak down Ruhn's face.

Lidia shot the car down the long, wide stone bridge between the palace and the towering iron gates at its far end. Another guard station threatened ahead.

"Copy, Emmet," Lidia said into the radio, wincing as she had to take the wheel with her bandaged arm. Whatever had happened to her had to be brutal if she was still in pain. Something in his chest twisted to think of it. "We're approaching the bridge gates."

"Camera feeds are wonky. We lost track of you in the elevator bay. All there?" Dec said.

"All here," Lidia said, glancing at Ruhn.

"Thank fuck," Dec said, and Ruhn choked on a sob. Then Dec said, "Camera's showing twelve guards at the gate. Do not stop, Daybright. Go. I repeat, go, go, *go*."

They sped toward the guard station, headed directly for the array of soldiers with guns aimed at them. They looked uncertain at the sight of the Hind driving the car. Everyone knew that to piss her off was to die.

"Lidia," Baxian warned. There were too many to shoot at once, no matter how uncertain they were.

Lidia punched the jeep into the highest gear.

The nearest soldier—an angel—catapulted himself into the sky, aiming his rifle down at them. Athalar's lightning sparked, a feeble attempt to halt the death about to come down.

But it was Baxian, unleashing the machine gun again, who downed the soldier. The angel's wings flared as he plummeted, blood showering them in a ruby rain.

Lidia charged through the fray, ducking low as bullets flew. They careened through the barricade, wood exploding, the crystal palace of the Asteri looming behind them, a grim reminder of what they fled.

Then they were past the gates, splinters of wood still falling into the jeep as they cut hard down the nearest avenue. Tearing out of a nondescript alley, a white van fell in line with them, the sliding door open to reveal—

"Where *the fuck* is your hand?" Tristan Flynn shouted to Ruhn over the gunfire, a rifle at his shoulder. He fired behind them, again and again, and Baxian pivoted the gunner to the rear, unloading bullets onto the pursuing enemy.

Ruhn was well and truly crying then.

The van veered, and Flynn shouted, "Shit!" as it narrowly dodged a pedestrian—a draki female who shrieked, falling back against the wall of a building.

The radio crackled again, and a stranger's voice filled it. "Daybright, we're a go at Meridan."

Another voice: "We're a go at Alcene."

Another: "Ready at Ravilis."

On and on. Eleven locations total.

Then a soft female voice said, "This is Irithys. Set to ignite at the Eternal City."

"What the fuck is happening, Lidia?" Hunt breathed. They raced through the narrow city streets, the van with Flynn falling into line behind them. Hunt grunted, "Those are all places on the Spine."

Athalar was right: Every single city mentioned was a major depot along the vital railway that funneled imperial weapons to the front.

Lidia didn't take her eyes off the road as she picked up the radio. "This is Daybright. Blast it to Hel, Irithys."

Ruhn knew that name. He remembered the three sprites telling Bryce just a few weeks ago that their queen, Irithys, would want to hear of Lehabah's bravery. The lost Queen of the Fire Sprites.

"Consider it done," Irithys said.

And as they took another sharp turn onto a broad street, Ruhn's body bleating with pain as he again collided with the car door, an explosion bloomed on the other end of the city. An explosion so big that only someone made of fire might have caused it—

In the distance, another eruption sounded.

Ruhn could see it in his mind's eye: The line of exploding orange and red that raced up the continent. One depot after another after another, all exploding into nothing. The Hind had broken the Spine of Pangera with one fatal blow, ignited by the fire from the lost Sprite Queen.

Ruhn couldn't help but admire the symbolism of it, for the only race of Vanir who'd universally stood with Athalar during the Fallen rebellion to have lit this match. He caught a glimpse of Athalar's face—the awe and grief and pride shining there.

The entire land seemed to be rumbling with the impact from

the explosions. Lidia said, "We needed a distraction. Ophion and Irithys obliged."

Indeed, not one pedestrian or driver looked at the jeep or the van racing for the city walls. All eyes had turned to the north, to the train station.

Angels in imperial uniforms flew for it, blotting out the sun. Sirens wailed.

Even if word had gone out about their escape, the Eternal City—and all of Pangera—had bigger things to deal with.

"And Ophion needed a shot at survival," Lidia added. "So long as the Spine remained intact, they couldn't gain any ground."

She'd once told Ruhn that Ophion had been trying and failing to blow up the Spine for years now. Yet she'd done it. Somehow, she'd done it . . . for all of them.

They turned onto an even larger avenue, this one leading right out of the city, and Flynn's van pulled up beside them again. "We'll cover the highway. Get to the port!" he shouted. Lidia saluted the male, and Flynn winked at Ruhn before the van peeled away and the Fae lord slid the door shut.

But ahead of them, at the gate through the city walls, a light began flashing. An alarm blaring atop another guard station.

From the massive stone archway, a metal grate began to descend, preparing to seal the city. Trapping those responsible for the station attack inside—or trapping *them*.

The guards, all wolves in imperial uniforms, whirled toward them, and Ruhn winced as Baxian unleashed his bullets before they could draw their weapons. People shrieked along the sidewalks, fleeing into buildings and ducking behind parked cars.

"We're not going to make it," Baxian called as Lidia zoomed toward the guard station.

"Lidia," Athalar warned.

"Get down!" Lidia barked, and Ruhn shut his eyes, sinking low as the grate lowered at an alarming rate. Metal screamed and exploded right above them, the car rocking, shuddering—

Yet Lidia kept driving. She raced onto the open road beyond the city as the grate slammed shut behind them.

"Cutting it a little close, don't you think?" Hunt shouted to Lidia, and Ruhn opened his eyes to find that the gunner had been ripped clean off. Baxian was clinging for dear life to the back of the jeep, a manic grin on his face.

They had made it, and the closure of the city gate had sealed in any land-bound cars or patrols. Precisely as Lidia had planned, no doubt.

"That was the easy part," Lidia called over the wind, and the jeep sailed out into the countryside, into the olive groves and rolling hills beyond.

Ruhn stirred from where he'd collapsed against the side paneling. His wrist bled—the wound had reopened.

Declan said over the radio, "Let me talk to him."

For a heartbeat, Ruhn met Lidia's bright, golden eyes. Then she extended the radio to him. It was all Ruhn could do to clutch the radio in his good hand. *Good* being relative. His fingernails were gone.

"Hey, Dec," he groaned.

Declan laughed thickly—like he might have been holding back tears. "It's so fucking good to hear your voice."

Ruhn squeezed his eyes shut, throat working. "I love you. You know that?"

"Tell me again when I see you in an hour. You've got a Hel of a drive ahead. Put Daybright back on."

Ruhn silently handed the radio to Lidia, careful not to touch her. Not to look at her.

"This is Daybright," Lidia said, and Ruhn glanced behind them. A pillar of smoke rose from the part of the city where the glass domes of the train depot used to gleam.

"You want good news or bad news first?" Dec asked over the radio.

"Good."

"Most of the imperial security forces are at the train station, and the city is under lockdown. Irithys made it out—she vanished into the countryside. Off to wherever."

"I gave her instructions on where to go—what to do," Lidia said quietly. But then asked, "What's the bad news?"

"Mordoc and two dozen dreadwolves also made it out of the southwestern gate before it shut. I think they've figured out you're headed for the coast."

"Fuck," Athalar spat from the back seat.

"Flynn?" Lidia asked.

"Flynn's behind them. Mordoc and company are crossing onto your road. They'll be on your tail within ten minutes at your current speed. So go faster."

"I'm already driving at top speed."

"Then you'll have to find a way to ditch them."

Cold washed through Ruhn that had nothing to do with his injuries or bleeding arm. He dared himself to look at Lidia—really look at her.

She merely stared at the road ahead. The wind ripped strands of her golden hair free from the chignon high on her head. Calculation swirled in her eyes.

Baxian said over the wind, "They'll have every guard between here and the coast watching the road."

And they'd just lost their machine gun. Lidia reached for the holster at her thigh and handed her sidearm back to Athalar.

"That's all we have?" Athalar demanded, checking the bullets. Ruhn didn't need to look to know there weren't enough in the gun to get them through this.

"If I'd packed more, someone would have been suspicious," Lidia said coolly.

Declan's voice crackled over the radio. "What's the plan, Daybright?"

Ruhn watched her beautiful, perfect face. Watched as determination set her features. "Have the ship at the planned coordinates," she told Declan. "Ready the hatch for an aerial landing."

34

The Autumn King stayed holed up in his study for the rest of the day, so Bryce took the opportunity to go poking about. First in the kitchen, which was utilitarian enough that it was clearly built for a team of chefs. The walk-in fridge was, thankfully, stocked with freshly cooked food. She helped herself to some poached trout and herbed rice for lunch, along with a glass of the fanciest champagne she could find—swiped from a cold case in the massive wine cellar—and tried all the door handles to the outside once before settling for a walk through the villa halls.

She wandered past white columns and soaring atriums, expanses of floor-to-ceiling windows, and artfully concealed panels for tech. She'd opened a few of the latter as she walked, hoping for something to connect her to the outside world, but so far they had revealed only controls for the radiant flooring, the automatic blinds, and the air conditioner.

Bryce swigged directly from the bottle as she meandered through the basement. A gym, steam room, massage room, and a sauna occupied one wing. The other wing held an indoor lap pool, a screening room, and what seemed to be the Autumn King's security office. All the computers and cameras were dark and locked. No amount of trying to turn them on worked.

He'd thought of everything.

Cursing him to darkest Hel, she wandered through the ground level: a formal living room, the dining room, his study—doors shut in a quiet message to keep the fuck out—the kitchen again, a den, and a game room complete with a pool table and shuffleboard table.

None of the TVs worked. A check revealed that their power cords were missing. No interweb routers to be found, either.

She tried not to picture her mom here, young and innocent and trusting.

On the next level up, doors had been left open to reveal various guest rooms, all as beautiful and bland as her own. One wing was locked—surely her father's private suite.

Yet the double doors at the end of the other wing had been left unlocked. She opened them to a familiar scent that had her heart clenching.

Ruhn.

Posters of rock bands still hung on the walls. The massive four-poster bed with its black silk sheets was really the only sign of princely wealth. The rest screamed rebellious youth: ticket stubs taped by the mirror, a record of all the concerts he'd ever been to. A closet full of black shirts and jeans and boots, mixed with a jumble of discarded knives and swords.

It was a time capsule, frozen right before Ruhn returned from Avallen after enduring his Ordeal and emerging victorious with the Starsword. Had he even come back here, or had he immediately found a new place to live, knowing the sword gave him some degree of leverage over his father?

Or maybe it hadn't gone down like that at all. Maybe the Autumn King had kicked him out, jealous and bitter over the Starsword. Or maybe Ruhn had just up and left one day.

She'd never asked Ruhn about it. About so many things.

She opened the drawers of the desk by the window to discover a lighter, various drug paraphernalia, chewed-up cheap pens, and . . .

Her chest tightened as she pulled out the tub of silver nitrate balm. Grade A medwitch stuff—to treat burns. Her fingers clenched around the plastic, so hard it groaned. She set the tub carefully back into the drawer and sank onto Ruhn's bed. The gorsian shackles at her wrists shone faintly in the dim light.

Ruhn had gotten out of this festering place, and she was glad of it. She offered up a silent prayer to Cthona that she'd get to tell her brother that.

For right now, though, she was alone in this. And it was only a matter of time until the Autumn King's patience wore thin.

It was nothing short of miraculous, what the Hind had done. Declan, Flynn, and Ophion had helped, but Hunt knew that the female driving the car had orchestrated it all.

She'd somehow found Irithys, Queen of the Fire Sprites . . . and convinced her to be the spark to ignite this enormous, unheard-of attack. For the Fallen, for the sprites who had become Lowers for standing with them—the smallest among the Vanir, the outcasts—this blow had been for them. Struck by the person who would hold the most meaning to those looking for a sign.

Irithys was not only free in the world. She was on the attack.

Hunt shook his head in wonder and glanced to Ruhn, slumped against the passenger-side door.

The strike had been for the rebellion, Hunt knew, but the escape—the escape had been entirely for Ruhn.

"What do you mean, *aerial landing*?" Baxian demanded, panting heavily.

Lidia veered the car off the paved road, down a dirt lane that wended between the dry hills, and toward the mountains near the shore. The car bumped and shook on the dusty ground, and each of Hunt's injuries screamed. Ruhn moaned.

Lidia didn't answer, and pushed the car to its limit, winding up and around the hills, through the patchy shade of the olive trees flanking the road, the wind in their faces hot and dry.

Without warning, Lidia slammed on the brakes, the car skidding on the loose gravel. Hunt crashed into the back of the driver's seat, grimacing at the impact.

"Shit," Lidia hissed amid the swirling dust. "*Shit.*"

The dust cleared enough that Hunt could finally see what had triggered her sudden stop. A few feet ahead, the road had ended. A thick grove of olive trees blocked the way, too dense to even try to drive through.

"Lidia," Baxian demanded, and she twisted in her seat, looking at them.

"I'd hoped this road would take us closer to the water," she said, out of breath for the first time since Hunt had known her. She peered over a shoulder at Hunt, then at Baxian. "You'll have to get into the skies from here."

"What?" Ruhn demanded, trying to push himself up from where he'd been thrown against the passenger door.

But Lidia leapt out of the car without opening her own door. Her eyes were wild as she asked Hunt and Baxian, flinging open the back door, "Do you think you can fly?"

Hunt managed to crawl out of the back seat and stand, head spinning with pain and exhaustion. With a hand braced on the side of the car, he spread his newly formed wings.

Pain lanced down his back, sharp and deep. Gritting his teeth, Hunt made them move. Made them flap—once, twice. Their beats stirred the dirt and dust into clouds that gathered at their feet. "Yeah," he said roughly, fighting through the agony. "I think so."

On the other side of the jeep, Baxian was doing the same, black wings coated in dust. The Helhound nodded in agreement.

Lidia rushed over to the passenger door, dirt crunching beneath her boots, and heaved it open. Ruhn nearly fell into the dirt at her feet, but she caught him with her good arm. Hauled him over to Hunt, earning a glare from the Fae Prince as he fought to regain his footing. Lidia didn't so much as look down at Ruhn as she ordered Hunt and Baxian, "Carry him between you. The *Depth Charger* is waiting."

Hunt blinked, stepping up to help Ruhn stand. Pain again tore through him at the effort.

"What about you?" Baxian demanded, limping to Ruhn's other side. His dark wings dragged in the dirt.

Lidia lifted her chin. The sunlight danced over the silver of her torque as she did so. "I'm the bigger prize. Mordoc will go after me. It'll buy you time."

"I can carry you," Baxian insisted, even as he slid an arm under Ruhn's shoulders. Hunt could have sighed with relief at having the burden lessened.

Ruhn said nothing. Didn't even move as Baxian and Hunt kept him upright.

Lidia shook her head at the Helhound. "You're both at death's door. Take Ruhn and go." Her expression held no room for argument. *"Now,"* she snarled, and apparently the discussion was over, because she shifted.

Hunt had never seen Lidia in her deer form. She was lovely—her coat a gold so pale it was nearly white. Her golden eyes were framed by thick, dark lashes. A slice of darker gold slashed up between her eyes like a lick of flame.

Lidia looked at Ruhn, though. Only at him.

Half-dangling between Hunt and Baxian, Ruhn stared at her. Still said nothing.

The world seemed to hold its breath as the elegant doe walked up to Ruhn and gently, lovingly, nuzzled his neck.

Ruhn didn't so much as move. Not a blink as Lidia pulled away, those golden eyes lingering on his face—just a moment longer.

Then she bounded off into the trees, a streak of sunlight that was there and gone.

Like she'd never been.

Ruhn scanned the forest where Lidia had vanished, his hand rising to his neck. The skin there was warm, as if her touch still lingered.

"Right," Athalar grunted, stooping to reach for Ruhn's legs. "On three." Baxian tightened his grip under Ruhn's shoulders.

Wings stirred, and Ruhn stirred with them. "Lidia," he croaked.

But Athalar and Baxian jumped into the skies, both males groaning in agony, the world tilting—and then they were airborne, Athalar holding Ruhn's legs, Baxian at his shoulders.

Ruhn hung like a sack of potatoes. His stomach flipped at the dizzying drop to the arid ground far below. The mountain rising before them. The glittering blue sea stretching beyond.

Behind them, shooting among the olive trees like a bolt of lightning, raced that beautiful, near-white doe. A hind.

To reach the sea, she'd have to ascend through the hilly groves, and then right up the rocky mountain itself.

Was there a way down on the other side? She'd only mentioned an aerial landing when she'd spoken to Dec. Not a sea rescue. Or a land rescue.

Lidia wasn't coming.

The realization clanged through Ruhn like a death knell.

"Oh fuck," Athalar spat, and Ruhn followed the direction of the angel's gaze behind them.

A pack of two dozen dreadwolves streamed like ants through the forest. All headed straight for that deer.

A wolf larger than the others led the pack—Mordoc. Closing in fast on Lidia as the hills slowed her.

"Stop," Ruhn rasped. "We have to go back."

"No," Athalar said coldly, his grip tightening on Ruhn's legs.

Which was faster—a deer or a wolf?

If they caught up to her, it'd be over. Lidia had known that, and gone anyway.

"Put me down," Ruhn snarled, but the malakim held him firm, so hard his bones ached.

The wolves narrowed the distance, as if the hills were nothing to them. But Athalar and Baxian had caught an air current and were soaring swiftly enough now that Lidia rapidly shrank in the distance—

"PUT ME DOWN!" Ruhn roared, or tried to. His voice, hoarse from screaming, could barely rise above a whisper.

"Aerial legion from the east," Baxian announced to Hunt.

Ruhn looked up, following Athalar's line of sight. Sure enough, like a cloud of locusts, soldiers surged for them.

"Fuckers," Athalar hissed, wings beating faster. Baxian kept pace as they swooped toward the sea.

Farther from Lidia, who now neared the top of the towering

mountain. That was the last Ruhn saw of her as they soared over the arid peak.

Open ocean spread before them. Ruhn twisted, trying to keep an eye on Lidia.

His stomach dropped.

As if Ogenas herself had sliced it in half, the mountain's seaward side had been shaved off. There was nothing waiting for Lidia but a straight, lethal plunge to the water hundreds of feet below.

35

Hunt blocked out Ruhn's screams and cursing. He knew he'd have been in the same state if it had been Bryce out there, being run aground by two dozen dreadwolves. He'd made those sounds once, long ago—when Shahar and Sandriel had plummeted toward the earth, Shahar's blood streaming—

The glare of the sun on the sea made his head throb. Or maybe that was his injuries and exhaustion. Each flap of his wings sent agony rocking through him, threatening to steal his breath. He took it into his heart, though. Embraced the pain. He deserved every pulse of it.

But there, emerging from the water like a breaching whale . . .

A shining metal hatch cleared the surface. Then a person burst through it, waving frantically. And Hunt could only wonder if he was hallucinating as he realized it was Tharion signaling to them, urging them on from the narrow exterior deck atop the *Depth Charger*.

Hunt and Baxian dove, and Ketos leapt onto the nose of the mighty ship, shouting something that the wind devoured.

Toward the coast, angels were gaining speed, closing in. The cool spray of waves stung every inch of Hunt, salt burning in his open wounds. He half fell the last ten feet onto the soaked metal of the ship.

Tharion raced forward, face stark with urgency. "I said land *in* the hatch!" the mer yelled.

Hunt ground his teeth, but Ruhn had shot to his feet, swaying, dangerously close to falling into the water. "Lidia," he gasped to Tharion, pointing to the cliffs. He swayed again, and Tharion caught him. Ruhn gripped the mer's muscled forearm with his good hand. Tharion's eyes dropped to the prince's missing hand. The mer paled.

But Ruhn groaned, "You have to help her."

"This ship can't get any closer to shore," Tharion said placatingly.

"Not this ship," Ruhn snarled with impressive menace. *"You."*

Hunt eyed the mountain—the cliff looming like a giant at the distant shore. "Ruhn, even if Lidia can make it to the edge . . . that's a deadly drop." She'd be splattered on the surface of the water.

"Please," Ruhn said, voice breaking as he scanned Tharion's face.

Tharion looked to Hunt. Then Baxian. Apparently realized they were in no shape to fly another foot.

Tharion sighed but declared, "Always happy to provide the heroics." The mer passed the prince over to Baxian, and stripped out of his clothes. Utterly unconcerned by his nudity, the mer leapt into the cobalt swells and, a heartbeat later, his massive tail splashed the surface. He didn't look back before he disappeared under the water, a flash of orange against the blue.

Baxian began murmuring a prayer to Ogenas. It was all Hunt could do to join him.

Maybe this was his fault, too. If he'd stopped Bryce, stopped the others, from going up against the Asteri . . . none of them would be in this position. None of this would have happened.

But Ruhn stayed silent throughout. Eyes fixed on the shore, face pale as death. As if he could see all the way to the shifter on the cliffs, racing for her life.

Every breath burned Lidia's lungs.

Each galloping step was uphill, nothing but dry, treacherous stones and snaking roots underneath. So many roots, all intent on tripping her delicate hooves.

This hadn't been part of the plan. She'd been a fool to take that road, not knowing where it would end, that it would strand her in the arid foothills with a mountain to climb.

But Ruhn and the angels had made it. Would be on the ship by now.

Irithys had made it out, to go do what needed doing. At least her trust in the queen hadn't been misplaced. At least that much had gone right.

Snarls filled the scrub behind her, and Lidia recognized them all.

Her dreadwolves. Her soldiers. The deepest snarl, unnervingly close behind, was Mordoc.

Lidia pushed herself faster, harder. Found a switchback trail—a deer path, ironically enough—up the mountain. A legion of angels loomed like thunderclouds in the sky.

She had to get to the water. If she could make it to the sea, she might stand a chance at swimming to the ship.

Brush snapped to her left, and Lidia leapt toward a boulder just as Mordoc crashed through the scrub and trees, jaws snapping.

He missed her by inches.

Mordoc rebounded against the rock below and leapt upward again. He'd clear the boulder and be on her soon. Right on his tail were Vespasian and Gedred, his favored torturers and hunters— *her* favored torturers and hunters. Foam streamed from their maws as they scaled the rocks.

Lidia leapt again, higher onto the boulder, then atop it. The wolves couldn't jump as far, but she didn't wait to see them try as she dashed across the rock's broad top, then upward again.

Branches and thorns ripped at her fur, her legs.

The scent of her own blood filled her nose, coppery and thick. Her hooves slipped against the loose stones, the sound like bones clacking. There had to be some path around the side of the mountain, some way to round it and get down its other side to the water below—

There. Up another quarter mile. A ledge that curved around the mountain. She plunged ahead, and the snarls behind her closed in again. She had to get to the ledge. Had to reach the water.

She couldn't cry in this body, but she nearly did as she at last reached the curve around the mountain. As the ledge jutted out before her.

Like a long finger, it stretched high above the sea and rock five hundred feet below. The rest of the mountain was a sheer cliff face.

There was no other way down. No way back.

From the way her hooves dug into the stone, she could tell the rock was some sort of soft material that would crumble in her hands if she tried to climb down the cliff in her humanoid form. That is, if Mordoc and the others didn't shoot her off it first.

Mordoc's vicious snarl sounded behind her, and Lidia looked back, then, right as he shifted. The wolves behind him did the same.

So Lidia shifted into her humanoid form as well. Panting hard, reorienting her senses to this body, she backed a step toward the edge.

Vespasian, at Mordoc's left, drew a rifle. Pointed it at her.

"This seems familiar," Mordoc panted, a wild light in his eyes. "What was it that you told that thunderbird bitch?"

Lidia backed away another step, as Gedred, too, drew and aimed her rifle.

Mordoc spat on the dry ground, then wiped his mouth with the back of his hand. "Are you faster than a bullet? That's what you asked Sofie Renast that night." Her captain laughed, too-large teeth flashing. "Let's see, *Lidia*. Let's see how fast you are now, you traitorous cunt."

Lidia's gaze darted between Vespasian and Gedred. She found no mercy on their faces. Only hate and rage. They were dread-wolves who had let a hind lead them. And she had betrayed them.

Now they'd make her pay.

The shots wouldn't be to kill her. They'd lame her, as she had done with Sofie Renast, so they could drag her back to the Asteri to be ripped to shreds. Either by them or Pollux.

The shouts of the aerial legion drew closer from above. Was Pollux with them? Leading the swarm of angels to grab her?

Death lay behind her, at the end of the ledge. Swift, forgiving death.

The sort she'd be denied by the Asteri. If she could make it to the end of the cliff . . . it would be fast.

She'd fall, and her head would splatter on the rocks, and she'd likely feel very little. Perhaps a swift burst of pain, then nothing.

Even if she would never see what she had worked for, hoped for.

Lidia shoved that thought behind her. As she had always done.

Gedred knelt, rifle braced against a shoulder. Ready to fire.

So Lidia reached up to the silver torque around her neck. A flick of her fingers and it snapped free. "Since we're repeating the past, I suppose I'll tell you what Sofie told me that night." She flung the torque, that hateful collar, into the dirt and smiled at Mordoc, at the dreadwolves. *"Go to Hel."*

Then she broke into a run. Faster than she'd ever sprinted in this human form, hurtling toward the cliff edge. Two bullets landed at her heels, and she veered to the side, easily dodging the third.

She'd taught these dreadwolves everything they knew. She used it against them now.

"Shoot that bitch!" Mordoc screamed at his snipers.

Lidia's life diluted into each step. Each pump of her arms. Bullets sprayed rock and shrapnel at her feet. Only a few more steps.

"END HER!" Mordoc roared.

But the cliff edge was there—and then she was over it.

Lidia sobbed as she leapt, as the open air embraced her. As the rocks and surf spread below.

For a heartbeat, she thought the water might be rising to meet her.

But that was her. Falling.

A gunshot cracked like a thunderhead breaking. Pain ruptured through her chest, bone shattering, red washing over her vision.

Lidia let out a choked, bloody laugh as she died.

36

Jesiba Roga moved Ithan from the bar pretty damn quickly after he'd said precisely who he wanted to raise from the dead. He found himself transported to an office—her office, apparently—crammed full of crates and boxes of what had to be relics for her business.

She shoved him into a chair in front of a massive black desk, took a seat on the other side in a tufted white velvet armchair, and ordered him to tell her everything.

Ithan did. He needed her help, and he knew he wouldn't get it without honesty.

When he finished, Roga leaned back in her seat, the dim golden light from her desk lamp gilding her short platinum hair.

"Well, this wasn't how I expected my evening to go," the sorceress said, rubbing her groomed brows. On the built-in bookshelf behind her sat three glass terrariums filled with various small creatures. People she had turned into animals? For their sake, he hoped not.

But maybe she could turn him into a worm and step on him. That'd be a mercy.

Jesiba's eyes gleamed, as if sensing his thoughts. But she said quietly, "So you want a necromancer to raise this Sigrid Fendyr."

"It hasn't been very long," Ithan said. "Her body is probably still fresh enough that—"

"I don't need a wolf to tell me the rules of necromancy."

"Please," Ithan rasped. "Look, I just . . . I fucked up."

"Did you?" A cold, curious question.

He swallowed against the dryness in his throat as he nodded. "I was supposed to rescue her—and she was supposed to make the Fendyrs better, to save everyone."

Roga crossed her arms. "From what?"

"From Sabine. From how fucking *awful* the wolves have become—"

"As far as I remember, the wolves were the ones who raced to Asphodel Meadows this spring."

"Sabine refused to let us go."

"Yet you defied her and went anyway. The others followed you."

"I'm not here to debate wolf politics."

"But this *is* politics. You raise Sigrid, and . . . what then? Have you thought that through?"

Ithan growled, "I need to fix it."

"And you think a necromancer will solve that problem."

He bared his teeth. "I know what you're thinking—"

"You don't even know what *you're* thinking, Ithan Holstrom."

"Don't talk to me like—"

She lifted a finger. "I will remind you that you are in *my* House, and asking for a gargantuan favor. You came here uninvited, which itself is a violation of our rules. So unless you want me to hand you over to the vamps to be sucked dry and left to rot on the dock, I suggest you check that tone, pup."

Ithan glared, but shut his mouth.

Roga smiled slightly. "Good dog."

Ithan reined in his growl. She smiled wider at that.

But after a moment she said, "Where's Quinlan?"

"I don't know."

Roga nodded to herself. "I do nothing for free, you know."

He met her stare, letting her see that he'd give her whatever she wanted. Her lips pursed with distaste at his desperation. He didn't care.

"Most necromancers," she continued, "are arrogant pricks who will fuck you over."

"Great," he muttered.

"But I know one who might be trustworthy."

"Name your price. And theirs."

"I told you already: I need a competent assistant. As far as memory serves, you were a history major at CCU." At his questioning look, she said, "Quinlan used to prattle on and *on* about how proud of you she was." His chest ached unbearably. Roga rolled her eyes, either at her words or at whatever was on his face, then gestured to the crates and boxes around her. "As you can see, I have goods that need sorting and shipping."

Ithan slowly blinked. "You mean . . . work for you, and you'll get me in touch with this necromancer?"

A dip of her chin.

"But I need it done *now*," he said, "while her body's still fresh—"

"I shall arrange to have the body transported from wherever the Viper Queen has thrown it, and keep it . . . on ice, as it were. Safe and sound. Until the necromancer becomes available."

"Which is how long?"

Her lips curved. "What's the rush?"

He couldn't answer. He didn't believe *The weight of my own guilt is killing me and I can't stand it another moment* would make any difference to her.

"Let's start with a couple days, Holstrom. A couple honest days of work . . . and we'll assess whether you do a good enough job to merit the aid you seek."

"I could walk right out of here and ask the nearest necromancer—"

"You could, but the vamps might take a bite before you can. Or you might ask the wrong necromancer and wind up . . . unsatisfied."

Jesiba opened her laptop. She typed in her password, then said without looking up from the screen, "That big crate marked *Lasivus* needs unpacking and cataloging. There's an extra laptop on the credenza over there. Password *JellyJubilee*. Both words capitalized, no spaces. Don't give me that look, Holstrom. Quinlan set it."

Ithan blinked again. But slowly got to his feet. Walked to the crate.

He summoned his claws, using them in lieu of a crowbar, and pried the lid off the crate. It landed on the carpeted floor with a dull thud and a spray of dust.

"You break it, Holstrom," the sorceress drawled from her desk as she typed away, "you buy it."

Wasn't that the truth.

Bryce didn't see the Autumn King for the rest of the day. She foraged dinner from the kitchen so she didn't need to endure another meal and game of twenty questions with him.

She was carrying her plate up to her bedroom when her captor appeared at the top of the stairs. "I was looking for you."

Bryce lifted the plate and the ham-and-butter sandwich atop it. "And I'm looking to eat. Bye."

The Autumn King remained directly in her path as she crested the stone steps. "I want to talk to you."

She peered up at him, hating that he stood taller than her. But she managed to give him a look down her nose—one that had worked wonders on irritating Hunt when they'd first met. And despite herself and all that had happened between them, she asked, "Why haven't you cleared out Ruhn's old room?"

He angled his head. Clearly, he hadn't been expecting a question like that. "Is there a reason I should have done so?"

"Seems awfully sentimental of you."

"I have ten other bedrooms in this house. Should I ever need his, I will have it cleared."

"That's not an answer."

"Is there a specific answer you're looking for?"

She opened her mouth to bite out a reply, but shut it. She surveyed him coolly.

He said a shade quietly, "Go ahead and ask."

"Do you ever wonder?" she blurted. "What might have happened if you hadn't sent your goons to hunt us down, or hadn't tossed me to the curb when I was thirteen?"

His eyes flickered. "Every single day."

"Then why?" Her voice cracked a bit. "You hit her, and then felt bad about it—you still feel bad about it. Yet you hunted us down, nearly killed her in the process. And when I showed up years later, you were nice to me for, like, two days before you kicked me out."

"I don't answer to you."

She shook her head, disgust chasing away any trace of appetite. "I don't get it—get *you*."

"What is there to get? I am a king. Kings do not need to explain themselves."

"Fathers do."

"I thought you wanted nothing to do with me."

"And that hasn't changed. But why not be a nice fucking person?"

He stared at her for a long, unbearable moment with that look she knew she so often had on her own face. The expression she'd inherited from him, cold and merciless.

He said, "Here I was, thinking you had a *real* father in Randall Silago and didn't have any need of me whatsoever."

She nearly dropped her plate. "Are you—are you *jealous* of Randall?"

His face was like stone, but his voice hoarsened as he said, "He got your mother in the end. And got to raise you."

"That sounds awfully close to regret."

"I have already told you: I live with that regret every day." He surveyed her, the plate of food in her hands. "But perhaps we might eventually move past it." He added after a moment, "Bryce."

She didn't know what to feel, to think, as he spoke her name.

Without her last name attached, without any sort of sneer. But she cleared her throat and replied, "You help me find a way to get Hunt and Ruhn out of the Asteri dungeons, and then we can talk about you becoming a better dad." She said the last words as she stepped around him, heading for her bedroom. Even if she no longer wanted to eat, she needed to put some distance between them, needed to think—

Her father called after her, "Who said Athalar and Ruhn are still in the dungeons? They haven't been since this morning."

Bryce halted and turned slowly.

"Where are they?" Her voice had gone dead—quiet. The way she knew his voice went when his temper flared.

But her father only crossed his arms, smug as a cat. "That's the big question, isn't it? They escaped. Vanished into the sea, if rumor is to be believed."

Bryce let the words sink in. "You . . . you let me think they were in the dungeons. When you knew all along they were free."

"They *were* in the dungeons when you arrived. Their status has now changed."

"Did you know it was about to change?" White, blinding fury filled her head, her eyes. Even as part of her wondered if he, too, had needed some distance between them after their conversation, and revealing this truth . . . it was his best way to shove her away again.

"I answered your questions, as you stipulated. You asked where the Asteri took them after your encounter. I told you the truth. You didn't ask for an update today, so—"

One heartbeat, the plate and sandwich were in her hands. The next, they were hurling through the air toward his head. "You *asshole.*"

Her father blasted away both plate and food with a wall of fire. Cinders of crisped bread and meat fell to the floor among shards of broken ceramic.

"Such tantrums," he said, surveying the mess on the carpet, "from someone who just learned her brother and mate are free."

"How about this," Bryce seethed, hating the gorsian shackles around her wrists more than ever. "You let me go right now, and I'll toss your ass straight through a portal and into the original Fae world. Go pack your bags."

He chuckled. "You'll bring me to that Fae world whether I let you go or not."

"Oh yeah?"

"I hear your mother and Randall have adopted a son. It'd be a shame if something happened to the boy."

She rolled her eyes. "Don't come crying to me when Mom and Randall kick your ass. They did it once—I'm sure they'll be happy to remind you what they're capable of."

"Oh, it wouldn't be me darkening their doorstep." He smirked, wholly confident. "A whisper to Rigelus, let's say, of your parents harboring a rebel boy . . ."

Bryce rolled her eyes again. "Did you take some sort of class in school? Intro to Bad Guys? Get fucking serious. You're not going to conquer any world."

"If you should open a door between worlds at my behest, Rigelus may be grateful enough to me that he grants me a good chunk of it."

Bryce eyed the shards of broken plate. Sharp enough to slit his throat.

He gave her a condescending smile, like he knew what she was contemplating.

Her father wasn't for or against the Asteri. He was just an opportunist. If removing them got him more power, he'd fight them. If bowing to the Asteri proved more lucrative, he'd prostrate himself before their crystal thrones. For all his talk of helping the Fae, he believed in nothing except advancing himself.

She said tightly, "You're already a king here."

"Of a continent. What is that to an entire planet?"

"You know, you might not be the Starborn Chosen One, but I think out of all of us, you've got the most in common with Theia. She thought the same damn thing. But she learned too late that Rigelus doesn't share."

"With the knife you brought back in play, he might find himself willing to bargain."

Bryce gave him a flat look. "What makes you think the blades will do anything to him?"

"Those blades, united, would end him."

"Trust me: I tried it on an Asteri and it didn't do anything." At least, not before Nesta had interfered.

If he was shocked by her confession, he didn't let on. "Did you *order* them to work?"

"Hard to order them, shithead, when I don't know what they can even do."

"Open a portal to nowhere," the Autumn King said, the flame guttering in his eyes.

"What do you mean?" Bryce demanded.

"The Starsword is Made, as you called it." He waved an idle hand, sparks at his fingertips. "The knife can Unmake things. Made and Unmade. Matter and antimatter. With the right influx of power—a command from the one destined to wield them—they can be merged. And they can create a place where no life, no light exists. A place that is nothing. Nowhere."

Her knees wobbled. "That's not . . . that's not possible."

"It is. I read about it in the Avallen Archives centuries ago."

"Then how do I do it? Just say 'merge into nowhere' and that's that?"

"I don't know," he admitted. "My research has not revealed the steps to merge the blades. Only what they could do."

Bryce stared at the male before her for a long moment. Glanced down the steps to the lower level—toward his study. "I want to see this research myself."

"It is on Avallen, and females are not allowed beyond the lobby of the archives."

"Yeah, our periods would probably get all over the books."

His lip curled. "Perhaps it is lucky you weaseled out of your engagement to Cormac. Your coarseness wouldn't have been well tolerated in Avallen."

"Oh, they'd warm up to me once they saw me swinging around the Starsword and remembered who and what I am."

"That would be an affront all on its own. A female has never possessed the blade."

"What?" She barked a laugh that echoed off the stone walls. "In fifteen thousand years, you mean to tell me only males have claimed it?"

"As females are not allowed in the Cave of Princes, they had no opportunity to attempt to claim it, even if they had the starlight in their veins."

Bryce gaped at him. "Are you fucking kidding me? They banned females from the Cave of Princes to keep us from getting our hands on the sword?"

His silence was answer enough.

She snapped, "I'm pretty sure there are rules, even in this shitty empire, against treating females like that."

"Avallen has long been left mostly to govern itself, its ways hidden from the modern world behind its mists."

"But there's information, somewhere on Avallen, about what these blades can do."

"Yes, but you must be invited in order to cross the mists. And considering where you stand with Morven . . ."

She was never getting in. Certainly not without the assistance of the male before her.

Her head swam, and for a heartbeat, everything that she had done and still had to do weighed so heavily she could barely breathe.

"I need to go lie down," she rasped.

The Autumn King didn't stop her as she again turned toward her bedroom. Like he knew he'd won.

She strode in silence down the hall, steps muffled by the stone.

But not to her room. Instead, she walked all the way to Ruhn's room, where she collapsed onto the bed. She didn't move for a long while.

37

Ruhn's life had become beeping machines and flickering monitors and an uncomfortable vinyl chair that served as both seat and bed.

He technically had a bed, but it was too far from this room. A few times, Flynn and Dec had come to sedate him and drag him there for a restorative treatment, as his hand was still recovering.

His fingers had formed again, but they were pale and weak. The medwitches had a small store of firstlight potions—a rarity on a ship where firstlight was banned and they relied on some sort of jacked-up bioluminescence to light everything—but Ruhn had refused them. Had demanded that they give every last drop to Lidia. His hand would heal the old-fashioned way. Whether he and Baxian would ever recover from the ordeal that had led to his hand being chewed off was another story.

But one he'd deal with later.

"Get some sleep," Flynn said from the doorway, a cup of what smelled like coffee in hand. His friend nodded to the bed and wires and machines before Ruhn. "I can take watch."

"I'm fine," Ruhn rasped. He'd barely spoken since yesterday. Didn't want to talk to anyone. Not even Flynn and Dec, though they'd come for him. Had saved him.

All because of this female before him.

While they'd been rebuilding what was left of her body, she'd flatlined twice. Even with the firstlight potion having healed the wounds to her heart. Both times, Ruhn had been sleeping in his own bed, halfway across the damned ship.

So he'd stopped leaving this room.

That there was anything left of Lidia at all was thanks to Tharion, whose cushioning plume of water had shielded her from the full impact of landing on the rocks—but the mer had still been far enough away that it hadn't stopped her plunge entirely.

It didn't matter though, because a hole as big as a fist had already been shot through her heart.

The hole was gone, healed now thanks to that rare, precious firstlight potion. And she had a functioning heart again, if the monitor marking every beat was any indication. Lungs: repaired. Ribs: rebuilt. Cracked skull: patched together. Brains stuffed back in.

Ruhn couldn't stop seeing it. How Lidia had looked when Tharion had hauled her onto the *Depth Charger.* Her limp body. So . . . small. He'd never realized how much smaller she was than him.

Or what the world might be like without her living in it.

Because Lidia had been dead. When Tharion had carried her back from the coast, she'd been completely dead. Even her Vanir healing abilities had been overtaxed.

Something had broken in Ruhn at the sight of it. Something even Pollux and the Hawk and the Asteri's dungeons hadn't managed to reach.

So the ship's medwitches had emptied their stores of firstlight potions on Lidia. Then Athalar had used his lightning to jumpstart her heart, because even liquid miracles weren't enough to get it beating again. Had used it three times now, because the crash cart had taken too long to fire up when she'd flatlined.

When Ruhn asked how he knew to try such a thing, the angel had muttered something about thanking Rigelus for the idea, and left it at that. Ruhn had been too relieved at the sound of Lidia's thumping heart to ask more.

"Ruhn, buddy—you gotta sleep." Flynn finally stepped into the room, dropping into the chair beside his. "If she gets up, I'll call you. If she even *moves*, I will call you."

Ruhn just stared at the too-pale female on the bed.

"Ruhn."

"The last thing I said to her," Ruhn whispered, "was that she was dead to me."

Flynn blew out a breath. "I'm sure she knew you didn't mean it."

"I did mean it."

His friend swallowed. "I didn't realize things between you guys had become so . . . intense."

"She did all this to save me anyway," he said, ignoring Flynn's unspoken request to fill him in.

The guilt of it would eat him alive. She'd done horrible things as the Hind, both before and after becoming Daybright, things he couldn't forget, yet . . . his head was spinning with it. The rage and guilt and that other thing.

Flynn squeezed his shoulder. "Go sleep, Ruhn. I've got your girl."

She wasn't his girl. She wasn't anything to him.

Yet he still ignored Flynn. Didn't move from the chair, though he closed his eyes. Focused on his breathing until sleep loomed.

"Stubborn asshole," Flynn muttered, but threw a blanket over Ruhn anyway.

Day, Ruhn said into the void between them, as he had nearly every hour now. *Day—can you hear me?*

No answer.

Lidia.

He'd never addressed her by her name before. Even in here.

He tried again, sending it out into the void like a plea. *Lidia.*

But the darkness only howled in answer.

"So," Hunt said to Tharion as they sat in the empty mess hall of the *Depth Charger,* "the Viper Queen, huh?"

Tharion picked at his poached fish and fine strands of seaweed salad. "Let's not get into it, Athalar." They'd missed lunch, but had been able to scrounge up plates of leftovers from the cooks.

"Fair enough." Hunt flexed his wings, now fully back to their usual strength, thanks to that firstlight Lidia had manipulated her way into giving him. "Thanks for coming to pick us up."

Tharion lifted his stare—bleak, empty.

Hunt knew the feeling. Was trying not to feel that way every second of every minute. Was drowning under it, now that he and his friends were here, safe, without the physical torture to distract him.

"Holstrom said we're a pack," Tharion said. "I don't necessarily appreciate the canine comparison, but I like the sentiment. As soon as Lidia told us you guys were days away from being executed . . . we had to do what was necessary." Sort of. It hadn't been as easy as that, of course, but once he'd been out of the Meat Market, he'd been all in.

Hunt had gotten the rundown yesterday of all that had happened. Or at least some of it. Considering that Lidia remained unconscious, he still had no idea what she'd done on her end to organize everything.

It was all so unlikely, so impossible.

He'd awoken last night, drenched in sweat, convinced he was back in those dungeons. It had taken him switching the lights on to accept the reality of his surroundings. Those initial seconds in the pitch black, when he couldn't tell where he was, were unbearable.

He wished Bryce were with him. Not just to sleep beside him, and to remind him that he'd made it out, but . . . he needed his best friend.

Bryce was gone, though. And that fact, too, woke him from slumber. Dreams of her tumbling through space, alone and lost forever.

Tharion seemed to sense the shift in his thoughts, because he asked quietly, "How you holding up, Athalar?"

"Wings are back to normal," Hunt said, folding them tightly behind him. "Emotionally . . . ?" He shrugged. He'd sat in the shower for an hour last night, the water near-scalding as it rinsed away the filth and blood of the dungeon. As he had in those days before Bryce, he'd let the water scourge the dirt and the darkness from him. But there was one marking that couldn't be washed away.

Tharion's eyes now drifted to Hunt's brow. "They're monsters to do that to you again." Hot anger sharpened the mer's face.

"They're monsters with or without putting the halo back on me." Hunt lifted his wrist, exposing the brand. The *C* that had been stamped there, negating it, was gone. "You think a slave can still be a prince?"

"I'm sure those Fae assholes have some regulations forbidding it," Tharion said with a wry smile, "but if there's anyone who could get around them, it's Bryce."

Hunt blocked out the pain in his chest. He couldn't bear to imagine the look of sorrow and rage that would creep over her face when she saw the halo, the brand. If she ever came back.

That last thought was more unbearable than any other.

Hunt forced himself past it and asked Tharion, "How are you doing?"

"About the same as you, but hanging in there." Tharion picked at his food again. Shadows seemed to swim in his brown eyes. "Taking it hour by hour."

"No word from Holstrom?"

Tharion shook his head, dark red hair shifting with the motion. The mer set down his fork at last. "What now?"

"Honestly?" Hunt braced his forearms on the metal table. "I don't know. Yesterday, my main goal was not dying. Today? All I can think about is where Bryce is, how to find her." And how he'd live with himself in the meantime.

"You really think she's in some other world?"

The blazing lights of the mess hall bounced off the metallic surface of the table in a bright blur. "If she's not in Hel, then yes—I hope she's in another world, and safely so."

"We'll figure out some way to get her back here."

Hunt didn't bother telling the mer it was likely impossible. Bryce was the one person on Midgard who could open a portal capable of bringing her home.

He just said, "Bryce would want me to get the word out—about what she learned regarding the Asteri. So I figure I'll start with the Ocean Queen. She's not allied with Ophion, but she seems to . . . help them." He gestured to the ship around them.

"Ah," Ketos said wryly. "And I thought you found me in my bunk to do lunch."

"I did. I wanted to see how you were," Hunt said, then admitted, "but I also wanted to see if you had any sort of in."

"With the Ocean Queen?" Tharion laughed, cold and hollow. "Might as well ask if I've got an in with Ogenas herself."

"She's gone to all this trouble to help the enemies of the Asteri," Hunt said, drumming his fingers on the table. "I want to know why."

Tharion studied his face with a scrutiny that reminded Hunt why Ketos had been made the River Queen's Captain of Intelligence. Hunt let the mer see the pure determination that flowed through him.

"All right," Tharion said gravely. "I'll see what I can do. Though . . ." He winced.

"What?"

"Considering what happened with her sister and niece . . . it might not go well."

"You're on this ship, and no one has tried to kill you or send you back to the River Queen—that must mean something."

"I think it has more to do with Lidia's importance than mine, much as that kills me to say." Tharion sighed through his nose. "And believe me, from the moment I got onto this ship, I've taken no shortage of shit about defecting from the River Queen. I'm pretty much a pariah."

"Well . . . maybe there's a way to use it to your advantage to lure the Ocean Queen here for a meeting."

Tharion crossed his muscular arms. "I'd rather not."

"Think about it," Hunt said. "Whatever you can stomach doing . . . I'd appreciate it."

Tharion dragged his long fingers through his red hair. "Yeah. Yeah, I know." Tharion shifted on the metal bench to pull a phone from his skintight wetsuit. He began typing. "I'll see if Sendes is free to talk." He got to his feet with fluid grace. "I'll let you know if I get anywhere."

Not an ember of the mer's usual spark lit his eyes.

"Thanks," Hunt said. "Keep me posted." Tharion nodded and strode off, still typing away.

Hunt finished his own plate of fish, then the rest of Tharion's, before he left the mess hall. The ship halls were quiet. Using the walk to stretch and test the strength of his healed wings, he strode in silence along the glass-lined corridors, nothing but dark ocean beyond. All that crushing water held back by the Ocean Queen's magic. Hunt could only marvel.

He hadn't gone back to the biodome a few levels up. Couldn't bear to see where he and Bryce had officially become mates.

He found Baxian in the gym they'd been assigned—one of dozens on this ship, and the closest to their living quarters—doing chest presses.

"You need a spotter for that much weight," Hunt warned, pausing near the bench where the angel shifter grunted under the bar, dark wings splayed beneath him. "You should have asked."

"You weren't in your room," Baxian said as he lowered the bar to his bare, muscled chest. Sweat dribbled down the groove between his pecs, his brown skin gleaming. Shreds of the tattoo across his heart— *Through love, all is possible*, inked in Danika's handwriting—remained. How he'd ever get it replaced . . . Hunt's own heart strained.

Baxian went on, "And when I asked the sprites if they'd seen you, they said you were off *doing lunch*."

Hunt had stopped by the small interior room where Malana, Sasa, and Rithi had holed up since arriving, to ask if they wanted to join him and Tharion. They were at a low, constant level of panic being down here, under the water. But they hadn't wanted to come to lunch. Didn't want to see the ship, or any indication that an endless ocean was all around them. So they stayed in their windowless room, binge-watching some inane reality TV show about realtors selling beach villas in the Coronal Islands, and pretended they weren't surrounded by a giant death trap for their kind.

It had pained him to see them gathered around the TV earlier. Lehabah would have loved them. Lehabah should have been there, with them. With all of them.

Baxian kept his eyes on the weights he'd been lifting. "I needed to get in here for a bit."

"Why?"

"Bad thoughts" was all Baxian said.

"Ah." Likely ones that included the taste of Ruhn's blood in his mouth. Hunt silently stepped behind the bench, within reach of the bar as Baxian lifted it again, arms shaking. He easily had six hundred pounds on it. "What number is this?"

"Eighty," Baxian grunted, arms straining, wings splayed beneath him. Hunt took it upon himself to guide the bar back to its posts. "I want to get to a hundred."

"Baby steps, buddy."

Baxian panted up at the ceiling, then his eyes slid toward Hunt, watching him upside down. "What's up?"

"Just checking in on a friend."

"I'm fine," Baxian said, curling upward and bracing his hands on his thighs. His wings drooped to the black plastic tiles.

Hunt knew it was a lie, but he nodded anyway. If Baxian wanted to talk, he'd talk.

He'd told Baxian everything while they'd lain in the medwitch's room yesterday, in between stitches and potions and pain. Told him about Bryce, and the Hind, and all the shit they'd learned.

Baxian had taken it well, though he clearly remained in shock about the Hind's involvement. Hunt didn't blame him. He still had trouble believing it himself. But Baxian had been working with Lidia for even longer than Hunt—it'd probably take longer to adjust his image of her.

Baxian nodded to Hunt's face. "Any luck getting that shit removed?"

Hunt didn't dare look at the wall of mirrors behind the Hel-hound. Hadn't been able to stand the sight of his face with that halo once again marring his brow. He could have sworn its ink seared him every now and then. It had never done that before—but this halo, inked by Rigelus, felt different. Worse. Alive, somehow.

"No," Hunt said. "Hypaxia Enador got rid of it the last time. So unless there's a witch-queen hiding on this ship, I've gotta learn to live with it for the time being."

"Rigelus is a fucking asshole. Always was." Baxian wiped the sweat from his brow with the back of his hand.

Hunt angled his head. "What changed with you, really? Is this new Baxian Argos just the result of learning Danika was your mate?"

It was a potential minefield, to bring up his dead mate. To lose a mate was to lose half of your soul; to live without them was torture.

"I don't want to talk about the past," Baxian said, wings snapping in tight to his body, and Hunt let it drop.

"Then let's talk about next steps," Hunt said, folding his own wings with a lingering whisper of tightness. Another day and he'd be totally back to normal.

"What's there to talk about? Big picture: the Asteri have to go."

Hunt snorted. "Glad we're on the same page." He could only pray that Tharion was able to get Sendes to contact the Ocean Queen—and that she might be on the same page as them, too.

He surveyed the male he thought he'd known for so many years. "Is it too much to hope that some of Sandriel's old triarii might also be secret anti-imperialists?"

"Don't push your luck. Two's already huge. Three, if we include you."

Thankfully, he'd never been in her actual triarii—just had to put up with their shit while surviving the years he'd been shackled to Sandriel. Hunt ignored the familiar shiver of dread at the memory of those years and asked, "But you and Lidia never had any idea that you both were—"

"No. None. I thought she was no better than Pollux." Baxian wiped more sweat from his brow, his breath steadying. "You think Lidia will make it?"

Hunt rubbed his jaw. "I hope so. We need her."

"For what?"

Hunt gave his old enemy—now friend, he supposed—a slash of a smile. "To make these fuckers pay for what they've done."

Tharion told himself to snap out of it. To focus on the fact that, against all odds, they'd succeeded in rescuing their friends from the Asteri dungeons—had even gone a step beyond and saved Lidia Cervos from certain death.

It didn't matter, though. Holstrom had stayed behind. Holstrom, whose life Tharion had wrecked.

And not only Holstrom's life, but the future of the wolves, too. That Fendyr heir was dead because of him. Technically because of Holstrom, but . . . none of it would have happened if it weren't for Tharion's own choices.

He hadn't let anyone catch wind of the past day he'd spent since getting on this ship puking up his guts. Partially from the withdrawal to the Viper Queen's venom, but also from sheer disgust at all he'd done, what he'd become.

Ariadne had been sold off, the gods knew where. To whom. And fine, she hadn't been technically *sold*, because the Viper Queen hadn't owned her, but . . . she'd left to avoid having to kill Holstrom. Or so the Viper Queen had let her believe, getting the advantageous trade while planning all along to put Sigrid in the ring against Ithan.

If there was a level below rock bottom, Tharion had found it.

He forced himself to stop grinding his teeth and concentrate on Sendes. She stood in the center of the bridge, taking a report from one of her soldiers.

None of the other technicians or officers on the bridge spoke to him. None even looked his way.

At least no one here called him a traitor. But they all knew he'd defected from the River Queen. And given how little she was liked on this ship, he knew it had more to do with the fact that he'd defected from the *mer*. From them.

He wanted to shout to this whole bridge that if he could, he'd defect from himself.

Sendes turned at last when she'd dismissed her soldier. "Sorry about that."

Tharion waved her off. Considering how much they owed Sendes and this ship, she never needed to apologize to him for anything. "I feel like this is all I say these days, but I wanted to ask for a favor."

She smiled faintly. "Go ahead."

He braced himself. "If I wanted to get in touch with the Ocean Queen, arrange a meeting between her, me, and Hunt Athalar . . . could you facilitate it?"

Sendes's throat bobbed. Not a good sign.

"If it'll put you in a weird position," Tharion amended, "don't worry about it. But I told Athalar I'd ask you, and—"

"You'll get your wish," she said ruefully. "The Ocean Queen is coming here tomorrow."

Tharion swallowed his surprise. "Okay," he said carefully. "You sound . . . worried?"

Sendes tugged at the neck of her collar. "She wants to see you. All of you."

His brows rose. "Then problem solved."

"I got the sense from her call that she isn't . . . entirely pleased you're here." Sendes grimaced. "Something to do with the Viper Queen *and* the River Queen threatening war for harboring you?"

Well, shit.

38

Ithan lunged for the book that had somehow skittered for the office doorway, landing atop it with a thud that echoed through his bones.

To his dismay, the book squirmed under him, trying to wriggle for the door and the world beyond.

"Keep it down over there," Jesiba growled above her typing.

Ithan grunted, pressing all his considerable weight onto the errant book—

"Enough," Jesiba snapped, and the book stilled at the command in her voice.

Yet Ithan didn't move until he was certain the book had fully obeyed its mistress. Uncurling to peer down at the blue leather-bound book, he tensed, then reached a hand for it.

But the book just lay there. Dormant. Like any other book—

It snapped for his fingers, and Ithan lunged again.

"Lehabah was much more effective—and ate far less. Where does all that food go, wolf?"

Ithan couldn't answer as he again wrestled the book into submission, wrapping the tome in his arms. Clutching it to his chest, he eased to his feet, then stomped toward the shelf where it was *supposed* to have stayed while he unpacked yet another crate—

"I said *enough,*" Jesiba snapped again, and the book froze in

Ithan's arms. He shoved it back on the shelf before it could get away. Then gave it another shove as a *fuck you.*

The book shoved back, as if it'd leap off the shelf and go at him for round three, but a golden ripple of light shimmered down its spine—a barrier falling back into place. Wards to seal the magical books in. The book thudded against it—and could go no further.

Jesiba said from the desk, "I thought I'd outsmarted it with the previous ward, but let's see it try to get through that one."

As if in answer, the book again rattled on the shelf. Ithan flipped it off, then faced the sorceress.

He'd been working nonstop for the past day, unpacking crates, inspecting the goods, cataloging the contents, rewrapping the artifacts inside, attaching new shipping labels . . . Busywork, but it kept him occupied.

Kept him from thinking about the blood on his hands. The body he could only hope was indeed on ice somewhere in this subterranean warren.

He didn't leave Roga's office. She had food delivered from the House's private kitchens—and if he needed to rest, she ordered him to curl up on the carpet like the dog he was.

He did, ignoring the insult, and slept deeply enough that she'd had to prod him with a foot to wake him.

He might have objected had she not been the bearer of good news: Hunt Athalar, Ruhn Danaan, and Baxian Argos had escaped from the Asteri's dungeons during a rescue operation that had incinerated the entirety of the Spine.

The Hind had done it. Tharion and Flynn and Dec had done it. Somehow, they'd pulled it off. Relief had tightened his throat to the point of pain, even as shame for not helping them twisted his gut.

Since then, Ithan and Jesiba had spoken little. Roga had mostly been on calls with clients or off at House meetings she didn't tell him about, but now . . . Ithan peered at the shelf, at the magic book again shuddering against the wards holding it in place.

"During the Summit," Ithan said, ignoring the belligerent volume, "Micah said your books were from the Library of Parthos."

Amelie had gossiped about it afterward. "That they're all that's left of it."

"Mmm," Jesiba murmured, continuing to clack away at her keyboard.

Ithan threw himself into the chair before her desk. "I thought Parthos was a myth."

"The books say otherwise, don't they?"

"What's the truth, then?"

"Not one that's easy to swallow for Vanir." But she stopped typing. Her eyes lifted above the computer screen to find his.

"Amelie Ravenscroft claimed that Micah said the library held two thousand years of human knowledge *before* the Asteri."

"And?" Her face revealed nothing.

He pointed to the pissed-off book. "So the humans had magic?"

She sighed through her nose. "No. The magic books here . . . they were *supposed* to be guardians of the library itself. At least, that's what I enchanted them to do, centuries ago. To attack those who tried to steal the books, to defend them." One such book, Ithan recalled Bryce telling him, had helped save her when she fought Micah. "But the volumes took on lives and desires of their own. They became . . . aware." She glared at the misbehaving book. "And by the time I tried to unweave the spells of life on them, their existence had become too permanent to undo. So I needed monitors such as Lehabah to guard the guardians. To make sure they didn't escape and become more of a nuisance."

"Why not sell them?"

She gave him a withering look. "Because *my* spells are written in there. I'm not letting that knowledge loose in the world." Roga had been a witch before she'd defected to the House of Flame and Shadow and called herself a sorceress instead. He could only imagine what she'd seen in her long, long life.

"So what do they say? The Parthos books?"

The clacking keys resumed. "Nothing. And everything."

Ithan snorted. "Cryptic, as usual."

Her typing stopped again. "They'd bore most people. Some are books on complex mathematics, entire volumes on imaginary numbers. Some are philosophical treatises. Some are plays—tragedies, comedies—and some are poetry."

"All from human life before the Asteri?"

"A great civilization lived on Midgard long before the Asteri conquered it." He could have sworn she sounded sad. "One that prized knowledge in all its forms. So much so that a hundred thousand humans marched at Parthos to save these books from the Asteri and Vanir who came to burn them." She shook her head, face distant. "A world where people loved and valued books and learning so much that they were willing to die for them. Can you imagine what such a civilization was like? A hundred thousand men and women marched to defend a *library*—it sounds like a bad joke these days." Her eyes blazed. "But they fought, and they died. All to buy the library priestesses enough time to smuggle the books out on ships. The Vanir armies intercepted most of them, and the priestesses were burned, their precious books used as kindling. But one ship . . ." Her lips curved upward. "The *Griffin*. It slipped through the Vanir nets. Sailed across the Haldren and found safe harbor in Valbara."

Ithan slowly shook his head. "How do you know all this, when no one else does?"

"The mer know some of it," she hedged. "The mer aided the *Griffin* across the sea, at the behest of the Ocean Queen."

"Why?"

"That's the mer's story to tell."

"But why do *you* know this? How do you have this collection?"

"I'll refrain from making the comparison to a dog with a bone." Jesiba closed her laptop with a soft click. Interlaced her fingers and set them upon the computer. "Quinlan knew when to keep her mouth shut, you know. She never asked why I have these books, why I have the Archesian amulets that the Parthos priestesses wore."

Ithan's mouth dried out. He whispered, "What—who are you?"

Jesiba burst out laughing, and several of the books on the shelf shuddered. Ithan was barely breathing as Jesiba snapped her fingers.

Her short hair flowed out—down into long, curling tresses that softened her face. Her makeup washed away, revealing features that somehow seemed younger . . . more innocent.

It was Jesiba, yet it wasn't. It was Jesiba, as if she'd been trapped in the bloom of youth. Of innocence. But her voice was as jaded as he'd always heard it as she said, "Lest you think me lying . . . This is the state I will always revert to—can revert to, at a mere wish."

"So you're . . . able to do magical makeovers?"

She didn't smile. "No. I was cursed by a demon. By a prince who intercepted my ship and the books on it."

Ithan's heart thundered.

"We had almost reached the Haldren Sea when Apollion found the *Griffin*." Her voice was flat. "He'd heard about the doomed stand at Parthos, and the ships, and the priestesses burned with their books. He was curious about what might be so valuable to the humans that we were willing to die for it. He didn't understand when I told him it was no power beyond knowledge—no weapon beyond learning." Her smile turned bitter. "He refused to believe me. And cursed me for my impudence in denying him the truth."

Ithan swallowed hard. "What kind of a curse?"

She gestured to her longer hair, her softer face. "To live, unchanging, until I showed him the true power of the books," she said simply. "He still believes they're a weapon, and that I'll one day grow tired enough of living that I'll hand them over and reveal all their supposed secret weapons."

"But . . . I thought you were a witch."

She shrugged. "I was, for a time. How do you categorize a human woman who stops aging? Who always reverts to the same age, the same physical condition as she was when she was cursed? I'd cherished my years with my fellow priestesses at Parthos. When the witch-dynasties rose, I thought I might find similar companionship with them. A home."

"You . . . you were a *priestess* at Parthos?"

She nodded. "Priestess, witch . . . and now sorceress."

"But if you were human, where'd your magic come from?" She'd said Apollion granted her long life, not power.

Her gray eyes darkened like the stormy sea she'd sailed across long ago. "When Apollion found my ship, he was ripe with power. He'd just consumed Sirius. I don't think he intended it, but when his magic . . . touched me, something transferred over."

From the way she said *touched*, Ithan knew exactly how she viewed what he'd done to her.

"It took me a while to realize I had powers beyond the stasis of eternal youth," she said blandly. "And fortunately, I've had fifteen thousand years to master them. To let them become part of me, take on a life of their own, as the books did."

Horror sluiced through him. "Do you want to . . . start aging again?"

It was a dangerously personal question, but to his surprise, she answered. "Not yet," Jesiba said a shade quietly. "Not until it's time."

"For what?" he dared ask.

She looked over a shoulder at the small library, at the feisty book that had at last simmered down, as if sulking. "For a world to emerge where these books will be truly safe at last."

39

Bryce found the Autumn King in his study, his red hair aglow in the morning light. Contemplating the Starsword and Truth-Teller on his desk.

What she'd said the other night must have struck a nerve, then. Good.

"So close," she purred as she shut the door and approached the desk, "but so far. So unworthy."

Flames danced in his eyes. "What is it you want, girl?"

She swept around the desk to stand beside his chair, peering at the weapons from his angle. He frowned, as if her mere proximity was distasteful. "Did my mom ever tell you what happened that night she was trying to get me to safety? When your goons caught up to her and Randall?"

"I'd consider your words carefully," he snarled.

Bryce smiled. "Randall hadn't picked up a gun in years. Not since he'd gotten home from the front and vowed he'd never use one again. He was on the verge of swearing his vows to Solas when he got the request from the High Priest to go help a single mom and her three year-old daughter get away from you. And that night your loser guards caught up with us . . . that was the first time Randall picked up a gun again. He put a bullet right through your chief security officer's head. Randall hated every single fucking second of it. But he did it. Because in that moment, even after only three days on the run, he knew that he was already in love with my mom. And that there was nothing he wouldn't do for her."

The Autumn King's nose crinkled with annoyance. "Is there a point to this story?"

"My point," she said, leaning closer to her father, "is that I didn't just learn about love from my mom. I learned about it from my dad, too. My *true* dad. My weak human dad who you're so jealous of that you can't stand it. He taught me to fight like Hel for the people I love."

"I grow bored of this." The Autumn King made to pull away, but Bryce grabbed his arm.

"Way ahead of you there. I grew bored of you the instant you opened your mouth."

Stone clicked.

The Autumn King reeled back, but too late. The gorsian shackle had already clamped on his wrist.

"You little bitch," he hissed, and Bryce let the shackle from her other wrist tumble to the ground. "You have no idea who you're fucking with—"

"I do. A useless, pathetic loser."

He lunged to his feet, but she'd already snatched up both Truth-Teller and the Starsword. He halted as she unsheathed the blades and pointed both at him.

Bryce said smoothly, the knife and sword steady in her hands, "Here's the bargain: you don't put up a fight, and I don't impale you with these and experiment on how to open a portal to nowhere in your gut."

Flame burned and then died out in his eyes as the shackle held him firm.

She smiled, inclining her head. "Thanks for that intel about the blades, by the way. I thought you might know something of use. It's really too bad that you sent all the servants away, isn't it? No one to hear you scream."

His face whitened with rage. "You arrived here intentionally."

"Guilty as charged," she said, shaking her hair over a shoulder with a toss of her head. "I knew you'd been doing all this research for centuries. You're the one person who's obsessed with the Starsword and its secrets, sad Chosen One reject that you are. So I came here for answers. To learn what, exactly, a weapon like this could do. How to get rid of our little intergalactic friends." She grinned. "And you assumed I landed here because . . . ?"

He glowered.

"Oh right," she said. "Because I'm your stupid, bumbling daughter. I landed here by accident—is that it?" She laughed, unable to help herself. "You probably even convinced yourself it was Luna sending you some sort of gift. That you were given the gods' favor and this was destined by Urd."

His silence was confirmation enough.

She made an exaggerated pout. "Tough luck. And *really* tough luck about the shackle. Though I guess it's fitting that I used the key Ruhn kept in his room. He told me about it once, you know. That's what he had to use when you'd bind him with these and burn him. You put these delightful things on him so he couldn't fight back. And it happened often enough that he invested in a disarming key that he left in his desk so he could free himself when you sent him back to his room to suffer."

Again, the Autumn King said nothing. The bastard wouldn't deny it.

Bryce flashed her teeth, searing white rage creeping over her vision. But her voice was cold as ice as she said, "To be honest, I'd really like to kill you right now. For my mom, but also for Ruhn. And for me, too, I guess." She nodded to the doorway. "But we do have a bargain, don't we? And I've got a hot date today."

Pure death loomed in his eyes. "The Asteri will kill you."

"Maybe. But you're not going to help them by telling them about this." She extended the Starsword toward his face. He didn't dare move as she bopped him on the nose with its tip. "It's a real shame that you unplugged all your electronics and shut off your interweb. There'll be no way to call for help from the basement closet."

He choked on his outrage. "The—"

"Oh, don't worry," she drawled. "I put a bucket and some water in there for you. Probably enough to last until one of your meathead guards wonders what's going on in here and comes to check." She pretended to think. "They might have a bitch of a time getting through your wards, though."

"As will you."

"Unfortunately for you, no, I won't. You didn't ward against teleporting. Such a rare gift here—you didn't even think to spell against it, did you? Lucky me."

"I would consider your next moves *very* carefully if—"

"Yeah, yeah." She pointed with the sword to the door. "Let's go. Your subterranean abode awaits."

He didn't try anything as she escorted him down, clearly wary of the power of the weapons she held.

Ever since Vesperus had writhed under the two blades, there had been a thought niggling at the back of Bryce's mind. Remembering all Ruhn had told her about the Autumn King's obsession with the Starsword, she'd gambled that he might know about the dagger, too.

It had been the hardest decision she'd ever made: to come here, to play this game, rather than to will the portal to take her right to Hunt. But Hunt, as she had feared, had still been in the dungeons, and to appear there would have been too risky. And this knowledge was too important.

But now she knew a little more. The Starsword and Truth-Teller could open a portal to nowhere, whatever that was. Now she just needed to learn how to make them do it.

Good thing he'd also told her where on Midgard to find more information about the blades.

The Autumn King balked as Bryce pointed with the sword to the open closet in the basement. Like so much of the house, it was fireproof. The heavy steel door would likely take him a while to break out of, if he even managed to free himself from the gorsian shackle.

The Autumn King growled as he backed into the closet, "I will kill you and your bitch mother for this."

She motioned him further inside. "I'll pencil you in for tomorrow."

With that, she slammed the door shut in his face and locked it. He barreled into it a second later, the door shuddering, but it held.

Whistling to herself, propping the Starsword on a shoulder, Bryce strode out of the basement.

There was so much more to do. Places to be. People to see.

And more to learn.

Five minutes later, Bryce pulled her phone out of the desk drawer in the Autumn King's study. It was dead, and a quick search of his office showed no hint of charging cords to get it working again. She slipped it into the band of her leggings, then picked up the Starsword and Truth-Teller from where she'd placed them on the desk.

The Autumn King's prism device sat where he'd left it. An idle beam of sunlight shone through the windows, catching in the prism and refracting a rainbow onto one of the golden planets of the orrery—on Midgard. Light pulled apart. Light stripped bare.

In the chaos of those final moments with Vesperus and these days with the Autumn King, she hadn't yet had a chance to explore the magic she'd taken from Silene's store.

She'd claimed the magic, she supposed, as Silene had surely left it there for future heirs to take. But why hadn't they? Why hadn't her son, who'd heard the truth directly from her mouth? Bryce knew she might never know the answer now. But she could try to learn something about the power she now held within her.

With a sharp inhale, Bryce rallied her magic. On the exhale, she sent a stream of her starlight into the prism, her power faster than ever before.

Starlight hit the prism, passed through it, and—

"Huh."

It wasn't a rainbow that emerged from the other side. Not even close.

It took her a moment to process what she was seeing: a gradient beam of starlight. Where the rainbow would have been full of color, this one began in shimmering white light and descended into shadow.

An anti-rainbow, as it were. Light falling into darkness, droplets of starlight raining from the highest beam into the shadowy band at the bottom, devoured by the darkness below.

Like the fading light of day—of dusk.

What did it mean? She was pretty sure her light had been pure before, but now, with Silene's power mixed in . . . there was darkness there, too. Hidden beneath.

Et in Avallen ego.

Did it make a difference to her power? To her? To now have that layer of darkness?

Bryce buried the questions. She could think about it later. Right now . . .

She took the notebook on the desk and slid it into the inside pocket of her athletic jacket.

Then she nudged the prism on the desk a few inches to the side, angling it toward the device across the room. The one the Autumn King said might be able to recapture the light, possibly with more power added to it. But what if light blasted from either prism, meeting in the middle? What would happen in the collision of all that magic?

All that smashing light, those little bits of magic bashing into each other, would produce energy. And fuel her up like a battery.

She hoped.

"Only one way to find out," she muttered to herself.

With a prayer to Cthona, she sent twin beams of light arcing around the prisms, shooting straight into them.

Twin bursts of that light flared from either prism, gunning for each other. Bands of light falling into darkness, her power stripped to its most elemental, basic form. They shot for each other, and where they met, light and darkness and darkness and light slamming into each other—

Bryce stepped into the explosion in the heart of it.

Stepped into her power.

It lit her up from the inside, lit up her very blood. Her hair drifted above her head, pens and papers and other office detritus flowing upward with it.

Such light and darkness—the power lay in the meeting of the

two of them. She understood it now, how the darkness shaped the light.

But all that colliding power . . . it was the boost she needed.

With a parting middle finger to the floor at her feet and the Autumn King sulking beneath it, she teleported out of the villa to the place she wanted to be the most.

Home. Wherever that was in Midgard.

Because her home was no longer just a physical place, but a person, too.

Silene had claimed as much when she spoke of Theia and Aidas—their souls had found each other across worlds, because they were mates. They were each other's homes.

And for Bryce, home was—and always would be—Hunt.

Exhaustion weighed so heavily on Ruhn that despite his aching neck, he couldn't be bothered to shift into a more comfortable position in the chair. Machines beeped endlessly, like metal crickets marking the passing of the night.

He had a vague sense of Declan replacing Flynn. Then Dec left and it was Flynn again.

He didn't know what woke him. Whether it was some hitch in the machine or some shift in the cadence of her breathing, but . . . a stillness went through him. He cracked his eyes open, sore and gritty, and looked to the bed.

Lidia still lay unconscious. Ghastly pale.

Lidia.

No answer. Ruhn leaned over his knees and rubbed his face. Maybe he could crash on the tiled floor. It'd be better than contorting himself in the chair.

"Morning," Flynn said. "Want some coffee?"

Ruhn grunted his assent. Flynn clapped him on the back and slipped out, the door hissing open and shut.

Gods, his whole body hurt. His hand . . . He examined the thin, strangely pale fingers, the lack of tattoos or scars. Still weak.

Like it was still rebuilding the strength stored in his immortal blood on the day of his Drop.

He flexed his fingers, wincing, then slowly sat up and rolled his neck. He was on his third rotation when he looked at the bed and noticed Lidia staring at him.

He went wholly still.

Her golden eyes were hazy with pain and exhaustion, but they were open, and she was . . . she was . . .

Ruhn blinked, making sure he wasn't dreaming.

Lidia rasped, "Am I dead or alive?"

His chest caved in. "Alive," he whispered, hands beginning to shake.

Lidia's lips curled faintly, like it took all her effort to do so. The weight of it hit him—of what she was and who she was and what she had done.

The Hind lay before him—the fucking *Hind*. How could he feel such relief about someone he hated so much? How could he hate someone whose life mattered more to him than his own?

Her glazed eyes shifted from his. Glanced around the windowless room, taking in the machines and her IV. Her nostrils flared, scenting the room beneath the antiseptics and various potions. Something sharpened in her stare. Something like recognition.

Then Lidia asked very quietly, "Where are we?"

The question surprised him. She'd planned this escape. Had her injury affected her mind? Gods, he hadn't even thought about the potential damage from going without oxygen for so long. Ruhn said softly, "On the *Depth Charger*—"

She moved.

Tubing and monitors came flying off her, ripped from her arm so fast blood sprayed. Machines blared, and Ruhn couldn't act quickly enough to stop her as she leapt out of the bed, feet slipping on the floor as she hurtled to the door.

The glass hissed open, revealing Flynn with two cups of coffee in hand. He dodged to the side with a "What the fuck!"

Lidia barreled out, hardly able to stand, and it was all Ruhn could do to race after her.

The few medwitches in the hall at this hour let out surprised cries at the deer shifter stumbling past in her pale blue medical gown, careening into the walls with the grace of a newborn colt. Her legs had been rebuilt—she'd never used these ones before.

"What the *Hel*," Flynn said, a step behind Ruhn, smelling of the coffee that had spilled on him when he'd dived out of Lidia's way.

Lidia hit the stairwell, and just before the door shut behind her, Ruhn saw her trip, falling to her knees on the steps, then surge up again.

"Lidia," he panted, each step singeing his lungs. *Fuck* his still-healing body—

He slammed into the stairwell door, but she was already halfway up, long legs pale and thin against the gray tiles.

She charged up and up, around and around, either unaware or uncaring that Ruhn ran close behind. She threw open an unmarked door, then bolted down the hall. People in civilian clothes pressed back against the walls at the sight of her—then him. The walls here were covered with bright art and flyers.

Sharp inhales came from Lidia. She was sobbing, craning her neck to see through the windows of the rooms she passed. Ruhn read the words on each wooden door: *Year Three. Year Seven. Year Five.*

She skidded to a halt, gripping a doorjamb. Ruhn reached her side as she shoved her face up to the glass.

Year Nine.

A group of teenagers—most of them mer, with striped skin and various coloring—sat in rows of desks in the classroom. Lidia pressed a hand against the door. Tears rolled down her cheeks.

And then a boy, golden-haired and blue-eyed, looked away from his teacher and toward the window. The kid wasn't mer.

The ground slid out from under Ruhn. The boy had Lidia's face. Her coloring.

Another boy to his left, also not mer, had dark hair and golden eyes. Lidia's eyes.

Behind them, Flynn grunted with surprise. "You've got brothers on this ship?"

"They're not my brothers," Lidia whispered. Her fingers curled on the glass. "They're my sons."

40

Hunt leaned against the wall of the massive tactical room on the *Depth Charger*, arms crossed. Tharion and Baxian flanked him, the former feigning nonchalance, the latter the portrait of menace.

Only a conference table occupied the room, and though they'd been told to take a seat upon walking in five minutes ago, they all remained standing.

Hunt ran through all the things he needed to say. The Ocean Queen had told Sendes that she wanted Tharion presented to her, but Hunt knew he wouldn't get a better opportunity to ask her his questions. Assuming Tharion wasn't turned into a bloody pulp before Hunt could start talking. That would throw a wrench in his plans.

If Tharion was nervous, the mer didn't show it. He just removed invisible flecks of lint from his aquatic suit and glanced at the digital clock on the far wall every now and then. But Hunt had noted his dead-eyed stare. A male prepared to face his end. Who might think he deserved it.

Power shuddered through the ship, like an undersea earthquake. As menacing and deadly as a tsunami. Ancient and cold as the bottom of an oceanic trench.

"She's here," Tharion murmured.

Baxian's dark wings tucked in tighter, and he glanced sidelong at Hunt. "You ever meet the Ocean Queen?"

"Nope," Hunt said, folding in his own wings. He wished he had a weapon—any weapon. Even with his lightning and brute strength, there was something comforting in the weight of a gun or sword at his side. Though neither would be helpful against the being who'd arrived on the ship. "Never even seen her. You?"

Baxian ran a hand over his tightly curled black hair. "No. Ketos?"

"No," was the mer's only reply, his eyes again fixed on the clock.

It was no surprise that even Tharion hadn't met the Ocean Queen. She was more of an enigma than the River Queen, rumored to have been born of Ogenas herself. The daughter of a goddess, who could likely bring the force of this entire ocean crashing down upon this ship and—

The door clicked open. Sendes appeared on the threshold and announced, "Her Depthless Majesty, the Ocean Queen." The commander stepped aside, bowing at the waist as a tiny female entered behind her.

Hunt blinked. Even Tharion seemed to be restraining his shock, his breath shallow.

Her luscious body measured barely more than four feet. Her skin was as pale as the belly of a fish; her angular eyes as dark as a shark's. Her heart-shaped face was neither pretty nor plain, and the rosebud-shaped lips were the reddish pink of a snapper. She walked with a strange sort of lightness—like she was unused to being on solid ground—and the gown of kelp and sea fans she wore trailed behind her, the shells and coral in the train tinkling as she moved.

Pushing off the wall, the three of them followed Sendes's lead and bowed.

Hunt watched the Ocean Queen as he did so, though, and noted the slow sweep of her eyes over them. She only moved her eyes—nothing else. An apex predator assessing her prey.

When she'd decided they had suitably worshipped her, she stalked to the head of the table. Each step left behind a wet footprint on the tiles, though she appeared entirely dry. Barnacles adorned some strands of her hair like beads.

"Sit," she ordered, voice deep and rolling and utterly chilling.

Wings rustled and chairs groaned as they obeyed. Hunt could only wonder if he'd pissed off Urd today as he realized *he* had claimed the chair nearest to the head of the table—to the monarch standing there. Baxian sat on his other side, and Tharion, the worm, had wriggled his way to the seat farthest away—within leaping distance of the door.

Adjusting his wings around the chair back, Hunt caught Baxian's eye. The Helhound gave him a look that pretty much said: *Well, I'm shitting my pants.*

Hunt glanced pointedly at his own chair, as if to say, *You're not the one sitting closest to her.*

The queen surveyed them with ageless, pitiless eyes.

Hunt couldn't help his swallow. He'd never felt so small, so insignificant. Even in front of the Asteri, he'd remembered that he was a warrior, and a damned good one, and might at least make a last stand against them. But before this female . . . He saw it in her eyes, sensed it in his blood: one thought from her, and she'd wipe him from existence with a tidal wave of power.

Sendes cleared her throat and said, voice shaking, "May I present Hunt Athalar, Baxian Argos, and Tharion Ketos."

"Our guests from Valbara," the Ocean Queen acknowledged. Squalls howled in her words, even as her tone remained mild. Hunt's entire body tensed.

As fast as a storm sweeping in over the sea, she seemed to grow—no, she *was* growing, taller and taller, until she towered over Sendes, nearly Hunt's own height.

Her power surged, filling the room, dragging their meager souls down into its airless heart like a maelstrom. The Ocean Queen slid her attention to Tharion and said with knee-trembling menace, "You have brought a heap of trouble to my doorstep."

* * *

Ruhn tried and failed to process what he'd heard. Lidia had . . . children?

A female voice behind them said, "Miss Cervos."

Lidia didn't turn. Just stared at the boys in the classroom.

But Ruhn looked, and found a full-bodied, dark-skinned mer female with a kind face standing there. She said to Ruhn, "I'm Director Kagani, the head of this school."

Lidia's fingers contracted on the glass of the door's window. "Can I meet them?" The question was very, very quiet. Broken.

Kagani sighed softly. "I think it would be disruptive, and too public, for them to be pulled out of class right now."

Lidia finally turned at that, teeth flashing. "I want to meet my children."

Ruhn's mind spun at her expression. Rage and pain and a mother's unbreaking ferocity.

"I know you do," Kagani said with unflappable calm. "But it would be best if we talk in my office after school. It's right down the hall."

The Hind didn't so much as move.

"Consider what is best for *them*, Lidia," Kagani encouraged. "I understand, I truly do—I'm a mother, myself. If I had . . ." Her throat worked. "I would want the same if I had made your choices. But I'm also an educator, and an advocate for these children. Please put the twins first today. Just as you have every day for the past fifteen years."

Lidia scanned the female's face with an openness Ruhn had never seen from her. She looked over a shoulder, back into the classroom. The blond boy now stood at his desk, staring at her with wide eyes. The dark-haired one watched carefully, but remained seated.

So much of Lidia was written all over their features. When they were away from her, it was unlikely that anyone would draw a connection, but it was impossible to miss the relation when seeing them in close proximity.

"All right," Lidia whispered, lowering her hand from the window. "All right."

Kagani let out a small sigh of relief. "Why don't you go get cleaned up. School isn't out for another five hours, so take your time. Have some food. Maybe get cleared by your medwitch." A nod to the half-healed holes in Lidia's arm where she'd torn out her IV.

"All right," Lidia said a third time, and stepped away. As if Ruhn and Flynn didn't exist.

Director Kagani added gently, "I'll contact Brann and Actaeon's adoptive parents to see if they can come in, too."

Lidia nodded silently, and kept walking.

Ruhn glanced to Flynn, whose brows were high. Ruhn raised his own brows in silent agreement.

A sudden movement snared his attention and Ruhn whirled toward Lidia, blindly reaching for her.

But he wasn't swift enough to catch her as she fainted, crumpling to the floor.

Tharion had never met anyone as petrifying and alluring as the Ocean Queen. Never wanted to cry and laugh and scream at the same time . . . though he was leaning toward the latter as the queen bestowed the full force of her displeasure upon him.

"Tharion Ketos." She spoke his name like it left a foul taste in her mouth. "How is it that you have not one, but *two* queens demanding your head?"

He winced and put forth his brightest charm—his first and best line of defense. "I tend to have that effect on females?"

The monarch didn't smile, but he could have sworn Sendes, stationed in the doorway, was trying not to.

The Ocean Queen folded her hands in front of her curved, soft belly. "I have received reports that the Viper Queen of Lunathion has put a bounty on your head for three million gold marks." Athalar, the bastard, let out a low whistle. "*Five* million if you're alive, so she can punish you herself."

Tharion choked on a breath. "For what?" He added hastily, "Your Majesty."

"I don't know the particulars, nor do I care to," the Ocean Queen said, pearlescent teeth flashing behind her vivid red lips. "But I believe it has something to do with your presence bringing certain individuals who then caused untold damage to her property. She holds *you* responsible."

He was so, so fucked.

"But that is not the end of my problems," the queen went on. He could have sworn those glistening teeth sharpened. "My so-called sister in the Istros is demanding your return as well. She is threatening war upon me—*me*—if you are not handed over. Presumably to be executed."

He could scarcely get a breath down. "Please," he whispered, "my parents—"

"Oh, I wouldn't worry about your family if I were you," the Ocean Queen seethed. Her teeth were now hooked and razor-like. Pure shark. "The River Queen and Viper Queen only want *you*. I would like one good reason why I shouldn't hand you over—let them squabble over your carcass."

He scrambled for some way to disarm the moment, to win her, but came up empty. His unnaturally deep pool of luck had finally and officially run dry—

"You hand him over," a female voice drawled from the open doorway, "and you'll have a third queen pissed at you."

Tharion's stomach bottomed out.

Bryce Quinlan swept through the doorway and winked at the Ocean Queen. "Tharion serves me."

41

Hunt had left his body. Maybe he'd died. That was *Bryce* in the doorway, smirking at the Ocean Queen.

She was Bryce and yet she was . . . not.

She wore her usual casual attire—skintight jeans and a soft white T-shirt topped with a navy athletic jacket. Hel, she even sported those neon-pink sneakers. But there was something different in her posture, in the way the light seemed to shimmer from her.

She was older, somehow. Not in any line or wrinkle, but in her eyes. Like she'd been through some major shit, good and bad. Hunt recognized it, because he knew it lay etched in his own face, too.

The Ocean Queen eyed Bryce unflinchingly. "And who, pray tell, are *you?*"

Bryce didn't miss a beat. "I'm Bryce Danaan, Queen of the Valbaran Fae."

Hunt let out a strangled sound—a sob.

Bryce looked at him then, scanning his face, the tears he couldn't stop. Her gaze flicked to the halo, then down to his wrist—but her expression yielded nothing. She just walked up to where he sat, and it *was* her, her fucking scent, and that was her soft skin brushing his hand as she peered down into his face.

"Hey," he said, voice rough, eyes stinging.

Bryce squeezed his hand, tears filling her eyes as well. "Hey." She blinked her tears away, twisting back to the Ocean Queen, who monitored every move. Every breath.

The Ocean Queen said to Bryce, shark's teeth flashing, "I recognize no queen bearing that title."

"I do," Hunt said, folding his wings behind him as he stood, coming to Bryce's side. Her fingers grazed his own, and a chill of pleasure soared through him. "She's my mate." He sketched a bow to the Ocean Queen. "Prince Hunt Athalar Danaan, at your service. I can testify that Tharion Ketos serves my queen and mate. Any other claims to him are false."

Bryce shot him a wry glance that seemed to say, *You're a big fucking liar, but I love you.*

The Ocean Queen still surveyed Bryce with a face as cold as the northern reaches of the Haldren Sea. "That remains to be seen." She pointed to Tharion, her fingernail made of pure nacre. "Tharion Ketos, you are confined to this ship until I decide otherwise."

Tharion bowed his head, but remained still and silent.

The Ocean Queen lowered her finger and shot a sharp glance at Bryce. It was instinct for Hunt's knees to bend, to prepare to leap between them, to shield his mate. But there was no amount of lightning, no gun, no weapon that could save Bryce, should the Ocean Queen bring the full wrath of the sea down upon them. This deep, they'd have no chance of reaching the surface in time. That is, if their bodies didn't explode first from the pressure.

But the near-divine being declared, a shade haughtily, "Queen or no queen, you are all now guests on my ship—and will leave only when I bid you to."

Hunt refrained from saying that her checkout policy wasn't very guest friendly. Especially as the Ocean Queen asked Bryce, dark eyes narrowing, "Does your father the Autumn King still draw breath?"

Bryce smiled slowly. "For the time being."

The Ocean Queen weighed the words—then answered Bryce's

smile with her own, revealing all those hooked shark's teeth. "I don't recall inviting you onto this ship."

Bryce checked her nails—it was such a thoroughly Bryce movement that Hunt's chest tightened. "Well, *someone* sent me an e-vite."

Hunt lowered his head to keep the grin from his face. He'd forgotten how fun it was—to see Bryce in her element. Leading these shitheads along by the nose. It lightened some of that weight in his chest, some of that primal terror—just a fraction.

The Ocean Queen said flatly, "I do not know of any such thing."

Amusement glimmered in Bryce's whiskey-colored eyes, but her tone was dead serious as she explained, "I teleported here. I needed to find my mate."

"You and your mate are dismissed," the Ocean Queen said, waving that nacre-tipped hand. A hermit crab skittered through her dark locks and then vanished again. "I have important matters to discuss with Captain Ketos."

Tharion looked up, grimacing. Maybe his death sentence hadn't been delayed after all.

But again, Bryce didn't miss a beat. "Yeah, see, *my* matters are a bit more pressing."

"I find that highly unlikely."

Two queens facing off. And there was no doubt in Hunt's mind that Bryce *was* a queen now. The poise, the strength radiating from her . . . She didn't need a crown to rule this room.

Bryce sucked in a breath, the only sign of nerves. And said to the ruler of the seas, "You're wrong."

It was only through sheer will that Bryce didn't throw her arms around Hunt immediately and kiss him silly. Only through sheer will that she didn't start raging and crying at the halo inked anew on his brow, the brand stamped on his wrist.

She'd kill the Asteri for this.

She'd already planned to, of course, but after what they'd done to Hunt while she'd been gone . . . she'd make sure they died slowly.

That is, once she figured out how to kill them.

And as soon as she held Hunt, she wasn't letting go. Ever. But they had so much shit to do right now that giving in wasn't an option, holding him and loving him weren't options.

She didn't dare ask where Ruhn was, not with the Ocean Queen present. Baxian was with Hunt, so maybe her brother was nearby, too. The Autumn King had said they were all rescued. Ruhn had to be here. Somewhere.

But she couldn't wait for her brother. He'd have to be filled in later.

"I journeyed to the original world of the Fae," she began, "through a Gate in the Eternal Palace. I possess Luna's Horn, which helped clear the pathway between worlds."

Stunned, breathless silence filled the room. Hunt practically thrummed with lightning and curiosity, but Bryce kept her eyes on the Ocean Queen as the female said neutrally, "I'm assuming you learned something."

Bryce gave a shallow nod. "I knew already that the Asteri are intergalactic parasites. But I learned that the Asteri infected Midgard's waters upon invading this world."

"Infected," the Ocean Queen mused.

Bryce nodded again. "The Asteri put an actual parasite in the water—or something like a parasite. I don't really know what it is, specifically. Whatever it is, it makes everyone on Midgard *have* to offer up firstlight via the Drop. Or else we'll lose our powers— we'll wither and die."

"Fuck," Hunt breathed. Bryce still didn't look at him, though. At Tharion or Baxian or Sendes, who were all gaping in absolute dread.

Only the Ocean Queen didn't appear surprised.

Bryce said, narrowing her eyes in realization, "You—you knew this."

The Ocean Queen shook her head. "No. I always wondered, though, why my people still needed to make the Drop, even down here. But now that you have revealed this terrible truth, what shall *you* do?"

"I guess I'll take on the Asteri," Bryce said. "Banish them from this world."

"How?" The Ocean Queen shifted, the coral beading on her gown tinkling.

Bryce hedged, not quite willing to lay out *everything* for this stranger. "I don't suppose an eviction notice would do the trick?"

The three males around them didn't bat an eye, but Sendes shifted on her feet.

The Ocean Queen said plainly, "This is folly. You'd need entire armies to fight the Asteri."

"Care to supply one?" Bryce countered.

"My people are skilled in the water, not on land. But Ophion has forces, what little remain. I believe Lidia Cervos mustered them the other day to devastating effect. Though I have not yet learned how many survived the mission."

Bryce said to the queen, "So you *do* work with Ophion?"

"We assist each other when we can—I harbor their agents if they make it here. But Ophion is as prejudiced against us as a Vanir against a mortal. They find accepting our help to be . . . unsavory."

"Plenty of Vanir have helped Ophion over the years," Baxian cut in with soft strength.

Bryce's heart tightened as Danika's face flashed through her mind. If Danika could not be here, it was only fitting that her mate stood here instead.

"And Ophion resents all of them," Commander Sendes said from where she still stood beside the doorway. "We'd need a solid bridge between us to get talks going about unifying armies."

Hunt turned to Bryce and asked quietly, "What about Briggs?"

Her blood chilled. "No fucking way. He'll turn around and kill us." The former rebel leader's gaunt, hollow face flashed in her mind, along with those deep blue eyes that had seemed to bore right through her.

"She is correct," the Ocean Queen said, folding her hands over her stomach once more in a portrait of regal poise. "Another route is required."

Bryce said as casually as she could, "Hel will aid us."

The Ocean Queen scoffed. "You trust those demons?"

"I do." At the ruler's raised brows, Bryce said, jaw clenching, "Hel's known all this stuff for millennia. And tried their best to make it right. To help liberate us. That's what they were trying to do during the First Wars."

Again, her friends were stunned into silence.

But the Ocean Queen let out a small, disbelieving snort. "You learned that in this other world as well?"

"Yes." Bryce kept her tone even, refusing to be baited.

"You trust Hel enough to fully open the Northern Rift to allow their armies through?"

"If it's our only shot at defeating the Asteri."

"You'd trade one evil for another."

Bryce couldn't stop the starlight that began pulsing under her skin, condensing and sharpening into that *thing* that could cleave through stone. "I'd hardly call the Princes of Hel evil, when they've refused to let the Asteri win all these years. When they've gone out of their way to try to help us, even though it'll cost them. Hel owes us nothing, yet they're so convinced of the importance of ridding the universe of the Asteri that they've been at this for thousands of years. I'd say that's a pretty solid commitment."

The Ocean Queen seemed to grow an inch, then another. She jerked her chin toward Hunt. "Your mate hunted demons for centuries—has seen their brutality and bloodlust up close. What does he have to say about their supposed altruism?"

Hunt squared his shoulders, utterly unshakable. Bryce's throat tightened to see it—to know even before he spoke that he had her back. "It's tough for me to accept, especially when they wrecked Lunathion this spring, but if Bryce trusts them, I trust them. Besides, we're out of options."

Bryce spared him from dwelling further on the topic by saying, "There is another thing."

All of them turned to her. Hunt, at least, had the good sense to look nervous.

Bryce kept her gaze on the Ocean Queen as she said, "We need to head to Avallen."

"Why?" the Ocean Queen demanded. A tsunami roared in her tone.

"There's some research I need to do in its archives that might help our cause." It was at least *partially* the truth. "About the First Wars and Hel's involvement."

Okay, the last part was a lie. But she wasn't about to explain what she really needed on the mist-shrouded isle.

The Ocean Queen drawled, "I don't recall becoming a ferry service. Do you assume my city-ship is at your disposal?"

"Do you want to win this war or not?"

Shock rippled through the room at her words. Hunt tensed, readying for a physical confrontation.

But Bryce blazed with starlight as she said, "Look, I know nothing is free. But for fuck's sake, let's talk plainly. Name your price. You've gone out of your way to try to help people for years, working toward bringing down the Asteri. So why are you making things more difficult when we finally have a chance at beating them?"

"This is becoming tedious," the Ocean Queen said. "I did not come here to be ordered about by an impostor queen."

"Call me what you want," Bryce said, "but the longer we don't act, the easier it will be for Rigelus and the rest of the Asteri to move against us."

"Everything seems urgent to the young."

"Yeah, I get that, but—"

"I was not done speaking."

Bryce hid her wince as the Ocean Queen surveyed her. "You *are* young. And idealistic. And inexperienced."

"Don't forget ill qualified and always inappropriately dressed."

The female cut her a warning glare. Bryce held up her hands in mock surrender.

The Ocean Queen loosed a long breath. "I do not know you, Bryce Danaan, and so far have seen little to recommend you as a reliable ally. My people have managed to evade the Asteri's influence for millennia now—to remain safe down here, fighting against them as best we can. And yet you have informed me that even here, we are not untouched. Even here, in my domain, the Asteri's parasite infects us all."

"I'm sorry to have been the bearer of bad news," Bryce said, "but would you rather I had kept it from you?"

"Honestly? I don't know." The Ocean Queen studied her hand—a banded sea krait twined around her wrist like a living black-and-white bracelet. Poisonous as Hel. The ruler said quietly, "Have you thought about an evacuation?"

Bryce started. "To where? There's nowhere on Midgard, except maybe this ship, that isn't under their control." Avallen was apparently shielded by its mists, yes, but King Morven still bowed to the Asteri.

The queen lifted her head. "To the home world of the Fae."

Hunt shifted, wings rustling. "You mean leave this planet completely?"

The Ocean Queen didn't take her eyes from Bryce's as she said, "Yes. Use the Horn, allow as many through as you can, and then seal the way forever."

Horror twisted through her. "And what—abandon the rest here? To be slaves and feeding troughs for the Asteri?" She'd be no better than Silene.

The Ocean Queen asked, "Isn't it better for some to be free, than for all to be dead?"

Hunt let out a low laugh, stepping closer to Bryce's side as he said to the Ocean Queen, "You can't mean that. Who the fuck would even get chosen to come? Your people? Our families? In what universe is that fair?"

Seated at the conference table, Baxian nodded his agreement, but Tharion kept still as stone. Maybe he didn't want to attract the queen's attention or ire once more. Spineless asshole. But Bryce squashed her distaste. She needed all the allies she could get.

"I do not say it is fair," the Ocean Queen said, stroking the sea krait on her wrist. "But it might be what is necessary."

Bryce swallowed the dryness in her mouth. "I came back here to help everyone, not to abandon them to the mercy of the Asteri."

"Perhaps Urd sent you to that other world to establish a safe harbor. Have you considered that?"

Bryce exploded, "What was all this for, then? The stealth, the ships, the Ophion contacts? What the fuck was it for if you just want to run away from the Asteri in the end?"

Eyes blacker than the Melinoë Trench pinned her to the spot. "Do not dare question my dedication, girl. I have fought and sacrificed for this world when no one else would. Once, my kingdom was vaster than you can imagine—but the Asteri came, and entire islands withered into the sea in despair, taking the very heart of this world with it. The very heart of the mer, too. If there is anyone who understands how futile it is to stand against the Asteri, it is I."

Bryce's breath caught in her throat. "Wait—you were here *before* the Asteri? The mer were here? I thought only humans lived on Midgard then."

The Ocean Queen's face became distant with memory. "They had the land—we had the seas. Our people met only occasionally, the root of the humans' legends about the mer." A wistful smile, then her eyes again focused on Bryce, sharp and calculating. "But yes, we have always been here. Midgard has always had magic, as all nature has inherent magic. The Asteri just did not deign to recognize it."

Bryce filed away the information. "Fine—you win the award for longest-suffering people on Midgard. That doesn't entitle you to jump to the front of the Evacuate Midgard line." Hunt touched her shoulder lightly, a gentle warning. But Bryce ignored him and laid her hands flat on the table, leaning over it to breathe in the Ocean Queen's face. "I *refuse* to open a gate like that. I won't help you condemn the majority of Midgard's people while a select few dance off into the sunset."

The sea krait on the Ocean Queen's wrist hissed at Bryce. Even as its mistress's face remained as cold as the ice floes of the north. "You will come around to the idea when your friends and loved ones start dying around you."

"Don't you dare condescend to her," Hunt growled at the queen.

Sendes cleared her throat, trying to bail them out of this

clusterfuck, but all Bryce could hear was a roaring in her ears, all she could see was a blinding white creeping over her vision—

"You're a coward," Bryce spat at the Ocean Queen. "You hide behind your power, but you're a *coward*."

The ship shuddered, as if the very sea tensed with rage.

But the Ocean Queen said, "Against my better instincts, I will deposit you and yours in Avallen, as requested. Consider that my last gift."

Bryce ground her teeth so hard her jaw hurt.

"But when you fail in whatever uprising you think you can muster," the Ocean Queen said by way of dismissal, striding for the door, leaving a trail of water in her wake, "when you realize that I am right and fleeing is the best option, I ask only this in exchange for my services: take as many of my people as you can."

42

Bryce couldn't help but be impressed that Hunt, Tharion, and Baxian held their shit together until they got back to a cabin barely big enough to fit all of them, let alone so many egos. She certainly had a Hel of a time with it.

But as soon as the door shut, absolute chaos erupted.

"What the *fuck*—" Hunt exploded.

"Are you all right—" she started.

"The *home world of the Fae*?" Tharion demanded at the same time Baxian chuckled, "That was epic."

Tharion sank onto one of the bunks, his normally tan skin pale. "Only you would tangle with the Ocean Queen, Legs."

Baxian said to the mer, "Confined to the ship, huh?"

Tharion winced. "I'm fucked."

Bryce turned to Hunt, who was leaning against the door he'd shut. She arched her brows at her mate, at his too-calm expression. She knew that look. He was no doubt debating how soon he could kick everyone out and fuck her senseless.

Her toes curled in her sneakers, and she gave him a wink. Hunt rolled his eyes, a corner of his mouth kicking up despite himself.

She hadn't failed to see that glimmer of darkness in his gaze, though. Whatever had happened to him while she'd been gone, it had left a mark on the inside, too.

But they'd talk about it later. Bryce asked, "Where's Ruhn?"

"With Lidia," Hunt said quietly.

"Lidia?"

Baxian nodded, sitting beside Tharion, his black wings gleaming like raven feathers. "Yeah. She got us all out. She's, uh . . . a bit worse for wear. Ruhn's been watching over her."

Bryce's chest tightened. "Will she—"

Before Bryce could finish, the door blasted open. Hunt's lightning was an instant crackling wall in front of her.

But Bryce let out a low sound of joy when she saw Ruhn panting in the doorway, her brother's eyes wide with shock.

Then they were hugging and laughing, and such joy poured from her that her starlight glowed brightly, casting stark shadows in the cramped room. "Bryce," he said, grinning, and the pride in his voice had her throat closing up. She grabbed his hand, unable to come up with the words, but then she saw his arms.

His tattoos were in ribbons. Like his skin had been split open so deep—

Her starlight winked out. "Ruhn," she breathed.

"All in one piece," Ruhn said, and glanced to Baxian. "Again."

"I don't want to know what that look means," Bryce said as Baxian winced apologetically.

"You really don't," Hunt said, sliding an arm around her shoulders and guiding her to the bunk opposite where Baxian and Tharion rested. He sat close enough that his thigh pressed into hers, and went so far as to drape a wing over her. Like he'd never let her out of his sight again.

She breathed in his scent, his warmth, over and over again. The most wonderful things in the universe.

Ruhn blinked at Bryce, as if not convinced she was really there. "I'm not hallucinating, right?" he asked.

"No." Bryce patted the bed beside her.

But Ruhn lingered by the door, his face grim. "It kills me to say this, but I can't stay long."

"What happened?" Baxian asked.

"Lidia woke up," Ruhn said. "And, ah . . . she had some surprises to share."

"So," Hunt said to Ruhn in the stunned quiet five minutes later. "Your girlfriend has . . . kids."

Bryce's mind reeled from all her brother had said.

Ruhn only lifted baleful eyes to Hunt. All right: no teasing. She let out a low whistle. "How the Hel did Lidia hide it? When did she even *have* these kids?"

Baxian said ominously, "I think the better question is whether they're Pollux's."

"They didn't have wings," Ruhn said tensely. "But that doesn't mean anything."

"She's all right, though?" Bryce asked. She owed the female everything. *Everything.* If there was anything she could do to help her—

"She's sleeping again," Ruhn said. "I think the run upstairs drained her."

"Adrenaline fueled it, probably," Tharion mused.

Ruhn's eyes went hazy, worried, so Bryce supposed Hunt did him a favor when he changed the subject. He turned to her. "Okay, let's hear it. How the *fuck* did you get onto this ship? How did you find us?"

To distract Ruhn, she could play along. "I told you: I teleported." She met Hunt's eyes, registering the love and pain there, and said quietly, "You're my home, Hunt. Our love spans across stars and worlds, remember?" She smiled slightly. "I'll always find you."

His throat worked, no doubt recalling that he'd said those same words to her before she'd jumped through the Gate in the Eternal Palace. But he dropped her stare like he couldn't bear it, and asked, "*Where* did you teleport from?"

Fine, then. She'd give him some space to sort out his shit. "From dear old Dad's house. Where he thought he was keeping me hostage."

"He *thought*?" Ruhn demanded.

Bryce shrugged.

Hunt threw her a bone this time. "Can you explain what you said to the Ocean Queen in there? About the parasites in the water and the Asteri?"

"What else is there to say? They infected the waters of Midgard with it. It's in all of us. It forces us to make the Drop, otherwise it sucks away our power."

"Excuse me?" Ruhn blurted.

Bryce sighed. And explained it again.

All of it, this time—from the start. Arriving in the other world, being held in the dungeon. Escaping and traveling the tunnels with Azriel and Nesta. Then what she'd learned in that secret chamber: of the world of the Fae, of the Daglan, of Theia and Fionn and Pelias, of Silene and Helena, of Hel's assistance. Of claiming Silene's power, and how her own starlight now felt different. Then the encounter with Vesperus and stealing Truth-Teller from Azriel.

It took an hour to explain it all, though she omitted any mention of the Mask or the Trove. The fewer people who knew about them, the better. When she got to the part about how she'd been able to zero in on Hunt and jump right to him, his eyes gleamed, so full of love that her chest ached.

Ruhn had been silent through all of it, though his phone buzzed frequently while she spoke. She had a feeling that he was getting updates from someone about Lidia's current state.

Hunt leaned forward, bracing his forearms on his thighs. He exhaled a long breath. "Okay. That is . . . a lot. Just give me a moment."

Bryce absently rubbed at her chest, the eight-pointed star scar there. She said quietly, "Tell me what happened here. Please."

Bryce needed a minute when they finished.

Ten minutes, actually.

She left the room with a quiet "I'm so sorry" and then she was in the hall, stomach churning, breath stalling—

"Bryce," Hunt said from a few steps behind, boots thudding on the tiled floor.

She couldn't turn to face him. She'd left them, and they had suffered so much—

"Quinlan," he growled. His hand wrapped around her elbow, halting her. The hall was empty, its window overlooking the crushing black sea beyond the glass.

"Bryce," he said again, and gently turned her. She couldn't stop her face from crumpling.

Hunt was there in an instant, wrapping her in his arms, wings folding around them, surrounding her with that familiar, beckoning scent of rain on cedar.

"Shhh," he whispered, and she realized she'd begun crying, the full force of all that had happened to him, to her, crashing down.

Bryce slid her arms around his waist, clinging tight. "I was so worried—"

"I'm fine."

She scanned his face, his silver-lined eyes. "Those dungeons weren't . . . fine, Hunt."

"I survived."

But shadows darkened his face with the words. He bowed his head, leaning his brow against hers. That hateful halo pressed against her skin. "Barely," he admitted. She tightened her arms around him, shaking. "The thought of you kept me going."

He might as well have punched her in the heart. "You kept me going, too."

"Yeah?" The love in his voice threatened to shatter her heart. "I knew these smoldering good looks would come in handy one day."

She laughed brokenly. Lifted a hand to his face and traced its strong, beautiful lines.

"I'm sorry," he breathed, and the pain in the words nearly knocked her to the ground.

"For *what*?"

He shut his eyes, throat bobbing. "For getting us into this mess."

She pulled back. "*You? You* got us into this mess?"

He opened his eyes again, his gaze bleak as the sea beyond the wall of windows at their backs. "I should have warned you, should have made us all think before we jumped into this nightmare—"

She gaped. "You did warn me. You warned us all." She cupped his cheek in a hand. "But the only ones to blame for any of this are the Asteri, Hunt."

"I should have tried harder. None of us would be in this situation—"

"I'm going to stop you right there," she said hotly, laying her palm on his chest. "Do I regret the pain and suffering that you all went through? Solas, yes. I can barely think about it. But do I regret that we took a stand, that we *are* taking a stand? No. Never. And you couldn't have stopped me from starting that fight." She frowned. "I thought we were on the same page about doing what needs to be done."

His expression shuttered. "We were—are."

"You don't sound too sure of that."

"You didn't have to see your friends carved apart."

The second the words were out, she knew from his wide eyes that he regretted them. But it didn't stop them from hurting, from pelting her heart like stones. From sending her anger boiling up within her.

But she stared at the black ocean pressing against the glass, all that death held a few inches away. She said quietly, "I had to live with the terror of possibly never getting home, never seeing you again, wondering if you were even alive, every second I was gone." She glanced at him sidelong in time to see something cold pass over his face. She hadn't seen that coldness in a long, long time.

The face of the Umbra Mortis.

His voice was chilled, too, as he said, "Good thing we both made it, then."

It wasn't a resolution. Not even close. But this wasn't the conversation she wanted to have with him. Not right now. So she said blandly, turning from the wall of windows, "Yeah. Good thing."

"So we're really headed to Avallen?" Hunt asked carefully,

letting it drop as well, that Umbra Mortis face vanishing. "You ready to deal with King Morven?"

Bryce nodded, crossing her arms. "We won't accomplish anything against the Asteri if I can't learn what that portal to nowhere is and how it could possibly kill them. The Autumn King suggested that the Avallen Archives have a trove of information about the blades. And as for Morven . . . I just spent a few days with one asshole Fae King. Morven won't be any worse."

Hunt shifted on his feet, wings tucking in tight. "I'm down with the plan and all, but . . . you really think there's anything in the Avallen Archives that hasn't already been discovered?"

"If there's any place on Midgard that might have clues, it's there. The heart of all things Starborn. And that's where the Autumn King said he read about the portal to nowhere in the first place."

"I'll take whatever edge we can get, but again: King Morven isn't exactly friendly."

Bryce glanced down at her chest, the star-shaped scar barely peeking above the dip of her T-shirt. "He'll welcome us."

"Why are you so sure?"

She reached a hand into the interior pocket of her black athletic jacket. With a flourish, she pulled out her father's notebook. "Because I've got the Autumn King's dirty little secrets."

43

Lidia Cervos stared at her sons. Their mer foster parents were seated on either side of them, watching her with predatory focus. Davit and Renki. She'd never learned their names until now. But judging by the way they sat poised to strike, her boys had been well cared for. Loved.

Director Kagani sat across her desk from them, hands interlaced before her. The silence was palpable. Lidia had no idea how to break it.

Had no idea who she was, sitting here in one of the *Depth Charger*'s dark blue tactical bodysuits. A far comfier uniform than her old one, designed for an aquatic lifestyle. No sign of her silver torque or imperial medals or any of the trappings of that fake life she'd created.

She'd woken again a few hours after collapsing, in a different hospital bed, free of tubes and ports. She hoped the medwitch who'd helped her out of bed assumed her shaking legs were from lingering weakness.

Even if the feeling continued now, as she sat before her sons.

Brann, golden-haired and blue-eyed, wearing a forest-green T-shirt and jeans with holes in the knees, held her stare. Didn't balk from it as Actaeon, dark-haired and golden-eyed, did. But it was to Actaeon, in his black T-shirt and matching jeans, that she spoke, gentling her voice as much as she could. "There is . . . a great deal to tell you. Both of you."

Actaeon glanced to the foster father on his left. Davit. The brown-skinned male in a dark blue officer's uniform nodded encouragingly. Lidia's chest tightened. This had been her choice. One she'd had no option but to accept, yet . . .

She looked to Brann, whose eyes glowed with inner fire. Fearless—reckless. A natural leader. She'd seen that look on his face before, even as a baby.

Brann said, "So, what—we're supposed to live with you now?"

Actaeon whipped his head to his parents in alarm. Lidia suppressed the sting at that expression, but answered, "No." It was all she could manage to say.

Renki, pale-skinned and dark-haired, assured Actaeon, "This doesn't change anything. You guys are staying with us. And besides that, your mom has to take care of some stuff." He was clad in the navy-blue coveralls of a ship medic—he must have run right over from work.

Brann's brows lifted, as if he'd ask what kind of stuff, but Actaeon said quietly, "She's not our mom."

The words landed in her gut like a physical blow.

Davit said a shade sharply, "Yes, she is, Ace."

An oily sort of jealousy wended its way through her at the nickname. Her dark-haired son lifted his head, and—

Pure power glimmered in his eyes. She'd seen that look on his face before, too—long, long ago. The thoughtful, quiet stone to Brann's wildfire.

Lidia couldn't help her smile, despite the hurtful words. She said to Actaeon, to Brann, "You're exactly as you were as infants."

Brann smiled back at her. Actaeon didn't.

Director Kagani interrupted, "We're not going to put labels on anything or anyone right now. Lidia does indeed have . . . work that will keep her from settling down yet, and even once she does, we will all have another discussion about what is best for you two. And your fathers."

Lidia met Renki's gaze. The dominance and protectiveness in it. She still saw the glimmer of pleading beneath it. *Please don't take my sons away from me.*

It was the same sentiment she'd once conveyed to the Ocean Queen. A plea that had fallen on deaf ears.

They were her boys, her babies for whom she had changed the course of her life, but they had been raised by these males. Actaeon and Brann *were* their sons. Not by blood, but through love and care. They had protected them, raised them well.

She could have asked for nothing more—that the boys possessed such an attachment to their parents went beyond any hope she'd harbored.

So Lidia said, even as something in her soul crumbled, "I have no intention of taking you away from your parents." Her heart thundered, and she knew they could all hear it. But she raised her chin anyway. "I don't know when my work will be over, if ever. But if it is, if I am allowed to return here . . . I would like to see you again." She looked to the twins' parents. "All of you."

Renki nodded, gratitude in his eyes. Davit put a hand on Actaeon's shoulder.

Brann said, "You mean the work you do . . . as the Hind?"

Lidia glanced to Director Kagani in alarm. She had made them promise not to tell the boys who and what she was—

"We have TV down here," Brann said, reading her surprise and dismay. "We recognized you today. Had no idea you were our birth mom until now, but we know what you do. Who you work for."

"I work for the Ocean Queen," Lidia said. "For Ophion."

"You serve the Asteri," Actaeon cut in coldly. "You kill rebels for them."

"Ace," Davit warned again.

But Actaeon didn't back down. He looked to his twin and demanded, "You're cool with this? With her? You know what she does to people?"

Fire sparked in Brann's gaze once more. "Yeah, asshole, I do."

"Language," Renki warned.

Actaeon ignored him and pressed Brann, "Her boyfriend's the *Hammer*."

"Pollux is not my boyfriend," Lidia cut in, back stiffening.

"Your fuck buddy, then," Actaeon snapped.

"*Actaeon*," Renki snarled.

Director Kagani said quellingly, "That is enough, Actaeon." The director sighed, facing Lidia. "And perhaps that is enough for all of us for one day."

Actaeon let out a humorless laugh. "I'm just getting started." He pointed to his brother. "You want to play loyal dog, go ahead. You'll fit right in with her dreadwolves."

"You're a dick, you know that?" Brann seethed.

"Boys," Davit said. "That is *enough*." The male winced at Lidia. "I'm really sorry about this. We raised them to behave better."

Lidia nodded, throat closing up. But she said to Actaeon, "I understand. I really do."

She stood, the weight of their stares threatening to send her to her knees. But she said to Davit and Renki, "Thank you for taking care of them. For loving them."

Her eyes stung, and something massive began to implode in her chest, so Lidia said nothing else before walking out of the director's office, shutting the door behind her. She nodded her farewell to the administrative assistant sitting beyond the door, then she was out in the hall, gasping down air, fighting that implosion—

"Lidia," said a male voice behind her, and she turned to find Renki walking after her.

The male's face was pained. "I'm so sorry about how that went down. Davit and I have discussed this possibility for years, and we never planned it to be like that." He ran a hand through his dark hair. "I don't want you to think we, like . . . tried to turn the boys against you."

She shook her head. "The thought never crossed my mind."

Renki shifted on his feet, black work boots squeaking softly on the tiled floor. "We didn't know who you were, either. Until today.

We knew their mom was deep undercover for Ophion, but we didn't know *how* undercover."

"Only Director Kagani and the Ocean Queen knew."

"I'd love to hear the full story, if you're allowed to tell it. Davit would, too."

She swallowed hard. "Perhaps another day."

"Yeah—definitely get some rest." He grimaced, surveying her. "I'm, ah, a medic here. I was on the team that brought you in, actually. I'm glad to see you're back on your feet."

She nodded, unsure what to say.

Renki went on, "Davit captains one of the submersible-pods that runs recon, so he's occasionally away for days or weeks at a time—sometimes it's just me and the boys." He added, "Well, me, and both sets of our parents, who help out a lot. They adore the boys."

Grandparents. Something the boys wouldn't have had otherwise.

"Do you have siblings?" she asked the male.

Renki nodded. "I have two brothers, and Davit has a sister. So there are lots of cousins running around. The boys grew up in a veritable pack of them."

She smiled slightly. "Was it hard for them to live here without being mer?"

"At times," Renki said. "When they were toddlers, they didn't get why they couldn't just jump into the water with the other kids. There were lots of tantrums. Especially from Brann." A soft, loving laugh. "But Actaeon's a bit of a genius. He devised helmets and fins for them to use so they can keep up with the others. Even in the depths."

Pride bloomed in her chest. "Is that why you call him Ace?"

Renki grinned. "Yeah. He's been taking things apart and putting them back together into something smarter and cooler since he was a baby."

"I remember that," she said softly. "He'd always pull apart every toy I gave him . . ." She cut herself off.

But Renki's smile remained. "Still does. It's the one downside to living on this ship. Director Kagani gets the best teachers she can, but we're limited in what kind of higher ed we can offer him."

"And Brann?"

Renki let out a laugh. "Brann is . . . Well, he's a what-you-see-is-what-you-get kind of guy. A natural athlete—fearless. Quick to anger, and quick to laugh. He does okay in school, but right now, he's more interested in hanging out with his buddies. He's the stereo-typical jock. We're both content to let him be who he is."

"They're like the sun and moon, then," she said quietly.

Renki's smile softened. "Yeah. Exactly." He reached into his pocket and pulled out a business card. "This has my contact infor-mation, in case you need anything. If you want to chat with me, or Davit, or have any questions . . ."

Lidia took his card, nodding her gratitude, unable to find words.

Renki said, "Ace might have said some . . . not-nice stuff in there, but don't for one moment think that he hasn't been won-dering about you all this time. The two of them have some foggy memories of you, I think. Director Kagani says they were too young at the time, but I swear they do. They told me once that you had hair like Brann's and eyes like Ace's. Since they never learned who you were until today, I'm going to finally believe them."

"You're very kind for saying that."

Renki held her stare, sorrow and something else in his gaze. "I'll work on Ace for you. But for now, give him time."

She bowed her head. "Thank you."

She didn't trust herself to say more before she turned away, walking down the hall.

Lidia had nearly reached the stairwell, nearly tamped down the tears threatening to rise within her, when hurrying feet scuffed behind her. She slowed her pace, and stopped before the stairwell door, not opening it.

Only when the messenger extended a folded piece of kelp to her did Lidia turn.

The messenger, a young mer male who regarded her with a

mix of curiosity and wariness, announced, "From Her Depthless Majesty," before stepping aside to wait for a response.

Lidia unfolded the broad, flat kelp leaf. She read what was within, then nodded to the messenger. "I'll go right to her."

She didn't let herself look back at the hall, toward her sons behind the office door halfway down it, before walking into the stairwell. But as the door slammed behind her, it echoed through her entire being.

Five minutes later and ten floors down, Lidia found herself before the ruler of the seas. The Ocean Queen stood at a wall of windows overlooking the eternal dark of the deep ocean, her black hair floating around her as if she were indeed underwater.

It had been fifteen years since Lidia had last seen her. Last spoken to her.

As she had then, the Ocean Queen stood no taller than Lidia's chest, but Lidia steeled her spine against the power that filled the room.

She'd spent decades enduring the Asteri's presence. This female's power, however mighty . . . she'd weather it, too. Maybe that was why the Ocean Queen had bothered with her in the first place, all those years ago: Lidia had been able to face her and not tremble.

"I heard you have been reunited with your young," the Ocean Queen said without turning.

Lidia inclined her head anyway. "I thank Ogenas for such a gift."

"I do not recall granting you leave to abandon your post."

Lidia lifted her chin, keeping her breathing steady as the Ocean Queen slowly, slowly pivoted. Her eyes were black as the ocean outside.

The Ocean Queen went on, "I do not recall granting you leave to bring all these fugitives onto one of my city-ships."

Lidia remained silent, well aware that she had not been given leave to speak, either.

The Ocean Queen's eyes flickered. She was pleased by this small show of obedience, at least. "Our work relies upon our secrecy—it relies upon the Asteri considering us too vague a threat to bother investigating. We evade the Omega-boats, we offer sanctuary to the occasional Ophion agent. Nothing more. No attacks, no direct conflict. But you have now given the Asteri cause to start wondering what, exactly, swims in the deep. What *I* am doing down here."

When Lidia didn't reply, the Ocean Queen waved a hand. Permission to speak.

"I had no choice," Lidia said, keeping her eyes on the tiled floor. "We could not risk losing such valuable assets to our cause. But I can assure you that before I left, Rigelus and the others still did not consider you and your people a priority."

"Perhaps not," the Ocean Queen said, growing a few inches taller, ripping away nearly all the air in the room. "But now their most wanted enemies are on this ship. It will be only a matter of days before his mystics find us."

"Then it should be a relief that they shall depart for Avallen tomorrow."

The insolent words were out before Lidia could rein them in. She'd overheard the news from a passing group of officers—who'd all given her a wide berth when they noticed who was walking down the hall toward them. But the Ocean Queen only smiled. A shark's smile.

"And *you*," the ruler said with menacing softness, "shall depart tomorrow, too."

Every word eddied out of Lidia's head. Despite her years of training, of self-restraint, all she could say was, "My sons—"

"You have seen them." The ruler's sharp teeth flashed. "Consider yourself Ogenas-blessed indeed for that. Now you will resume your duties."

The unbearable, soul-shredding departure had nearly broken Lidia fifteen years ago. And now . . .

"You loathe me," the Ocean Queen said, as if delighted.

Lidia shoved every bit of despair, every bit of defiance, down deep. Her feelings didn't matter. Only Actaeon and Brann mattered.

So her tone was bland, empty, when she spoke. As hollow and soulless as it had been all these years with the Asteri, with Pollux. "Tell me what I must do."

Ruhn paced his room, grinding his teeth until they ached. Bryce had gone to the home world of their people. And their father had held her hostage. Granted, she'd engineered it, but . . .

The true weight of it had only sunk in later, once they'd parted.

Maybe he should hit the gym. Work out some of this aggression roaring through his system, overriding any joy from seeing Bryce. To out-sweat the need to find his father and wipe him from the face of Midgard for what he'd tried to do to Bryce. For the fact that Ruhn hadn't been there to stop it, to shield her from him.

He untied his boots, then slung off his long-sleeved shirt, aiming for the small locker at the opposite end of his room, where he'd been provided with clothes and sneakers. A ten-mile run on the treadmill followed by a fuck-ton of weights would help. Maybe he'd get lucky and someone would be in the gym to spot him.

Ruhn yanked out a white T-shirt, carrying it with him as he flung open the door, intending to pull it on as he walked to the gym—

He ran smack into Lidia.

Her scent hit him, addling his senses, and he took a step back, out of it. "Hey," he said, then blurted, "You're up."

She lifted her chin, eyes a bit glassy. "Yes."

Ruhn twisted his shirt in his hands. She was wearing one of the ship's aquatic bodysuits that left nothing to the imagination. He might not have explored her body—on this plane, anyway—but their souls had definitely fucked, and he had no idea where the Hel that put them.

"I, um, was about to go to the gym," he said, and held up the shirt. His palms turned sweaty. "How are you feeling?"

"Stronger." It wasn't an answer, not really. She nodded to a door directly across the hall from his. "I've been moved to that room."

Ruhn stepped further into the corridor, shutting his door behind him. As he did, her smell wrapped around him, dizzying and heady and so fucking enticing that his mouth watered—and then he beheld the ice in her eyes.

He stepped back, brows lifting. "These are appropriate digs for Agent Daybright?"

Lidia looked at him without any humor, any sense that they'd shared their souls. Two passing officers skirted around them. He caught a few of their whispers as they headed for the elevator bay at the end of the hall. *There she is. Holy shit, it's her.*

Lidia ignored them.

The elevator opened down the hall, and Ruhn couldn't help but think of the last time he and Lidia had been in one. When she'd put a bullet through the Hawk's head and killed those dread-wolves. Then, her eyes had been open and pleading. None of that remained.

He couldn't stop himself from asking, "Did you see your sons yet?"

"Yes." She fit a key in her lock.

"How . . . ah . . . how'd it go?"

She didn't face him. "I am a stranger to them." Not one shred of emotion laced the words.

"How are the foster parents?"

The lock clicked. "A nice mer couple."

What happened? Who was the father? How did you wind up here? He wanted to know so many things. How had she ever kept this hidden? Her family—

Fuck, her family. These boys were male heirs to the Enador line. Hypaxia was their aunt.

But Lidia said distantly, turning to face him at last, "Every-thing I did was for them, you know."

His chest ached. "For your kids?"

She studied her hands, the imposing ruby ring on one of her

fingers. "I haven't seen them since they were eighteen months old. Not even a picture."

But she'd known them on sight today. Had known what grade they'd be in, remembered where the school was on this ship, and run directly there.

He lingered at his doorway. For a heartbeat, he allowed himself to look at her face. The impossible perfection of it, the light of her golden eyes, the glint of her hair. The most beautiful female he'd ever seen, and yet it didn't even fucking matter. None of that had ever mattered when it came to her.

He asked, "What happened?"

"What difference does it make?" she asked, wary and sharp. "I thought you didn't wish to hear my *sob story*, as you put it."

Well, he'd earned that. "Look," he said tightly, "you can't expect me to learn who you are, what you are, and be immediately cool with it, okay? I'm still processing all this shit."

"What is there to process? I am who I am, and I've done what I've done. The fact that I have children doesn't erase that."

All right. She was pissed off. "It's almost like you want me to resent you."

"I wanted you to *listen*," she snapped, "but you wouldn't. Yet now that I fit some sort of acceptably sad female backstory, you're willing to hear me out."

"That's bullshit." Fuck, she and Bryce would get along well. The fact that both of them were on this ship . . . Part of him wanted to run and hide.

Lidia went on, "Would you have listened if I had no backstory other than realizing what was right and wanting to fight for it? Of doing whatever it took to make sure that good prevailed against tyranny? Or does my being a mother somehow make my choices more palatable to you?"

"Most dudes run when they find out the female they're into has kids."

Her eyes flickered with cold fire. "That's male strength for you."

"You seemed to like my strength plenty, sweetheart."

She snorted, turning back toward her door. Dismissing him.

His temper coiled. "So what's the *sob story*, Lidia?"

Slowly, she looked back, her face a mask of utter contempt, and said before she shut the door in his face, "You don't deserve to hear it."

44

Ithan was carefully setting down a figurine of Cthona giving birth on all fours—the planet Midgard crowning between her legs—when Jesiba's phone rang. The shrill sound shattered the silence, but Ithan's sunball reflexes kept him from dropping the fragile marble.

"What."

Even Ithan's wolf-keen hearing couldn't make out the person on the other end.

"Fine."

She hung up, gaze instantly shooting to Ithan. He gently nestled the figurine into a crate, packing peanuts rustling. "What is it?" he asked carefully.

"Come with me." She got to her feet and strode across the room with surprising speed considering her dark blue four-inch heels. She hadn't bothered to change her hair back to its usual short length, and the sight of her swaying golden locks was . . . odd. So was the face free of its usual makeup. She might very well have been a few years older than Ithan for all she appeared.

She halted at the doorway and pointed to the wall adjacent to the bookshelf. "Bring that with you. It's loaded."

Ithan glanced over at the weapon mounted there. He'd heard what Bryce had done to Micah with it.

But Ithan didn't hesitate as he crossed the room and grabbed the Godslayer Rifle off the wall.

Jesiba led Ithan through a dark-stoned warren, lit by simmering golden fires. The hallways were strangely quiet, and it occurred to him that he had no idea what time it was. Judging by the quiet, he guessed it was the middle of the night. But in the House of Flame and Shadow, where so many nocturnal predators dwelled, that might not have been accurate.

It didn't matter, really.

The sounds of a gathered crowd rumbled down the stones long before he reached the round chamber.

Pillars had been formed from stalactites and stalagmites that had merged together—he scoured his brain and came up short on what *those* were called—and unlike the cut, polished glory of the other halls, the walls were raw stone. The domed ceiling was rough-hewn, and it echoed the murmuring and chattering of the crowd, too thick to identify individual words.

People quieted as Jesiba strutted through the natural archway into the room, Ithan a step behind her, that notorious gun in his hands. It was lighter than he'd thought it would be, yet he'd never held anything more electric.

The crowd parted to allow Jesiba through. She looked straight ahead as she strode into the center of the room, her dark blue skirt trailing behind her, heels beating a rolling, take-no-shit beat. If anyone was shocked by her new hairdo and lack of makeup, no one dared say anything. Or keep their stare on her for too long.

But Ithan glanced ahead to what—who—stood in the center of the chamber, and his heart stumbled.

The Astronomer lifted a knobbly finger and pointed at Ithan.

"*You're dead, thief,*" the old man snarled.

Tharion knew he'd dodged a bullet. Knew Bryce's arrival had spared him from the Ocean Queen sending him right back to Lunathion.

A bounty on his head. Fuck.

But to be confined to this ship . . . was it any better than being held by the River Queen or the Viper Queen? Confined as a *guest*, the Ocean Queen had claimed. But he knew what she'd meant.

"Avallen has always given me the creeps," Flynn was saying as they all squeezed around a table in their deck's mess hall, discussing the next day's arrival on the misty isle. At this hour of the evening, every table was crammed with people for dinner, their conversations and laughter so loud it made it nearly impossible for Tharion to hear his companions. "But Morven's terrible. I've known him since I was a kid, and he's a fucking snake. Him, and the Murder Twins."

"Murder Twins?" Athalar asked with a mix of alarm and amusement from where he sat beside Bryce, an arm looped around her waist, his fingers idly toying with the ends of her hair. Tharion knew that even if they hadn't been short on space around the table, the mates would have kept close together.

"A nickname we gave my distant cousins," Ruhn said around a mouthful of bread. "After they joined Cormac in trying to kill us multiple times in the Cave of Princes." The prince's eyes flickered with regret as he spoke Cormac's name.

Tharion blocked out the image that flashed—of Cormac's final moments, of running while the Fae male immolated himself. His grip clenched around his fork, so tight his knuckles turned white.

But Ruhn went on, "They can read minds . . . whether you want them to or not." He pointed with his half-eaten chunk of bread to Bryce. "They're not going to ask for permission like that Night Court dude."

Bryce grimaced. "Can anyone defend against their skills?"

"Yeah," Ruhn said, "but you have to be vigilant at all times, even when you can't see them near you. And they obey Morven unconditionally."

Bryce examined her nails. "I love me some good old-fashioned goons."

Tharion smiled, grip loosening on his fork.

But Ruhn shook his head. "They're not your usual goons, and Morven's not your usual sort of asshole. During my Ordeal—"

"I know," Bryce said, scooping up some rice, grown in one of the ship's many hydroponic gardens. "Big, bad uncle. You pissed him off, he sent you into the Cave of Princes to punish you, you showed him up . . ."

"He's Cormac's father," Declan said carefully. "Don't forget that he's just lost a son and heir."

Tharion stared down at his platter of rice and fish, though his appetite had vanished like seafoam on the sand.

"He was quick to disown him," Lidia Cervos said from the far end of the table.

Tharion had nearly keeled over in shock when she'd sat down with them. But . . . where else would she sit in the packed hall?

He didn't fail to note that Ruhn sat at the opposite end of the table.

Lidia added, "But I will echo the warning: King Morven only agrees to things that are advantageous to him. If you're going to convince him not to immediately sell you out to the Asteri, you need to spin it the right way."

"I'd planned to go right to the archives," Bryce said. "No royal visit required."

"The mists," Ruhn said, "tell him everything. He'll know we've arrived. It'll infuriate him if you don't . . . pay tribute."

"So we play nice," Athalar said, draining his glass of water. The other diners kept glancing toward their table—with awe, with dread, with curiosity. All of them pretended not to notice.

"And," Ruhn added, wincing, "females aren't permitted in the archives."

Tharion rolled his eyes. "Please," he muttered.

"Yeah, yeah," Bryce said, waving a dismissive hand. "The Autumn King made *sure* I was aware of their No Girls Allowed rules. But too bad for Morven: I'm going in."

Hunt nudged her with a gray wing. "I'm assuming you have some plan up your sleeve that you're going to spring on us at the worst possible moment."

"I think you mean the coolest possible moment," Bryce said, and Tharion, despite himself, smiled again.

"Note how she didn't answer that," Hunt said darkly to Baxian, who chuckled and said, "Danika was the same."

An undercurrent of longing and sorrow flowed beneath the Helhound's light tone. A male who'd lost his mate. It was, rumor claimed, worse than losing one's soul. Tharion couldn't decide whether he pitied the male for the loss, or envied him for being lucky enough to have found his mate in the first place. He wondered what Baxian would have preferred: to have never known Danika, or this, to have had their centuries together cut so brutally short.

Bryce reached across the table and squeezed the Helhound's hand, love and pain on her face. Tharion turned his gaze from the matching expression Baxian gave her as he squeezed her hand back. A private, intimate moment of grieving.

After a moment of silence for the two of them to mourn the wolf they'd both loved, Flynn said, "Avallen is an old and fucked-up place. We need to be fast so we can get the Hel out of there."

Bryce let go of Baxian's hand and said primly, "Research takes time." The perfect imitation of a schoolmarm. But she dropped the act as she added quickly, "Plus I want to visit the Cave of Princes."

Tharion had heard only legends regarding the famed caves—none of them good.

Ruhn gaped. "And you think you can do this without even saying hello to Morven? Females aren't allowed in there, either."

Bryce crossed her arms, leaning into Athalar's side. "Okay, maybe we'll drop in for tea."

Her brother was having none of it. "The Cave of Princes . . . why? What's that got to do with the portal-to-nowhere stuff?"

Bryce shrugged, going back to her food. "It's where the Starsword has always been held. I think there might be some information there."

"Again . . . not actually answering," Hunt said under his breath to Baxian. Tharion stifled his grin of amusement. Especially as Bryce glared at her mate. Athalar just pressed a kiss to her brow, a casual bit of love that had Baxian glancing away.

Tharion wished he had something to offer the Helhound, some sort of comfort. But the gods knew he wasn't the one to dispense any sort of advice regarding love. Loss, maybe—he'd learned to live with the hole in his chest after Lesia had been murdered—but he doubted Baxian wanted to hear someone try to liken losing a sister to losing one's mate.

"We shouldn't stay on Avallen a moment longer than necessary," Flynn insisted, drawing Tharion's attention once more. "I'm telling you, every time I've been on the island, it's made my magic . . . unhappy." In emphasis, a delicate vine wrapped around his hand, between his fingers. "It literally shrivels up and dies when I'm there." The vine did just that, withering into dust that sprinkled over his half-eaten plate of fish and rice. Flynn took a bite anyway.

"I always forget you actually have magic," Bryce said. "But I'll refrain from making the obvious dig about failing to perform on Avallen."

"Thanks," Flynn muttered, shoveling another forkful of food into his mouth.

"We should split up when we arrive," Declan declared, pushing around his own meal. "Some of us can hit up the archives, and the others can go to the Cave of Princes. We'll all look for any extra intel about the Starsword and its connection to the dagger."

With a glance to the massive window at the rear of the mess hall, overlooking the crushing black ocean beyond, Tharion said, "And I'll be here, praying to Ogenas that you find something useful about how to destroy the Asteri with those blades."

Ogenas—Keeper of Mysteries. If there was a god to beg for knowledge, it'd be her.

"Archives," Ruhn, Flynn, and Declan said, raising their hands.

Bryce glowered at them. "Shitheads. I was counting on some guidance from you, since you've actually been in the Cave of Princes before." She turned to Athalar and Baxian and sighed. "Looks like we get to do some spelunking."

"Just so you know," Ruhn said, "during our Ordeal, it took the three of us a while to get to Pelias's tomb and the Starsword. But that was also because we were being chased and hunted by ghouls and

Cormac and the Murder Twins. So there might be a more direct route—though there are mists that try to confuse you every step of the way."

"Great," Bryce said, but Tharion didn't miss how her eyes had seemed to brighten, as if her brother's words had sparked something.

"And," Ruhn added, "there are carvings throughout the caves— including in the burial chamber. It could take you a while to find anything. Make sure you bring a few days' worth of supplies with you."

"Noted," Athalar said grimly.

"Fantastic," Baxian grumbled beside him.

Tharion's heart strained, his own words from a moment ago sinking in. He *would* be here, on this ship. While they left. Tomorrow they'd part ways. These people Urd had brought into his life, who he didn't deserve . . .

"I'm going with you," Lidia said. "To Avallen." She'd been so silent that Tharion had forgotten she sat at the other end of the table.

Ruhn didn't so much as look at her as she spoke. Tharion noted that the Hind was deliberately not looking at him, either. Only at Bryce.

"Why?" Bryce asked. "You, ah . . . Your kids are on this ship."

Lidia's spine stiffened. "The Ocean Queen has made it very clear that if I do not resume my duties as Agent Daybright, the protection she has given them will . . . cease." They all looked at her in surprise, but Lidia continued, "The Asteri have created a new, worse type of mech-suit—worse than the hybrids from a few weeks ago. This one no longer requires a pilot to operate it, only techs in a distant room. Rigelus has ordered the suits stationed atop Mount Hermon." A glance toward Hunt, whose face was stony at the news. "The Ocean Queen wants me to learn how to stop them, but I fear there's little that I can glean beyond what the news networks have all been reporting. The suits are already built, and ready to be unleashed. We can do nothing."

"Avallen's the opposite direction from the Eternal City," Hunt growled. "We'd be taking you way too far north."

Lidia shook her head. "It is useless to expend my time looking for a way to stop the mech-suits—a solution that in all odds probably doesn't exist. I convinced the Ocean Queen that I'm of better use to her if I accompany you to Avallen and learn whatever you uncover there."

"So," Bryce said, "you've offered to—what, spy on us for the Ocean Queen? And are telling us about it?"

A shallow nod. "You've made her nervous, Bryce Quinlan, and that is not a good thing. But because I have . . . connections to your group, she's seen the advantage in sending me." A glance toward Ruhn at last. The Fae Prince continued to ignore her.

"Do you really think nothing can be done about those new suits?" Bryce asked. "They sound dangerous."

Lidia's face remained solemn. "Destroying them would require assembling a force to march on the Eternal City. A force we do not have. So I will be going with you, for the time being. Until we figure out how we're all going to end this."

Stunned silence filled the room. Tharion's breathing hitched at the thought of what Lidia was implying.

"Well, great," Flynn muttered, earning a sharp look from Lidia. "Are you on Team Archives or Team Caves?"

"That remains to be seen," Lidia said coolly. "As it remains to be seen whether you can convince Morven to even allow you to enter either place. *Especially* if females are not allowed."

"We'll convince him," Bryce said, flashing that disarming smile. Tharion didn't fail to catch the suspicious look Hunt slid her way.

Tharion would worry about it later. His friends were leaving. And he'd remain on this ship, under the control of the Ocean Queen. It didn't matter if Bryce claimed him as her subject—there was no standing up to the ruler of the seas.

It wouldn't have surprised him to glance down and find his chest caving in.

But his friends continued talking, and Tharion tried to savor it—the easy camaraderie, the tones and rhythms of their voices.

Too soon, he'd likely never see them again.

"This ship is just one big version of the Astronomer's ring," Sasa said quietly from where she floated above the glass conference table. "Malana's been sick about it since we got on board." Indeed, there was no sign of the third sprite.

"Is she okay?" Bryce asked.

"She'll be okay when we leave," Rithi said, admiring her reflection in the glass surface of the table. But the sprite suddenly peered up at Bryce's face. "When we're in open air again."

"That's what we came to talk about," Lidia said, glancing between the sisters from where she sat on the other side of the table. "Your next move."

Bryce had been surprised and a little unnerved when Lidia had pulled her aside after dinner and explained her plan. Bryce had an intimate connection to the sprite community, and Lidia needed the triplets sent on an essential task. It would be best if that request came from someone they trusted, the Hind insisted.

The sprites now swapped looks. "We had planned to follow you to Avallen," Sasa said, chin lifting. "Unless you would rather not have three sprites—"

"It would be an honor and a joy to have three sprites with me," Bryce said, hoping her earnest tone proved how much she meant it. How her heart had been aching since Lidia had grabbed her earlier, and the memory of Lehabah's beautiful face had glowed brightly in her mind. "And honestly, where we're going, you guys would be super useful." In the darkness of the Cave of Princes, even with Bryce's starlight, three extra flames would have been *very* helpful. "But . . ." She considered her next words carefully.

Lidia spared her the effort. "Irithys is free."

The sprites gasped, both going vibrant orange. "Free?" Rithi breathed.

"Escaped," Lidia amended. "I helped her get out of the Asteri palace, in exchange for her assistance with rescuing our friends from the dungeons."

"Where is she now?" Sasa demanded, flame warming—paling to a lighter hue.

"That is why we came to talk to you," Bryce said. "We don't know where she is."

"You . . . lost our queen?" Sasa said softly.

"When we parted ways," Lidia added quickly, as Rithi and Sasa were now turning white-hot with anger, "I suggested that Irithys go find a stronghold of your people. She seemed . . . hesitant to do so. I think she might be worried about how she'll be received."

The sprites bristled with anger.

"So," Bryce cut in quickly, "we were wondering if you guys would go find her. Make sure she's, ah . . . safe. And offer her your companionship."

"Our queen doesn't want to see her people?" Rithi's voice was dangerously low, her flame still a simmering white.

"Irithys," Lidia said calmly, "has spent the majority of her existence locked within a crystal ball. As you, perhaps, can understand better than anyone else on Midgard . . . to suddenly be free of captivity, to be alone in the world, is no easy thing. So I"—a glance at Bryce—"*we* are asking you to find her. To offer her companionship and guidance, yes, but also . . ."

"To help us," Bryce finished. "We need you three to advocate for Midgard—help her understand what we're fighting for. And maybe convince her to help against the Asteri again. When the time's right."

The sprites studied them for a long moment.

Sasa said, "You would trust Lowers and slaves with this?"

"We would trust no one else for so important a task," Lidia said.

There weren't many Vanir on Midgard who would say it—and believe it. Bryce felt herself slide dangerously toward liking the Hind.

But Rithi asked, "You can't believe that some fire sprites would make a difference against the Asteri. Our ancestors didn't during the battle with the Fallen . . . and that was against malakim."

"Lehabah made a difference against Micah," Bryce said, throat unbearably tight. "One fire sprite took on an Archangel and handed his ass to him. Her presence bought me the time to kill him. To kill an Archangel."

The sprites' eyes widened. "You *killed* Micah?" Rithi breathed.

Lidia didn't seem surprised—as the Hind, she'd probably heard about the whole thing right after it happened. "With Lehabah's help," Bryce said. "*Because* of Lehabah's help." She swallowed down the ache in her throat. "So yes—I believe that the fire sprites can and will make a difference against the Asteri."

The sisters looked at each other, as if they could mind-speak like Ruhn.

Then Sasa met Bryce's stare. And said without an ounce of fear, "We will find Irithys." The sprites burned to a deep, true blue. "And fight with her against the Asteri when the time comes."

"That went well," Bryce said minutes later as she and Lidia walked down the hall, back toward their sleeping quarters. "I'm glad you had me talk to them."

The Hind said nothing, gaze fixed on the passage ahead.

"You all right?" Bryce dared ask. The Hind had sat with them at dinner, but had been mostly quiet. And definitely hadn't even looked once at Ruhn. Nor had her brother acknowledged Lidia's presence.

"Fine," Lidia said, and Bryce knew it for the lie it was.

They said nothing more for the rest of the way, stopping only when they reached the sleeping quarters. Hunt was waiting for Bryce in their room. But Bryce paused and said before Lidia could walk into her own cabin, "Thank you."

Lidia halted, turning her way. "For what?"

"Saving my mate. My brother. My best friend's mate. You know, three of the most important people in my life." She offered a tentative smile.

Lidia inclined her head, regal and graceful. "It was the least I could do." She turned back to open her door.

"Hey," Bryce said. Lidia paused again. Bryce jerked her chin at Lidia, and the cabin beyond the Hind—where she'd be staying alone. "I know we don't, uh, know each other or anything, but if you need someone to talk to . . . Someone who's *not* Ruhn . . ." She shrugged. "I'm a door away."

Gods, that sounded stupid.

But Lidia's mouth quirked upward, something like surprise in her eyes. "Thank you," she said, and walked into her room, quietly shutting the door behind her.

All day, Hunt had been practically counting down the minutes until he could get Bryce alone in their room, then get her naked. But now that he was lying in the too-narrow bunk with her, lights out and the only sound their breathing . . . he didn't know where to start.

That fucked-up conversation between them earlier didn't help. He'd told her his truth, and she didn't want to hear it. Couldn't accept it.

But it *was* his fault—out of all of them, he should have known better than to lead them down this road again. He didn't get how she couldn't see that.

"Can I be honest about something?" she said into the darkness. She didn't wait for his answer before she said, "Aside from dangling the Autumn King's notes in front of Morven, I don't have a solid game plan for dealing with him. Or a solid backup plan should he not go for the notebooks."

Hunt put aside thoughts of their earlier fight and said, "Oh, I know. You didn't have nearly as much insufferable swagger about this as you usually do when you have a genius secret plan."

She whacked his shoulder. "I mean it. Aside from the Autumn King's notes, my only other bargaining chip with him is my breeding potential. And since you and I are married . . ."

"Are you asking for a divorce?"

She chuckled. "No. I'm saying that I've got no worth to these shitheads. Since my uterus is . . . spoken for."

"Mmm. Sexy." He nipped at her ear. "I missed you." They could get into the nitty-gritty of their argument later. Tomorrow. Never.

He trailed a hand down her hip, her thigh. His cock stirred at the softness of her, the sweet smell of lilac and nutmeg.

"As much as I want to bang your brains out, Athalar," she said, and Hunt laughed into her hair, "can we just . . . hold each other tonight?"

"Always," he said, heart aching. He tucked her in tighter, so fucking grateful for her scent in his nose, the lushness of her body against his. He didn't deserve it. "I love you."

She pressed even closer, arm wrapping around his waist. "I love you, too," she whispered back. "Team Caves, all the way."

He huffed a laugh. "Let's get T-shirts."

"Don't tempt me. If Avallen wasn't a backwater island with no interweb, I would have already ordered them to arrive at Morven's castle."

He grinned, that weight in his chest lifting for a precious moment. "There's really no interweb?"

"Nope. The mists block all. Legend has it that even the Asteri can't pierce them." She made a silly little eerie *woooooo* noise and wriggled her fingers. Then she paused, as if considering, before adding, "Vesperus mentioned things called *thin places*—wreathed in mist. The Prison in the Fae world was one. And it seems too coincidental that the ancient Starborn Fae *also* established a strong-hold in a place wreathed by mist that keeps out enemies."

Hunt's brows rose. "How can the mists possibly keep a wall up against the Asteri?"

"The better question is why would the Asteri leave Avallen alone for so long if it *is* capable of keeping them out."

Hunt pressed a kiss to the top of her head. "I suspect you'll find out the answers in the most dramatic way possible."

She snuggled closer to him, and he held her tighter. "You know me well, Athalar."

Ithan didn't dare point the Godslayer Rifle at the Astronomer. But he remained poised to do so as Jesiba said, "What is this about?"

The crowd—draki, vamps, daemonaki, and many others he couldn't name—was silent as death. They had all come to witness this retribution. Ithan's mouth dried out.

The Astronomer's slate-gray eyes blazed with hatred. "The wolf stole something of mine."

Jesiba shrugged. "The matter of the sprites and the dragon has been settled between us."

"Do not toy with me, Jesiba," the Astronomer snapped. "We both know he took more than those firelings."

Ithan stepped up. His hands grew sweaty against the sleek wood and metal of the rifle. "A tank is no place for a wolf." *Or anyone,* he thought. "And besides, she wasn't yours to begin with. She had no slave mark."

"Her father sold her to me. It was an unofficial passing of ownership."

"She was a child, and you had no right—"

Ithan had killed her. *He* had no right to speak of her like he wasn't as bad as this man before him—

"You are a *thief*, wolf, and I demand payment! I demand her returned to me!"

Words were suddenly impossible. Ithan couldn't speak.

But a lovely, lilting female voice said from behind the crowd, "The Fendyr heir shall never again be yours, Astronomer."

The crowd hissed, and parted to reveal Queen Hypaxia Enador walking into the chamber, robes floating behind her on a phantom wind.

From the corner of his eye, Ithan caught Jesiba's smirk. "Hypaxia," the sorceress said. "Just the necromancer I was looking for."

45

That Jesiba was able to clear the crowd without so much as a word was testament to her grip on this place, this House.

Ithan found himself torn between looking at Hypaxia and the Astronomer—and avoiding both of their gazes.

The Astronomer waited until the crowd had left before saying to the witch-queen, "If you know where the wolf is and withhold that information, then the law says you are—"

"No law applies here," Hypaxia cut in, "as the Fendyr heir was not a legal slave. Just as you said." Gods, Ithan wished he had one fraction of her steadiness, that serene intelligence. Hypaxia went on, "So there was nothing for Ithan Holstrom to steal. He merely allowed a free civitas to make a choice about whether to remain in that wretched tank . . . or to leave."

And then he'd killed her.

Jesiba was giving him a warning look, as if to say, *Do not fucking breathe a word about that*. Ithan returned her a look, as if to say, *Do you think I'm that dumb?*

She glanced pointedly at his *CCU SUNBALL* T-shirt.

He rolled his eyes and turned to the witch-queen facing off against the Astronomer.

"That wolf cost me untold sums of gold. The loss of one mystic—"

"I'll pay it," Ithan said hoarsely. His parents had made some wise investments before their deaths. He had more money than he knew what to do with.

"I require ten million gold marks."

Ithan burst out coughing. He was well off, but—

"Paid," Jesiba said coolly.

Ithan whirled to her, but the sorceress was smiling blandly at the Astronomer. "Add it to my monthly tab."

The Astronomer glared at her, then at Ithan, and finally at Hypaxia, who looked at him with icy disdain. But he only spat on the ground and stalked out, long stringy hair flowing behind him.

In the silence, Jesiba faced Hypaxia and said, "I called you days ago and told you to come *immediately*. Is your broom not working?"

Ithan whirled on Jesiba. "*This* is the necromancer you had in mind?"

Honestly, he didn't know why he hadn't thought of it himself. He'd just worked with her, for fuck's sake, when they'd tried to conjure Connor at the Autumn Equinox. Maybe because it *hadn't* worked and the Under-King had arrived instead, he'd written her off, but—

"Hypaxia's father was the finest necromancer I've ever known," Jesiba said, crossing her arms. "She has his gift. If there's anyone to trust with your task, Holstrom, it's her."

Hypaxia's brows lifted in faint surprise—as if the praise was unusual. But she said to Jesiba, "We should talk in your office."

"Why?"

Hypaxia seemed to debate whether to answer, but finally said, "You want to know what delayed me these days? What I feared this fall has come to pass. Morganthia Dragas and her coven have staged a coup in the name of what they consider the preservation of witchkind's old ways. I am Queen of the Valbaran Witches no longer." She touched her breast, where her usual golden pin of Cthona was broken in two. "To escape their executioners, I have sworn fealty to the House of Flame and Shadow."

* * *

Lidia had let Renki decide on the place for this early-morning meeting. Somewhere neutral, somewhere private, somewhere "chill," as the mer male had described it.

Lidia wished she had some *chill* herself as she sat on the couch in the quiet student rec area—Director Kagani had closed it to everyone else for an hour—and looked at her sons. They sat on the opposite couch, which was stained and sagging, befitting a student lounge.

Davit had been called away for work late last night, so only Renki had come. The male now sat at the beverage counter on the opposite end of the room. Giving them space. An illusion of privacy.

She wished he'd sat with them.

There was a good chance Morven wouldn't let them leave Avallen alive. She'd needed to see her boys before she left, just one more time, but that didn't mean this was comfortable.

Ace leaned back against the cushions, arms crossed, staring at the TV blasting sunball highlights above the foosball table. But Brann surveyed her frankly, gaze bright with his keen intellect and fighting nature. A warrior indeed. He said without preamble, "Why did you want to meet us so early?"

Lidia subtly wiped her sweaty palms on the legs of her tactical bodysuit. She knew both boys marked the motion. "I thought I might make myself available to you, in case you had any questions about me. My past."

She'd faced down horrors without flinching, and yet this—this had her heart thundering.

Brann's mouth twisted to the side as he thought about it. Without taking his eyes off the TV, Actaeon said, "It's because she's leaving."

Too smart for his own good. Lidia looked at him, though Ace wouldn't acknowledge her, and said, "Yes. Today."

Brann glanced between them. "Where?"

Ace answered before she could. "She's not going to tell you. Don't bother asking. She doesn't know what the word *honesty* means."

Lidia clenched her jaw. "I wish I could tell you. But our mission relies on secrecy."

Ace slid his eyes to her then. "And us kids will go blabbing your location to everyone, right?"

Gods help her. "I wish I could tell you," she repeated.

Brann asked, voice thick, "Are you coming back?"

Lidia said frankly, "I hope so."

Actaeon returned to the TV. "You've managed to slither out of every scrape so far. I don't see why this would be any different."

The words hit like a blow to some soft, unguarded part of her.

Brann gave his twin a warning glare. "Come on, Ace." Clearly, they'd had some sort of conversation beforehand. About how they'd behave.

And clearly, Ace hated her.

Fine. She could live with that. He was safe, and loved. For that, she could endure his resentment.

"We're at war," Lidia told them. "And it's about to get uglier. I cannot tell you where I am going, but I can tell you I may not come back. Every time I venture out, especially now that my enemies know the truth about me, there is a good chance I will not return."

Ace snapped, "Are we supposed to feel bad and cry for our mommy?"

It took all her will not to break down. Mustering that coolness she'd perfected over the years, she said, "You claimed I didn't know what honesty was a moment ago. Well, I'm giving it to you. If you interpret this as manipulation, I cannot help that. But I wanted to see you—both of you—before I left today. To say goodbye."

Brann again glanced between them. Then said, "I guess my biggest question is why. Why you left us here."

"I didn't have a choice," she said plainly, keenly aware of Renki across the room. "It was either leave you here, safe and with people who would love you, or risk bringing you into a world that would have offered the opposite. I . . . I've thought about you every single day since."

This was veering into territory she wanted to avoid. She hadn't planned on approaching it during this visit. Maybe ever. And she knew that if she stayed for one more moment, she'd likely say more than was wise, things she wasn't ready to say aloud—things the boys might not be ready to hear.

Instead, with slightly trembling fingers, she pulled her ruby ring from her finger and laid it on the table between them. "I want you to have this." She fought past the tightness in her throat. "It's an heirloom of my father's household. He's not anyone worth remembering, but that ruby . . ." She couldn't bear to see what expression might be on their faces. "It's very valuable. You can sell it to pay for university, housing . . . when you're old enough, I mean. If you ever leave this ship. Not that you should." She was rambling. She swallowed, and at last looked at them. Ace's face was blank, but Brann was staring with wide eyes at the obscenely huge ruby. "Or if you want to keep it," she said quietly, "that's fine, too."

She wished she had something else to leave them, some other piece of her that wasn't connected to the monster who'd sired her, but this was all she possessed.

Task complete, Lidia stood, and Renki glanced her way. She nodded to him.

She faced her sons—fierce and strong and capable, no thanks to her. "I know it won't matter to you," she said, staring at Ace as he again pointedly watched the TV, "but I'm so very proud of how you turned out. Of the males you are, and are still becoming. I look at you both and know that . . . that I made the right choice." She smiled softly at Brann.

Brann's eyes gleamed. "Thanks for that. For giving us our parents." He motioned to Renki. Lidia bowed her head. "Good luck out there," Brann said. "Wherever you're going."

She put a hand on her heart.

Brann jabbed Ace with an elbow. Ace slid his golden eyes back to her and said, "Bye."

Lidia kept her hand on her heart, tapping it once, and turned away.

She left, not knowing where she was going, only that she had to keep moving or else she'd find some place to crumple up and die.

She walked through the gleaming halls of the ship. Walked and walked and walked, and did not let herself look back.

Ithan only waited until the door to Jesiba's office shut before he whirled on Hypaxia.

"What happened?" Ithan demanded.

Jesiba had warned him before setting off through the halls to *keep quiet*, and he'd obeyed, even while they'd stopped in the dark dining hall for the former witch-queen to get some food. Apparently, she hadn't eaten in days—that alone had banked his rising impatience. But now, safely behind the locked doors to Jesiba's office, they'd get answers.

"It's as I said," Hypaxia replied, voice a bit flat as she laid the tray of food on the table. "My mother's former general, Morganthia, had her forces surround my fortress. They gave me their terms: yield the cloudberry crown or die. I offered the crown, but they somehow heard *die*."

"Can they do that?" Ithan demanded. "Just . . . kick you out?"

"Yes," Jesiba said, claiming her leather desk chair. "The witch-dynasties were founded in fairness, in the right to remove an unfit ruler. It was meant to protect the people, but Morganthia has used it to her advantage."

Hypaxia sank into one of the chairs before Jesiba's desk and rubbed her eyes with her thumb and forefinger. It was the most normal-looking gesture Ithan had ever seen the queen make. "Morganthia's first act as queen was to order my execution. Her second was to undo my mother's animation spell for my tutors." She added at Ithan's raised brows, "They are—were—ghosts."

How it was possible, he had no idea, but he still said, "I'm sorry."

She nodded her thanks, voice weighted with grief. "The spell was bound to the crown. And once that crown was hers . . ." She looked up at Jesiba, her face full of pleading.

"You mourn for three people long dead," Jesiba said coolly, and Ithan hated her for it. "Mourn for your people instead, now beholden to an unhinged queen and her coven."

Hypaxia straightened. "You sound as if you think I should have fought her."

"You should have," Jesiba shot back, dark fire flashing in her eyes. A seed of Apollion's power—transformed into something new. "Did you even try to hold on to your crown before conceding?"

"I would have died."

"And retained your honor. Your mother would have been proud."

"A bloodless coup was a better alternative to fighting, to bringing in innocents to die in my name—"

"Once she gets her reign underway, Morganthia will spill far more blood than what might have been shed for you." Jesiba closed her eyes and shook her head with pure disgust.

"I did not come here for your judgment, Jesiba," Hypaxia hissed, wilder than Ithan had ever witnessed her.

"As I am second in command of this House, you now answer to me."

Ithan reined in the shock that reared through him. Jesiba was *second* in command of the House of Flame and Shadow?

And she thought *Hypaxia* was the best necromancer for Ithan? When she had all those others at her disposal?

"And," Jesiba went on to Hypaxia, heedless of Ithan's surprise, "as someone who spent centuries with the witches, I have insights worthy of your attention."

Hypaxia snapped, "You abandoned our people."

"So did you."

Fraught, miserable silence filled the room. Hypaxia took one bite—just one—of her ham-and-cheese sandwich.

Hypaxia didn't know, Ithan realized, what Jesiba was, deep down. She still thought her a witch defector. "Look," he said, "I know you guys have some baggage to sort out, but . . . I do have a pressing matter."

The former witch-queen turned to him, and her eyes softened. She took another bite of her sandwich, and said after she'd swallowed, "Jesiba apprised me of the situation when she called. I must admit, I was surprised by my sister's involvement. But I am sorry for what happened."

He bowed his head, shame washing through him.

Hypaxia went on, finishing off the sandwich in a few more bites, "But necromancy is no easy thing, Ithan."

"I remember," he said.

Her lips thinned. Yeah, she remembered every minute of their little encounter with the Under-King, too. But Hypaxia said, eyes bright with determination, "I will try to help you."

The breath nearly went out of him.

Hypaxia added, "I'll begin tomorrow. Today I have obligations. Oaths to swear."

Oaths to the Under-King, who'd been impressed enough by her skill at the Autumn Equinox that he'd told her he'd welcome her here. Even Morganthia Dragas would hesitate before tangling with the Under-King.

"I don't have much time," Ithan said.

"These oaths cannot wait," Jesiba said. She pointed to the door of her office, an order to Hypaxia. "They must be sworn at the Black Dock before sunup, girl. You had your last meal. Now go."

Hypaxia didn't hesitate. She left, robes flowing behind her, and shut the door.

"Fool," Jesiba said, slumping in her chair. "Innocent, idealistic fool."

Ithan stayed still, wondering if she'd forgotten he was there.

But Jesiba raised her eyes to him. "She's always been that way. Worse than Quinlan. Letting her heart lead her around like a dog on a leash. I blame her mother for keeping her locked away. No wonder Celestina swept her off her feet when—"

Ithan started. "Wait. Hypaxia and Celestina?" Jesiba nodded. Ithan angled his head to one side. "The Hind said that Celestina was the reason the Asteri knew Bryce was headed for the Eternal City. Hypaxia wouldn't—"

"It's over now," Jesiba said shortly. "I have it on good authority that Hypaxia was . . . not pleased when she found out that Celestina had sold out your friends. But even that betrayal didn't open Hypaxia's eyes enough to see Morganthia's move coming."

"She saw it," Ithan said. "She came here this spring, asking Ruhn for protection from Morganthia. I guarded her—"

"*Protection*," Jesiba snapped. "*Guarding*. Not *acting*. She knew Morganthia was a threat and chose to wait for her to attack rather than strike her own blow against her. Rather than find allies, she played medwitch in the city, made love to that Archangel. Rather than gather power, she ran to a Fae Prince and a wolf to shield her." She shook her head again. "Hecuba meant to protect her all these years by keeping her isolated from the corrupt covens. She hobbled her in the process." Jesiba crossed her arms and stared at nothing, fury and disdain tightening her face.

Ithan dared ask, "Why did you defect from the witches?"

"I didn't like the direction they were headed."

"Was this when Hecuba was queen?"

"Long before that. The witches have been in decline for generations. A magical and moral rot." She leaned her head against the back of her chair. "Naïve girl," Jesiba murmured to herself.

"What sort of oaths does Hypaxia need to swear at the Black Dock before sunrise?"

"Old ones."

"That's not—"

"The mysteries of the House of Flame and Shadow are not for you to know."

"Will Hypaxia . . . change?"

"No. Her oaths are nothing like those the Reapers swear. The establishment of allegiance is a legal process, but one that must be honored as the Under-King has decreed."

The Under-King . . . whom Jesiba served as second in command. "I didn't know you were so important here."

"I'm flattered. And before you ask, no, Quinlan isn't aware. People in this House don't talk. But the City Heads know."

"And the Astronomer . . . he knows." She nodded. "What's your deal with him? You said you have a monthly bill." He blew out a breath. "Fuck, I can't pay you all that money—"

"It's a tax write-off for the House," Jesiba said, waving a hand.

"And I'm growing tired of all these questions from you. You're asking things you have no right to know."

"Then stop telling me so much."

She smirked. "You're not as boring as you seem."

"I'm flattered," he echoed.

Jesiba laughed quietly. And then said, "A few centuries after Apollion changed me, he heard whispers that I had . . . powers. Being a lazy wretch, he sent his brother Aidas to investigate. And presumably to kill me if I was indeed a threat."

She spoke the names of the demon princes like they were people she knew well.

"But Aidas found that I posed no threat, and discovered that I still had the library and remained defiant to his brother's demands to reveal its so-called power. In the strange way of things, Aidas and I became friends, of a sort. We still are. I suppose it's because we're so used to each other now. It's been . . . a long time."

"So what did he report to Apollion?"

"That I was to be respected, but left alone."

"And did Apollion listen?"

A half shrug. "He sends Aidas to check in every once in a while."

"What does this have to do with the Astronomer?"

"I've paid the Astronomer for years now to look for a way to undo Apollion's grip on my soul."

Disgust roiled through him. "So you pay him and he does your bidding?"

"I pay him," she said blandly, "but he also stands to benefit from any discovery."

"Why?"

"He wants to find the answer so he might use it to become young himself. He is human—or used to be, before so much foul magic tainted his soul. He fears death more than anything. He stands to gain a great deal should he succeed in his search. I suppose we're two miserable creatures feeding off each other." She cut Ithan a look. "He might seem frail, but he's slippery. He'll be seeking other ways to fuck you over."

He nodded to where he'd replaced the Godslayer Rifle on the wall. "Would you have given me the order to kill him today?"

"No," Jesiba said. "The rifle was just a threat. I still need him."

"I think scientists call it a symbiotic relationship."

"Well, it's one I've been building toward long before he came into existence."

"So you've been using this creep and his hold on innocents—"

"You didn't seem to have any qualms about using him when you went for information about your brother."

The Astronomer must have told her about that visit. Ithan pressed on. "Can you . . . elaborate?" At her flat look, he added, "Please? Why did you even use the Astronomer in the first place?"

"I thought it was the cats who had a problem with curiosity."

"Blame it on the part of me that chose to be a history major in college."

Her lips curled upward, but she sighed at the ceiling and said, "In my own research over the millennia, I learned that dragon fire is one of the few things that can make a Prince of Hel balk."

"You meant to use it against *Apollion*?" Ithan couldn't help but gape at her sheer audacity.

She studied her manicured nails. "I thought it might be a good . . . negotiating tool."

Ithan let out an impressed laugh. "Wow. So what happened?"

"Rumor spread in the city that the Astronomer had possession of a dragon. I sought him out and offered to buy Ariadne on the spot." She crossed her arms again. "The bastard wouldn't sell her, not for anything in the world. But I realized that day that I might have another opportunity on my hands: I could use his mystics to hunt in Hel for answers on how to free me, and have the mystics guarded by Ariadne while they did so."

"But you said you wanted to wait to . . . not be young until the books were safe."

"Yes. But when that time comes, I want the solution in hand."

"Why?"

"So I don't talk myself out of it." He felt, more than saw, the weight of all those years bowing her shoulders. "You're not like most wolves I've known."

"Is that an insult or a compliment?" He honestly couldn't tell.

She uncrossed her arms and drummed her fingers on the desk. "There's a lot you don't know, Ithan Holstrom, about the truth. Too much for me to delve into here and now." Her fingers halted, and her gaze simmered with ancient pain and anger. "But it was the wolf packs who reached Parthos first. Who started the slaughter and burnings. It was the wolf packs, led by Asteri-bred bloodhounds, who hunted down my sisters. I've never forgotten that."

Ithan's stomach churned at the shameful history of his people, but he asked, "Bred?"

A wry smile. "The gift already existed amongst the wolves, but the Asteri encouraged it. Bred it into certain lines. They still do."

"Like Danika."

Jesiba's fingers resumed their drumming. "The Fendyrs have been a . . . carefully cultivated line for the Asteri."

"How so?"

She fixed her blazing eyes on him. This female had lived through all of Midgard's Asteri history. He could hardly wrap his mind around it. "Didn't you ever wonder why the Fendyrs are so dominant? Generation after generation?"

"Genetics."

"Yes, genetics bred by the Asteri. Sabine and Mordoc were ordered to breed."

"But Sabine took the title from her brother—"

"At whose urging? She's an angry, small-minded female. Her brother was smarter, but clearly no male of worth, if he sold his daughter to the Astronomer. He was likely deemed unfit by the Asteri, who coaxed Sabine into challenging him. And when Sabine's dominance won out, they made sure Mordoc was sent to produce a line of more . . . *competent* Fendyrs."

"Well, Micah fucked that up for them."

"And who do you think pulled Micah's strings?"

Ithan was glad he was sitting. "You think the Asteri had Micah kill Danika? After all that trouble to breed her into existence?"

Never mind that Connor and the Pack of Devils had been destroyed as a result of that scheming—

"I think Danika was reckless and willful, and the Asteri knew they could never control her as they could Sabine. I think they realized that with Danika, they'd produced a wolf so powerful she rivaled the ones I faced in the First Wars. *True* wolves. And she was not on their side. She had to be eliminated."

Ithan sagged in his seat, but then a thought struck him. "The Under-King told Hypaxia and me that Connor . . . that the Under-King had been given a command not to touch my brother. Why?"

Jesiba's face was unreadable. "I don't know. In all likelihood, it's because he was an asset in life, and remains so in death."

"To who?"

"The Asteri. They know what Connor means to Quinlan, to you—that makes his soul very, very valuable."

Ithan reeled. "I'm nobody."

Jesiba gave him a disdainful look, but her phone rang before she could answer him. She picked up after one trill.

She listened silently until she said in a clipped tone, "Fine." The sorceress hung up and fixed Ithan with a stare. "You're wanted downstairs at the morgue."

"You guys have a private morgue here?"

She rolled her eyes. "Hypaxia finished her vows in record time—she's waiting down there for you. With Sigrid's corpse."

46

This is as far as the ship can take you," Commander Sendes said as Bryce and Hunt steadied themselves on the wave-tossed top of the *Depth Charger*. A gray sea crashed around them, the damp, howling wind blasting right through Bryce's feeble jacket to bite at her bones.

It wasn't exactly how Bryce had pictured the entrance to the fabled Fae homeland.

Hunt's wings, nearly the same hue as the water, stretched wide, as if testing the air currents. On his other side, Baxian peered out over the water, his black wings braced against the wind.

Not that they had far to fly.

The wall of mist rose from the sea itself, stretching all the way into the clouds. Perhaps it continued above them. It was impossible to see.

As she'd suspected, the mists were nearly identical to those around the Bone Quarter. Impenetrable, ominous . . . Were these truly thin places between worlds? And what the Hel was it about *these* mists that the Asteri couldn't cross?

"You can't cruise under the mist?" Hunt asked Sendes, nodding toward the swirling mass ahead.

Sendes shook her head, the bitter wind ripping strands of her dark hair free from its tight braid. "No. There's no mist under the water, but there is a barrier—invisible, yet solid as stone."

"So they're wards?" Bryce asked, shivering again. The fire sprites, who had been perched on her shoulders when she climbed into the freezing air, had left moments ago, three flames zooming out across the waves toward the distant landmass of Pangera. She'd offered up a prayer to Solas as they quickly vanished over the horizon.

"Not wards in the way we know them," Sendes explained, barely flinching at the frigid wave that slammed into the side of the ship, showering her. Bryce, a few steps away, hissed at the spray, leaping back a step. "They seem . . . naturally occurring, rather than spell-made. Even the Ocean Queen's never given the order to attempt to breach the mists here. It's like Midgard itself made these."

Bryce slid her chilled, wet hands into the pockets of her jacket. It did little to warm them. "Told you the mists are worth looking at."

Last night in bed, she'd wanted to talk to him about their quarrel. But she'd been exhausted, and so grateful to just be lying next to him, that she hadn't said anything.

Hunt peered up at the towering barrier of mist, feathers rippling in the wind. "So how'd the Fae get access in the first place?"

"Those sleazeballs can wriggle their way into anything. The ancient ones were no different," Bryce said.

Sendes grunted in agreement, but her phone pinged, and the commander stepped away to read whatever message had come in.

Baxian stepped up to Hunt's other side, grimacing as another wave roared, showering them all this time. *Fuck* it was cold. "So what's the plan?" the Helhound asked them. He jerked his chin to Hunt. "You and I fly recon along the wall, looking for a way in?"

Hunt nodded grimly and said, "Maybe we'll find a doorbell somewhere."

"Your brother's late," Baxian said to Bryce. "We shouldn't stay here any longer than necessary. There are probably Omega-boats nearby."

"The ship knows how to avoid them," Bryce countered, dodging behind Hunt to avoid another shower of icy water.

"Yeah, but we don't want them tipped off that we're heading into Avallen," Baxian said. He spread his wings, flapping them once, spraying droplets off his black feathers. "I'll head west along the wall," the Helhound said to Hunt. "Meet back here in ten?"

Before Baxian could leap into the skies, the hatch behind them groaned, and Ruhn appeared through it, Flynn and Dec behind him. All three armed, as Bryce, Hunt, and Baxian were, with weapons from the *Depth Charger*'s arsenal. Handguns and knives, mostly—but better than nothing.

"Sorry, sorry," Ruhn said upon seeing Hunt's frown. "Flynn and Dec discovered the waffle station in the mess hall and went crazy."

Flynn patted his stomach. "You mer know how to do breakfast," he said to Sendes, who slid her phone into her pocket and sauntered over.

Bryce might have laughed if Tharion hadn't emerged from the hatch behind them, tight-faced and pale. He met Bryce's stare as he came to her side—bleak and exhausted.

Bryce reached out and cupped the mer's strong jaw. "Hang in there," she murmured.

"Thanks, Legs." Tharion stepped back to the rail's edge, his face becoming unreadable.

She wished she had more to say, more comfort to offer him. After all he'd done to help them these past several months, this was the best she could do? Leave him behind?

Movement in the hatch caught her eye again, and Lidia's golden head emerged. Though Ruhn and his friends continued to debate whether waffles went better with syrup or whipped cream—of all the fucking things to talk about right now—she could have sworn her brother tensed.

Lidia didn't look at Ruhn, though. Didn't say anything, only stared up at the swirling mist. If she was surprised at its ominous presence, her face revealed nothing. She offered no explanation, no apology for her own tardiness.

The Hind glanced back at the open hatch. No doubt thinking about her sons far below.

Baxian was watching her—like she puzzled him. Bryce didn't blame him. The Helhound had worked closely with her as the Hind, and yet here she stood, so different underneath the same exterior he'd always known. Even if he, too, had hidden his true allegiances behind his own mask.

She couldn't begin to imagine how Lidia might feel, though. Bryce walked up to her and said quietly, "I'm sorry you can't stay with them."

Lidia's golden eyes snapped to her face. For a moment, Bryce steadied herself for a biting response. But then Lidia's shoulders slumped slightly, and she said, "Thank you." Her gaze softened, like she remembered Bryce's offer to talk last night, and she said again, quieter this time, "Thank you."

Bryce nodded, and turned to find Ruhn watching them closely. His face instantly became as unreadable as stone. Whatever was between him and Lidia, she wouldn't poke it with a ten-foot pole. A hundred-foot pole.

Bryce instead said to her brother, to Flynn and Dec, "We were about to run some recon, but it occurs to me that you three have actually been here before." She gestured to the mists. "How do we get in?"

A particularly large wave rocked the *Depth Charger*, and Hunt was instantly there, a hand at Bryce's back to steady her.

"Alphahole," she muttered up at him, but let him see the light dancing in her eyes.

Ruhn and his two friends were frowning at each other, though. Her brother said, "Normally, you need an invite from Morven. But I learned during my Ordeal that having the Starsword grants you . . . entry privileges."

Bryce's brows lifted, but she winced as another blast of cold, wet wind slammed into her. She stepped closer into Hunt's warmth, her mate curling a gray wing around her to block the gusts. "How?"

Ruhn jerked his chin to where the sword was sheathed down her back. "Draw it and you'll see." Bryce and Hunt swapped wary glances, and Ruhn sighed. "What, you think this is some sort of prank?"

Bryce said, "I don't know! You're being awfully cryptic!"

Baxian chuckled from Hunt's other side, enjoying the show. Gods, he and Danika had been made for each other.

Despite the pang of loss at the thought, Bryce glared at the Helhound, then drew the sword in one smooth movement. The black blade didn't so much as gleam in the gray light. The dagger at her side seemed to weigh heavier, as if being dragged toward the blade—

"Well, look at that," Tharion drawled, peering up at the wall of mist.

"Doorbell indeed," Hunt murmured.

A triangle of a door—like the one in Silene's caves—had slid open.

The hair on Bryce's arms rose as a white boat, the opposite of those at the Black Dock, sailed out. The arching prow had been carved like a stag's head, twin lanterns hanging from the branches of its mighty horns.

And then the stag itself spoke, eyes glowing, its mouth moving as a deep male voice came from inside it—no doubt broadcast from a king miles away.

"Welcome, Bryce Danaan. I've been expecting you."

Tharion watched his friends climb into the white boat, the angels furling their wings tightly. The boat held steady on the bobbing waves, guided by whatever magic had sent it here in the first place. Flynn kept a wary eye on Lidia as she leapt in after Ruhn, but hesitated before jumping himself. He turned back to Tharion and offered a hand. "See you around, mer."

Tharion studied the male's broad, callused hand, its golden skin flecked with sea spray. Behind Tharion, Sendes had already waved to his friends and was now heading for the hatch.

If he was to make his move, it had to be now. Because if he stayed on this ship another day . . . it wouldn't end well for him.

Which left him with one choice, really.

Sendes paused at the open hatch and beckoned Tharion below. Places to be and all that.

Flynn frowned at the hand he still held extended, at Tharion, standing there—

Tharion moved.

Bracing his hands on the rail, he vaulted over the side, landing in the white boat with a thud that had the others cursing at him.

"Ketos," Athalar demanded, a steadying hand on the side of the boat as it rocked, "what the fuck?"

But Flynn landed behind Tharion a second later, saying, *"Go, go, go,"* to the boat or whatever magic controlled it.

Tharion's blood raced in his veins as the boat began to pull away from the *Depth Charger*, and then Sendes was at the rail, her eyes wide with shock.

"She'll *kill* you," Sendes cried. "Tharion—"

Tharion flashed the commander a grin. "She'll have to breach the mists first."

He barely got the last word out before the prow of the boat entered the famed mists.

Yet he could have sworn a shudder went through the ocean behind them, as if a great leviathan of power was already surging, rising for him—

They crossed into the dense mists. The sense of pure power vanished. Nothing remained except the gray water around the boat and the drifting mists, too thick to see more than a few feet beyond the glow of the stag's eyes.

Tharion faced forward at last and found his friends staring at him in varying degrees of alarm. Lidia Cervos was slowly shaking her head—like she understood the gravity of what he'd done better than any of them.

"Well," he said as casually as he could, sitting down and crossing his legs, "not to invite myself to the party, but I'm coming with you guys as well."

47

"You have no idea how many people I had to convince not to eat her carcass on her way down here," Jesiba drawled as Ithan stared blankly at the shape of the body beneath the white sheet in the morgue.

At the sagging place between neck and head.

Hypaxia, working on something at the counter, called over, "This might take a while."

Ithan peered around the sterile, tiled morgue and managed to say, "Why *do* you guys have a morgue down here?"

Jesiba sat on a medical-looking stool, back straight. "Where else are we supposed to raise dead bodies?"

"I don't know why I asked."

"You did a number on her, you know."

Ithan glared at the sorceress. Jesiba winked at him.

But Hypaxia turned to them, and Ithan got his first good look at her face since coming down here. Exhaustion etched deep lines into it, and her eyes were bleak. Hopeless.

What had swearing her allegiance to this House cost her? Jesiba had claimed the ritual had been unusually fast—was that why she looked so drained? Part of him didn't want to know.

He opened his mouth to tell her she didn't have to do this for him, that she should rest, but . . . he didn't have time. The longer they waited, the less chance they had to be successful at raising the decapitated—

Decapitated—

Nausea churned in his gut.

"Take a seat, Ithan," Hypaxia said gently. Greenish light wreathed her fingers as she approached the table holding a bundle in her hands.

"Is that a sewing kit?" He was going to puke everywhere.

Jesiba snorted. "You'd better hope her head's back on when Hypaxia wakes her."

The former witch-queen pulled a glowing syringe of firstlight from a cabinet and laid it on a tray atop a wheeled cart. "As soon as she wakes, an injection of firstlight will heal the damage. But the head needs to be attached first so that the tendons can regrow and latch on."

"Okay," Ithan said, taking a deep breath against his rising nausea. "Okay." Fuck, he was a monster for having made this necessary.

"Here we go," Hypaxia said.

Jesiba caught Ithan's eye. "Sure you want to resurrect a Fendyr?"

He didn't answer. Couldn't face the answer. So he said nothing.

Hypaxia began chanting.

Hunt had been in Morven Donnall's throne room for all of ten seconds and he already hated it.

After the shining white boat had guided them through the mists, he'd expected some sort of summer paradise to lie beyond. Not a cloudy sky above a land of dense green hills and a gray-stoned castle perched on a cliff above a winding—also gray—river. In the distance, thatched-roof cottages marked farmsteads, and a small city of two- and three-story buildings crusted the hill, up to the castle itself.

No skyscrapers. No highways. No cars. The lamps he could make out were flame, not firstlight.

The boat sailed down the river toward the cliff, entering the castle through a yawning cave at its base. Everyone had stayed silent throughout the journey, assuming the stag on the prow had ears that worked as well as its mouth, and could broadcast every word to the male waiting in the castle for them.

A male now seated before them, on a throne seemingly crafted from a single set of antlers. The beast who'd grown them had to have been colossal, the likes of which didn't exist elsewhere on Midgard. Did stags that big roam around here? The thought was . . . not comforting.

But neither were the shadows that curled like snakes around the king, wild and twining. A coiled crown of them sat atop Morven's dark head, blacker than the Pit.

Bryce and Ruhn stood at the head of their little group, and Hunt swapped a look with Baxian, whose frown told Hunt he was deeply unimpressed by this place.

"Could use a reno, if you ask me," Tharion muttered from Hunt's other side, and Hunt's mouth twitched upward.

The mer had some nerve, cracking jokes when he'd just acted directly against the Ocean Queen's orders. Yeah, Hunt was glad to have Ketos with them, but fuck—what had the mer been thinking, jumping into the boat?

Hunt knew what he'd been thinking, actually. And didn't blame the mer for his choice, but they had enough enemies out there as it was. If this somehow provoked the Ocean Queen to work against them . . .

From the glares the others kept throwing Ketos's way, they weren't happy about this development, either. But right now, they had another ruler to deal with.

"You bring traitors and enemies of the empire to my home," the Fae King intoned. The shadows around him halted their twining—predators readying to attack.

But Bryce pointed to herself, then to Ruhn, the portrait of innocent confusion, and said, "Are you talking to me or him?"

Baxian ducked his head, as if trying not to smile. Hunt felt inclined to do the same, but he didn't dare take his focus off the stone-faced ruler or the shadows at his command.

"This male"—a disdainful look at Ruhn—"has been disowned by his father. You are the only royal standing before me."

"Oof," Bryce said to Ruhn. "So harsh." Ruhn's eyes glittered, but he said nothing. She gestured to the dim, small castle around them. "You know, I'm surprised by all this doom and gloom. Cormac said it'd be nicer."

Morven's dark eyes flashed. The shadow-crown atop his head seemed to darken further. "That name is no longer recognized or acknowledged here."

"Yeah?" Ruhn said, crossing his arms. "Well, it is with us. Cormac gave his life to make this world a better place."

"He was a liar and a traitor—not just to the empire, but to his birthright."

"And we can't have that," Bryce crooned. "All that precious breeding stock—gone."

"I will remind you that royal you might be, but you are still female. And Fae females speak only when spoken to."

Bryce smiled slowly.

"Now you've done it," Hunt grumbled, and decided it was a good time to step up to his mate's side. He said to the king, "Telling her to shut up doesn't end well for anyone. Trust me."

"I will not be addressed by a slave," Morven seethed, nodding toward Hunt's wrist, the mark barely visible past his black sleeve. Then he nodded to Hunt's haloed brow. "Least of all a Fallen angel, disgraced by the world."

"Oh boy," Bryce said, sighing at the ceiling. She whirled to their group. "Okay, let's do a head count. If you're disowned, disgraced, or both, raise your hand."

Tharion, Baxian, Lidia, Hunt, and Ruhn raised their hands. Bryce surveyed Flynn and Dec, both still in their usual black jeans and T-shirts, and sighed again. She gestured expansively, giving them the floor.

Flynn smirked, sauntering to Bryce's side. "Far as I know, I'm still my father's heir. Good to see you again, Morven."

Hunt could have sworn Morven's shadows hissed. "It would be in your best interests, Tristan Flynn, to speak to me with the utmost respect."

"Oh?" Flynn crossed his arms, brimming with entitled arrogance.

Morven motioned to someone behind them, the delicate silver embroidery along the wrists and collar of his immaculately cut black jacket gleaming in the firelight, and Hunt whirled as two hulking guards prowled from the shadows. He hadn't sensed them, hadn't heard them—

From Tharion's and Baxian's shocked faces, he knew they were equally surprised.

But Ruhn, Flynn, and Declan glowered. Like they recognized the approaching males, both towering and armed to the teeth. They were clearly twins.

The Murder Twins Ruhn had mentioned, capable of prying into minds as they saw fit.

But that wasn't Hunt's top concern—not yet.

Because between them, in black leggings and a white sweater, light brown hair down around her face . . . Hunt had no idea who the Fae female was. She was fuming, though, outright seething at the guards, the king, and—

"What the fuck?" Flynn exploded.

"Sathia?" Declan said, gaping.

"It seems," Morven drawled as the Murder Twins dragged the Fae female forward, their grips white-knuckled on her arms, hard enough to bruise, "that your sister has landed in a heap of trouble, Tristan Flynn."

48

Bryce didn't know who to focus on: Sathia Flynn bristling with fury in Morven's throne room, or Tristan's shocked face as he processed the scene before them. Bryce opted for the latter, especially as Flynn snapped at the King of Avallen, "What do you mean, *trouble?*"

Morven drawled, "Many of the Valbaran Fae sense . . . unrest on the horizon, and have been seeking shelter within my lands." Those serpentine shadows writhed around his neck, over his shoulders, with unnerving menace. The king's shadows, the Murder Twins' . . . they felt different from Ruhn's: wilder, meaner. Ruhn's shadows were gentle, stealthy night; theirs were the dark of lightless caves.

"If you pitched this place as a luxury vacation, you're about to get a bunch of one-star reviews," Bryce muttered, earning a chuckle from Tharion. She didn't smile at the mer, though. He'd added another nearly all-powerful ruler to their list of enemies—she didn't want to talk to him right now. From the way Tharion's chuckle quickly died off, he knew she wasn't happy.

So Bryce watched as Flynn, dead serious perhaps for the first time in his life, said to the Stag King, voice dripping with disdain, "Let me guess, my parents came running right over." He glanced around the throne room. "Where's my oh-so-brave father? And everyone else, for that matter?"

Morven's face might as well have been carved from stone. "A select few have been allowed in. Most have been sent back to Lunathion. But for those who remain here, there is a price to be paid, of course."

Flynn slowly turned toward his sister. "What did you promise him?" Pure rage and a hint of fear laced his question. But Flynn didn't go for the female or the twins holding her.

Bryce sized them up, and found both males already smiling at her. And then, deep in her mind, twin dark shadows snarled, readying to strike—

She incinerated them with a mental wall of starlight.

The twins hissed, one of them blinking as if that light had physically blinded him. Bryce bared her teeth, and kept that shining wall in her mind. A second later, there was a polite tap against it and Ruhn said, *Keep this up. No matter what.*

Tell Hunt and the others to put up a wall as well, Bryce replied, glaring daggers at the twins.

Already did, Ruhn replied. *You should see the lightning around Athalar's mind. He burned their probes into crisps.*

Yuck. Don't say probes.

Ruhn snorted, and his presence faded from her mind just as Morven continued, "Sathia has promised me nothing. In fact, she has refused to pay my asking price. A generous one, at that: her choice between the males who stand beside her. And as a female has no worth here beyond the offspring she might bear Avallen, I don't see a reason why your sister should remain in this haven another moment."

Morven's words sank in. "I'm sorry," Bryce said, glancing between Sathia's outraged, pretty face and the Stag King and his feral shadows, "but to clarify: Are you saying you're requiring any females who seek refuge here to *marry*?"

"It would be unsafe for so many unwed females to be running about without a male relative or husband," Morven said, picking at an invisible fleck of dirt on his night-black pants.

"Yeah," Bryce said, "the gods know what would happen if all us females were unsupervised. Absolute anarchy. Cities would crumble."

But Flynn said to Morven, "So bring their brothers and husbands over."

Bryce glared at him, but Morven declared, "I have no need for more males in this land."

Bryce ground her teeth hard enough to hurt. This was the male who'd agreed with her father that Bryce and Cormac should marry, injecting more power and dignity into the Fae royal line.

Flynn said, "And my parents?"

Morven sniffed. "I have allowed Lord and Lady Hawthorne to remain here, as our ties date back to the First Wars. They are currently residing at my private hunting lodge up north."

"So send Sathia to my dad," Flynn snapped.

"He won't," Sathia said at last. Though her Fae voice was soft and cultured, Bryce didn't miss the backbone of steel running through it. "It's either marry here, or go back to Lunathion."

"So go back," Flynn ordered his sister.

Sathia slowly shook her head. "It's not safe."

"You've got your cushy villa," Ruhn said with unusual harshness. "You'll be fine."

Sathia shook her head again, gaze fixing on her brother. "It's not safe because of *you*."

"What?" Flynn blurted.

"Word has spread," Morven said from his antler-and-shadow throne, "of your assistance in that one's"—a nod toward Ruhn—"escape. Along with the escape of two other enemies of the empire." A flick of his cold eyes to Baxian and Hunt, who glared back with impressive menace. "The entire Hawthorne family is now wanted by the Asteri for questioning."

"They want to kill us to punish you," Sathia burst out, pointing a damning finger at Flynn. "We had to leave in the middle of the night, when we got an alert that the 33rd was coming to bring us in. These clothes are the only ones I have with me."

"What a sacrifice for you," Flynn sneered. But Bryce caught the guilt darkening his eyes. Declan had already pulled out his phone, no doubt to check on his family and Marc—

"There's no reception here, thanks to the mists," Sathia said to Declan.

The male's face paled, and he muttered, "I forgot."

But Sathia added quietly, "I put in a call to your parents before we left. They said they'd get in touch with your boyfriend, too."

Flynn gaped at her, but Declan bowed his head in thanks.

"What?" Sathia glared at her brother. "You think I'm that much of a monster?"

Flynn gave her another sneer that said, *Yes*, and Bryce stepped in to spare everyone from their bickering. "Okay," she said to Morven, "so you're insisting that Flynn's sister marry one of . . . these creeps?" Bryce gestured to the Murder Twins holding Sathia, making sure that mental wall of starlight was still intact. She wasn't letting their minds anywhere near hers.

"Seamus and Duncan are lords of the Fae," Morven snapped at Bryce. "You will address them with a female's proper tone of deference."

For fuck's sake. "You didn't answer my question," Bryce said. Sathia's expression had become downright panicked. "You're really forcing her into marriage or deporting her to be killed by the Asteri?"

Morven twirled a shadow around one of his long, broad fingers. "Her father has agreed it is in her best interest to wed. And has agreed that should she refuse, she shall be sent back to Lunathion." He clenched his fist, crushing the shadow within. "For too long, she has refused any males he has presented to her for marriage. Her father's patience has come to an end, and he has begged me to oversee this matter."

"Dad of the year," Baxian growled.

Bryce grunted her agreement.

Sathia said with impressive coldness, "It is within my rights to refuse any suitor presented to me."

Morven gave her a look dripping with distaste. "It is, girl. Just as it is within your father's rights to disown you for failing in your duty to continue the family bloodline."

Bryce grumbled, "So what's the point of giving females refusal rights at all if you punish them for it?"

"This isn't our problem," Flynn grumbled, and even Ruhn whirled to him in shock. "We didn't come here to deal with this."

"So you're not here to beg asylum as well?" Morven asked, propping his chin on a fist.

"No," Hunt growled, stepping forward, wings flaring. "We're not." He glanced to Bryce, motioning her forward again.

Swapping a look with Ruhn that said they'd deal with the issue of Sathia later, Bryce set aside her concern and lifted her chin as she stepped to Hunt's side. "I'm here to access the Avallen Archives and the Cave of Princes."

"Access denied," Morven said.

"You mistake me," Bryce said in that voice that brooked no argument. "I wasn't asking your permission." The star on her chest began to glow, illuminating her T-shirt and athletic jacket. "As a Starborn Princess, no part of Avallen is denied to me."

"I shall decide who is worthy of accessing my realm," Morven snarled.

"The starlight says otherwise," Bryce said. She drew the Starsword—and the dagger. "And so do these."

As if their sheaths had kept their power contained, the naked metal now throbbed against her palm, up her arms, tugging toward each other so violently it took all her strength to keep them apart.

Morven paled. Even his shadows receded. "What is that in your left hand?" Even the Murder Twins and Sathia had their eyes trained on her, as if they couldn't look away.

"Some major prophecy fulfillment," Bryce said, hoping to Hel she was hiding the tremble in her arms from keeping the black blades steady, from ignoring that instinct murmuring to her to bring them together, not keep them apart.

"Where did you get that knife?" Morven hissed.

"So you know what it is, then?" Bryce said.

"Yes," he seethed. "I can feel its power."

"Well, that makes it easier," Bryce said. She sheathed both weapons. Mercifully, the pulling eased with the action. "Less explaining for me." She nodded to Morven, and he glowered. "I'll be in and out of here before you know it."

His shadows returned, darkening the air behind his antler-throne until it seemed Morven sat before a void. "Females are forbidden in both the Avallen Archives and the Cave of Princes."

"I don't really care," Bryce said.

"You spit on our sacred traditions."

"Get over it."

Morven's nostrils flared. "I'll remind you, girl, that one word from me and the Asteri will have you in their grasp."

"You'd have to open the mists to them first," Bryce countered. "And it seems like you've worked *really* hard not to do that—or give them a reason to come here at all."

"You can be removed by guards."

Bryce gestured to Hunt, then Baxian, then the others. "My own guards might make that difficult."

"This is *my* kingdom—"

"I'm not challenging that. I just want to look through your archives. A few days, then we'll all be out of your hair." She pulled the Autumn King's notebook from her jacket. "I'll even sweeten the deal: Here's my sire's private journal. Well, his most current one. All his recent scheming, written down. It's pretty stupid, if you ask me. *Dear Diary, today I made a list of all my enemies and how I plan to kill them. It's so hard being king—I wish I had a friend!*"

She grinned as Morven's eyes narrowed on the leather-bound notebook, and she flashed him the first page, where her father's distinctive handwriting was visible. He'd know it well, as the two old losers communicated mostly through written letters, since Avallen had no computers. "You let us stay here and it's yours when we leave."

Morven's fingers drummed on the arm of his throne. Fish on a line.

But he said, shadows lightening at last, "Your presence here threatens to bring the Asteri's wrath upon me."

Bryce considered, blinking. "Well, it seems you've got no problem harboring fugitives, if you're letting in Flynn's parents."

He glared, pure darkness in his eyes.

Bryce went on, "I mean, you could probably make up for Cormac's *dishonor* by selling us out to the Asteri . . . but if you hand us over, you'd have to turn in Flynn's parents and the other nobles, too. And I doubt it'd win you any points with your own people if you betrayed some fancy-ass nobles." She crossed her arms. "You're in a real pickle, huh?"

Morven tapped his booted foot on the ground.

"It's super hard," Bryce commiserated, "to try to play both sides, isn't it?"

"I am not playing either side," Morven said. "I am loyal to the Asteri."

"Then open the mists—invite them here. Let's have them over for brunch."

Morven's silence was damning.

Bryce smiled. "I thought so." She nodded to Sathia. "One more thing: she doesn't marry anyone, and she comes with us."

Sathia gaped at Bryce. But Bryce threw the Fae female a warning look. Bryce had only seen Sathia Flynn from a distance at parties. Usually, the female's hair was dyed varying shades of shining dark brown or blond. Now her locks were an ordinary light brown—her natural color, perhaps. It was like seeing a glimpse of the real female beneath.

"I cannot allow that," Morven said. "She is an unwed female."

"Her brother is here," Bryce said, nodding to Flynn. "Irresponsible party boy that he is, at least he has the parts that matter to you."

Flynn glared, but Dec elbowed him hard enough that he stepped up and said, "I'll, uh, take responsibility for Sathia."

Sathia bristled like an angry cat, but kept her mouth shut.

"No," Morven said, a shadow wrapping itself around his wrist like a bracelet. An idle, bored bit of magic. "You are an unsuitable chaperone, as you have demonstrated time and again."

Hunt gave Bryce a look, and she knew what he was thinking. It was the same thing Ruhn said into her mind a heartbeat later:

As much as it kills me to say this . . . we might have to let this go. Sathia is Flynn's sister and all, but it's not our battle to fight.

Bryce subtly shook her head. *You really want to leave her to Morven's mercy?*

Trust me, Bryce, Sathia can handle herself.

But Bryce glanced back at Lidia, who'd been watching all this with a cold, clear focus. Staying completely silent in that way of hers that made others forget her presence. Even Morven, it seemed, hadn't noticed who stood in his throne room—because he now let out a low grunt of surprise at the sight of her.

Yet the Hind met Bryce's gaze. *What would you do?* Bryce tried to convey.

Lidia seemed to grasp the general direction of her thoughts, because she said quietly, "I never had anyone to fight for me."

Well, that did it.

Bryce opened her mouth, rallying power to her star, but Tharion spoke from behind them.

"I'll marry Sathia."

It took Hypaxia seven hours, seven minutes, and seven seconds to raise Sigrid.

Ithan barely moved from his stool the entire time Hypaxia stood over the corpse and chanted. Jesiba left, came back with her laptop, and worked for some of the time. She even offered Ithan some food, which he refused.

He had no appetite. If this didn't work . . .

Hypaxia's now-hoarse chanting stopped suddenly. "I—"

Ithan hadn't been able to watch as she'd sewed Sigrid's head back on. Only when she'd covered the body again had he returned his gaze to the spectacle.

Hypaxia staggered back from the examination table. From the shape under the sheet. Ithan was instantly up, catching her smoothly.

"What have you done?" Jesiba demanded, laptop shutting with a click.

Ithan set Hypaxia on her feet, and the former witch-queen

looked between them, helpless and—terrified. Out of the corner of his eye, something white shifted.

Ithan turned as the body on the table sat up. As the sheet rippled away, revealing Sigrid's grayish face, her eyes closed. The thick, unforgiving stitches in an uneven line along her neck. She still wore her clothes, stiff with old blood.

Stitches popping, Sigrid slowly turned her head.

But her chest . . . it didn't rise and fall. She wasn't breathing.

The lost Fendyr heir opened her eyes. They burned an acid green.

"Reaper," Jesiba breathed.

49

I'm telling you, Ketos, she is the *worst*," Flynn growled at Tharion in the shadows of the pillars flanking one side of the throne room. Normal shadows, thankfully. Not the awful ones the Fae King commanded. "This is a terrible idea. It will ruin your life."

"My life is already ruined," Tharion said, voice as hollow as he felt. "If we live through this, we can get a divorce."

"The Fae don't divorce." Flynn gripped his arm hard. "It's literally marriage until death."

"Well, I'm not Fae—"

"She is. If you divorce her, she won't have any chance of ever marrying again. She'll be sullied goods. After the first marriage, the only ways out are death or widowhood. A widow can remarry, but a divorcée . . . it's not even a thing. She'd be persona non grata."

On the opposite side of the room, Declan and Ruhn were talking to Sathia in hushed tones. Likely having the same conversation.

Morven glowered away on his throne, shadows like a hissing nest of asps around him, the monstrous twins now flanking him on either side. Tharion had detected the oily shadows creeping toward his mind the moment the twins had arrived. He'd instinctively thrown up a roaring river of water, creating a mental moat around himself. He had no idea what he was doing, but it had worked. The shadows had drowned.

It only made this decision easier. To have anyone forced to endure the Murder Twins' presence, to *marry* someone who could pry into minds—

Tharion now said to Flynn, "Your sister would be a pariah amongst the Fae only. Normal people won't have a problem with divorce."

Flynn didn't back down one inch, his teeth flashing. "She is the daughter of *Lord Hawthorne*. She's always going to want to marry within the Fae."

"She accepted my offer." With the quietest and blandest *yes* he'd ever heard, but still. A clear acceptance.

Flynn snapped, "Because she's desperate and scared—you think that's a good state of mind to make an informed decision?"

Tharion held the male's stare. "I don't see anyone else stepping forward to help her."

Flynn growled. "Look, she's spoiled and petty and mean as a snake, but she's my little sister."

"So find some alternative that doesn't involve her death to get her out of this."

Flynn glared, and Tharion glared right back.

Across the way, Sathia shoved past Dec and Ruhn and stormed toward them. She was short—but stood with a presence that commanded the room. Her dark eyes were pure fire as they met Tharion's. "Are we doing this?"

Gone was that quiet, bland tone.

Bryce, Athalar, and Baxian were watching from the rear of the room, the Hind a few steps to the side.

None of them had expected the day to go this way. Starting with Tharion bailing on the Ocean Queen, and culminating in this shitshow. But if it had been Lesia in Sathia's stead . . . he would have wanted someone to step up to help her, faithless soldier or no.

So Tharion said to Sathia, "Yeah. Let's do it."

Morven wasted no time in summoning a Priestess of Cthona. Like the bastard was trying to call Tharion's bluff.

Not five minutes later, Tharion found himself with a wife.

"You," Sigrid growled at Ithan, her rasping voice barely more than a whisper.

Ithan could hardly process what he was hearing—seeing.

"What happened?" Jesiba shouted at Hypaxia, who was still clinging to Ithan—who, in turn, was backing them toward the door.

But it was Sigrid who answered, more stitches popping as her neck moved, revealing a brutal scar now etched there. "We came to a doorway. *She* wanted to go one way . . ." A smile twisted her face. "I went the other."

Hypaxia shook her head, frantic. "She wouldn't come, she slipped through my fingers—"

"I had no interest in letting such a prize go," intoned a cold voice.

Even Jesiba got to her feet as the Under-King appeared in the morgue doorway.

As he had on the night of the Autumnal Equinox, he wore dark, fraying robes that floated on a phantom breeze.

"You had no right," Hypaxia challenged, pushing past Ithan as his every sense went into overdrive at the Under-King's unearthly presence, his ageless might. "No right to turn her—"

"Am I not lord of the dead?" He remained in the doorway, hovering as if standing on air. "She had no Sailing. Her soul was there for the claiming. You offered her one option, witch. I gave her another."

He beckoned to Sigrid, who moved off the table as if she were alive. As if she had never been dead. Were it not for the acid-green eyes, the scars, Ithan might have believed it.

A Fendyr was a *Reaper.* A half-life, a walking corpse—

It was sacrilege. A disgrace.

And it was all his fault.

"Which is the more attractive choice?" the Under-King mused

as Sigrid took his hand. "To have been raised by you, Hypaxia, to be under your command and thrall . . . or to be free?"

"To be your servant," Hypaxia corrected with impressive steel.

"Better mine than yours," the Under-King countered. He then inclined his head to Ithan. "Young Holstrom. You have my gratitude. Her soul might have drifted forever. She's in capable hands now."

"What—what are you going to do?" Ithan dared ask.

The Under-King peered down at Sigrid and smiled, revealing too-large, brown teeth. "Come, my pet. You have much to learn."

But Sigrid turned to Ithan, and he'd never known such self-loathing as he did when she said in that rasping Reaper's voice, "You killed me."

"I'm sorry." The words didn't even cover it. Would never cover it.

"I won't forget this."

Neither would he. As long as he lived. He held her stare, hating those acid-green eyes, the deadness in them—

"We will speak soon," the Under-King said to Jesiba, more warning than invitation. Before Jesiba could reply, the Under-King and Sigrid vanished on a dark wind.

Only when its scraps of shadow had faded from the morgue did Jesiba say, "What a disaster."

Hypaxia was staring at her hands, as if trying to walk herself through her mistake.

Ithan couldn't stop the shaking that overtook him from head to toe, right down to his very bones. "Fix this."

Hypaxia didn't look up.

Ithan growled, his heart racing swiftly, "*Fix* this."

Jesiba clicked her tongue. "What's done is done, pup."

"I don't accept that." Ithan bared his teeth at her, then pointed at Hypaxia. "Undo what you just did."

Slowly, Hypaxia lifted her eyes to his. Bleak, pleading, tired. "Ithan—"

"FIX IT!" Ithan roared, the witch's necromantic instruments rattling in the wake of the sound. He didn't care. Nothing fucking mattered but this. *"FIX HER!"* He whirled on Jesiba. "Did you know this would happen?" His voice broke.

Jesiba gave him a flat look. "No. And if you take that tone with me again—"

"There might be a way," Hypaxia said quietly.

Even Jesiba blinked, turning with Ithan to survey the former witch-queen. "Once the dead have crossed that threshold into Reaperdom—"

Hypaxia's gaze met Ithan's and held, the pain bleeding away to pure determination. "Necromancy can lead her to that threshold; it can haul her back again, too."

"How?" Jesiba asked. Ithan could barely breathe.

"We need a thunderbird."

Jesiba threw up her hands. "There are none left."

"Sofie Renast was a thunderbird," Ithan said, more to himself than to the others. "We thought her brother might be one, too, but—"

"Sofie Renast is dead," Jesiba said.

Hypaxia only asked, "Where's her body?" The question rang like a death knell through the morgue.

Jesiba got it before Ithan did. "After that debacle," she said, pointing to the examination table where Sigrid had laid moments before, the sheet now discarded on the floor beside it, "you really want to try raising the dead again?"

"Sofie's been dead for too long to raise," Ithan said, nausea churning in his gut. And, he didn't add, he couldn't help but agree with Roga about Hypaxia's track record.

"If she hasn't been given a Sailing, then it should work—though the decayed state of her body will be . . . gruesome." Hypaxia paced the room. "She should still have enough lightning lingering in her veins to bridge the gap between life and death. The thunderbirds were once able to aid necromancers, to use their lightning to hold the souls of the dead. They could even imbue their power into ordinary objects, like weapons, and give them magical properties—"

"And you think it can somehow undo Sigrid becoming a Reaper?" Ithan said.

"I think the lightning might be able to pull her soul back toward life," Hypaxia said. "And give her the chance to make the choice again. A few days as a Reaper might change her mind."

Silence fell. Ithan looked to Jesiba, but the sorceress was silent, as if weighing Hypaxia's every word.

Ithan swallowed hard. "Will it work?"

Jesiba didn't take her eyes from Hypaxia as she said quietly, "It might."

"But where's her body?" Ithan pushed. "The last I heard from my friends, the Ocean Queen had it on her ship. She could have sent it out the air lock for all we know—"

"Give me thirty minutes," Jesiba said, and didn't wait for a reply before stalking out of the room.

There was nothing to do but wait. Ithan didn't feel like doing anything except sitting at the desk and looking at his hands.

His inept, bloodstained hands.

He'd tried to save Sigrid from the Astronomer, and had only succeeded in killing her. And then turning her corpse into a Reaper. Every choice he'd made had led them from bad to worse to catastrophic.

Jesiba breezed through the metal doors of the morgue exactly thirty minutes later. "Well, it took more bribes than I'd have liked, but I have good news and bad news," she declared.

"Good first," Ithan said, looking up from his hands at last. Hypaxia had sat in the other desk chair the entire time, silent and thoughtful.

"I know where Sofie's body is," Jesiba said.

"And the bad news?" Hypaxia asked quietly.

Jesiba glanced between them, gray eyes blazing. "It's on Avallen. With the Stag King."

50

Ruhn had no idea how Bryce managed to not kill Morven. He honestly had no idea how he didn't, either.

But they wasted no time getting to work. Though Bryce was apparently on Team Caves, she insisted on checking out the archives first.

The Avallen Archives were as imposing and massive as Ruhn remembered from his last and only visit to Avallen. Granted, he'd never been allowed inside, but from its looming gray exterior, the building rivaled the *Depth Charger* in sheer size. A city of learning, locked behind the lead doors.

Only for the royal bloodlines—the royal males—to access.

"We really have to *work*?" Flynn groused, rubbing his head. "Can't we relax for a bit? This place gives me the creeps—I need to decompress."

Athalar gave Flynn a look. "It gives all of us the creeps."

"No," Flynn said gravely, shaking his head. "I told you—my magic *hates* this place."

"What do you mean?" Bryce asked, peering at him over a shoulder.

Flynn shrugged. "The earth feels . . . rotted. Like there's nothing for my magic to grab on to, or identify with. It's weird. It bothered me the first time we were here, too."

"He whined about it the entire time," Declan agreed, earning an elbow in the ribs from Flynn.

But Flynn jerked his chin at Sathia, standing by herself a few feet away. "You sense it, too, right?"

His sister twisted her rosebud mouth to the side, then admitted, "My magic is also uneasy on Avallen. My brother's claims are not totally without merit."

"Well," Bryce said, "buck up, Flynn. I think a big, tough Fae male like you can power through. We'll *decompress* tonight. Tomorrow we split into Team Archives and Team Caves and work as fast as we can."

She lifted a hand to one of the lead doors, but didn't touch it yet. "Trust me, though, I don't want to stay on this miserable island for a moment more than necessary."

"Agreed," Athalar muttered, stepping up beside Bryce. "Let's find what we need and get the fuck out."

"What are we looking for, exactly?" Sathia asked. "Everything you told me about the other Fae world and all you've learned . . . I'm sorry, but I need a bit more direction to go on when we get in there."

Since we're all known enemies of the Asteri, what's another person who knows our shit? Bryce had asked when Flynn had demanded that Sathia stay behind.

And Sathia had refused to be left alone, even with the safety of her married status now granting her the right to move freely. *I'm not going to be locked up in some room to rot,* she'd said, and stomped after Bryce, who had begun explaining everything she'd learned about Theia and her daughters and the Fae history in and outside of Midgard. She hadn't spoken a word to Tharion since they'd exchanged their vows—and the mer had seemed just fine about that, too.

It was all fucking nuts. But Ruhn had heard what Lidia had said to Bryce—about never having had anyone to fight for her. It hadn't sat well.

Ruhn dared a look over at where Lidia stood, peering up at the towering entrance to the archives. He hadn't failed to note

Morven's shock upon realizing she stood in his throne room. And as they'd departed, the Stag King had seemed poised to speak to Lidia, but the Hind had breezed past him before he could.

Her golden eyes slid to Ruhn's, and he could have sworn pure fire pulsed through him—

He quickly looked away.

Sathia asked Bryce, "What if you don't find the answers you seek?"

"Then we're fucked," Bryce said plainly, and finally laid her palm flat against the doors to the archives. A shudder seemed to go through the metal.

On a groan, the doors swung inward, revealing nothing but sunlight-dappled gloom beyond. Ruhn swapped glances with Dec, whose brows were high at the display of submission from the building. But Bryce breezed through, Athalar and Baxian on her heels.

"So you really intend to go into the Cave of Princes?" Sathia asked Bryce as they entered the dim space.

"I know my female presence will probably cause the caves to collapse from sheer outrage," Bryce said, voice echoing off the massive dome above them, "but yes."

Ruhn snickered and peered up at the dome. It was a mosaic of onyx stones, interrupted by bits of opal and diamond—stars. A crescent moon of pure nacre occupied the apex of it, gleaming in the dimness. Eerily similar to the Ocean Queen's sharp nails.

Sathia trailed Bryce and asked softly, "And—that's really it? The knife?"

"Shocking, I know," Bryce said. "Party girl bearing the prophesied—"

"No," Sathia said. "I wasn't thinking that."

Bryce paused, turning, and Ruhn knew Athalar was monitoring every word, every move from Sathia as Flynn's sister clarified, "I was thinking about what it means. Not just in regard to the Asteri and your conflict with them. But what it means for the Fae."

"Whole lot of nothing," Flynn snorted.

"We were told our people would be united with the return of that knife," Sathia countered sharply. Her tone gentled as she asked Bryce, "Is that part of . . . whatever plan you have? To unite the Fae?"

Bryce surveyed the rows and rows of shelves and said coldly, "The Fae don't deserve to be united."

Even Ruhn froze. He'd never thought about what Bryce might do as leader, but . . .

"Come on, Quinlan," Athalar said, slinging his arm around her shoulders and decisively changing the subject, "let's get to exploring."

"Yeah, yeah," Bryce muttered. "I suppose it's too much to hope for a digital catalog here, so . . . I guess we'll have to do it the old-fashioned way." She pointed ahead, to the entire wall taken up by a card catalog. "Look for any mention of the sword and knife, anything about the mists guarding this place, Pelias and Helena . . . Maybe even stuff about the earliest days of Avallen, either during the First Wars or right after."

"That is . . . a lot to look for," Flynn said.

"Bet you're wishing you'd learned to read," Sathia trilled, striding for the catalog.

"I can read!" Flynn sulked. Then mumbled, "It's just boring."

Ruhn snorted, and the sound was echoed nearby—Lidia.

Again, that look between them. Ruhn said a shade awkwardly to her, "We should get cracking."

A catalog that massive could take days to comb through. Especially since there was no librarian or scholar in sight. Come to think of it, the entire place had an air of neglect. Emptiness. The castle did, too, as well as the small city and surrounding lands.

It had all seemed so mysterious, so strange when he'd come here decades ago: the famed misty isle of Avallen. Now he could only think of Cormac, growing up in the gloom and quiet. All that fire, dampened by this place.

And yet he'd loved his people—wanted to do right by them. By everyone on Midgard, too.

There had to be something good here, if Cormac had come out of it. Ruhn just couldn't for the life of him figure out what.

The Fae don't deserve to be united.

Bryce's words hung in the air, as if they still echoed off the dome above. And Ruhn didn't know why, but as the words settled into the darkness . . . they made him sad.

After a few tense minutes, Declan declared, "Well, *this* is interesting."

He stood at the nearest table, what looked like a stack of maps unrolled before him. A large one—of Midgard—was spread across the top.

Ruhn strode for his friend, grateful for the break. "What is?" The others followed suit, gathering around the table.

Dec pointed at Avallen on the map, the paper yellow with age despite the preserving spells upon it. "I thought looking at old maps might give us some hints about the mists—you know, see how old cartographers represented them and stuff. And then I found this."

Athalar rubbed his neck and said, "At the risk of being ridiculed . . . what am I looking at?"

"There are islands here," Declan said. "Dozens."

It clicked. "There shouldn't be any islands around Avallen," Ruhn said.

Bryce leaned closer, running her fingers across the archipelago. "When's this map from?"

"The First Wars," Dec said, and pulled another map from the bottom of the pile. "This is Midgard now. No islands in this area except the one we're on."

"So . . . ," Baxian said.

"*So,*" Dec said, annoyed, "isn't it weird that there *were* islands fifteen thousand years ago, and now they're gone?"

Tharion cleared his throat. "I mean, sea levels do rise—"

Dec gave them all a withering look, and pulled out a third map. "This map's from a hundred years after the First Wars." Ruhn scanned it. No islands at all.

Across the table, Lidia was silently assessing the different maps. She lifted her eyes to Ruhn's, and he couldn't stop his heartbeat from jacking up, his blood from thrumming at her nearness—

"All those islands," Bryce murmured, "disappeared within a hundred years."

"Right after the Asteri arrived," Athalar added, and Ruhn looked away from Lidia long enough to consider what was before them.

He said, "Well, despite its mists, Avallen clearly has had no problem revealing its shape and coastline to the Asteri for the empire's official maps. Why hide the islands?"

"There are no islands," Sathia said quietly. "The ones on that first map . . ." She pointed along the northwestern coast. "We sailed in from that direction. We didn't see a single island. The mists could have obscured some of them, but we should have seen at least a few."

"I've never seen or heard any mention of additional islands here," Flynn agreed.

Silence fell, and they all glanced between the three maps as if they'd reveal some big secret.

Dec finally shook his head. Something happened here a long time ago—something big. But what?"

"And," Lidia murmured, the cadence of her voice sending shivers of pleasure down Ruhn's spine, "is this knowledge at all useful to us?"

Bryce tapped a hand on the oldest map, and Ruhn could practically see the wheels turning in her head.

"Silene said something in her memories about the island that had once been her court." Bryce's face took on a faraway look, as if she were trying to remember the exact words. "She said that the land . . . shriveled. That when she started to house those monsters to hide the Harp's presence, the island of the Prison became barren. And the Ocean Queen said islands literally withered into the sea in despair when the Asteri arrived."

"So?" Flynn asked.

Bryce's gaze sharpened again. "It seems weird that two Fae strongholds, both islands, were once archipelagos, and then *both* lost all but the central island in the wake of the arrival of . . . unpleasant forces."

Ruhn raised his eyebrows. "I can't believe you actually told us what you were thinking, for once."

Bryce flipped him off as Athalar snickered. She nodded decisively. "Team Archives: keep looking into this."

The others dispersed again to resume their researching, but Bryce grabbed Ruhn by the elbow before he could move. "What?" he asked, glancing down at her grip.

Bryce's look was resolute. "We don't have the luxury of time."

"I know," Ruhn said. "We'll search as quickly as we can."

"A few days," Bryce said, letting go of his arm. She glanced toward the sealed front doors of the archives, the island beyond. "I don't think we have more than that before Morven decides it's in his best interest to tell the Asteri we're here, risks to his people be damned. Or before the Asteri's mystics pinpoint our location."

"Maybe the mists can keep out mystic eyes as well," Ruhn suggested.

"Maybe, but I'd rather we not find out the hard way. A few days, Ruhn—then we're out of here."

"The caves could take longer than that to navigate," Ruhn warned. "You sure there's anything in there worth finding? As far as I could tell, it was some decorative crap on the walls and a lot of misty tunnels. We'd get through the archives way faster if we all tackled the catalog together."

"I have to look at the caves," Bryce said quietly. "Just in case."

It hit him then, like a bucket of ice water. Bryce wasn't entirely sure she *could* find anything to help her unite the blades. To kill the Asteri.

So Ruhn squeezed her shoulder. "We'll figure it out, Bryce."

She offered him a grim smile. It was all Ruhn could do to offer one back.

They found nothing else regarding the missing islands, the mists, or the sword and the knife in the hours they spent combing through the catalog. They'd barely made a dent in the collection by the time Bryce called it quits for dinner, her hands so achingly dry from all the dust that they burned.

In silence, the group walked to the castle dining room. What a long, fucking day. Each of their trudging steps seemed to echo the sentiment.

The dining room was empty, though a small buffet of food had been laid out for them.

"Guess we're early," Tharion said as the group surveyed the firelit room, its faded tapestries depicting long-ago Fae hunts. Their quarry lay at the center of one: a chained, collared white horse.

Bryce jolted. It wasn't a horse. It was a *winged* horse.

So they'd survived here, then—at least for a few generations. Before they'd either died out or the Fae had hunted them to extinction.

"We're not early," Sathia said beside Tharion, her face tight. "The formal dinner started fifteen minutes ago. If I were to guess, it's been moved to another location for everyone else."

"No one wants to eat with us?" Hunt asked.

Bryce said, "They probably consider it beneath them to mingle with our ilk." Hunt, Baxian, and Tharion turned to her with incredulous expressions. Bryce shrugged. "Welcome to my life." Hunt was frowning deeply, and Bryce added to him, unable to help herself, "You don't need to feel guilty about that one, you know."

He glared at her, and the others made themselves scarce.

"What does that mean?" Hunt asked quietly.

It wasn't the time or place, but Bryce said, "I can't get a read on you. Like, if you even want to be here or not."

"Of course I do," Hunt growled, eyes flashing.

She didn't back down. "One moment you're all in, the next you're all broody and guilty—"

"Don't I have the right to feel that way?" he hissed. The others had already reached the table.

"You do," she said, keeping her voice low, though she knew the others could hear them. One of the downfalls of hanging with Vanir. "But each of us made choices that led us to all this. The weight of that's not only on you, and it isn't—"

"I don't want to talk about this." He started walking toward the center of the room.

"Hunt," she started. He kept walking, wings tucking in tight.

Across the room, she met Baxian's stare from where he was pulling out a chair at the table. *Give him time,* the Helhound's look seemed to say. *Be gentle with him.*

Bryce sighed, nodding. She could do that.

They served themselves, and sat at random spots along the massive table, large enough to seat forty: Ruhn, Flynn, Sathia, and Dec in one cluster; Tharion, Baxian, Hunt, and Bryce in another. Lidia claimed a chair beside Bryce, definitely *not* looking to where Ruhn watched them from down the table.

"So this is Avallen," Lidia said, breaking the awkward silence.

"I know," Bryce muttered. "I'm trying to scrape my jaw off the floor."

"It reminds me of my father's house," Lidia said quietly, digging into her potatoes and mutton. Hearty, simple food. Definitely not the fine feast Morven and his court were indulging in elsewhere.

"They must both have a subscription to *Medieval Living,*" Bryce said, and Lidia's mouth curved toward a smile.

It was so weird to see the *Hind* smile. Like a person.

The males must have been thinking the same thing, because Baxian asked, "How long, Lidia? How long since you turned spy?"

Lidia gracefully carved her meat. "How long since *you* started believing in the cause?"

"Since I met my mate, Danika Fendyr. Four years ago."

Bryce's chest ached at the pride in his voice—and the pain. Her fingers itched with the urge to reach across the table to take his hand, just as she had last night.

But Lidia blinked slowly. And said softly, "I'm sorry, Baxian."

Baxian nodded in acknowledgment. Then said to Lidia and Hunt, "I kind of can't get over being here with the two of you. Considering where we were not that long ago. Who we were."

"I bet," Bryce murmured.

Hunt tested the edge of a knife with his thumb, then cut into his own meat. "Urd works in mysterious ways, I guess."

Lidia's eyes glimmered. Hunt lifted his glass of water to her. "Thanks for saving our asses."

"It was nothing," she replied, slicing into the mutton again.

Baxian put down his fork. "You put everything on the line. We owe you."

Bryce glanced down the table and noticed Ruhn watching them. She gave him a pointed glance, as if to say, *Chime in, asshole*, but Ruhn ignored her.

Lidia's mouth kicked into a half smile. "Find a way to kill the Asteri, and we're even."

The rest of dinner was mostly quiet, and Bryce found herself growing weary enough that by the time she'd finished her plate, she just wanted to lie down somewhere. Thankfully, *one* person in the castle deigned to engage with them: an older Fae woman who gruffly said she'd show them to their rooms.

Even if they weren't welcome, at least they were given decent accommodations, all along the same hall. Bryce didn't really mark who bunked with whom, focusing solely on being shown to her own room, but she didn't fail to notice the awkward beat when Tharion and Sathia were shown through a door together halfway down the hall.

Bryce sighed once she and Hunt entered their own chamber. She wished she'd had the energy to talk to Ruhn, to really delve into what it had been like for him here, what he was feeling, but . . .

"I need to lie down," Bryce said, and slumped face-first onto the bed.

"Today was weird," Hunt said, helping to remove her sheathed sword and dagger. He placed them with expert care at the side of the bed, then gently turned her over. "You all right?"

Bryce peered up into his face—the halo on his brow. "I really hope we find something here to make it worthwhile."

Hunt sat beside her, removing his own weapons and setting them on a side table. "You're suddenly worried we won't?"

Bryce got to her feet, unable to sit still despite her exhaustion. She paced in front of the crackling fire. "I don't know. It's not like I was expecting a giant neon sign in the archives that said *Answers Here!* But if the Asteri are going after Flynn's family . . ." She hadn't let herself think about it earlier. There was nothing she could do from here, without phone or interweb service. "Then they're going after mine."

"Randall and Ember can look after themselves." But Hunt rose, walking to her and taking her hands. "They'll be okay." His hands were warm around hers, solid. She closed her eyes at the touch, savoring its love and comfort. "We'll get there, Quinlan. You traveled between worlds, for fuck's sake. This is nothing by comparison."

"Don't tempt Urd."

"I'm not. I'm just telling you the truth. Don't lose faith now."

Bryce sighed, examining his tattooed brow again. "We need to find some way to get this off you."

"Not a big priority."

"It is. I need you at your full power." The words came out wrong, and she amended, "I need you to be free of them."

"I will be. We all will be."

Staring into his dark eyes, she believed him. "I'm sorry about earlier. If I pushed you too hard."

"I'm fine." His voice didn't sound fine.

"I wasn't trying to tell you how to feel," she said. "I just want you to know that none of us, especially me, hold you responsible for all this shit. We're a team."

He lowered his stare, and she hated the weight pressing on his head, drooping his wings. "I don't know if I can do this again, Bryce."

Her heart strained. "Do what?"

"Make choices that cost people their lives." His eyes lifted to hers again, bleak. "It was easier for Shahar, you know. She didn't care about other people's lives, not really. And she died so fast, she didn't have to endure the weight of the guilt that might have come later. Sometimes I envy her for it. I did envy her for it, back then. For escaping it all by dying."

"That's the old Umbra Mortis talking," Bryce said, fumbling for humor amid the cold wash of pain and worry at his words, his dead tone.

"Maybe we need the Umbra Mortis right now."

She didn't like that. Not one bit. "I need Hunt, not some hel-meted assassin. I need my mate." She kissed his cheek. "I need *you*."

The darkness in his eyes lightened, and it eased her heart, relief washing through her.

She kissed his cheek again. "I know we should go wash up for bed and use the chamber pot or whatever excuse they have for a toilet in this museum, but . . ."

"But?" He lifted his brows.

Bryce rose onto her toes, brushing her mouth against his. And the taste of him . . . Gods, yes. "But I need to feel you first."

His hands tightened around her waist. "Thank fuck."

There was more to be discussed, of course. But right now . . .

He lowered his face to hers, and Bryce met him, the kiss thor-ough and open, and just . . . bliss. Home and eternity and all she'd fought for. All she'd keep fighting for.

From the way he returned the kiss, she knew he realized it, too. Hoped he let it burn through any lingering scraps of remorse.

"I love you," he said against her mouth, and deepened the kiss. She stifled a sob of relief, arms winding around his neck. Hunt's hands slid around to her ass and he hefted her up, smoothly walk-ing them over to the enormous, curtained bed.

Clothes were peeled away. Mouths met, and explored, and tasted. Fingers caressed and stroked. Then Hunt was over her, and Bryce let her joy, her magic shine through her.

"Look at you," Hunt breathed, hips flexing beneath her hands, cock teasing her entrance. "Look at you."

Bryce smiled as she let more of that power shine through her: Starborn light so silvery bright it cast shadows upon the bed. "Like it?"

Hunt's thrust, driving himself in to the hilt, was his response. "You're so fucking beautiful," he whispered. Lightning gathered around his wings, his brow. Like his power couldn't help but answer hers, even with the halo's damper on it.

Bryce moaned as he withdrew, nearly pulling out of her, then plunged back in.

Hunt angled her hips to drive himself deeper. And as his cock brushed her innermost wall, as lightning flickered above her, in her . . .

Mate. Husband. Prince. *Hunt.*

"Yes," Hunt said, and she must have voiced her thoughts aloud, because his thrusts turned deeper, harder. "I fucking love you, Bryce."

Her magic rose at his words, a surging wave. Or maybe that was her climax, rising along with it. She couldn't get enough of him, couldn't get close enough to him, needed to be *in* him, his very blood—

"Solas, Bryce," Hunt growled, pumping into her in a long, luxurious stroke. "I can't—" She didn't want him to. She gripped his ass, nails digging in deep in silent urging. "Bryce," he warned, but he didn't stop moving in her. Lightning crackled and snaked around them, an avalanche racing toward her.

"Don't stop," she pleaded.

Their magics collided—their souls. She scattered across the stars, across galaxies, lightning skittering in her wake.

She had the dim sense of Hunt being thrown with her, of his shout of ecstasy and surprise. Knew that their bodies remained joined in some distant world, but here, in this place between places, all they were melted into one, crossed over and transferred and becoming something *more.*

Stars and planets and rainbow clouds of nebulas swirled around them, darkness cut with lightning brighter than the sun. Sun and moon held together in perfect balance, suspended in the same sky. And beneath them, far below, she could see Avallen, thrumming with their magic, so much magic, as if Avallen were the very source of it, as if *they* were the very source of all magic and light and love—

Then it ebbed away. Receded into muted color and warm air and heavy breathing. The weight of Hunt's body atop hers, his cock pulsing inside her, his wings splayed open above them.

"Holy shit," Hunt said, lifting himself enough to look at her. "Holy . . . *shit.*"

It had been more then fucking, or sex, or lovemaking. Hunt stared down at her, starlight shimmering in his hair. Just as she knew lightning licked through her own.

"It felt like my power went into you," Hunt said, eyes tracking the lightning as it slithered down her body. "It's . . . yours."

"As mine is yours," she said, touching a fleck of starlight glittering between the sable locks of his hair.

"I feel weird," he admitted, but didn't move. "I feel . . ."

She sensed it, then. Understood it at last. What it had always been, what she'd learned to call it in that other world.

"Made," Bryce whispered with a shade of fear. "That's what it feels like. Whatever power can flow between us . . . my Made power from the Horn can, too."

Hunt looked down at himself, at where their bodies remained joined. She had a pang of guilt, then, for not telling him all she knew yet about the other Made objects in the universe—about the Mask, the Trove. "I guess it flows both ways: my power into you, and yours into me."

Hunt smiled and surveyed the room around them. "At least we seem to be past ending up somewhere new every time we fuck."

Bryce snorted. "That's a relief. I don't think Morven would have appreciated our naked asses landing in his room."

"Definitely not," Hunt agreed, kissing her brow. He brushed back a strand of her hair. "But what difference does it make? That we're connected this way?"

Bryce lifted her head to kiss him. "Another thing for us to figure out."

"Team Caves all the way," he said against her mouth.

She laughed, their breath mingling, twining together like their souls. "I told you I should have ordered T-shirts."

51

Tharion stood in the old-timey stone bedroom, complete with a curtained bed and tapestries on the wall, and had no idea what to say to his wife.

Apparently, Sathia Flynn had no idea what to say to him, either, because she took a seat in a carved wooden chair before the crackling hearth and stared at the fire.

They'd barely exchanged more than a word all day. But now, having to share a room—

"You can take the bed," he said, the words too loud, too big in the chamber.

"Thank you," she said, arms wrapping around herself. The firelight danced on her light brown hair, setting golden strands within it shining.

"I don't, uh—I don't expect anything."

That earned him a wry look over her shoulder. "Good. Neither do I."

"Good," he echoed, and winced, walking to the window. The starless night was a black wall beyond, interrupted only by a few glimmering fires at farmstead cottages. "Does it ever get . . . not gloomy here?"

"This is my first visit, so I can't say." Her tone was a bit sharp, as if unused to speaking normally to people, but she added, "I hope so."

Tharion walked to the wooden chair opposite hers and sank onto it. The damn thing was hard as Hel. He shifted, trying to find a more comfortable angle, but gave up after a second and said, "Let's start from the beginning. I'm Tharion Ketos. Former Captain of Intelligence for the River Queen—"

"I know who you are," she said quietly, her soft tone belied by the steely calm in her eyes.

He arched a brow. "Oh? Good or bad?"

She shook her head. "I'm Sathia Flynn, daughter of Lord Hawthorne."

"And?"

She cocked her head to the side, strands of her long hair slipping over a shoulder. "What else is there?" ·

He feigned contemplation. "Favorite color?"

"Blue."

"Favorite food?"

"Raspberry tarts."

He let out a laugh. "Really?"

She frowned. "What's wrong with that?"

"Nothing," he said, then added, "Mine's cheese puffs."

She let out a hint of a laugh. But it faded as she said, "Why?"

He ticked the reasons off on his fingers. "They're crispy, they're cheesy—"

"No. I mean—why did you do this?" She gestured between them.

Tharion debated how to spin his story, but . . . "This arrangement of ours might as well be an honest one." He sighed. "I'm a wanted male. The Viper Queen has a bounty of five million gold marks on my head."

She choked. "What?"

"Surprise," he said. Then added, "Sorry. I feel like . . . maybe I should have mentioned that before."

"You think?" But she mastered herself, a practiced, calm

demeanor stealing over her pale features before she said for a third time, "Why?"

"I . . . may have been indirectly responsible for burning down the Meat Market, and now she wants to kill me. That was after I defected from the River Queen, who, uh, also wants to kill me. And then the Ocean Queen harbored me and forbade me from leaving her ship, but I disobeyed her order and bailed, and now here I am and . . . I'm really not doing a good job of making myself seem appealing, am I?"

"My father is going to keel over dead," Sathia said. Something like wicked amusement glinted in her eyes.

He could work with a sense of humor.

"As glad as I am to hear that," Tharion said, earning another few millimeters of smile, "it's a long way of saying . . . I've fucked up a lot." Sigrid's dead body flashed before his eyes, and he shoved it away. "Too much," he amended.

"So this is some attempt at redemption?" Any amusement faded from her face.

"It's an attempt to be able to look at myself in the mirror again," he said plainly. "To know I did something good, at some point, for someone else."

"All right," she said, then looked back at the fire.

"You seem, uh . . . relatively cool with this whole marriage thing."

"I've grown up knowing my fate would lead me to the marriage altar." The words were flat.

"But you thought that would be marriage to a Fae—"

"I don't particularly want to talk about the things that have been expected of me my entire life," she said with the imperiousness of a queen. "Or the doors that are now closed to me. I am alive, and I didn't have to marry Goon One or Goon Two, so—yes, I'm *cool* with that."

"The mind-prying thing didn't woo you, huh?"

"They're brutes and bullies, even without their mind gifts. I abhor them."

"Good to know you have standards." Tharion extended his hand to her. "It's nice to meet you, Sathia."

She gingerly took the offered hand, her fingers delicate against his. But her handshake was firm—unflinching. "It's nice to meet you, too . . . husband."

Dawn broke over Avallen, though Lidia had never seen such a gloomy sunrise. Granted, given her fitful sleep last night, she wasn't exactly in the mood to appreciate any sunrise, clear or cloudy. But as she stood on one of the small castle balconies overlooking the hilly countryside, her arms braced against the lichen-crusted stone rail, she couldn't help but wonder if Avallen ever saw sunshine.

The city—more of a town, really—had been built atop a craggy hill, and offered views from every street of the surrounding green countryside, the land a patchwork of small farms and quaint homesteads. A land lost in time, and not in a good way.

Even Ravilis, Sandriel's former stronghold, had been more modern than this. There wasn't so much as a trace of firstlight anywhere. The Fae here used candles.

And had apparently been given an order, considering the unusually quiet streets, to shun the visitors at every turn. But she could have sworn that countless Fae were watching her from the shuttered windows of the ancient-looking town houses flanking the streets winding up to the castle. She'd always known Morven ruled with an iron fist, but this submission was beyond what she'd expected.

She'd barely been able to sleep last night. Hadn't been able to stop seeing her sons' faces as she'd left that room, or how they'd blended with the memory of their faces as babies, how they'd been sleeping so peacefully, so beautifully, in their cribs that last night, when she'd looked at them one final time and left. Walked off the *Depth Charger* and into the submersible pod.

It had felt like dying, both then and now. Felt like Luna had shot her with a poisoned arrow and she was bleeding out, an invisible wound leaking into the world, and there was nothing that could ever be done to heal it.

Lidia scrubbed her hands over her face, finding her cheeks chilled. Maybe it would have been better to have not seen them again. To have never returned to the ship, and not reopened that wound.

There was no torture that Pollux or Rigelus could have devised for her that hurt worse than this. The chill wind whipped past, moaning through the narrow streets of the ancient, mist-wreathed city.

Below her, in the courtyard, Bryce and Athalar, Baxian, Tharion, and the mer's new bride were preparing to leave. Ruhn and his two friends stood with them, speaking in low voices. No doubt running over all they knew regarding the Cave of Princes once more.

She didn't really know why she'd come out here—they hadn't bothered to tell her they'd be leaving, or invite her to the send-off. Baxian at last looked up, either sensing or spotting Lidia, and lifted a hand in farewell. Lidia returned the gesture.

The rest of the group turned, too, Bryce waving a bit more enthusiastically than the others.

Flynn and Dec just nodded to her. Ruhn merely glanced up before averting his eyes. With a final embrace for his sister, the Fae Prince stalked back into the castle and disappeared from view, his two friends with him. Bryce and her crew aimed for the castle gates. For the countryside beyond, still half asleep under the grayish light.

Shadows whispered over the stones of the balcony, and Lidia didn't turn to acknowledge Morven as he stepped up beside her. "So sentimental of you, to see them off."

Lidia kept her gaze on the departing group, headed for a cluster of taller hills rising against the horizon. "Is there something you want?"

A hiss at her impudence. "You're a filthy traitor."

Lidia slid her stare to the Fae King at last. Beheld his pale, hateful face. "And you're a spineless coward who disavowed his own child at the first sign of trouble."

"Had you any honor, any understanding of royal duty, you would understand why I did so." Shadows twined over the shoulders of his fine black jacket, the silver embroidery. The Stag King, they called him. It was an insult to deer shifters. The Fae male had no affinity for the beasts, despite his throne, crafted from the bones of some noble, butchered beast. "You would know there are more important things than even one's own children."

There was nothing more important. Nothing. She was here today, on this island, back in the field once more, because there would never be anything more important than the two boys she'd left on the *Depth Charger*.

"I enjoyed watching you grovel, you know," Lidia said. And she had—despite everything, she'd loved every second of Morven kneeling before the Asteri. Just as she loved seeing him bristle with fury as she threw his humiliation in his face.

"I have no doubt a blackheart like you did," Morven sneered. "But I wonder: Should a better offer come along, will you betray these friends as easily as you did your masters?"

Lidia's fingers curled at her sides, but she kept her face impassive. "Are you sulking because you did not see me for what I truly am, Morven, or because I witnessed you in your moment of shame? In the moment you traded loyalty to your son for your own life?"

He seethed, shadows poised to strike. "You know nothing of loyalty."

Lidia let out a low laugh, and glanced toward the five figures heading out into the greenery of the countryside. Toward the red-haired female in the center of the group. "I've never had a leader to stir the sentiment."

Morven noted the direction of her gaze and scowled. "You're a fool to follow her."

Lidia gave him a sidelong look, pushing off the stone wall of the balcony. "You're a fool not to," she said quietly, striding for the archway into the castle proper. "It will be your doom. And Avallen's."

Morven snarled, "Is that a threat?"

Lidia kept walking, leaving her enemy and the miserable dawn behind. "Just some professional advice."

"So all that talk, all those myths and hand-wringing about the Cave of Princes," Hunt said to Bryce, sweating lightly from their hours-long trek across the rolling fields to this craggy cluster of hills, the castle now a lone spike on the horizon behind them, "and *this* is it?"

Bryce looked around. "Underwhelming, isn't it?"

The entrance to the cave was little more than a sliver between two boulders. Ancient, weatherworn runes were etched into the stones, but that was all that set this place apart from any other crack in the rock face.

That, and the tongue of mist slithering out from the gloom.

"Morven needs a decorator," Tharion said, peering into the darkness beyond. "I think he could really move beyond his ancestors' shadows-and-misery theme."

"This is how he likes it," Sathia said. "The way Avallen was when it was first built—right after the First Wars ended. His father kept it that way, and his father before him, going all the way back to Pelias himself."

Hunt swapped a look with Bryce. That was precisely why they'd come. If there was a place any bit of truth might be preserved, it was here. He didn't relish the thought of going into a cave; some intrinsic part of him bucked at the idea of being so far from the wind, so far belowground, trapped once again. But he forced himself past the bolt of fear and dread and said to Sathia, "Do *you* have any idea how the mists keep the Asteri out of Avallen?" She hadn't volunteered the information yesterday, but maybe it was because they hadn't thought to ask.

"No," Sathia said. "The rumor is that the magic of the mists is so old, it predates even the Asteri's arrival."

"Well," Tharion said, gesturing dramatically, "ladies first, Legs."

"Such chivalry," Bryce retorted.

"You're the one with a built-in flashlight," Hunt reminded her.

She rolled her eyes and said to a wary Sathia, "Word of advice: don't let them push you around."

"I won't," Sathia said. For some reason, Hunt believed her.

Bryce was looking at Flynn's sister as if she was thinking the same thing. "It's good to have another female around here." She nodded to Baxian, Tharion, and Hunt. "The Alphahole Club was getting too crowded for my liking."

Bryce halted at the line between light and shadow. The mist trickling along the cave floor reached for her pink sneakers with white, curving claws. Her starlight didn't pierce the darkness beyond a few feet ahead. It only illuminated a thicker cloud of mist. Masking any threats waiting beyond.

She couldn't bring herself to cross that line.

"This place feels wrong," Baxian murmured, coming up beside Bryce.

"Here's hoping we see daylight again," Tharion said with equal quiet from a step behind them.

"We will," Hunt said, adjusting the heavy pack strapped between his wings. "Nothing to worry about except some ghouls. And wraiths. And 'scary shit,' Ruhn claimed."

"Oh, just that," Bryce said, throwing him a wry glance. She added to Sathia, pointing to the spires barely poking over the green horizon, "It's not too late to head back to the castle."

"I'm not going to sit around with those mind-reading bastards lurking about," Sathia hissed.

They all turned toward her.

"Did something . . . happen?" Hunt asked carefully. Tharion was watching her closely.

"I'm not going to be left alone in that castle," Sathia insisted, wrapping her arms around herself, fingers digging into her white sweater, and Bryce knew she didn't want to discuss it further.

"Fair enough," Hunt said, reading Sathia's tone, too. "But Ruhn warned me that most of what's in here is old, and wicked, and likes to drink blood. And eat souls. I'm not sure of the order, though."

"Sounds like your run-of-the-mill Fae nobility, then," Bryce said, hefting her heavy pack higher. She winked at Sathia. "You'll be right at home."

The Fae female gave her a watery smile, but to her credit, didn't run screaming from the cave and its grasping, misty fingers. If Sathia did indeed prefer to face what lurked in this cave over the Murder Twins, maybe Bryce owed it to her and females every-where to kick some ass when they got back.

If they got back.

"Right," Hunt said. "According to Declan, Pelias's tomb and the Starsword's resting place lie right in the center of the cave network." They'd swiped food and water from the surprised-looking kitchen staff, preparing for a few days' journey. "But there are lots of things that will try to eat us along the way."

Bryce ignored the twisting in her stomach. She'd gone to another world, she'd faced an Asteri—she could deal with a few ghouls and wraiths. She had three badasses with her. Plus Sathia. She could do this.

Bryce faced the others and held out her hand at waist level. "Go Team Caves on three?"

They all looked at her, but didn't cover her hand with theirs. Not even Hunt, the bastard. After the way they'd fucked last night, the least he could do was indulge her with some team spirit. But he gave her a look, as if to say, *Gravitas, Quinlan.*

Fuck that. She lifted her hand in the air and shouted, "Gooooo Team Caves!"

The words echoed off the boulders, down the passage, and into the misty darkness beyond. Where they suddenly cut off, as if the caves themselves had devoured them.

"That's not creepy at all," Hunt murmured.

"Totally normal," Baxian agreed.

"Don't worry," Bryce crooned. "I'll protect you from the scary cave." And with that, she strode into the dark.

Morven cornered Ruhn outside the dining hall just before he and his friends left for the archives again after breakfast.

"A word," Morven said, hooking a finger toward him. The mass of shadows from the day before was gone, but the crown of them remained floating atop his head.

"Here I was," Ruhn drawled, nodding at Flynn and Dec to keep going down the hall, "thinking I didn't exist to you."

Morven leveled a cold look at him—it made Ruhn's father seem downright cheerful. But Ruhn noticed that the king waited to speak until Lidia had walked past, out the door, not sparing a glance for either of them.

"What are your sister's intentions in coming here?"

"Bryce told you," Ruhn said tightly. "She wants information."

"On what?"

"The sword and knife, for one thing. The rest is classified." *Asshole,* he didn't need to add.

Morven's eyes darkened to blackest night. "And does she plan to claim Avallen for herself?"

Ruhn burst out laughing. "What? No. If she did, I wouldn't tell you, but trust me: this place . . ." He surveyed the dark, crypt-like hall. "This isn't her style. Just ask my father."

"That is another thing: Your sister must have done something to him. How else would she come to possess his journal?"

"If she has, it didn't involve trying to claim his crown. She's said nothing about it." Ruhn glared at the king. "And again: If she was planning some sort of Fae coup, why the Hel would I tell you about it?"

"Because you are *true* Fae, not some half-breed—"

"I'd mind how you speak about my sister."

Morven's shadows gathered at his fingers, his shoulders. Wild, angry shadows that Ruhn's own balked to meet. They seemed corrupted somehow, like those Seamus and Duncan wielded mentally. "You are Starborn. You have an obligation to our people."

"To do what?"

"To ensure they survive."

"Bryce is Starborn, too."

Ruhn, Dec, and Flynn had given his sister and the others all the pointers they could regarding what they'd face in the dark labyrinth of the Cave of Princes, but their own journey through the misty cave network had been so chaotic that they had little to offer when it came to a direct route to Pelias's tomb. Bryce hadn't seemed too concerned, despite her comment last night about time running out. But maybe she was putting on a brave face.

"Yes," Morven sneered, "and what has your sister done with her Starborn heritage except show contempt for the Fae?"

"You don't know a damn thing about her."

"I know she spat on her Fae lineage when she announced her union with that *angel*." His shadows quivered with rage.

"All right," Ruhn said, turning to go. "I'm officially done. Bye."

Morven grabbed him by the arm. Shadows slithered up from his hand onto Ruhn's forearm, squeezing tight. "After dealing with your sister yesterday, I prayed all night to Luna for guidance." His eyes gleamed with a fanatic's fervor. "She allowed me to see that you, despite your . . . transgressions . . . are our people's only hope of regaining some credibility in future generations."

Ruhn sent his own shadows racing down his arm, biting at Morven's and snapping free of their grip with satisfying ease. "Luna doesn't strike me as the type who'd stoop to talking to assholes like you."

Despite his shredded shadows, Morven's fingers dug into his arm. "There are females here who—"

"Nope." Ruhn shrugged off his uncle's hand. Kept a wall of shadows at his back as he walked away. *"Bye."*

"Selfish fool," Morven hissed. Ruhn could have sworn the king's shadows hissed, too.

But Ruhn lifted his arm above his head and flipped him off without looking back. He found Dec and Flynn waiting by a courtyard fountain outside, a safe distance from Lidia.

"What was that all about?" Flynn asked, falling into step beside Ruhn.

"Not worth explaining," Ruhn replied, keeping his eyes on the archives dome a few streets away.

Declan asked Lidia, "Any chance Morven will run to the Asteri?"

"Not yet," she said quietly. "Bryce's claims yesterday were true—she handled him well." She added, turning toward Ruhn, "You could learn a thing or two from your sister."

"What's that supposed to mean?" Ruhn demanded.

Flynn and Dec pretended to be busy looking into a closed butcher shop as they passed by.

"You're a prince," Lidia said coolly. "Start acting like one."

52

You're a prince. Start acting like one.

Fuck, Lidia knew precisely what to say to piss him off. To keep him thinking about her in the hours that passed, during all the fruitless searching for anything about the missing islands, the Starsword, the dagger, or the mists.

She'd gone on a walk for half an hour and then come back, smelling of the sea, and still hadn't said anything to him.

"You could, uh, talk to her," Flynn said from beside Ruhn, shutting yet another useless drawer full of catalog cards. "I can literally feel you brooding."

"I'm not brooding."

"You're brooding," Declan said from Ruhn's other side.

"*You're* brooding," Ruhn said, nodding to Dec's taut face.

"I have good reason to. I can't get in touch with my family or Marc—"

Ruhn softened. "I'm sure they're fine. You warned them to lie low before all that shit at the Meat Market, and Sathia said she reached out to them. Marc will make sure they stay safe."

"It doesn't make it any easier, knowing I can't even check in with them thanks to this medieval playland."

Ruhn and Flynn grunted their agreement.

"This place sucks," Dec said, and slammed the drawer he'd

been combing through closed. "And so does this library's cataloging system." Dec peered down the long, long row and called, "Anything?"

Ruhn tried but failed not to look at Lidia. She'd taken the far end of the catalog, definitely on purpose, and had yet to say a word to them in the hours they'd been here together. "No," she said, and continued her work.

Fine.

Just fine.

"Well," Hunt whispered, voice echoing off the slick black stone before being swallowed by the dense mists, "this is terrifying."

The reek of mold and rot was already giving him a headache, unsettling every instinct that told him to get out of the misty enclosed space and into the skies, into the safety of the wind and clouds—

"Once you've seen a Middengard Wyrm feeding," Bryce muttered in the soupy darkness, waving away the mist in front of her face to no avail, "nothing's as bad."

"I don't want to know what that is," Baxian said.

Hunt appreciated that Baxian hadn't needed to be asked before flanking Bryce's exposed side. Tharion and Sathia walked close behind, saying little as the pathway descended. Ruhn had said the carvings on the walls started a little ways in, but they hadn't found a hint of them yet. Just rock—and mist, so thick they could only see a few feet ahead.

Bryce said, "Think an earthworm with a mouth full of double rows of teeth. The size of two city buses."

"I *said* I didn't want to know what that was," Baxian grumbled.

"It's not even that bad, compared to some of the other shit I saw," Bryce went on. And then admitted, if only because they had followed her into the deadly dark and deserved to know the whole truth, "They have a thing called the Mask—a tool that can literally raise the dead. No necromancers needed. No fresh bodies, either."

They all stared at her. "Really?" Tharion asked.

Bryce nodded gravely. "I saw the Mask used to animate a skeleton that had been dead for ages. And give it enough strength that it could take on the Wyrm."

Hunt blew out a whistle. "That's some mighty powerful death-magic."

He refrained from complaining that she hadn't mentioned it until now, because he certainly wasn't mentioning how Rigelus had taken his lightning to do something similar, and Baxian, thankfully, didn't say anything, either. They'd heard nothing about what had come of it, but it couldn't be good.

Another thing he'd have to atone for.

He'd heard what Bryce was trying to tell him last night, about all of them bearing a piece of the blame for their collective actions. But it didn't stop him from harboring the guilt. He didn't want to talk about it anymore. Didn't want to feel it anymore.

"Yeah," Bryce said, continuing into the dark, "the powers in that Fae world are . . . off the charts."

"And yet the Asteri want to tangle with them again," Baxian said.

"Rigelus knows how to hold a grudge," Bryce said. She halted abruptly.

Hunt's every instinct went on alert. "What?" he asked, scanning the misty darkness ahead. But Bryce's gaze was on the wall to her left, where a carving had been etched into the stone with startling precision.

"An eight-pointed star," Baxian said.

Bryce's hand drifted to her chest, fingers silhouetted against the brightness shining there.

Hunt surveyed the star, then the images that began a few feet beyond it, plunging onward into the mists, as if this place marked the beginning of a formal walkway. Bryce merely began walking again, head swiveling from side to side as she took in the ornate, artistic carvings along the black rock. It was all Hunt could do to keep up with her, not letting the mists veil her from sight.

Fae in elaborate armor had been carved into the walls, many holding what seemed to be ropes of stars. Ropes that had been looped around the necks of flying horses, the beasts screaming in fury as they were hauled toward the ground. Some sank into what looked like the sea, drowning.

"A hunt," Bryce said quietly. "So the early Fae did kill all of Theia's pegasuses, then."

"Why?" Sathia asked.

"They weren't fans of the Starlight Fancy dolls," Hunt answered.

But Bryce didn't smile. "These carvings are like the ones in Silene's caves. Different art, but the storytelling style is similar."

"It'd make sense," Tharion said, running his fingers over a thrashing, drowning horse, "considering that the art's from the same time period."

"Yeah," Bryce muttered, and pressed on, her starlight now flaring a beam through the mists. Pointing straight ahead. There was no privacy to corner her and ask what the Hel she was *really* thinking—certainly not as something shifted in the shadows to Hunt's left.

He reached over a shoulder for his sword, lightning at the ready. Or as ready as it could be with the gods-damned halo suppressing it—

"Ghouls," Baxian said, drawing his sword in an easy motion. The shadows writhed, hissing like a nest of snakes.

"They're not coming any closer," Sathia whispered, her fear thick as the fog around them.

Hunt wrapped his lightning around his fist, the sparks making the damp walls glisten like the surface of a pond. But light flared from Bryce, and the ghouls shrank back further.

"Benefits of being the Super Powerful and Special Magic Starborn Princess," Bryce drawled, sashaying past the nooks and alcoves in the stone where the ghouls teemed. "Ruhn said they ran from his starlight during his Ordeal. Looks like they're not fans of mine, either."

Sathia inched past the nearest cluster of ghouls, keeping a step behind Bryce.

A scabbed, jet-colored hand skittered from a deep pocket of shadows, its nails long and cracked, digging into the stone—

Before Hunt's lightning could strike, Bryce's starlight flared again. The hand fell back, a low hiss skimming over the rocks. "Super Powerful and Special Magic Starborn Princess, indeed," Hunt said, impressed.

But Bryce turned toward the lines the ghoul had gouged into the rock, running a hand over them. She rubbed the bits of dust and debris between her forefinger and thumb, sniffed it once, then slid her gaze to Hunt. "Flynn's right: I don't like it here." She licked—fucking *licked*—the dark substance on her fingers and grimaced. "Nope. Not at all."

Sathia, still a few steps behind Bryce, shivered. "Can you feel it, then? How . . . dead it all seems? Like there's something festering here."

Hunt had no idea what the Hel either female was talking about, and from Tharion's and Baxian's baffled expressions, they didn't, either.

Bryce only moved on into the dark and mists. They had no choice but to keep pace with her, to stay in that protective bubble of starlight.

"There's water ahead," Baxian said, his advanced hearing picking it up before Hunt could detect it. "A river—a big one, from the sound of it."

Bryce slid Hunt a look. "Good thing we've got two hunky dudes with wings."

And there it was again—that gleam in her eyes. There and gone, but . . . he could almost hear her brain working. Connecting some dots he couldn't see.

"Stay close," Bryce murmured, leading them deeper into the cave. "I've spent a disgusting amount of time underground lately, and I can tell you there's nothing good coming our way."

Flynn and Dec left to grab everyone lunch, and Ruhn resigned himself to working in silence with Lidia, only the rustle of paper and slamming of fruitless drawers for sound.

He found nothing. Neither did she, he concluded from her occasional sighs of frustration. So different from the contented, near-purring sighs she'd made in his arms that time their souls had merged, as he'd moved in her—

Cousin.

Ruhn slowly, slowly turned toward the towering open doorway. No one stood there. Only the gray day lay beyond.

On your left.

Seamus leaned against a nearby stack, arms crossed. A dagger was buckled over his broad chest, just as it had been all those decades ago. As it had been then, the male's dark hair was cut close to his head—to avoid an enemy getting a grip on it, Ruhn knew. And if Seamus was there, then that meant—

On your right, Duncan said into his mind, and Ruhn glanced the other way to find Seamus's brother leaning in a mirror position on the opposite stack. In lieu of a dagger, Duncan carried a slender sword strapped down his spine.

Ruhn kept both of them in his line of sight. *What do you want?*

Instinct had already kept his mind veiled in stars and shadows, but he did a quick mental scan to ensure his walls were intact.

Duncan sneered. *Our uncle sent us to make sure the female was behaving herself.*

Ruhn glanced at Lidia, still searching the catalog. *Fuck,* her mind was unguarded—

It was second nature, really, to leap for her mind. As if he could somehow shield her from them.

But on the other end of that mental bridge, a wall of fire smoldered. It wasn't just fire—it was a conflagration that swirled sky-high, as if generating its own winds and weather. Magma seemed to churn beneath it, visible through cracks in the whirling storm of flame.

Well, he didn't need to worry about her, then.

You spoil our fun, cousin, Seamus said.

She'd be fun to rummage through, Duncan added.

Ruhn eyed the males. *Get lost.*

Her presence defiles this place, Seamus said, attention sliding to

Lidia and fixing on her shoulder blades with an intensity Ruhn didn't like one fucking bit.

So does yours, Ruhn shot back.

Seamus's dark eyes shifted toward Ruhn once more. *We can smell you on her, you know.* Seamus's teeth flashed. *Tell me: Was it like fucking a Reaper?*

A low growl slipped out of Ruhn, and Lidia turned at the sound. She showed no surprise. As if she'd been aware of their presence this whole time, and had been waiting for some sort of signal to interfere.

She looked coolly between his cousins. "Seamus. Duncan. I'll thank you to stay out of my mind."

Seamus bristled, pure Fae menace. "Did we talk to you, bitch?"

Ruhn clenched his jaw so hard it hurt, but Lidia lifted those golden eyes to the twin princes and said, "Shall I demonstrate how I *make* males like you talk to me?"

Duncan snarled. "You're lucky our uncle gave the word to stand down. Or else we'd have already told the Asteri you're here, Hind."

"Good dogs," Lidia said. "I'll be sure to advise Morven to give you both a treat."

Ruhn's lips twitched upward. But—she'd told him to act like the prince he was. So he schooled his face into icy neutrality. A mask as hard as Lidia's. "Tell Morven we'll send word if we require his assistance," he said to his cousins.

The dismissal found its mark better than any taunt. Duncan pushed off the bookshelf, hand curling at his side—shadows wrapping around his knuckles. Darker, wilder than Ruhn's. As if they'd been captured from a storm-tossed night.

"You're an embarrassment to our people," Duncan said. "A disgrace."

Seamus stalked over to his twin, his identical face displaying matching disdain. "Don't waste your breath on him."

Seamus said into Ruhn's mind, *You'll get what's coming to you.*

Ruhn kept his face impassive—*princely,* some might say. "Good to see you both."

Again, his failure to snap back at them only riled them further, and both of his cousins growled before turning as one and striding from the archives.

Only when they'd vanished through the massive doors did Ruhn say quietly to Lidia, "You all right?"

"Yes," she said, her golden eyes meeting his. Ruhn's breath caught in his throat. "They're no different from any other brute I've encountered." Like Pollux. She turned back to the catalog. "They'd get along with Sandriel's triarii."

"I'll remind you that a good chunk of that triarii has since proved to be on our side," Ruhn said. But he could think of nothing else to say, and silence once more fell—inside his head and in the archives—so he began to search again.

After several long minutes, it became unbearable. The silence. The tension. And simply to say something, to break that misery, he blurted, "Why fire?"

She slowly turned toward him. "What?"

"You always appeared as a ball of fire to me. Why?"

She angled her head, eyes gleaming faintly. "Stars and night were already taken." She smirked, and something eased in his chest at this bit of normalcy. Of what it had been like when they were just Day and Night. Despite himself, he found himself smiling back.

But she studied him. "How . . ."

He met her wide, searching stare. "How what?"

"How did you wind up like this?" she asked, voice soft. "Your father is . . ."

"A psychotic dickbag."

She laughed. "Yes. How did you escape his influence?"

"My friends," he said, nodding toward the door they'd exited through. "Flynn and Dec kept me sane. Gave me perspective. Well, maybe not Flynn, but Dec did. Still does."

"Ah."

He allowed himself the luxury of taking in her face, her expression. Noted the kernel of worry there and asked, "How did it go with your sons before we left yesterday?" He'd heard she'd gone to say goodbye, but nothing about the encounter. And given how haunted her face had looked when they'd left the *Depth Charger* . . .

"Great." The word was terse enough that he thought she wouldn't go on, but then she amended, "Terrible." A muscle ticked in her jaw. "I think Brann would want to get to know me, but Ace— Actaeon . . . He loathes me."

"It'll take time."

She changed the subject. "Do you think your sister will actually find something of use against the Asteri?"

Given how many people over the centuries had probably looked for such a thing, Ruhn didn't resent her question. "Knowing Bryce, she's up to something. She always has a few cards up her sleeve. But . . ." He blew out a breath. "Now that she's in the fucking Cave of Princes, part of me doesn't want to know what those cards might entail."

"Your sister is a force of nature." Nothing but admiration shone through the words.

Pride glimmered in his chest at the praise, but Ruhn merely said, "She is." He let that be that.

But the silence that followed was different. Lighter. And he could have sworn he caught Lidia glancing toward him as often as he looked toward her.

Ithan strode down the halls of the House of Flame and Shadow, Hypaxia at his side, his stomach full and contented after a surprisingly good breakfast in its dim dining hall. They'd been early enough that most people hadn't yet arrived.

He'd eaten an insane amount, even for him, but given that they were leaving for Avallen tomorrow, he'd wanted to fuel up as much as possible. He'd demanded that they go *now*, but Jesiba apparently had to arrange transportation and permission for them to enter the island, and since they weren't telling anyone the truth about why they were going, she also had to weave a web of lies to whoever her contact on the Fae island was.

But soon he could right this awful wrong. They'd find Sofie's body, get her lightning, and then fix this. It was a slim shard of hope, but one he clung to. One that kept him from crumbling into absolute ruin.

One he could only thank the female beside him for—the female who hadn't thought twice before helping him so many times. It was for her sake that he made himself keep his tone light as he patted his rock-hard stomach and said, "Did you know they had such good food here?"

Hypaxia smirked. "Why do you think I defected so easily?"

"In it for the food, huh?"

Hypaxia grinned, and he knew the expression was rare for the solemn queen. "I'm *always* in it for the—"

A shudder rumbled through the black halls, clouds of dust drifting from the ceiling. Ithan kept his footing, wrapping a hand around Hypaxia's elbow to steady her.

"What the Hel was that?" Ithan murmured, scanning the dark stone above them.

Another *boom*, and Ithan began running, Hypaxia hurrying behind him, aiming for Jesiba's office. He was through the double doors a moment later, revealing Jesiba at her desk, her face taut, eyes wide—

"What the Hel is going on?" Ithan demanded, rushing over to where she had a feed up on her computer, showing exploding bombs.

Another impact hit, and Ithan motioned Hypaxia to get under the desk. But the former witch-queen did no such thing, instead asking, "Is that feed right above us?"

"No," Jesiba said, her voice so hoarse she almost sounded like a Reaper. "Omega-boats pulled into the Istros." On the feed, buildings crumbled. "Their deck launchers just fired brimstone missiles into Asphodel Meadows."

53

Ithan and Hypaxia raced across the city, the blocks either full of panicking residents and tourists or deathly, eerie quiet. People sat on the sidewalks in stunned shock. Ithan steeled himself for what he'd find in the northeastern quarter, but it wasn't enough to prepare him for the bloodied humans, ghostlike with all the dust and ash on them, streaming out of it. Children screamed in their arms. As he crossed into Asphodel Meadows, the cracked streets were filled with bodies, lying still and silent.

Further into the smoldering ruin, cars had been melted. Piles of rubble remained where buildings had stood. Bodies lay charred. Some of those bodies were unbearably small.

He drifted someplace far, far away from himself. Didn't hear the screams or the sirens or the still-collapsing buildings. At his side, Hypaxia said nothing, her grave face streaked with silent tears.

Closer to the origin of the blasts, there was nothing. No bodies, no cars, no buildings.

There was nothing left in the heart of Asphodel Meadows beyond a giant crater, still smoldering.

The brimstone missiles had been so hot, so deadly, that they'd melted everything away. Anyone who'd taken a direct hit would have died instantly. Perhaps it had been a small mercy to be taken out that fast. To be wiped away before understanding the nightmare that was unfolding. To not be scared.

Ithan's wolf instinct had him focusing. Had him snapping to attention as Hypaxia pulled a vial of firstlight healing potion from her bag and ran to the nearest humans beyond the blast radius—two young parents and a small child, covered head to toe in gray dust, huddling in the doorway of a partially collapsed building.

Hypaxia might have defected from being queen, but she was, first and foremost, a healer. And with his Aux and pack training, Ithan could make a difference, too. Even though he was a wolf without a pack, a disgraced exile and murderer. He could still help. *Would* still help, no matter what the world called him. No matter what unforgivable things he'd done.

So Ithan sprinted for the nearest human, a teenage girl in her school uniform. The fuckers had chosen to strike in the morning, when most people would be out in the streets on their way to work, kids on their way to school, all of them defenseless in the open air—

A snarl slipped out of him, and the girl, bleeding from her forehead, half-pinned under a chunk of cement, cringed away. She scrambled to push the cement block off her lower legs, and it was him—*his* presence that was terrifying her—

He shoved the wolf, the rage down. "Hey," he said, kneeling beside her, reaching for the chunk of cement. "I'm here to help."

The girl stopped her frantic shoving against the block, and lifted her bloodied eyes to him as he easily hauled it off her shins. Her left leg had been shredded down to the bone.

"Hypaxia!" he called to the witch, who was already rising to her feet.

But the girl grabbed Ithan's hand, her face ghastly white as she asked him, "Why?"

Ithan shook his head, unable to find the words. Hypaxia threw herself to her knees before the girl, fishing another firstlight vial from her satchel. One of a scant few, Ithan saw with a jolt. They'd need so many more.

But even if all the medwitches of Crescent City showed up . . . would it be enough?

Would it ever be enough to heal what had been done here?

"You getting anything?" Hunt asked Tharion as they stood on the bank of a deep, wide river rushing through the cave system. Bryce, standing a few feet away, let the males talk as she studied the river, the mists blocking its origin and terminus; the carved walls continuing on the other side of the river; the musty, wet scent of this place.

Nothing so far that would tell her anything new about the blades, mist, or how to kick some Asteri ass, but she filed away everything she saw.

"No," the mer said. Bryce was half listening to him. "My magic just senses that it's . . . cold. And flows all through these caves."

"I guess that's good," Baxian said, tucking in his wings. He winked at Bryce, drawing her attention. "No Wyrms swimming about."

Bryce glowered. "You wouldn't be joking if you'd seen one." She didn't give the Helhound time to reply before she said to him and Hunt, "Wings up to carry us?"

Her mind was racing too much for conversation as they awkwardly crossed the river, Hunt flying Sathia and Bryce together, Baxian carrying Tharion. Bryce extended her bubble of starlight so they could all remain within it, which was about as much extra activity as she could be bothered with while she took in the carvings.

They didn't tell the story that Silene's carvings had narrated—there was no mention of a slumbering evil beneath their feet. Just a river of starlight, into which the long-ago Fae had apparently dragged those pegasuses and drowned them.

Yeah, the Fae here had been no better than the ones in Nesta's world.

They walked for hours and hours—miles and miles. There were occasional stops, alternating who took watch, but sleep was difficult.

The ghouls lurked in crevices and alcoves all around, scraps of malevolent shadow. They hissed with hunger for warm blood—and in abject fear of her starlight. Only someone with the Starborn gift—or someone under their protection—could survive here.

The Starsword pressed on her back; the dagger dug into her hip. They burdened each step, locked in some strange battle to be near each other that intensified as she got farther into the cave.

Bryce ignored them, and instead tracked the carvings on the walls. On the ceilings. Brutal images carved with care and precision: Merciless, unending battles and bloodshed. Cities in ruins. Lands crumbling away. All falling into that river of starlight, as if the Starborn power had swept it away in a tide of destruction.

"I have a question." Sathia's voice echoed through the tunnel. "It might be considered impertinent."

Bryce snorted. "Didn't you know? That's the motto of Team Caves."

Sathia increased her pace until she was at Bryce's side. "Well, you don't seem to want anything to do with the Fae."

"Bingo," Bryce said.

"Yet you're here, bearing our two most sacred artifacts—"

"Three, if you count the Horn in my back."

Sathia's stunned silence seemed to bounce through the cave. "The . . . the *Horn*? How?"

"Fancy magic tattoo," Bryce said, waving a hand. "But go on."

Sathia's throat worked. "You bear *three* of our most sacred artifacts. Yet you plan to . . . do what with the Fae?"

"Nothing," Bryce said. "You're right: I want nothing to do with them." The carvings around them only strengthened that resolve. Especially the ones of the pegasus slaughter. She glanced sidelong at the female. "No offense."

But Sathia said, "Why?"

This really wasn't a conversation Bryce felt like having, and she gave the female a look that said as much. But Sathia held her stare, frank and unafraid.

So Bryce sighed. "The Fae are . . . not my favorite people. They never have been, but after this spring even more so. I *really* don't want to associate with a group of cowards who locked out innocents the day demons poured into our city, and who seem intent on doing that again on a larger scale here on Avallen."

"Some of us had no choice but to be locked in our villas," Sathia said tightly. "My parents forbade me from—"

"I never let something being forbidden stop me from doing it," Bryce said.

Sathia glared, but went on. "If you . . . if we . . . survive all this, what then?"

"What do you mean, *what then?*"

"What do you do with the sword and knife? With the Horn? Let's say your wildest hopes about the Asteri come true, and we find the knowledge here or in the archives to help defeat them. Once they're gone, do you keep these objects, when you want nothing to do with our people?"

"Are you saying I shouldn't keep them?"

"I'm asking you what *you* plan to do—with them, and yourself."

"I'm changing the motto of Team Caves," Bryce announced. "It's now *Mind Your Own Business.*"

"I mean it," Sathia said, not taking Bryce's shit for one second. "You'll walk away from it all?"

"I don't see much of a reason to hang around," Bryce said coldly. "I don't see why you'd want to, either. You're chattel to them. To the Autumn King, to Morven, to your dad. Your only value comes from your breeding potential. They don't give a fuck if you're smart or brave or kind. They only want you for your uterus, and Luna spare you if you have any troubles with it."

"I know that," Sathia answered with equal ice. "I've known that since I was a child."

"And you're cool with it?" Bryce countered, unable to stop the sharpness in her voice. "You're cool with being used and treated like that? Like you're lesser than them? You're cool with having no rights, no say in your future? You're cool with a life where you either belong to your male relatives or your husband?"

"No, but it is the life I was born into."

"Well, you're Mrs. Ketos now," Bryce said, nodding back at Tharion, who was watching them carefully. "So brace yourself for all that entails."

"What does *that* mean?" Tharion demanded.

But Sathia ignored her taunts and said, "What are you going to do to the Fae?"

"*Do?*" Bryce asked, halting.

Sathia didn't back down. "With all that power you have. With who you are, what you bear."

Hunt let out a low whistle of warning.

But Bryce seethed at Sathia, "I just want the Fae to leave me the fuck alone. And I'll leave them the fuck alone."

Sathia pointed at the Starsword on Bryce's back. "But the prophecy—when those blades are reunited, so shall our people be. That has to mean you, uniting all the Fae peoples—"

"I already did that," Bryce cut in. "I connected the Fae of Midgard to the ones in our home world. Prophecy fulfilled. Or were you hoping for something else?"

Sathia's gaze simmered. An unbroken female, despite the life she'd led. "I was hoping for a Fae Queen. Someone who might change things for the better."

"Well, you got me instead," Bryce said, and continued into the dark, fingers curling at her sides. Maybe she'd use her laser power to wipe these carvings from the walls. As easily as Rigelus had shattered the statues in the Eternal Palace. Maybe she'd send out a blast of her light so vicious it would obliterate all the hissing ghouls around them. "The Fae dug their own graves. They can lie in them."

Sathia let it drop.

Hunt fell into step beside Bryce, putting a hand on her shoulder as if to offer his support, but she could have sworn that even her mate was disappointed in her.

Whatever. If they wanted to preserve a long, fucked-up line of Fae tyrants, that was on them.

Flynn and Dec abandoned Ruhn the moment they called it quits at the archives, leaving him and Lidia to share a painfully quiet meal in the castle's empty dining room.

There was so much he wanted to ask her, to talk to her about, to know. He couldn't find the words. So he ate, fork unbearably loud against his plate, each bite like crunching glass. And when they finished, they walked back to their rooms in silence, each step echoing in the hallway, loud as a thunderclap.

But before they parted ways, as Ruhn was about to enter his room, he blurted, "You think my sister's okay?"

"You're the one who's been in the Cave of Princes," Lidia said, but turned toward him. "You tell me."

He shook his head. "Honestly, I don't know. Bryce has got a lot of shit going on right now. Those caves are confusing on a good day. If you're not focused, they can be deadly."

Lidia crossed her arms. "Well, I have faith that between her, Athalar, and Baxian, your sister will be fine."

"Tharion will be insulted."

"I don't know Ketos well enough as a warrior to judge him."

"Ithan Holstrom calls him Captain Whatever, but I think it's selling him a bit short. Tharion's a badass when he feels like it."

She smiled, and damn if it didn't do funny things to Ruhn's chest. She said again, "Your sister will be fine."

He nodded, blowing out a breath. "Do you and Hypaxia have any contact?"

"No. Not since the ball."

His mouth moved before he could think through his next question. "That night . . . were you ever going to meet me in the garden?"

Surprise flickered in her eyes, then vanished. Her mouth pursed, like she was debating her answer. "The Harpy got there before I did," she said finally.

He stepped toward her, the hall suddenly too small. "But were you going to show up like we'd planned?"

"Does it matter?"

He dared another step. He hadn't realized how her hips swelled so invitingly before dipping to her waist.

His hands curled, and he hated himself for the punch of lust that went through him, nearly knocking the breath from his lungs. He wanted her. Wanted her naked and under him and moaning his name, wanted her to tell him *everything*, and wanted . . . wanted his friend back. The friend he could speak honestly to, who knew things about him that no one else knew.

He took one more step, and he could see her trembling. With fear or restraint, he had no idea.

"Lidia," he murmured, in front of her at last, and she closed her eyes, the pulse in her throat fluttering.

Her scent shifted—like flowers unfurling under the morning sun. That scent was pure arousal. His cock tightened painfully.

He didn't care that they were in the middle of a hallway with his awful cousins running amok. He slid a hand onto her waist, nearly groaning at the steep curve, the way it fit his hand perfectly.

She kept her eyes closed, her pulse still flickering. So he took his other hand and tilted her head to the side. Leaned down and brushed his mouth over that fluttering spot.

Her breathing hitched, and his eyes nearly rolled back in his head. She tasted . . . fuck. He needed more. His teeth grazed the soft skin of her throat, and his tongue skimmed along the space just under her ear. His cock throbbed in answer.

Her body loosened, pliant in his hands, and her head tipped a little further to the side. An invitation. He licked up the column of her throat, hand drifting from her waist down to her ass—

She stiffened. Pulled away.

Like she'd caught herself. Remembered who she was. Who he was.

He stood there like a fucking moron, panting slightly, cock fully hard and straining against his pants, and she just . . . stared at him. Wide-eyed.

"I . . ." He had no idea what to say. What to do.

His head swam. This female had so much blood on her hands, yet—

"Good night," he rasped, and turned to his own room before he could make a greater fool of himself.

She didn't stop him.

54

Bryce lay on the hard, cold ground and tried to pretend she was back in her bed, that a rock wasn't poking into her hip bone, that her arm was the *most* comfortable pillow—

From Sathia's tossing and turning nearby, she knew the female was having the same amount of success getting settled for the night.

Hunt had fallen asleep right away, his deep breathing now a gentle rhythm that she tried to focus on, to lure her to sleep. She supposed his warrior days had made him used to rougher conditions, but . . . no. She didn't want to think about all the things Hunt had endured so that sleeping on this unforgiving surface was easy for him. Especially when the misplaced guilt from so many of those things was now clearly eating him alive.

It had been easier in the Fae world, as exhaustion had been riding her so hard that she'd had no choice *but* to pass out. But here, even well protected by Baxian on watch, sleep remained elusive.

Bryce flipped onto her back, her starlight shifting with her, broadcasting every one of her movements like a lighthouse beacon. Fuck, how she'd sleep with *that* blazing in her eyes—

She stared miserably up at the ceiling, carved here to resemble the branches of a forest. Beautiful, remarkable work that had never been documented, never been revealed to the world at large. Only to the few Fae royal males who'd sought the Starsword.

That blade was currently lying to her left, a thrumming, pulsing presence made worse by Truth-Teller on her right, which pulsed in a counter-beat. Like the blades were talking.

Just fucking great. It was a regular old sleepover here. Bryce ignored the chattering blades as best she could, focusing instead on the caves, the carvings.

Females had never been allowed in here. Now *two* Fae females had entered. She hoped all the long-dead princes buried in the caves were thrashing in their sarcophagi.

Such fear of females—such hatred. Why? Because of Theia? Pelias had been the one to found the Starborn line here on Midgard. Had all the bans and restrictions stemmed from his fear of someone like her rising again?

Bryce supposed scholars and activists had spent centuries researching and debating it, so the likelihood of finding an answer herself, even knowing the truth about Theia, was slim to none. It didn't make it any easier to swallow, though.

So she curled on her side, gazing at the carved river of stars that her starlight illuminated. The river of her lineage, meant to last through the millennia. Her bloodline, in its literal, starry form. Her bloodline, running straight through these caves. An inheritance of cruelty and pain.

She wished Danika were with her. If there was one person who might have understood the complexity of such a fucked-up inheritance, of having the future of a people weighing on her, it would have been Danika.

Danika, who'd wanted more for this world, for Bryce.

Light it up.

But maybe the Fae and their bloodline didn't deserve Bryce's light. Maybe they deserved to fall forever into darkness.

Flynn and Dec, the bastards, didn't show up to breakfast. Leaving Ruhn and Lidia to dine alone again.

Ruhn had lain awake most of the night, hard and aching—then fretting about what Bryce and the others were facing in the Cave of Princes. Maybe he should have gone with them. Maybe staying here had been cowardly, even if they did need information from the archives. Flynn and Dec could have found it.

The dining room doors opened as they were finishing their meal, and Ruhn braced himself for his asshole cousins. But a tall Fae male walked in, glancing about before quietly shutting the door behind him. As if he didn't want to be seen.

"Lidia Cervos." The male's voice shook.

Ruhn reached a hand toward the knife in his boot as the male approached the table. Lidia watched him, expression unreadable. Ruhn tried and failed to control his thundering heart. He opened his mouth. To order the stranger to announce himself, to demand he leave—

"I came to thank you," the male said, and reached for his pocket. Ruhn drew his knife, but the male only pulled out a piece of paper. A small portrait of a female and three young children. All Fae.

But Lidia didn't look. Like she couldn't bear to.

The male said, "Ten years ago, you saved my life."

Ruhn didn't know what to do with his body. Lidia just stared at the floor.

The male went on, "My unit was up in the base at Kelun. It was the middle of the night when you burst in, and I thought we were all dead. But you told us that the Hammer was coming—that we had to run. All seven of us are alive today, with our families, because of you."

Lidia nodded, but it seemed like a *thank you, please stop* motion. Not from any humility or embarrassment—it was pain on her lowered face. Like she couldn't endure listening.

He extended the portrait of his family again.

"I thought you might like to see what your choice that night achieved."

Still, Lidia didn't look up. Ruhn couldn't move. Couldn't get a breath down.

The male went on, "There are a few of us from my unit still

here, in secret. Prince Cormac convinced us all to join the cause. But we never told him, or anyone, who saved us. We didn't want to jeopardize whatever you were doing. But when we heard through the rumor mill that you—the Hind, I mean—had defied the Asteri, some of us contacted each other again."

The male at last noticed Lidia's discomfort and said, "Perhaps it is too soon for you to acknowledge all you have done, the lives you saved, but . . . I wanted to tell you that we are grateful. We owe you a debt."

"There is no debt," Lidia said, finally meeting the male's eyes. "You should go."

Ruhn blinked at the dismissal, but Lidia clarified to the stranger, "I assume you have kept your activities and associations secret from Morven. Don't risk his wrath now."

The male nodded, understanding. "Thank you," he said again, and was gone.

In the silence that followed, Ruhn asked, "You let them see who you really were?"

"It was either risk my identity being revealed to the world, or let them die," Lidia said quietly as they headed for the door. "I couldn't have lived with myself if I'd chosen the latter."

Ruhn arched a brow. "Not to sound totally callous, but why? There were only seven of them. It wouldn't have made a difference in the rebellion."

"Maybe not for Ophion as a whole, but it would have made a difference for their families." She didn't look at him. "Partners, children, parents—all hoping for their safe return."

"There had to be more to it than that," he pushed. "There was way more than that on the line for you."

She opened the door, and didn't speak again until they'd stepped into the hallway. "I guess I hoped that . . . that if my sons were ever in a similar situation, someone would do the same for them."

His heart twisted at the words, her truth. "Your path was difficult, Lidia—Hel, I don't think I could have endured any of it. But what you did was incredible. Don't lose sight of that."

"I could have saved more," she said softly, eyes on the floor as they strode down the empty hall. "I should have saved more."

Lidia had no idea what to make of the encounter with the former rebel this morning.

Maybe Urd had sent him to her, to remind her that her choices and sacrifices had, in fact, made some difference in the world. Even if they had gutted her.

The Ocean Queen hadn't given her a choice in leaving the ship, both all those years ago and now. But here, on this cheerless Fae island . . . here, at least, were some people who'd benefitted from that impossible position.

Flynn and Declan hadn't yet arrived in the archives, and as the silence became unbearable while she and Ruhn started their search, the only scents the musty catalog cards and Ruhn's inviting, reassuring smell, Lidia found herself calling down the line of the card catalog, "I'm going to go hunt for some coffee. Want to join me?"

Ruhn looked over, and gods, he was handsome. She'd never really let herself think about the sheer beauty of him. Even with his tattoos in ribbons, proof of what Pollux had done—

His blue eyes flickered, as if noting the direction of her thoughts. "Sure, let's go."

Even the way he spoke, the timbre of his voice . . . she could luxuriate in that all day. And when he'd touched her last night, licked her—

Did he have any idea how close she'd come to begging him to strip her naked, to lick her from head to toe and spend a long while between her legs?

"What's that look about?" Ruhn asked, voice low, thick. She noted every shifting muscle in his shoulders, his arms, his powerful thighs as he walked toward her. The way the sunlight gleamed on his long dark hair, turning it into a silken cascade of night. That buzzed side of his head seemed to be begging for her fingers to slide over the velvet-soft hair while she nipped at his pointed ear—

She began walking as he reached her, because the alternative was to wrap herself around him. "Brain fog. I need a cup of coffee."

She'd slept poorly again last night. At first, it had been thanks to the memory of what they'd done in the hallway, but then her thoughts had shifted to Brann and Actaeon, to that last conversation with them, and she'd wished that she could find herself on that mental bridge, her friend Night sitting in his armchair beside her.

Not just to have someone to talk to, but to have *him* to talk to. About . . . everything.

Ruhn fell into step beside her. "Who would have thought the Hind had a caffeine addiction?"

His half smile did something funny to her knees. But he said nothing more as they explored the back hallway of the archives, opening and closing doors. A closet crammed with half-rotted brooms and mops, another closest adorned with trays of various quartz crystals—no doubt some sort of scholarly recording device needed for this technology-free island—and a few empty cells with chipped desks that must have once been private studies.

"Morven really needs to invest in a new break room," Ruhn said as they finally beheld the kitchen. "This can't be good for employee morale."

Lidia took in the dark, dusty space, the wooden counter against the wall littered with mouse droppings, the cobwebs spun under the row of cabinetry. "This is like some bad medieval cliché," she said, approaching the filth-crusted cauldron in the darkened hearth. "Is this . . . gruel?"

Ruhn stepped up beside her, and his scent had her going molten between her legs. "I don't know why everyone thought Avallen would be some fairy-tale paradise. I've been telling Bryce for years that it's horrible here."

Lidia turned from the days-old goop in the cauldron and began opening cabinets. A mouse had made a home in a box of stale crackers, but at least there was a sealed jar of tea bags. "I should have known there would be no coffee." She peered around for a kettle and found Ruhn standing with one by the ancient sink, pumping water into it.

"Your sister," Lidia said, "was right to wonder what was going on with this place. Do you think Morven's hiding anything?"

"You're the super spy-breaker," Ruhn said, going to the hearth and tossing a few logs into the ashes. "You tell me."

The muscles in his forearm shifted as he grabbed some kindling and flint and lit the fire with a sort of efficiency that shouldn't have made her mouth water. He glanced over a shoulder, those blazingly blue eyes curious, and she realized he'd asked her a question, and she'd just been . . . staring at him. At his arms.

She cleared her throat and went about hunting for two mugs. "Morven never gave the Asteri or me cause to look into this place. He always appeared when summoned, and offered his services without question. He was, as far as Rigelus was concerned, a perfect minion."

"So there was never any discussion about these mists and Morven getting to hide behind them whenever he wanted?" The fire sparked to life, and Ruhn rose, stepping back to monitor it.

"No," Lidia said. "I think Rigelus believes the mists to be some . . . charming quirk of Midgard and the Fae. Something that added a bit of personality to this world. And since Morven and his forefathers played nice, they were left alone."

Ruhn slid his hands into the pockets of his black jeans. "I guess I'm surprised that after the truth about Cormac came out, the Asteri still didn't come poking around Avallen to see what might have caused the prince to turn rebel."

"Morven slithered right to the Eternal City," Lidia said, clenching her jaw. "And disavowed his son immediately."

"Right, with my dad in tow."

She scanned his face, the pain and anger that he didn't hide. "Yesterday, when I said you should act more like a prince . . ."

"Don't worry about it."

"I know the kind of monsters you're going up against." She dipped her eyes to his forearms, where the childhood burn scars were now mostly gone, but a few shiny pink streaks remained, untouched even by Pollux's ministrations.

"I can look after myself," he said tightly, fitting the kettle onto the hook over the fire and swinging it above the flame.

"I know you can," she tried, failing miserably at explaining. "I'm just . . . I see how good you are, Ruhn. You wear your emotions on your face because you *feel* in a way that Morven and the Autumn King do not. I don't want them to use that against you. To figure out how to hurt you."

He slowly faced her, those beautiful blue eyes wary, yet tender. "I think that's a compliment?"

She huffed a laugh, and plopped two tea bags into the least dusty mugs she'd found. "It's a compliment, Ruhn." She met his gaze, and offered him a small smile. "Take it and move on."

They found nothing new that day. Flynn and Dec seemed content to let them do the work, because they didn't show up. Or perhaps they'd gone off on some important errand and couldn't let them know, with no way to text or call.

"Listen to this," Lidia said, and Ruhn stopped his endless browsing to walk over to where she'd opened an ancient scroll. He'd noticed the way she'd been looking at him earlier—the pure desire in her eyes, her scent. It had distracted him so much that he'd barely been able to light the fire in that sorry excuse for a kitchen.

But Ruhn reined in the urge to scent her, to bury his face in her neck and lick that soft skin. Lidia pointed at the unfurled scroll before her. "The catalog listed this scroll's title as *The Roots of Earthen Magic.*"

"And?"

Her mouth quirked to the side. "I think it's strange that both Flynn and Sathia can't stand Avallen."

"What does that have to do with defeating the Asteri?"

"I figured it might be worthwhile to pull out some of the

earliest writings about earth magic—what role it played in the First Wars, or soon after. This scroll was the oldest I could find."

Flynn had picked a Hel of a time to not show up. "And . . . ?"

"This doesn't offer more than what we already know about the usual sort of earth magic the Fae possess, but it *does* mention that those with earth magic were sent ahead to scout lands, to sense where to build. Not only the best geographical locations, but magical ones, too. They could sense the ley lines—the channels of energy running throughout the land, throughout Midgard. They told the Asteri to build their cities where several of the lines met, at natural crossroads of power, and picked those places for the Fae to settle, too. But they selected Avallen *just* for the Fae. To be their personal, eternal stronghold."

Ruhn considered. "Okay, so if Flynn and Sathia say this place is dead and rotting . . ."

"It doesn't line up with the claims recorded here about Avallen."

"But why would the ancient Fae lie about there being ley lines here?"

"I don't think they lied," Lidia said, and pointed to the maps on the other table, where Dec had discarded them. "I think the Avallen they first visited, with all those ley lines and magic . . . I think it existed. But then something changed."

"We knew that already, though," Ruhn said carefully. "That something changed."

"Yes," Lidia said, "but the mists haven't. Could that be intentional? They left the mists intact, but the rest was altered—entire islands gone, the earth itself festering."

"But that would only have hurt the Fae—and we all know they're self-serving bastards. They'd never willingly part with any sort of power."

"Maybe they weren't willing," Lidia mused. "Whatever happened, the mists kept it hidden from the Asteri."

"What do you think they wanted to hide? Why rot their own land?"

Lidia gestured to the catalog behind them. "Maybe the answer's in there somewhere."

Ruhn nodded. Even as he wondered if they'd be ready for whatever that answer might be.

Bryce stood with Baxian on the bank of a second river, surveying the path on its distant side, her star glowing dimly toward it. The river passageway was narrow enough that she would have to teleport them across. She kept her starlight blazing bright, the ghouls a whispering malice around them.

There had been nothing helpful in the carvings so far. Fae slaying dragons, Fae dancing in circles, Fae basking in their own glory. Nothing of use. All surface-level shit. Bryce ground her teeth.

"Danika was the same, you know," Baxian said quietly so the others wouldn't hear. "With the wolves. She hated what so many of them were, and wanted to understand how they had become that way."

Bryce turned toward him, her starlight flaring a bit brighter as it illuminated the downward sweep of the river. It dimmed as she faced the Helhound fully. "The wolves are by and large *way* better than the Fae."

"Maybe." Baxian glanced to her. "But what of your brother? Or Flynn and Declan?" A nod to where Sathia, Tharion, and Hunt sat together. "What of her? Do you think they're all a lost cause?"

"No," Bryce admitted. Baxian waited. She let out a long breath. "And the Fae I met in the other world weren't so bad, either. I might have even been friends with them if circumstances had been different."

"So the Fae aren't inherently bad."

"Of course not," Bryce hissed. "But most of the ones in this world—"

"You know every Fae on Midgard?"

"I can judge them by their collective actions," Bryce snapped. "How they locked people out during the attack—"

"Yeah, that was fucked up. But until Holstrom defied orders, the wolves weren't helping, either."

"What's your point?"

"That the right leader makes all the difference."

Bryce recoiled at the words: *the right leader.* Baxian went on, "The Valbaran Fae might not be the most charitable people in our world, but think about who's led them for the last five hundred years. And long before that. Same with the wolves. The Prime isn't bad, but he's only one decent guy in a string of brutal leaders. Danika was working to change that, and she was killed for it."

"Rigelus told me they killed her to keep the information about their true nature contained," Bryce said.

Baxian cut her a look. "And you believe everything Rigelus says? Besides, why can't it be both? They wanted to keep their secrets to themselves, yes, but also to destroy the kernel of hope Danika offered. Not only to the wolves, but all of Midgard. That things could be different. Better."

Bryce massaged her aching chest, the starlight unusually dim. "They definitely would have killed her for that, too."

Baxian's face tightened with pain. "Then make her death count for something, Bryce."

He might as well have punched her in the face. "And what," she demanded, "try to redeem the *Fae*? Get them some self-help books and make them sit in circles to talk about their feelings?"

His face was like stone. "If you think that would be effective, sure."

Bryce glowered. But she loosed a long breath. "If we survive this shit with the Asteri, I'll think about it."

"They might go hand in hand," he said.

"If you start spewing some bullshit about rallying a Fae army to take on the Asteri—"

"No. This isn't some epic movie." He cocked his head. "But if you think you could manage—"

Bryce, despite herself, laughed. "Sure. I'll add it to my to-do list."

Baxian smiled slightly. "I just wanted you to know that Danika was thinking about a lot of the same things."

"I wish she'd talked to me about it." Bryce sighed. "About a lot of stuff."

"She wanted to," he said gently. "And I think putting that Horn in your back was her way of perhaps . . . manipulating you onto a similar path."

"Typical Danika."

"She saw it in you—what you could mean for the Fae." His voice grew unbearably sad. "She was good about seeing that kind of thing in people."

Bryce touched his arm. "I'm glad she had you to talk to. I really am."

He gave her a sorrowful smile. "I'm glad she had you, too. I couldn't be there with her, couldn't leave Sandriel, and I'm so fucking grateful that she had someone there who loved her unconditionally."

Bryce's throat closed up. She might have offered some platitude about them reuniting in the afterlife, but . . . the afterlife was a sham. And Danika's soul was already gone.

"Guys," Hunt said from where he and the others had risen to their feet. "We need to keep going."

"Why?" Bryce asked, walking over. Her starlight dimmed, as if telling her she was headed in the wrong direction. *I know,* she told it silently.

"We shouldn't linger, even with the Magical Starborn Princess watching over us," Tharion said, winking. "I think it's getting too tempting for the ghouls." He jerked his head toward the writhing mass of shadows barely visible within the mists. Their hissing had risen to such a level that it reverberated against her bones.

"All right," Bryce said, resisting the urge to plug her ears against the unholy din. "Let's go."

"That's the first wise decision you've made," drawled a deep male voice from the tunnel behind them.

And there was nowhere to run, nothing to do but stand and face the threat, as Morven stalked out of the mists. And behind him, flame simmering in his eyes, strode the Autumn King.

55

Hunt let his lightning gather at his fingers, let it wind through his hair as the two Fae Kings approached, one wreathed in flame, the other in shadow. The hissing of the ghouls, their stench, had veiled the kings' approach. Unless Morven had *willed* the ghouls to make such a racket, so they could creep up this close without even Baxian's hearing picking it up.

Hunt's lightning was a spark of what he'd command without the halo, but it was enough to fry these fuckers—

The Autumn King only stared at Bryce, pure hatred twisting his face. "Did you think that closet could hold me?"

Hunt's lightning sizzled around him, twining up his forearm. He was dimly aware of Tharion forming a plume of water straight from the river they'd been about to cross and aiming it at the kings. Of Baxian, sword out and snarling—

Seeming supremely unconcerned, Bryce said to her father, "I imprisoned Micah in a bathroom, so a closet seemed good enough for you. I have to admit that I'd hoped you'd stay in there a bit longer, though."

Morven's shadows thrashed around him like hounds straining at the leash. "You will return to my castle with us to face the consequences for treating your sovereign so outrageously."

Bryce laughed. "We're not going anywhere with you."

Morven smiled, and his shadows stilled. "I think you will."

Dark, scabby hands dragged Flynn and Declan out of the shadows. The males struggled, but the ghouls held them in check. Only the creatures' hands were visible—the rest of their bodies remained hidden in the shadows, as if unable to stand being so close to Bryce's starlight.

Sathia let out a low noise of shock. But Hunt demanded, "Where the fuck is Ruhn?"

"Occupied with wooing that traitorous bitch," Morven said. "He didn't even notice my nephews stealing these idiots away."

Two voices said into Hunt's mind, *We'll kill you and then breed your mate until she's—*

Starlight flared, silencing the voices but revealing the Murder Twins lurking behind the two kings. Steps away from Dec and Flynn, like the brothers commanded the ghouls to hold the males.

Bryce blazed, bright white against the blue and gold of the Autumn King's flames, the impenetrable dark of Morven's shadows. "What the fuck do you want?"

Flynn and Declan let out high, keening sounds. Though the ghouls' hands hadn't shifted, blood was trickling from her friends' noses. Dripping onto the ground.

Seamus and Duncan smiled. Whatever those fucks were doing to Dec's and Flynn's minds—

"You treacherous little brat," Morven spat at Bryce, shadows now at the ready once more. "Trying to win me over with your sire's research. He would never have let you get your dirty hands on it if you hadn't incapacitated him somehow. I went to investigate immediately."

Hunt could only gape as Bryce feigned a yawn. "My mistake. I assumed you'd want a leg up on this asshole here." She pointed with her thumb at the Autumn King. "But I didn't bargain on you being too dumb to interpret what was in his notes without his help."

Hunt had to stifle a chuckle, despite the danger they were in. Morven's affronted look was a little too forced—Bryce had clearly hit home. The Autumn King shot him a nasty glare.

"Let them go," Bryce said, "and then we'll talk like adults."

"They will be released when you have returned to my castle," Morven said.

"Then kill them now, because I'm not going back with you."

Flynn and Dec turned outraged eyes on her, but the ghouls held them firm. Morven said nothing. Even his shadows didn't move. The Murder Twins just eyed Bryce, readying for a fight.

Bring it, fuckers, Hunt wanted to say. From the way the twins glared at him, he wondered if they'd picked up his thoughts.

Yet Bryce smiled mockingly at Morven. "But I know you won't kill them. They're too valuable as breeding assets. Which is what all this comes down to, right? Breeding."

The Autumn King said coldly, even as red-hot flame simmered at his fingertips, "The Fae must retain our power and birthright. The royal bloodlines have been fading, turning watery and weak in your generation."

"Cormac proved that with his spinelessness," Morven bit out. "We must do everything we can to strengthen them."

"Cormac was more of a warrior than you'll ever be," Tharion snapped, that plume of water narrowing to needle-like sharpness. It'd punch a hole through the face of whoever got in front of it.

"Too bad I'm married now," Bryce mused. "And you guys don't do divorce."

Morven sneered. "Exceptions can be made for the sake of breeding."

Hunt's rage roared through him.

"All this breeding talk is *awfully* familiar," Bryce said, yawning again. "And come to think of it, this whole Fae King versus Fae Queen thing seems like history repeating itself, too." She scrunched up her features, pretending to think. "But you know . . ." She patted Truth-Teller's hilt. "Some things might be different these days." Hunt could have sworn the Starsword hummed faintly, as if in answer.

"You disgrace our people and history by bearing those blades," Morven accused.

"Don't forget that I also bear this," Bryce said, and held up a hand. Light—pure, concentrated light—fizzed there.

"Oh, you believe mere light can best true darkness?" Morven seethed, shadows rising behind him in a black wave. They were deep, suffocating—lifeless.

Hunt gathered his lightning again, a chain twining around his wrist and forearm. One whip of it, and he'd fry the ghouls holding Dec and Flynn, freeing up two more allies in this fight—

But the Autumn King beheld that concentrated seed of light at Bryce's finger. His flames banked. Any amusement or rage leached from his expression as he murmured to Morven, "Run."

"Now *that's* the first wise decision *you've* made," Bryce mocked.

A beam of slicing, burning light shot from her hand toward the ceiling.

Then solid rock rained down upon them all.

Ruhn had just decided that he really should go see where his friends had disappeared to all day, and was about to do so after leaving the archives that night when he found himself walking back toward the bedrooms with Lidia.

"I know it's an unusual situation," she said when they reached his door, "but I liked working with you today."

He halted, throat working before he managed to say, "Must be nice, to finally get to . . . be yourself. Out in the open."

"It's complicated," she said quietly.

She shifted on her feet, like she wanted to say more but didn't know how, so Ruhn decided to do her a favor and asked, "Wanna come in for a minute?" At her arched brow, he added, "Just to talk."

Her lips curved, but she nodded. He opened his door, stepping aside to let her in. They found seats in the threadbare armchairs before the crackling fire, and for a moment, Lidia stared at the flames as if they were speaking to her.

Ruhn was about to offer her a drink when she said, "Everything in my life is complicated. All the relationships, real and faked . . . sometimes I can't even tell them apart." Her voice was soft—sad. And utterly exhausted.

Ruhn cleared his throat. "When you and I . . ." *Fucked.* "Slept together, you knew who I was. Beyond the code name, I mean."

Her eyes found his, dancing with flame. "Yes."

"Did it complicate things for you?"

She held his stare, her eyes as gold as the flames before them, and his heart thundered. "No. I was shocked, but it didn't complicate anything."

"Shocked?"

She gestured to him. "You're . . . you."

"And that's . . . bad?"

She huffed a laugh, and it was so much like Day that he couldn't get a breath down.

"You're the defiant, partying prince. You have all those piercings and tattoos. I didn't have you down for being a rebel."

"Trust me, it wasn't on my five-year plan, either."

She laughed again, and the breathy sound went right to his cock, wrapping tight. Her voice had always done that. "Why risk it?"

"At first?" He shrugged, fighting past the rising lust pounding through his body. "Cormac blackmailed me. Said he'd tell my father about my mind-speaking abilities. But then I realized it was . . . it was the right thing to do."

"Agent Silverbow will be sorely missed. He already is."

"You knew Cormac, then?"

"No, but I knew of the things he accomplished for Ophion, and the people caught up in the war. He was a good male." She glanced to the shut door. "His father did not deserve a son like him."

Ruhn nodded.

She looked at him intently. "Your father, too—he does not deserve a son like you."

The words shouldn't have meant anything, especially coming from the Hind, but Ruhn's throat tightened at the raw honesty in her voice.

"Can I ask," he ventured, "about your deal with the Ocean Queen?"

Lidia's jaw tightened. "I was young, and afraid, when I made my bargain with her. But even now, I'd make the same choices. For my sons."

"What happened?" He met her eyes. "I know it's not my business, but . . ."

"Pollux isn't their father." He nearly sighed with relief. "It . . ." She struggled for words. "I come from a long line of powerful stag shifters. We have rituals. Secret ones, old ones. We don't necessarily worship the same gods that you do. I think our gods predate this world, but I've never confirmed it."

"Let me guess: You participated in some kind of secret sex rite and got pregnant?"

Her eyes widened, then she laughed—a full, throaty sound this time. "Essentially, yes. A fertility rite, deep in the Aldosian Forest. I was selected from the females of my family. A male from another family was chosen. Neither of our identities were known to each other, or to each other's families. It was quick, and not particularly interesting, and if there was fertility magic, I couldn't tell you what the Hel it was."

"Were you already with Pollux then?"

"Ruhn . . ." She looked at her hands. "My father took me from my mother when I was three. I remember being taken, and not understanding, and only learning later, when I was old enough, that my father was a power-hungry monster. He's not worth the breath it takes to speak of him, and I blamed my mother for letting him take me away. I became his little protégé, I think out of some hope that it would wound her when she heard I had turned out exactly like him."

She took a shaky breath. "I trained, and I schemed, and I wound up in Sandriel's triarii, a high honor for my family. I'd been serving Sandriel for ten years when my father chose me for this ritual. I had become adept at . . . getting people to talk. Pollux and I were dancing around each other, but I had not yet decided to let him into my bed. So I went to the ritual."

Ruhn couldn't move, couldn't have spoken even if he wanted to.

"A few weeks later, I knew I was pregnant. A baby from a sacred ritual would have been celebrated. I should have rushed right to my father to announce the good news, but I hesitated. For the first time in my life, I hesitated. And I didn't know *why* I couldn't tell him. Why, when I thought of the baby inside of me, when I thought of handing that child over to him, I couldn't."

She hooked a stray lock of hair behind her ear, the restless motion at odds with her usual poised demeanor. Ruhn refrained from putting a hand on her shoulder.

"I knew that within a matter of days, Pollux or the others—Athalar was still with us then—would scent the pregnancy. So I staged my own kidnapping and disappearance. I made it look like Ophion had grabbed me. I didn't even know where I was running to. But I couldn't stop thinking of the babies—I knew it was twins, by that point—and how I would do anything to keep them out of my father's hands. Out of Sandriel's hands. I knew, deep down, what sort of monsters I served. I had always known. And I didn't want to be like them. Not just for the babies' sake, but my own. So I ran."

"And that's when the Ocean Queen found you?" His voice was hoarse.

"I found her. When I finally paused to breathe, I remembered what some rebels had claimed while I . . . interrogated them. That the ocean itself would come to help them. It seemed strange enough that I took a chance. I walked into a known rebel base and surrendered. I begged to be taken to the ocean."

He couldn't imagine what she'd felt in that moment—knowing her children's lives hung in the balance.

"Their highest commanders understood, and got me onto the *Depth Charger*. The Ocean Queen welcomed me, but with a caveat. I could stay on her ship, bear the babies, and remain for a time. But in exchange for her protection, and the continued protection of my children . . . I had to go back. I would spin a lie about being interrogated and held prisoner for more than two years, and I would go back. Work my way up in the Asteri's esteem, gain their trust. I would feed any intel to Ophion—and by extension, the Ocean Queen."

"And you could not see your sons."

"No. I would not see my sons again. At least, not until the Ocean Queen allowed me to."

"That's terrible."

"It kept them safe."

"And kept you in her service."

"Yes. I tried to save the rebels who crossed my path, though."

"Was it your idea or hers to save them?" He didn't realize how vital her answer was until he asked the question.

"I told you, my eyes had been opened. And while I had to play the part of interrogator and loyal servant, I did everything I could to mitigate the damage. There were agents who were about to talk, to spill vital secrets. Those, I had to kill. 'Accidents' during torture. But I gave them swift, merciful deaths. The ones who held out, or who stood a chance . . . I tried to get them out. Sometimes it didn't work."

"Like Sofie Renast."

"Like Sofie Renast," she said quietly. "I did not intend for her to drown. The mistake in timing . . . I carry that."

He took her hand—slowly, making sure she'd allow the touch. "What happened when you returned?"

"Pollux confessed his feelings. Said he'd been frantic to find me for the two years I'd been gone. That he'd slaughtered countless rebels trying to find me. The old Lidia would have slept with him. And I knew it would make my cover complete. The rest is history."

She lifted her gaze to his. "I'm not wholly innocent, you see," she said. "Had it not been for my sons, I might very well have become the person the world believes me to be, forever ignoring that small voice whispering that it was wrong."

"It must have been so . . . lonely," he said.

Surprise lit her eyes at his understanding. It shamed him. "Then you came along," she said. "This nearly inept, reckless agent."

He snickered.

She smiled. "And you saw me. For the first time, you saw *me*.

I could talk to you as I hadn't spoken to anyone. You reminded me that I was—I am—alive. I hadn't felt that way in a very long time."

He scanned her face. Saw past that remarkable beauty and into the burning soul inside.

"Don't look at me like that," she whispered.

"Like what?" he murmured.

But she shook her head and got to her feet, walking to the door.

Ruhn caught up to her before she could reach for the knob. "Lidia."

She paused, but didn't look at him.

He laid a hand on her cheek. Gently turned her face back to his. Her skin was so soft, so warm. "Lidia," he said roughly. "Finding out who you are . . . it fucked with my head. To know you're the Hind, but also Lidia—also Day. *My* Day. But now . . ." He swallowed.

"Now?" Her gaze dipped to his mouth.

His cock tightened at that gaze. He said, voice near guttural, "Now I don't fucking care who you are, so long as you're mine." Her eyes shot to his, again full of surprise. "Because I'm yours, Day. I'm fucking yours."

Her face crumpled. And he couldn't stand the sight of her crying, the relief and joy. So he leaned forward, bringing his mouth to hers.

The kiss didn't start sweetly. It was openmouthed—teeth clacking, tongues clashing. Her hands wrapped around his neck, and he hauled her to him, pulling her flush against his chest.

Yes, yes, yes.

His hand coasted over her ass and he squeezed, drawing a moan from deep in her throat. She pulled her mouth from his, though. "Ruhn."

He stilled. "What?" If she wanted to stop, he'd stop. Whatever she wanted, he'd give her.

She ran her fingers over his pecs. He shuddered as she asked, "Are you sure?"

"Yes," he breathed, nipping at her bottom lip. He guided her toward the bed, then onto it. She traced her finger over where his lip ring had been ripped out. Then his brow ring.

"I couldn't stand it," she whispered, putting her mouth to his brow. "I couldn't . . ." She began shaking. He tightened his arms around her.

"I'm here," he said. "We made it."

She trembled harder, as if all that she had experienced and done were now breaking free in aftershocks.

"I'm here," he said again, and leaned down to kiss the side of her neck. "I'm here." He kissed below her ear. Her hands came up, caressing a line down his back. She stopped shaking. "I'm here," he said, kissing the base of her throat. Tugging down the zipper on the front of her tactical bodysuit.

She wasn't wearing a bra. Her breasts, lush, high palmfuls tipped in rosy pink, spilled out into his hands. He swore, and couldn't stop himself from dipping his head to suck one into his mouth.

She inhaled sharply, and the sound was kindling to his cock. He grazed his teeth over her nipple, tugging lightly.

Her hands wandered around his waist, aiming toward his front, and—yeah, not happening. He wanted to explore first. Not removing his mouth from that delicious breast, he grabbed her wrists in one hand and pinned them above her head, settling more firmly between her legs.

She flinched.

It was barely more than a flicker, but he felt it. The slight tightening in her body. He halted, raised his head. Looked down at her. At the hands he'd pinned—

That *fucker.*

Ruhn let go immediately.

He'd kill him. He'd rip Pollux limb from limb, feather by feather for putting that flinch there, for hurting her—

Her eyes softened. She laid her palms on either side of his face and whispered, "Just an old memory."

One that shouldn't be there. One that Pollux had put there.

"Ruhn."

He took her wrists in his hands and gently pressed a kiss to each one. Then laid them on her chest, hands over her heart, kissing her as he did so.

"Ruhn," she said again, but he sprawled out beside her. Looped an arm over her middle.

"Stay here with me tonight," he said quietly. A tendril of his shadows curled around the flames of the sconces, dimming them. "No sex. Just . . . stay with me."

He could feel her eyes on him in the dark. But then she moved—zippers hissing as she shrugged out of her clothes. He tugged off his pants, nestling under the blankets.

Then her warm, soft, lush body curled into his.

And yeah, he wanted to be inside of her so badly he had to grind his teeth, but her scent soothed him. Steadied him. He slid a hand over her bare waist, tucking her in close, her breasts flush against his chest. His hand drifted lower, to her ass, and all it would have taken was a shift in angle and he would have been between her legs.

But this wasn't about sex. And as their breathing evened out, as they stared at each other in the near-dark, he'd never felt more seen.

Eventually, her eyes closed. Her breathing deepened.

But Ruhn lay awake, holding her tight, and did not let go until dawn.

"Is that a *laser*?" Tharion shouted as rock crumbled from where the light had sliced into it, the cave-in now cutting off access to the two Fae Kings, Flynn and Dec, and the Murder Twins. And a bunch of ghouls. But Bryce ordered, "The river!"

"What?" Hunt barked. Bryce was already running for the dark, rushing water.

"Jump in," Bryce called, starlight bobbing with each step.

"Teleport us across!" Hunt countered. Flynn and Declan had been stranded on the other side of that cave-in, and they needed to figure out how to get them away from the kings and the twins—

"Jump in *now*," Bryce ordered, and didn't wait before she ran for the ledge. Hunt grabbed for her, to stop her from this pure insanity—

She leapt. Right into the river. He could have sworn the starlight glowed brighter as she did, as if agreeing with her decision.

Then the light in her chest went out.

And in the sudden dark, with only Hunt's lightning flickering around them, the ghouls began to hiss, drawing nearer, as if coming through the rock itself.

"River," Tharion said, grabbing Sathia and racing for it. He dove, and she shrieked as he dragged her with him. The roar of the river swallowed the sound—and them—in half a second.

There was no choice left, really. Hunt met Baxian's stare and saw his own annoyance mirrored there. They could have taken the kings. Bryce surely knew that. And yet . . .

If Bryce had chosen to cause a cave-in, to block the kings but not kill them, to opt for going downriver instead of teleporting across . . . she hadn't told him why, likely due to their fight. She hadn't told him, which meant his mate probably no longer trusted him, and he had no idea how to start fixing that—

"Athalar," Baxian growled. "Snap out of it!"

Hunt blinked. He'd been frozen in place, reeling. Baxian's eyes were wide. Hunt shook off his shame. It pissed him off to no end, but Bryce did nothing without reason.

Hunt didn't wait to see if Baxian followed before he tucked his wings in tight and leapt.

56

Hunt shuddered with cold, teeth chattering, as he hauled himself onto a dark bank illuminated dimly by Bryce's star.

After a rushing, disorienting downhill journey, the river had calmed and emptied into the pool around them, a small bank providing the lone path of escape. Tharion was already near Bryce, a shivering Sathia between them, and Baxian was just crawling onto the shore a few feet from Hunt, dark wings dragging on the rock beside him.

Hunt exploded at his mate, "What the *fuck*?"

"Later, Athalar," Bryce murmured, turning from the pool and facing a natural archway of stone, with a tunnel beyond. Her star blazed bright—brighter than it had upriver.

"No, *now*," he warned, scrambling to his feet, water sloshing from his boots, his waterlogged wings impossibly heavy. "You say we're all in this together, making decisions *together*, and then you go and pull that shit?"

She whirled, teeth bared. "Well, *someone* has to lead."

His temper flared. "What the fuck does that mean?"

"It means that I'm not letting my fear and guilt swallow me whole." The others stayed silent, several feet away. "It means that I'm putting all that shit aside and focusing on what needs to be done!"

"And I'm not?" He splayed his arms, motioning to the caves around them. Lightning flickered over his hands. "I'm here, aren't I?"

"Do you even *want* to be?" Her voice echoed off the rocks. "Because it seems like your fear of the consequences outweighs your desire to defeat the Asteri."

"It *does*," he snarled, unable to stop the words from coming out. "It will be hard to enjoy freedom if we're *dead*."

"I'd rather die trying to bring them down than spend the rest of my life knowing the truth and doing nothing."

He could barely hear above the roaring in his head. "Everyone we love will die, too. You're willing to risk that? Your mom and dad? Cooper? Syrinx? Fury and June? You're willing to let them be tortured and killed?"

She stiffened, shaking with anger.

Hunt took a deep breath, collecting himself, and shook the water out of his wings. "Look, I'm sorry." He took another deep breath. "I know this isn't the time to pick a fight. This whole thing might be a colossal fucking mistake, might get everyone we know killed, but . . . I'll go along with it. I have your back. I promise."

She blinked. Then blinked again. "That's not good enough for me," she said quietly. "That isn't good enough for me—that you'll just go along with it."

"Well, get used to the feeling," he said.

"Get over yourself, *Umbra Mortis*." With that, she stormed into the misty gloom, star illuminating the way.

"Yeesh," Tharion said lightly to Sathia and Baxian, but Hunt didn't smile as they continued after Bryce, trailing water everywhere.

"How the fuck did you know to get out here, anyway?" Baxian asked Bryce, likely trying to lighten the tension now filling the caves as surely as the mist smothering them.

"Because I've been here before," Bryce said, her voice still a little rough around the edges.

Even Hunt's anger eased enough for him to wonder if she'd hit her head in the river. Especially as they approached a solid wall of rock.

Bryce pushed a hand against the wall. A wedge of an archway opened beneath her palm. Her starlight flared, lighting up the wall and the carving that surrounded the triangular doorway.

An eight-pointed star. Twin to the scar on her chest.

"These caves," Bryce said, pointedly not looking at him, "are nearly identical to the ones I walked through in the original world of the Fae." She took a step into the star's doorway. "The river there flowed throughout them—provided shortcuts. The Wyrm used them to sneak up on us. But my star glowed brighter whenever it wanted me to go a certain way, like it does here. It guided me into one of the rivers in the Fae world. I listened to it, jumped in, and it led me down to a passage that took me exactly where I needed to be to learn Silene's truth. Just now, my star was glowing brighter when I faced downriver. I figured this river might lead down to another passage. Maybe one that's got another bit of truth. Anything to help against the Asteri."

"That was an insane leap of logic," Tharion said. "And what about Flynn and Dec? The Autumn King and Morven and the Murder Twins still have them, those fucking *ghouls* still have them—"

"That confrontation will come." Bryce walked calmly into the waiting darkness and swirling mist, adjusting Truth-Teller at her side. "But not yet."

They had no choice but to follow her. "What does it all mean?" Baxian asked Hunt, almost plaintively.

Hunt cast aside his lingering anger and kept his focus pinned on his mate. "I think we're about to find out."

Flynn and Dec still weren't at breakfast the next morning. And Ruhn's quick jog through the castle and its grounds revealed no sign of them. Or of the Murder Twins. Just some Fae nobles and servants, unsure what to make of him, whether to sneer or bow. He ignored them, and was hurrying back to his room when Lidia emerged from it.

She took one look at his face and asked, "What's wrong?"

He didn't wonder how she'd guessed it—she'd had to be

excellent at reading people her whole adult life. Her survival had depended on it.

Ruhn checked that his various blades were in place. "Flynn and Dec . . . I don't think they're here. And neither are my creep cousins. Or Morven."

Her eyes sharpened with caution. "It might be unconnected."

"It's not. My friends don't bail on me." And he'd been so fucking distracted by her, by wanting her, that he hadn't let himself think about it.

She put a hand on his arm. "Where do you think they went?"

Ruhn sucked in a breath. "Morven and the twins have to be involved. They must have taken Flynn and Dec to the Cave of Princes."

"To make a move against Bryce?"

Ruhn's stomach churned. "Maybe. But I think Morven took them as bait—for me. He expects me to follow."

"If it's a trap, then we shouldn't rush in—"

"My friends rushed to save me from the Asteri dungeons," he said, holding her beautiful gaze. "You found them, and they ran to help. I can't leave them in Morven's hands."

"I wasn't suggesting we leave them," she said, striding to her own room. She left the door open so he could see her as she grabbed two guns off her night table and holstered them at her thighs. "I'm saying let's think through a strategy before we go rescue them."

Something burned in Ruhn's chest, and he didn't dare name it.

But he felt it all the same as they armed themselves and went to save his friends.

Hunt didn't let his guard down, not for one second. Even with every word of his fight with Quinlan hanging in the air like the residue of fireworks. Lightning flickered in one fist; his sword was clenched in another. He didn't put either aside as they entered a chamber at the other end of the tunnel.

He scanned its intricately carved walls of black stone, the exquisite landscapes depicted there, as they stepped in—

Stone grated against itself, and before Hunt could whirl, faster even than his lightning, the triangular door shut behind them. Tharion, a step ahead, let out a low whistle.

Baxian just swapped a look with Hunt that told him the Hel-hound suspected the same thing he did: only Bryce could get that door to open. It wasn't a calming thought. Not as Hunt surveyed what lay ahead.

The lone object in the chamber was a sarcophagus carved from white marble, the hue striking against the deep black of the stone walls. A statue of an armored Fae male lay atop the sarcophagus, hands clasped around a missing object.

Bryce nodded to it. "That must be where the Starsword lies when not in use." Her voice was flat, as if drained from their argument.

Sathia staggered a step closer. "Prince Pelias's tomb," she breathed.

"Ruhn told me his creepster descendants line the walls of the main passages in here," Bryce said, pointing to the only other way out: another archway of stone across the chamber, barely visible through the mists. She adjusted the Starsword across her back, and a hand fidgeted with Truth-Teller at her side—like the blades were bothering her.

Hunt surveyed the domed space, examining the stories told on the walls: an archipelago nestled above a sea of starlight, an idyllic, serene land—all that the world believed Avallen to be. "I don't see anything about the Starsword or Truth-Teller, let alone how to unify them," Hunt admitted. "Or the mists. The islands are here, but nothing else." Maybe this was a dead end for information.

"There could be something out in the main passage," Tharion offered.

But Bryce approached the sarcophagus. Peered down at the perfectly carved, handsome face of the first Starborn Prince.

"Hello, you rapist fuck," she said, her voice cold with fury.

Hunt barely breathed. He wondered if Urd were watching, if the heaviness in the room wasn't the mists, but rather the god-dess's presence, having guided them here.

"You thought you won," Bryce whispered to the sarcophagus. "But she got one over on you in the end. She got the last laugh."

"Bryce?" Hunt ventured.

She looked up from Pelias's carved rendering, and there was nothing of her human heart in those eyes. Only icy, Fae hatred for the long-dead male before her.

Offering a rope of neutral ground, Hunt said, "Can you, uh, fill us in?"

Yet it was Tharion who gestured to the empty death chamber. "Maybe Pelias built another chamber around here that's actually got something about the sword and dagger and that portal to nowhere—"

"No," Bryce said quietly. "We're exactly where we need to be." She pointed to the floor, the carving of rivers of stars winding throughout. "And this place wasn't built by Pelias. He had nothing to do with these tunnels, the carvings." She laid a hand on the floor. Her starlight flowed through the carvings in the stone, the walls, the ceiling—

What had looked like etched seas or rivers of stars now filled in with starlight, became . . . alive. Moving, cascading, coursing. A secret illustration, only for those with the gifts and vision to see it.

The rippling river of starlight flowed right to the sarcophagus in the center of the chamber. Swirled around it like an eddy.

Bryce threw herself against the coffin, legs straining as she pushed—

And the sarcophagus slid away. Revealing a small, secret staircase beneath.

Bryce panted for a moment, and then smiled grimly. "This place was built by Helena."

57

The sword and knife pulsed more strongly with each step downward into the secret stairwell. Like they wanted to be here—*needed* to be here. Just when Bryce thought she honestly might chuck them off her for a moment of relief, her feet touched the bottom.

Amid the mists, trickling water sounded from a narrow stream in the center of the chamber. Some offshoot of the river a level up, filtered through the black rock. And beside the stream, a black ewer and bowl rested upon an etching of an eight-pointed star.

"What the fuck is this?" Hunt murmured, sticking close to her. As if, despite their fight, he still wanted to protect her. But maybe it was that need to protect her that was leading to the guilt, the fear devouring him whole.

She'd meant every word she'd said to him—it wasn't good enough for him to go along with things. She needed Hunt, all of him, fighting at her side. She didn't know how to convey that. How to make him understand and embrace that.

Her teeth chattered with the cold, but even that seemed secondary as Bryce surveyed the stream and pitcher and bowl. The eight-pointed star. Two of its points had been hollowed out into slits—one small, one larger.

There was nothing else in the room.

"You don't know what this is?" she asked Hunt. She could play Situation Normal with him—at least for now.

"I'm getting really fucking sick of surprises," Tharion burst out, arriving at the bottom of the stairs with Sathia in tow.

Bryce held up a finger, and let her light condense there.

"And then there's *that*," Tharion said, but Bryce held Hunt's stare as she pointed it at the ground and sliced a small line. An inch, and that was it.

"Helena used the same gifts to carve this place as her sister, Silene, used in their home world. But there's one big difference. One reason why she chose this place for the caves."

She knelt, and rubbed her fingers through the debris she'd left on either side of the cut. Brought it up to Hunt's face. "Do you recognize it?"

Hunt studied the black, glittering dust on her fingers and paled. "That's black salt."

Bryce nodded slowly. Baxian blew out a breath that sounded suspiciously like *Oh fuck.*

"These caves are made entirely of black salt," Bryce said. She'd seen it as soon as the ghoul had gouged lines in the wall. Knew its smell, its rotting, oily feel. A taste of it had confirmed her suspicions.

Hunt frowned. "You think Helena was trying to summon her sister from their home world?"

"No," Bryce said, shaking her head. "She sent Silene back to be safe—she was an asshole, but she would never have done anything to jeopardize that."

"So what is this place, then?" Tharion asked.

It was Sathia who got it first. "It's to summon demons. To commune with Hel."

Stunned silence rocked the room.

"They were her only remaining allies," Bryce explained.

Helena might have done some unforgivable things, but Bryce could admit the female had been a fighter. Until the very end, if this chamber was any indication.

Hunt asked, wings twitching, "But why make an entire underground warren of caves? And why dedicate it to her rapist husband?"

Bryce shrugged. "As a reason to keep coming here. She built him a tomb that would last, where his sword might lie forever until a worthy successor came along."

"You can't possibly know that," Hunt said carefully. Like he was afraid of getting into another fight.

It did something to her heart, that caution, but Bryce said, "The caves are nearly identical to the ones in her home world—caves she grew up navigating. And Avallen, like her childhood home, is wreathed in mist. It's a thin place as well. Judging by all the mists in here, maybe Avallen, these caves, are an even *stronger* thin place than the one in the Fae world. The Prison—the court it had been before that . . . Vesperus said that she chose it originally because it was a thin place, good for traveling between worlds. Theia knew this, too. She must have told Helena."

Tharion cleared his throat. "So Helena made all these caves just to have a private line to Hel?"

"Pretty much," Bryce said. "Avallen had everything she needed. But for her to have built the caves this way suggests resources. Helena couldn't have done it in secret. She had to have had approval from Pelias. And what better way to hide this, to protect it through the ages, than to wrap it up in a temple to the patriarchy?" Bryce pointed to the sarcophagus room above them. To the bones she'd have liked to scatter into a septic tank. "She knew the Fae males would never tear this place down or disturb it—for fuck's sake, Morven refuses to update Avallen in *any way* because he wants it to stay the same as it was when Pelias was alive. Helena knew these males well. She knew if she hid this under here, it'd be preserved, and remain undisturbed."

"Okay, assuming for a moment that we believe all that," Tharion said, "how do you know this was some secret chamber she used to commune with Hel, of all places? What do the pitcher and bowl mean?"

"She'd get thirsty with all the salt down here?" Baxian quipped, and Hunt grunted.

But Sathia walked up to the stream. "That water filters straight through the black salt, and this chamber is thick with it." She met Bryce's stare, brows knotting. "Can you summon a demon if you drink water laced with black salt?"

"I've never heard of anything like that, even during my demon-hunting years," Hunt said.

"If Helena was summoning demons here, someone would have noticed," Baxian said. "The temperature would have dropped enough that anyone else in the caves would have felt it, even a level above."

"Maybe she wasn't summoning them *here*," Bryce said, walking to the pitcher and bowl, to the eight-pointed star they sat upon. The slits in two of the points had been deeply carved—too deep for her to see how far into the rock they went. But Bryce tapped the side of her head. "But in here."

"What?" Hunt asked.

Bryce knelt and dipped the ewer into the dark, icy water. The vessel and bowl, too, had been carved from black salt. "The Starborn could mind-speak. Still can." She nodded up toward the river a level above, with the Murder Twins lurking somewhere on its other side. "Maybe the salt helped her mind-speak with Hel. Maybe someone in Hel can tell us how to kill the Asteri. Apollion himself ate Sirius . . . Maybe he's had the answer all along."

Hunt blurted, "Don't you dare—"

Bryce lifted the jug to her lips, but lightning smashed the vessel apart before she could drink.

She whirled, temper searing through her.

Hunt was glowing with lightning, furious as he advanced on her. "Do *not* drink from that—"

"This is *not* the time to go Alphahole!"

"—without me," he finished.

Bryce could only gape at her mate as he grabbed the drinking bowl and held it out to her.

Ready to follow her into Hel.

* * *

Together, then. As their powers, their souls, were linked, so they'd drink the salt-laced water together.

"This . . . might be a very bad idea," Tharion said as Bryce and Hunt sat facing each other, knee to knee and hand to hand.

Hunt was inclined to agree. But he said, "Apollion appeared to both me and to Bryce in dream states. Maybe he was using the same communication method he'd used with Helena."

"So, what," Baxian said as Sathia gathered the water in the drinking bowl. "You're going to drink and hope you pass out and . . . talk to Hel? Ask them for answers about the sword and knife that they might have somehow forgotten to tell you until now?"

"Helena left this here," Bryce said, holding Hunt's stare. No doubt or fear—only steely focus gleamed in his mate's eyes. "Just as Silene left everything in the caves of her home world. For someone to find. Someone who could bear the Starsword, and whose starlight would lead them down here. Someone who might also have learned the truth . . . and known where to look." Bryce turned her gaze to the ceiling, the stairs upward. "I think Helena left this to help us."

"Helena and Silene weren't . . . good people," Baxian warned.

"No, but they hated the Asteri," Bryce said. "They wanted to get rid of them as much as we do." And it was hope that brimmed in her eyes then, so bright it nearly stole Hunt's breath away. For a moment, not even a full heartbeat, he nearly believed they might succeed. "If this buys us a shot, whatever it might be, we have to try. I want answers. I want the truth."

Bryce lifted the bowl to her lips and drank.

Bryce was falling backward, and yet not moving. Her body remained kneeling, yet her soul fell, icing over, into the dark, into nothing and nowhere. A presence around her, beside her, flickered with lightning. Hunt.

He was with her. Soul-falling alongside her.

It was a leap. All of it was a leap, but she had to believe that Urd had led her here. That Helena had been as smart as her sister, and would have fought the male who abused her until the very end. That Helena had played the game not only for her lifetime, but for future generations.

Hoping that maybe one day, millennia from her death, another female might come along with starlight—Theia's starlight—in her veins. Passed down not from Pelias, but from Helena herself. Theia's starlight.

Passed down to her. Bryce Adelaide Quinlan.

And maybe she wasn't who Helena or Silene would have chosen, certainly not with their anti-human bullshit, but that wasn't her problem.

The falling sensation stopped. There was only blackness, frigid and dry. Her starlight flickered, a pale, feeble light in the impenetrable dark. A hand found hers, and she didn't need to look to know Hunt stood beside her in . . . whatever this place was. This dreamworld.

Two blue lights glowed in the distance, closing in on them. Hunt's fingers tightened on hers in warning. His lightning flickered. But the lights drew nearer. And nearer. And when they crossed into the light of her star . . .

Aidas was smiling faintly—joy and hope brightening his remarkable eyes. "It seems you got a little lost on your way to find me, Bryce Quinlan. But welcome to Hel."

58

It took two days of working without rest to help the people of the Meadows. But Ithan didn't mind, barely thought about the need to go to Avallen to find Sofie's body or the exhaustion as he dug through the rubble, or carried out the dead or dying, or held down the wounded long enough for Hypaxia or another medwitch to save them. And still there were more. So many more humans, hurt or dead.

There was no sign of the Governor, but the 33rd showed up, at least. The Aux—Fae and a scant number of wolves—arrived soon after. Ithan kept clear of the latter, both to avoid conflict and to avoid being spotted by any Asteri sympathizers who might have come to gloat over the ruins.

But he kept his head down. Kept working. Doing what little he could to help or clear or at least respectfully move the fallen.

There were no Sailings, not for the humans. There'd never been Sailings for them. So their bodies were laid out in rows upon rows inside the lobby of the nearest intact office building.

Barely a dozen wolves had shown up. Only the equivalent of two packs had come to help. It was a disgrace.

Something in this world had to change. And as Ithan piled up the dead, as he laid child after child in that building lobby, he realized that change had to start with him.

Make your brother proud.

He had to get to Avallen. Had to get Sigrid back. Only with her, with an alternate Fendyr heir to lead the wolves . . . Only then could changes begin.

A new future. For all of them.

For the first five minutes, Tharion didn't stop monitoring Bryce's and Hunt's breathing.

Baxian and Tharion had caught them as they'd suddenly toppled backward, unconscious, and laid them gently on the black salt ground. They didn't move. Only the rise and fall of their chests showed any signs of life. Whatever was happening, it indeed took place in their minds.

Tharion, Sathia, and Baxian sat a few cautious feet away from their friends. "How long do we give them?" Sathia asked. "Until we try to wake them, I mean."

Tharion swapped a look with Baxian. "Fifteen minutes?"

"Give them thirty," Baxian said. Then added, "We'll keep monitoring them, though."

Silence fell, interrupted only by their breathing and the sound of the stream trickling through the cavern. Beside Tharion, Sathia was turning the black salt drinking bowl over in her slender hands, again and again. Lost in thought.

"You ever done anything like this?" Baxian asked, noting her unease.

"No," she said. "I'm not the adventurous sort."

"Have you gone through your Ordeal?" Baxian asked.

She nodded shallowly. Not a good experience, then.

Part of Tharion wanted to ask about it, but he said, "What happened with you and your brother to put such a divide between you?"

Her eyes slashed to his. "What happened between you and the River Queen to put such a high bounty on your head?"

He gave her an indolent smile. "You don't know?"

"I've pieced bits of it together. You upset her prissy daughter, and had to run. But what did you do to upset her in the first place?"

Tharion drummed his fingers on the cold stone floor. "I wanted to call off our engagement. She didn't."

Sathia straightened. "You were *engaged*? To the River Queen's daughter?"

"For ten years."

She set the bowl on the ground. "And she didn't realize that after ten years, you didn't want to marry her?"

Tharion glanced to where Bryce and Hunt lay, deathly still. "I don't really feel like talking about this."

Yet Sathia pushed, "So you called it off, but she . . . tried to keep it?"

"And keep me. Beneath. Forever."

The dismay on her face set him laughing. Laughter was the sole alternative to crying. "Yeah."

"But you could have swum away."

"You can't just *swim away* from the River Queen. She denies her daughter nothing. She'd have locked me in my humanoid form, to ensure I couldn't swim out."

Again, that dismay on her face. "She'd do that to one of her own kind? Destroy your fins to confine you?"

"She isn't mer," he said. "She's an elemental. And yes, she does it to punish mer all the time."

"That's barbaric."

"So is treating Fae females like broodmares and forcing them to marry."

Sathia only angled her head. "You ran away from marriage to the River Queen's daughter . . . only to wind up married to a stranger."

He knew Baxian was listening closely, though the Helhound kept his focus on Bryce and Athalar. "It seemed like a better option."

"It doesn't make sense."

He sighed. And maybe because they were on some cursed island in the middle of the Haldren, maybe because they were hundreds of feet underground with only Cthona to witness it, he said, "My little sister. Lesia. She, ah, died last year."

Sathia seemed taken aback at the turn the conversation had taken. "I'm sorry, Tharion," she said gently. She sounded sincere.

Baxian murmured, "I didn't know that. My condolences, Ketos."

Tharion couldn't stop the memory of Lesia from flashing bright in his mind. Red-haired and beautiful and alive. His chest ached, threatening to cave in on itself.

But it was better than the other memory of her—of the photographs her murderer had snapped of her body. What he'd done to her when Tharion hadn't been there to protect her.

Tharion went on, "I know you and Flynn have a . . . tense relationship. But you're still his little sister. You were in trouble. And I knew that if Lesia had been in the same spot, I'd have wanted a decent male to help her out."

Sathia's eyes softened. "Well, thank you. If we make it through all this"—she waved a hand to the caves, the world beyond—"I'll see if there's a way to liberate you from this . . . situation."

"Trust me, it's in my best interest to stay married to you until the River Queen's daughter moves on to some other poor bastard. If I'm single . . ."

"She'll come after you."

Tharion nodded. "It's cowardly and pathetic, I know. And I mean, her mother will probably come after me and kill me anyway. But at least I won't have to spend my life as a royal concubine."

"All right." Sathia squared her shoulders. "Marriage it is, then." She gave him a small smile. "For now." Then she glanced to Bryce and Hunt. "You think they're really in Hel?"

"Part of me hopes yes, the other part hopes no," Tharion answered.

"They're in Hel," Baxian said quietly.

Sathia twisted toward him. "How do you know?"

Baxian pointed to their slumbering friends. "Look."

Bryce and Hunt lay peacefully on the black salt ground, hands entwined, their bodies covered in a thin layer of frost.

The black boat that Aidas led Bryce and Hunt into was a cross between the one that had brought them into Avallen and the ones that carried bodies to the Bone Quarter. But in lieu of a stag's head, it was a stag's skull at the prow, greenish flame dancing in its eyes as it sailed through the cave. The eerie green light illuminated black rock carved into pillars and buildings, walkways and temples.

Ancient. And empty.

Bryce had never seen a place so void of life. So . . . still. Even the Bone Quarter had a sense of being lived in, albeit by the dead. But here, nothing stirred.

The river was wide, yet placid. The lap of water against the hull seemed to echo too loudly over the stones, over the ceiling so far above that it faded into the gloom.

"It's like a city of the dead," Hunt murmured, draping a wing around Bryce.

Aidas turned from where he stood at the prow, holding in his hands a long pole that he'd used to guide them. "That's because it is." He gestured with a pale hand to the buildings and temples and avenues. "This is where our beloved dead come to rest, with all the comforts of life around them."

"But we're not . . . here-here," Bryce said. "Right? We're just dreaming?"

"In a sense," Aidas said. "Your physical body remains in your world." He glanced over a shoulder. "In Helena's cave."

"You knew about it this whole time," Hunt accused.

Aidas's eyes gleamed. "Would you have believed me?"

This close to Hunt, Bryce felt every muscle in his body tense. Her mate said, "The truth might have been a good start toward that."

Before Aidas could answer, the boat approached a small quay leading to what appeared to be a temple. A figure emerged from between the pillars of the temple and descended its front steps. Golden-haired, golden-skinned.

Hunt's lightning sparked, illuminating the whole city and river.

Apollion lifted a hand. Pure, sizzling lightning danced around it, arcing out to meet Hunt's.

"Welcome, son," said the Prince of the Pit.

59

Every word eddied from Hunt's head. Apollion, Prince of the Pit, had called him—

Bryce leapt out of the boat and onto the shore, chest blazing with starlight. "What the Hel did you just say?"

No matter what tension or argument might lie between them, she'd go down swinging for him. Hunt jumped after her, wings steadying him as his boots hit the loose black stones. Apollion had called him *son*—

The Prince of the Pit swept down the stairs, his every step seeming to echo through the vast cavern. Another male in dark armor followed him, his tightly curled hair almost hidden by his war helmet.

"Thanatos," Bryce said, drawing up short, pebbles skittering under her neon-pink sneakers.

Hunt had enough sense left in him to get to his mate's side, but Aidas was already there, lifting a hand. "We are here to talk. There will be no violence."

From within the ornate helm, Thanatos's eyes blazed with murderous rage.

"Do as he says," Apollion ordered the Prince of the Ravine, halting at the base of the temple steps.

Hunt's lightning twined up his forearms, ready to strike as

he growled at the Prince of the Pit, "What the fuck did you mean by—"

He didn't finish his words as Aidas reached to touch Bryce's shoulder. Acting on instinct, Hunt lunged, intending to shove the Prince of the Chasm away from his mate.

He went right through the demon prince.

Hunt stumbled and lifted his hands. His fingers shimmered faintly with a pale, bluish light. Bryce had the same aura around her.

They were ghosts here.

Apollion let out a low chuckle as Hunt backed toward Bryce's side once more. "You will find that you cannot harm us, nor we you, in such a state." His deep voice pealed like thunder off the walls.

Son. It wasn't possible—

"Helena planned it that way," Aidas said. His gaze remained fixed on Bryce while he explained, "During my time with Theia, Helena was a quiet girl, but she always listened."

"You spoke too much," Thanatos snapped.

Aidas ignored him. "Helena learned black salt would allow her to commune with us while protecting her mind and her soul."

Just like the barrier of it that Bryce had sprinkled in her apartment, that day she'd summoned Aidas. When Hunt had still thought her a frivolous party girl, playing with fire.

"Fine," Hunt cut in. "Great, we're protected." He eyed the Prince of the Pit. His very bones shook, but he forced himself past his fear, his dread. "What the fuck did you mean by calling me son?"

Thanatos scoffed. "You are no son of his." He yanked off his war helmet, cradling it under an arm. "If anything, you are mine."

Hunt's knees buckled. *"What?"*

"Let us sit and be civilized about this," Aidas said to Bryce, but she was peering into the shadows of the temple looming at the top of the steps.

"I think we're good here," she hedged. Hunt cleared his reeling thoughts enough to follow her line of vision.

He saw them, then. The dogs. Their milky eyes glowed from the gloom between the pillars.

"They will not harm you," Aidas said, nodding toward the hounds that looked an awful lot like the Shepherd that Bryce and Hunt had fought in the Bone Quarter. "They are Thanatos's companions."

Hunt reached for his lightning, little that it could do in this insubstantial form. It zapped against his fingers, normally a familiar, comforting presence, but . . .

No one had ever known who had sired him. Where this lightning had come from.

"My concern exactly," Bryce said, not taking her attention off the hounds. She nodded to Thanatos. "He eats *souls*—"

"The Temple of Chaos is a sacred place," Apollion said sharply. "We shall never defile it with violence." The words rumbled like thunder again.

Hunt sized up Apollion, then Thanatos. What the fucking *fuck*—

But Thanatos sniffed toward Bryce, almost as canine as the hounds in the shadows, and said, "Your starlight smells . . . fresher."

The hunger lacing the male's words stilled Hunt's chaotic mind—honing him into a weapon primed for violence. He didn't give a shit if he never got answers about his parentage. If that asshole made one move against Bryce, ghostly forms or no—

Bryce said nonchalantly, "New deodorant."

"No," Thanatos said, missing the joke entirely, "I can smell it on your spirit. I am the Prince of Souls—such things are known to me. Your power has been touched by something new."

Bryce rolled her eyes, but for a heartbeat, Hunt wondered if Thanatos was right: Bryce had explained how the prism in the Autumn King's office had revealed her light to now be laced with darkness, as if it had become the fading light of day, of twilight—

"We don't have much time," Aidas said irritably. "The dreaming draft will only last so long. Please—come into the temple." He inclined his head in a half bow. "On my honor, no harm shall come to you."

Hunt opened his mouth to say the Prince of the Chasm's honor meant shit, but Bryce's whiskey eyes assessed Aidas in a long, unhurried sweep. And then she said, "All right."

Pushing aside every raging thought and question for the moment, Hunt kept one eye on the exit behind them as they traded the pebbled shore for the smooth temple steps. As they walked up those steps and entered a space that was a near-mirror to temples back home—indeed, its layout was identical to the last temple Hunt had stood in: Urd's Temple.

He shut down the memory of Pippa Spetsos's ambush, the desperate scramble for their lives. How they'd hidden behind the altar, barely escaping. In lieu of the black stone altar in the center of the temple, a bottomless pit was the main focal point. Five chairs of carved black wood encircled it.

Hunt and Bryce claimed the chairs closest to the stairs behind them—closest to the river and the boat still idling at the shore. Aidas took the one on Bryce's other side, sitting with a smooth, feline grace. The braziers bounced their bluish light off his blond hair.

Apollion's eyes glimmered like coals as he said to Hunt, "I am disappointed to see that you have not yet freed yourself from the black crown, Orion Athalar."

"Someone explain what the fuck that is," Hunt snapped. Of all the things he'd ever imagined for his life, sitting in a circle with three Princes of Hel hadn't been anywhere on the list.

"The black crowns were collars in Hel," Thanatos answered darkly. His powerful body seemed primed to leap across that pit to attack. Hunt monitored his every breath. "Spells, crafted by the Asteri to enslave us. They were a binding, one the Asteri adapted in their next war—upon Midgard."

Hunt turned to Aidas. "You seemed surprised to see one on me that first time we met. Why?"

But before Aidas could begin, Apollion answered, "Because the Princes of Hel cannot be contained by the black crowns. The Asteri learned that—it was their downfall. As you were made by Hel's princes, it should not be able to hold you."

Made by them? By these fuckers?

Hunt had no idea what to say, what to do as everything in his life swirled and diluted, his heartbeat ratcheting up to a thunderous beat. "I—I don't . . ."

"Start talking," Bryce snapped at Apollion, scooting her chair an inch or two closer to Hunt's. Not from fear, Hunt knew—but from solidarity. It settled something in him, soothed a jagged edge. "Hunt's mother was an angel."

His mother's loving, tired face flashed before Hunt's eyes, twisting his heart.

"She was," Apollion said, and the way he smiled . . .

White rage blinded every one of Hunt's senses. "Did you *dare*—"

"She was not ill used," Aidas said, holding up an elegant hand. "We might command nightmares, but we are not monsters."

"Explain," Bryce ordered the demon princes, starlight rippling from her. Thanatos sniffed the air once more, savoring it, and earned a glare from Aidas. "From the beginning."

Despite the heated words they'd exchanged earlier, Hunt had never loved her more—had never been so grateful that Urd had chosen such a loyal, fierce badass for his mate. He could trust her to get the answers they needed.

"How much do you know?" Aidas asked her. "Not just about Athalar, but about the whole history of Midgard."

"Rigelus has a little conquest room," Bryce said, the softness fading from her face as she crossed her arms. "He's got a whole section about invading your planet. And I know Hel once had warring factions, but you sorted out your shit and marched as one to kick the Asteri out of Hel. A year later, you hunted them down across the stars and found them on Midgard. You fought them again, and it didn't go well that time. You got jettisoned from Midgard and have been trying to creep back through the Northern Rift ever since."

"Is that all?" Apollion drawled.

Bryce said warily to Aidas, "I know you loved Theia. That you fought for her."

The Prince of the Chasm studied his long, slender hands. "I did. I continue to do so, long after her death."

Hunt had a feeling that the darkness in the pit before them was breathing.

"Even though she was hardly any better than the Asteri?" Bryce challenged.

Aidas lifted his head. "There is no denying how Theia spent most of her existence. But there was goodness in her, Bryce Quinlan. And love. She came to regret her actions, both in her home world and on Midgard. She tried to make things right."

"Too little, too late," Bryce said.

"I know," Aidas admitted. "Believe me, I know. But there is much that I regret, too." He swallowed, the strong column of his throat working.

"What happened?" Bryce pressed. Hunt almost didn't want to know.

Aidas sighed, the sound weighted with the passing of countless millennia. "The Asteri ordered Pelias to use the Horn to close the Northern Rift, to defend themselves against attack. He did, sealing out all the other worlds in the process, but the Horn broke before he could close it entirely on Hel. The tiniest of wedges was left in the Rift for my kind to sneak through. Helena used black salt to contact me, hoping to launch another offensive against the Asteri, but we couldn't find a way. Unless the Rift was fully opened, we could not strike. And our numbers were so depleted that we would not have stood a chance."

Thanatos picked up the narrative, resting his helmet on a knee. "The vampyrs and Reapers had defected to the Asteri. They betrayed us, the cowards." From the shadows behind him, his hounds snarled, as if in agreement. "They'd been our captains and lieutenants, for the most part. Our armies were in shambles without them. We needed time to rebuild."

"I believe Helena realized," Aidas went on, "that the war would not be won in her lifetime. Nor by any of her sons. They had too much of their father in them. And they, too, greatly enjoyed the benefits of being in the Asteri's favor."

Bryce uncrossed her arms, leaning forward. "I'm sorry, but I still don't understand why Helena built the Cave of Princes. Just to talk to you guys like long-distance pen pals?"

Aidas's full mouth kicked up at a corner. "In a way, yes. Helena needed our counsel. But by that point, she'd also figured out what Theia had done in her last moments alive."

60

The Cave of Princes was as foul and disorienting as Ruhn remembered. But at least he had a kernel of starlight to keep the ghouls at bay in the misty dark. Even if it took most of his concentration to summon it and keep it glimmering.

He and Lidia had entered hours ago, and he'd immediately smelled Flynn's and Dec's scents hanging in the air. Along with Morven's and the Murder Twins'. But it was the sixth scent that had sent Ruhn running down the passages, Lidia easily keeping pace with him. A scent that haunted his nightmares, waking and asleep.

Somehow, the Autumn King was here. And his father wasn't lying in wait for Ruhn, but heading deeper into the caves, after Bryce. Ruhn pushed ahead, even when his legs demanded a break.

Morven's and his father's scents—with the others in tow—cut through nearly hidden tunnels and steeply descending passageways, as if the Stag King knew every secret, direct route. He probably did, as King of Avallen. Or maybe the ghouls showed him the way.

Eventually, Ruhn's body screamed for water, and he paused. Lidia didn't complain—didn't do anything but follow him, always alert to any threat. Yet as they once again rushed down the passage, Lidia said quietly, "I apologize for last night."

Despite every instinct roaring at him to hurry, Ruhn halted. "What do you mean?"

Her throat worked, her face almost luminous in his starlight. "When I . . . flinched."

He blinked. "Why the Hel would you apologize for that?" Pollux should be the one to apologize. Hel, Ruhn would *make* the fucker apologize to Lidia—on his knees—before putting a bullet in his head.

Color stained her cheeks, a rosy glow against the misty darkness behind them. "I like to think myself immune to . . . lingering memories."

Ruhn shook his head, about to object, when she went on. "Everything I did with Pollux, I did willingly. Even if I found his brand of entertainment hard to stomach at times."

"I get it," Ruhn said a shade hoarsely. "I really do. I'm not judging, Lidia. We don't have to do anything you don't want to do. Ever."

"I want to, though." Lidia glanced at his mouth.

"Want to what?" he asked, voice dropping an octave.

"Know what your body feels like. Your mouth. In reality. Not in some dreamworld."

His cock hardened, and he shifted on his feet. He didn't mask the arousal in his tone, his scent, when he said, "Anytime you want, Lidia."

Except, of course, right now. But after he sorted through whatever shitshow was about to go down in these caves—

The pulse in her throat seemed to flutter in answer. "I want you all the time."

Gods damn. Ruhn leaned in. Ran his mouth, his tongue, up her neck. Lidia let out a breathy little sound that had his balls drawing tight.

Ruhn said against her soft skin, "When we get out of these caves, you'll show me exactly where you want me, and how you want me."

She squirmed a little, and he knew that if he slid his hand between her legs, he'd find her wet. "Ruhn," she murmured.

He kissed her neck again, watching through heavily lidded eyes as her nipples pebbled, poking against the thin material of her shirt. He'd explore *those* a lot. Maybe do a little exploring right now—

A rasping, ancient *hiss* sounded from the rocks nearby.

And this was so not the place. Ruhn peeled away from Lidia, meeting her eyes. They were glazed with lust.

But she cleared her throat. "We have to keep going."

"Yeah," he said.

"Maybe you should, ah, take a moment," she said, smirking at the bulge in his pants.

He threw her a wry look. "You don't think the ghouls will appreciate it?"

Lidia snickered. Then grabbed his hand, tugging him back into a steady, paced run. "I want to be the only one who gets to appreciate it from now on."

He couldn't stop the purely male smugness that flooded him. "I can live with that."

"I know what Theia did," Bryce said, shaking her head. "She tried to send her daughters back to their home world, but only Silene made it."

Aidas arched a brow. "I'm assuming you have gleaned something of the truth, if you know of Silene by name. Did you learn what happened to her?"

"She left a . . . a magical video that explained everything." Bryce pulled Truth-Teller from the sheath at her side. Here, at least, the blades didn't pull at each other. "Silene had this with her when she returned to her home world. And now I've brought it back to Midgard."

Aidas started at the sight of the dagger. "Did Silene account for what happened during that last encounter with her mother?"

Bryce rolled her eyes. "Just tell me, Aidas."

Thanatos and Apollion shifted in their seats, annoyed at her irreverence, but Aidas's mouth curved toward a smile. "It took me—and Helena—years to understand what Theia actually did with her magic."

"She shielded her daughters," Bryce said, recalling how Theia's star had split in three, with an orb going to each of her children. "She used the Harp to carry her magic over to them as a protection spell of sorts."

Aidas nodded. "Theia used the Harp to divide her magic—*all* her magic—between the three of them. A third to Silene. A third to Helena. And the remainder stayed with Theia." His eyes dimmed with an old sorrow. "But she did not keep enough to protect herself. Why do you think Theia fell to Pelias that day? With only a third of her power, she did not stand a chance against him."

"And the sword and knife?" Bryce asked.

"Theia endeavored to keep the Asteri from being able to wield her power to use the sword and knife. Both weapons were keyed to her power, thanks to Theia's assistance in their Making," Aidas explained calmly. "It is why the Starsword calls to the descendants of Helena—of Theia. But only to those with enough of Theia's starlight to trigger its power. Your ancestors called these Fae Starborn. The Asteri have no power over the blades; they lack Theia's connection to the weapons. Since the Starsword and the knife were both Made by Theia at the same moment, their bond has always linked them. They have long sought to be reunited, as they were in their moment of their Making."

"Like calls to like," Bryce murmured. "That's why the Starsword and Truth-Teller keep wanting to be close to each other. Why they keep freaking out."

Aidas nodded. "I believe that when you opened the Gate, despite your desire to come to Hel, the Starsword's desire to reach the knife—and vice versa—was so strong that the portal was redirected to the world where they were Made. With the door closed between worlds, they had been unable to reunite. But once you opened it, the blades' pull toward each other was stronger than your untrained will."

With the Starsword in hand, she'd gone right to Truth-Teller, landing on that lawn mere feet away from Azriel and the dagger.

Bryce winced down at the blades. "I'm trying not to be creeped out that these things are, like . . . sentient." But she'd felt it, hadn't she? That pull, that call between them. She'd sworn they were *talking* last night, for fuck's sake. Like two friends who'd been apart, now rushing to catch up on every detail of their lives.

Over fifteen thousand years of separation.

Aidas went on, "But it wasn't just the blades that you reunited in the home world of the Fae, was it?"

Bryce's hands glowed faintly with that ghostly aura. "No," she admitted. "I think . . . I think I claimed some of Theia's magic. Silene left it waiting there." She'd thought it was another star, not a piece of a larger one.

Aidas did not seem surprised, but the other two princes wore such similar expressions of confusion that she almost smiled. Bryce glanced to Hunt, who nodded shallowly. *Go ahead,* he seemed to say.

So Bryce explained how she had claimed the power from the Prison, what she'd seen and learned from Silene's memory, her confrontation with Vesperus.

Bryce finished, "I thought Silene had left *her* power, yet she still had magic afterward. It must have been Theia's power that she left in the stones. It absorbed into mine—like it *was* mine. And when my light shone through the Autumn King's prism, it had transformed. Become . . . fuller. Now tinged with dark."

Aidas mused, "I'd say you had a third of Theia's power already, the part that originally was given to Helena—that came down to you through Helena's bloodline, and you took another third from where Silene stashed it. But if you can find the last third, the part that Theia originally kept for herself . . . I wonder how your light might appear then. What it might do."

"You knew Theia," Bryce said. "You tell me."

"I believe you've already begun to see some glimpses of it," Aidas said, "once you attained what Silene had hidden."

Bryce considered. "The laser power?"

Aidas laughed. "Theia called it starfire. But yes."

Bryce frowned. "Is it—is it the same as the Asteri's?" She hadn't realized how much the question had been weighing on her. Eating at her.

"No," Apollion cut in, scowling. "They are similar in their ability to destroy, but the Asteri's power is a blunt, wicked tool of destruction."

Aidas added, eyes shining with sympathy, "Starfire's ability to destroy is but one facet of a wonderous gift. The greatest difference, of course, lies in how the bearer chooses to use it."

Bryce offered him a small smile as that weight lifted.

Hunt cut in, "So just to clarify: There's still a third well of Theia's power out there—or was?"

"Helena knew that her own portion of her mother's magic would be passed down to future generations," Aidas said. "But when Theia died, all that remained of Theia's power lay in the Starsword. Theia put it into the blade after she parted from her daughters."

Bryce shook her head. "Let me get this straight. Theia divided her power into three parts: one to each of her daughters, and she transferred the last part to the Starsword. So the final piece of her magic is . . . in this blade? It's been waiting all this time?"

"No," Aidas said. "Helena removed it."

Bryce groaned. "Really? It can't be easy?"

Aidas snorted. "Helena did not deem it wise to leave what remained of Theia's star in the sword, even in secret."

"But how would the Asteri have been able to wield Theia's power to use the sword and knife," Bryce protested, "if she was dead?"

"They could have resurrected her," Hunt said quietly.

Aidas nodded gravely. "Theia didn't want them to be able to access the full strength of the star in her bloodline, even through her corpse. So she split it in three, putting only enough into the Starsword for her to face Pelias—long enough to buy her daughters time to run. She gave her magic to her daughters, thinking they would both escape to their home world and be beyond the reach of the Asteri forever."

"Why not send the Starsword with them, too?"

"Because then the knife and sword would have been together," Thanatos said.

"But what sort of threat do they pose?" Bryce said, practically shouting with impatience. "The Autumn King said they can open a portal to nowhere—is that it?"

"Yes," Aidas confirmed. "And together, they can unleash ultimate destruction. Theia separated them to keep the Asteri from ever having that ability. She did not know of a way they could be united by someone not of her bloodline, but the Asteri have been known to be . . . creative."

"How did Helena transfer the power out of the sword? She didn't have the Harp," Bryce said.

"No," Aidas agreed. "But Helena knew that Midgard possessed its own magic. A raw, weaker sort of magic than that in her home world, but one that could be potent in high concentrations. She learned that it flowed across the world in great highways, natural conduits for magic."

"Ley lines," Bryce breathed.

Aidas nodded. "These lines are capable of moving magic, but also carrying communications across great distances." Like those between the Gates of Crescent City, the way she'd spoken to Danika the day she'd made the Drop. "There are ley lines across the whole of the universe. And the planets—like Midgard, like Hel, like the home world of the Fae—atop those lines are joined by time and space and the Void itself. It thins the veils separating us. The Asteri have long chosen worlds that are on the ley lines for that exact purpose. It made it easier to move between them, to colonize those planets. There are certain places on each of these worlds where the most ley lines overlap, and thus the barrier between worlds is at its weakest."

Everything slotted together. *Thin places,* Bryce said with sudden certainty.

"Precisely," Apollion answered for Aidas with an approving nod. "The Northern Rift, the Southern Rift—both lie atop a tremendous knot of ley lines. And while those under Avallen are not as strong, the island is unique as a thin place thanks to the presence of black salt—which ties it to Hel."

"And the mists?" Hunt asked. "What's the deal with them?"

"The mists are a result of the ley lines' power," Aidas said. "They're an indication of a thin place. Hoping to find a ley line strong enough to help her transfer and hide Theia's power, Helena sent a fleet of Fae with earth magic to scour every misty place they could find on Midgard. When they told her of a place wreathed in mists so thick they could not pierce them, Helena went to investigate. The mists parted for her—as if they had been waiting. She found the small network of caves on Avallen . . . and the black salt beneath the surface."

Aidas smiled darkly. "She returned to the Eternal City and convinced Pelias that only such a place would be a worthy burial location for him. He was vain and arrogant enough to believe her. So they established the Fae kingdom on Avallen, and she carved his royal tomb into the rock. She spun lies about wanting future generations to worship him, to have to be born with the *right* blood to have the privilege of attaining his sword, which would be buried with him."

Aidas gestured toward the Starsword, sheathed down Bryce's back. "Helena knew Pelias would never part with his trophy, not until he died. And when he did, she at last drew upon the raw power of Avallen's ley lines to take the star her mother had imbued in the Starsword and hide it."

"So why the prophecy about the sword and knife?" Hunt asked. "If Theia was so scared of them being reunited, why all this crap about trying to get them back together?"

Aidas crossed his legs. "Helena planted that prophecy, seeded it in Fae lore. She knew that despite her mother's fears, the sword and knife *are* needed to destroy the Asteri. She knew that if a scion came along who could claim all three pieces of magic, they'd need the sword and knife to make that power *count*. Theia's power, when whole, is the only thing that can unite and activate the true power of those blades and stop the Asteri's tyranny."

Bryce's mouth dried out. A real path to ending the Asteri, at last.

"So where is it?" Bryce asked. "Where's the last part of Theia's power?"

"I don't know," Aidas said sadly. "Helena told no one, not even me."

Bryce let out a long, frustrated breath, but Hunt kept pushing the princes. "So to unite the sword and knife, Bryce needs to find the starlight Helena took from the Starsword—the last third of Theia's power—which is stashed somewhere on Avallen?"

"Yes," Aidas said simply.

"But how do I make them open that portal to nowhere—and what the Hel does that mean, anyway?" Bryce griped.

Thanatos said roughly, "We've been wondering that for eons."

Aidas dragged a hand through his golden hair. "*Ultimate destruction* was the best any of us could guess."

"Fantastic," Bryce grumbled.

Yet Hunt asked, "If Avallen is one of the stronger thin places, why did the Asteri even allow the Fae to live here?"

"The black salt, in such high quantity, keeps them away. They never realized that its presence drew us as much as it repelled them," Apollion said with satisfaction. "It has the same properties that made us immune to the thrall of their black crowns."

Bryce tensed at that, glancing at Hunt, but her mate asked, setting aside his own questions for now, "Did Helena know the Asteri were repelled from this place?"

Aidas nodded. "Once she figured it out, it confirmed her decision to hide Theia's power here."

Bryce angled her head. "But why did the mists open for Helena to get through in the first place?"

"The black salt only repels the Asteri; the mists repel everyone else. But certain people, with certain gifts, can access the power of thin places—on any world. World-walkers." Aidas gestured gracefully to Bryce. "You are one of them. So were Helena and Theia. Their natural abilities lent themselves to moving through the mists."

Bryce brushed invisible dirt off her shoulders,

"Add it to Bryce's list of Magical Starborn Princess crap," Hunt said, chuckling. But then he frowned deeply. "If the sword and knife could open a portal to nowhere all along, why didn't Theia use them herself in the First Wars?"

"Because she was scared," Aidas said, his voice suddenly tense. "For everyone."

"Right," Bryce said. "Ultimate destruction."

"Yes," Aidas said. Thanatos gave a disdainful snort, but Apollion looked at Aidas with something like compassion. "Theia," Aidas explained, "had theorized about what uniting the blades would do, but never put it into practice. She was afraid that if she opened a portal to nowhere, all of Midgard might get drawn in. She might succeed in trapping the Asteri in another world only to damn this world to follow them right in. So she opted for caution. And by the time she should have damned caution to the wind . . . it was too late for her. For us. It was safer, wiser, for her to separate the blades, and her power."

"But Helena felt differently," Bryce said.

"Helena believed the risk worthwhile," Aidas said. "She suffered greatly in the years following the First Wars—and saw the suffering of others, too. I came to agree with her. She wouldn't tell me where she moved Theia's power, but I know she left it accessible for the future scion who might emerge, bearing Helena's own third of Theia's light. The person who could somehow, against all odds, unite the pieces of Theia's power—and then the two blades."

"What blinds an Oracle?" Bryce whispered.

"Theia's star," Aidas said softly. "I told you: The Oracle did not see that day . . . but I did. I saw you, so young and bright and brave, and the starlight Helena had told me to wait for. That third of Theia's power, passed down through Helena's line."

Hunt demanded, "But what is Bryce supposed to *do*? Find that last piece of Theia's power, use it on the blades, and open this portal to nowhere while praying we don't all get locked in with the Asteri, too?"

"That's about the sum of it," Aidas said, his eyes fixed on Bryce.

"But there was one thing Theia and Helena did not anticipate: that you would bear the Horn, reborn, in your body. Another way to open doors between worlds."

"And what's she supposed to do with that?" Hunt snarled.

Aidas smiled slightly. "Fully open the Northern Rift, of course."

61

So," Bryce said slowly, as if letting the words sink in, "why not use the Horn to open the portal to nowhere?"

"Because no one knows what that is—*where* it is. The sword and knife are pinpointed to its location, somehow. They are the only way to get to that nowhere-place."

Hunt's head spun. Hel, his head had been spinning nonstop for the past ten minutes. But Bryce was having none of it. "What if I never got the knife back? What if I never came to Avallen? What if I never got the chance, or refused to come here, or whatever?"

Apollion and Thanatos shifted in their seats, either bored or on edge, but Aidas continued speaking. "I do not know how Helena hoped you would be able to retrieve the knife from her home world. As for Avallen . . . Helena wanted me to nudge you along. But you harbored such hatred for the Fae—you would never have trusted me if I had pushed you to travel to their stronghold."

"That's true," Bryce muttered.

"My brothers and I had doubts about Helena's plans. We continued to rest our hopes on reopening the Northern Rift so that we could continue the fight against the Asteri. If someone like you, a world-walker, did come along and Avallen was somehow not accessible for you to claim Theia's power, we still needed a way to . . . fuel you up, as it were." He faced Hunt at last.

Hunt could barely breathe. Here—after all this waiting . . . here were the answers.

"You are the son of my two brothers only in the vaguest sense," Aidas said.

Something in Hunt's chest eased—even as his stomach roiled.

"Thanatos refused to help at first," Apollion added, glaring at his brother.

"I did not approve of the plan," Thanatos snapped, gripping his helmet tight. "I still do not."

"My brother," Aidas said, nodding to Thanatos, "has long excelled at crafting things."

"Funny," Bryce said, "I didn't take you for a quilter."

Hunt gave her an incredulous look, but Aidas smiled before he said to Hunt, "During the First Wars, as you call them, Thanatos helped Apollion breed new types of demons to fight on our side. The kristallos, designed to hunt for the Horn—so we might find a way into Midgard unobstructed. The Shepherd. The deathstalkers." A nod to Hunt, like he knew of the scar down Hunt's back from one of them. "They were but a few of my brothers' creations."

Bryce shook her head. "But the kristallos venom can negate magic. If you knew how to do that, why did you not use it against the Asteri in the war?"

"We tried," Aidas said. "It did not have the same effect on their powers."

"I'm sorry," Hunt interrupted, "but are you implying that I was made by *you two assholes*? As some sort of pet?" He pointed to Thanatos, then to Apollion.

"Not a pet," Apollion said darkly. "A weapon." He nodded to Bryce. "For her, whenever she might come along."

"But you didn't know the timelines would overlap," Bryce said a bit breathlessly.

"No. There were previous experiments," Apollion said. "We hoped they would spread and multiply throughout Midgard, but the Asteri caught wind of our plan and removed them."

"The thunderbirds," Bryce said, gaping. "You guys made them, too?"

"We did," Aidas said matter-of-factly, "and sent them through the cracks in the Northern Rift. But they were hunted to near-extinction generations ago. Blessing an angel with their power, a perfect soldier . . . it was a gift of poisoned honey. The Asteri believed they had somehow, through their selective breeding of the malakim, finally achieved a flawless soldier to serve them. That it was their own brilliance that brought someone like Hunt Athalar into the world."

"But you rebelled," Apollion said to Hunt with no small hint of pride. "You were too valuable to kill, but they wanted you broken. Your servitude was that attempt."

Hunt could barely feel his body.

"Can we please rewind for a moment?" Bryce cut in. "You guys made the thunderbirds to complement my power—in case I never got the sword and knife, and if I ever needed a boost to open the Rift. But when they were hunted down, you . . . made Hunt, and then I was born . . ."

"Athalar was already enslaved by then," Aidas said, "but we kept a close watch."

Apollion nodded to Hunt. "Why do you think you're so adept at hunting demons? It's in your blood—part of *me* is in your blood."

Nausea clawed its way up Hunt's throat. The thought of owing anything at all to the Prince of the Pit . . .

"Just as he gave over some of his essence for the kristallos," Thanatos said, "so he gave something to me for you. His Helfire."

"Helfire?" Bryce demanded.

"The lightning," Thanatos said, waving an irritated hand. "Capable of killing almost anything. Even an Asteri."

"That's how you killed Sirius?" Bryce asked. "With your . . . Helfire?"

"Yes," Apollion said, then added to Hunt, "Your name was a nod to that, whispered in your mother's ear as you were born. Orion . . . master of Sirius."

"Clever," Hunt snapped, then demanded, "Wait—my lightning can kill the Asteri?" Hope bloomed, bright and beautiful in his chest.

"No," Apollion said. "It is . . . diluted from my own. It could harm them, but not kill them. I believe your mother's angelic blood tempered my power."

That hope withered. And something darker took its place as he asked, "How did my mother play into this?" He could handle some genetic meddling, but—

"There was a scientist at the Asteri Archives," Aidas said. "An angel who was delving into the origins of the thunderbirds, how strange their power was. He named the project after a near-forgotten god of storms."

"Project Thurr," Bryce said. "Was Danika investigating it, too? I found mentions of it, after she died."

"I don't know," Aidas said, "but the angel was researching thunderbirds at the behest of the Asteri, who worried they might return. It led him to us instead. When we told him the truth, he offered to help in whatever way he could. Thanatos was finishing up his work then. And with a male volunteer, only a female to breed with was needed."

Hunt couldn't breathe. Bryce laid a hand on his knee.

"Your father knew your mother briefly," Aidas said. "And he knew having a partner would help lift her from her poverty. He had every intention of staying. Of leaving behind his life and raising you in secret."

Hunt could barely ask, "What happened?"

"The mystics told Rigelus of your father's connection to us. They didn't discover everything—nothing about you or your mother. Only that he had been speaking to us. Rigelus had him brought in, tortured, and executed."

Hunt's heart stalled.

"He didn't break," Apollion said with something like kindness. "He never mentioned your mother, or her pregnancy. The Asteri never knew you were tied to him in any way."

"What . . . what was his name?"

"Hyrieus," Aidas answered. "He was a good male, Hunt Athalar. As you are."

Bryce squeezed his knee, her hand so warm—or was he unnaturally cold? "Okay, so Hunt was made to be a backup battery for me—"

"Can I do the same for Ruhn, then?" Hunt interrupted.

"No," Thanatos said. "The prince's light, his affinity for these thin places, isn't strong enough. Not like hers."

Hunt gripped Bryce's hand atop his knee. "Is it in my DNA that Bryce and I are mates? Was that engineered, too?"

"No," Aidas said quickly, "that was never intended. I think that was left to higher powers. Whatever they may be."

Hunt turned to Bryce and found nothing but love in her eyes. He couldn't stand it.

Horror cracked through him, as chilled as hoarfrost. He'd been created by these males to give and to suffer, and where the fuck did that leave him? Who the fuck did that make him?

"Okay," Bryce said, "Helfire and starfire: a potent combination. But Helena left all this shit to help end this conflict. It sounds like *you guys* just want me to open a gods-damned door for you to come in and save the day instead."

"Is it so bad," Thanatos purred, "to have us do your dirty work?"

Bryce glowered at him. "This is my world. I want to fight for it."

"Then fight alongside us," Thanatos challenged.

Tense silence stretched between them. Hunt had no idea how to even begin processing this insanity. But that cold in his veins . . . that felt good. Numbing.

"I could have used a bit more time to prepare," Bryce muttered.

Aidas only shook his head. "You weren't ready before. And what if you had told the wrong person? You know what the Asteri do to those who challenge their divinity. I could not risk it. Risk you. I had to wait for you to find the answers for yourself. But haven't I told you from the start to find me? That I will help you? That is what Apollion was attempting to do, too, in his misguided way: to ready you both for all this—to battle the Asteri."

"But how," Hunt asked, fighting past that numbing, blissful

chill in his chest, "did you kick the Asteri out of Hel the first time?"

"They had trouble feeding off our magic," Thanatos said, voice thick with disgust. "And found that our powers rivaled their own. They fled before we could kill them."

Bryce swallowed audibly as she surveyed Apollion. "And you really *ate* Sirius? Like, ingested her?"

But it was Aidas who answered, pride flaring on his face. Apollion slew her with his Helfire when she attacked him—he pulled her burning heart from her chest and ate it."

Hunt shuddered. But Bryce said, "How is that even possible?"

"I am darkness itself," Apollion said softly. "True darkness. The kind that exists in the bowels of a black hole."

Hunt's bones quaked. The male wasn't boasting.

"So why can't you just . . . eat the rest of them?" Bryce asked.

"It requires proximity," Aidas said. "And the Asteri are well aware of my brother's talents. They will avoid him at all costs."

The princes flickered, like they were on a screen that had glitched.

"We're running low on time," Thanatos said. "The black salt is wearing off."

Bryce focused on Apollion. "You guys have been telling me nonstop about having your armies ready to go." She gestured to the temple, the dead city beyond. "This place looks pretty empty."

Apollion's eyes grew ever darker. "We have allowed you to see only a fraction of Hel. Our lands and armies are elsewhere. They are ready."

"So if I open the Northern Rift with the Horn . . . ," Bryce said. Hunt cleared his throat in warning. "All seven of you and your armies will come through?"

"The three of us," Aidas amended. "Our four other brothers are currently engaged in other conflicts, helping other worlds."

"I didn't realize you guys were, like, intergalactic saviors," Bryce said.

Aidas's mouth quirked upward. She could have sworn Apollion's did, too.

"But yes," Aidas went on, "opening the Northern Rift is the only way for our armies to fully and quickly enter Midgard."

"After what happened this spring," Hunt said to his mate, "you trust them not to fucking *eat* everyone?"

"Those were our pets," Aidas insisted, "not our armies. And they have been severely punished for it. They will stay in line this time, and follow our orders on the battlefield."

Bryce glanced to Hunt, but he couldn't read the expression on her face. The princes flickered once more, the temple shimmering and paling. A tug pulled at Hunt's gut, yanking him back toward the body he'd left in Avallen.

"I'll think about it," Bryce answered.

"This is no game, girl," Thanatos snapped.

Bryce leveled a cool look at the Prince of the Ravine. "I'm sick and tired of people using *girl* as an insult."

Thanatos opened his mouth to respond, but abruptly vanished—his connection had been severed.

Apollion said to Hunt, "Do not squander the gifts that have been given to you—by me, by my brother." His gaze drifted to the halo on Hunt's brow. "No true son of Hel can be caged."

Then he was gone, too.

Son of Hel. Hunt's very soul iced over at the thought.

Only Aidas remained, seeming to cling to the connection as he spoke to Bryce, his blue eyes intense on her face. "If you find that final piece of Theia's power . . . if the cost of uniting the sword and knife is too much, Bryce Quinlan, then don't do it. Choose life." He glanced to Hunt. "Choose each other. I have lived with the alternative for millennia—the loss never gets easier to bear."

Bryce reached a ghostly hand toward Aidas, but the Prince of the Chasm was gone.

And all of Hel with him.

62

Bryce opened her eyes to fire. Blazing, white-hot fire.

Hunt's lightning instantly surrounded her, but it was too late.

The Autumn King and Morven stood in the chamber, somehow having caught up with them. Shadows wreathed the latter, but her father raged with flame.

And in the center of the room, surrounded by fire that even Tharion's water could not extinguish, stood her friends.

Bryce gave herself one breath to take in the sight: Tharion, Baxian, Sathia, Flynn, and Declan, all huddled close and ringed by fire. There was no sign of the ghouls in the shadows, but the Murder Twins stood just outside the perimeter, smirking like the assholes they were.

The Autumn King didn't bother to encircle her and Hunt with fire, knowing that even Hunt's lightning couldn't stop him if he chose to burn their prisoners to ashes. It was protection enough.

"Get up," Morven ordered Bryce, shadows like whips in the Stag King's hands. "We've been waiting long enough for you to snap out of that stupor."

Hunt hissed, and Bryce glanced over to find angry, blistered weals along her mate's forearm. They'd been *burning* Hunt to try to wake him up—

Bryce lifted her eyes to the shadow-crowned King of Avallen. To her sire, standing cold-faced beside him despite the fire at his fingertips. "What did you do with that black salt?" the Autumn King asked quietly. "Who did you see?"

Bryce drew the Starsword and Truth-Teller.

"Relinquish those weapons," Morven snapped. "You've sullied them long enough."

The fire closed in tighter around their friends. Baxian swore as a lick of it singed his black feathers.

"Sorry," Bryce said to the kings, not lowering her weapons, "but the blades don't work for rejected losers."

The Autumn King sneered, "Their taste is questionable. We shall remedy that at last."

"Right," Bryce said thoughtfully. "I forgot that you killed the last Starborn Prince because you couldn't deal with how jealous you were of him."

The Autumn King, as he had the last time she'd accused him of this, only chuckled. Morven glanced at him, as if in sudden doubt.

But the Autumn King said, "Jealous? Of that sniveling whelp? He was unworthy of that sword, but no more unworthy than *you*."

Bryce flashed him a winning smile. "I'll take that as a compliment."

The Autumn King went on, "I killed the boy because he wanted to put an end to the bloodline. To all that the Fae are." The male jerked his chin at Bryce. "Like you, no doubt."

She shrugged. "Not gonna deny it."

"Oh, I know your heart, Bryce *Quinlan*," the Autumn King seethed. "I know what you'd do, if left to your own devices."

"Binge an obscene amount of TV?"

His flame rose higher, herding her friends closer together. Dangerously little space remained between their bodies and the fire. "You are a threat to the Fae. Raised by your mother to abhor us, you are not fit to bear the royal name."

Bryce let out a harsh, bitter laugh. "You think my mom turned me against you? I turned against you the moment you sent your goons after us to kill her and Randall. And every moment since then, you pathetic loser. You want someone to blame for me thinking the Fae are worthless pieces of shit? Look in the mirror."

"Ignore her hysterical prattling," Morven warned the Autumn King.

The Autumn King bared his teeth at her. "You've let a little bit of inherited power and a title go to your head."

Morven's shadows rose behind him, ready to obliterate all in their path. "You'll wish for death when the Asteri get their hands on you."

Bryce tightened her grip on the blades. They hummed, pulling toward each other. Like they were begging her for that final reunification. She ignored them, and instead asked the Fae Kings, "Finally going to hand us over?"

"The worms you associate with, yes," the Autumn King said without an ounce of pity. "But you . . ."

"Right, breeding," Bryce said, and didn't miss Hunt's incredulous look at her tone. Her arms strained with the effort of keeping the blades apart. "I'm assuming Sathia, Flynn, and Dec will be kept for breeding, too, but any non-Fae are out of luck. Sorry, guys."

"This is not a joke," Morven spat.

"No, it's not," Bryce said, and met his stare. "And I'm done laughing at you fools."

Morven didn't flinch. "That little light show might have surprised us last time, but one spark from you, and your friends burn. Or shall we demonstrate an alternate method?" Morven gestured with a shadow-wreathed hand to the Murder Twins.

Bryce checked that her mental wall of starlight was intact, but like the bullies they were, the twins struck the person they assumed was weakest.

One heartbeat, Sathia was wide-eyed and monitoring the showdown. The next, she'd snatched a knife from Tharion's side.

And held it against her own throat.

"Stop it," Tharion snarled toward the twins, who were snickering.

Sathia's hand shook, and she pressed the dagger into her neck a little harder, drawing a trickle of blood.

"You make one move toward her, fish, and that knife slides home," Morven said.

"Leave her alone," Bryce said, and stepped forward—just one foot. The sword and dagger in her hands now seemed to tug forward, too—toward the center of the room. She tightened her grip on them.

Fire blazed brighter around her friends. One of Baxian's feathers caught fire, and Dec only just managed to pat it out before it could spread. "Drop the blades, and they'll release her mind," the Autumn King countered.

Bryce glanced to the sword and knife, fighting that tug from both weapons toward the center of the room.

Sathia stood on the other side of that burning ring, pure, helpless terror on her face, blood streaming down her neck. One thought from Seamus or Duncan, one motion, and that knife would slide into her throat.

Bryce tossed the blades to the ground.

Their dark metal clanked against the stone with brutal finality as they skittered to a stop nearly atop the eight-pointed star. Out of reach.

Neither king advanced, though, as if afraid to pick them up— or even walk over to them.

The Murder Twins pouted at their spoiled fun, but Sathia lowered the knife. Her fingers still clenched it at her side, though— clearly at the twins' direction. None of the others dared to pry it from her fingers.

But Bryce only stared at the Autumn King as she snarled, "You were giving me all that bullshit about how much you loved my mom and regretted having hit her—yet this is what you're doing to your own daughter? And to the daughter of one of your Fae buddies?"

"You stopped being my daughter the moment you locked me in my own home."

"Ouch," Bryce said. "That hit me right in the heart." She tapped on her chest for emphasis, and the star glowed in answer.

"She is stalling for time," the Autumn King said to Morven. "She did precisely this with Micah—"

"Oh yeah," Bryce said, advancing a step, "when I kicked his ass. Did he tell you?" she asked Morven. "It's supposed to be a big secret." She stage-whispered, taking another step closer, "I cut that fucker into pieces for what he did to Danika."

The Murder Twins seemed to start in surprise.

Bryce smiled at them, at Morven, at the Autumn King, and said, "But what I did to Micah is *nothing* compared to what I'll do to you."

She extended her hands. Starsword and Truth-Teller flew to them, as they had in the Fae world. Like calling to like.

But she hadn't been stalling for time for herself. She'd been stalling for Hunt.

As the sword and dagger flew to her, Hunt's lightning, gathering in a wave behind her, launched for the Murder Twins.

They had a choice, then: let go of their hold on Sathia to intercept the two whips of lightning that lashed for them, or allow Hunt's lightning to obliterate them.

The twins opted to live. A shield of shadows slammed against the reaching spears of lightning. It was all Bryce needed to see before she burst into motion.

The Autumn King shouted in warning, but Bryce was already running for them. For him.

She didn't hold back as she erupted with starlight.

The entire cave shook as lightning and shadow collided. Hunt gritted his teeth.

Tharion had managed to get the knife away from Sathia before she dropped it and impaled her own foot, and now the female crouched in the circle of fire, head gripped in her hands.

The blast of starlight that shot from Bryce as she ran for their enemies threatened to bring down the cavern. Her hair rose above her head, her fingertips shining white-hot with starfire.

Hunt gaped at her power, the beauty and condensed might of it.

But one of the Murder Twins laughed, a spiteful sound that promised his mate would suffer. Six ghouls burst from the shadows, little more than shadows themselves in their dark, tattered robes and reaching, scabbed hands.

What unholy things had the twins done, to become masters of these wretched beings?

Hunt glimpsed jaws stocked with three-inch, curving teeth opening wide, aiming for a distracted Bryce—

With a roar of fury, he sent half a dozen spears of lightning crackling for the ghouls and a seventh—a lucky one—for the twins' shadows.

Where lightning met ancient malice, the ghouls exploded into sizzling dust. But his lightning fractured against the twins' wall of darkness. It kept them from joining the fight with Bryce, though it didn't destroy their shield.

"Help her," Baxian hissed over the crackling flame, but Hunt shook his head, throwing more of his lightning at the twins, who were now pushing back with a slowly advancing wall of shadow. Hunt dared a glance at Sathia, who watched with wide eyes as Bryce launched herself at the two Fae Kings.

Bryce flew like a shooting star through the dim cavern.

"She doesn't need my help," Hunt whispered.

Fire met starlight met shadows, and Bryce loosed herself on the world.

It ended today. Here. Now.

This had nothing to do with the Asteri, or Midgard. The Fae had festered under leaders like these males, but her people could be so much more.

Bryce carried the weight of that with each punch of starfire toward the Autumn King that had him dancing away, with each smothering spate of shadows Morven sent to herd her back toward the stream.

She hadn't gone to that other world only because of the sword and knife, or to find some magic bullet to stop the rot in her own world. She knew that now.

Urd had sent her there to see, even in the small fraction of their world that she'd witnessed, that Fae existed who were kind and brave. She might have had to betray Nesta and Azriel, trick them . . . but she knew that at their cores, they were good people.

The Fae of Midgard were capable of more.

Ruhn proved it. Flynn and Dec proved it. Even Sathia proved it, in the short time Bryce had known her.

Bryce launched a line of pure starfire at Morven, gouging deep in the black-salt floor. He dodged, rolling out of reach with a warrior's skill.

It stopped today.

The pettiness and chauvinism and arrogance that had been the hallmarks of the Fae of Midgard for generations. Pelias's legacy.

It all fucking stopped *today*.

The starlight flared around Bryce, the darkness of Silene's—Theia's—dusk power giving it shape, transforming it into that starfire. If she could find that final third piece and make the star whole—

She was already whole. What she had—who she was . . . it was enough. She'd always been enough to take on these bastards, power or no power. Starborn crap or no.

She was enough.

The Murder Twins were returning Hunt's ambush now. From his angle, Bryce knew Hunt couldn't see what they were up to behind their wall of shadows, pushing his way, blasting apart his lightning.

But from over here . . . Bryce could see how they used that wall against Hunt. Used it to shield themselves from view as they turned her way.

Even Hunt's lightning wasn't fast enough as the Murder Twins sprang for her with swords drawn. Right as their shadowy talons scraped down the wall of her mind.

It stopped today.

Bryce exploded—into the twins's minds, their bodies. Flooding them with starfire. A part of her recoiled in horror as their huge forms crumpled to the ground, steaming holes where their eyes had been. Where their brains had been. She'd melted their minds.

Morven screamed in fury—and something like fear.

She'd done that. With only two-thirds of Theia's star, she'd managed to—

"Bryce!" Hunt shouted, but he was too late—Morven had sent a whip of shadow, hidden beneath a plume of the Autumn King's flame, for her. It wrapped around her legs and *yanked*. Bryce slammed into stone, starlight blinking out.

The impact cracked through her skull, setting the world spinning. Or maybe that was the shadows, dragging her closer to the wall of flame.

Bryce slashed down at the leash of shadows with a hand wreathed in starfire.

It tore the darkness into ribbons. Bryce was up in a heartbeat, but not fast enough to dodge the punch of flame the Autumn King sent toward her gut—

Bryce teleported, swift and instinctive as a breath. Right to the Autumn King.

It ended now.

The Autumn King staggered in shock as she grabbed his burning fist in one hand. As she held firm, her nails digging in hard. His fire singed into her skin, blinding her with pain, but she dug her nails in deeper and sent her starfire blasting into him.

Her father roared in agony, falling to his knees. Morven, so stunned he'd been frozen in place, swore brutally.

Bryce stared at what she had done to the Autumn King's fist. What had once been his hand.

Only melted flesh and bone remained.

The Autumn King retched at the pain, bowing over his knees, hand cradled to his chest.

"Do you think those gifts make you special?" Morven raged, shaking free of his stupor. A swarming nest of shadows teemed around him. "My son could do the same—and he was trash in the end. Just like you."

Morven's shadows launched for her like a flock of ravens.

Bryce blasted out a wall of starlight, destroying those shadow birds, but more came, from everywhere and nowhere, from below—

The Autumn King got to his feet, face gray with agony, cradling his charred remnant of a hand. "I'm going to teach you a new definition of pain," he spat.

And there was no amount of training that could have prepared Bryce, no time to teleport to avoid the two swift attacks from the Fae Kings, matched in power.

She dodged the bone-searing blast of fire from her father, only to have Morven's shadows grab her again. Hands of pure darkness hurled her onto the stone so hard the breath went out of her. The Starsword and Truth-Teller flew from her fingers.

A female cried out, and for a moment, Bryce thought it might have been Cthona, maybe Luna herself.

But it was Sathia.

It was Sathia, on her feet again, and yet it wasn't. It was every Fae female who'd come before them.

Bryce exploded her light outward, shredding Morven's shadows apart. They cleared to reveal the Autumn King standing above her, a sword of flame in his undamaged hand.

"I should have done this a long time ago," her father snarled, and plunged his burning sword toward her exposed heart.

The Autumn King only made it halfway before light burst from his chest.

Hunt's lightning had—

No.

It wasn't Hunt's lightning that shone through the Autumn King's rib cage.

It was the Starsword. And it was Ruhn wielding it, standing behind him.

Ruhn, who had driven the sword right through their father's cold heart.

Ruhn knew in his bones why he'd walked through these caves. He was a Starborn Prince, and he'd come to right an ancient wrong.

With the Starsword in his hand, piercing his father's heart . . . Ruhn knew he was exactly where he was meant to be.

The Autumn King let out a shocked grunt, blood dribbling from his mouth.

"I know *every* definition of pain thanks to you," Ruhn spat, and yanked out the sword.

His father collapsed face-first onto the stone floor.

Even Morven's shadows halted as the Autumn King struggled to raise himself onto his hands. Lidia, guarding Ruhn's back against the Stag King, said nothing.

No pity stirred in Ruhn's heart as his father gurgled blood. As it dribbled onto the stones. The Autumn King lifted his head to meet Ruhn's stare.

Betrayal and hatred burned in his face.

Ruhn said into his mind, into all their minds, *I lied about what the Oracle said to me.*

His father's eyes flared with shock at Ruhn's voice in his head, the secret his son had kept all these years. Ruhn didn't care what Morven made of it, didn't even bother to look at the Stag King. Bryce and Athalar could handle the shadows, if Morven was dumb enough to attack.

So Ruhn stared into his father's hateful face and said, *The Oracle didn't tell me that I would be a fair and just king. She told me that the royal bloodline would end with me.*

He had the sense that his friends were watching with wide eyes. But he only had words for the pathetic male before him.

I thought it meant your *bloodline.*

Ruhn lifted the bloodied Starsword. Flame simmered along his father's body, limning his powerful form. But Ruhn was no longer a cowering boy, inking himself with tattoos to hide the scarring.

I was wrong. I think the Oracle meant all of them, Ruhn went on, mind-to-mind. *The* male *lines. The Starborn Princes included—all you fucks who have corrupted and stolen and never once apologized for it. The entire system. This bullshit of crowns and inheritance.*

His father's sneering voice filled his mind. *You're a spoiled, ungrateful brat who never deserved to carry my crown—*

I don't want it, Ruhn snapped, and shut down the bridge between their minds that allowed his father to speak. He'd had enough of listening to this male.

Blood trickled from his father's lips as his Vanir body sought to heal him—to rally his strength to attack.

The line will end with me, you fucking prick, Ruhn said into his father's mind, *because I yield my crown, my title, to the queen.*

True fear turned his father's face ashen. And out of the corner of his eye, Ruhn saw Bryce's star begin to glow.

A serene peace bloomed in him. *I always assumed the Oracle's prophecy meant that I would die.* He let his kernel of starlight flicker down the blade, an answer to Bryce's beckoning blaze. One last time.

But I am going to live, he said to his father. *And I am going to live well—without you.*

Even Morven's shadows weren't fast enough as Ruhn whipped the Starsword through the air again. And sliced clean through his father's neck.

Bryce had no words as Ruhn severed the Autumn King's head. As her brother skewered the skull on the Starsword before it even hit the stone.

She got to her feet. Came up beside Ruhn where he stood rigid, still holding the bloodied sword, their father's head impaled on it.

The fire around their friends remained, an impenetrable prison. As if the Autumn King had imbued the flames with energy he'd cast outside himself, to linger even past his death. A final punishment. Lidia rushed over, as if she could somehow find a way to undo the flames—

"Let them go," Bryce said to Morven in a voice she didn't entirely recognize. "Before we skewer you as well."

Morven bared his teeth. But despite the blazing hate in his eyes, he lowered himself to his knees and lifted his hands in submission. "I yield."

The fire vanished. Morven blinked, as if surprised, but said nothing.

Their friends were instantly on their feet, Hunt putting a hand on Sathia's back to steady her. Then they all came to stand, as one, behind Bryce and Ruhn. And she saw it, for a glimmering heartbeat. Not a world divided into Houses . . . but a world united.

Bryce walked a few steps to pick up Truth-Teller from where it lay near the Autumn King's decapitated corpse. She didn't look at the body, at the blood still pooling outward, as she said to Ruhn, "Helena created the prophecy to explain what these weapons could do, the power needed to take on the Asteri. But I think, in her own way, the prophecy was also her hope for *me*. What I might do, beyond wielding the power."

Confusion swirled in Ruhn's bright blue eyes.

"Sword," Bryce said, nodding to the Starsword in his hand. She lifted Truth-Teller in her own. "Knife." And then she pointed to their friends, to the Fae and angel and mer and shifter behind them. "People."

"It wasn't only about the Fae," Ruhn said quietly.

"It doesn't have to be," Bryce amended. "It can mean what we want it to." She smiled slightly. "*Our* people," she said to Ruhn, to the others. "The people of Midgard. United against the Asteri."

It had taken all this time, a journey through the stars and under the earth . . . but here they were.

Morven spat on the ground. "If you plan to fight the Asteri, you will fail. It doesn't matter if you unify every House. You will be wiped from the face of Midgard."

Bryce surveyed the king on his knees. "I appreciate your confidence."

Morven's shadows began to seethe along his shoulders again. Rippling down his arms. "I yield now, girl, but the Fae shall never accept a half-breed by-blow as queen, even a Starborn one."

Ruhn lunged for him, Starsword angling, but Bryce blocked him with an arm. For a long moment, she stared down into Morven's face. Really, truly looked at it. At the male beneath the crown of shadows.

She found only hate.

"If we win," Bryce said quietly, "this new world will be a fair one. No more hierarchies and bullshit." The very things Hunt had fought for. That he and the Fallen had suffered for. "But right now," Bryce said, "I'm Queen of the Valbaran Fae." She nodded to the Autumn King's body cooling on the ground, then smirked at Morven. "And of Avallen."

Morven hissed, "You'll be Queen of Avallen over my dead . . ." He trailed off at the smile on her face. And paled.

"As I was saying," Bryce drawled, "for the moment, I'm queen. I'm judge, jury . . ."

Bryce looked to Sathia, still shaken and wide-eyed from the twins' attack—yet unafraid. Unbroken, despite what the males in her life, what this male, had tried to do to her.

So Bryce peered down at Morven and finished sweetly, "And I'm your motherfucking executioner."

The King of Avallen was still blazing with hate when Bryce slid Truth-Teller into his heart.

It was a matter of a few strokes of Truth-Teller through Morven's neck for Bryce to behead him. And as she rose to her feet, it was a Fae Queen who stood before Ruhn, wreathed in starlight, unflinching before her enemies. From the love shining on Athalar's face as he beheld Bryce, Ruhn knew the angel saw it as well.

But it was Sathia who approached Bryce. Who knelt at her feet, bowing her head, and declared, "Hail Bryce, Queen of the Midgardian Fae."

"Oof," Bryce said, wincing. "Let's start with Avallen and Valbara and see where we wind up."

But Flynn and Declan knelt, too. And Ruhn turned to his sister and knelt as well, offering up the Starsword with both hands.

"To right an old wrong," Ruhn said, "and on behalf of all the Starborn Princes before me. This is yours."

No words had ever sounded so right. Nor had anything felt so right as when Bryce took the Starsword from him, a formal claiming, and weighed it in her hands.

Ruhn watched his sister glance between the Starsword and Truth-Teller, one blade blazing with starlight, the other with darkness. "What now?" she asked quietly.

"Other than taking a moment to process the deaths of those two assholes over there?" Ruhn said. He nodded toward Morven and his father.

Bryce offered a watery smile. "We learned some things, at least."

"Yeah?" The others were all crowding around them now, listening.

"Turns out," Athalar said with what Ruhn could have sworn was forced casualness, "Theia did some weird shit with her star magic, divvying it up between herself and her daughters. Long story short, Bryce has two of those pieces, but Helena used Avallen's nexus of ley lines and natural magic to hide the third piece somewhere on Avallen. If Bryce can get that piece, the sword and knife will be able to open a portal to nowhere, and we can trap the Asteri inside it."

Bryce gave Hunt a look as if to say there was a *lot* more to it than that, but she said, "So . . . new mission: find the power Helena hid. Aidas claimed that Helena used Midgard's ley lines to hide it in these caves after Pelias died." She sighed, scanning all their faces. "Any thoughts on where it might be?"

Ruhn blinked at her. "Yeah," he said hoarsely. "I do have a thought."

"Really?" Athalar said, frowning.

"Don't look so shocked," Ruhn grumbled.

Lidia came up to his side, adding, "After Pelias died, you say?"

"Yeah. It's complicated—"

"I think it's part of the land," Lidia interrupted. "In the very bones of Avallen."

Bryce and Athalar raised their eyebrows, but Ruhn glanced to Lidia and nodded. "It explains a lot."

Bryce cut in, "Like . . . ?"

"Like why Avallen was once part of an archipelago, but now it's only one island," Ruhn said. "You said Helena drew upon Avallen's ley lines to contain her mother's star—to hide it here, right? I think doing so drained *all* the land's magic from its ley lines, and repurposed it to encage Theia's power. It made the land wither. Just as you said Silene's own lands withered around the Prison while it held her own share of power."

Bryce mused, "Silene had the Horn, but Helena had to use the ley lines instead. Yet both had a disastrous effect on the land itself." She peered down at the blades again.

"How do you propose getting the magic out?" Lidia challenged. "We have no idea how to access it."

No one answered. And, fuck, Morven and the Autumn King were lying there, dead and dismembered, and—

"Anyone got any bright ideas?" Tharion asked into the fraught silence.

Ruhn stifled his laugh, but Bryce slowly turned toward the mer, as if in surprise.

"Bright," she murmured. Then looked at Athalar, scanning his face. "Light it up," she whispered. As if it was the answer to everything.

Bright.

Light.

Light it up.

The world seemed to pause, as if Urd herself had slowed time as each thought pelted Bryce.

She glanced at the walls. At the river of starlight that Helena had depicted at the bottom of every carving.

Mere hours ago, she'd thought it was the bloodline of the Starborn in artistic form.

But Silene had depicted the evil running beneath the Prison in her carvings, unwittingly warning about Vesperus . . . Perhaps Helena, too, had left a clue.

A final challenge.

Bryce peered down at the eight-pointed star in the center of the room. The two strange slits in the points. One small, one larger.

She looked at the weapons in her hands: a small dagger, and a large sword. They'd fit right into the slits in the floor, like keys in a lock.

Keys to unlock the power stored beneath. The last bit of power she needed to open the portal to nowhere.

That power had originally belonged to the worst sort of Fae, but it didn't have to. It could belong to anyone. It could be Bryce's for the taking.

To light up this world.

"Bryce?" Hunt asked, a hand on her back.

Bryce rallied herself, breathing deep. Bits of debris and rock from her battle with the Fae Kings began drifting upward.

She walked through it, right to that eight-pointed star on the ground, identical to the one on her chest. The debris and rock swirled, a maelstrom with her at its center.

Bryce inhaled deeply, bracing herself as she whispered, "I'm ready."

"For *what*?" Hunt demanded, but Bryce ignored him.

On an exhale, she plunged the weapons into the slits in the eight-pointed star. The small one for the knife. The larger one for the sword.

And like a key turning in a lock, they released what lay beneath.

63

Light blasted up through the blades into her hands, her arms, her heart. Bryce could hear it through her feet, through the stone. The song of the land beneath her. Quiet and old and forgotten, but there.

She heard how Avallen had yielded its joy, its bright green lands and skies and flowers, so it might hold the power as it was bid, waiting all this time for someone to unleash it. To free it.

"Bryce!" Hunt shouted, and she met her mate's eyes.

None of what the Princes of Hel had said about him scared her. They hadn't made Hunt's soul. That was all hers, just as her own soul was his.

Helena had bound the soul of this land in magical chains. No more. No more would Bryce allow the Fae to lay claim over anything.

"You're free," Bryce whispered to Avallen, to the land and the pure, inherent magic beneath it. "Be free."

And it was.

Light burst from the star, and the caves shook again. They rolled and rattled and trembled—

The walls were buckling, and she had the sense that Hunt lunged for her, but fell to his knees as the ground moved upward. Stone crumbled away around them, burying Pelias's sarcophagus, the corpses of the two newly dead kings, and all their other hateful ancestors below. It churned them into dust. Sunlight broke through, the very earth parting as Bryce and the others were thrust upward.

Sunlight—not gray skies.

They emerged in the hills less than a mile from the castle and royal city. As if the caves had been backtracking all this way.

And from the rocky ground beneath them, spreading from the star at Bryce's feet, grass and flowers bloomed. The river from the caverns burst forth, dancing down the newly formed hill.

Sathia and Flynn laughed, and both siblings knelt, putting their fingers in the grass. The earth magic in their veins surged forth as an oak burst from Flynn's hands, shooting high over them, and from Sathia's hands tumbled runners of strawberry and brambles of blackberry, tangles of raspberries and thickets of blueberries—

"Holy gods," Tharion said, and pointed out to the sea.

It was no longer gray and thrashing, but a vibrant, clear turquoise. And rising from the water, just as they had seen on the map Declan had found, were islands, large and small. Lush and green with life.

Forests erupted on the island they stood on, soon joined by mountains and rivers.

So much life, so much magic, freed at last of Vanir control. A place not only for the Fae, but for everyone. All of them.

Bryce could feel it—the joy of the land at being seen, at being freed. She looked at Ruhn, and her brother's face was bright with awe. As if their father didn't lie beneath the earth, lost forever to the dark, his bones to be eaten by worms.

It was only awe, and freedom, lighting Ruhn's face.

No more pain. No more fear.

Bryce didn't know when she started crying, only that the next moment Ruhn was there, his arms around her, and they were both sobbing.

Their friends gave them space, understanding that it wasn't pure joy that coursed through them—that their joy was tempered by grief for the years of pain, and hope for the years ahead.

The world might very well end soon, Bryce knew, and they

might all die with it, but right now the paradise blooming around them, this awakened land, was proof of what life had been like before the Asteri, before the Fae and the Vanir.

Proof of what might be afterward.

Ruhn pulled back, cupping her face in his hands. Tears ran down his face. She couldn't stop crying—crying and laughing—with all that flowed from her heart.

Her brother only pressed a kiss to her brow and said, "Long live the queen."

64

The land had awoken, and the Fae of Avallen were terrified.

Hunt tried not to be smug at the sight of the destroyed castle. The occupants and the town had been spared, but vines and trees had burst through Morven's castle and turned it into rubble.

"A last *fuck you* from the land," Bryce murmured to Hunt as the two of them arrived at a hill overlooking the ruins. At their far end, a group of Fae stood in apprehensive silence around the demolished building.

Beside him, Bryce thrummed with power—from Helena and her cursed bloodline, but also from whatever lingering soul-wound had healed the moment Ruhn had cut off their father's head.

Hunt slid an arm around his mate's waist, taking in the Fae who were gawking at the ruins, the island of Avallen—and the new islands surrounding it.

Bryce peered up at him. "Are you . . . okay?"

He was silent for a long moment, looking out at the landscape. "No."

She pressed closer into his side.

His throat worked for a moment. "I'm some weird demonic test-tube baby."

"Maybe that's where you came from, Hunt," she said, offering him a gentle smile, "but it's not who you are—who you became."

He glanced at her. "Earlier, you seemed to not like the person I became."

She sighed. "Hunt, I get it—all the shit you're feeling. I really do. But I can't do this without you. *All* of you."

His heart ached as he looked at her fully. "I know. I'm trying. It's just . . ." He struggled for the words. "My worst nightmare would be to see you in the Asteri's hands. To see you dead."

"And avoiding that fate is worth letting them rule forever?" There was no sharpness to her question—just curiosity.

"Part of me says yes. A very, very loud part of me," he admitted. "But another part of me says that we need to do whatever it takes to end this. So future generations, future mates . . . they don't have to make the same choices, suffer the same fates, as we have."

He *would* try to put his fear behind him. For her, for Midgard.

"I know," she said gently. "If you need to talk, if you need someone to listen . . . I'm here."

He scanned her face, pure love aching in his heart. Some of that lingering darkness and pain remained, yes, but he'd fight through it. And he knew she'd give him the space he needed to do so. "Thanks, Quinlan."

She rose up on her toes to kiss his cheek. A sweet, soft brush of her lips that warmed the final numbed shards of his soul.

Then she surveyed the ruins once more, taking his hand as they began walking down toward their friends gathered at the foot of the hill. "I got the last piece of Theia's power, but what now? How do we take on the Asteri? How do we get close enough to them to use the knife and sword and toss them through that portal?"

He kissed her temple. "Give it a rest for today. For now, enjoy being leveled up."

She snorted. "That doesn't sound like a strategy from the Umbra Mortis."

"I can't tell if that's an insult or not." He nudged her with a wing. "We've got some other urgent stuff to sort out first, Bryce."

"Yeah, I know," she said as they came to a stop among their friends. She addressed all of them. "Since this place can hold out against the Asteri, we need to get as many people here as possible. Without tipping off imperial forces."

"The *Depth Charger* could help," Flynn suggested. Tharion grimaced but didn't object.

Lidia asked, "But how would they pierce the mists?"

Bryce lifted a hand, and in the distance, the mists parted—then sealed. "Didn't you hear? I'm a fancy world-walker who can do this shit innately. Plus . . ." She gave a crooked grin. "I'm now Queen of Avallen. Wielding the mists is a perk of the job."

"Of course," Hunt said, rolling his eyes and earning a jab to the ribs.

But Ruhn warned, "The Fae won't be happy to share."

Bryce motioned to the ruins, the damage she'd unleashed, however unknowingly. "They don't have any choice."

Ruhn snorted. "Long live the queen, indeed."

Declan gave a shout from up on the hill, and they all turned toward him.

"Whatever you did with those mists, Bryce," Declan shouted, "I got service!" He lifted his phone in triumph, and then lowered his head to read whatever messages he had.

"Small victories," Bryce said. Lidia and Tharion laughed.

The Hind's amusement faded, though, as she turned to Tharion, as if drawn by the mer's own chuckle. "You could hide here, you know. The Ocean Queen can't pass through these mists unless Bryce allows it."

"Hide," Tharion said, as if the word tasted foul.

"The alternative is begging her not to kill you," Lidia said, "and then doing everything she says for the rest of your life."

"No different from the River Queen," Tharion said. Sathia was watching him carefully—curiously. The mer shrugged, and asked Lidia baldly, "How do you live with it? Being at her mercy?"

Lidia's mouth tightened, and they all pretended they weren't listening to her every word as she said at last, "I had no other choice." She looked to Ruhn, eyes bright. "But I'm not going to anymore."

Ruhn started, whirling to her. "What?"

Lidia said to him, to all of them, "If we survive the Asteri, I'm not going back."

Hunt had seen enough of the Ocean Queen to know how well that would go down.

Bryce said cautiously, "But your sons . . ."

"If we survive, my enemies will be dead," Lidia said, chin lifting with queenly grace. "And surely she will have no need of my services anymore." She nodded to Tharion. "I'm not going back, and neither should you. The age of unchecked rulers is over." She motioned to the ruins. "This is the first step."

A chill went down Hunt's spine at the surety of her words. Bryce opened her mouth like she might say something.

But Baxian pivoted toward Declan, as if he'd sensed something off. A second later, Declan's head snapped up.

A foreboding quiet settled over Hunt. Over all of them.

No one spoke as Declan approached. As the male's throat bobbed. And when he looked at Ruhn, at Bryce, tears shone in his eyes.

"The Asteri made their move."

Bryce grabbed Hunt's arm, as if it would keep her from falling.

"Tell me," Lidia said, pushing through them to get to Declan.

Declan glanced at the Hind, then back to Bryce. "The Asteri organized a hit, led by Pollux and Mordoc, on every Ophion base. They wiped them off the map."

"Fuck," Hunt breathed.

But Declan was shaking his head. "They wiped out everyone in their camps, too."

Hunt's knees shook.

And when Declan looked to Bryce, Hunt knew immediately that it would be bad. Wished he could undo it, whatever it was—

"And they dispatched their Asterian Guard to Asphodel Meadows. They . . . they said it was a hotbed of rebel activity."

Bryce began shaking her head, backing away.

Declan's voice broke as he said, "They unleashed ten brimstone missiles on the Meadows. On everyone living there."

PART III
THE ASCENT

65

Ithan stood on the deck of a fishing boat that had seen better decades, Hypaxia at his side. Apparently, Jesiba Roga didn't think the two of them needed to travel in style.

But at least the shark-shifter crew hadn't asked questions. And had kept their own counsel as they cut the engine and the boat bobbed in the gray swells of the Haldren, right in front of the impenetrable, sky-high wall of mist.

Ithan nodded to the broken brooch on Hypaxia's cloak. "Any chance your broom still works? We could fly over them."

"No," Hypaxia said. "And besides, only Morven can let us through."

Ithan reached a hand toward the mists, twining it through his fingers. "So how do we contact him? Knock on the barrier? Send up a flare?"

His tone was more cheerful than he felt. Somewhere beyond these mists lay Sofie's body. Apparently, Morven had told Jesiba they could have it—his late son had shipped it to his home, and the Fae King hadn't yet bothered to have it tossed into the garbage. A stroke of luck sent from Urd herself. Jesiba had promised that Morven wouldn't touch it—that he'd be glad to dump the body into their hands.

That is, if they could get through the barrier. Hypaxia lifted a light brown hand to the mists, as if testing them. "They feel . . ."

As if in answer, the curtain of the mists shuddered and parted.

Sunlight flooded through. Gray seas turned turquoise. The wind warmed to a balmy, gentle breeze. A paradise lay beyond.

Even the gruff shark shifters gasped in shock. But Ithan glanced at Hypaxia, who was wide-eyed as well. "What's wrong?"

Hypaxia slowly shook her head. "This is not the Avallen I have visited before."

"What do you mean?" Every instinct went on alert, his wolf at the ready.

Hypaxia motioned to the captain to start sailing through the parted mists, toward the lush, beckoning land. Prettier than even the Coronal Islands. The former witch-queen breathed, "Something tremendous has occurred here."

Ithan sighed. "Please tell me it was a *good* tremendous change?"

Her silence wasn't reassuring.

Hunt found Bryce sitting atop the ruins of what had once been a tower, tangles of blooming vines and roses all around her. A beautiful, surreal place for a Fae Queen to rest.

The land seemed to know her, small blooming flowers nestling around her body, some of them even curling in the long strands of her hair.

Yet her face when Hunt sat beside her was hollow. Devastated.

Dried tears had left salty tracks down her cheeks. And her whiskey-colored eyes, usually so full of life and fire, were vacant. Vacant in a way he hadn't seen since that time he'd found her at Lethe, drinking away her grief at Danika's death, the wound reopened when she realized her father had withheld vital information that would have helped with the investigation.

Hunt sat at her side on an uneven bit of tumbled stone and slid a wing around her. From up here, he could see the scattering of islands amid the vibrant teal of the ocean. Avallen had awoken into a paradise, and part of him ached to leap into the skies and explore every inch of it, but . . .

"All that new power from Theia," Bryce said hoarsely, "and it didn't amount to shit. I didn't find it in time to help anyone—save anyone."

Hunt kissed her temple and promised, "We'll make it count, Bryce."

"I'm sorry," she said quietly. "For being a dick to you about what you're going through."

"Bryce . . . ," he began, scrambling for the words.

"I apologize for everything I said to you about getting over it," she went on. "But . . ." Her lips pressed into a thin line, as if keeping in a sob that wanted to work itself free.

"What just happened," he said roughly, "isn't your fault. It's no one's fault but the Asteri's. You've always been right about that."

She said dully, as if she hadn't heard a word he'd said, "Fury and June are getting into a helicopter with my parents, Emile—Cooper, I mean—and Syrinx," A glance down at where she'd discarded her phone in the blossoms beside her. "The Asteri didn't find them before the attack, but I want them all here, kept safe."

"Good," Hunt said. They'd all spent the past hour making frantic phone calls to family and friends. Hunt had debated for a long while about whether to risk calling Isaiah and Naomi, but had opted not to in the end, lest it raise any trouble if their phones were tapped. Which was part of why he'd sought Bryce out now, even though he knew she'd come up here to be alone.

The others were finding lodgings for the night, now that Morven's castle lay in ruins. From Ruhn's grim face, it seemed the Fae weren't being welcoming. *Tough fucking luck,* Hunt wanted to say. They were about to get a whole influx of people.

"We could stay here," Bryce murmured, and Hunt knew that the words were ones she'd only speak in front of him. "We could get all our friends and family, anyone who can make it across the Haldren—and just . . . stay here, protected. Forever. It's basically what the Ocean Queen asked for. And would make me little better than my ancestors—to hide like that. But at least people would be safe. Some people on Midgard, at least." While the majority remained at the mercy of the Asteri.

Hunt leaned forward to peer at her face. "Is that what you want to do?"

"No," Bryce said, and her eyes lifted to the island-dotted horizon. To the wall of mist beyond it. "I mean, anyone who can make it here, any refugees, they'll be allowed in. I willed the mists to make it so."

He would normally have ribbed her about how very Super Powerful and Special Magic Starborn Fae Queen that was, but he kept his mouth shut. Let her keep talking.

"But us . . ." The bleak look on her face had him folding his wing more tightly around her. "We can't hide here forever."

"No," he agreed. "We can't." He let her see how much he meant it. That he'd fight until the very end.

She leaned her head against his shoulder. "I can't even think about what they did. To Ophion and the camps . . . to the Meadows . . ." Her voice broke.

He couldn't process it, either. The innocents killed. The children.

"We have an obligation," Bryce said, and lifted her head. "To those people. To Midgard. And to other worlds, too. We have an obligation to end this."

It was Bryce's beloved face looking at him, but it was also the face of a queen. His lightning stirred in answer. And it didn't matter to him if those fucks Apollion and Thanatos had made him, made his power. If his lightning could help her, save her, save Midgard from the Asteri . . . that was all that mattered.

Bryce said, "*I* have an obligation to end this."

Her gaze swept over the peaceful archipelago, and for a moment, Hunt could see it: a life here, with their kids and their friends. A life they could build for themselves in this untouched place.

It shimmered there, so close he could nearly touch it.

Bryce said, as if thinking the same thing, "I think Urd needed me to come here."

"To know it could be a refuge?"

She shook her head. "I wondered why the mists kept out the Asteri, how we could use those mists against them. I thought we'd come here and find answers, maybe some secret weapon—like some major Asteri-repelling device."

She slid her exhausted gaze to him at last.

"But it's the sheer quantity of black salt that keeps the Asteri out, not the mists, and we can't replicate that. I think Urd wanted me to see that a society could thrive here. That I could be safe here, along with everyone I love."

Her mouth trembled, but she pressed it into a thin line.

"I think Urd wanted me to see and learn all that," she went on, "and have to decide whether to stay, or leave this safety behind and fight. Urd wanted to tempt me."

"Maybe it was a gift," Hunt offered. "Not a test or challenge, Bryce, but a gift." At her raised eyebrows, he explained, "For Urd to let the people you love be safe here—while you go kick some Asteri ass."

Her smile was unspeakably sad. "To know they'll be protected here . . . even if we fail."

He didn't try to reassure her that they'd succeed. Instead, he promised gently, "We'll do it together. You and me—we'll end it together." He brushed a strand of her hair behind a delicately pointed ear. "I'm with you. All of me. You and I, we'll finish this."

Her chin lifted, and he could have sworn a crown of stars glimmered around her head. "I want to wipe them off the face of the planet," she said, and though her voice was soft, nothing but pure, predatory rage filled it.

"I'll get the mop and bucket," he said, and flashed her a smile.

She looked at him, all regal fury and poise—and laughed. The first moment of normalcy between them, joyous and beautiful. Another thing for him to fight for. Until the very end.

Tendrils of night-blooming purple flowers unfurled around her in answer, despite the daylight. Had it always been leading toward this? In the night garden, before they were attacked by the kristallos all those months ago, he could have sworn the flowers had opened for her. Were they sensing this power, the dusk-born heritage in her veins?

"This is remarkable," he said, nodding to the island that seemed to respond to her every emotion.

"I think it's what the Prison—the island in the Fae's home world—once was. When Theia ruled it, I mean. Before Silene fucked it all up. Maybe they're linked in some way through being thin places and spilled over to each other a bit. Maybe back in that other world . . . maybe I woke up the land around the Prison, too."

Hunt's brows rose. "Only one way to find out, I guess."

She huffed. "I don't think they'll ever let me set foot back in that world."

"Do you think there's any chance we could recruit them to fight for us?"

"No. I mean, I don't know what they'd say, but . . . I wouldn't ask that of them. Of anyone."

"I take back what I said earlier, about giving the planning a rest: we need to start thinking through our strategy." He hated putting the burden on her, but they had to make a move. She was right—they couldn't hide here. "The Asteri clearly want us to retaliate for what they did. Rigelus probably expects us to try to rally an army and attack them, but it'll never work. We'll always be out-gunned and outnumbered." He took her hand. "I . . . Bryce, I lost one army already."

"I know," she said.

But he pushed, "We're also talking about taking on *six* Asteri. If it was us versus Rigelus, maybe . . . but all six? Do we separate them? Pick them off one by one?"

"No. It'd give the others time to rally. We strike them all at once—together."

He considered. "It's time to let Hel in, isn't it?"

The sweet breeze ruffled her hair as she nodded.

"So where does that leave us?" he asked.

The star on her chest glowed. "We're going to Nena. To open the Northern Rift."

"Fuck. Okay. Ignoring the enormity of that, and assuming it all goes right, what happens next? Do we walk into the palace and start fighting?"

Her gaze had again lifted to the islands and glimmering sea. That regal expression spread over her face, and he knew he was getting a glimpse of the leader she'd become. If they got through this.

"What is the one thing Rigelus has constantly told us?" Bryce asked.

"That we suck?"

She chuckled. "He went out of his way to offer you freedom," she said, nodding to where the brand was back on his wrist, "as a way to entice me to keep my mouth shut about killing Micah. And keep you quiet about killing Sandriel."

He angled his head. "You want to go public about it?"

"I think Rigelus and the Asteri are nervous about the world finding out what we did. That their precious Archangels could be killed. By two apparent randos, no less."

It was Hunt's turn to chuckle. "We're not exactly randos."

"Yeah, but I'm still going to show Midgard that even Archangels can be killed."

"Okay, that's . . . that's awesome," Hunt said, his blood pumping at the thought. Rigelus would lose his fucking mind. "But what will it accomplish?"

"They'll be so busy dealing with the media they won't think about us for a little while," Bryce said, smiling cruelly. Just a hint of the father who now lay dead beneath the earth here. "It will be more of a distraction than any army from Hel."

"I think it's a good idea," Hunt said, mulling it over. "I really do. But how are you going to prove it? Everyone would have to take your word for it, and the Asteri would deny it immediately."

"That's why I need to talk to Jesiba."

"Oh?"

She got to her feet and offered him a hand to rise. "Because she has the video footage of what I did to Micah."

* * *

What lay before Ithan was truly a paradise on Midgard. Crystal clear water, lush vegetation, streams and waterfalls pouring into the sea, powdery sand, birds singing . . .

He remained on alert, however, as the boat pulled up to a cove, close enough to the shore that he and Hypaxia jumped out and waded the few feet onto the beach.

"Which way?" he asked the former queen, scanning the dense foliage bordering the beach, the rising hills. "Jesiba said the castle was a few miles inland, but I didn't see anything while we were sailing in—"

Wings flapped above, and Ithan shifted on instinct, his powerful wolf's body nudging Hypaxia behind him as he snarled up at the sky.

Two scents hit him a heartbeat later.

And Ithan's head emptied out entirely as Hunt Athalar landed in the sand, Bryce in his arms.

66

Back in his humanoid form, Ithan sat across from Bryce and Hunt in the grass, unable to get words out. Hypaxia, seated beside him, gave him space to think.

Beyond Bryce sat Ruhn, Flynn, Dec, and Tharion—and Lidia and Baxian. Along with a female who was apparently Tharion's wife and Flynn's sister.

Some crazy shit had happened. Ithan knew that. But they didn't offer any explanations, instead waiting for him to get into why he'd come here. What had happened.

His throat became unbearably tight.

"I . . ." They were all staring at him. Waiting. "I need Sofie Renast's body."

"Well," Hunt said, whistling, "that wasn't what I expected to hear."

Ithan lifted pleading eyes to the Umbra Mortis. "Jesiba said King Morven has the body—"

"Had the body," Ruhn amended, crossing his arms. His tattoos looked like they'd been put through a paper shredder. Ithan had noticed that immediately upon seeing his friends, upon hugging them all so tightly they'd complained about his grip. Ruhn went on, "The body is now technically Bryce's."

Ithan shook his head, not understanding.

Hunt drawled, "Morven is dead, and Bryce is Queen of Avallen."

Ithan just blinked at Bryce, who was watching him. Carefully. Like she knew something had—

"The Meadows," he blurted. Had they heard about it here? Had they—

"We know," Flynn said.

"Fucking bastards," Tharion murmured.

Bryce only asked Ithan, "How bad?"

Ithan couldn't talk about the small bodies, so many of them—

"As one might expect," Hypaxia answered grimly, "and then some." Heavy silence fell.

"Whatever took you away from helping the city," Lidia said, eyes on her sister, "must be important indeed. Why do you need Sofie's body?"

Again, they all looked at him. And he couldn't contain his misery as he said, "Because I fucked up."

It all came out. How he'd found an alternate heir to the Fendyr line, freed her from the Astronomer . . . and then killed her.

None of it was news to Tharion, Flynn, or Dec. But judging from the way Bryce and Ruhn were glowering at the trio . . . Apparently, they had forgotten to mention this information in the chaos of the last few days.

How they'd forgotten to mention the thing that had literally shredded apart Ithan's life was beyond him, but he didn't dwell on it. He plowed on to the part of his story that was news for all of them: How he and Hypaxia had attempted to raise Sigrid. And now the Fendyr heir was a Reaper.

When he reached the end of his account, they were all staring at him wide-eyed. No one more so than Bryce, who hadn't said anything when he'd spoken of an alternative to Sabine, someone Danika might have liked.

Ithan finished, "So if Sofie's body is intact—"

"It's not," Bryce said quietly.

Something crumpled in Ithan's chest as he met her whiskey-colored eyes.

"Morven's castle collapsed," Bryce said sadly. "Sofie's body is underneath tons of rubble, even if it *is* intact."

Ithan put his face in his hands and breathed hard.

Flynn put a consoling arm around his shoulders, squeezing. "Maybe there's another way—"

"We needed a thunderbird," Ithan said through his hands. There was no fixing this. No undoing it. He'd brought this upon an innocent wolf, upon his people—

"Look," Bryce said, and the gentleness in her tone almost killed him. She blew out a long breath. "An alternate Fendyr heir would have been amazing. But . . ."

Ithan lowered his hands from his face. "But *what*?"

Hunt's eyes flashed at Ithan's snarl. But Bryce didn't back down as she said, "We have bigger problems right now. And time isn't our ally."

"I killed her," Ithan said, voice cracking. "I fucking *killed* her—"

But Athalar said to Hypaxia, "Rigelus collected some of my lightning—for a similar purpose, I think." Bryce started, as if this was news to her. "Are you sure it wouldn't help with Sigrid?"

"It might be worth a try," Hypaxia admitted, "but I don't have any of the supplies I'd need to contain your sort of power."

Ruhn's head lifted. "Like a bunch of crystals?"

They all turned to the prince, but he was looking at Lidia. The Hind explained, "We found a cache of them in the archives."

Ruhn added, "Rigelus used one to grab Athalar's power in the dungeons. Would it work for you, too?"

Hypaxia nodded slowly and said to Hunt, "I wouldn't require much."

Bryce glanced around at the others. Ruhn took her meaning and motioned to his friends. "Come on. Let's grab those crystals from the archives. Hopefully it's still standing."

Flynn, Dec, Lidia, Baxian, and Tharion—his wife in tow—headed down the hill with Ruhn. Only Tharion glanced back, just once, his eyes full of pity. Like the mer understood what it was to have fucked up so royally. To regret.

But Bryce grabbed Ithan's hand, bringing his attention back to her. "What's done is done, Ithan."

"Jesiba said the same thing," he said glumly.

"And she's right," Bryce said. At her side, Athalar nodded. But Bryce motioned with a hand to Hypaxia. "The whole fucking world's changing so rapidly—we're all changing, faster than we can process. For Cthona's sake, Hypaxia isn't even queen anymore. Have either of you really reflected on that?" A punch of guilt went through Ithan. He'd been so focused on himself that he hadn't thought to check in with the witch. But Hypaxia's face remained grave, determined. And Bryce went on to Ithan, "So look: you killed Sigrid, and she's a Reaper, and I think it's . . . really admirable that you're trying to raise her—"

"Don't patronize me," he snarled, and again Athalar threw him that warning glare.

"I'm not," Bryce said. She was the Queen of Avallen, and Ithan could see it in her eyes: the leader glimmering there. "Part of why I love you is because you'll stop at nothing to do the right thing."

"Trying to do the right thing led me to the debacle with Sigrid," he said, shaking his head in disgust.

"Maybe," Bryce said, and glanced at Hypaxia. "But the two of you . . . I need your help. I have to believe that Urd sent you here for this."

"For what?" Hypaxia said, head angling.

Bryce and Hunt swapped glances. The angel motioned to his mate, as if to say, *Your story to tell.*

"I, uh," Bryce said, pulling at some blades of grass, "have a lot to update you guys about."

"You weren't kidding about the big update," Ithan said when Bryce had finished.

"Where do we factor into this, though?" Hypaxia asked. "If

you're thinking to raise an army to aid Hel, I have no sway with the witches, and Ithan wouldn't be able to muster the wolves—"

"No armies from Midgard," Bryce said. "We don't have the time for that, anyway."

Hypaxia pulled on a tightly coiled curl. "What, then?"

Bryce's eyes seemed to glow. "I need you to make an antidote for the Asteri's parasite."

Hypaxia blinked slowly. That bit of Bryce's story had been the hardest to swallow. That they were all infected by something in the water, their magic cut off at the knees.

Bryce pushed on, "You figured out an antidote for the synth, Hypaxia. I need you to do it again. Help us level up before we take on the Asteri. Get us free of their restraints."

"You place an awful lot of faith in my abilities. I'll need to study the parasite before I can even start mapping out the properties of an antidote—"

"We don't have time for the full-blown scientific method," Bryce said.

"I'd hesitate to give you anything that hadn't been fully tested," Hypaxia countered.

"We don't have that luxury," Athalar said firmly. "Anything you can rig up, even if it's temporary, even if it just holds the parasite at bay for a bit . . ."

"I don't know if that's possible," Hypaxia said, but Ithan could see the ideas gleaming in her eyes. "And I'd need a lab. Considering the state of Avallen after your . . . claiming of it, I don't think there's anything here I could use."

"And no power, anyway," Bryce said. "So you'll have to head back to the Lunathion House of Flame and Shadow—it seems like you guys will be hidden and protected there. Especially if Jesiba's around."

Ithan hadn't told Bryce about who—what—Jesiba really was. That was Jesiba's secret to tell.

Her words settled. Ithan said, "What do you mean *you guys*? I don't know shit about science. I can't help Hypaxia with this."

"You know how to fight," Athalar said. "And defend. Hypaxia will need someone to guard her while she works."

Ithan turned to Bryce, who was watching him with a grim expression. "But Sigrid—"

"We need that antidote, Ithan," Bryce said gently, but firmly. "More than anything. Hunt will give you the lightning for Sigrid, but we need that antidote first." She added to Hypaxia, "As fast as you can make it."

Hypaxia and Bryce stared at each other for a long moment. "Very well," Hypaxia said, inclining her head.

Ithan closed his eyes. To abandon his quest, to leave Sigrid as a Reaper . . .

But his friends needed him. They were asking for his help. To deny them, even if it was to save Sigrid . . . He'd already screwed up Sigrid's life. He wouldn't do the same to his friends.

So Ithan opened his eyes and said, "When do we head back to Crescent City?"

Bryce's face remained grim as she said, "Right now."

"Now?" Hypaxia said, the first bit of shock she'd shown.

"That boat's still waiting for you," Athalar said, pointing to the ocean in the distance. "We'll go get the crystals from the others, and I'll fire up the stones. Once I bring them back here, get on that boat and sail for Lunathion."

"And if—when—I come up with an antidote to the parasite?" Hypaxia asked Bryce and Hunt. "How do I contact you?"

"Call us," Bryce said. "If you can't reach us, get the antidote to the Eternal City. There's a fleet of mech-suits on Mount Hermon— hide near there, and we'll find you."

"When, though?"

Bryce's face hardened. "You'll know when it's too late to help us."

Ithan started, "Bryce—"

But Bryce nodded toward the glimmering sea. "As fast as you can," she repeated to the former witch-queen. "I'm begging you."

With that, she walked to Athalar, and he leapt into the skies, flying them in the direction the others had headed.

There was no chance to talk to Tharion or Flynn or Dec. No

chance to even say goodbye. From the way Hypaxia was watching the angel and Bryce vanish toward the distant ruins, he suspected she was thinking the same thing about Lidia.

Twenty minutes later, Bryce and Athalar were back, half a dozen quartz crystals sizzling in the angel's hands. Bottled lightning.

Hypaxia pocketed them, promising to use them well. Bryce kissed her cheek, then Ithan's.

Once, he would have done anything for that kiss. But now it left him hollow, reeling.

Athalar only clapped Ithan on the shoulder before launching skyward with Bryce again, soon no more than a speck against the blue.

When they were alone, Hypaxia motioned to the path they'd taken up from the beach. "We must rise to meet this challenge, Ithan," she said, her voice sure. She patted the lightning-filled crystals now glowing through the pockets of her dark blue robes.

With that, she started off for the boat and the task before them.

Ithan lingered for a moment longer. He'd failed in this quest, too. He'd had a second shot at fixing Sigrid, and he'd failed. It was important to help their friends—and all of Midgard—but the decision weighed on him.

He'd always thought of himself as a good guy, but maybe he wasn't. Maybe he'd been deluding himself.

He didn't know where that left him.

Ithan followed Hypaxia, turning his back on Avallen and the sliver of hope it had offered. To have the lightning in hand, but to have to postpone any effort to help Sigrid . . .

He had no choice but to keep putting one foot in front of the other.

Maybe at some point, he'd stop leaving a trail of absolute destruction in his wake.

67

Hunt found Baxian arranging fresh bundles of hay in the castle stables. They remained intact, located just far enough away from the castle to have been spared during its collapse. "You got the lightning to the wolf and the witch?" Baxian asked by way of greeting.

"They're on their way back to Lunathion with it. But the priority is to try to find a cure for the parasite."

"Good," Baxian grunted. "I hope they have more success than I've had with finding us housing for tonight."

"That bad, huh?" Hunt said, leaning against the doorway.

"No one wants to loan us a room or even a bed, so short of kicking people out of their homes . . ." The Helhound gestured grandly to the stables. "Welcome to Hotel Horseshit."

Hunt chuckled, surveying the woodwork. "Honestly, I've slept in way worse. These horses have a nicer home than the one I grew up in."

Sad, but true.

"Same," Baxian said, and it surprised Hunt enough that he lifted a brow. Baxian said, "I, ah . . . grew up in one of the poorer parts of Ravilis. Being half-shifter—half–*Helhound* shifter—and half-angel . . . it didn't make my parents popular with either the

House of Earth and Blood or the House of Sky and Breath. Made it hard for them to keep their jobs."

"Which one of your parents was the angel?"

"My dad," Baxian said. "He served as a captain in Sandriel's 45th. He had it easier than my mom, who was shunned by everyone she ever knew for 'sullying' herself with an angel. But they both paid the price for being together."

From the way his tone darkened, Hunt knew it had to have been bad. "I'm sorry," he said.

"I was eight. I still don't know how the mob started, but . . ." Baxian's throat worked, yet he finished one pallet of hay and moved on to start another. "It ended with my mom torn to shreds by her fellow Helhounds, and my father seized by the very angels he commanded and given the Living Death."

Hunt blew out a breath. "Fuck."

"They were in such a frenzy, they, ah . . ." Baxian shook his head. "They kept cutting off his wings every time they tried to heal. He lost so much blood in the end that he didn't make it."

"I'm sorry," Hunt said again. "I never knew."

"No one did. Not even Sandriel." Baxian laid a blanket over the next pallet. "From then on, I was on my own. Neither side of the family would take a *half-breed*, as they made sure to call me, so I learned how to fend for myself in the slums. How to keep hidden, how to listen for valuable information—how to sell that information to interested parties. I became good enough at it that I made a name for myself. The Snake, they called me, because I fucked over so many people. And Sandriel eventually heard about me and recruited me for her triarii—to be her spy-master and tracker. The Snake became the Helhound, but . . . I kept a few touches."

The memory of Baxian's reptilian armor flashed through Hunt's mind.

"I hated it, hated Sandriel, hated Lidia, who I always thought could see through me, but . . . what else was I going to do with myself?" Baxian finished with all the pallets and faced Hunt. "Serving in Sandriel's triarii was better than living in the slums, always looking over my shoulder for whoever wanted to knife me. But the shit she had us do . . ." He tapped his neck, the scar Hunt had given him. "I deserved this."

"We all did fucked-up shit for Sandriel," Hunt said roughly.

"Yeah, but you didn't have a choice. I did."

"You chose to turn away from it, to mitigate the damage when you could."

"Thanks to Danika," Baxian said.

"What better excuse than love?" Hunt asked.

Baxian smiled sadly. "I told her everything, you know. Danika, I mean. And she understood—she didn't judge. She told me she had a half-human, half-Fae friend who had faced similar troubles. I think her love for Bryce allowed her to see past all my shit and still love me."

Hunt smiled. "You should tell Bryce that."

Baxian eyed him. "You guys . . . ah, you guys okay? Things seemed kind of rough for a while, down in the caves."

"Yeah," Hunt said, letting out a long breath. "Yeah, we are. We talked."

"And the Hel stuff . . ." Bryce had filled everyone in about what the Princes of Hel had claimed about Hunt's origins. "You doing okay with that?"

Hunt considered. "It seems secondary to everything else that's going on, you know? Poor me, with my daddy issues. Daddies? I don't even know."

Baxian huffed a laugh. "Does it matter? Your exact genetic makeup?"

Hunt considered again. "No. That's just stuff in my blood, my magic. It's not who I am." He shrugged. "That's what Bryce says, anyway. I'm working on believing it."

Baxian nodded to the halo on Hunt's brow. "So how come you haven't taken it off yet? They claimed you've had the power all along."

Hunt glanced toward the raftered ceiling. "I will," he hedged.

Baxian gave Hunt a look that said he saw right through him. That right now, Hunt needed a breather. Just some time to process everything. He wanted to be free of the halo, but to go full Prince of Hel or whatever . . . he wasn't ready for that. Not yet.

But Baxian said, "Bryce is right, though. Who you are isn't about what's biologically in your system. It's about who raised you. Who you are now."

Hunt's mother's face flashed before his eyes, and he fixed the memory of her close to his heart. "Have you and Bryce been exchanging notes on how to give me a pep talk?"

Baxian laughed, then glanced around. "Where is she, anyway? Off making more gardens?"

Hunt laughed quietly. "Probably. But I came here to find you—we're having a council of war in a minute, but I wanted to ask you something first."

Baxian crossed his powerful arms, giving Hunt his full attention. "What?"

"Some shit's going down soon. I need someone to run things if I'm not around."

"And where would you be?"

"You'll hear about everything from Bryce," Hunt said, holding his stare. "But I need a second in command right now."

Baxian raised his brows. For a moment, Hunt was in a war tent again, giving orders to his soldiers before battle. He shook off the chill of the memory and folded his wings.

Baxian smirked, though. "Who said you're in charge?"

Hunt rolled his eyes. "My wife, that's who." But he pressed, "So . . . will you? I need someone who can fight. On the ground and in the air."

"Oh, you're only asking because I have wings?" Baxian ruffled his black feathers for emphasis.

"I'm asking," Hunt said, noting the spark of amusement on the Helhound's face, "because I trust you, asshole. For some weird reason."

"Asteri dungeon bonding at its finest." The tone was light, though the shadows of all they'd been through darkened Baxian's eyes. "But I'm honored. Yeah—you can trust me. Tell me what needs to get done and I'll do it."

"Thanks," Hunt said, and motioned to the exit. "You might regret that in a few minutes . . . but thanks."

"Let me get this straight," Ruhn said. They had all gathered around a campfire in the middle of an open plain—about the only privacy they could find from spying ears. Just for the Hel of it, Flynn had grown a small grove of oak trees around them. His earth-based magic seemed to be exploding here now, as if the reborn land were calling to him to fill it, adorn it.

But Ruhn fixed his stare on his sister as he said, "We're going to *Nena*. To open the *Northern Rift*."

Bryce, seated on a large stone with Hunt beside her, said, "*I* am going to Nena. With Hunt. And my parents—I need Randall's particular brand of expertise. Baxian will stay here with Cooper until they get back. *You* are going to take those two buzzards"—she nodded to Flynn and Declan, who glared at her—"and go back to Lunathion."

Ruhn blinked slowly. "To . . . die? Because that's what will happen if we're caught."

"To find Isaiah and Naomi. See if they can come join us. Their phones and emails are no doubt tapped—we don't have any other way to contact them."

"You want us to go convince two members of Celestina's triarii to go rogue?" Dec said.

Hunt said, "They won't need much convincing, but yes. We need them."

Ruhn shook his head. "If you're thinking of rallying some sort of angelic host to take on the Asteri, forget it. No angel is going to follow any of us—even Athalar—into battle."

Bryce held her ground. This was her plan, and there'd be no shaking her or Athalar from it, Ruhn knew. He opened his mouth to keep arguing anyway, but Dec cut him off.

"What about him?" Dec asked, pointing to Baxian. "He's got a better in with the angels."

Bryce shook her head. "Baxian will stay here to help coordinate the arriving refugees, and lead in our stead." Bryce gestured to herself and Hunt.

"We could do that," Flynn said.

"No," Bryce said coolly. "You can't. The Fae are more scared of him, so he'll be the most effective."

"Says who?" Flynn demanded. "We're plenty scary."

"Says the fact that he, at least, was able to get us the stables to sleep in," Hunt growled. Baxian waggled his eyebrows at the Fae lord. "The rest of you struck out completely."

Flynn and Dec scowled. But Ruhn's breath caught as Bryce looked to Lidia. "I'm not going to presume to give you orders. I know you have an obligation to the Ocean Queen. Do what you must."

"I go with Ruhn," Lidia said quietly, and something in his chest sparked at that.

Bryce just nodded, and he didn't miss the gratitude in his sister's eyes.

"And me?" Tharion asked at last, brows high.

"I need you to go back to the River Queen," Bryce said softly. "And convince her to shelter as many people Beneath as possible."

Tharion paled. "Legs, I'd love to do that, but she'll kill me."

"Then find some way to convince her not to," Athalar said, nothing but pure general as he fixed his stare on the mer. "Use those Captain Whatever skills and figure out something she wants more than killing you."

Tharion glanced to Sathia, who was watching attentively. "She, uh . . . won't be pleased by my new marital status."

"Then find something," Hunt said again, "to please her."

Tharion's jaw clenched, but Ruhn could see him thinking through his options.

"The Blue Court was the only faction in Crescent City that sheltered people during the attack this spring," Bryce said. "You guys went out of your way to help innocents get to safety. Appeal to that side of the River Queen. Tell her a storm is coming, and that after what went down in Asphodel Meadows, we need her to take in as many people as the Blue Court can accommodate. If there's anyone who's got the charm to sway her, it's you, Tharion."

"Ah, Legs," Tharion said, rubbing his face. "How can I resist when you ask like that?"

Sathia, to Ruhn's surprise, laid a hand on the mer's knee and promised Bryce, "We'll both go."

"Then she'll definitely kill Tharion," Flynn said.

Sathia glared at her brother. "I know a thing or two about dealing with arrogant rulers." Her chin lifted. "I'm not afraid of the River Queen." Tharion looked like he might warn her against that, but kept his mouth shut.

"Good," Bryce said to Sathia. "And thank you."

"So that's it, then," Ruhn said. "Come dawn, we're scattering to the winds?"

"Come dawn," Bryce said, and her chest flared with starlight that lit up the entire countryside, "we're retaliating."

Ruhn was still mulling it over—what Bryce wanted to do. Opening the Northern Rift to *Hel*. She had to be insane . . . yet he trusted her. And Athalar. They surely had some other sneaky-ass shit up their sleeves, but they'd reveal it when the time was right.

Ruhn tossed and turned on his crunchy, spiky pallet of hay, unable to sleep. Perhaps that was because Lidia lay across from him, staring up at the raftered ceiling.

Her eyes slid over to his, and Ruhn said into her mind, *Can't sleep?*

I'm thinking about all the Ophion agents I encountered over the years. I never knew them in person, but the people who helped me organize the strike on the Spine, and worked with me for years before that . . . they're all gone now.

It wasn't your fault.

Asphodel Meadows was aimed at your sister. But butchering Ophion, the people in the camps . . . that was to punish me. Ophion aided me in your escape, and Rigelus wanted revenge.

Ruhn's heart ached. *We'll make the Asteri pay for it.*

She turned on her side, looking at him full in the face. Gods, she was beautiful.

How are you feeling? Her question was gentle. *After . . . what happened with your father.*

I don't know, Ruhn said. *It felt right in the moment, felt good, even. But now . . .* He shook his head. *I keep thinking about my mother, of all people. And what she'll say. She might be the only person who'll mourn him.*

She loved him?

She was attached to him, even if he treated her as little more than a broodmare. But he kept her in comfort all these years, as a reward for birthing him a son. She was always grateful for that.

Lidia reached a hand across the narrow space between them and found his own—his fingers still strangely pale and uncalloused. But her skin was so soft and warm, the bones beneath so strong. *You'll find a way to live with what you did to your father. I did.*

Ruhn lifted a brow. *You . . . ?*

I killed him, yes. The words were frank, yet weary.

Why?

Because he was a monster—to me, and to so many others. I made it look like a rebel attack. Told Ophion to get their mech-suits and be waiting for him when his car drove through a mountain pass on its way to a meeting with me. They left a flattened vehicle and a corpse in their wake. Then burned the whole thing.

Ruhn blinked. *Beheading my father seems like it was much . . . faster.*

It certainly was. Her eyes held nothing but cold anger. *I told the Ophion agents in the mech-suits to take their time squashing him in his car. They did.*

Cthona, Lidia.

But I, too, wondered, about my mother after that, she said quietly. *About Hecuba. Wondered what the Queen of the Valbaran Witches made of her ex-lover's death. If she thought of me. If she had any interest, any at all, in reaching out to me after he died. But I never heard from her. Not once.*

I'm sorry, he offered, and squeezed her hand. After a beat he asked, *So you're really not going back to the Ocean Queen?*

No. Not as her spy. I meant every word earlier. I serve no one.

Is it weird to say I'm proud of you? Because I am.

She huffed a laugh and interlaced their fingers, her thumb stroking over the back of his hand. *I see you, Ruhn,* she said gently. *All of you.*

The words were a gift. His chest tightened. He couldn't stop himself from leaning across the space and quietly, so no one around them might hear, pressing his mouth to hers.

The kiss was gentle, near silent. He pulled away after a heart-beat, but her free hand slid to his cheek. Her eyes glowed golden, even in the moonlit dimness of the stables. *When we're not sleeping in a stable surrounded by people,* she said, mind-voice low—a purr that curled around his cock and gripped tight—*I want to touch you.*

His cock hardened at that, aching. He shut his eyes, fighting it, but her lips brushed his, silently teasing.

I want to ride you, she whispered into his mind, and slipped her hand from his to palm him through his pants. Ruhn bit down on his lower lip to keep from groaning. Her fingers slid down the length of him. *I want this inside of me.* She dug the heel of her palm along him, and he stifled a moan. *I want you inside of me.*

Fuck yeah was all he could manage to say, to think.

Her laughter echoed in his mind, and her lips slid from his to find the spot beneath his ear. Her teeth grazed over his too-hot skin, and he writhed against the hand she still had on him, the crackling hay so gods-damned loud—

"Please don't fuck right next to us," Flynn muttered from a few feet away.

"Ugh," Bryce called from across the stables. "Really?"

Ruhn squeezed his eyes shut, fighting his arousal.

But Lidia laughed quietly. "Sorry."

"Pervs," Declan muttered, hay crinkling as he turned over.

Ruhn looked back to Lidia and saw her smiling, delight and mischief brightening her face.

And damn if it wasn't the most beautiful thing he'd ever seen.

68

Y ou're hovering."

"Sorry, sorry." Ithan paced the morgue that Hypaxia had swiftly converted into a lab. "I just don't know what to *do* with myself while you're working on all that science stuff."

Hunched over the desk, Hypaxia was setting up the things she'd need to begin her experiments.

She said idly, without lifting her head, "I could use a sample of the parasite."

He halted. "How?" He answered his own question. "Oh. A glass of water." He glanced to the sink. "You think there are tons of them swimming around?"

"I doubt it's that obvious, considering how many scientists and medwitches have studied our water over the years. But it must be in there somewhere, if we're all infected."

Ithan sighed and walked over to the sink, grabbing a mug that said *Korinth University College of Mortuary Science*. He filled it with water and plunked it down beside Hypaxia. "There. The Istros's finest."

"That mug could be contaminated," Hypaxia said, using a ruler to sketch out a grid on a piece of paper. "We need a sterile container first. And samples from several different water sources."

"Did I mention that I hate science?"

"Well, I love it," Hypaxia said, still without looking up. "There are sterile cups in the cabinet along the back wall. Get multiple samples from this tap, from the Istros itself, and one from a bottle of store-bought water. We'll need a wider sample base, but that'll do for the initial phases." Ithan gathered a bunch of the sterile containers and headed for the door.

He was a glorified water boy. He'd never hear the end of it from his sunball buddies. That is, if he ever talked to them again.

But Ithan said nothing before slipping out, and Hypaxia didn't call after him.

Ithan bottled and labeled the various samples, gave Hypaxia a few vials of his blood as a base for an infected person, and then she sent him back out for *more* water samples from different sources. The dining hall, a nearby restaurant, and—best of all—the sewers.

He was on his way back through the dark door of the House of Flame and Shadow when the hair on the back of his neck rose. He knew that eerie, unsettled feeling. He whirled—

It wasn't Sigrid. A different female Reaper, veiled head to toe in black, glided smoothly over the quay. People outright fled—the street behind her was wholly empty.

But she continued toward the door, where Ithan stood frozen. He had no option, really, but to hold the door open for her.

The Reaper drifted by, black veils billowing. Acid-green eyes gleamed beneath the dark fabric over her face, and her rasping voice turned his bowels watery as she said, "Thank you," and continued into the stairwell.

Ithan waited five whole minutes before following. She had no scent at all. Not even the reek of a corpse. As if she'd ceased to exist in any earthly way. It drove his wolf nuts.

But—

Ithan sniffed the air of the stairwell again as he descended toward the lowest levels of the House and the morgue-lab. As he slipped into the lab and shut the door behind him, he asked, "What happens to the parasite when we die?"

Hypaxia finally looked up from her papers and vials and forms. "What?"

"I just saw a Reaper," he said. "They're dead. Well, they died. So do they still have the parasite? They don't eat or drink, so they couldn't be reinfected, right? But does the parasite disappear when we die? Does it die, too?"

Hypaxia blinked slowly. "That's an interesting question. And if the parasite does indeed die when the host does, then Reapers might provide a way to locate the parasite simply by the lack of it in their own bodies."

"Why do I feel like you're going to ask me to—"

"I need you to get me a Reaper."

Dawn broke, purple and golden, over the islands of Avallen. But Bryce only had eyes for the helicopter making its descent onto the grassy, blooming field before the ruins of Morven's castle. She smiled grimly.

The roar was deafening to her Fae ears, but she had insisted on being here. On seeing this: Fury waving from the pilot's seat, June waving frantically from beside her.

Bryce waved back, her throat tight to the point of pain, and then the side door to the helicopter slid open, and a yip cut through the air.

There was no stopping Syrinx as he bounded off the helicopter and raced for her through the high grasses. She dropped to her knees to hug him, kiss him, let him lick all over her face as he wiggled his little lion's tail and yowled with joy.

Boots crunched in the grass, and Randall was walking toward her, a pack on his back and a rifle slung over his shoulder. His eyes were bright as he beheld her, and he clapped the tall boy at his side—Emile, now Cooper—on the shoulder.

And Bryce couldn't stop her laugh of pure joy as her mother leapt out of the helicopter behind them, took one look at Bryce kneeling in the meadow, and said, "Bryce Adelaide Quinlan, what's all this talk about you jumping around between worlds?"

69

Ithan knew he'd have no luck convincing a Reaper on his own. At least without risking getting his soul sucked out and eaten. But fortunately, there were plenty of Reapers who would answer Jesiba Roga's summons. Unfortunately, one arrived at the morgue within an hour of Jesiba's request to the Under-King.

Ithan kept reminding himself of every exit, of his strength, of where the knife in his boot was, of how quickly he could summon claws or shift—

The male Reaper was relatively fresh, judging by the way he'd strutted—only a hint of a glide—into the morgue. This one seemed inclined to play rock star, with his torn black jeans dangling precariously off his prominent hip bones and an array of tattoos scattered over his unnervingly pale torso. No shirt to be seen. He'd bothered with ass-kicking black boots, left partially untied at the tops, and he'd strapped twin black leather bracelets at his wrists.

Gods, Bryce would have had a field day with this guy—his long golden hair was *very* carefully mussed. That is, until she beheld the acid-green eyes, and the throat that revealed precisely where his death blow had been. The wound had sealed over, but the scars remained.

"Thank you for coming," Hypaxia said, standing beside the

examination table with queenly grace. "This will only take a few moments."

The Reaper glanced between her and Ithan, but sauntered over to the table, hopping on with a thud that set the metal shuddering. "Heard you defected, witchy-witch." His voice was a hoarse, wicked rasp. It might have been dismissed as a result of the death wound to his throat, but it was typical of a Reaper. Exactly how Sigrid's voice had sounded—

"Welcome to the House," the Reaper continued, bluish lips quirking up in a sneer. He nodded to Ithan. "What's a wolf pup doing here?"

Ithan mastered his primal fear of the creature before them and crossed his arms. "What's it to you?"

"You're Holstrom, right?" That sneer didn't fade. If this shithead said anything about Connor—

"I was in the Aux," the Reaper said, tapping one of his tattoos. "Lion-shifter pack."

Oh shit. Ithan had heard of this guy. A low-level lion who'd shown up with his pack a few months ago on a routine Aux inspection of a vampyr nest in the Meat Market. The wounds on his neck corresponded with what the vamps had done to the guy. But to have chosen to become a Reaper, in the same House as the ones who'd killed him . . .

From the gleam in the Reaper's eyes, Ithan couldn't help but wonder if he had turned Reaper not to elude true death, but to one day exact vengeance.

Hypaxia approached the Reaper and said, "May I touch your head?"

The Reaper kept his eyes on the former queen. "Touch me all you want, sweetheart."

For fuck's sake. Ithan suppressed a growl, but Hypaxia remained unruffled as she placed her brown hands on his shining golden hair.

Ithan refrained from reaching for the knife in his boot as the Reaper inhaled deeply. Getting a whiff of her scent? Or preparing to eat her spirit? "Your soul smells like rain clouds and mountain berries." The creep licked his lips. "Anyone ever tell you that?"

How Hypaxia kept her hands on his head, Ithan had no idea. He was half inclined to rip the shithead's arms out of their sockets and use them to beat the guy senseless.

The Reaper inhaled again. "A little bit of witch, a little bit of necromancer, huh?"

"She needs to concentrate," Ithan said through his teeth.

The Reaper slid those acid-green eyes over to him. He asked Hypaxia, "Am I distracting you, honey?"

She didn't answer. The expression on her face was distant as she focused on what lay within the Reaper's mind.

The Reaper inhaled deeply again, his eyes rolling back in his head. "Gods, your scent's like fucking *wine*—"

"We're done, thank you," Hypaxia said politely, stepping back and making notes on the papers stacked on her desk. "Please give my regards to your master."

The Reaper stared at her for a long moment, practically feral. Ithan barely breathed, ready to pounce, even though this lowlife was unkillable—

"I'll see you around," the Reaper said, more of a promise than a parting, and hopped off the table. He strutted again for the doors, this time with a bit of that Reaper's floating gait, as if trying to show off for the witch.

Only when he left did Ithan let out a long breath. "What a fucking creep."

Hypaxia leaned against the examination table. "Your guess was right, though. He didn't have the parasite." She crossed her arms. "I didn't sense anything like one, anyway. I didn't sense anything living inside him at all."

"So what now?"

"I compare what I detected in him to what I discovered in your blood. See what stands out. See if I can isolate where in *you* the parasite lies."

Good. At least he'd contributed that much.

"How could you stand it?" Ithan asked, unable to contain his curiosity. "Being that close to him?"

"I've had to endure plenty of uncomfortable situations and difficult people in my life," Hypaxia said, pushing off the table and walking to the computer. She clicked the monitor on. "A lonely, scared Reaper, new to the afterlife, doesn't bother me."

"Lonely? Scared?" Ithan choked on a laugh.

But Hypaxia glanced over a shoulder, her face unreadable. "You couldn't see it? What lay beneath the bravado? His clothes and attitude show how desperately he's trying to cling to his mortal life. He's frightened out of his mind."

"You pity him."

"Yes." She turned back to her computer. "I pity him, and all Reapers."

Sigrid included, no doubt. Guilt tightened his chest, but Ithan said, "Most half-lifes seem to enjoy terrorizing the rest of us."

"They might, but their existence is what their name implies: It is half a life. Not true living. It seems sad to me."

Ithan considered. "You're . . . you're a really good person." She chuckled. "I mean it," he insisted. "The witches are worse off without you."

She glanced over a shoulder again, and this time her eyes were full of sorrow. "Thank you." She nodded to the door. "I need to focus for a while. Without your, ah . . . hovering."

He saluted her. "Message received. I'll be down the hall if you need me."

"Queen of all this, huh?"

Bryce didn't stop sorting through the trunks of supplies Fury had brought on the helicopter, even though her friend's question came with a shit-eating grin.

"Did you get the goggles?" Bryce asked, pushing past a layer of winter hats. All the snow gear was there, just as she'd requested. On short notice, Fury had pieced together a remarkable array of jackets, pants, hats, gloves, underlayers—everything they'd need to survive the subzero temperatures of Nena.

Bryce intended to leave Avallen as soon as her parents had a rest from the helicopter journey—as soon as they were able to get Cooper settled with Baxian, and process all she'd told them upon their arrival.

Her parents sat in the grass on the other side of the field, talking quietly, Syrinx lounging in Randall's lap. So Bryce gave them space, using the time to check the gear Fury had brought—not that she didn't trust Fury to have thought of every detail.

But she should check, anyway. Just to make sure that they had all the gear they might need. So many things could go wrong, and she was taking her human parents with her, she was really going to do this—

A slender brown hand touched Bryce's wrist. "B—you okay?"

Bryce looked up at last, finding Juniper standing beside her, a deep frown on her beautiful face. A few feet away, Fury stood with crossed arms, brows high.

Bryce sighed, turning from the three massive trunks that would be loaded onto the helicopter looming behind them.

Her friends were safe here. It should have eased something in her chest—a gift from Urd, Hunt had claimed—but seeing them here . . .

There was a fourth trunk, resting in the grass close to the helicopter. Fury had only been able to gather so much before the quick takeoff from Valbara, but still . . . there were a considerable number of weapons here.

Handguns. Rifles. Knives.

A joke, really, considering that they were going up against six intergalactic, nearly all-powerful beings. Most of the weapons would be for the others—to buy them any shot at surviving.

Everything else would come down to her.

Fury and Juniper were watching. Waiting. Like they could see all of that on her face. Just as Juniper, that bleak winter, had sensed from Bryce's tone alone that despair had pushed her to the brink.

Juniper—whose last audiomail to Bryce had been so angry, after Bryce had done such an unforgivable thing by calling the director of the Crescent City Ballet. Only love and relief showed on her face now.

Juniper silently opened her arms, and Bryce rushed into them.

Her throat closed up, eyes stinging, at her friend's warmth, her scent. Fury's scent and arms wrapped around them a moment later, and Bryce shut her eyes, savoring it.

"I'm so sorry you both got dragged into this," Bryce said hoarsely. "June, I'm sorry for all of it. I'm so fucking sorry."

Juniper's arms tightened around her. "We've got bigger problems to face—you and I are good."

Bryce pulled back, glancing between her two friends. She'd updated them, and her parents—Cooper in tow—about as much as she could.

Fury frowned. "I should be coming with you guys. I'm of more use in the field."

Bryce would have given anything to have someone as talented as Fury watching her back. But this wasn't about Bryce's own safety, her own comfort.

"You're precisely where you should be," Bryce insisted. "When people hear that Fury Axtar's guarding Avallen, they'll think twice before fucking with this place."

Fury rolled her eyes. "Babysitting."

Bryce shook her head. "It's not. I need you guys here—helping any of the people who can make it. Helping Baxian."

"Yeah, yeah," Fury said, jerking her chin toward the rest of their friends, standing on the other side of the helicopter. "I'll admit, I'm looking forward to grilling Baxian about him and Danika."

They stared toward the handsome male, who must have sensed their attention and turned from where he'd been talking to Tharion and Ruhn. Baxian winced.

Juniper laughed. "We won't bite!" she called to the Helhound.

"Liar," Fury muttered, earning another laugh from Juniper.

Baxian wisely went back to his conversation. Though Bryce didn't fail to notice how Tharion poked the angel shifter in the side, grinning.

"I can't believe she never told us about him," Juniper said quietly, sadly.

"Danika didn't tell us a lot of stuff," Bryce said with equal softness.

"Neither did you," Fury teased, nudging Bryce with an elbow. "And again: Queen of Avallen?"

Bryce rolled her eyes. "If you want the job, it's yours."

"Oh, not for all the gold in the world," Fury said, dark eyes dancing with amusement. "This is your shitshow to run."

Juniper scowled at her girlfriend. "What Fury means is that we have your back."

Bryce kissed June's velvet-soft cheek. "Thanks." She looked between her friends again. "If we don't make it back . . ."

"Don't think like that, B," Juniper insisted, but Fury said nothing.

Fury had dealt in the shadows of the empire for years. She was well aware of the odds.

Bryce went on, "If I don't make it back, you'll be safe here. The mists will allow any true refugee through—but I'd still keep an eye out for any Asteri agents. There are plenty of natural resources to sustain everyone, and yeah, there's no firstlight to fuel your tech, but—"

Juniper laid a hand on Bryce's wrist again. "We got this, B. You go do . . . what you need to do."

"Save the world," Fury said, chuckling.

Bryce grimaced. "Yeah. Basically."

"We got this," Juniper repeated, hand tightening on Bryce's wrist. "And so do you, Bryce."

Bryce took out her phone. Popped it free of the case, revealing the photograph she'd tucked in there of them. Of how it had been when there were four. "Keep this for me," she said, handing it to Fury. "I don't want to lose it."

Fury studied the photo—how happy they'd all been, how

seemingly young. She folded Bryce's fingers around the photo. "Take it." Fury's eyes shone bright. "So we'll all be with you."

Bryce's throat tightened again, but she slid the photo into the back pocket of her jeans. And allowed herself to look at June and Fury one last time, to memorize every line of their faces.

Friends worth fighting for. Worth dying for.

Ember Quinlan was waiting on the hill where Bryce and her friends had risen from beneath the Cave of Princes.

Ember peered at the grassy ground, face tight. No trace of the caves remained. "So his body is just . . . under there."

Bryce nodded. She knew who her mother meant. "Ruhn decapitated him and, um, impaled his head before the ground swallowed him. There's no chance of him coming back."

Ember didn't smile as she stared at the earth, the Autumn King's corpse far beneath it.

"I spent so long running from him, fearing him. To imagine a world where he doesn't exist . . ." Her mom lifted her eyes to Bryce's face, and at the pain and relief in them, Bryce threw her arms around her and held tight.

"I'm so proud of you," Ember whispered. "Not for . . . dealing with him, but for all of it. I'm so, so proud, Bryce."

Bryce couldn't stop the stinging in her eyes. "I could only do it because I was raised by a badass mom."

Ember chuckled, pulling back to clasp Bryce's face in both hands. "You look different."

"Good different or bad different?"

"Good. Like a functioning adult."

Bryce smiled. "Thanks, Mom."

Ember wrapped her arms around Bryce and squeezed. "But it doesn't matter if you're Queen of the Fae or the Universe or whatever crap . . ." Bryce laughed at that, but Ember said, "You'll always be my sweet baby."

Bryce hugged her mother tightly, all thoughts of the hateful male lying dead far below them fading away.

In the distance, the helicopter started roaring again, this time piloted by Randall, thanks to his compulsory years in the peregrini army. All humans were forced to serve. The skills he'd learned during those years remained useful, especially now, but Bryce knew the experience weighed on his soul.

Bryce looked up at last from her mother's embrace and saw Hunt motioning for them to get on board—obnoxiously tapping his wrist, as if to say, *Time is of the essence, Quinlan!*

Bryce scowled, knowing that with his angel-sharp eyes he could see it from this distance, but she held her mom for another moment. Breathed in her mom's smell, so familiar and calming. Like home.

Ember hugged her back, content to be there—to hold her daughter for one moment longer.

This was what really mattered in the end.

70

Ithan was thoroughly sick of playing bodyguard, even from a floor below. While Hypaxia had been comparing what she'd observed in the Reaper to the water samples and Ithan's own blood, he'd been packing up artifacts in Jesiba's office. And glancing at the door every other minute as if Hypaxia would burst in and declare that she'd developed an antidote to the parasite. She never did.

When he entered the morgue, he found Hypaxia at the desk, head in her hands. Vials of all sizes and shapes littered the metal surface beside her.

Ithan dared to lay a hand on her shoulder. "Don't give up. You're exhausted—you've been working for hours. You'll find a cure."

"I already found it."

It took him a moment to process what she'd said. "You . . . Really?"

Her head bobbed, and she nudged a vial of clear liquid with a fingertip. "It went faster than I had even dared to hope. I was able to use the synth antidote as a template. Synth and the parasite have magic-altering properties in common—I'll spare you the details. With the changes I made, though, I think this will isolate the parasite and kill it the same way the synth antidote worked." She pointed at more small vials on a low table behind her. "I made as much as I could. But . . ."

"But?" He could barely breathe.

She sighed. "But it's far from perfect. I had to use Athalar's lightning to bind it together. I had to use all of it, I'm afraid."

She motioned to her desk, where six quartz crystals now lay. Dormant. Empty.

His heart twisted. "It's okay." Sigrid would remain a Reaper for the time being, but he wouldn't give up on trying to help her.

"Athalar's lightning holds it together, but not permanently," Hypaxia went on. "The antidote is highly unstable—a little jostling, and it might go completely stale. If I had more time, I might find a way to stabilize it, but for right now . . ."

He squeezed her shoulder. "Just tell me."

Her mouth twisted to the side before she said, "The antidote's not a permanent fix. Its effect will wear off—and since the water of Midgard is still contaminated with the parasite, we will be reinfected as soon as it does."

"How long will a dose work?"

"I don't know. A few weeks? Months? Longer than a few days, I think, but I'll need to keep refining it. Find some way to make it permanent."

"But it'll work for now?"

"In theory. So long as Athalar's lightning binds it together. But I haven't gathered the nerve to test it on myself. To see if it works and is safe, but also . . . to find out who I might be without this thing feeding on me." She raised her head and met his stare, her face bleak and exhausted. "If we remove this parasite, what will it accomplish? What will *you* do with the extra power?"

"I'll help my friends, for whatever good it'll do."

"And the wolves?"

"What about them?"

"If you get more power, it could put you beyond Sabine's abilities. Make you strong enough that you could challenge her." She looked at him seriously. "You might be able to end Sabine's tyranny, Ithan."

"I . . ." He couldn't find the right words. "I didn't really think about what we'd do next."

She wasn't impressed. "You need to. All of us do."

He stiffened. "I'm not a planner. I'm a sunball player, for fuck's sake—"

"You *were* a sunball player," she said. "And I suspect you haven't thought about the implications of having the most power among the wolves because you're avoiding thinking about what you really want."

He glared at her. "And what is that?"

"You want Sabine gone. No one but you is going to come along and do it."

He felt sick. "I don't want to lead anyone."

She gave him a look, as if seeing through him. But she said, with a disappointment that cut right to his heart, "All this arguing's of no use. We don't even know if the antidote works." She eyed the vial.

She would do it, he knew. She'd try it, risk herself—

Ithan didn't broadcast his moves before he snatched up the vial. Before he lifted it to his mouth and swallowed.

Hypaxia whirled toward him, eyes wide with apprehension—

Then there was only black.

There was his body . . . and more than his body.

His wolf, and him, and power, like he could leap between entire continents in one bound—

Ithan's eyes flew open. Had the world always been so sharp, so clear? Had the morgue smelled so strongly of antiseptic? Was there a body rotting away in one of the boxes? When had *that* arrived? Or had it been lying there all along?

And that smell, of lavender and eucalyptus . . .

Hypaxia was kneeling over him, breathing hard. "Ithan—"

A blink, and a flash, and he shifted. She staggered back at the wolf that appeared, faster than he'd ever changed before.

Another blink and flash, and he was back in his humanoid body.

As easy as breathing. Fast as the wind. Something was different, something was . . .

His blood howled toward an unseen moon. His fingers curled on the floor as he sat up, claws scraping.

"Ithan?" The witch's voice was a whisper.

"It worked." The words echoed through the room, the world. "It's gone—I can tell."

Somehow, a barrier had been removed. One that had ordered him to stand down, to obey . . . It was nothing but ashes now. Only dominance remained. Untethered.

But filling the void of that barrier with a rising, raging force—

Ithan held out his hand and willed the *thing* under his skin to come forward. Ice and snow appeared in his palm. They did not melt against his skin.

He could fucking summon *snow*. The magic sang in him, an old and strange melody.

Wolves didn't have magic like this. Never had, as far as he'd heard. Shifting and strength, yes, but this elemental power . . . it shouldn't exist in a wolf, yet there it was. Rising in him, filling the place where he'd never realized the parasite had existed.

Ithan said roughly, "We need to get this to our friends."

Hypaxia smiled grimly. "What are you going to do?"

Ithan eyed the door to the hall. "I think it's time for me to start making some plans."

"Only my daughter would drag us up to Nena," Ember groused, shivering against the cold that stole even Hunt's breath away. "You couldn't have done this in, oh, I don't know, the Coronal Islands?"

"The Northern Rift, Mom," Bryce said through chattering teeth, "is in the *north*."

"There's a southern one," Ember muttered.

"It's even colder down there," Bryce said, and looked to Hunt and Randall for help.

Hunt chuckled despite the frigid temperatures and howling wind that had hit them from the moment they'd stepped out of the helicopter.

They could fly no further. The massive black wall stretched for miles in either direction before curving northward, with wards protecting the airspace above it. Hunt knew from maps that the area the wall encircled was forty-nine miles in diameter—seven times seven, the holiest of numbers—and that at its center, somewhere in the barren, snow-blasted terrain, lay the Northern Rift, shrouded in mist. Barriers upon barriers protected Midgard from the Rift, and Hel beyond it.

"We better get going," Randall said, nodding to the lead doors in the wall before them.

"There aren't any sentries," Hunt observed, falling into step beside the male, grateful for the snow gear Axtar had somehow procured for all of them. "There should be at least fifteen here."

"Maybe they bailed because it was too fucking cold," Bryce said, shivering miserably.

"An angelic guard never *bails*," Randall said, tugging the faux-fur-lined hood of his parka further over his face. "If they're not here . . . it's not a good sign."

Hunt nodded to the rifle in Randall's gloved hands. "That work in these temperatures?"

"It'd better," Ember grumbled.

But Hunt caught Bryce's look, and summoned his lightning to the ready. He knew her starfire was already warming beneath her gloves. With Theia's power now united within her . . . he couldn't decide if he was eager to see what that starfire could do, or dreading it.

"Is it a trap?" Ember said as they approached the towering, sealed gates and abandoned guard post.

Hunt peered into the frosted window of the booth, then yanked open the door. The ice was crusted so thickly he had to use a considerable amount of strength to pry it free. A swift examination of the interior revealed rime coating the controls, the chairs, the water station. "No one's been here for a while."

"I don't like this," Ember said. "It's too easy."

Hunt glanced to Bryce, her eyes teary with cold, the tip of her nose bright red. In these temperatures, they wouldn't last ten more minutes before frostbite set in. He and his mate would recover, but Ember and Randall, with their human blood . . .

"Let's get this booth warmed up," Bryce said. She stepped inside and began brushing frost off the switches. "Maybe the heater still works."

Ember gave her daughter a look that said she was well aware Bryce and Hunt had avoided addressing her concerns, but stepped inside as well.

They got the heater working—just one of them. The others were too frosted over to sputter to life. But it was enough to warm the small space and offer her parents a sliver of shelter as Bryce and Hunt again explored the frigid terrain, studying the wall and its gate.

"You think it's a trap?" Bryce said through the scarf she'd tugged up over her mouth and nose. She'd found some pairs of snow goggles in the booth, and the world was sharp through the stark clarity of the lenses. Was this how it had looked through Hunt's Umbra Mortis helmet?

Hunt said, wearing polarized goggles of his own, "I've never known the guard station at the Northern Rift to be empty, so . . . something's up, for sure."

"Maybe Apollion did us a favor and sent a few deathstalkers to clear it out." As she spoke the demon prince's name, the wind seemed to quiet. "Well, that's not spooky at all."

"This far north," Hunt said, turning in place to survey the terrain, "maybe all those bullshit warnings about not speaking his name on this side of the Rift are true."

Bryce didn't dare test it out again. But she walked to the lead gates in the wall and laid a gloved hand on them. "I heard the wall and the gates both had white salt built into them." For protection against Hel.

"Hasn't stopped the demons from slipping through," Hunt noted, face unreadable with the goggles and his own scarf over his mouth. "I hunted down enough of them to know how fallible the wall is. And the guards, I suppose."

"I hate to imagine what's been getting past *without* guards here." Hunt said nothing, which wasn't remotely comforting. "So how do we get through?" Bryce asked.

"There's a button inside the booth," Hunt said. "Nothing fancy."

Bryce nudged him. "Easy-peasy, for once." A blast of icy wind slammed into her back, as if throwing her toward the wall. Even with the layers of winter gear, she could have sworn the cold bit her very bones.

"We should go before we lose the light." Hunt nodded at the sun already sinking toward the horizon. "Daylight's only a few hours up here."

"Bryce?" her dad called from the booth. "You guys need to see this."

They found Ember and Randall in front of a flickering monitor.

"The security footage." Ember pointed with a shaking gloved finger. Bryce knew the trembling wasn't from cold. Her mom hit a key on the computer and the footage began rolling.

"Is that . . . ," Bryce breathed.

"We need to get to the Rift," Hunt growled. *"Now."*

71

"You set foot in that Den without an invitation from the Prime or Sabine and you're dead, pup."

"I know," Ithan said, packing yet another crate for Jesiba. The task was stupidly mundane given all the shit that was going down. But when he'd burst into the office moments ago to tell her the good news, Jesiba had refused to speak to him until he *earned his keep* for a few minutes. So here he was, packing and talking at the same time. "But if Hypaxia and I are heading off to the Eternal City, we might . . . die." He choked on the word. "I want them to know the truth."

"And what truth is that?"

Ithan straightened from where he'd been bent over the crate. "The truth of what I did to Sigrid. That Sigrid exists, I guess, even if she is a Reaper. That—"

"So it's about you easing your guilty conscience."

Ithan cut her a look. "I want them to know what happened. That yeah, Sigrid is a Reaper, and I totally failed at trying to undo that, but . . . they do technically have an alternative to Sabine— even if it's a half-life. It'd be radical and unheard of to accept a Reaper as Prime, but stranger things have happened, right?"

Jesiba began typing away on her computer. "Why do you care?"

"Because the wolves have to change. They need to know they

can choose someone other than Sabine." He looked down at his palm, willing ice to form there. It cracked over his skin in a thin film before melting away. "They need to know there's an antidote that might grant them powers beyond hers. That they don't need to be subservient to her."

"The wolves will need proof regarding that bit," Jesiba said, "or you won't walk out of there alive."

"Isn't this enough?" He formed a shard of ice on his fingertip, as much as he could reliably control. He supposed he'd need to seek out the Fae or some sort of ice sprite to teach him how to command this new ability.

Hypaxia had taken the antidote minutes after him. She'd blacked out, as he had, but awoken thrumming with power. He could have sworn a light, playful breeze now played about her hair constantly—and that a steady sort of power seemed to emanate from her, even when she wasn't using it.

He'd offered Jesiba a vial upon telling her the news, but the sorceress had said, *It won't help me, pup.* And then ordered him to begin this miserable work while he explained the rest.

Jesiba now said, "Knowing the wolves, they'll think Quinlan asked me to do something to you that made you . . . unnatural."

"They know Bryce is a good person."

"Do they? As far as I recall, they've been anything but kind to her since Danika and the Pack died. You included."

Ithan's cheeks warmed. "It was a rough time. For all of us."

"Danika Fendyr would have skewered all of you to the front gates of the Den for how you treated Quinlan."

"Danika would have . . ." Ithan trailed off as a thought struck him. "Danika questioned the wolf power structure, you know. Even she thought it was weird that the Fendyrs went unchecked for so long."

"Did she?"

Ithan turned toward the sorceress's desk. "Bryce and I found some research papers Danika had hidden. She wanted to know why the Fendyrs were so dominant—I don't think she approved of it, either." He nodded to himself. "She would have encouraged the others to take the antidote. To kick Sabine to the curb."

Jesiba's brows rose. "If you say so. You knew Danika far better than I ever did."

"I know she hated her mother—and thought the hierarchies were grossly unfair." Ithan paced a few steps. "I have to get those papers. I'll bring them to the Den to show everyone that it's not just *me* questioning this, but that even one of the Fendyrs disagreed with their unchecked dominance. It might help sway them toward accepting an alternative to Sabine. Sigrid's a Fendyr, but she's not in the direct line. That might help them accept her as an alternative."

"They'll say you forged them." Jesiba typed away at her keyboard.

"That's a risk I have to take," Ithan said, striding to the door. "The days of Sabine keeping the wolves down, of making us stand by while innocents suffer . . . that has to end. We need a change. A big one. And maybe, if Urd's got our backs, what's most important within Sigrid still remains intact, unchanged by becoming a Reaper. If that's the case, I'll take Sigrid over Sabine any day."

Maybe it wasn't a matter of undoing what had been done, but rather of playing the bad hand that had been dealt to him. Of adapting.

"Open-minded as that is, Holstrom," Jesiba said, shutting her laptop, "do you really think it's a wise decision to not only go to the Den utterly defenseless, but to start preaching that they accept a *Reaper* as their Prime Apparent? Let's not forget that some of the wolves might still like Sabine and her style of leadership. Many probably do, in fact."

"Yeah, but it's time to give them the chance to choose otherwise. To break free of her control."

"You forget," Jesiba said darkly, "that from the very start, they've been the Asteri's chief enforcers. They've never shown any inclination to *break free* of anyone's control."

"It's a risk I have to take," he insisted. "And I can't sit around."

"Quinlan told you to protect Hypaxia."

"This won't take long. Keep an eye on her for me—please."

He walked to the door, and Jesiba spoke as he wrapped his

fingers around the knob. Her voice was heavy, resigned. "Be careful, pup."

Ithan snuck over to Bryce's apartment using the House of Flame and Shadow's unnervingly accurate map of the sewers. He didn't want to think about who else made regular use of those tunnels.

Even with the access that Danika had long ago granted him, he entered the building through the roof door. There was no doubt the building was being watched, and he kept to the shadows as much as he could. If the guard downstairs saw him on the cameras, no one came to investigate.

Danika's papers remained where he and Bryce had left them: in the junk mail drawer. He leafed through them just to make sure they did indeed say all he'd remembered.

They did. It could be a convenient bit of backup for his claims. *See? Even Danika wanted all this to change. And, yes, Sigrid is a Fendyr—but she's also* different—*she could be a step in the right direction.*

He'd find some way to say it more eloquently, but Danika's name still carried weight.

Ithan gently folded the pile of papers and slid them into the back pocket of his jeans. Outside, the city remained quiet—hushed. Grieving.

And inside this building . . .

Gods, it was weird to see this apartment, so empty and stale without its occupants.

Ithan glanced to the white sectional, like he'd find Athalar and Bryce sitting there, Syrinx curled up with them.

How far away that existence seemed now. He doubted it'd ever return. Wondered if his friends would ever return. If Bryce was—

He didn't let himself finish the thought.

He had no choice but to keep going. However it played out. And Jesiba was right. To walk into the Den was likely suicide, but . . . He glanced down the hall. To Bryce's bedroom door.

Maybe he didn't need to go in unarmed.

72

It took too long—way too fucking long—for the gates to yawn open, ice and snow cracking off and falling to the ground. Bryce wedged through them first, starfire blazing under her gloves.

"I don't understand," Ember was saying as she squeezed through behind Bryce, Randall hot on her tail. Hunt came last. "What is the *Harpy* doing out here?"

"She's not the Harpy anymore," Bryce said. "She's like . . . some weird necromantically raised thing made by the Asteri thanks to whatever they managed to do with some of Hunt's lightning. I don't know, but we don't want to meet whatever she is now."

Bryce caught the worry and guilt on Hunt's face. They didn't have the time, though, for her to assure him that this wasn't his fault. He'd had no choice but to give Rigelus his lightning. It had been used for some fucked-up shit, but that wasn't on him.

Ember protested, "But the Harpy *ate* the guards—"

"Which is why we're going to the Rift," Bryce said, nodding to Hunt, whose eyes shone with steely determination. "Right fucking now."

Hunt didn't wait before lifting her mother in his arms and spreading his wings. Bryce grabbed Randall and said, "Surprise: I can teleport. Don't barf."

Thankfully, Randall didn't vomit as she teleported them the

twenty-four and a half miles to the center of the walled ring. But he did when they arrived.

They beat Hunt and her mother there, leaving Bryce with nothing to do but watch her dad puke his guts up in the snow as the dizziness of teleporting hit him again and again.

"That is . . . ," Randall said, and retched again. "Useful, but horrible."

"I think that sums me up in a nutshell," Bryce said.

Randall laughed, vomited again, then wiped his mouth and stood. "You're not horrible, Bryce. Not by a long shot."

"I guess. But this is," she said, and gestured up at the structure before them. At the swirling mists.

A massive arch of clear quartz rose forty feet into the air, its uppermost part nearly hidden by the drifting mist. They could see straight through the archway, though, and nothing lay within it except what could only be described as a ripple in the world. Between worlds. And more mist on its other side.

"The Asteri must have built the archway around the Rift to try to contain it," Bryce said. "Or try to control it, I guess."

"I'll say this once, and that's it," Randall said. Behind him, closing in, Hunt and Ember approached from above. "But is opening the Rift . . . the best idea?"

Bryce blew out a long, hot breath that faded into the mists wafting past. "No. But it's the only idea I have."

There wasn't one black ribbon of mourning in the Den. No keening dirges offered up to Cthona, beseeching the goddess to guide the newly dead. In fact, somewhere in the compound, a stereo was blasting a thumping dance beat.

Trust Sabine to proceed as if nothing had changed. As if an atrocity hadn't occurred in a neighboring district.

At this time of year, it was tradition for many of the Den families to scatter into the countryside to enjoy the changing of the leaves and the crisp autumn mountains, so only a skeleton crew of packs remained. Ithan knew which ones would be there—just as he knew that only Perry Ravenscroft, the Black Rose's Omega and Amelie's little sister, would be on guard duty at the gates.

A bronze rendering of the Embrace—the sun sinking or rising out of two mountains—was displayed in the window of the guard station. And it was because he knew Perry so well that he understood that this small decoration was her way of telling the city that there were some in the Den who mourned, who were praying to Cthona to comfort the dead.

Perry's large emerald eyes widened at the sight of Ithan as he prowled up to the guard booth. To her, it must have seemed like he'd materialized out of thin air. In fact, his stealth was courtesy of his new speed and preternatural quiet—furthered by the fact that he'd traveled through the sewers, needing to remain out of sight until the last possible minute.

Perry lunged for the radio on the desk, long brown hair flashing in the afternoon sunlight, but Ithan held up a hand. She paused.

"I need to talk," he said through the glass.

Those green eyes scanned his face, then drifted to a spot over his shoulder, to the sword he carried. Perry stared at him—then opened the door to the booth. Her cinnamon-and-strawberry scent hit him a heartbeat later.

This close, he could count the smattering of freckles across the bridge of her nose. The pale skin beneath them seemed to blanch further as she processed what he'd said.

"Sabine's in a meeting—"

"Not Sabine. I need to talk to everyone else." Ithan pushed, "You were the only one who checked in to see if I was alive after . . . everything." She'd texted him occasionally—not much, but with Amelie as her Alpha and sister, he knew she didn't dare risk more communication than that. "Please, Perry. Just let me into the courtyard."

"Tell me what you want to talk to us about, and I'll consider it." Even as Omega, the lowest of the Black Rose Pack, she didn't back down.

It was for that courage alone that Ithan told her his secret first. "A new future for the wolves."

Ithan knew it was due to how loved and trusted Perry was within the Den that so many wolves arrived in the courtyard quickly, as soon as her message went out about a last-minute announcement.

He kept to the shadows of the pillars under the building's north wing, watching the people he'd counted as friends, almost family, congregate in the grassy space. The red and gold trees of the small park behind them swayed in the crisp autumn breeze, the wind luckily keeping his scent hidden from the wolves.

When enough of a crowd had assembled—a hundred wolves, or so—Perry stepped out onto the few steps in front of the building doors and said, "So, uh . . . almost everyone's here."

People smiled at her, bemused yet indulgent. It'd always been that way for Perry, the resident artist of the Den, who at age four had painted her room every color of the rainbow despite her parents' order to pick one hue.

Perry glanced toward him, eyes bright with fear. For him or for herself, he had no idea.

"Go ahead," she said quietly, and stepped off the stairs and into the grass.

Make your brother proud.

Though those words had come from the Viper Queen, Ithan held them close to his heart as he stepped out of the shadows.

Snarls and growls and shouts of surprise rose. Ithan held up his hands. "I'm not here to start trouble."

"Then get the fuck out!" someone—Gideon, Amelie's third—shouted from the back. Amelie herself was striding through the crowd, fury twisting her face—

"Everything we are is a lie," Ithan said before Amelie could reach him and start swinging.

Some people quieted. Ithan plunged on, because Amelie's canines were lengthening, and he knew she'd be making the full shift soon.

"Danika Fendyr questioned this, too. She died before she could find the truth."

The words had their desired effect. The crowd went silent. But Amelie still charged forward, shoving people out of the way now, Gideon a menacing, hulking mass close behind—

Ithan looked at Perry, standing at the front of the crowd, her green eyes trained on him. It was to her that he said, "The Asteri planted a parasite in our brains that repressed our inherent magic, reducing it to its most basic components: shifting and strength. Yet even those abilities have been cut off at the knees. All so we can remain their faithful enforcers, as we've been since the Northern Rift opened."

Amelie was ten feet away, muscles tensing to jump onto the stairs, to pin him and shred him—

"Look," Ithan said, and held out a hand. Ice swirled in his palm.

A gasp went through the crowd. Even Amelie stumbled in shock.

Ithan said, letting the ice crust his fingers, "Magic—*elemental* magic. It was lying there, dormant in my veins all this time." He found Perry's eyes again, noted the shock and something like yearning in them. "A friend of mine, a medwitch, made an antidote for me. I took it and discovered what I really am. *Who* I really am. What sleeps in the bloodline of all wolves, repressed by the Asteri for fifteen thousand years."

"It's a witch-trick," Amelie spat, making to shove past her little sister. "Move," she ordered Perry. Not as her sister, but as her Alpha.

But Perry, despite her slim frame, held firm. And said to Amelie, her voice carrying, "I want to hear what he has to say."

Ithan spoke as quickly as he could, giving the wolves an overview of the parasite and what it did to their magic. And then, because they were still looking doubtful, he explained what really happened in the Bone Quarter: Secondlight. The meat grinder of souls.

When he was done, Ithan found Perry's face again. She'd gone ghostly white.

"Queen Hypaxia Enador can verify all I've told you," Ithan said.

"She's not queen anymore!" a wolf called. "She's been kicked out—like you, Holstrom."

Ithan bared his teeth. "She's brilliant. She figured out how to fix this *thing* in our brains, to give us this magic back. So don't you take that fucking tone about her."

And at the snarl in his voice, the order, the wolves in the crowd straightened. Not with anger or fear, but . . .

"What did you do?" Perry said, staggering forward a step. "Ithan, you're—"

"There is another Fendyr," Ithan said, plowing ahead, bracing himself.

The crowd stirred. Perry gaped at him. "What do you mean?" she asked. He couldn't stand the confusion and hope in her voice, her bright eyes.

"Her name is Sigrid," Ithan said, throat tightening painfully. "She . . . she's the daughter of Sabine's late brother. And she—"

"That is enough," Amelie spat, shoving forward at last. "This insane rambling stops *now*."

Ithan growled, low and deep, and even Amelie halted, one foot on the step.

He held her gaze, let her see everything in it.

"Why is this traitor still alive?" Sabine's voice slithered over the courtyard.

Ithan pivoted, carefully keeping Amelie in his sights as he surveyed the approaching Prime Apparent.

A step behind her, emerging from the shadows, strode Sigrid and the Astronomer.

73

Reaper," Perry breathed, falling back. Not to run, but to protect a young wolf a few steps behind her, who shook in pure terror at the acid-green eyes of the Reaper in their midst.

Judging by Sigrid's fairly normal gait, she was still in the middle of her transition. But there was an oddness to her movements already. The beginnings of that unnaturally smooth glide that only Reapers could effect.

And she'd left on her wrecked, bloodied clothes. As proof, he realized—because his blood was also on them. And the wolves would know that with one sniff.

Struggling for the right words as he pointed at Sigrid, Ithan said, "It's—she's no threat to you all."

"That is a *Reaper*!" someone shouted at him from the back.

The Astronomer was grinning at Ithan. How had the old bastard managed to get her away from the Under-King? He'd somehow orchestrated this, right down to bringing his former mystic to Sabine. All for vengeance on Ithan.

"Whatever story Holstrom is spinning for you," Sabine said loudly, "don't listen to a word of it." The crowd was recoiling, desperate to get away from the Reaper at Sabine's side. "Ithan Holstrom is a liar," Sabine declared, "and a traitor to all we stand for."

"That's not true," Ithan growled.

"Isn't it?" Sabine pointed to where Sigrid stood beside her, gazing out at the crowd with an impassive face. "Look at what you did to my dear niece."

The word hit the crowd like a rogue wave. He practically felt them piecing it together—that the Reaper before them was the same Fendyr heir he'd been telling them about moments ago.

Niece, people whispered. *Is it possible that*—

The Astronomer folded his withered hands before him, the portrait of serene old age. "It is true," he announced. "Twenty years ago, Lars Fendyr sought me out and sold his eldest pup into my service." He motioned to Sigrid. "She was my faithful companion, as dear to me as my own daughter." His dark eyes slid to Ithan, sharp with hate. "Until that boy kidnapped her and turned her into *that.*"

The crowd shifted away, all their focus now on Ithan, their eyes distrusting, damning—

"My brother's daughter," Sabine said, raising her voice to be heard over the murmuring, shifting crowd. "Killed in cold blood by that male." She pointed to Ithan. "Just as he and his Fae friends tried to kill me."

"That's—" Ithan started, noting how pale Perry had become.

"It's the truth," Sabine sneered. "I have the video footage of it, courtesy of the Viper Queen. I'd be happy to show everyone how brutally you executed a defenseless young wolf."

Horror stole any words from Ithan's throat.

It had always been a long game for the Viper Queen. Not only to amuse herself, but to use the knowledge of what he'd done to her advantage. Her relationship with Sabine was strained—so why not sweeten it with a little peace offering?

Marc had even told Ithan that the Viper Queen dealt not in money, but in favors and intel. He'd walked right into that trap.

"He then tried to have a necromancer raise her from the dead," Sabine went on, gesturing to the Reaper. "So she might be his puppet for usurping me."

"That is *not*—"

The Astronomer added, "And when I heard what had befallen

— 635 —

her . . ." The Astronomer gave Sigrid a pitying look. "I petitioned the Under-King for her release so that I could immediately bring her to the Den, to you good people."

This couldn't be happening.

Sabine grinned. It sure as fuck was happening. "This morning, Sigrid informed me that when she was faced with this unspeakable enslavement," Sabine said, "she wanted to protect her people, so she chose the existence of a Reaper instead. And she has made her way here at last, to be my heir."

There was a shocked silence.

He'd been a stupid fucking fool to think that Sigrid would be like Danika, that she might have chosen to be a Reaper and still want joy and peace and what was best for the wolves—instead of the pure hate that now gleamed in her eyes as she glowered at Ithan.

But Amelie was blinking at Sabine. *She* was Sabine's heir. To name another, and a Reaper, at that . . .

Perry glanced between her sister and Sabine, then at the Reaper. "Why don't you let your new heir speak for herself, Sabine?"

Sabine snarled at Perry, and Perry backed away a step.

Ithan's hackles rose at the fear, the submission.

"Everyone knows the Holstroms have long desired to replace the Fendyrs," Sabine went on.

"Bullshit," Ithan spat.

"Our traditions continue because they are *strong*," Sabine said to the crowd. The Astronomer stepped closer to Sigrid's side, eyeing the wolves. "To listen to this boy spew the propaganda of a renegade witch—"

"Go to the Bone Quarter," Ithan cut in. "Plead with the Under-King to grant you an audience with my brother. Connor will tell you—"

"Only the scum of the House of Flame and Shadow can do such things," Sabine sneered.

"Your *heir*," Perry said with quiet authority, "is in that House, Sabine."

Sabine gave Perry a simpering smile that made Ithan see red. "Sigrid has defected to Earth and Blood." The crowd murmured again. "And," Sabine continued, "she will dwell here from now on. As your future Prime Apparent."

The Astronomer nodded, his long beard grazing the belt around his draped robes. "After convincing the Under-King to release her into my care, it pains me to again part with my daughter-of-the-heart, but for your benefit, I shall. Sigrid is henceforth a part of your Den—a true wolf."

"I don't recall approving the request," said an old, withered voice. The crowd hushed as the Prime hobbled through the doors. Even the Astronomer lowered his head in deference.

Sabine must have coached Sigrid, because the wolf dropped to her knees before the Prime and bowed her head. "Grandfather," she rasped.

People gasped at the sound of her voice. The hoarse whisper of a Reaper.

The Prime peered down at Sigrid's sallow face. Her acid-green eyes. The wounds on her throat, her neck.

He said nothing as his milky eyes slid to Ithan. Sorrow and pain filled them.

Ithan swallowed hard, but held his ground. "I'm sorry. I . . . I didn't mean for it to turn out like this." The attention of the crowd pushed on his skin like a weight. "I was trying to make things right."

"At the expense of the wolves' future," Sabine snapped.

Ithan reached over his shoulder and drew the weapon he'd brought from Bryce's bedroom.

The Fendyr sword whined as it came free of its sheath. Sabine's eyes flared with fury and longing—

But Ithan knelt before the ancient Prime and bowed his head, lifting the blade in offering.

"I have no intention of usurping the Fendyrs," Ithan said, keeping his gaze on the ground. "I only want what's best for our people. I thought Sigrid might be . . . different, but I was wrong. I was so wrong, and I am so sorry."

Sabine seethed, "Father, don't listen to this trash—"

"Silence," the Prime ordered, in a voice Ithan had not heard in years. He dared to look up at the old male. "I heard what you said," the Prime told Ithan. "Over the cameras." His milky eyes seemed to clear for a heartbeat, revealing a glimpse of the powerful, righteous wolf he'd been. "Danika did indeed guess at what you have told everyone. She suspected it, and asked me about it, and though I had long thought the same, I shied away from the truth. It was . . . easier to continue than to face a painful reality. To keep stability, rather than risk an uncertain future."

The Prime took the sword Ithan offered, his withered hand shaking with the effort of holding the heavy blade. "I allowed our people to be forced to serve in the Aux," he continued, looking now to Perry, "even when their artist's souls abhor it." Perry's eyes shone with pain. "What Ithan has said to you is true. It has always been true, going back to the First Wars and the unspeakable atrocities our people committed on behalf of the Asteri. My daughter"—a glance at Sabine, who was snarling softly—"did not care to listen when I mentioned that the wolves might be more—better—than we have been. But my granddaughter did."

The old wolf let out a heavy sigh. "Danika might have led us back to what we were before we allowed ourselves to be collared by the Asteri. I have long believed that she was killed for this goal—by the powers who wish the status quo to remain in place." The Prime looked down at the wolf kneeling at his feet. "But it must be broken." He extended the sword to Ithan. "Ithan Holstrom is my heir."

Stunned silence rippled through the crowd, the world. Ithan couldn't get a breath down.

"And no one else," the Prime finished.

Sabine had gone white as death. "Father—"

The Prime leveled a cold look at his daughter. "For too long I've left you unchecked."

"I've kept our people, this city safe—"

"You are hereby stripped of your title, your rank, and your authority."

Sabine just stared. At her side, Sigrid's blazing green eyes darted between the two wolves.

The Astronomer was now glancing at the distant eastern gates, as if starting to wonder if he'd backed the wrong horse.

"Take it," the Prime said to Ithan. He extended the sword again.

Ithan shook his head. "I didn't come here to—"

"I offered to make you Alpha once, Ithan Holstrom. I now offer to make you Prime. Don't walk away from it."

Ithan didn't reach for the sword. "I—"

He didn't get the chance to finish his refusal.

One moment, he was staring at the sword. The next, Sabine had snatched it from her father's hands.

She plunged it through the Prime's ancient face.

The crowd exploded into screams and shouts. From the corner of his eye, Ithan saw Amelie dragging a struggling Perry away, out of range.

The Prime crumpled to the ground before Ithan, eyes unseeing, coated with blood. If a medwitch got here soon enough, maybe—

Sigrid moved.

Ithan couldn't contain his cry of dismay as she leapt onto her grandfather's body and pressed her mouth to his withered lips. She inhaled deeply.

Light flared up through the Prime's mouth, illumining his hollowed cheeks, and then Sigrid was breathing it in, drinking it.

His soul, his firstlight—

She cocked her head back and swallowed that light, his essence. Her skin gleamed as the light passed down the column of her throat, inch by inch.

There was no coming back for the Prime.

Sabine cut off his head anyway. The Astronomer, slack-jawed and sprayed with blood, had stumbled back a step, gaping at Sigrid as she leveled her green stare on him, ravenous—

Ithan had only a heartbeat to pivot, to leap off the stairs before Sabine swung the bloodied sword at him. He couldn't take his eyes off the Prime, though. Off Sigrid, the Reaper he'd created who had eaten the old wolf's soul, as hungry as a vampyr—

"Ithan!" Perry shouted, and he snapped to attention as Sabine launched for him again, sword arcing.

He leapt back, narrowly missing being gutted.

"This sword," Sabine panted, brandishing it, "is mine. The title is *mine*."

Ithan shifted, so fast even Sabine blinked.

Make your brother proud.

Sabine swung the sword as Ithan charged, a powerful blow that would cleave even his wolf's skull in two.

Ithan leapt straight at the blade. His jaws closed around it.

Sabine's eyes flared with shock as Ithan bit down, tasting metal.

And shattered the Fendyr sword between his teeth.

74

Most of the crowd had fled as soon as Sigrid had started feeding on the Prime's soul. But Perry and Amelie, Gideon with them, remained near the trees, watching Sabine and Ithan.

Sabine stared down at the seven shards the Fendyr sword had broken into, then lifted her furious gaze to Ithan.

Ithan shifted back into his humanoid body with a near-instant flash. "It's just a piece of steel," he said, panting, the metallic tang of the blade lingering in his mouth. "All those years you obsessed over it, resented Danika for having it . . . It's just a piece of metal."

Sabine's claws glinted. Her lips curled back from her fangs as she snarled.

But behind her, Sigrid was closing in on the Astronomer, who had fallen to the ground and was now crawling backward, hands up. The male pleaded, "Did I not treat you well, deliver you from the Under-King's grasp—"

The Astronomer didn't get the chance to plead his case. Sigrid, either from spite or lost to her hunger, left the old man no time to scream as she leapt upon him and fitted her mouth against his.

Even Sabine paused to watch as Sigrid plunged her clawed hand into his chest, ripping out his still-beating heart in the same moment that she inhaled deeply, and that glimmering light—the secondlight—of his soul rose up through his body, into their fused mouths—

Not Ithan's problem. Not right now. He whipped his head back to Sabine, and let out a long, deep snarl of his own.

Sabine's nose crinkled. "You are no Alpha, pup," she growled, and lunged.

Ithan charged. A straight sprint into death's awaiting claws.

Sabine leapt for him, and Ithan ducked low, sliding, grabbing the longest of the sword's shards and lifting it high—

Blood rained down, and Sabine screamed as she hit the grass with a thud. Ithan sprang to his feet and whirled. Sabine crouched on the ground, a hand pressed to her gut. As if it'd keep the organs now spilling on the grass from tumbling out.

He had a dim awareness of Sigrid, behind him, swallowing down the Astronomer's dying soul and dropping his limp corpse to the stones of the stairs.

But Ithan slowly approached Sabine, and there was no one else in the world, no task but this. Sabine lifted raging, pain-filled eyes to him.

"Everything I have done," Sabine panted up at him, "has been for the wolves."

"It's been for yourself," Ithan spat, stopping before her.

She sneered, revealing blood-coated teeth. "You will lead them to ruin."

"We'll see" was all Ithan said before shifting once more into his wolf's body with that preternatural speed.

Sabine looked his wolf in the eyes—and beheld her death there. She opened her mouth to speak, but Ithan didn't give her the chance. Enough of her vitriol had poisoned the world.

A leap, a crunch of his impossibly strong jaws, and it was done.

With that extra strength he'd gained, he'd broken through the steel of the sword. Breaking through flesh and bone was nothing by comparison.

But once her blood hit his tongue, red washed over his vision, blazing, burning. He was rage and snarls and fangs. He was blood and entrails and primal fury—

"Ithan."

Perry's quavering voice shook him from the daze. From what he'd done to Sabine's body. Her blood coated his mouth, her flesh was stuck between his teeth—

"They're watching," Perry breathed, stepping up to him.

Still in his wolf form, Ithan started to turn toward the witnesses of his savagery, but Perry said, "Don't look," and dropped to her knees before him. Tilted back her head and exposed her neck. "I yield." She added a heartbeat later, "I yield to the Prime."

The words struck a chord in him, one of despair and suffocation. But he couldn't stop it—the instinct to reach forward and lightly clamp his teeth around Perry's slender throat. To take that cinnamon-and-strawberry taste into his mouth.

To accept her submission to him. Her recognition.

Footsteps thudded nearby. Then Amelie stood there, shock paling her face—

But she, too, dropped to her knees. Exposed her neck.

It was either submit to him, or die. As a potential rival, he'd have had no choice but to kill her. A glance behind him revealed the corpse of the Astronomer sprawled across the stairs, leaking blood that trickled down the steps. But Sigrid had vanished. As if she knew he would be coming for her.

Something relaxed in him as he gently closed his jaws around Amelie's throat, too, accepting her surrender. A bitterer, staler taste than Perry's sweetness. But he accepted it all the same.

"Hail Ithan," Amelie said, loud enough for all to hear, "Prime of the Valbaran Wolves."

In answer, a chorus of howls went up from around the Den. Then the city. Then the wilderness beyond the city walls. As if all of Midgard hailed him.

When it ceased, Ithan tipped his wolf's head to the sky and loosed a howl of his own. Triumph and pain and mourning.

Make your brother proud.

And as his howl finished echoing, he could have sworn he heard a male wolf's cry float up from the Bone Quarter itself.

75

Ruhn didn't recognize his city.

Imperial battleships filled the Istros. Dreadwolves prowled the streets. The 33rd had been joined by the Asterian Guard.

And the Meadows still smoldered in the north, lines of smoke rising to the jarringly blue sky.

But it was the quiet that unnerved him the most as he and Lidia crept through the sewers, making their way toward the Comitium. Flynn and Dec had peeled off a few blocks back to go scope out the Aux headquarters for any whisper of where Isaiah and Naomi might be. If they could intercept Isaiah and Naomi at the Comitium, they'd save themselves hours of searching.

Then came the hard part: finding a secure place to meet with them, long enough to explain everything. But for right now, his focus was on finding the two members of Celestina's triarii. And trying not to get caught in the process.

"This should open up into a tunnel that will lead right under the Comitium," Ruhn told Lidia, keeping his voice low. The sewers appeared empty, but in Crescent City there was always someone watching. Listening.

"Once we're in the building," she said, "I can get us to their barracks."

"You're sure you know where the cameras—"

She gave him a look. "It was my job when Ephraim visited to know where they were. Both as the Hind and as Agent Daybright. I could navigate this place blindfolded."

Ruhn blew out a breath. "All right. But when we get to the barracks—"

"Then those shadows of yours come into play, and we hide until Isaiah and Naomi appear. Unless they're already there and we can get them alone."

"Right. Got it." He rolled his neck.

She eyed him. "You seem . . . nervous."

He snorted. "It's my first mission with my girlfriend. I want to impress her."

Her lips quirked up, and Ruhn led the way down another tunnel. "Am I your girlfriend, then?" she asked.

"Is that . . . okay with you?"

She gave him a true smile. It made her seem younger, lighter— the person she might have been if Urd hadn't taken her down her particular fucked-up life path. It knocked the breath from him. "*Yeah*, Ruhn. It's okay with me."

He smiled back, remembering how she'd chastised him when they'd first met for saying "Yeah," for being so casual.

Ahead, Ruhn saw that they were approaching a dented metal door marked *Do Not Enter*. "Now, that's practically an invitation," he said, earning a laugh from Lidia as he kicked in the door.

The sight of the imperial battleships in the Istros robbed Tharion of any joy at the river's familiar, beckoning scent. So did the presence of the Omega-boats docked with them. And right by the Black Dock . . . the *SPQM Faustus*. The very Omega-boat they'd barely outrun that day on Ydra.

He hadn't dared venture into the northernmost part of the city to see the damage to Asphodel Meadows. They weren't here for that, and he knew he'd see nothing that would make him feel any better. The city was eerily quiet. As if in mourning.

Face and hair hidden under a sunball cap, Tharion glowered at the armada for long enough as he stood on the quay that Sathia warned, "You'll draw attention to us with all that glaring."

"I should slip into the water and blast holes in all their hulls," Tharion snarled.

"Focus," she said. "You do that, and we won't accomplish what we came here to do." She frowned at the ships. "Which is clearly still necessary."

"They're holding the city hostage."

"All the more reason to plead with the River Queen to take people in."

Tharion found only cool determination on Sathia's heart-shaped face. "You're right," he said. He let out a low whistle, and waited.

An otter in a bright yellow vest leapt onto the quay, dripping everywhere. It rose onto its hind legs in front of Tharion, whiskers twitching, spraying droplets of water.

Sathia grinned.

"Stop it," Tharion muttered. "It only encourages them to be cuter."

She bit her lip, and though it was thoroughly distracting, Tharion got his act together enough to say to the otter, "Tell the River Queen that Tharion Ketos wants a meeting."

The whiskers twitched again.

Sathia added, "Please."

Tharion avoided the urge to roll his eyes, but also added, "Please." He fished out a gold coin. "And make it speedy, friend."

The otter took the coin in his little black fingers and turned it over, eyes brightening at the outrageous sum. With a flick of his long tail, he leapt back into the clear turquoise water with barely a ripple and was gone.

Tharion watched him gracefully swim out into the depths, then vanish over the drop into the dark, to the Blue Court Beneath. Only tiny, glimmering lights showed any signs of life there.

"What now?" Sathia asked, again eyeing the warships docked in the river. If just one of the soldiers on them recognized Tharion . . .

He tugged his sunball hat over his hair. "Now we lurk in the shadows and wait."

"This doesn't seem safe," Ember said for the fifth time as Bryce stood before the Northern Rift's archway. Hunt waited ten paces behind her, freezing his feathers off. "This seems like the opposite of safe. You're opening *the Northern Rift to Hel.* And we're supposed to believe these demons—the princes, for Urd's sake—are *good*?"

"I'm not sure they're good," Bryce said. "But they're on our side. Just trust me, Mom."

"Trust her, Ember," Randall said, but from the tightness in his voice, Hunt knew the man wasn't too happy, either.

"When you're ready, Athalar," Bryce called to him.

"I thought you didn't need me to fuel you up anymore," Hunt said. "Especially with all that extra power you've got now."

"I don't want to try it on my own for this," Bryce said. "Seems like a high-stakes situation to test out my new abilities."

"I bet you could do it," Hunt called over the wind, "but all right. On three." Bryce stilled, squaring her shoulders.

Hunt rallied his lightning. Prayed to every god, even if they'd mostly fucked him over until this point. The power of his lightning was familiar, yet suddenly foreign. *Helfire,* Apollion had called it.

Answers—at long last, answers about why he was what he was, about why he and no one else had the lightning. Even the thunderbirds, made by Hel, had been hunted to extinction by the Asteri. With Sofie's death, they were truly gone.

Though the Harpy's resurrection—another thing that was his fucking fault—suggested that the Asteri now had other methods of raising the dead.

Only if they could get their hands on more of his lightning. He'd sooner die.

"One . . . ," Hunt breathed, and lifted a hand wreathed in lightning.

Lord of Lightning, the Oracle had called him.

"Two . . ."

Had the Oracle seen what he was, where his power came from, that day?

You remind me of that which was lost long ago. The thunderbirds, hunted to extinction.

Was that the wind ruffling her parka, or was Bryce shaking as she waited for the blow? Hunt didn't give himself a moment to reconsider. To halt.

"Three."

He launched a spear of lightning at his mate.

76

As it had that day at the Asteri's palace, when she had leapt from her own world to another, Hunt's lightning lanced through Bryce's back, through the Horn, into the star on her chest—and out into the Gate.

Ember shouted in fear, and even Randall stumbled back a step, but Hunt let his lightning flow into Bryce, kept a steady stream of it surging between them.

"Open," Bryce said, her voice carrying on the wind. A sliver of darkness began to spread in the middle of the Gate.

Hunt funneled more lightning into her, and the sliver widened, inch by inch.

The Northern Rift had been fixed on Hel—until now. Until his power had passed through not only the Horn on Bryce, but the star on her chest, too—that link to a different world. Reorienting the Gate, as it had that day in the Eternal Palace, to open elsewhere. That was their theory, at least. No one had ever tried to manipulate the Northern Rift to open somewhere other than Hel, but—

"That's enough, Hunt," Ember warned.

Hunt ignored her and sent another spike of power into his mate. Bryce's hair floated up, snow and ice drifting with it, but she maintained an eerie calm until the void filled the entirety of the massive Gate.

Hunt cut off his lightning, running to where Bryce stood before the wall of darkness.

Darkness—flecked by starlight.

A female with golden-brown hair sat in an armchair before a fireplace on the other side of it. All that darkness was the starry night beyond her windows.

And her face was a portrait of pure shock as Bryce lifted a hand in greeting and said, "Hello, Nesta."

The River Queen sat in a chair before a computer panel in the control room connected to the west air lock, a makeshift throne in the sterile, utilitarian space. The tech who operated the computer had vacated the chamber in a near-sprint at the queen's snapped command.

Tharion was well aware that the air lock could be easily hosed down to remove any and all traces of blood. A body flushed out through it would go straight to the sobeks circling outside like Reapers.

If Sathia noted those details, if she understood that she and Tharion had been brought here purely for the convenience of getting rid of his corpse, she didn't let on.

His wife simply curtsied, a graceful swoop downward, at odds with her casual leggings and white sweater, the cashmere now streaked with dirt and torn along the bottom hem. "Your Majesty," Sathia said, her voice cultured yet unthreatening. "It is an honor to meet you."

The River Queen's dark eyes swept over Sathia. "Am I supposed to open my arms to the female who usurped my daughter?"

Sathia didn't so much as flinch. "If my union with Tharion has brought you grief or offense, then I offer my wholehearted apologies."

A beat, too long to be comforting. Tharion lifted his gaze to the River Queen and found her watching him. Her gaze was cold, cruel. Unimpressed.

"I take it," the River Queen said, "you want something very badly from me, if you have come back to risk my wrath."

Tharion bowed his head. "Yes, Your Majesty."

"And yet you have brought your *wife*—for what? To soften me? Or as a shield to hide behind?"

"Considering she's barely up to my chest," Tharion said dryly, "I don't think she'd make much of a shield."

Sathia glared at him, but the River Queen frowned. "Always making jokes. Always playing the fool." She waved a hand adorned in rings of shell and coral toward Sathia. "I suppose I should wish you congratulations on your nuptials, but I instead wish you luck. With a male like that for a husband, you'll need it in droves."

"I thank you," Sathia said with such sincerity that Tharion nearly bought it, too. "May your good wishes fly straight to Urd's ears."

Okay, maybe he'd underestimated his wife. She seemed more comfortable in this setting than he was.

Indeed, the River Queen seemed intrigued enough by Sathia's grace under fire that she said, "Well, Tharion. Let's hear what was so important that you dared enter my realm again."

He clasped his hands behind his back, exposing his chest like he knew the River Queen preferred. He didn't see her jagged sea-glass knife anywhere, but she always had it on her. "I am here on behalf of Bryce Quinlan, Queen of the Fae of Valbara and Avallen, to request asylum in the Blue Court for the people of Crescent City."

Another long pause.

"Queen, is it?" the River Queen said. "Of Valbaran and Avallen Fae?" Her eyes slid to Sathia—the Fae representative, he supposed.

Sathia's chin dipped. "Bryce Quinlan now rules both territories. I serve her, as does Tharion."

Eyes as black and depthless as a shark's slid to Tharion. The same eyes as her sister, the Ocean Queen, he realized. "Am I supposed to be pleased to hear you have yet again defected?"

"I did what my morals demanded," Tharion said.

"Morals," the River Queen mused. "What morals do you have other than ensuring your own survival at any cost? Was it your *morals* that guided you when you took my daughter's maidenhead, swearing to love her until you died, and then toyed with her affections for the next decade?"

Fuck. But Sathia answered for him with that unflinching calm, "These are the mistakes of youth—ones Tharion has reflected upon and learned from."

The River Queen fixed her attention on Sathia again. "Has he? Or was that the poisoned honey he poured into your ear to woo you?"

"He brought me before you," Sathia countered. "Proof that he is willing to own up to his actions."

It took a special sort of person to talk like that to the River Queen. To not back down one inch, not tremble at her power, her ageless face.

The River Queen's eyes narrowed, clearly thinking along the same lines. "And this *Queen Bryce* thought Tharion the best emissary to beg me for such an enormous favor?"

Sathia's chin didn't lower. "She remembered how Tharion and your people so bravely and selflessly carried innocents down here to safety during the attack this spring."

Damn, she was good.

The River Queen waved a hand toward the window overlooking the depths and the monsters prowling beyond. "And does she have a good reason why I shouldn't kill Tharion where he stands and send his body out to the river beasts?"

Sathia didn't even glance toward the circling sobeks. "Because he is now in Queen Bryce's employ. You strike him down, and you shall have the Fae to deal with."

A flash of little pointed teeth. "They'll have to get Beneath first."

Sathia didn't miss a beat. "I believe it would not be in your best interest to become a city under siege."

Holy gods, his wife had balls. Tharion wisely wiped any sort of reaction from his face, but Ogenas damn him, if they survived this meeting, he wanted Sathia to teach him everything she knew.

The River Queen scoffed, but angled her head before changing the subject. "How does the girl suddenly wield such power?"

"That is her own story to tell," Sathia said, folding her hands behind her back, "but she has powerful allies. In this world and in others."

"Others?"

Tharion dared say, turning his voice into a mirror of his wife's poised calm, "Bryce counts the Princes of Hel as allies."

"Then she is an enemy to Midgard. And an imbecile as well, if she is seeking to hide the people of this city from the demons she'd ally with."

"She doesn't seek to hide people from Hel," Tharion said, "but from the Asteri's wrath."

The River Queen blinked slowly. "You ask me to take a stand against the Republic itself."

"What happened in Asphodel Meadows was a disgrace," Tharion said, voice dangerously low. "If you don't stand against the Republic for something of this nature, then you're complicit in their slaughter."

Sathia cut him a warning glance, but the River Queen studied him. Like she hadn't really seen him until this point.

She opened her mouth, and hope surged in Tharion's chest—

But then the interior door to the room hissed open, and the River Queen's daughter was charging in, rage and sorrow crumpling her beautiful face as she screamed, *"How could you?"*

"Is that a Prince of Hel?" Ember whispered from a few steps behind Bryce, her teeth clacking with cold.

"Does she *look* like a prince?" Randall hissed back, snow crunching as he hopped from one foot to another to keep warm.

"Bryce said Aidas appeared to her as a cat, so who's to say—"

"Guys," Bryce murmured as Nesta slowly, slowly rose from her chair by the fireplace. A dagger had somehow appeared in the female's hand, as if it had been concealed under the cushion.

It had worked. They'd managed to make the Northern Rift open to a place other than Hel.

"What are you doing?" Nesta said, and it occurred to Bryce in that moment that none of the others could understand her. Which left Bryce as translator.

So Bryce muttered to Hunt, wide-eyed but poised to leap into action, "Give me a minute," and faced Nesta.

"I'm not going to harm you, or your world," Bryce said in Nesta's own language.

"Then why is there a giant portal in my living room?" Nesta's blue-gray eyes were gleaming with predatory violence. Some of that silver flame was starting to build at her fingertips. Would it withstand Bryce's starfire? Especially with the force of that leveled-up power in her body behind it?

But she hadn't come here for that. "I needed to talk to you."

"How did you know I'd be alone?"

"I didn't. Urd threw me a bone."

The dagger and the silver flame didn't vanish. "Shut that portal."

"Not until I say what I need to say."

The silver flame now flickered in Nesta's eyes. "Then say it, and be gone." Her gaze lowered to Bryce's side. "And leave the dagger you stole."

Bryce ignored that and swallowed hard.

Ember hissed to Randall, *"I don't think it's going well."* Randall hushed her.

But Nesta's eyes slid to Hunt—to the feathered wings, the lightning dancing at his hand, the halo on his brow. "Is that your mate?"

Bryce nodded, and motioned Hunt to step forward. "Hunt Athalar." She'd never fucking use *Danaan* again. For either of them.

Hunt approached and inclined his head. Bryce could have sworn lightning lashed across his eyes, as if the power he'd summoned, enough to open the Northern Rift, was riding him hard.

But Nesta only observed him imperiously, then turned to Bryce. "What do you want?"

Bryce squared her shoulders. "I need you to give me the Mask."

77

Is that a request or a threat?" Nesta asked quietly, and even with a portal between them, the ground seemed to shudder at the female's power.

"It's a plea. A desperate fucking plea," Bryce said, and exposed her palms to the female in supplication. "I need it to give me an edge against the Asteri. To destroy them."

"No." Nesta's eyes held no mercy. "Now shut the portal and be gone." She glanced over a shoulder, where the stars seemed to be winking out in the far distance. "Before the High Lord gets here and rips you to shreds."

"What is that?" Hunt murmured, marking the darkness sweeping in.

"Rhysand," Bryce murmured back, then said to Nesta, "Please. I don't need the Mask forever. Just . . . until it's done. Then I'll return it."

Nesta laughed, pure ice. "You expect me to trust a female who tried to deceive and outsmart us at every turn?"

"I *did* outsmart you," Bryce said coolly, and Nesta's eyes sparked at the challenge. "But that's neither here nor there. Look, I get it— the Mask is insanely powerful and dangerous. I wouldn't trust someone who asked me to use the Horn, either. But my world needs this."

Nesta said nothing.

The darkness crept closer. Fury leaked from it, along with a primal rage. Bryce took a step forward, and Nesta's dagger angled upward.

"Please," Bryce said again. "I promise I'll return the Mask—and Truth-Teller. After I've done what I need to do here."

"You must think me a fool if you believe I'd hand over one of the deadliest weapons in my world. Especially when the monsters in *your* world have wanted to get their hands on it and the rest of the Dread Trove for millennia. Not to mention that few people can use the Mask and live. You put it on, and you might very well die."

"That's a risk I'm willing to take," Bryce said calmly.

"And I'm supposed to trust that you, after all you did here, are going to return the Mask out of the goodness of your heart?"

Bryce nodded. "Yes."

Nesta laughed joylessly, glancing at the approaching darkness. "All I have to do is wait until he gets here, you know. Then you'll wish you'd shut that portal."

"I know," Bryce said, and her throat tightened. "But I'm begging you. The Asteri just exterminated an entire human community in my city. Families." Her eyes burned with tears, and the frigid wind threatened to freeze them. "They killed *children*. To punish me. To punish my mate"—Bryce gestured to Hunt—"for escaping their clutches. This has to end—it has to stop *somewhere*."

The cold anger in Nesta's eyes flickered.

Bryce couldn't stop the tears that slid down her cheeks, turning instantly to ice. "I know you don't trust me. You have no reason to. But I promise I'll return the Mask. I brought collateral—to prove that my intentions are good. That I *will* give it back."

And with that, Bryce ushered her parents forward. Ember and Randall gave her wary glances, but edged closer to the portal.

It tore Bryce's heart out to do it, but she said firmly to Nesta, "These are my parents. Ember Quinlan and Randall Silago. I'm giving them to you—to stay in your world, until I destroy the Asteri and return the Mask to you."

Nesta's eyes flared with shock, but she mastered it instantly, squaring her shoulders. "And if you die in the process?"

"Then my parents will be safer stuck in your world than in mine."

"But the Mask will be in yours. In the hands of the Asteri."

"I don't have anything greater to offer you than this," Bryce said, voice cracking.

"It's not about offering me anything."

Bryce bit back her sob, and her parents turned to her, confused and trusting, angry on her behalf without knowing why.

"Bryce," Hunt said, eyeing that approaching storm. "We should shut the connection." Only Hunt knew the horrible thing she was doing. How it had killed her to leave Cooper behind, because it would have been too suspicious to insist he come on so dangerous a mission. But Baxian, Fury, and June would look after him—and Syrinx.

"Bryce?" her mom asked. "What's going on?"

Bryce couldn't stop her tears as she looked at her mom, at her dad. Possibly for the last time. "Nothing," she said, and faced Nesta again.

"If you won't give me the Mask," she said to the female, "then take them anyway."

Nesta blinked.

"Take my parents," Bryce said, voice breaking. "They have no idea why they're here or who you are or what your world is. They think I'm talking to someone in Hel. But take them, and keep them safe. I ask only that."

Nesta studied Bryce, then Bryce's mother and father. She set her dagger down on the side table near her chair. "You'd leave them in my world . . . and possibly never see them again."

"Yes," Bryce said. "I need Hunt to help me against the Asteri. But my parents are human. They'll be easy targets for the Asteri— they're already being hunted by them. They're good people." She fought back another sob. "They're the best people."

"Bryce," Randall said, enough warning in his voice that she knew he'd spied the encroaching darkness and could tell that something was not right with this plan.

But Bryce couldn't look at her parents. Only at Nesta.

The silver fire in the female's gray-blue eyes banked. Then vanished.

Nesta extended her hand toward Bryce. Something golden glittered in it.

The Mask.

"For whatever good it can do you," Nesta said quietly, "it's yours to borrow." A glance at her parents told Bryce enough: she'd take the collateral.

Bryce's throat bobbed. Hunt murmured, "What the fuck *is* that thing?" As if he could sense the ancient, depthless power leaking from the Mask in Nesta's hand.

But Bryce said, "Thank you," and reached toward Nesta. She could have sworn the very world—all worlds—shuddered as Nesta's hand crossed into Midgard and passed the Mask to Bryce.

Then it was in Bryce's gloved fingers, and it was unholy and empty and cruel—but the star in her chest seemed to purr in its presence.

Bryce tucked it into her jacket, zipping it up inside. It thrummed against her body, its ancient beat echoing in her bones. Her starlight seemed to flicker in answer. Like whatever piece of Theia remained in it knew the Mask, and was glad to see it once more.

"Thank you," Bryce said again. The darkness was now blotting out the city below Nesta's window.

"Good luck," Nesta whispered.

Bryce inclined her head in thanks. And with a subtle nod to Hunt . . .

His power struck her parents. Not lightning, but a storm wind at their backs. Shoving them through the portal, through the Northern Rift, and into Nesta's world.

"Bryce!" her mother shouted, stumbling—but Bryce didn't wait. Didn't say anything as she willed the Horn to sever the connection, to collapse the bridge between their worlds. The last image she had was of the darkness, of Rhysand's power, slamming into the windows of Nesta's room, her mother's outraged face, Randall reaching for his rifle—

Snow and mist returned. The Rift was shut. And her parents were on the other side of it.

Bryce's knees wobbled. Hunt put a hand to her elbow. "We have to get out of here."

She had the Mask. And the Horn. And Theia's star. And the blades. It would have to be enough to take on living gods.

"Bryce, we have to go," Hunt said, stronger now. "Can you teleport us back to the wall?"

It should have been a relief, to know her parents were in that other world, with people who she had learned were decent and kind, but her mom would never forgive her. Randall would never forgive her. Not just for throwing them into that world, but for leaving Cooper behind.

"What the *fuck*," Hunt hissed, and Bryce whirled as he hauled her behind him.

Right as the Harpy, clad in white to camouflage her against the snow, dove from the mists. Even her black wings had been painted white to blend in.

Amid the swirling mists, she was as awful as Bryce remembered, yet her face . . . There was nothing alive there, nothing remotely aware. She was a husk. A host. With one mission: *kill*.

78

Any hope of succeeding died in Tharion as the River Queen's daughter threw herself into her mother's lap and sobbed. "You married *her*?"

They were the only words he could discern among the weeping.

Sathia just stared at the girl. Like she was completely out of politesse to spin to their advantage. The River Queen stroked her daughter's dark hair, murmuring gentle reassurances, but her eyes blazed with pure hate for Tharion.

Tharion began, "I . . ." He couldn't find the right words.

The River Queen's daughter lifted her head at his voice, her face streaked with tears. The river outside trembled, shaking the Blue Court. "You sold yourself to some Fae harlot?" She sniffed at Sathia. "With *dirt* in her veins? Not even a drop of water to call to you?"

Sathia took the insults, stone-faced, granting him a window into the way she'd been treated in her life. It didn't sit well.

It was enough to goad him into responding, "Her magic is that of growing things, of life and beauty. Not of drowning and stifling."

The River Queen's daughter stood slowly. "You *dare* speak to me in such a way?"

And at her petulant fury, at her mother's rage . . . he'd had it. He'd fucking *had* it.

Tharion pointed to the window. Not at the sobeks, but at the surface too far above to see. "There are *imperial battleships* in this river! Asphodel Meadows is a smoldering *ruin*, with the bodies of children strewn in the streets!"

He'd never yelled like this. At anyone, least of all his former queen and princess.

But he couldn't stop it, the pure rage and desperation that ruptured from him. "And all you care about is who one stupid fucking male is married to? There are babies in that rubble! And you cry only for *yourself*!"

Sathia was gaping, warning etched on her face, but Tharion spoke directly to the River Queen. "Bryce sent me to beg you to help, but I'm asking you personally, too. Not as mer, not as someone in the Blue Court, but as a living being who loves this city. There is nowhere else on Valbara that might weather the storm. This place, Beneath . . . it can withstand at least the initial brunt. Give the children of Crescent City a safe harbor. A chance. If you won't let all the people come, then at least take the children."

"No," the River Queen's daughter sniveled. "You used and discarded me. You don't have the right to ask such favors of us, of the Blue Court."

"I'm *sorry*," Tharion burst out. "I am sorry that I misled you, and slept with you, and realized too late that I had gone too far. I'm sorry I strung you along for years—I didn't know how to talk to you, or be an adult, and I'm sorry. It wasn't right of me, and it was immature, and I hate that I did that to you, to anyone."

She glowered at him, sniffling.

Tharion said, "And I married Sathia to bail her out of a shitty situation. King Morven of Avallen was forcing her into marriage with a Fae brute, and the only options were face the Asteri's wrath and die, or wed. I offered her a way out. Marriage to me. I owed it to my sister to help a female in trouble. Our marriage isn't a comment on how I feel about you *or* her."

"And the fact that she is a Fae beauty held no sway over you?" sneered the River Queen's daughter.

"No," Tharion said honestly. "I . . ." He looked toward his wife, who was indeed pretty. Beautiful. But that hadn't entered into his decision to offer his aid. "She was a person in trouble, who needed help."

The River Queen's daughter seethed.

Tharion said, voice breaking, "But if you take in the people of this city, if you shelter them against whatever storm the Asteri might bring . . . when this is over, if I am alive . . ." He held her stare. "I will divorce my wife and marry you."

Sathia whirled to him, but he couldn't face her, couldn't bear to see her reaction to how he'd abandon her, too—

The River Queen's daughter sniffed, a child calming from a tantrum. "I accept. I shall marry you once you're rid of her."

"You shall not." The River Queen's voice shook the room, the river. "My daughter does not accept this offer. Nor do I."

Tharion's chest crumpled. "Please," he begged. "If you could just—"

"I am not done speaking," she said, and held up a hand. Tharion obeyed. "I no longer wish my daughter to be tied to the likes of you, in truth or in promise. As far as marriage between you is concerned, it shall never happen."

"*Mother*—"

"You are your wife's problem now," the River Queen said to Tharion.

Tharion shut his eyes against the stinging in them, hating this, hating that he'd lost this opportunity, this safe haven for the people of Crescent City, due to his own bullshit.

"But your willingness to sacrifice your freedom to live Above is no small thing," the River Queen went on. She tilted her head to the side, and one of the shells in her hair sprouted legs and skittered under the tresses. A hermit crab. "You never asked me why I sent you to look for Sofie Renast's body, and to find her brother."

Tharion opened his eyes and found her staring curiously at him. Not with kindness, but with something like respect. "It . . . it wasn't my place to question," he said.

"You are frightened of me, as all wise beings are," she said a shade smugly. "But I have fears, too. Of this world, at the mercy of the Asteri."

Tharion tried not to gape.

"Our people are ancient," the River Queen said. "My sisters and I remember a world before the Asteri arrived and caused the land's magic to wither. Entire islands vanished into the sea, our civilizations with them. And though we were limited in our power to stop them . . . we have tried, each in our own way."

Her daughter was staring at her like she didn't know her.

But the River Queen went on, "We remember the power the thunderbirds wielded. How the Asteri hunted them down. Because they *feared* them. And when I learned one had been killed, her thunderbird brother on the loose . . . I knew those were assets the Asteri would seek to recover at any cost. I might not have known why, but I had no intention of letting them attain either Sofie or her brother."

Tharion blinked. "You . . . you wanted them in order to stop the Asteri?"

A shallow nod. "It might not have made a difference in the greater sense, but keeping them safe was my attempt, however small, at thwarting the Asteri's plans."

Tharion had no idea what to do other than bow his head and admit, "Emile wasn't a thunderbird. Only a human. He's in hiding now."

"And yet you kept this from me." The river shuddered at her displeasure.

"I thought it would be best for the boy to disappear from the world completely."

The ruler scanned his face again for a long, long moment.

"I see the male that you are," the River Queen said, and it was more gentle than he'd ever heard her. "I see the male that you shall become." She nodded to Sathia. "Who sees a female in trouble and does not think of the consequences to his own life before helping." A nod, grave and contemplative. "I wish I had seen more of that male here. I wish you had been that male for my daughter. But if you are that male now, and you are that male for the sake of this city . . ."

She waved a hand, and the sobeks swam away on a silent command.

"Then the Blue Court shall help. Any who we can bring down here before the warships catch wind of it . . . any person, from any House: I shall harbor them."

The Harpy was a horror. Hunt could *feel* her lack of presence. The emptiness leaking from her.

The Asteri had raised her from the dead, but left her soul by the wayside.

They'd bypassed the necromancers, who used one's soul for resurrection, and instead created a perfect soldier to station here: one who did not feel cold, who did not need to eat, and who had no scruples whatsoever.

And it had all come from his lightning. His Helfire. He knew, deep down, that it wasn't his fault, but . . . he'd given Rigelus that lightning.

And it had created this nightmare.

Rigelus had to have guessed they'd come to the Northern Rift, and planted the Harpy to lie in wait.

Hunt rallied his lightning, making the mists glow eerily around him, but Bryce said, "What did they do to you?"

The Harpy didn't answer. She didn't show any sign that she'd heard or cared. As if she'd lost her voice. Her very identity.

"Fry the bitch," Bryce muttered to Hunt, and he didn't wait before sending a plume of lightning for the Harpy.

She dodged it, those white-painted wings as fast as they had ever been—

No, they hadn't been painted white. They'd *turned* white. As if whatever the Asteri had done to her with Hunt's lightning had bleached the color out of them.

Hunt threw another bolt of lightning, then another, and he might have lit up the whole fucking sky if not for that gods-damned halo—

"Athalar!" A familiar male voice rang from the mists above

them. Hunt didn't dare take his focus off the Harpy as the voice clicked.

Isaiah.

"What the *Hel*—" an equally familiar female voice said. Naomi.

But it was the third voice, coming from behind him as its owner landed in the snow, that made Hunt's blood go cold. "What new evil is this?"

The Governor of Valbara had arrived.

Bryce didn't know which was worse: Celestina or the Harpy. The female who'd stabbed them in the back, or the one who'd literally tried to slit Ruhn's throat.

She and Hunt couldn't take on two enemies at once—not in subfreezing temperatures, totally drained from opening the Rift, with the mists obscuring almost everything.

The Harpy swooped, and Hunt launched his lightning, so fast only the swiftest of angels could evade the strike. The Harpy did, and plunged earthward, mist streaming off her white wings, straight for Bryce. Bryce rolled out of the way and the Harpy hit the ground, snow exploding around her, but she was instantly up, lunging for Bryce again.

Isaiah blasted the Harpy with a wall of wind, knocking her back. But Celestina stood three yards away, and Hunt was already whirling to face her—

Bryce unzipped her thick jacket, the cold wind instantly biting into her skin. She grabbed the Mask.

And gave no warning at all as she fitted the icy gold to her face.

Wearing the Mask was like being underwater, or at a very high altitude. Her head was full of its power, her blood thrumming, pulsing in time with the presence in her head, her bones. The world seemed to dilute into its basics: alive or dead. She was alive, but with the Mask, she might escape even death itself and live forever.

The star in her chest hummed, welcoming that power like an old friend.

Bryce shoved aside her revulsion. Hunt was readying his lightning for Celestina, the mists glowing with each crackle, and the Harpy had broken through Isaiah's power and was diving for Bryce again—

"Stop," Bryce said to the Harpy. It was her voice, but not.

The Harpy halted.

Everyone halted.

"Bryce," Hunt breathed, but he was far away. He was alive, and her business was with the dead.

"Kneel."

The Harpy fell to her knees in the snow.

Celestina started, "What evil weapon have you—"

"I shall deal with you later," Bryce said in that voice that resonated through her and created ripples in the mist.

Even the Archangel fell silent as Bryce approached the Harpy. Peered down into her narrow, hateful face. Truly soulless.

A body with no pilot.

Cold horror lurched through Bryce, despite the Mask's unholy embrace. Maybe it was a mercy, she thought as she stared into the vacant, raging face of the Harpy. Maybe it was a mercy to do this.

There was no soul to grab onto, to command. Only the body. But the Mask seemed to understand what was needed. "Your work is done," Bryce said, her voice reverberating through the frozen landscape. "Be at rest."

It was sickening—and yet it was a relief as the Harpy's eyes closed and she collapsed to the ground. As her skin began to wither, her body reclaiming the form it had known in death.

The cheekbones sank, decaying over the Harpy's face. Bryce knew that beneath the angel's white gear, her body would be doing the same.

When the Harpy lay desiccated in the snow, Bryce finally peeled the Mask off—only to find Naomi, Isaiah, and Celestina staring at her, awash in shock and dread.

79

Nah," Ruhn said into the phone as he and Lidia once again wended through the sewers, "they weren't at the triarii's private barracks. We waited for hours, but they're deserted. No one came or went. From the look of Isaiah's and Naomi's rooms, no one's been there for days."

Lidia trudged ahead, neck bent forward as she checked a burner phone she'd brought with her from the *Depth Charger*—years ago, it seemed.

"So what do we do?" Flynn asked. "Keep waiting? Dec was able to hack into the Aux's computers while I scouted around the area, but he found nothing about their movements, either. It doesn't seem like the Aux even knows they're gone." With the Asteri out to punish anyone caught associating with them, it had been safest to observe the Aux from a distance, rather than directly talk to anyone. Not to mention the risk of being sold out to the Asteri by any enterprising sorts.

Ruhn considered. "If Isaiah and Naomi are missing, Celestina probably wants to keep their absence unnoticed."

In the background, Declan said, "You think she killed them?"

"It's possible," Ruhn said as Flynn switched him to speaker-phone. "We're going to circle back there tomorrow. See if we can pick up anything else. You two be on the lookout for any sign of them. Check the squares where they do the crucifixions."

"Fuck," Flynn said.

"I'll try to access the security footage from the Comitium," Dec volunteered. "Maybe there's something there that can point us in the right direction."

Ruhn sighed. "Be careful. Let's rendezvous at sunset—the northeastern corner of the intersection just past the shooting range."

"Copy," Flynn and Dec said, and hung up.

Ruhn and Lidia walked another block or so in the reeking quiet before he said, "You lulled me to sleep with a story once. About a witch who turned into a monster."

"What of it?" She glanced sidelong at him.

"Is it a real story, or did you make it up?"

"It was a story my mother told me," she said softly. "The only story I remember her telling me as a child before she . . . let me go."

He'd been about to ask if the similarities between the evil prince and Pollux, the kind knight and himself, had been meant prophetically, but at the sadness in her voice . . . "I'm really sorry you went through that, Lidia. I can't imagine doing that to a child. The thought of letting my own kid go into the arms of a stranger—"

"I did it, though," she said, staring ahead at nothing. "What my mother did to me, I did exactly the same thing to my sons."

His heart ached at the pain and guilt in her voice. "You entrusted your sons to a loving family—"

"I didn't know that. I had no idea who they were going to be living with."

"But the alternative was taking them with you."

"Maybe I should have. Maybe I should have run into the wilds and hidden forever with them."

"What kind of life would that have been? You gave them a real life, and a happy one, on the *Depth Charger*."

"A true mother would have—"

"You *are* a true mother," he said, and grabbed her hand, turning her to face him. "Lidia, you made an impossible choice—you decided to protect your children, even if it meant you wouldn't see them grow up. Fuck, if that doesn't make you a true mother, then I don't know what does."

Pain rippled across her face, and he wrapped his arms around her as she leaned against his chest. "They were the one thing that kept me going," she said. "Through every horror, it was just knowing that they were there, and safe, and that my choices were keeping them that way."

He slid a hand down her back, luxuriating in the feel of her, offering up whatever comfort he could. They stood there for long minutes, just holding each other.

"I told you before," she said against his chest, "that you remind me that I'm alive."

He kissed the top of her head in answer, her golden hair silky against his mouth.

"For a long time, I wasn't," she said. "I did my work as the Hind, as Daybright—all to keep my sons safe and do what I thought was right. But I felt nothing. I was essentially a wraith most days, occupying a shell of a body. But then I met you, and it was like I was back in my body again. Like I was . . . awake." She pulled back, scanning his face. "I don't think I'd ever been truly awake," she said, "until I met you."

He smiled down at her, his heart too full for words. So he kissed her, gently, lovingly.

She slid her hand into his as they continued onward. But Ruhn paused her again, long enough to tip her head back and kiss her once more. "I know we have some shit to sort out still," he said against her mouth, "but . . . girlfriend, lover, whatever you want to be, I'm all in."

Her lips curved against his in a smile. "I thank Urd every single day that Cormac asked you to be my contact."

He pulled away, grinning. "I still owe you a beer."

"If we get through this, Ruhn," she said, "I'll buy *you* a beer."

Ruhn grinned again, and slid an arm around her waist as they walked on into the gloom. They strode in warm, companionable quiet for several blocks before Lidia's phone buzzed, and she pulled it from her pocket to glance at the screen. "It's from the *Depth Charger*," she said, and paused to open the message.

He watched her eyes dart over the screen—then halt. Her hands shook.

"Pollux," Lidia breathed, and Ruhn stilled. Her eyes lifted to his, and pure panic filled them as she whispered, "He's taken my sons."

Hunt didn't let himself dwell on it—the unholy majesty that was Bryce wearing the Mask. On what she'd been able to do to the Harpy.

He faced Celestina, Isaiah and Naomi behind her, all clad in heavy winter gear. Isaiah's and the Governor's white wings were nearly invisible against the snow. All their faces, however, were taut with shock. "What are you doing here?" Hunt said.

"What is that?" Naomi breathed, ignoring his question, eyes on the golden object in Bryce's hands.

"Death," Isaiah answered, face ashen. "That mask . . . it's death."

Hunt demanded again, "What are you doing here?"

Isaiah's eyes shot to Hunt's. "We've been tracking that *thing*." He gestured to the pile of clothes that had been the resurrected Harpy moments before. "Celestina's old contacts up here reported that the guard station at the wall had been attacked by some new terror, so we all raced up here, fearing it was something from Hel—"

"Why not send a legion?" Hunt asked, eyeing the two angels who'd once been his closest companions. "Why come yourselves?"

"Because the Asteri ordered us to stand down," Naomi said. "But someone still had to stop this carnage."

Hunt met Celestina's eyes, the Archangel's flawless face a mask of stone. "Going off-leash, huh?"

Temper sparked in her gaze. "I regret what I did to you and yours, Hunt Athalar, but it was necessary to—"

"Spare me," Hunt snapped. "You fucking betrayed us to the Asteri—"

"Hunt," Isaiah said, holding up a hand, "look, there's a lot of bad blood here—"

"Bad blood?" Hunt exploded. "I fucking went to the *dungeons* because of her!" He pointed at the Governor. Bryce moved closer to him, a comforting presence at his side. He gestured to his forehead, barely visible with his gear. "I have this *halo* on my fucking head again because of her!"

Celestina just stood there, shivering. "As I said, I regret what I did. It has cost me more than you know." She seemed to blink back tears. "Hypaxia has . . . ended things between us."

"What, your girlfriend didn't like that you're a two-faced snake?" Hunt said.

"Hunt," Bryce murmured, but he didn't fucking care.

"You were supposed to be *good*," Hunt said, voice breaking. "You were supposed to be the good Archangel. And you're even worse than Micah." He spat, and it turned to ice before it could hit the snow. "At least he made it clear when he was fucking someone over."

His lightning thrashed in his veins, looking for a way out.

"Hunt," Naomi said, "what the Governor did was fucked up, but—"

"She went against Asteri orders to be here," Isaiah finished. "Let's get out of the cold and talk—"

"I'm done fucking talking," Hunt said, and his power stirred. "I am *done* with Archangels and your fucking *bullshit*."

His lightning hissed along the snow. And as his vision flashed, he knew lightning forked across his eyes.

Celestina held up her gloved hands. "I want no quarrel with you, Athalar."

"Too bad," Hunt said, and lightning skittered over his tongue. "I want one with you."

He didn't give any further warning before he hurled his power at the Archangel. He gave everything, yet it wasn't enough. His power choked at its limits, restrained by the halo.

A leash to hold demons in check.

It hadn't worked on the princes. He'd be damned if he allowed it to keep working on him.

Hunt let his power build and build and build. The snow around him melted away.

Apollion had given his essence, his Helfire, to Hunt. And if that made him a son of Hel, so be it.

Hunt closed his eyes, and saw it there—the black band of the halo, imprinted across his very soul. Its scrolling vine of thorns. The spell to contain him.

Everyone knew the enslavement spell couldn't be undone. Hunt had never even tried. But he was done playing by the Asteri's rules. By anyone's rules.

Hunt reached a mental hand toward the black thorns of the halo. Wreathed his fingers in lightning, in Helfire, in the power that was his and only his.

And sliced through it.

The thorns of the halo shivered and bled. Black ink dripped down, dissolving into nothing, gobbled up by the power that was now surging in him, rising up—

Hunt opened his eyes to see Isaiah gaping at him in fear and awe. The halo still marred his friend's brow.

No more.

Knowing where it was, how to destroy it, made it easier. Hunt reached out a tendril of his power for Isaiah, and before his friend could recoil, he sliced a line through the halo on his brow.

Isaiah hissed, staggering back. A roaring, raging wind rose from his feet as his halo, too, crumbled away from his brow.

Celestina was looking between them, terror stark on her face. "That's not—that's not—"

"I suggest you run," Hunt said, his voice as frozen as the wind that bit at their faces.

But Celestina straightened. Held her ground. And with bravery he didn't expect, she said, "Why are *you* here?"

As if he'd be distracted by the question, as if it'd keep her fate at bay—

Bryce answered for him. "To open the Northern Rift to Hel."

Naomi whirled on Bryce and said, "What?"

Isaiah, too stunned at his halo's removal to pay much attention to the conversation, was staring at his hands—as if he could see the unleashed power they now commanded.

Celestina shook her head. "You've lost your minds." She planted her feet, and white, shining power glowed around her. "You want to fight me, Athalar, go ahead. But you're not opening the Rift."

"Oh, I think we are," Hunt said, and launched his lightning at her.

The world ruptured as it collided with a wall of her power, and Hunt poured more lightning in, snow melting away, the very stone beneath them buckling and warping as his lightning struck and struck and struck—

"Athalar!" Naomi shouted. "What the fuck—"

Celestina blasted out her power, a wall of glowing wind.

Hunt snapped his lightning through it. He was done with the Archangels. With their hierarchies. Done with—

Isaiah stepped into the fray, hands up.

"Stop," he said, and power glowed in his friend's eyes. "Athalar, stop."

"She deserves to die—every fucking Archangel deserves to die for what they do to us," Hunt said through his teeth. But it registered, suddenly, that Bryce was no longer by his side.

She was running back toward the Rift, her star blazing. So bright—with the two other pieces of Theia's star now united with what Bryce had been born with, her star blazed as bright as the sun. The sun *was* a star, for fuck's sake—

"No!" Celestina shouted, and her power flared.

Hunt slammed his lightning into the Archangel so hard it shattered her power, sending her flying back into the snow with a satisfying thud.

Celestina's wings splayed wide, flinging snow in all directions, blood leaking from her nose and mouth. "Don't!" she cried to Bryce. "I've dedicated *years* of my life to preventing the Rift from opening," she panted. "Find another way. Don't do this."

Bryce halted, snow spraying with the swiftness of her stop.

That magnificent star blazed from her chest, casting a brilliant glimmer over the snow. Breathing hard, Bryce said to the Archangel, "The Princes of Hel have offered their help, and Midgard needs it, whether you know it or not. Hunt and I have already killed two Archangels. Don't make us kill you, too."

Hunt glanced to Bryce in question. As if there was an alternative to killing Celestina—

"You . . . ," Celestina said. "You killed Micah and Sandriel," she whispered.

"They were stronger than you," Hunt said, "so I don't think much of your chances."

Hunt's lightning flared around him, poised to strike, to flay her from the inside out, as he had done with Sandriel.

But Celestina's brown eyes widened at his lightning, released from its bonds and spreading through the world. She'd never seen the full extent of what he could do—she'd never had the chance during those weeks they'd worked together. "How is it . . . how is it that you have the power of Archangels but are not one yourself?" she asked.

"Because I'm the Umbra Mortis," Hunt said, voice unyielding as the ice around them. And he'd never felt more like it as he stared at Celestina, and knew that with one strike to her heart, she'd be smoldering, bloody ruins.

Celestina's gaze lowered, and she dropped to her knees. Like she knew it, too.

A plume of pure, uncut lightning rose above Hunt's shoulder, an asp ready to strike true. He looked to Bryce, waiting for the nod to incinerate her.

But Bryce was staring at him sadly. Softly, lovingly, she said, "You're not, Hunt."

He didn't understand the words. He blinked at her.

Bryce stepped forward, snow crunching under her feet. "You're not the Umbra Mortis," she said. "You never were, deep down. And you never will be."

Hunt pointed a lightning-wreathed finger at Celestina. "She and all her kind should be blasted off the face of Midgard."

"Maybe," Bryce said gently, taking another step. Her starlight faded into nothing. "But not by you."

Disgust roiled through him. He'd never once hated Bryce, but in that moment, as she doubted him, he did.

"She doesn't deserve to die, Hunt."

"Yes, she fucking does," Hunt spat. "I remember each and every one of them—all the angels who marched against us on Mount Hermon, all the Senate, the Asteri, and the Archangels at my sentencing. I remember *all* of them, and she's no better than they were. She's no better than Sandriel. Than Micah."

"Maybe," Bryce said again, her voice still gentle, soothing. He hated that, too. "No one is forgiving her. But she doesn't deserve to die. And I don't want her blood on your hands."

"Where was this mercy when it came to the Autumn King? You didn't stop Ruhn then."

"The Autumn King had done nothing in his long, miserable life except inflict pain. He didn't merit my notice, let alone my mercy. She does."

"Why?" He looked to his mate, his rage slipping a notch. *"Why?"*

"Because she made a mistake," Naomi said, stepping forward, expression pained. "And has been trying to make it right ever since. Isaiah and I didn't come up here with her because she ordered us to. We wanted to help her."

Hunt pointed to the Rift mere feet from Bryce. "She's going to stop you from opening it."

"I will not," Celestina promised, keeping her head bowed. "I yield."

"Let her go, Hunt," Bryce said.

"Morven yielded, and you killed him," Hunt snapped at her.

"I know," Bryce said. "And I'll live with that. I wouldn't wish the same burden on you. Hunt . . . We have enough enemies. Let her go."

"I swear upon Solas himself," Celestina said, the highest oath an angel could invoke, "that I will help you, if it is within my power."

"I'm not going to take the word of an Archangel."

"Well, we're going to need this Archangel," Bryce said, and Hunt's rage slipped further as he looked to her again.

"What?"

Bryce glanced at the Harpy's body, half-melted from Hunt's lightning clashing with Celestina's power. The rock around it had been warped—his lightning had altered the stone itself. Bryce closed the distance between her and Hunt, reaching out to take his hand.

His lightning crawled over her skin, but he didn't let it hurt. He could never hurt her.

"You said you're with me—all of you," Bryce murmured, staring at him and only him. "Put the past behind you. Focus on what's ahead. We have a world to save, and I need my mate at my side to do it. No one else—not a son of Hel, not the Umbra Mortis, not even Hunt fucking Athalar. I need my *mate*. Just Hunt."

He saw it all in her eyes—that no matter what had happened, who he'd been and what he'd done . . . it really didn't matter to her. Being made in Hel didn't matter to her. But she'd captured who he was, deep down, in those photos last spring. The person she'd brought into the world. The person she loved.

Just Hunt.

So he let go. Let go of the lightning, of the death singing in his veins. Let go of Apollion's and Thanatos's smirking faces. Let go of his rage at the Archangel before him, and the Archangels who'd existed before her.

Just Hunt. He liked that.

His lightning faded, fizzling away entirely. And he said to Bryce, as if she were the only person on Midgard, in any galaxy, "I love you, Just Bryce."

She snickered, and kissed him lightly on the cheek. "Now, if you don't plan on killing Celestina anymore . . ." Bryce pulled the Mask from her jacket again. "We're going to raise an army."

"What army?" Isaiah whispered.

"We're going to raise the Fallen," Bryce said, tossing the Mask in the air and catching it like it was a fucking sunball.

Hunt's knees buckled. "You said we were going to use the Mask to fight the Asteri."

"And we are," Bryce said, pitching the Mask up and catching it once more. "It's your fault you didn't ask for specifics on *how* we'd use it against them."

No, he'd assumed she'd put it on and it would give her some edge to kill them.

Hunt shook his head. "You're out of your mind."

Bryce halted her tossing at that, voice gentling. "We need a distraction for the Asteri. Hel won't be enough. But an army of the dead, an army of the Fallen, will work nicely. An army that won't have to die again. And Isaiah and Naomi are going to lead them."

"That's why you sent Ruhn and Lidia to get them," Hunt said quietly, fighting through his shock.

Isaiah gave him a questioning look, but Bryce replied, "Yes. I thought if we could get them, and get the Mask from Nesta . . . it might work."

"But how can you raise them?" Hunt demanded. Nesta had used the bones of a beast, Bryce had told him. "Their bodies are gone—"

"The Asteri kept their wings," Bryce said, disgust lacing every word. "They kept *your* wings, like trophies. But because they didn't have Sailings, I think part of their souls might still be attached."

Hunt rubbed at his frozen face. "And what—you're just going to have a bunch of wings flying around?"

She cut him a sharp look. "No. Well, yes—but only to get them to where we need their souls."

"You said the Mask can reanimate dead bodies—not give souls new ones."

"That's what I saw Nesta do," Bryce said. "But Theia's star . . ."

Cupping her hands before her chest, she drew out the blazing, beautiful star. It illuminated the mists, set the snow at their feet sparkling.

"Wow," Naomi breathed.

What Bryce had taken from her chest that day during the

attack last spring was a fraction of the star she now held between her palms.

"This," Bryce said, face glowing in the starlight, "seems to recognize the Mask, somehow. When I put the Mask on, I could feel the pull between the two powers. Maybe it's something about Theia's star. I think it can command the Mask to do . . . different things."

"This isn't the time to experiment," Hunt warned.

"I know," Bryce conceded. "But I think all it would take is a bit of the deceased, and I could Make them anew. Not give them true life, but their souls would be returned—given new forms. Unlike . . . unlike what the Asteri did to the Harpy."

"That mask can truly raise the dead, then," Naomi said hoarsely.

Bryce nodded. "The Fallen wouldn't be given new, breathing bodies, but yes—they'd be able to help us."

"What sort of bodies, then?" Isaiah asked, glancing nervously at Hunt.

"Ones the Asteri already made for us," Bryce said a shade quietly. "Perfect blends of magic and tech."

"The new mech-suits," Hunt realized. "The ones the Asteri stationed on Mount Hermon."

Bryce nodded gravely. "I think Rigelus stationed those suits up there to taunt you guys, but it's about to blow up in his stupid fucking face. Lidia said the suits don't need pilots to operate, so we don't have to worry about any physical interference. Dec can hack into their computer system and block imperial access while the souls of the Fallen fuse with the mech-suits and pilot them under Naomi and Isaiah's command."

But to do what she was suggesting . . .

"We can't," Hunt rasped, wings slumping. "*I can't* ask them to die for us again. Even if they're already dead. The Fallen have given too much."

Bryce walked over to him. Took his hand. "We need those suits piloted by the Fallen, or they'll be used against *us* by the Asteri. We need the Asteri and their forces entirely occupied."

But Hunt's heart twisted. "Bryce."

"It will be their choice whether to return, to pilot those suits. I'll give them that choice, when I raise them. And I'll be with you for every moment of it." She nodded to Isaiah and Naomi. "They'll command the Fallen. You don't need to shoulder that burden anymore. I'll need you with me—in the Asteri's palace."

He closed his eyes, breathing in her scent. Celestina could have struck, he supposed, but she remained kneeling.

And just as he had that day when Hunt had given Sandriel her due, Isaiah suddenly knelt before him. Naomi joined him on her knees.

"I'm not an Archangel," Hunt blurted. "And I haven't agreed to lead you two. So get up."

It was Celestina who said, "Perhaps the age of Archangels is over."

"You sound happy about it."

"I would be, if it were to come to pass," Celestina said, and got to her feet. "I told you once: Shahar was my friend. I might not have had the courage to fight alongside her then . . ." Her chin lifted. "But I do now."

He was having none of it. "And what are *you* going to do during all this?"

Bryce answered before Celestina could reply. "She's going to Ephraim's fortress." At Hunt's surprised look, echoed by Celestina, Bryce explained, "He's the closest Archangel to the Eternal City. We need him occupied. If Ephraim joins the fight, it will complicate everything."

Celestina nodded gravely. "I will make sure he does not come within a hundred miles of the capital."

"How?" Hunt demanded. "Tie him up?"

"I will do whatever is necessary to end this," Celestina said, chin high.

Hunt pointed to the Rift. "We're going to open the Rift to *Hel*. You didn't seem too keen on that a moment ago."

Celestina glanced between Hunt and Bryce. "It goes against everything I've worked for, but . . . it does seem that all you two have done has been in the best interest of the innocents of

Midgard. I don't believe that you would open the Rift if it would jeopardize the most vulnerable."

"Yeah?" Hunt snapped. "And where the fuck were *you* when Asphodel Meadows was blasted into nothing?"

That brought a measure of ice to Bryce's stare. True grief filled Celestina's eyes.

"It was the final straw, Hunt," Isaiah said. "Why we—she— disobeyed the Asteri. They gave no warning. The ships pulled into the Istros, and they said it was for our protection. I didn't even know the ships could send aerial missiles that far."

Naomi's lashes were pearled with tears that quickly turned to ice as she added, "It was the most cowardly, unforgivable . . . We don't stand for that. None of us. Not Celestina, and certainly not the 33rd."

Hunt looked back to Bryce, and found only pain and cold resolve staring back at him. She was right. They had enough enemies. Ones who had to pay.

And he might not have trusted one word out of an Archangel's mouth, but if Isaiah and Naomi believed Celestina, that meant something. Isaiah, who had suffered under Archangels as much as Hunt had, was here, helping Celestina, knowing she had betrayed his friend. Isaiah wasn't some spineless asshole—he was good and smart and brave.

And Isaiah was here.

So Hunt said, "All right. Let's ring Hel's doorbell."

Hunt had enough lightning left to blast Bryce again. It passed through her and into the Gate—into the heart of the Northern Rift.

Her will, blazing with that undiluted starlight, changed its location once more.

Celestina, Isaiah, and Naomi held back a step, all glowing with power, readying for the worst.

Impenetrable darkness spread within the archway, broken only by two glowing blue eyes.

Prince Aidas stood there, impeccably dressed in his jet-black clothes, not one golden hair on his head out of place. He surveyed the icy terrain, the sun now setting after a brief window of daylight.

Bryce swung her arm out in a grand, sweeping gesture as the Prince of the Chasm stepped through the Northern Rift. "Welcome back to Midgard," she said. "Hope you have a pleasant stay."

80

So," Jesiba said, drumming her fingers on her desk, "the pup goes to pitch a deworming medicine to a bunch of wolves and comes home Prime."

Ithan ignored the jab. "I need you to get me in with the Under-King," he said. He'd showered in the barracks at the Den and changed into nondescript Aux clothes, then swiftly checked on Perry and the others before running back to the House of Flame and Shadow. He was Prime, yes, and all that entailed, but—

"Why?"

"I need to see my brother. And considering that it was a fucking disaster the last two times I tangled with the dead . . . I'm not going to make mistakes this time. I need the Under-King's help." Ithan paced her office.

"Again: Why?"

He looked straight at her. "Because Connor is trying to reach me." He'd heard that howl from the Bone Quarter and known whose it was. Who was calling to him.

While Ithan had changed, Hypaxia had handed out the anti-dote at the Den, to those who'd take it. Perry had been first in line, apparently. And it hadn't been an Omega standing before Ithan when he'd checked on her as he left the Den.

Ithan hadn't stayed long enough to find out what Perry was—what powers she and the others had gained, long buried in the wolves' bloodline. He'd given the order that this new knowledge was to be contained to the Den, and the wolves had agreed.

Obeyed him.

"You were right," Ithan said to Jesiba, "about needing a plan. I have no idea what I'm doing."

"You could take some lessons from Quinlan about thinking two steps ahead."

Ithan glared at her. "Any updates from Avallen?"

"She called two hours ago. Wanting a favor, as always. And an update on your progress." The sorceress smirked. "And when I told her what Hypaxia had accomplished, of course, she requested that you bring that antidote to her."

"When—where?"

Jesiba smirked again. "The Eternal City. Tomorrow. I think Quinlan's had enough of being pushed around. She said to bring some wolves, if you have any to back you up."

Ithan stared. To not only *be* Prime, but to *act* as Prime . . . "Is there going to be a battle?"

"I don't know." Jesiba fixed him with a grave look. "But if I were you, I'd get the pups and vulnerable wolves to safe hiding places. Not the Den, not in Lunathion. Get them evacuated deep into the wild. Go to ground. And then take the best fighters you have to the Eternal City."

"There aren't many at the Den—most are away."

"Then take whoever's around. It will be better than nothing."

Ithan paced a step, then another. "Maybe I should have left Sigrid in that tank. It'd be better than being a Reaper." There was no one to blame for her predicament but himself. Ithan rubbed his forehead. "Look, I need to see my brother. One last time."

"That's impossible."

Ithan's teeth flashed. "I know you can ask the Under-King." He didn't wait for her reply before he asked, "Do you know—about the secondlight? That our souls are food for the Under-King and the Asteri?"

"Yes."

Ithan shook his head. "And it doesn't bother you?"

"Of course it bothers me. It's bothered me for fifteen thousand years. But it is just one branch of the many-headed beast of the Asteri rule."

Ithan scrubbed at his face. "Can you help me or not?" He'd need all the help he could get. He wasn't a leader. Judging by the mess he'd brought upon Sigrid, he wasn't fit to make decisions for anyone. He'd tried to save her and failed—utterly and completely failed. That had been only one life. With all the Valbaran wolves now his responsibility . . .

He pushed back against the crushing panic and dread.

Jesiba was silent for a moment. Then she said quietly, "Let me see what I can do, pup." Her mouth twisted to the side. "Bring Hypaxia with you."

Bryce had just entered the guard booth when her phone rang. She'd needed one second—one fucking moment by herself—to process the enormity of what she'd done.

She'd thrown her parents into the Fae world.

Bryce had always found a sense of comfort in knowing that no matter what she did, or where she was, Ember Quinlan and Randall Silago were in Nidaros—that Ember and Randall *existed* and would always be there to fight for her. Fight *with* her, if she was being honest about her mom. Knowing that was a comfort, too.

And now they were . . . gone. Alive, yes, but on the other side of the universe.

They could have stayed on Avallen, safe with everyone else, with Cooper . . . but she'd needed them. Needed them to bargain with Nesta, but she also needed to know that her parents were forever beyond the Asteri's reach.

It was selfish, she knew. Cowardly. But she didn't regret it.

Though she really wanted *one second* to process it all. Hence the guard booth.

Until the phone rang.

She'd been out of range beyond the wall, so she had no idea if it was Urd's timing or if her brother had been trying to reach her nonstop. She answered on the first ring.

"Ruhn?"

"I need you back here."

"What's wrong?"

Panic edged his every word. "Pollux intercepted the *Depth Charger* as it dropped people off at the edge of Avallen's mists. He slaughtered a bunch of mer, and . . . I don't know how, but he knew about Lidia's sons. He took them. He's holding them at the palace."

Bryce nearly dropped her phone. Outside, Hunt was a shadow against the darkness and snow, their companions more shadows around him.

"I guess the Asteri figured out how to lure us to them," Bryce said quietly.

"The *Depth Charger* sent us a transport pod—we're about to get on it with Flynn and Dec and head to the Eternal City," Ruhn said hoarsely. "But if those kids are in the dungeons—"

Her stomach flipped. "Okay," she breathed. "Yes, of course. Okay. We'll get on the helicopter immediately."

Ruhn let out a shaking breath. "Did you . . . do what you needed to up there?"

"Yes," Bryce said, and stepped out into the howling wind and brutal cold. Hunt and Aidas were huddled together, planning. Isaiah and Naomi stood a few feet away, chiming in, but keeping their distance, as if not quite comfortable with the idea that they were in the presence of a Prince of Hel. Celestina had flown off to Ephraim's fortress in Ravilis moments ago, her white wings blindingly bright with the light off the snow. She'd keep him occupied, she'd promised again before leaving—with a final nod to Hunt that he hadn't returned.

Beyond Hunt and the others, stretching into the distance, marched the armies of Hel. They covered all twenty-four and a half miles from the wall to the still-open Rift.

Unholy terrors—especially those pets that had been unleashed in Crescent City this spring. Bryce had never been more glad to have the Archesian amulet around her neck—though she wondered if it could hold off *this* many demons, should they choose to have a little snack.

From Hunt's tense shoulders, she knew the horde was as unnerving for him as it was for her. Leathery-winged, horned humanoids that seemed to be grunt soldiers. Bone-white reptilian beasts that crawled on all fours—hounds of war. Skeletal beings with too-large jaws, stacked with needlelike teeth that gleamed with greenish slime. There were more—so many more: things that slithered, things that flew, things that surveyed Midgard with milky, sightless eyes and bayed at the anticipated bloodlust.

Hunt offered no commentary on the endless lines of nightmares. He'd spent a lifetime hunting down the very creatures now fighting for them—how many of Hel's marching forces knew that, too? How many of them had crossed into Crescent City just a few months ago and gleefully unleashed pain and death?

But this time, true to the princes' word, the beasts stayed in line. As for the soldiers, Bryce didn't look too closely at the faces beneath their armor. At the spiky wings poking above the lines, the taloned hands gripping spears. But they did not speak, did not snarl. Their breath curled from beneath the visors of their helmets with each step through the frigid air. Each step deeper into Midgard.

All of Hel, ready to strike.

She had to trust that it would prove to be the right choice.

"Tell Lidia we're coming," Bryce said to Ruhn, still on the line. The thundering of their feet and hooves and claws shook the snowy earth. "And tell her we're not coming alone."

81

This seems familiar," Ithan muttered to Hypaxia as they stood on the Black Dock, each clutching a Death Mark in their hands. "You, me, the Under-King . . ."

"Our best friend," Hypaxia said wryly, the mists from the Bone Quarter an impenetrable wall across the river. She gestured to the water. "Shall we?"

Ithan nodded, and they flicked their Death Marks into the river. They landed with a soft plunk, and ripples spread outward in only one direction—south. Toward the Bone Quarter. They vanished into the mist.

In the ensuing silence, Ithan dared say, "Jesiba said you and the Governor were, ah . . . together. How long?"

She threw him a pained wince. "A while. But not anymore."

"Even while she was with Ephraim?"

"Her arrangement with Ephraim is a political contract. What she and I have . . . had . . ." She shook her head, the moonlight silvering her dark curls. "I'm sure Jesiba said I was naïve."

"Maybe," he hedged.

Hypaxia looked at where her Death Mark had disappeared under the surface. "Everyone told me, you know. That Archangels aren't to be trusted. That they've got those secret training camps that indoctrinate them, that they're puppets for the Asteri. But she spent all that time in Nena, and I thought it had removed her from their influence." She chewed on her lip, then added, "Apparently it gave her incentive to do whatever it took to get her off that frozen bit of land."

"We . . . we all make bad decisions." He blew out a breath. "Gods, that sounded dumb."

Hypaxia laughed quietly. "It's appreciated nonetheless." She sobered. "But when I learned what she'd done . . . Well. I miss my mother most days, but especially lately. Especially after everything with Celestina." She indicated the mists across the way. "So I understand why you seek out your brother."

"I'm sorry about your mother," he offered.

"Most people tell me I should be over her passing. But . . ." Her shoulders bowed. "I don't know if there will ever come a day when I don't feel like there's a hole in my heart where she used to be."

"Yeah," he said quietly, his own chest aching. "I know the feeling." He cleared his throat. "So you couldn't, uh, raise your mom with your necromancy?"

"No," Hypaxia said gravely. "She took steps to ensure that her soul did not fall into the clutches of the Under-King. And even if I could, she would resent me for using it for something so . . . selfish."

"She's your mom, though."

"She was also my queen." Hypaxia's chin lifted. "And she would be ashamed to learn that I have defected from the witches and yielded my crown. So, no. I don't want to see her. I couldn't face her, even if I had the chance."

"Aren't you still a witch, though? I mean, yeah—you're now in Flame and Shadow, but you didn't stop being a witch." Jesiba may have rejected the title, but that had been her choice.

"I'm still a witch," Hypaxia said, hands curling at her sides. "That can never be taken away from me."

Ithan surveyed the black planks beneath his feet. He had to arrange the Sailing for the Prime. For Sabine, too, he supposed.

Did he, though? The Prime's soul was gone. There was nothing to offer up to the Bone Quarter beyond an empty body. And if the people of Lunathion saw the Prime's boat tip, not understanding why . . . he couldn't allow it.

He'd gladly give Sabine the indignity of letting everyone see her boat tip. He'd also be glad to let her soul live on in the Bone Quarter until it was time to be turned into mystery meat for the Asteri, but he'd have to decide whether she deserved a Sailing in the first place.

Gods, he wished Bryce was with him. She'd have an idea. *Just cut her up real small and shove her down the garbage disposal.*

Ithan snorted and offered up a prayer to Luna's bright face above him that his friend was indeed safe—and on the move.

A black boat glided out of the mists ahead, aiming straight for Ithan and Hypaxia, waiting on the dock. Exactly as Jesiba had promised it would.

Ithan swallowed hard. "Cab's here."

Ithan knew he was Prime of the Valbaran Wolves, but he certainly didn't feel like it. The whole thing was a joke. He was just . . . a dude. Granted, one with more power than he'd realized, but now there were people depending on him. He had to make decisions.

At least as sunball captain, he'd had coaches telling him what to do. Now he was coach and captain rolled into one.

And, given how much he'd fucked up lately, how every choice to help Sigrid had only led her toward an absolutely disastrous fate . . . Gods, he really didn't feel like Prime at all.

But he tried to at least look like it—back straight, shoulders squared—as he and Hypaxia stood before the Under-King in a gray-stoned temple to Urd.

The Under-King lounged on a throne beneath a behemoth statue of a figure holding a black metal bowl between her upraised hands. Symbols were carved all over the bowl, continuing down her fingers, her arms, her body. Ithan could only assume it was meant to represent Urd. No other temples ever depicted the goddess, no one even dared—most people claimed that fate was impossible to portray in any one form. But it seemed that the dead, unlike the living, had a vision of her. And those symbols running from the bowl onto her skin . . . they were like tattoos.

They looked oddly familiar. Ithan didn't have time to ponder it as he and Hypaxia inclined their heads to the Under-King.

"Thank you for the audience," Ithan said, trying to keep his breathing normal. Praying that none of those hounds the Under-King had sent after them on the Autumnal Equinox were lurking around in the misty shadows.

At least there weren't any Reapers. No sign of Sigrid, wherever she'd gone. One more clusterfuck for him to deal with—but another day. If he managed to live another day, of course.

The Under-King's bony, withered fingers clicked on the stone arms of his throne. "Prime," he said to Ithan, "I'm honored to be your first political visit. Though I believe protocol dictates that a meeting with the Governor should have been your priority." A knowing glance at Hypaxia. "Unless present company makes such things . . . uncomfortable."

Hypaxia's eyes flickered, but she said nothing.

They'd come here for a reason, so Ithan ignored the Under-King's mocking and said, "Look, uh . . . Your Majesty." The Under-King gave him a smile that was all browned, aged teeth. Ithan tried not to shudder. "Jesiba Roga said you agreed that we could make a request. I'd like to speak to my brother, Connor Holstrom."

The Under-King turned to Hypaxia. "Did I not give you duties to attend to?"

"Handing out blood bags to vampyrs isn't a good use of my time," Hypaxia said with impressive authority.

"Shall I reassign you to waiting on the Reapers?" A cruel smile. "They'd enjoy a taste or two of you, girl."

"I only want five minutes with my brother," Ithan interrupted.

"To do what?" The Under-King leaned forward.

"I need to tell him a few things."

"The goodbye you never got to say," the Under-King taunted.

"Yes," Ithan said sharply.

The Under-King angled his head. "And you promise not to warn him of what awaits?"

"Does it matter if I do? He's trapped here already," Ithan said, gesturing to the temple, the barren land beyond.

"I have no interest in civil unrest—even amongst the dead," the Under-King said. "And too much unrest would bring unwanted attention and questions." From the Asteri, no doubt.

Ithan crossed his arms. "That didn't seem to be your position when you sold my friends out to Pippa Spetsos."

"Pippa Spetsos stood to assist in expanding my kingdom significantly," the creature said. "It was an investment for my Reapers—to keep them contented and fed."

Ithan blocked out the flash of the Prime's broken body, the way Sigrid had sucked out his soul.

Hypaxia said calmly, "Why did the Reapers first defect from Apollion and join you?"

The Under-King flinched. "Do not speak his name here."

"My apologies," Hypaxia murmured. She didn't sound at all sorry.

But the Under-King settled himself. "In Hel, the Reapers fed on and ruled the vampyrs, and when the vampyrs defected to this world, the Reapers followed their food source. And found the other beings on Midgard to be a veritable feast. So they have left the vampyrs to themselves, feeding as they please on the rest of the populace."

Ithan couldn't stop his shudder this time. He couldn't imagine what Hel was like, if Reapers and vampyrs had just been walking about—

"But you are not from Hel," Hypaxia said.

"No." The Under-King's milky eyes settled on Ithan. "I was birthed by the Void, but my people . . ." He smiled cruelly at Ithan. "They were not unknown to your own ancestors, wolf. I crept through when they charged so blindly into Midgard. This place is much better suited to my needs than the caves and barrows I was confined to."

Ithan reeled. "You came from the shifters' world?"

"You were not known as shifters then, boy."

"Then what—"

"And she," the Under-King went on, gesturing to that unusual depiction of Urd towering above him, "was not a goddess, but a force that governed worlds. A cauldron of life, brimming with the language of creation. Urd, they call her here—a bastardized version of her true name. Wyrd, we called her in that old world."

"That is all well and good," Hypaxia said, "but my friend's request—"

"Go speak to your brother, boy," the Under-King drawled, almost melancholy. As if all the talk of his old world had exhausted him. "You have seven minutes."

Ithan's mouth dried out. "But where—"

The Under-King pointed to the exit behind them. "There."

Ithan turned. And there was Connor, as vibrant as he'd ever been in life, standing in the temple doorway.

82

Ithan didn't know whether to laugh or cry as he sat beside his brother on the front steps of the temple. Hypaxia remained inside, speaking quietly with the Under-King.

Connor appeared exactly as he had the day Ithan had last seen him, cheering in the stands at his sunball game . . . except for the bluish light around his body. The mark of a ghost.

Ithan had found out the hard way what that meant—he'd tried to hug his brother, but his arms went right through him.

Seven minutes. Less than that now.

"There's so much I wanted to say to you," Ithan began.

Connor opened his mouth, but no sound came out.

Ithan blinked. "You can't . . . you can't talk?"

Connor shook his head.

"Ever? Or just—now?"

Connor mouthed *ever*.

"But Danika talked to Bryce—"

Connor tapped his chest. As if to say, *In here.*

Ithan rubbed at his face. "The Under-King fucking *knew* you couldn't talk, and—"

Blue glowed in his vision as Connor laid a hand on his shoulder. It didn't have any weight. But the look his brother gave him, pitying and worried—

"I'm sorry I wasn't there," Ithan said, voice breaking.

Connor slowly shook his head.

"I should have been there."

Connor laid a finger on his lips. *Don't say another word.*

Ithan swallowed down the tightness in his throat. "I miss you every single day. I wish you were with me. I . . . Fuck, I'm knee-deep in shit, and I could really use my brother right now."

Connor angled his head. *Tell me.*

Ithan did. As succinctly as he could, aware of each second counting down. About Sigrid and Sabine and the Prime. About what he was now. About the parasite and its antidote.

Ithan glanced at his phone when he finished. Only two minutes left. Connor was smiling faintly.

"What?" Ithan said.

His brother laid a hand on his heart and bowed his head, a mark of respect to the Prime.

Ithan glowered. "It's not funny."

Connor lifted his head, shaking it. There was nothing but pride in his eyes.

Ithan's throat closed up. "I don't know what to do now. How to be Prime. How to fix this shit with Sigrid—if it can even *be* fixed. We're all out of Athalar's lightning now, anyway. Maybe I'm an asshole for not making Sigrid a priority. But I need to help Bryce and the others first. I'm so fucking far out of my league. And . . . there's more I can't tell you. I wish I could, but—"

Connor glanced behind them, to the temple and the Under-King inside it.

When he was assured that they were truly alone, he extended a hand toward Ithan. A sparkling seed of light filled it. Connor lifted it to his mouth and mimicked eating it.

"You know?" Ithan whispered. "About the secondlight?"

Connor nodded once.

Ithan snorted. "Trust the Pack of Devils to figure it out."

But Connor reached into a pocket and laid something on the ground between them.

A bullet.

It was crafted of the same reeking metal as a Death Mark. As if it had been created from all those coins tossed into the river. Whatever properties its metal held must have allowed it to be touched and moved by the dead.

"I don't understand," Ithan said. "What is it?"

Connor began gesturing, too fast for Ithan to follow.

But robes rustled on stone, and Ithan grabbed the black bullet before the Under-King appeared from between the temple pillars and declared, "Your time has come to an end."

Connor looked to Ithan's hand, then up at him, eyes pleading with him to catch his meaning.

"Just one more minute," Ithan begged. "Please."

"You have already been granted more than most mortals ever receive. Be grateful."

"Be grateful," Ithan breathed as Hypaxia stepped beside the Under-King. "For what? For my brother being *here*?" His shout echoed off the gray pillars, the gravel, the empty mists.

Connor signaled to shut up. Ithan ignored him.

"I refuse to accept this," Ithan seethed, claws glinting at his fingertips. "That *this* is the best it gets—"

"Remember your vow, pup," the Under-King warned.

Ithan bristled. "What are you but some freak alien from another world who capitalized on this one?"

Connor was staring at him now—eyes wide, urging him to be quiet, to stand down.

But that thing that had awoken in Ithan the moment the parasite had vanished wouldn't go away. It stared down this creature, this *thing* from his people's home world, and it knew the Under-King for what he truly was.

Enemy, his blood sang, and it spoke of caves beneath hills, of plundered graves and musty darkness. *Enemy.*

Ithan's snarl cleaved the mists, bounced off the temple. Frost curled at his fingertips. Even Connor backed away in surprise.

"What is that?" the Under-King said, backing away a step as well, toward the temple interior. Ithan peered down at his hands. The ice crusting them.

Enemy.

The silent dead, the suffering—Ithan would stand for it no more.

"Get out of my realm," the Under-King said, and Ithan scented his fear. His surprise and dread. Like he knew Ithan for that ancient enemy as well.

The Under-King backed away another step, nearly inside the temple now, and slipped on pure ice. Righting himself, robes fluttering, he lifted a bony hand, and Ithan knew in his gut it would be to summon the hunting hounds.

Ithan didn't give him the chance.

Ice crusted the Under-King's withered hand. Then his arm. Then his shoulder—

"Stop this *now!*" the Under-King bellowed.

But the ice kept crawling over him. Ithan let it. Let this male see what a ruthless fucking murderer he was, let him see that he wouldn't tolerate this shit for his brother, for his parents, for *anyone* he loved.

No more Sailings. He'd never go to another.

He'd single-handedly destroyed the Fendyr line. Why not destroy Death, too?

The Under-King opened his mouth to shout, but Ithan's ice covered his face, his body. An encasing cold so complete, Ithan could feel it in his heart. Hear its frigid wind, capable of killing in seconds.

Ithan yielded to it. Poured it into the being now trapped on the stairs before him like a statue.

He knew Connor was watching in horror. And he didn't dare take his focus off the Under-King long enough to read Hypaxia's face.

Ithan became so cold he forgot what warmth was. Forgot fire and sun and—

Connor got in front of him. Snarling.

Ithan's focus slipped. But instead of the disgust and dismay he thought would be on Connor's face, there was only sorrow and worry.

"Well, that's one way to shut the old windbag up," Jesiba Roga said, stalking from the shadows of the temple interior.

Ithan whirled. But Jesiba said to Hypaxia, who was tense and thrumming with power by the nearest pillar, "Do it."

The former witch-queen didn't strike with her shimmering power. She merely lifted an unlit brazier from beside the temple entrance. With a face like stone, Hypaxia swung the dark metal.

And the Under-King exploded into sparkling shards of ice.

83

There was a ringing silence as Ithan took in the pile of ice that had once been the Under-King . . . and felt nothing.

The Under-King was dead. Gone.

Ithan had killed him.

"Looks like we'll need a new Head of House," Jesiba said calmly to Hypaxia, who was staring down at the Under-King, clearly appalled at what she'd done.

What they'd done.

"When I swung at him," Hypaxia said quietly to Ithan, ignoring Jesiba, "I put a bit of my power behind the blow."

Hypaxia held out a bloodied hand to Ithan, and he realized that he, too, was bleeding all over, from the explosion of razor-like ice shrapnel. Rivers of red ran down his hands, his face. Hypaxia didn't look much better.

He slid his bloodied hand into hers. Her hand glowed, and they were both healed. The cuts on her face vanished—along with his, judging by the tingle that washed over his skin. Faster than he'd ever seen any other medwitch work.

"Play later," Jesiba said. "We have work to do."

"What work?" Ithan asked.

"You kill it, you become it," Jesiba said to Hypaxia. "You are now, for all intents and purposes, Head of the House of Flame and Shadow. And this place."

Her face paled. "That's not possible. I don't want that burden."

"Too bad. You killed him."

Hypaxia advanced on Jesiba, her face twisted in anguish and fury. "You knew this would happen," she accused. "You made me escort Ithan not to help him, but—"

"I suspected things might shake out in your favor," Jesiba said mildly. "But even though you've inherited this place by right, you must make some decisions quickly. Before Rigelus becomes aware."

"Like what?" Ithan demanded, looking to Connor, who still stood nearby at the top of the stairs, watching them all with awe on his ghostly face.

"Like what to do with the souls here," Jesiba said, nodding to Connor.

"We let them go," Ithan said. "We don't even need the Quiet Realms at all, do we?"

"No," Jesiba said. "Death worked just fine without them before the Asteri came."

But Connor was shaking his head.

"No?" Ithan asked.

His brother nodded to Ithan's clenched fist, clutching the black bullet. Connor opened his mouth, but still, no sound emerged.

"Oh, please," Jesiba said, and turned to Hypaxia. "Order him to speak already."

Hypaxia's brows rose. "Speak."

Connor blew out a breath, distinctly audible. Hypaxia was truly the mistress of this place. Ithan marveled at it.

And it was his brother's voice, the voice he'd known his whole life, that insisted, "Don't send us off into the ether."

"Connor . . . ," Ithan started.

Connor held Hypaxia's stare. "Don't miss this opportunity." He began walking down the stairs—nearly running—and it was all they could do to follow him. With that strong, sure grace, his brother stalked down the empty avenue flanked with strangely carved obelisks. All the way to the Dead Gate, its crystal muted in the dimness.

Only when they stood before it did Connor speak again. "That bullet," Connor said, nodding to where Ithan held it, "was made by us—the dead. For Bryce." A soft, pained smile crossed his face at her name. "To use with the Godslayer Rifle."

"What's so special about it?" Jesiba demanded.

"Nothing yet. But it was crafted to hold us. Our secondlight." As if in answer, the Gate began to glow. "We had planned to make contact with Jesiba—to ask her, through her role in Flame in Shadow, to get in touch with one of you." Connor shrugged with one shoulder. "But when you appeared earlier, Ithan, with the Under-King distracted . . . Well, it was a little earlier than we'd planned, but everyone was ready. I think Urd made it so." After all Ithan had heard and experienced, he didn't doubt his brother's claim. "So they began the exodus through this Gate. They were finishing when I was summoned to you."

A conduit, like the one Bryce had drawn from in the spring.

"All of our secondlight, from every soul here," Connor said quietly. "It's yours to put in that bullet. Use it well."

Ithan's throat constricted. "But if you . . . if you turn into secondlight—"

"I'm already gone, Ithan," Connor said gently. "And I can think of no better way to end my existence than by striking a blow for all our ancestors who've been trapped and consumed by the Asteri." He nodded to the bullet, the glowing Gate illuminating his face. "Look at the engraving."

Memento Mori. The letters gleamed in the Gate's pale light.

Jesiba let out a quiet laugh. "Got the idea from me, did you?"

Connor's mouth quirked up at a corner. Ithan nearly broke down at that half smile. Gods, he'd missed it. Missed his big brother.

But the Dead Gate glowed brighter—as if the time had come. As if it couldn't hold all those souls, the secondlight they'd become, much longer.

Connor said to Ithan, "You do make me proud, you know. Every day before now, and every day after. Nothing you do will ever change that."

Something ruptured in Ithan's chest. "Connor—"

"Tell Bryce," Connor said, eyes shining as he stepped toward the glowing Gate, a wall of light now shimmering in the empty arch, "to make the shot count."

Connor stepped into the archway and faded into that wall of light.

He was gone. And this time it was just as unbearable, as unfathomable to have had his brother here, to see him and speak to him and lose him again—

The light began shrinking and contracting, pulsating, and Ithan could have sworn he heard the hissing of Reapers rushing toward them in the distance. The light shivered and imploded, condensing into a tiny seed of pure light.

It floated in the Gate's archway, thrumming with such power that the hair on Ithan's arms rose.

"Put it in the bullet," Jesiba ordered Ithan, who unscrewed its cap and gingerly approached the seed.

All the souls of the people here . . . the dreams of the dead, their love for the living . . .

Ithan gently slid the bullet around the seed of light and replaced the cap. He lifted the bullet between his thumb and forefinger, its point digging into his skin.

As the light floated up through the bullet, *Memento Mori* was briefly illuminated, letter by letter.

Then it faded, the dark metal stark in the gray light.

"What now?" Ithan rasped, barely able to speak.

Connor had been here, and now he was gone. Forever.

"I have Reapers to sort out," Hypaxia murmured, staring off into the distant mists, to where the hissing was growing louder.

Ithan mastered the hole in his heart enough to ask, "What about Sigrid?"

Hypaxia said carefully, "What would you like me to do with her?"

"Just, ah . . ." Fuck, he had no idea. "Tell her I want to talk to her." He clarified, "I need to talk to her. But only once I'm back from the Eternal City." If he ever came back.

Hypaxia nodded solemnly. "If I encounter her, I will convey the message."

"The Reapers won't take the power shift well," Jesiba warned Hypaxia.

"Then I appoint you my second in command and order you to help me," Hypaxia said flatly.

"Happy to oblige," Jesiba said, examining her red-painted nails.

"You can't kill them," Hypaxia warned the sorceress.

Jesiba gave the witch a wry smile, and nodded to Ithan, who pulled himself from his grief long enough to meet her steely gaze. "Get your ass to Pangera, Prime. And get that bullet to Bryce Quinlan."

Tharion didn't speak, barely breathed, until he and Sathia were back in the open air. It had taken a few hours to coordinate with his former colleagues about how they'd conduct the exodus from the city, how they'd get the message around without alerting anyone to the plan. Word was bound to leak at some point about the Blue Court harboring refugees, but hopefully by then they'd have a good number of people Beneath. And then the Blue Court would go into lockdown, praying that the River Queen's power could hold out against the brimstone torpedoes of the Omega-boats docked in the river. It was risky . . . but it was a plan.

Only when they'd ducked for cover in a shadowy alley did Tharion say to Sathia, "We did it. We fucking did it—"

She smiled, and it was beautiful. *She* was beautiful.

But a voice crooned from the shadows of the alley, "Isn't this an interesting turn of events?"

It was all Tharion could do to draw the knife at his side and step in front of Sathia as the Viper Queen emerged into the light, her drugged-out, hulking Fae assassins flanking her.

"I don't have any quarrel with you," Tharion said to the Viper Queen, who was clad in one of her usual jumpsuits—ocean blue this time, with high-top sneakers in an amethyst suede with maroon laces.

"You burned my house down," the Viper Queen said, her snake's eyes glowing green. Like a Reaper's eyes. The Fae assassins behind her shifted, as if they were an extension of her wrath.

"Colin?" Sathia blurted, and Tharion found her gaping at one of the Fae males. "*Colin? I thought you . . .*"

The Viper Queen glanced between the towering Fae male and Sathia and said to the latter, "Who the fuck are you?"

"Sathia Flynn, daughter of Padraig, Lord Hawthorne." Sathia's chin rose, pure disdain in every word. "I know who you are, so don't bother to introduce yourself, but I want to know why my friend is in your employ."

It was a different face from the one of courtly grace she'd poured on for the River Queen. This one was imperious and icy and a little bit terrifying.

The Viper Queen snorted.

Sathia bared her teeth. "Colin. Get away from this trash and come home."

The towering Fae male stared blankly ahead. As he had this whole time. Like he didn't hear her.

"Colin," Sathia said, voice sharpening with something like panic.

"McCarthy won't respond unless I give him the order," the Viper Queen drawled, walking to the male and running her manicured hands over his broad chest. Her metallic gold nails glinted against the black leather of his jacket. "But let me guess: Childhood friend? Handsome, poor Fae guard, spoiled little rich girl . . ." Her purple-painted lips curved in a smile, and she patted the male's cheek, purring to him, "Is that why you came crawling to me? Would her daddy not let you court her?"

Tharion's heart stalled at the pain that washed over Sathia's face as she breathed, more to herself than to anyone, "Father said you had found a new position in Korinth."

"Padraig Flynn has always been an excellent liar," the Viper Queen said. "And a better client. He introduced me to McCarthy, of course." She gestured to the blank-faced assassin.

Sathia paled. "Come home, Colin." Her voice broke. "Please."

Tharion had no idea how anyone, the drugged-out male included, could resist the pleading in that voice. Her face.

"It's too late for that," the Viper Queen said, and nodded to Tharion. "But you and I have unfinished business, mer."

"Leave him alone," Sathia snapped, teeth flashing as she stepped closer to Tharion. "Don't you *dare* touch him."

Tharion's fingers slid toward hers, squeezing once in warning to be quiet.

"And what authority do you have, girl, to order me away from him?"

"I'm his wife," Sathia spat.

The Viper Queen burst out laughing. And Tharion could have sworn that something like pain shown in McCarthy's bright blue eyes—just a glimmer.

"You leave him alone," Sathia said again, and vines curled at her fingers. "Him *and* Colin."

"That's not an option I'm interested in, girl," the Viper Queen said, and inclined her head to one side. The assassins, Colin included, aimed their guns. Did he imagine it, or was McCarthy's weapon trembling slightly?

Tharion sheathed his knife and held up his hands, again stepping in front of Sathia. "Your business is with me."

He'd accomplished what he needed to with the River Queen. And if Sathia became a widow . . . she could remarry, by Fae law. Maybe even find some way to save that poor bastard McCarthy and marry him. So Tharion said, "Let her walk out of here before you put a bullet in my head."

"Oh, I'm not going to kill you that quickly," the Viper Queen said. "Not a chance, Ketos."

She advanced a step, her assassins flowing with her.

"You take one more step toward my friend," said a familiar female voice, "and you die."

Tharion's knees wobbled as he glanced over a shoulder—and found Hypaxia Enador striding in from the quay, Ithan Holstrom bristling with menace at her side.

84

I don't take orders from former witch-queens," the Viper Queen said. Her guards didn't back down an inch. But Colin McCarthy's gun was definitely trembling, like he was fighting the order with everything he had.

"What about from the Head of the House of Flame and Shadow?" Hypaxia countered. Tharion's knees gave out abruptly at the greenish light that flared in her eyes.

Sathia caught him around the waist, grunting as she held him up.

Tharion whispered, "Pax?"

But his friend—this female who had been his friend from the moment they'd met each other at the Summit, who always seemed to see the real male beneath his veneer of charm—only glowered at the Viper Queen. "You touch him, or his friend, and you bring down the wrath of Flame and Shadow upon you."

Holstrom stepped up to her side, brimming with power—with *magic*, cold and foreign—and added, "And the wrath of all Valbaran Wolves."

There was only one person who could claim that.

The male before him was Prime. There was no doubt about it. But that strange power rippling from him . . . what the Hel was *that*?

The Viper Queen stared long and hard at Ithan, then at Hypaxia.

"Power shift," she murmured, pulling a cigarette from her jumpsuit pocket and putting it in her mouth. "Interesting." The cigarette bobbed with the word, and she lit it, taking a long drag. She fixed her snake's eyes on Tharion. "Your bounty still stands."

"Drop the bounty," Ithan ordered, pure Alpha echoing in his voice.

"I won't forgive or forget what Ketos did to me and mine. But he'll walk out of here today—I'll allow that much."

Hypaxia gave her a look dripping with disdain. "*You* will walk out of here today. *We* will allow that much."

The Viper Queen took another long drag of her cigarette and blew the air toward Hypaxia. "Give a witch a scrap of true power and it goes right to her pretty little head."

"Fuck you," Ithan snarled.

But the Viper Queen stepped back into the alley, whistling sharply to her assassins before striding away. They turned as one and marched after her.

Colin McCarthy didn't so much as look back.

"What the *fuck*?" Tharion exploded at Ithan, at Hypaxia. The Prime of the Valbaran Wolves and the Head of the House of Flame and Shadow. "What happened?"

"What happened to *you*?" Ithan countered. "Where are the others? Is Bryce here?"

"Bryce? No—she's in Nena. She . . ." Now wasn't the time for a catch-up.

But Ithan said, "Nena?" He dragged his hands through his hair. "Fuck."

"Why?" Tharion asked.

Hypaxia said gravely, "We need to get to Bryce. Immediately."

"Okay," Tharion said. "I'll see if I can reach her or Athalar."

Hypaxia and Ithan began walking, and Tharion followed, Sathia a few feet behind. When the door to the House of Flame and Shadow loomed before them, Hypaxia lifted a hand and it swung open silently. Hers to command.

Ithan walked right in. But Tharion at last mastered his shock enough to ask Hypaxia, "How did you wind up—"

"It's a long story," she said, tucking a dark curl behind her ear. "But get inside first. It's the only safe place in this city."

Tharion glanced back at Sathia, who was pale-faced at the open door before them. "Give me a minute," he said, and Hypaxia nodded and walked into the gloom.

"Hypaxia is a friend," Tharion explained softly to Sathia. "No harm will come to you in there."

Sathia lifted her gaze, bleak and despairing, to his face. Like she'd seen a ghost.

And maybe she had. "It was my Ordeal." Her lips were so, so white. "I only realized it afterward," she murmured. "After Colin . . . left. Losing him was my Ordeal."

Tharion laid a gentle hand on her back, surprised by the strange tightness in his gut, and eased her toward the doorway. "I'm sorry," he said, and led his wife into the gloom.

It was all he could offer her.

"The reception in Nena is shit—there's some weird interference happening right now," Tharion announced. They stood in Jesiba Roga's office, of all places. "But from the few words I managed to make out, they're heading for the Eternal City immediately."

"Good," Holstrom said, pacing in front of Roga's desk. "That's what Jesiba told me earlier. But where do we rendezvous?"

"That's the tough part," Tharion admitted, sliding into one of the chairs. Sathia sat quietly in the other one, lost in thought. "The reception cut off before we could get to that. I tried calling him back, and Quinlan, and her parents, but . . . nothing."

"Maybe they got the Rift open," Hypaxia mused. "Magic pouring into Midgard from Hel could be disrupting the connection. Demons cause power outages sometimes with their presence. Imagine what a lot of them all at once might do."

"It's possible, but doesn't change the issue at hand," Holstrom said. The wolf had changed—somehow, in the span of a day, he'd gone from lost to focused. From lone wolf to Prime. Tharion had gotten a vague story out of him about facing Sabine, and Hypaxia taking on the Under-King to become Head of the House of Flame and Shadow, but even beyond that, they seemed like they'd leveled up. Majorly.

Especially Ithan. Even the most powerful of wolves only had shifting abilities and super strength—not actual *magic*. And yet Holstrom, suddenly, had the ability to wield ice. Like the power had been locked in his bloodline all this time. But Tharion put aside the thought as Holstrom added, "We need to figure out how to link up with them."

"I'm sure if the Rift is open, we'll see them coming a mile off," Tharion said.

"We need to find Hunt and Bryce *before* they enter into any kind of confrontation with the Asteri," Ithan insisted. He picked up a vial of clear liquid from the desk. "Hypaxia found a cure for the Asteri's parasite. We need to distribute it to everyone we can."

Tharion blinked in shock. Sathia stopped her brooding to listen.

Then Ithan pulled out a long, dark bullet from his pocket. "And we need to get this to Bryce as soon as possible."

"What is that?" Tharion asked as a strange, ancient sort of power thrummed from the black bullet.

Ithan's face was grim. "A gift from the dead."

85

"Well, friends," Bryce said to Hunt, to Declan and Flynn, to Ruhn and Lidia. They had all gathered in a nondescript white van—one of a fleet Ophion had kept stashed throughout Pangera should an agent on the run ever need an escape vehicle—on the edge of the Eternal City. And though Lidia was frantic with urgency to rescue her sons, this step was necessary. "Ready to change the world?"

Jesiba had just sent over the footage of Micah's demise.

"Let's burn this fucker down," Flynn said, and Dec nodded, typing away on his laptop.

"We're recording in thirty seconds," Dec warned Bryce, and she looked to where Hunt sat next to her, so quiet, so thoughtful. Terrified, she realized.

He glanced up, bleak fear in his eyes as he said hoarsely, "The last time I took a stand like this, with the Fallen . . . it cost me everything." He swallowed hard, but he kept his gaze on her. She could have sworn lightning sparked along his wings. "But this time I have Bryce Adelaide Quinlan at my side."

She took his hand in hers, squeezing tightly. "I've got you, sweetheart," she whispered to him, and his eyes flickered in recognition. He'd said the same thing to her once—that day she'd had the kristallos venom removed from her leg.

He squeezed her hand back. "Let's light it up."

Declan signaled, and the red light on his laptop camera turned on.

Bryce stared into the camera's lens and said, "I am Bryce Quinlan. Heir to the Starborn Fae, Queen of the Fae in Avallen and Valbara, but most importantly . . . the half-human daughter of Ember Quinlan and Randall Silago."

Hunt barely seemed to be breathing as Bryce said, "This is my mate and husband, Hunt Athalar. And we're here to show you . . ."

It hit her, right then—a wave of nerves.

Hunt sensed it and picked up her thread without missing a beat. "We're here to show you that the Republic is not as all-powerful as you've been led to believe." He lifted his chin. "Centuries ago, I led a legion—the Fallen—against the Archangels, against the Asteri. You know how it ended. That day on Mount Hermon, only one other group of Vanir came to our aid: the sprites. We all suffered for it, and those of us who survived are still punished to this day." His throat worked, and Bryce had never loved him more as he continued, "But today we're here to tell you that it's worth it. Fighting back. That it's possible to defy them and live. That their hierarchies, their rules . . . it's all bullshit. And it's time to put a stop to it."

Bryce might have smiled had she not finally found the right words. "What happened in Asphodel Meadows was an atrocity. What happened to those innocent families . . ." She bared her teeth. "It must never be allowed to happen again. *We*, the people of Midgard, can never allow it to happen again."

She looked the camera dead in its dark eye, looked at the world beyond. "The Asteri lie to you, all of you, every second of every single day. For the past fifteen thousand years, they've lied to us, enslaved us, and we haven't even known the half of it. They use a parasite in the water to control and harvest our magic under the guise of the Drop. Because they need that magic—they need *us*, our power. Without the power from the people of Midgard, the Asteri are nothing."

She squared her shoulders. Hunt's pride was a warmth that practically seeped into her side, but he let her keep talking, let her take the lead as she said, "The Asteri don't want you to know this. They have schemed and murdered to keep their secrets." Danika's face, the faces of the Pack of Devils, flashed before her eyes. It was for them that she spoke, for Lehabah, for all those in the Meadows. "We've been told we're too weak, and they're too powerful, for us to fight back. But that's just another lie."

Bryce continued, "So we're here to show you that it can be done. I fought back, and I killed an Archangel who the Asteri used like a puppet to murder Danika Fendyr and the Pack of Devils. I fought back, and I won—I have the footage to prove it."

And with a flick of a switch from Declan, the video played.

Bryce peered around the small, bare-bones room in the safe house near the northernmost section of wall around the Eternal City. "Lidia's certain this is secure?"

Hunt, wings tucked in tight in the cramped space, nodded to the sliver of a bed. "Yeah. And I'm pretty sure all the five-star hotels would report our asses to the Asteri anyway."

"That's not what I meant," Bryce grumbled, plopping onto the creaky, lumpy bed. More of a cot, really. "I mean, all of Ophion's . . . dead." She choked on the word. "Who's to say this place hasn't been compromised? Lidia's not exactly in a calm state of mind. She might not be thinking clearly."

"Dec and Flynn are on guard," Hunt said, sitting down beside her with a groan. "I think we're good to rest tonight."

Bryce scrubbed at her face. "I'm not sure I can sleep, knowing that video's going out soon." And soon after that, Hel would begin its journey to the Eternal City. She could only pray the armies' presence would remain unnoticed until the right moment. She'd taken steps to ensure that.

Hunt waggled his eyebrows at her. "Want to do something other than sleeping?"

Despite all that weighed on her, despite what awaited them the next day, Bryce smirked. "Oh?" She half reclined, leaning back on her elbows. The bed let out a wailing *creaaak*.

"Oof," Bryce said, wincing. "If anyone has any doubt that we're about to fuck each other's brains out, this bed will clue them right in."

Hunt's mouth kicked up at a corner, but his eyes had darkened, going right to her mouth. "I'm down for some noisy sex." He braced a hand on one side of her, bringing his lips within grazing distance of her own. "Might be our last night on—"

She put a hand over his mouth. "Don't." Her throat closed up. "Don't say that."

He pulled back, his own gaze unbearably tender. "We're going to survive, Quinlan. All of us. I promise."

She leaned forward, brushing her mouth against his. "I don't want to think about tomorrow right now."

It was his turn to say, "Oh?"

She traced her tongue over the seam of his lips, and he opened for her. She swept her tongue in, tasting the essence that was Hunt, her mate and husband—"I want to think about you," she said, pulling back, grazing a hand over his pecs, his rock-hard stomach. "About you on top of me."

He shuddered, head bowing. She kissed the place where his halo had been, where he'd freed himself from its grasp.

Her hand trailed lower, to his black jeans and the hardness already pushing against them. "I want to think about this," she said, palming him, "inside of me."

"Fuck," he breathed, and pivoted them, laying her out flat beneath him. "I love you."

She lifted her hand to cup his face, drawing his gaze to her own. "I love you more than anything in this world—or any other."

He closed his eyes, pressing a kiss to her temple. "I thought you said no goodbyes."

"It's not a goodbye." She ran her hands down the groove of his spine, his wings like velvet against her fingertips. "It's the truth."

His mouth found her neck, and his teeth grazed over her pulse. "You're my best friend, you know that?" He pulled away, staring down at her, and she couldn't stop her star from flaring with light. "I mean, you're my mate and wife—fuck, that still sounds weird—but you're my best friend, too. I never thought I'd have one of those."

She ran her fingers over his strong jaw, his cheeks. "After Danika, I didn't think . . ." Her eyes prickled, and she reached up to kiss him again. "You're my best friend, too, Hunt. You saved me— literally, I guess, but also . . ." She tapped her heart, the glowing star. Another reference to this past spring, to all that had grown between them, the words spoken during what she'd thought had been her final phone call. "In here."

He scanned her eyes, and there was so much love in her that she couldn't stand it, so much love that it washed over any fear and dread of what tonight and tomorrow would bring. For the moment, it was just them—Bryce and Hunt. For the moment, it was only their souls, their bodies, and nothing else mattered.

Just Hunt. And Just Bryce.

So she kissed him again, and there was no more talking after that.

Hunt met her tongue stroke for stroke, and the weight of his body on hers was joy and comfort and home. Home—he *was* home. Her ability to teleport to him had only proved that. Home wasn't a place or a thing, but *him*. Wherever Hunt was . . . that was where home was. She'd find him across galaxies, if need be.

He tugged off her long-sleeved shirt, gently, lovingly. Bryce practically ripped his black shirt off his shoulders.

Hunt chuckled, rising up to unbuckle his belt, then unzipping his pants. "So impatient."

She rubbed her thighs together, desperate for any friction. Especially as his impressive length sprang free, and—

"Commando?" Bryce said, choking.

Hunt smirked. "All the underwear they gave me on the *Depth Charger* was too small for this." He palmed himself, pumping, and she groaned at the sight of the small bead of moisture at the tip of his cock. "Now let's see what underwear *you're* wearing, Quinlan," he said, eyes dark with lust, and tugged down her leggings. She lifted her hips off the bed, coils screeching, and Hunt laughed at the sound.

But his laugh died in his throat as he beheld the cherry-red thong. "*This* is what they gave you on the *Depth Charger*?"

"Not the *Depth Charger*." She grinned as he peeled off her leggings, exposing the tiny red lace thong. "I grabbed these from Morven's castle—the guest rooms had whole unopened packs of them."

Hunt's booming laugh set her star glowing, and the breath whooshed out of her as he gripped her knees in either hand and spread her legs wide. "If that asshole wasn't dead, I'd send him a thank-you note."

Hunt pressed his mouth to the front of her underwear and huffed a hot breath.

"Damn, Quinlan," he said against her, and she buried a hand in his silken hair. He slipped a finger around the front of her underwear, toying with her entrance. "Gods-damn."

She clawed at her underwear, beyond words.

Hunt obliged her by removing the thong with cruel, brutal slowness. She growled, but he dangled the underwear on one finger before setting it aside. "I wouldn't want to damage this precious thing."

"I'm going to damage *you* if you don't get in me right now," she managed to say, opening her legs wider.

She nearly climaxed at the raw need, the ravenous hunger on Hunt's face. Especially as he slowly, slowly lifted his gaze to hers, filled with pure lightning.

"Hunt," she begged, and he lunged for her.

He gripped her hips, lifting her off the mattress, angling her precisely how he wanted as he slid into her in a long, smooth glide.

Bryce moaned at the size of him, filling every part of her, and she dug her fingers into the hard muscles of his ass, pinning him there for a moment. Luxuriating in the stretch of herself around him, the weight of his body against hers.

"How?" he panted against her hair. "How the fuck can it feel this good every time?"

Her fingers clenched harder, urging him to move. He withdrew almost to the tip, and plunged back in, hard enough that another moan slipped out of her.

"You like that?" He angled her hips again, his to play with. "You like my cock this deep in you?"

She couldn't manage anything more than a nod. He rewarded her with another long stroke that had her seeing stars.

Those were . . . those were *actual* stars dancing around them, filling the room.

"Quinlan," he breathed, eyes wide at the stars floating by. But she needed more friction, more pleasure. She palmed her breast, squeezing, rolling her hard nipple between her fingers.

"*Fuck,*" he exploded, and thrust into her again, so deep and strong that it pushed them up the bed. Another stroke, and then his lightning was sparking over his shoulders, across his wings, a band of it over his brow like a crown—

She lifted a glowing hand, and his lightning twined over her fingers, zapping her delicately.

He withdrew, and her moan of protest turned into one of pure pleasure as he flipped her onto her front and plunged into her again, the fit of his cock so tight in her that she could barely stand it.

Starlight poured out of her, and his lightning skittered over her spine, ecstasy in its wake.

"Hunt," she cried, release hovering just over the horizon.

His fingers dug into her hips. "Come for me, Bryce."

Release crashed into her, out of her, her starlight flaring, and the room was blindingly bright. Hunt pounded into her in sure, steady strokes, and his lightning was between her thighs, his lightning was in her very blood, and all that she was and he was blended into such light, such power—

His hoarse shout was the only warning before he spilled into her, and it sent her climaxing again, knowing how deeply he was seated in her, marking her.

His fingers slid to her clit, stroking her through the throes, amplifying it. She reared up against him, pressing back into his chest as his fingers circled and swirled, and nothing had ever felt so perfect as wave after wave of pleasure washed over and out of her.

And then the world stilled, the light fading, and they were kneeling on the bed, Bryce leaning fully back against Hunt, one of his hands resting between her legs, the other looped around her middle. He pressed kiss after kiss to the space between her neck and shoulder. "Bryce," he murmured against her skin, his chest heaving into her spine. "Bryce."

She slid a hand over his, holding him between her legs, as if she could freeze this moment, stop the next sunrise from coming.

He shuddered, kissing her again. "I can . . . Fuck, I can *feel* you. Like, in me."

She twisted enough to peer up at his stunned, devastated face.

"It's like that part of you that's . . . Made, or whatever you called it," he breathed. "It's in me. Like this piece of you is nestled there."

"Good," she said, kissing his jaw. Inside her, his lightning lingered, fueling her up like a small sun. "No matter what happens tomorrow," she said, breathing hard, "I'll have this piece of you with me. Strengthening me." She could almost summon it, that lightning. It flowed under her skin, so full of possibility that she had no idea how she'd sleep.

Hunt tugged her back against him, holding her tight as he brought them both down onto the creaky bed. "Sleep, Quinlan," he whispered into her hair. "I'm with you no matter what."

86

Ithan left Tharion recovering from the dose of the antidote the mer had taken. His reaction had been strong enough that the pipes in the House of Flame and Shadow had burst from the surge in his water magic. Hypaxia had her hands full, keeping her House in order.

So Ithan had come to the Den. Which was now . . . his.

Well, it would never be his, since it belonged to all the wolves who called it home, but it was his responsibility.

He found Perry in the guard booth again, doodling in a notebook. He rapped on the glass, drawing her attention, and at her wide eyes, he gave her a half smile.

"Hard at work or hardly working?" he teased.

But she jumped to her feet, flinging open the door. "Sorry, I was just—"

"Per, it's me," he said, alarmed.

She straightened, standing at attention, as Sabine had liked. For fuck's sake. He'd deal with that later. For now . . . He sniffed, trying to read the subtle change in her scent. It remained that strawberries-and-cinnamon blend he'd known his whole life, but with the antidote . . . He couldn't put a finger on it. It had been so strong, right in those moments after she'd taken the antidote, yet now it had dimmed.

There wasn't time to ponder it, to wonder why an Omega once again stood before him. Ithan peered through the open gates of the Den. "Where is everyone?"

Perry shifted on her feet. "They, uh . . . they left."

Ithan slowly blinked. "What do you mean they left?" Had the River Queen started her evacuation already? He'd come here to inform everyone that it might be best to lie low in the Blue Court for a few weeks, but maybe she had already gotten a message to them.

"What happened shook them," Perry said. "They're loyal to you, Ithan, but they're worried. They all headed out of town. Said they wanted to wait until after the new year to see how things, um . . . turned out." In a few *months*.

Ithan weighed the fear in her eyes. Not for him, but . . . "And where's your sister?" he asked quietly. The wolf in him began bristling, snarling for the opponent he knew was coming.

"Amelie led them out," Perry said, throat bobbing. "I think she wanted to make sure everyone got to where they're going." But her eyes dropped to the pavement.

"Sure," Ithan said. Perry shifted on her feet. "Why didn't you go?"

"Someone had to stay to tell you," she mumbled, a blush creeping over her cheeks.

"I have a hard time believing your sister made you stay."

"She wanted me to go, but . . . I couldn't abandon the Den. They moved the Prime into the lobby—I think some wanted to stay for the Sailing, but the spooked ones wanted to leave. It didn't feel right to abandon his body there. Alone." Tears gleamed in her emerald eyes, genuine grief for the old wolf.

Any aggression rising in Ithan stalled out at the pain, the loyalty in her face. He squeezed her shoulder. "Thanks for staying, Per."

She followed him into the Den, hitting an interior button to shut the gates behind them. Ithan paused in the grassy meadow, watching the trees of the park bend in the cool breeze. The blood had been cleaned away from the building's entrance. The bodies of Sabine and the Astronomer—

"I dumped them in the sewer," Perry said with quiet rage,

reading Ithan's glance toward where the corpses had been. "They don't deserve a Sailing. Especially Sabine."

Surprise sparked in him at the normally peaceful wolf's act of defiance, but he nodded. "Rotting in the shit of the city seems like a good place for Sabine to wind up," he said, and Perry huffed a laugh. It wasn't real amusement. They were both far beyond that.

"Where did you go?" Perry asked, tentatively enough that he knew she was still feeling him out. As a friend, and as her Alpha and Prime. Learning how much she could push.

"It's a long story," he said. "But I came back here to get everyone to safety." He explained about the River Queen and the Blue Court.

"But now," he finished, "I have to head to the Eternal City."

Perry studied him, clearly understanding more than he'd said. "So we're going up against the Asteri?"

"*We* aren't doing anything," he said. "I'm going up against them."

"But you're Prime," she insisted. "You speak for all Valbaran wolves. Your choices are our choices. If you stand against the Asteri, *we* stand against the Asteri."

"Then disavow me," he said. "But I'm going."

"That's not what I'm saying," she said. "I don't disagree with you—things have to change, and change for the better. But the wolves are scattered at the moment. At vacation homes, on trips . . . too far to reach the Blue Court before you go off to the Eternal City."

"So?"

"So get the word out to them before you go. Give them a few hours to find shelter, either by getting to the Blue Court, or by finding somewhere in the wilds to lie low. The second the Asteri see you, the Prime, standing against them in any capacity, they'll go after the wolves to punish you. And after what happened at the Meadows . . ." Her eyes flooded with pain. "I don't think there's any atrocity they wouldn't commit."

Ithan opened his mouth to object. He had to get that bullet and antidote to Bryce *now*. It might even be too late already.

But he couldn't live with one more wolf death on his conscience.

And if a single pup were harmed because he hadn't given them time to hide . . .

"Three hours," Ithan agreed. "You know how to send encrypted messages?"

Perry nodded.

"Then start getting the word out." He looked to the building lobby beyond the pillars and the stairs up to it. "And I'll start digging a grave."

"A grave?" Perry protested. "But the Sailing—"

"There are no more Sailings," Ithan said quietly. "The Under-King is dead."

He was met with stunned silence. Then Perry said, "But—the Bone Quarter."

"Is a lie. All of it." Ithan gestured to the phone already in her hand. "Get the word out, then we'll talk. I'll tell you everything I know."

Perry held his stare, her own full of worry and shock and determination. Then she began typing into her phone. "I'm glad, Ithan," she said quietly, "that you're Prime."

That makes one of us, he almost said, but just nodded his thanks.

Tharion shoved the last gun into a rucksack and turned to where Hypaxia was nesting vials of the antidote into a satchel. "How many do you have?" he asked.

Water whispered in his ears, his heart, his veins. A steady flow of magic, as if a raging river coursed through him. Half a thought and it'd be unleashed.

"Two dozen, give or take a few," she said quietly. "Not enough."

"You're going to need entire factories dedicated to getting it out there," Tharion said.

She handed him the bag. "Here. Don't jostle it too much on the trip. Athalar's lightning holds them together—a little agitation can destabilize the doses to the point where they won't work."

He angled his head. "You're not coming?" He planned to make his way to the Asteri's palace itself—the most likely place for a confrontation between Bryce and the Asteri. Gods, the very notion of it was insane. Suicidal. But for his friends, for Midgard, he'd go, antidote in tow.

Hypaxia's eyes gleamed with that greenish light. "No—I'm staying here."

Tharion weighed the heaviness in that one word and took a seat on the edge of Roga's desk. The sorceress was off handling some squabble between vampyrs and city medwitches over the vampyrs' raid of a blood bank, apparently. "Why?"

"Someone has to deal with all the broken pipes in this House," Hypaxia teased.

Tharion blushed slightly. His eruption after ingesting the antidote would take a long while to live down. But there had been so much *power*—all of a sudden, he'd been overflowing with water, and it was music and rage and destruction and life. But he said, "Come on, Pax. Tell me why."

Her gaze lowered to her hands. "Because if all goes poorly over there, someone needs to remain here. To help Lunathion."

"If it goes poorly over there, everyone is fucked anyway," he said. "You being here, I'm sorry to say, won't make much of a difference."

"I want to keep making the antidote," she added. "We need a better way to stabilize it. I want to start on it *now*."

He looked at his friend—really looked at her. "You okay?"

Her eyes, so changed since taking Flame and Shadow's throne for herself, dipped to the floor. "No."

"Pax—"

"But I have no choice," she said, and squared her shoulders. She nodded to the doors. "You should get your wife and go."

"Is that a note of disapproval I detect?"

Hypaxia smiled gently. "No. Well, I disapprove of much of what led you to marry her, but not . . . the marriage itself."

"Yeah, yeah, get in line to lecture me."

"I think Sathia might be good for you, Tharion."

"Oh?"

Her smile turned secretive. "Yes."

Tharion gave her a smile of his own. "Knock 'em dead, Pax."

"Hopefully not literally," Hypaxia said with a wink.

Grinning despite himself, Tharion exited Roga's office. He'd left Sathia in a small guest room to wash up and rest, though they both knew that no amount of rest would prepare her for the insanity they were about to face.

He'd offered to send her down to the Blue Court, but she'd refused. And dropping her off in Avallen would have taken them too far out of their way. So she'd be coming with him.

Tharion knocked on the door to the guest room and didn't wait for her to reply before he opened it.

The room was empty. There was only a note on the bed, laced with her lingering scent. Tharion read it once. Then a second time, before it really set in.

I can't leave Colin in her hands. I hope you understand.

Good luck. And thank you for all you've done for me.

Sathia had left him. That's what the *thank you* at the end was. It was fitting—he'd done worse to the River Queen's daughter, and yet . . .

Tharion carefully laid the note back on the bed. He didn't blame her. It was her choice to go save her ex-boyfriend from being a drugged-out assassin—and a noble choice, at that. No, he didn't blame her at all.

It was better she didn't come with him to the Eternal City, in any case. She'd be safer that way.

Still, Tharion looked at the note on the bed for a long, long moment.

And though he knew he was heading off to challenge the Asteri, likely to die in the attempt . . . as Tharion left the House of Flame and Shadow, then Lunathion itself, he couldn't stop thinking about her.

The video Hunt and Bryce had recorded was due to go out at any moment. Ruhn was so fucking proud of his sister. She knew how to make the most of a bad hand.

That moment came soon after midnight, with a stroke of a key from Declan.

And now, sitting on the floor of the windowless bedroom in the safe house Lidia had procured for them, Ruhn peered over at where she sat beside him and said, "Just a few hours until dawn, then we'll make our move."

Lidia stared at nothing, knee bobbing nervously. She'd spoken little since they'd gotten the news of her sons' abduction. And though Ruhn had been aching to touch her in the quiet moments, he'd kept his hands to himself. She had other things on her mind.

"I never should have gone back onto the *Depth Charger*," Lidia said at last.

"If Pollux was able to learn about your kids," Ruhn objected, "he would have found out whether you were on the ship or off it."

"You should have let me die in the Haldren Sea," she said. "Then he'd have had no reason to go after them."

"Hey." Ruhn grabbed her hand, squeezing tight. She dragged her gaze over to him. "None of this is your fault."

She shook her head, and Ruhn gently touched her face. "You are allowed to feel whatever you need to right now. But come dawn, when we walk out of here, you'll have to bury it and become the Hind again. One last time. Without the Hind, we're not going to get into that palace."

She scanned his gaze, and leaned forward, her brow pressing against his.

Ruhn breathed in her scent, taking it deep into his body—but he found it already marking him. It had been there, hidden in him, since that first time.

"Can I . . ." She swallowed hard. "Can we . . ."

"Tell me what you want," he said, kissing her cheek.

She pulled back, and slid a hand against his jaw. "You. I want you."

"You sure?" She had so much burdening her. With her sons in the Asteri's hands, he didn't blame her if—

"I need to not think for a while," she said, then added, "and . . ."

I need to touch you." She traced her fingers over his lips. "Your real body."

He closed his eyes against her touch. "Tell me what you want, Lidia."

Her lips grazed his, and he shuddered. "I want you—all of you. In me."

A grin spread across Ruhn's face. "Happy to oblige."

He followed her lead, letting her set the pace. Each kiss, he answered with his own. Let her show him where she wanted him to touch, to lick, to savor.

Thankfully, the parts where she wanted him to *really* focus were the ones Ruhn had been especially interested in. The taste of her sweetness on his tongue had him nearly coming in his pants—and that was before her breathy moans filled his ears like the most beautiful music he'd ever heard.

"Ruhn," she said, but didn't give him the order to halt, so he kept working her in long strokes of his tongue, wishing to the gods he still had his lip piercing, knowing he could have driven her to distraction with it—but there would be time later.

She arched off the bed, and her orgasm sent him writhing, desperate for any sensation against his cock.

She put him out of his misery a moment later, her eyes nearly pure flame as she unzipped him, and her slender hand wrapped around him—

He bucked against her first stroke, and was about to start begging when she pushed him back onto the bed. When she climbed over him, straddling him, and that hand around his cock guided him to her entrance.

Ruhn slid his hands into Lidia's golden hair, the silken strands spilling through his fingers, and held her gaze as she sank down onto him.

He gritted his teeth at the warmth and tightness of her, panting through the rush of pleasure, the sense of perfection, the flawless fit—

She settled against him, seated fully, and her chest rose and fell so rapidly that Ruhn grabbed her hands, pressing kisses to her fingertips. Her eyes fluttered shut, and then her hips moved—and there was nothing more to say, to do, as she rode him.

He lifted his hips, and her moans heightened. He wished he could devour the sound. He made do by rising up, kissing her thoroughly, her legs wrapping around his middle. It plunged him impossibly deeper, and he lost it. Went positively feral at being so far inside her, at the smell and taste of her—

Lidia met him stroke for stroke, met his savagery with her own, teeth grazing his neck, his chest. Every thrust had him rubbing an inner wall, and fuck, he was going to *die* from this pleasure—

Then her head tipped back, and her delicate muscles tightened around him as she came, sending him spiraling after her. He pounded into her through it, that feral part of him relishing spilling into her, and she was *his* and he was hers, and there was a word for it, but it eluded him.

She stilled, and Ruhn took her weight as she leaned against him, their bodies now a tangle of arms and legs, his cock still buried to the hilt. Her every breath pushed against him, and he stroked his fingers down the column of her spine, over and over.

She was here. He was here.

For as long as Urd would allow them to be.

Lidia lay in Ruhn's arms as the hours passed, sleep eluding her.

It had been everything she'd wanted, needed, this joining with him. She'd never felt so safe, so cherished. And yet her sons remained in the Asteri's hands. In Pollux's hands.

The hours dripped by. Lidia shut down the part of her that cataloged every possible torment that might be inflicted on Brann and Actaeon. The torments that she herself had inflicted on so many others.

Maybe this was her punishment for that. Her punishment for so many things.

Ruhn stirred, and Lidia nestled closer to him, breathing in his scent, savoring the strength of his body around hers.

And tried not to think about tomorrow.

87

Hiding out in the unmarked van parked in a dusty alley of the Eternal City the next morning, Ruhn peered over at where Lidia sat stone-faced against the metal siding, and slid closer.

She'd barely slept, and Ruhn didn't blame her. A glimpse at her haggard face this morning as they'd crept out of the safe house and back into the van had kept him close to her, offering what comfort he could. Now he laid a hand on her knee and said, "Another hour or so. Then we'll head into the palace."

Another hour until Declan could confirm that the Asteri were well and truly distracted by the video they'd unleashed into the world. From Dec's initial reports this morning, it was a giant clusterfuck. The footage had been blasted on every news channel and social media site. Dec had also confirmed that he'd hacked into the imperial network and learned that this morning, the Asteri and their advisors would all be meeting to discuss the fallout. The news about the parasite had really resonated. All media outlets were abuzz with chatter about it. And the footage of Bryce killing Micah, her claims about how Danika and the pack had died . . .

It didn't matter that the imperial network had pulled the footage almost immediately. It was already out there, circulating on private servers, being downloaded onto phones. Being watched and analyzed over and over again. Imperial trolls tried to insist it was fake, planting comments that it was a manipulated video, but Dec made sure that footage of Bryce running through the streets of Lunathion this spring, saving the whole city, made it out, too.

And there were people out there who remembered that, who had seen her running to save them. They vouched for her, confirming not only that she had saved the city from Hel, but also from the brimstone missiles the Asteri had launched.

The Asteri had a lot on their hands that morning. Exactly as planned. And once their emergency meeting had begun, it would be time to make a move.

"A single misstep and my sons . . . ," Lidia began, swallowing hard.

"Set the fear aside," Ruhn said, offering her the honesty she'd so often given him. "Focus on the task, not the what-ifs."

"He's right," Bryce added from where she and Athalar sat nearby, leaning against each other. Flynn and Dec sat in the front, the former monitoring the streets, the latter with a laptop on his knees, hacking his way into the imperial military controls for the mech-suits. Another few hours, and they'd be in. "Leave the baggage behind today."

Lidia straightened. "My sons are not *baggage*—"

"No," Bryce amended, "they're not. But you know that palace better than anyone. Any distractions are going to cost us."

"I know Pollux better than anyone," Lidia said, staring ahead at nothing. "And that's why it's unbearable to sit here."

"Rest up while you can, Lidia," Athalar advised. "All Hel is going to break loose pretty damn soon."

"Literally," Bryce said with unnerving cheer.

Ithan buried the Prime in the heart of the meadow, so his soul might feel the romping joy of pups for generations to come.

If any of them survived this.

Tharion had called him, asking where the fuck he was, and Ithan told the mer to head to the Eternal City without him. To try to find Bryce and Athalar and get the antidote to them or any of their friends before they went full-tilt at the Asteri. If the antidote had leveled him up, then he couldn't even imagine what it would do to Bryce and Athalar.

Ithan shouldered his backpack and the Godslayer Rifle that Roga had loaned, and left the main building of the Den. Perry was again standing guard at the booth outside the gates.

"Did you get any rest?" Ithan asked, poking his head in. From the bruises under her eyes, he knew the answer before she nodded. "I told you to get some sleep."

"I wanted to be here," she said, "in case anyone came looking for help or had questions."

His chest tightened at her thoughtfulness—her kindness. "And did anyone?"

"No," she said, rubbing her eyes.

"You should get down to the Blue Court."

Her gaze found his. "You're leaving?"

"Yeah," he said. He hadn't slept much either, but he'd forced his body to rest. He knew he had to be at full strength for what was to come.

Perry's phone buzzed, and she glanced at the screen. Her brows knitted.

"What is it?"

She opened up her phone and read aloud, "'Bryce Quinlan and Hunt Athalar killed the Archangels Micah and Sandriel this spring.' There's . . . there's video footage of Bryce . . ."

Ithan's heart began racing. He was too late. Bryce was already making her move.

"I need to go," he said. "I have to help her however I can."

Perry rose from her seat in the booth. "Good luck, Ithan. I . . . I really hope I see you again."

He wrapped his arms around her in a tight hug, her cinnamon-and-strawberry scent washing over him. Just as it always had—like she hadn't taken the antidote. He set aside his curiosity about it again. "I hope I see you again, too," he said against her hair, and pulled back.

Her eyes shone with tears. "Please be careful."

He adjusted the straps on his backpack. "Get to the Blue Court, Perry."

"I'm in the imperial network," Declan announced a couple hours later.

Hunt finished arming himself with the few weapons he'd taken from what Fury Axtar had managed to bring in that helicopter: two handguns and a long knife. It wasn't much, but Axtar had chosen the weapons well. They were all solid, reliable pieces.

"Those mech-suits are no fucking joke." Dec shuddered. "But I'm ready to go when you guys are."

Hunt checked the gun holstered at his thigh. The clip was loaded. Reloads sat in his back pocket. He could have used the comfort of his Umbra Mortis suit with its twin swords nestled in the sheaths down its back. But two handguns, a knife in his boot, and his lightning would have to do. *He* would have to do.

Just Hunt. He could live with that.

He ran an eye over Bryce. The hilt of the Starsword rose above her ponytail, and Truth-Teller had been strapped on one thigh. She had a handgun on the other, only one clip for a reload.

Hel had brought its armies, but they fought with power and fangs and teeth and brute strength.

"Right," Bryce said, "we all clear on the plan?"

"Which one?" Ruhn muttered. "You have, like, seven."

"Better to over-prepare," Bryce trilled. "Plan's simple: keep the Asteri distracted by unleashing Hel and the Fallen . . . while Athalar and I sneak into the palace and destroy that firstlight core."

"Don't forget," Hunt cut in wryly, "rescue Lidia's sons, destroy Pollux, get close enough to the Asteri to eliminate them from the planet . . ." He ticked off the items on his fingers.

"Yeah, yeah," Bryce said, waving a hand. She winked at Lidia, flashing a grin that Hunt knew was designed to put the Hind at ease. "You ready to beat the shit out of these assholes?"

Lidia's chin lifted. She had a knife at her side and a handgun. That was it.

It was laughable that they were heading into the fucking Asteri's palace armed so lightly, but it didn't bear dwelling upon. They didn't have a choice.

"The moment we leave this truck, we have two minutes until the street cameras alert the Asteri's techs that we're in the city if they identify us," Lidia said.

"Which is why it's my job," Declan said from his station in the back of the van, "to keep those cameras away from you guys."

"And my job," Flynn said from the driver's seat, "to keep us moving around the city to avoid detection."

"As soon as I message you," Ruhn said, "be ready for a pickup."

"We did this once before, remember?" Flynn said to Ruhn. "Meeting up with Lidia once she'd sprung you and Athalar was a trial run for the big show."

"I don't care what you have to do," Lidia said to Flynn, to Dec, "or who you have to leave behind. But you get my sons out of this city and to the coast." She met their stare and added, "Please."

Dec nodded. "We've got you covered, Lidia." The name seemed to trip Dec up, but he got over it and said, "We'll protect your kids. Just do what you have to do, and we'll be where you need us."

She nodded back, eyes glittering. "Thank you."

Hunt glanced to Bryce, who was watching all this silently. Not a good sign.

Lidia noted Bryce's look and said, "You remember the way to their throne room?"

"Yes," Bryce said, and faced Hunt. "The wings were all still there a couple weeks ago—let's hope Rigelus hasn't redecorated."

"He won't have touched them," Lidia answered. "He abhors change."

The words hung in the air. Hunt swallowed against the dryness in his throat. They were doing this. He was doing this.

Hadn't he learned his fucking lesson *twice* now? With the Fallen, then with recent events? To go back for a third helping . . .

"I remember," Bryce said quietly—just to him, even with the

others listening. "Every movement of Micah's sword when he cut off your wings. How there was nothing we could do to stop him—stop *them*. I remember how they sold you back to Sandriel, and that time, too, there was nothing we could do to stop them. I remember every fucking moment of it, Hunt." Her eyes glimmered with pure rage and focus. "But today we finally fucking *stop them*."

Hunt held his mate's stare, and let her courage be his courage, let her strength be his guiding light.

"I promised myself that day Micah cut off your wings," Bryce said, still just for him, "that they'd pay for it. For what they've done." Starlight flickered around her head in a shadow of that crown of stars.

No one spoke. Bryce got to her feet, heading for the back doors of the van. The world, the Asteri, the end waited beyond.

She looked back at all of them. Her eyes met Hunt's.

And Bryce said before she stepped into the light, "Through love, all is possible."

88

It was too easy to get into the Asteri's palace. Lidia knew every entrance, but even with her unrivaled knowledge, it was too easy for them to get in through the service doors that led to the extensive garbage-processing dock.

Too easy to slip down one of the reeking chutes and land in a trash room a level below.

But only when the four of them were in the tiny, malodorous closet on the sublevel did they pause. Look at each other.

"Good luck," Ruhn said to his sister, perhaps for the last time.

But Bryce smiled gently, softly, and though she had been all fierce determination in the van a few minutes ago, it was love in her face now as she said to him, "You brought so much joy into my life, too, Ruhn."

He remembered, then, saying those words to her before she'd vanished through the Gate. *You brought so much joy into my life, Bryce.* It felt like a lifetime ago.

She said nothing more, and Ruhn had no words in him as Bryce, Athalar in tow, cracked open the door and slipped out.

Ruhn waited a moment in silence with Lidia, the reek of the trash threatening to send his meager breakfast of bread and olive oil back up. He met Lidia's stare in the dimness, though.

And while she might need to be the Hind today, might need to become that stone-cold female again, he leaned in to brush his mouth to hers. Only once, and then he whispered, at last naming that feeling he hadn't dared acknowledge until now, "If I don't get the chance to tell you later . . . I love you."

Lidia blinked, golden eyes glimmering. "Ruhn."

But he didn't wait for a response or a refusal or a denial. He eased open the door an inch and peered into the hallway.

"Clear," he murmured, drawing his handgun. With any luck, Dec was doing his job.

Praying that the Asteri, distracted with trying to tamp down the effects of Bryce and Hunt's message, wouldn't even consider that Hel was about to be unleashed in their own home, Ruhn stepped into the hall, Lidia right behind them.

And then, wreathed in his shadows as they stole through the heart of the empire, they began the hunt to find her sons.

They had a few close calls, and Hunt wished again for his Umbra Mortis suit, if only for the helmet's heightened hearing to detect any passing politicians or workers.

The politicians could get fucked for all Hunt cared. But the workers . . . Gods willing, when the time came, the workers would be able to escape. That when Declan hacked into the Asteri alert system, their phones would buzz with the evacuation order to get the fuck out of the palace, and they would heed the warning.

Hunt's heart was thundering through every inch of him as he and Bryce hid in the shadows of a massive statue of Polaris, the female's hands upraised in victory.

Beyond the statue rose a familiar set of doors. The whole hallway was precisely as it had been the last time Hunt had seen it, before his lightning and Rigelus's power had blasted it to smithereens: busts of the Asteri lining one wall, the windows overlooking the seven hills of the Eternal City on the other. And somewhere out there, inching along the main road of the Sacra Via . . . Dec and Flynn would be waiting.

But not for them. Hunt knew he and Bryce might never come back from this fight.

If they succeeded in destroying the firstlight core and cutting off the Asteri's renewable source of power, then they'd have to get close enough to those bastards for Bryce to use the sword and knife. To unite them using that star, and risk whatever might happen with a portal to nowhere.

Theia had been afraid of it. Aidas had warned them to *choose life*, for fuck's sake, if the portal was too dangerous. It didn't bode well. But what other options did they have?

There were too many ifs, too many unknowns. It was an even flimsier plan than the last time they'd snuck into this palace. And while they'd all agreed on the plan together, if it failed, if Bryce or any of them died . . .

No. He wouldn't go down that road again. He had made mistakes in the past, bad calls, but fighting against tyranny, against brutality, would never be the wrong choice.

Hunt glanced to his mate, her attention fixed on the hallway. On the Gate at its far end. Sensing his attention, she mouthed, *Go*, and motioned him along. And Hunt went, as he'd go anywhere, so long as it was with her.

For the first time in his life, it seemed that Urd was listening as he and Bryce slipped past the doors into the empty throne room. He gazed at the towering wall of the Fallen's wings behind the seven crystal thrones.

And there, at its center, pinned like a new trophy, was his Umbra Mortis helmet and suit.

Bryce held the Mask in her hands, its gold surface shimmering among the crystal of the sterile throne room. The wings of the Fallen hung on the wall, a fluttering array of colors and shapes and sizes. So many lives, given toward this moment.

Hunt buckled the last bit of his suit into place, fitting the Umbra Mortis helmet over his head. Bryce hadn't questioned him when he took it off the wall. She knew why he wanted it.

Just as she knew that his wings, pinned right above Rigelus's throne, could not remain.

He'd wear that suit and helmet one more time. It wouldn't be the Umbra Mortis wearing that suit, but Hunt. Her Hunt.

And together they would end this.

She wished Ithan had made it in time with Hypaxia's antidote. But they couldn't delay this—not by a single minute.

Bryce ran her thumbs over the Mask's smooth brow. It looked like a death mask for some long-dead king. Had it been crafted around the mold of some Asteri's face? Fashioned after the hateful visage of a Daglan in that other world?

"Bryce," Hunt warned, his voice low and warped through the helmet.

She beheld the Shadow of Death standing there. He drew his twin swords from the back of his suit, flipping them in his hands. "Do it now."

All she'd ever done in her life, every step . . . it had led here.

Here, to this chamber, with the wings of the noble Fallen around her. With Hunt, one of the few remaining warriors.

But no longer.

Bryce lifted the Mask to her face, and closed her eyes as she slid it on. The metal adhered to her skin. It sucked at her face, her soul—

The world diluted again. Alive, not-alive. Breathing, not-breathing. Dead . . . undead.

The star inside her flared brightly, as if to say, *Hello, old friend.* Yes, the ancient magic knew the Mask. It understood its deepest secrets.

Bryce turned to the wings. And in the shadow-vision of the Mask, where the wings were pinned, most held a twinkling light. The kernel of a soul. The last scraps of their existences, shining like a wall of stars.

She'd been right: They had never been given Sailings. It had been the final insult to the dead warriors, the shame of being denied a blessed afterlife. It would prove to be the Asteri's downfall. These souls, left to wander for centuries, were now hers to claim.

A thought, and her will was their will. The Mask called, and the souls of the Fallen answered, drifting from the wall like a swarm of fireflies.

Rustling filled the air. The wings began to beat slowly at first, like butterflies testing out their new bodies. The flapping of wings filled the throne room, the world. A storm wind from Hunt had the pins ripping free. All but two sets—one a familiar gray, one shiningly white—loosed into the world.

And then the throne room was full of wings—white and gray and black, soaring, their sparks of soul shining brightly within them, visible only to Bryce as she looked through the Mask.

Hunt and Bryce stood in the center of the storm, her hair whipped about by their wind, skin grazed by their downy feathers.

A spark of Hunt's lightning struck the two pairs of wings still pinned to the wall. His own wings, and Isaiah's. They caught fire, burning until they were nothing but ashes floating on the breeze of a thousand wings, freed at last from this place.

Another storm wind from Hunt and the doors to the hall opened. The windows lining the hall exploded.

And the wings of the Fallen soared for the open blue sky beyond.

The throne room emptied of them, like water down a drain, leaving a lone figure in the doorway. Staring at them.

Rigelus.

Feathers floated in the air around him.

"What," the Bright Hand seethed, glowing with power, "do you think you're doing?"

He stepped in, and his eyes went right to Bryce's face. Maybe it was the Mask, maybe she had been pushed beyond her limits, but she felt no fear, absolutely none, as she looked at the Bright Hand of the Asteri and said, "Righting a wrong."

But Rigelus narrowed his eyes at the Mask. "You bear a weapon you have no business wielding."

In the streets beyond, people were shouting at the sight of the host of wings flying overhead.

Dead and undead—Rigelus's nature confused the Mask. Alive and not-alive. Breathing and not-breathing. It couldn't get a grip

on the Bright Hand, and it seemed to be recoiling, pulling away
from Bryce—

She focused. *You obey me.*

The Mask halted. And remained in her thrall.

Rigelus eyed Hunt in his battle-suit and helmet. But he said to
Bryce, "You traveled a long way from home, Bryce Quinlan." He
advanced one step. That he hadn't attacked yet was proof of his
wariness.

Hunt's lightning slithered over the floor.

But Bryce pointed behind Rigelus. To one of the hills beyond
the city walls, where the wings had landed in the dry grass. They
coated the hilltop, wings flapping idly, a flock of butterflies come
down to rest.

And Bryce commanded them, *Rise, as you once were.*

Ice colder than that in Nena flowed through her, toward the
now-distant wings. She could sense Hunt's pain, but Bryce didn't
take her eyes from Rigelus.

"You have no idea what powers you toy with, girl," Rigelus said.
"The Mask will curse your very soul—"

"Let's spare ourselves the idle threats this time," Bryce said,
and pointed out the window again. This time to the army that had
crept up to stand among the wings bearing those souls. "I think
you have bigger issues to deal with."

She smiled then—a predator's smile, a queen's smile—as the
armies of Hel crested the hill.

"Right on time," Bryce said.

Rigelus said nothing as more and more of those dark figures
appeared atop the hill. Spilling out from the portal she'd opened
for them just over its other side, hidden from view.

At the sight of the teeming hordes cresting the hills, seemingly
from nowhere, at the sight of the three princes marching at their
front . . .

People began screaming in the streets. Another signal—for
Declan. To get the evacuation order out under the guise of an
Imperial Emergency Alert. Every phone in this city would buzz

with the command to escape beyond the city walls—to the coast, if they could.

Rigelus stared toward the armies of Hel now assembled on his doorstep.

"Surprise," Hunt said.

Rigelus slowly, slowly turned back toward Bryce and Hunt. And smiled.

"Did you think I didn't know the moment you opened the Northern Rift?" Bryce braced herself, rallied her power as Rigelus lifted a glowingly bright hand and said, "I have been waiting for your arrival. And have prepared accordingly."

A horn sounded, a clear note echoing across the city.

And in answer, the Asterian Guard exploded into the streets of the Eternal City.

89

"I knew as soon as you reached the Rift—my Harpy told me, and I watched you through her eyes before you ended her." Rigelus advanced another step into the throne room, power brewing in his hand, dancing along the golden rings on each long finger.

Bryce and Hunt tensed, eyeing the distance to the exit. A smaller door lay behind the thrones, but to reach it they'd have to put their backs to Rigelus.

In the city, light sparked and boomed—brimstone missiles. Made and fired by the Asterian Guard on the rooftops, spearing toward the demons of Hel's armies. Arcing, golden, the missiles slammed into the dark ranks atop Mount Hermon. Earth and rock shattered, light blooming upward.

"And like the rodents you are," Rigelus said, "I knew you'd leave an escape route for yourselves and your allies. Right to Hel. I knew you'd leave the Rift open."

Hunt grabbed Bryce's hand, preparing to get them out.

"So I sent three legions of my Asterian Guard to the Rift last night. I think they and their brimstone missiles will find Hel quite unguarded, with all its armies here."

"We have to warn Aidas," Hunt said, squeezing her hand. Bryce looked at Rigelus once more—at his smirk of triumph at outwitting them—

And with a shove of her power, she teleported herself and Hunt out of the palace.

Right to the chaos of the hills beyond the city.

Ruhn and Lidia raced along the palace corridors, veiled in his shadows.

They'd found no sign of her sons. Nothing in the dungeons, the sight of which had given Ruhn such a jolt of pure terror he had nearly dropped their concealing shadows. And nothing in any of the holding cells. They'd made their way through the palace as quickly as they could while staying undetected. Dec had disabled many of the cameras, and Ruhn's shadows took care of the rest. But after twenty minutes of fruitless searching, Ruhn grabbed Lidia's arm before they could race down yet another hallway.

"We need to stop and reconsider where they might be," Ruhn said, breathing hard.

"They're here—he's got them *here*," Lidia snarled, struggling against his grip.

Ruhn held firm, though. "We can't keep running around blindly. Think: Where would Pollux take them?"

She panted, eyes wide with panic, but took a breath. Another.

And that cold, Hind's mask slid over her face. "I know how to find them," she said. And Ruhn didn't question her as she took off again, this time heading back down the stairs, down, down, down until—

The heat and humidity hit him first. Then the smell of salt.

The one thousand mystics of the Asteri slumbered in their sunken tubs, in regimented lines between the pillars of the seemingly endless hall.

"*Traitor*," a withered, veiled female hissed from a desk in front of the doors, rising to her feet.

Lidia pulled out her handgun and sent a bullet through the female's skull without hesitation. The blast rocked like thunder through the hall, but the mystics didn't stir.

Ruhn stared at Lidia, at the place where the old female had been standing, at the blood now sprayed on the stones—

But Lidia was already heading for the nearest tank, for the controls beside it. She began typing. Then moved to the next mystic, then the next, and the next.

"We don't have long until someone comes down here to investigate that gunshot," Ruhn warned. But Lidia kept moving from tank to tank, and he peered at the first monitor to see the question she'd written. *Where are Lidia Cervos's sons?*

She stopped typing at the seventh mystic, and stalked along the rows of tubs.

Ruhn moved to the doorway to keep watch, hiding himself in shadows as he monitored the hall, the stairs at their far end. They'd be lucky if it took even a minute for inquiring ears to get down here—

Lidia gasped. Ruhn whirled toward her, but she was already running.

"Pollux has got them under the palace," she said as she reached the door and raced out, Ruhn running alongside her.

"Under?" Ruhn asked, trailing her down the stairs.

"In the hall with the firstlight core that your sister discovered—under the archives."

"Lidia," Ruhn said, grabbing her arm. "It has to be a trap. To have them at the core—"

She pointed the gun at his head. "I'm going. If it's a trap, then it's a trap. But I'm going."

Ruhn held up his hands. "I know, and I'm going with you, but we have to think through the—"

She was already sprinting again, the gun back at her side. The castle had filled with sound now, a cacophony of shouting, scared people trying to get out as fast as possible. It masked the sound of their creeping about, but . . . Lidia was frantic—desperate. Which made for a dangerous ally, Hind or no. She'd get herself killed, and her sons, too.

He couldn't let her jeopardize herself like that. If anyone was going to put themselves in that lethal danger . . .

It'd be him.

Ruhn vaulted down the stairs behind Lidia. And when he caught up to her, he clicked the safety off his gun.

Lidia heard that click and halted. Turned to him—slow, disbelieving. She didn't glance at the gun. She already knew it was there. Her eyes were on his. Unreadable, cold. The eyes of the Hind.

Ruhn rasped, "I can't let you get yourself killed."

"I will never forgive you for this," she said, voice like ice itself. *"Never."*

"I know," Ruhn said. And fired.

One shot, right to her thigh.

She shouted in pain as she crumpled, the bullet passing through the wound and ricocheting off the stairs behind her, the thunder of the gun and her scream spinning into a chorus that shredded his soul. A chorus that, thankfully, was muffled by the chaos unfolding levels above.

She pressed her palm to the open wound, which he'd inflicted far from any dangerous artery, and her eyes blazed with pure, flaming rage. "I will *kill* you—"

She reached for the gun at her other thigh, as if she really would blast his face off.

Ruhn bolted down the stairs before she could take aim. Holstering his own gun, he raced onward, leaving her to bleed behind him.

The waterways of the Eternal City were old, and strange, and unfriendly.

Tharion hated them. Especially with the amplified power in his veins, freed from its bonds. His body and soul recognized the very essence of his surroundings. They did not like what they encountered.

There was no mer court in the river wending like a snake through the city. There was barely any life at all beyond bottom-feeders and skittering things that clung to the shadows.

Above, the world was chaos. Armies and missiles and wings.

Here, the sounds were muffled. The water whispered to him where to go, where to bring the bag of sealed antidotes. Flowed with him, guided his powerful tail, right to the grate in the river-bank. His gills flared as he hauled away the metal. As he swam into the dark, lightless tunnel and switched on the aquatic headlamp he'd had the good sense to bring.

And with the water guiding him, Tharion swam like Hel for the Asteri's palace.

Bombs ruptured, and it was so much worse than the past spring. Brimstone missiles rose from the city, from the Asterian Guard hidden within it, from the mech-suits stirring to life atop Mount Hermon—

So much destruction. Hyperconcentrated angelic wrath.

Atop one of the hills beyond the city, Bryce was gasping for breath, a bit dizzy, as she yanked the Mask from her face. Hunt ran for where the Prince of the Chasm stood overlooking the dark beasts swarming toward the city walls and said, "Phase Two starts now."

Bryce mastered herself enough to stagger up to Aidas and Hunt. The armies of Hel, both terrestrial and airborne, all hungry and raging, were no fucking joke.

She knew it had been the only way. To stand a chance, unleashing Hel had been the only way. Even so, its army was petrifying, allies or not. She had to trust that Aidas and the other princes had them on tight leashes.

"They're almost close enough," Aidas said, clad in black armor akin to Thanatos's. Bryce could only assume that his brothers were either among the fray or overseeing their own divisions of the teeming black mass.

There was nothing to do for a moment but watch the Asterian Guard decide they had the beasts on the run and begin advancing beyond the city walls.

Wings fluttered nearby, and Isaiah and Naomi touched down beside Hunt.

"Ready?" Isaiah asked, clad in the black battle-suit of the 33rd.

"Soon," Aidas said. The angels still maintained a healthy distance from him, but had at least lost their disbelieving, wary expressions in his presence.

The Asterian Guard swept out into the hills and valleys below, their mech-suits marching among them, and where they struck, demons died.

"Do you think," Aidas mused, "that they have any idea what's about to happen to them?"

"No," Hunt said, smiling darkly. "And neither does Rigelus."

Bryce slid the Mask back on, and its ungodly, leeching presence ate into her soul. But the star inside her seemed to hold the Mask at bay.

"That'll teach him to think he can outsmart us," Naomi said.

The Asterian Guard, white plumes of horsehair on their helmets shining bright in the daylight, advanced through the field of demons. The feet of the scores of mech-suits among them shook the earth.

"I think the three legions he sent to Nena," Naomi said, "will be in for quite a surprise when they find that half of Hel's army is still there and waiting for them."

Isaiah said, with no small amount of satisfaction, "They should be getting word to the Asteri right about"—he checked his phone—"now."

"Perfect," Aidas purred. "Then we're ready."

"Messaging Declan," Naomi said, typing into her phone. The Fae warrior was waiting in the van, the hacked imperial military network laid bare at his fingertips.

The Asteri's mech-suits halted mid-stride. The Asterian Guard paused, glancing at the fancy new machines that had malfunctioned all at once. The glowing eyes of the mech-suits faded and died out.

"Magic and machines," Isaiah said. "Never a good combination."

"It's a go," Naomi said, reading a message on her phone. "Do your thing, Quinlan."

They all looked to Bryce.

Alive and not-alive. Dead and undead. Bryce reached out a hand toward the stilled metal army below. Cold, awful power went through her. But her will was their will. Her will was everything.

Rise, Bryce said, blasting the thought out. *Fight. Obey Isaiah Tiberian and Naomi Boreas. Hel is your ally—you fight beside them.*

Only she could see the twinkling souls of the Fallen, drifting toward those suits from the nearby hilltop, alighting on them one by one by one.

The eyes of the suits blazed again. Bryce saw the nearest mech-suit lift its metal arm in front of its face. Watch its fingers wriggle with something like wonder.

Then it turned to the closest Asterian Guard and bashed the soldier's head in.

"Holy gods," Naomi breathed as the mech-suits, one after another, began to march away from the Asterian Guard.

The souls of the Fallen had waited for the moment the Asterian Guard and their mech-suits had begun to march toward the city below.

And the remaining souls of the Fallen that didn't have a mech-suit to slip into . . . Well, there were plenty of dead demons and Asterian Guards with bodies intact enough for occupying. Twitching, as if adjusting to the new limbs, those corpses lurched to their feet. Came to stand beside their Fallen brethren in their mech-suit hosts.

"You're up," Hunt said to Isaiah and Naomi. "Time to get into the city."

The angels bowed their heads. And with a great thrust of their wings, they launched skyward. Isaiah's voice boomed out. *"Fallen, you are now Risen! To the gates!"*

Isaiah looked back at Hunt, his eyes brimming with pride and determination. The warrior touched his heart and flew off. Hunt lifted his arm in salute and farewell, as if beyond words.

It was indeed a sight beyond words—beyond any description. An army of the undead, of machines and demons, marched for the city walls.

"Incoming," Hunt said. "Seems like that footage kept them distracted until now."

"Right on time," Aidas confirmed, as the glowing figures approached the battlefield spread before the northern gates of the Eternal City, come to exterminate this threat themselves.

The Asteri.

And walking toward them, the armies parting before him, was the Prince of the Ravine, with the Prince of the Pit trailing close behind.

90

Hunt refrained from heaving a sigh of relief, even if his helmet would have masked the sound.

Bryce had freed the souls of the Fallen from the throne room and placed them into those mech-suit bodies, but the hardest and most dangerous part of their plan started now. Hunt fought to keep his breathing steady, his focus on the unfolding battle and chaos. His helmet blared with alerts and assessments.

Aidas unsheathed a shining silver blade that seemed to glow with bluish light. "My turn," the demon prince said, the dry breeze whipping his pale blond hair. He asked Bryce, "A ride?"

Hunt had only a moment to glimpse the worry, the fear in her eyes as she grabbed Aidas's hand, then Hunt's, and teleported them. With the power of Theia's star, it barely took a moment. Barely seemed to drain her. But what arose around them as they reappeared on the battlefield was a scene straight from a nightmare.

Kristallos demons, deathstalkers, hounds like the Shepherd, and worse . . . the pets of Thanatos, all racing past the Asteri and into the city itself. Hunt's helmet turned them all into distant figures, the world awash in red and black.

But the Asteri had bigger fish to fry: The three princes now before them. Especially Apollion, standing between his brothers.

There was no sign of Rigelus. He'd sent the other five Asteri to do his dirty work.

"You shall pay for marching on our city," Polaris snapped at them.

Hunt unfurled his power, lightning bright even from behind the visor of his helmet. Beside him, Bryce had already peeled off the Mask. And beyond them, around them, the Fallen—*his* Fallen, now in bodies of metal and nightmares, all still bound by the command to follow Isaiah and Naomi—engaged the Asterian Guard. Swarmed them.

Miniature brimstone missiles launched from the mech-suits' shoulder guns, fired at the Asterian Guard. Floating feathers and cinders were all that remained.

It had been Hunt's idea to play on Rigelus's arrogance. He thought them reckless and stupid—thought they'd be dumb enough to believe that they could somehow smuggle an army down from Nena and launch a surprise attack on the Eternal City. That they'd be dumb enough to leave Hel open and vulnerable.

So they'd let the Asteri split their Asterian Guard in two, sending half to Nena to conquer Hel . . . only to be slaughtered by a host of demons awaiting them there, under the command of one of Apollion's captains.

And this half of the guard, the most elite and trained of all angels . . .

They wouldn't stand a chance, either.

Three Princes of Hel faced off against five Asteri in the dry scrub beyond the city walls, war exploding all around them.

It was Polaris who looked to Bryce. "You shall die for this impertinence," she sneered, and launched a blinding blast of raw power for her. Apollion stepped forward, a hand raised. Pure, devouring darkness destroyed Polaris's light.

And satisfaction like Hunt had never known coursed through him at the way the Asteri halted. Stepped back.

Apollion inclined his golden head to the Asteri. "It has been an age."

"Do not let him get any closer," Polaris hissed to the others, and as one, the Asteri attacked.

The ground ruptured, and light met dark met light—

Hunt whirled to Bryce, a shield of pure lightning crackling between them and the fighting. His voice was partially muffled by his helmet. "We need to get out of here—"

"No," Bryce said, eyes on the Asteri.

"That's not the plan," Hunt growled, reaching for her elbow, intending to fly them away from the battlefield if she wouldn't teleport them. They needed to destroy the firstlight core, or else all this would be pointless. With it still functional, the Asteri could run back to the palace, regenerate their powers, their bodies. "Bryce," Hunt warned.

But Bryce drew the Starsword and Truth-Teller, starlight and darkness flowing down the black blades. She didn't unite them, though. At least there was still time to stick to the plan—

Polaris burst through the fray, eyes burning with white light fixed on Bryce. "You should have run when you had the chance," the North Star snarled.

The air seemed to pulse with the power from those blades, from Bryce. Like they knew the time to unite had come at last.

No running, then. Only adapting.

So Hunt rallied his own power, rising to meet his mate.

Polaris launched herself toward them, and Hunt struck: a blast of pure lightning at her feet, warping the very stone there, opening a pit for her to trip into—

Bryce teleported. Slowly enough that Hunt knew she was already tiring, despite the extra power from the star, but then she was there, in front of Polaris as the Asteri hit the ground, and only Hunt's lightning shield kept the blast of power from frying Bryce as she lifted the sword and the dagger above her head.

Polaris's eyes widened as Bryce plunged the blades into her chest. And as those blades thrust through skin and bone, the star in Bryce's own chest flared out to meet them.

It collided with the blades, and both sword and knife blazed bright, as if white-hot. The light extended up through Bryce's hands, her arms, her body, turning her incandescent—

Into a star. A sun.

Polaris screamed, her mouth opening unnaturally wide.

The slowing of the world when a great power died was familiar to Hunt from Micah's death, from Shahar's, from Sandriel's, but this was so much worse.

With the helmet, Hunt could truly see everything: the particles of dust drifting by, the droplets of Polaris's blood rising upward like a red rain as Bryce shoved her blades deeper and deeper—

The demon princes were turning toward them, their Asteri opponents with them.

Gone were the princes' humanoid skins. Creatures of darkness and decay stood there, mouths full of sharp teeth, leathery wings splayed. A great black mass lay within Apollion's yawning open mouth as he surged for Octartis—

The Asteri male flung up a wall of light.

The brimstone missiles from the shoulders and forearms of the mech-suit hybrids sparked again, ember by ember by ember, and Hunt could see with perfect clarity as the spiraling missiles launched into the world, toward the panicking Asterian Guard.

A deathstalker raced past, one galloping step lasting an age, a lifetime, an eon as it seemed to balance on one foot mid-stride.

And Bryce was still there, falling with Polaris, those two black blades meeting in the Asteri's chest, Theia's star uniting them in power and purpose—

Debris skittered toward Bryce, toward Polaris. Like whatever was happening at that intersection of the blades was drawing the world in, in, in.

To the portal to nowhere.

A primal chill sang down Hunt's spine. Theia had been right; Aidas was right. That portal to nowhere, opening somehow inside Polaris, was dangerous not just to the Asteri, but to anyone in its reach.

He had to stop it. He had to shut it fast, or else he knew, instinctively, that all of them would perish—

Time dripped by as Polaris contorted in pain. Bryce's hair was sucked toward the Asteri, toward the blades and wherever they were opening to—

Too slow. Whatever Theia's star was summoning, the portal was opening too slowly, and every second that it yawned wider threatened to swallow Bryce, too.

He'd been made by Hel to help her. To end this. *Helfire and starfire: a potent combination*, Bryce had said in Hel.

It was pure instinct. Pure desperation, too. Hunt unleashed his lightning, directed it toward the nexus where those blades met. It flowed like a sizzling ribbon through the world, past the death-stalkers, past the Princes of Hel, past the mech-suits—

Hunt watched it collide with the sword and dagger right where they crossed, where Theia's star still glowed between them, binding them in unholy union. And where his Helfire met starfire, where lightning met blades, it bloomed with blinding light.

Polaris's face twisted with agony. And still the world kept slowing, slowing—

Tendrils of Hunt's Helfire twined down the blade, into Polaris herself. Lightning danced over Bryce's teeth, over her shocked eyes.

He expected an outward explosion, expected to see every last bit of Asteri bone and brain rupture, shard by shard.

But instead, Polaris imploded. Her chest caved in, sucked into the blades as if by a powerful vacuum. Followed by her abdomen and shoulders, and Polaris was screaming and screaming—

Until he saw it, just a flash, so fast that in real time he'd never have witnessed it: the tiny, inky dot the two blades had made, right where they met.

The *thing* Polaris had been sucked into. A black dot.

It was there and then gone as Bryce stumbled forward, and the blades separated, and time resumed, so fast Hunt lost his breath. He touched a button on the side of his helmet, raising his visor, offering him lungfuls of fresh air.

One of the Asteri roared, and the world itself shook, the city walls with it.

But Bryce was staring down at the place where Polaris had been. At the blades in her hands, still wreathed in his Helfire and her starlight.

A portal to nowhere. To a black hole.

No wonder it had started to suck in Bryce as well. And the rest of the world. No wonder Theia had hesitated, if that was what she'd suspected would happen at the joining of the blades.

Hunt's body was vibrating with power as Bryce lifted her face to his. Pure, savage delight lit her eyes. She'd seen it, too—she knew she'd sent Polaris straight into the nothingness of a black hole.

And—there. A kernel of worry sparked. Like it was setting in how dangerous it would be to open another one, let alone five more. What they'd risk each time.

Still, they stared at each other, just for a moment. They'd killed a gods-damned Asteri.

Hunt's power buzzed through him again, in his very bones—

No. That wasn't his power buzzing through him. It was his phone. The interior speakers on his helmet patched Ruhn through.

"Danaan."

"You need to get to the hall with the firstlight core," Ruhn said. "We've . . . We need help." The line went dead.

"Bryce—" Hunt began, but when he turned to her, he found that pure light had again filled her eyes.

He'd seen that face only once before—the day she'd killed Micah. When she'd looked at the cameras and shown the world what lurked under the freckles and smile: the apex predator beneath. Wrath's bruised heart.

Whatever it took to end this . . . she'd do it. His blood pumped through him, sparking at that look, at what she had done—

"Go," shouted the thing Aidas had become, identifiable only by those blazing blue eyes as he faced Octartis beside Apollion.

The princes looked like the worst of horrors, but Hunt knew their true nature now. They had come to help. And for a single heartbeat, pride at being a son of Hel threaded through him.

Hunt looked back to Bryce, shutting the helmet's visor over his eyes again. "We have to get to the hall with the firstlight core," he said, but she was already reaching for him. Grabbing his hand, primal fury blazing on her face, the Starsword and Truth-Teller again sheathed.

A blink, and they were gone.

She was draining fast. They landed in a hallway three levels up, if the number on the nearby stairwell entrance was any indication.

Blood leaked from her nose, and Hunt might have fretted had he not heard the snarls surrounding them. Had his helmet not blared with alerts.

They'd teleported into a corridor full of deathstalkers.

Thanatos had sent his pets into the palace to distract and occupy any Asteri who might have stayed away from the battle-field, but his grip on them must have been weak, or he simply did not care.

Taking on just one had left a scar down Hunt's back. Granted, he'd been bound by the halo, but even at full power, taking on this many would be no mean feat. Beside him, Bryce panted. She needed a breather. After her fight with Polaris, after managing to avoid the black hole she'd opened, after the teleporting . . . his mate needed rest.

Hunt eyed the snarling pack. The thought of wasting his power to kill an ally's beast rankled him.

But in the end, he didn't have to decide—a wall of water crashed through the corridor.

And roared straight for him and Bryce.

91

There was no way out. No window, no exit, no place to breathe as water flooded the hall up to the ceiling.

Hunt grabbed Bryce, his lightning rendered useless in the water, and swam toward where he guessed the stairs might be in the tumbling dark. His helmet filled with water, warping his vision—

A light shone. He hadn't thought Bryce had that kind of power left—but no. It wasn't Bryce. Tharion was swimming toward them through the hall. Ketos had never commanded enough power to control this much water, and with such force, yet here he was, clearly the master of this flood.

An air bubble formed around Hunt and Bryce. He yanked off his helmet, splashing water down his front. "What the fuck," Hunt spat, choking on the water.

But Bryce got it before Hunt did, and yelled at Tharion through the air bubble now saving their asses, "Don't drown them all! We need them on the battlefield!"

"I had a bag of antidotes," Tharion shouted, his powerful, tiger-striped tail thrashing, "but the force of the water snapped the strap. It's down here somewhere, just wait for me to—"

"No time!" Bryce shouted back. "Find it, then find us!"

Bryce was right: to delay getting to that room, cutting off the Asteri's power at the knees . . . it wasn't a risk worth taking, even for the antidote.

The water roared past, into the stairwell. "Go!" Tharion called as the water vanished from the hall, the mer and the demons swept upward in its current. "I'll be right behind you!"

Hunt and Bryce landed hard on the stones, soaking wet and sputtering, but they didn't wait.

"Hurry," Bryce said, grabbing his arm to haul him to his feet. "The firstlight core's below us."

It was all Hunt could do to shake the water from his eyes, grab his helmet, and race after her.

Ruhn had fucked up. In so many ways, he'd fucked up.

He could think of nothing else as he stood before Pollux, hands raised, before the door down to the hall with the firstlight core running underneath it.

There was no sign of Actaeon or Brann.

"Where's Lidia?" Pollux sneered, pointing a gun at Ruhn's face, his white wings glowing with power.

Ruhn had left her bleeding and wounded on the stairs, utterly vulnerable, hating him—

"Where are the boys?" he growled.

"Someplace else," Pollux said, and Ruhn's stomach churned at what that might imply. "Rigelus guessed you'd seek out his mystics, so he instructed them to feed the lie to you. Which you swallowed so fucking easily, because you're a gullible fool." The Hammer stepped forward and jerked his chin at Ruhn. "Move. I know Lidia's around here somewhere."

Ruhn had little choice but to obey. To let the Hammer lead him away from the firstlight core, out of the archives, then back down that hall to where Lidia would be lying bleeding on the stairs.

Pollux's breathing hitched as the scent of her blood filled the hall. "Lidia," he called in a singsong. Her scent became overpowering as they turned the corner to where Ruhn had left her—

There was no trace of her.

Tharion helped Lidia limp along, a band of living water wrapped around the hole in her thigh. Chasing down the satchel and antidotes, he'd found both bag and Hind on the stairs, right before they'd heard the Hammer snarling.

Only two vials had made it. The rest had burst, thanks to either the impact or the volatility of Athalar's lightning. But Lidia had been shot—by Ruhn, she'd told him. Tharion didn't know whether to admire or curse Danaan for it. The idiot had done it to keep her from harm, so he'd face Pollux alone.

Tharion hadn't needed to ask what she and Ruhn were doing down here in the first place. Why they'd risked everything to be here, why they'd separated from Bryce and Hunt.

Pollux had gloated about Lidia's sons to Ruhn, how the mystics had been ordered to lie about where they were, leading her into a trap. But that meant her sons remained captive elsewhere in this palace—and Pollux knew how to find them.

"Lidia . . . ," the Hammer crooned. "Lidia . . ." He practically sang her name.

Lidia gritted her teeth. With a surge upward, she launched for the hall, for the Hammer, but Tharion grabbed her, hauling her back down beside him.

"We need to regroup," he hissed.

"I need to get to my *sons*," she hissed back, and tried to move again. They spoke so quietly that their words were barely more than whispers of breath.

Tharion held her still. "You're in no shape—"

She tried once more, and Tharion decided to Hel with it. He willed the water band around her thigh to push in tighter, to send a tendril into the hole in her skin for emphasis.

She clapped a hand over her mouth, swallowing a scream.

Tharion pulled back the tendril, hating himself for the pain he'd caused, but he held his magic in place to keep any hint of her blood from showing where she'd gone. Her eyes widened, surprise replacing pain as the water eased up at his command. A simple, normal bit of magic, but he knew his eyes blazed with power—with the raging rapids of the Istros itself.

He said, low and swift, "Hypaxia managed to develop an antidote for the parasite. It temporarily returns the magic the Drop took from us—more than that, actually."

Tharion could have sworn something like pride gleamed in her eyes. "I knew she'd figure it out," Lidia murmured.

"Here." He used a plume of water to free the case of antidotes from his pack. He lifted one of the precious two remaining vials. "Take it. You'll black out for a sec, but . . ."

But to face the monster in that hallway, she would need to be fully healed. Need that wound gone. Lidia didn't hesitate as she grabbed the vial, uncorked it, and drank.

She swayed, and gold flashed in her eyes. He caught her as she blacked out, counting the breaths: one, two—

Her gunshot wound healed instantly. Lidia's eyes flew open, blazing gold. She looked down at her hands, flexing her fingers. "I knew she'd figure it out," Lidia repeated, more to herself than to him.

Tharion gently set her down and motioned for her to keep quiet as steps sounded once more, far closer than before.

"We do this slow and smart," Tharion warned, and helped her to her feet. She rose without a grimace or wince, all traces of pain now gone. But she nodded.

On silent feet, with Tharion's magic sending little particles of mist to evaporate the trail of their scent, they descended the steps.

"Lidia . . . ," Pollux crooned again.

A glance between them, and they halted at the bottom of the stairwell. Tharion peered around the corner to the long hall beyond, where Pollux held Danaan at gunpoint in front of him.

"Lidia . . . ," Pollux sang again. "I found your *companion*, so you can't be far away . . ."

Tharion withdrew. Lidia shook with rage and power. Tharion could feel it shuddering around him, rising up like a behemoth from the deep.

What had that antidote woken in her? What had been taken during the Drop? And what had lain dormant, all this time? His water seemed to quail at it—like it knew something he didn't.

"You're here," Pollux said. "I can sense your soul nearby. It is entwined with mine, you know."

Lidia's teeth flashed, her power growing around them like a physical presence. Tharion sliced his hand in front of them, indicating that she should stand down. Until he had a clear shot at the Hammer, they couldn't give away their position—

"Very well," Pollux said. A whistle through his teeth, and a door down the hall groaned open. Footsteps sounded, approaching them, approaching Pollux.

Tharion dared risk another glance around the corner. Two angels in imperial armor had stepped out. And between them . . .

Two teenage boys, both bound and gagged.

Lidia didn't need to look. She inhaled, scenting whatever was coming—

Her eyes flared as she recognized her sons' scents. Pure, murderous rage filled her gaze, and Tharion was suddenly very, very glad she was on their side.

So he knew better than to stop Lidia as she emerged from their hiding spot, rounded the corner, and said, power ringing through her voice, "Let them go."

Bryce had enough strength to make it to a hall a level above the archives. From there, she and Hunt snuck down on foot, trailing water, as quickly and quietly as they could. She might have pushed herself to teleport them down to the hallway with the firstlight core, but she needed to conserve her strength. Only one Asteri was currently down—

She'd killed Polaris.

The realization kept rippling through her. How it had felt,

how Polaris's blood had felt, showering her, the primal, raging satisfaction in seeing the other Asteri's outrage as Bryce impaled their sister with the sword and dagger, ignited by Hunt's Helfire.

And then Polaris had been sucked into nothing.

Into *nowhere*. The blades, fueled by her starlight and sped along by Hunt's Helfire, had opened a portal to a place that wasn't a place.

One Asteri had been banished from Midgard. But would she be lucky enough to get near the others? Now that they knew what she could do, what she bore, they'd avoid her, as they'd avoided Apollion.

The thoughts shot through Bryce's mind, dread sinking in her stomach, as they ran through the palace.

There was no point in staying hidden. Everyone knew they were here. A nod to Hunt, and her mate blasted open the doors into the archives.

Glass shattered, spraying everywhere, and a shield of Hunt's lightning kept the shards from shredding them as they raced through it, Bryce leading them toward the door to the hallway where the power of Midgard was held—

The glow of the room spilled up the stairs, leading the way down.

There was no sign of Lidia's sons. Indeed, the hall was exactly as it had been before. A crystal floor. The seven pipes, each with an Asteri's name on an engraved plaque beneath, and next to the plaques, small screens showing their power levels.

Sirius and Polaris were now dark. But the others were nearly full.

One of them, the seventh, was at full power. And standing before it was its bearer, smiling faintly at them.

Rigelus.

92

Rigelus unleashed a wall of white-hot power, and Bryce had enough sense to blast up a wall of her own, matching the lightning Hunt hurled between them and the Asteri.

The entire palace above them shook at the impact.

And as it cleared, Bryce drew the Starsword and Truth-Teller. "It didn't end well for Polaris," she told the Bright Hand, sending starfire rippling down the blades. "It won't end well for you."

"Polaris was weak," Rigelus said. "And a fool to let you draw close with those blades." Without warning, he launched his power at them again.

Bryce grabbed Hunt this time and teleported to the other side of the room.

Rigelus's power hit the stairs behind them, and they buckled. A true blow from the Bright Hand might collapse the entire palace, but that strike still would have seared their skin down to the bone.

"We have to get to that core under the crystal," Bryce said, and Rigelus attacked again.

"Kill him first," Hunt grunted, nodding toward the blades in her hands.

"He won't let us get near enough." She gathered her strength to teleport them to the core, and Hunt erupted with his lightning as they reappeared, firing right for Rigelus—

It hit a barrier of light and scattered.

"Your lightning," Bryce said quickly. "It warped stone earlier when you shot it at Polaris. Do you think it can warp crystal?" They stood about thirty feet above the glowing core below. To even get through that block of crystal, they'd need precious, uninterrupted minutes. She'd thought her starfire could eventually chisel away at it, but they didn't have the luxury of time.

"I need a good shot at the floor—a few, probably," Hunt said, as Rigelus attacked once more. Again, Bryce teleported. "Can you buy me time?"

Her mouth had dried out, and blood was dribbling from her nose again, but she nodded.

"What is it you're whispering?" Rigelus said calmly from where he stood in front of the pipes, but Bryce teleported them again.

They appeared right in front of Rigelus, and from his shocked face, he hadn't expected that. No, he'd thought her power tapped out.

The distraction cost him.

Hunt's Helfire slammed into the crystal floor. Bryce didn't wait to see what happened, how Rigelus reacted, before teleporting them back to the center of the room, and Hunt's Helfire boomed as it collided with the stone, which had indeed warped, and was now splintering under the monstrous heat.

Crystal peeled away, melting.

And beneath it, a tunnel to the core of firstlight began to form.

The Eternal City was a chaos of brimstone missiles, mech-suits, demons, the Asterian Guard, and every imaginable nightmare. Light and darkness warred across every inch of the city.

But Ithan sprinted through the streets, heading toward the crystal palace. Toward the white light flashing from it like some massive strobe.

It had to be Bryce. But the palace was massive, as big as the Comitium, and to find her in it . . .

No one had answered his phone calls. With the battle, he didn't think they would, but he'd kept trying, all the way here on the boat he'd quickly hired, then running from the coast without rest, without food or water.

A brimstone missile sailed overhead, sparking with golden light. It hit a building nearby, and the world ruptured.

Even Ithan, with his speed and grace, was thrown. His bones cracked against the building, the Godslayer Rifle swinging from his shoulder. And something else had cracked behind him, not bone but—

Ithan slid to the ground among the screaming people, reaching for his pack. Frantically, he pulled out the container with the vials of antidote for Bryce and Hunt.

Liquid leaked from them. Only shards of the vials remained.

Tharion had more, but Luna knew where the mer was in this mess. The rifle, at least, was unharmed—scraped up along the barrel, but nothing that would affect its usefulness.

He struggled to his feet, but a strong hand gripped him. Helped him up.

Ithan whirled, teeth out, only to find a human woman standing there, her eyes blazing with determination. And behind her, helping the wounded or running for the battle, were more humans. Some in their work clothes, some unarmed, but all heading for the conflict. For this first and possibly last shot against the Asteri.

And he knew. Bryce's message hadn't only been a distraction for the Asteri. It had been a rallying cry. For the people who had suffered most at the Asteri's hands.

So Ithan began hurtling for the palace again. Past all those humans, valiantly helping and fighting—despite the odds, despite the cost. The antidotes for his friends were gone. But he still had the rifle and its bullet.

Make your brother proud.

Lidia didn't bother with bullets. She holstered her gun and drew her sword.

She knew the odds against Pollux. But she'd been studying him for years now. Had learned his moves, his arrogance, his tricks.

She hadn't let him learn hers.

So Lidia glanced sidelong at Ruhn and said, "Get out of here. This is between him and me."

She wanted nothing to do with Ruhn. He'd shot her—he'd *shot* her, in some male fit of dominance, and it had kept her from her sons. She'd never forgive him—

"No fucking way." Ruhn eyed the two guards flanking her sons. As if he could take them, as if Pollux's gun wasn't pointed right at the back of his skull.

It'd be a bullet for Ruhn, but Pollux wouldn't blast her apart with a gun, or with his power. Not right away. He'd want to bloody her up right. Hurt her slow and hard and make her beg for mercy.

The palace shuddered.

"Lidia," Pollux said with hideous satisfaction. "You look well for someone who's been knee-deep in trash lately."

"Fuck you," Ruhn spat.

Behind Pollux, still several feet down the hallway, her sons stood tall, even as they trembled. The sight short-circuited something in her brain.

But Pollux sneered at Ruhn. "Was it for you that she left, then? Betrayed all she knew? For a Fae princeling?"

"Don't give him that much credit," Lidia snarled. She'd say anything to keep Pollux's attention on her—away from the boys. Ruhn could go to Hel for all she cared. But Lidia gestured between herself and Pollux. "This reckoning was years in the making."

"Oh, I know," Pollux said, and motioned to the two angels behind him. "See, the Ocean Queen's fleet isn't all that secure. Catch a mer spy, threaten to fillet them, and they'll tell you anything. Including where the *Depth Charger* is headed. And the two *very* interesting children aboard it—their true heritage at last revealed and the talk of the ship."

Lidia considered every scenario in which she could take on Pollux and get her sons out of here. Few of them ended with her walking out of here alive, too.

"They put up an admirable fight, you know," Pollux said. "But they couldn't keep their mouths *shut*, could they?" He glared at Actaeon. A bruise bloomed on his temple. "You learned quick enough how effective a gag is."

A flame lit deep inside her, crackling and blazing.

"After all the trouble these two brats gave me," Pollux said, white wings glimmering with brute power, "I'm really going to enjoy killing them in front of you."

93

Ruhn kept perfectly still as Brann and Actaeon, bound in gorsian shackles, were shoved to their knees before Pollux by those two imperial guards.

The Hammer smiled at Lidia, who'd gone utterly still and pale. "I knew instantly that they weren't mine, of course. No sons of my blood could be captured so easily. Pathetic," he sneered at a seething Brann, who was sporting a bloody nose. The kid would take on the Hammer with his bare hands.

Actaeon, however, watched Pollux carefully, though the boy was equally battered. His golden eyes missing nothing. Assessing all. Trying to find an opening.

Lidia rasped, "Please."

Pollux laughed. "Too late for niceties now, Lidia."

Ruhn's mind raced, sifting through every angle and advantage they might have. The math was damning.

Even if Pollux lowered the gun pointed at Ruhn's head, he still stood close enough to kill the boys with one strike. There was no way either Lidia or Ruhn could reach the boys in time, physically or magically. A bullet would be slower than the striking Hammer.

And even with Tharion at Lidia's side . . . No, there was no chance.

"Go get Rigelus," Pollux said to the two guards, not taking his gaze off Lidia, off Ruhn. "He'll enjoy watching this, I think."

Without question, without so much as a blink at the atrocities they were leaving behind, the guards departed down the hall. Turned into the stairwell and out of sight.

Tharion struck.

A blast of water, so concentrated it could have shattered stone, speared for Pollux. Ruhn darted to the left as Pollux fired his gun. But not for him, he realized as the bullet raced, faster than it should have, borne on a wave of angelic power—

Pollux dove aside, the plume of water missing his wing. But his bullet and power struck true.

Tharion grunted, going down before Ruhn could see where the mer had been hit. Somewhere in the chest—

As water dripped off the walls and ceiling around them, Lidia said, "Let them go, Pollux. Your quarrel is with me."

He snickered. "And what better way to destroy you? I suppose I can make one allowance: you can choose which boy dies first."

Brann snarled through his gag at Pollux, but Actaeon looked at his mother, eyes sharp, as if telling her to kill this asshole.

"They're children," Lidia said, voice cracking. Ruhn couldn't stand it—the pure desperation in her face. The agony.

"They're *your* children," Pollux said, power flickering at his hand. "Ordinarily, I'd like to make this last a while, but sacrifices must be made in battle." As if in answer, the very building around them shuddered. "I hear there are deathstalkers loose in here. Perhaps I'll feed the brats to them."

"Don't," Lidia said, falling to her knees. "Tell me what you want, what I must do, and I'll do it—anything—"

Ruhn's heart cleaved in two. For the boys; for her, debasing herself for this prick.

He rallied his shadows. But if Tharion hadn't been able to hit his mark . . .

Pollux smiled at Lidia. "I always liked you on your knees, you know."

"Whatever you want," Lidia pleaded. "Please, Pollux. I am *begging* you—"

She'd do it. Give Pollux whatever he wanted.

Her boys stiffened. Seeing that, too. Perhaps finally under-standing what—who—their mother was. What had guided her all these years, and would continue to guide her in her final moments.

Ruhn just saw Lidia. Lidia, who had given so much, too much. Who would do this without a thought.

So Ruhn stepped forward. "I'll trade you. Me, for them."

Any other opponent would have dismissed it. But Pollux looked him over with a cruel, hungry sort of curiosity.

Ruhn snarled, saying the words he hadn't dared voice until now, "She's my mate, you fucker."

Lidia inhaled a sharp breath.

Ruhn taunted the Hammer, "You want me to tell you how she said we measured up?" Crass, crude words—but ones he knew would strike the Hammer's fragile ego.

The blow landed. "I'll kill the lot of you," Pollux seethed, his beautiful face ugly with rage.

"Nah," Ruhn said. "You touch her or the boys, and your atten-tion will be split. Giving me the opening I need to blast you to Hel."

He should have taken that shot when Tharion attacked. He'd wasted the mer's blow—and now Tharion was lying on the ground, alarmingly still, blood leaking from a hole in his chest.

"Ruhn," Lidia warned.

"But," Ruhn went on smoothly, "you hand over the boys unharmed, you let them and Lidia and Tharion go, and I'll walk right up to you. With no guns, no magic. You can pull me apart piece by piece. Take all the time you want."

"*Ruhn*," Lidia's voice broke.

He didn't look at her. Didn't have the strength to see whatever was in her eyes. He knew she hated him for putting that bullet in her thigh—but it had been to save her. To keep them from this ter-rible fate that they'd all arrived at anyway.

So he said to her, mind-to-mind, *I love you. I fell in love with you in the depths of my soul, and it's my soul that will find yours again in the next life.*

He shut off the connection between them before she could reply.

Then Ruhn faced the white-winged angel, lifting his hands. "All yours, Hammer."

94

Unarmed, Ruhn kept his gaze on the Malleus. "What's it gonna be, Pollux?"

Lidia's sons were watching him closely. Lidia said nothing. But the Hammer looked toward her. "I don't see why I can't have everything I want," the angel said. Then grinned at Ruhn. "Wait your turn, princeling."

It happened so fast.

Pollux pivoted to the boys. Fixed his stare on Brann. Pure, brute power flared around the angel.

Lidia screamed as Pollux unleashed a lethal spear of his power toward Brann.

Ruhn couldn't turn away. Didn't want to watch, and yet he knew he had to witness this crime, this unforgivable atrocity—

But Lidia ran, swift as the wind. Swifter than a bullet.

Ruhn didn't understand what he saw next: How Lidia reached Brann in time. How she threw herself over her son, knocking him to the ground as she burst into white-hot flames.

They erupted from her like a brimstone missile, blasting Pollux off his feet. Not some freak accident or bomb, but fire magic, pouring out of Lidia. Searing from her.

"Brann," she was panting down at her son, the boy untouched by the flame, scanning his stunned face, tugging the gag from his mouth. *"Brannon."* She stifled a sob around the boy's full name, but then Actaeon was there, hauling his brother away as best he could with the bonds still restraining them.

"What are you?" Ace breathed.

Still panting, blazing with fire, Lidia said, "An old bloodline," and got to her feet.

It was Daybright, as Ruhn had seen her in his mind. She'd presented herself—her *true* self—to him all this time.

"Get them out of here," Lidia said to Ruhn, hair floating up in a golden halo, embers swirling around her head. "Get the mer to a healer." It was a miracle that Tharion wasn't already dead, given the hole blasted through him.

Pollux got to his feet. "You cunt," he spat. "What the fuck is this?"

"Shifters, as they used to be," Lidia said, fire rippling from her mouth. "As Danika Fendyr told me we were. Now free of the Asteri's parasite."

Ruhn gaped at her. She was free of the parasite? She must have gotten that antidote, somehow—from Tharion?

Lidia was glorious, wreathed in flame and blazing with fury.

Pollux's power surged again. "I'll kill you all the same, bitch."

"You can try," Lidia said, smiling.

Pollux ran at her, striking with his magic. The hallway shook, debris raining down—

A wall of blue fire leapt between them. Pollux collided with it, then stuck. A fly in a burning web.

Lidia stalked toward the angel as Pollux struggled against the flames.

"You signed your death warrant when you touched my sons," she said. And exhaled a breath.

Flame rippled from her mouth into Pollux's flesh. The angel screamed—or tried to.

Freed of any secrets, of any need to keep them, Lidia seemed to unleash all that she was. Ruhn could only watch as fire poured down Pollux's throat. Into his body. Roasting him from the inside out until he was nothing but smoldering cinders, a pillar of brimstone standing mid-strike, mouth still open.

She'd incinerated him.

Lidia held out a finger. And poked the towering pillar that had once been Pollux.

It sent Pollux's ash-statue crumbling to the ground.

Her sons got to their feet, shock stark on their battered faces. The knife in Ruhn's boot helped him make quick work of prying open their gorsian shackles, but it was Actaeon who whispered to Lidia, "Mom?"

She looked over a shoulder to her son. Her lips curved upward—at what he'd called her, Ruhn guessed.

The palace shook again—whatever was going on outside, it had to be bad.

"Get the mer to Declan to be healed. Even after taking the antidote, I don't think Ketos's own body can save him," Lidia ordered. "And that's the last vial of the antidote in his bag. My sister figured it out. Don't jostle it, though—it's volatile."

"Lidia," Ruhn said, but her eyes blazed with true fire.

"I need to help the others." She launched into a run for the stairs. "Get my sons to safety, and we're even. Save them, and I forgive you for shooting me."

She glanced back at her boys, and then vanished up into the palace. Into the battle-torn world beyond.

Lidia had known, even as a child, that she was pure power, and she'd kept that power buried in her veins.

Not witch-power. She knew her flames were . . . different. Her father didn't have them, either.

She'd kept them secret, even from the Asteri. Especially from the Asteri. No other shifters had them, to her knowledge, and she knew what revealing them would mean: becoming an experiment to be pulled apart by the Asteri.

Then she had run into Danika Fendyr, who had somehow learned things about Lidia's paternal bloodline, and wanted to know if Lidia had any strange gifts. Fae-like, elemental gifts.

She'd debated killing Danika then and there to keep the gift secret. And what else did Danika know—could she know about her sons?

The shifters were Fae from another world, Danika had explained. Blessed with a Fae form and a humanoid one, gifted with elemental powers.

It confirmed what Lidia had long guessed. Why she had named Brannon after the oldest legends from her family's bloodline: of a Fae King from another world, fire in his veins, who had created stags with the power of flame to be his sacred guards.

Lidia hadn't mentioned any of that as Danika had filled her in on how they'd become shifters, and the Asteri's experimentation with them on Midgard, which had eventually erased their pointed ears. She'd been glad when Danika had died, all her questions with her.

No longer.

After ingesting the antidote that her brilliant, brave sister had made, the fire had surged so close to the surface that she couldn't deny it. Didn't want to deny it.

Flame rippled from Lidia as she raced out of the palace, through the city, and onto the battlefield beyond. Untethered, unconquerable.

The dreadwolves scented her first, no doubt thanks to Mordoc's keen bloodhound senses. Spotted her standing before the gates to the city. They knew her, even with the fire, and they raced for her in humanoid form, teeth bared. Mordoc led the pack, the hate practically radiating off him. Behind him, as always, ran Gedred and Vespasian, sniper rifles aimed.

It was time for Lidia to clean house.

"You—" Mordoc barked.

Lidia didn't give him the chance to finish. No longer would this male, Danika Fendyr's sire, spew his vitriol into the world. He was done inflicting pain upon Midgard.

Lidia turned Mordoc and the two snipers into ashes with a thought. Until all that remained of them was the molten silver from the darts in their collars, pooled on the ground. Another thought, and the pack of dreadwolves, now skidding to a halt in panic, met the same fate.

Angels in the Asterian Guard shot from the skies, power blasting. Lidia obliterated them, too.

Demons paused, their long-dead Fallen allies with them, mech-suits going utterly still.

The Asterian Guard's war-machines shifted directions and rumbled toward her, each mammoth tank armed with brimstone missiles. The angels manning them aimed their rifles at her and unleashed a barrage of bullets.

Her fire a song in her blood, Lidia walked across the battlefield. Bullets melted before they could reach her.

It was so much more natural than it had ever been. In the Cave of Princes, it had taken nearly all her concentration to douse the flames of the Autumn King around her companions. Only Morven had seemed to be surprised—the others hadn't questioned how the flames had disappeared. There had been too much chaos for anyone to piece it together.

Now her fire flowed and flowed. Her truth was freed.

The war-machines halted. Angled their guns and bombers toward her. They'd wipe her from Midgard.

But she'd keep going until the end. She didn't look behind her at the palace, where she could only pray that Ruhn—her mate—was getting her sons to safety.

For the first time in her miserable existence, she let the world see her for what she was. Let herself see all that she was.

The missile launchers turned white-hot. Lidia rallied her flames. Even if she intercepted the missiles in midair, the shrapnel alone could kill her allies—

There was one way to stop it. To get there first. Before the missiles launched. And take them all out, herself included.

She began running.

She wished she'd been able to say goodbye to her sons. To Ruhn. To tell him her answer to what he'd said.

I love you.

She cast the thought behind her, toward the Fae Prince she knew would keep her sons safe.

The war-machines followed her movements with their launchers. They'd try to blast her into Hel before she could reach them.

Emphasis on *try*.

It had been a short life, as far as Vanir were concerned, and a bad one, but there had been moments of joy. Moments that she now gathered and held close to her heart: cradling her newborn sons, smelling their baby-sweet scents. Talking with Ruhn for hours, when she knew him only as Night. Lying in his arms.

So few happy memories, but she wouldn't have traded them for anything.

Would have done it all again, just for those memories.

Lidia dove deep, all the way into the simmering dregs of her power.

The war-machines loomed, black and blazing with power. Ready for her. Launch barrels stared her down, brimstone missiles glowing golden in their throats.

Lidia unleashed her own fire, ready for her final incineration.

But before her flame could touch those war-machines, before the brimstone missiles could fire, the launch barrels melted. Iron dripped away, sizzling on the dry earth.

And those brimstone missiles, caught in the melting machinery . . .

The explosions shook the very world as the missiles ruptured, turning the war-machines into death traps for the soldiers within. They melted into nothing. The heat of it singed Lidia's face, and amid the burning and billowing smoke—

Three tiny white lights burned bright.

Fire sprites. Simmering with power.

Through the fire and smoke and drifting embers, Lidia recognized them. Sasa. Rithi. Malana. Blazing, raging with fire. They must have crept up unseen from behind enemy lines. Too small to be noticed, to ever be counted by arrogant Vanir.

Another war-machine rumbled forward, rolling over the ruins of the front line.

A stupid mistake. The metal treads melted, too, pinning the machine in place. Trapping the soldiers and pilots within it.

They tried to fire their missiles at Lidia, at the three sprites now coming to her side, but they never got the chance. One moment, the war-machine was there, missile launchers primed with their payload. The next, the metal of the machine flared white, and then melted.

Where the machine had been, a fourth sprite glowed, a hot, intense blue.

Irithys.

She lifted a small hand in greeting.

Lidia raised one back.

"We found her," Sasa said to Lidia, breathless with adrenaline or hope or fear or all of them at once. "We told her what you and Bryce said."

Malana added as Irithys zoomed for them, leaving a trail of blue embers in her wake, "But it did not take much convincing to get her here."

"How did you know to come today?" Lidia asked as Irithys joined them, a blue star in the midst of the three shimmering lights of the others.

Irithys grinned, the first true smile Lidia had seen from the Sprite Queen. "We didn't. They reached me yesterday, and we talked long into the night." A fond smile at the three sprites, who turned raspberry pink with pleasure. "We were still awake when Bryce Quinlan and Hunt Athalar's video went out. We raced down from Ravilis, hoping to help in any way we could."

"We arrived in the nick of time, it seems," Sasa said, nodding to the smoldering ruins.

"We wouldn't have wanted to miss all the fun," Rithi added with a wicked smile.

Irithys's smile was more subdued as she studied Lidia. The queen's flame set Lidia's own sparking in answer. Dancing over her fingertips, her hair, in joyful recognition. "I sensed the fire in you the moment we met," the queen said. "I didn't think yours would manifest so brilliantly, though."

Lidia sketched a bow, but refrained from telling the queen about the antidote just yet, how it would make Irithys's flame even more lethal. Later—if they survived. But right now . . . Lidia smirked at the queen, at their gathering enemies. "Let's burn it all down."

Because ahead of them, dozens strong, an entire line of war-machines headed their way. Missile launchers groaned into position. All aiming for where they stood.

"With pleasure," Irithys said, and even from a few feet away, Lidia's skin seared with the heat of the queen's flame. "We shall build a new world atop their ashes."

Rithi, Sasa, and Malana turned blue, matching their queen's fire with their own. The four fire sprites unleashed their power on the war-machines and the Vanir powering them. Lidia's white-hot flames joined theirs, twining and dancing around it, as if every moment of recognition until now had built toward this, as if her flames had known theirs for millennia.

And as one flame, one unified people, as Bryce Quinlan had promised, their fire struck the enemy line.

Machines ruptured. Lidia staggered back, back, back with the force of it, still unfamiliar with the fire in her veins, after it had been so long suppressed.

But the sprites kept their fire concentrated on the machines and their pilots. And as Lidia hit the ground, as the missiles exploded upon contact with the flames, she cast the last of her power upward. To shield the allied forces fighting behind them and the fire sprites now ahead of her from the shrapnel, which melted until it became raining, molten metal.

It hissed where it hit the earth.

Irithys blazed like a blue star, shooting from machine to machine, leaving burning death in her wake. The three other sprites followed suit. Where they shimmered, imperial forces died.

And as the enemy melted at their fingertips . . . for a moment, just one, Lidia allowed herself to kindle a spark of hope.

* * *

"I'm okay," Tharion panted, blood leaking from his mouth. "I'm okay."

"I call bullshit," Ruhn said, kneeling beside the mer, fumbling through his pack for the vial Lidia had mentioned. The mer would be dead already without the antidote in his veins. But if Ruhn didn't do something to help Tharion now, he'd surely be dead in a few minutes.

"Get him into a sitting position," Actaeon was saying to his brother. "Get his head above his chest so the blood doesn't go out too fast."

"We have to help her," Brann said. "She's out on the battlefield—"

"You guys aren't going anywhere," Ruhn said to the boys. He found the clear vial and knocked it back. "Help me get Ketos up. We've got two seconds before those shithead guards come back, maybe with Rigelus in tow—"

They didn't have two seconds.

From the stairwell at the far end of the hall, the two angels who'd held the boys captive emerged. No sign of Rigelus, thank the gods, but right then, whatever was in that potion hit Ruhn's stomach, his body, and the world tilted, surging, blacking out—

A moment, long enough so that when his vision returned, it was to see the two angels reaching for their guns.

Ruhn exploded.

Starlight, two beams of it straight to their eyes, blinded them. Just as Bryce had done to the Murder Twins. Twin whips of his shadows wrapped around their necks and squeezed.

"What the fuck," Brann said, but Ruhn barely heard him. There was only power, surging as it never had before. His mind was starkly clear as he willed the shadows to begin slicing through angelic flesh.

Blood spurted. Bone cracked. Two heads rolled to the ground.

"Holy shit," Brann breathed. Actaeon was gaping at Ruhn.

"The mer," the kid said, whirling back to where Tharion had passed out again.

"*Fuck,*" Ruhn spat, and put a hand to Tharion's chest to staunch the bleeding—

Warm, bright magic answered. *Healing* magic, rising to the surface as if it had been dormant in his blood.

He had no idea how to use it, how to do anything other than will it with a simple *Save him.*

In answer, light poured from his hands, and he could *feel* Tharion's flesh and bone knitting back together beneath his fingers, mending, healing . . .

It had been a clean shot through the chest and out the back. And this new healing magic seemed to know what to do, how to close both entry and exit wounds. It couldn't replace the blood, but if Ketos was no longer leaking . . . he might survive.

A shudder rocked the palace, and time slowed.

For a heartbeat, Ruhn thought it might be his own power, but no. He'd felt this before. Just a short time ago, when the world had rippled with what he knew, deep in his bones, was the impact of an Asteri dying. Like an Archangel's death, but worse.

Another Asteri must be going down.

He willed that lovely, bright power to keep healing Ketos, though. To use the stretch of time to buy more of it for the mer, to heal, heal, heal—

It was eternity, and yet it was nothing. Time resumed, so fast that the boys lost their grip on Tharion, but the wound had healed over. Ruhn grunted as he hoisted the unconscious mer over a shoulder and said to the boys, "We gotta get out of here."

Half of him wanted to dump the twins somewhere safe and race to wherever Lidia was, but his mate had asked him to protect the two most precious people in her world.

He wouldn't break a gesture of trust so great. Not for anything.

They tore through the palace, its halls eerily empty. People must have gotten the evacuation order and fled. The guards had even left their stations at the doors and the front gates.

Ruhn and the boys made it into the city streets, and Ruhn reached for his phone to dial Flynn, praying the male had the van nearby. Only then did he get a look at the battlefield beyond the city. The cloud of darkness above the glowing lights.

That darkness was pure Pit. Fires blazed on the other side of the field—that had to be Lidia.

"Ruhn!" He knew that voice.

He turned, Tharion a limp weight on his shoulder, and found Ithan Holstrom sprinting toward them, a rifle over his shoulder.

He knew that rifle, too. The Godslayer Rifle.

Ithan's face was splattered with dirt and blood, like he'd fought his way up here. "Is Ketos alive?" At Ruhn's nod, Ithan asked, "Where's Bryce?"

As if in answer, light flared from the palace above and behind them.

Ruhn's blood turned to ice. "We told her and Athalar to meet us. But it was a trap . . . fuck."

"I need to get to Bryce," Ithan said urgently.

Ruhn pointed to the palace, and couldn't find the words, any words, to say that the wolf might already be too late.

Ace and Brann looked up at him, at the palace, at the battlefield.

His charges. His to protect through the storm.

"Run," Ruhn told Ithan, and motioned to the twins. "Keep close, and follow my lead."

95

Bryce's breath sawed through her lungs, but she gave herself over to it. To the wind and movement and propulsion of herself and Hunt through the small space as Rigelus launched strike after strike.

She was not the scared female she'd been a week ago, running from him down the hall. She knew Theia's star gave her enough of an edge to keep one step ahead of Rigelus as she teleported again and again and again.

They just had to deactivate the core, and then she'd take the sword and knife and go after the Asteri. One by one.

Hunt's lightning slammed continuously into the floor. But she and Hunt kept moving, so fast that one boom hadn't finished sounding before another began. The sound was monstrous, all-consuming, and the room rained stone and crystal.

But in the center of the room, the tunnel of warped, melted crystal was almost complete.

Minutes had passed, maybe years. It was a dance, keeping one step ahead of Rigelus, and she knew that it would come to its crashing finale soon enough.

Another blow, and the glow of the firstlight core blazed, casting Rigelus's furious face in stark relief.

Bryce teleported them away, but it was slower—too slow—

Rigelus snapped his power at them.

A wall like burning acid sent them careening into the stairwell, and Bryce knew only Hunt's lightning kept it from being fatal. She rallied her power to teleport, but it sputtered out.

"Perhaps you should not have expended so much of your strength against Polaris." Rigelus smirked, and lifted his gleaming hand—

It was a choice of death or survival.

Bryce teleported herself and Hunt—but not to the center of the room. They crashed to the floor a level above, clear of the core.

"One more strike!" Hunt was shouting. "Bryce, one more fucking strike and we're through—"

Bryce's knees buckled, and her head swam. Her power had dissolved into stardust in her veins.

Hunt caught her as she swayed. "Bryce." Her nose stung; she could taste the blood in her mouth, metallic and sharp. "Fuck," Hunt hissed, and grabbed her face in his hands. "Bryce—look at me."

It took effort. Too much effort.

"I'm sorry," she panted, and the words were barely a rasp. "I'm sorry." All that power she'd attained . . . what good had it done? And what good would having the Starsword and the knife be if she had no starlight left to unite them?

"One more, Bryce," Hunt said, breathing hard. Blood leaked from his own nostrils. The cost of all that power, without cease. "Just one more blow, I can feel it . . ."

"Okay," she said. "Okay."

They had to get back down there before Rigelus could find some way to repair the damage they'd done. "Okay," she said again, but her power wouldn't rally. She looked to Hunt. "A boost?"

From the concern in his eyes, she knew he didn't have much left, either. But his lightning sparked, a crown about his head, making a primal god of him.

Rather than strike her with his Helfire, he hauled her to him and kissed her.

Lightning flowed from him into her, a living river of song and power. She pulled back, panting hard, and it hadn't been much, but it was there, it was enough—

"Stop," called an exhausted male voice from down the hall.

And though she'd leapt between worlds and ended Archangels and Asteri, nothing had prepared her to see Ithan Holstrom racing down the palace hallway with the Godslayer Rifle slung over his shoulder.

Hunt had no energy left to dwell on the fact that Holstrom seemed . . . leveled up. Older, more powerful somehow, even though he'd just seen the wolf. He didn't fucking care about any of it as the wolf reached them and said to Bryce, "I was sent to give you this." He handed her the rifle.

With shaking hands, Bryce took it. "Jesiba gave it to you?"

"No. I mean, yes, but . . ." Ithan's eyes were wide. "There's a bullet in there, full of the secondlight of the dead of Crescent City. Connor gave it to me. For you."

"Connor?" Bryce swayed again, and Hunt caught her.

"There's no time to explain," Ithan said, "but the dead sent me to give you that rifle, and that bullet." Ithan's eyes shone bright. "Connor said to make it count, Bryce."

Bryce looked down at the rifle in her hands, weighing it. Hunt asked, "What use is one bullet of secondlight against an Asteri?"

"Not against an Asteri," Bryce said. "That bullet is a secondlight bomb."

Ithan nodded, apparently getting what she meant more than Hunt did.

"I don't have enough strength to teleport both of us back to the core," Bryce said, and took Hunt's hand. She pressed something cold into it.

Her words struck, and Hunt spat, "Fuck that." His temper flared. "Fuck that, Bryce, let's go blast that monster to Hel—"

"Get out of the palace," Bryce warned, and teleported. Alone.

Taking the Godslayer Rifle with her, and leaving the Mask in Hunt's hand.

She had one shot.

Last time, Lehabah had bought her the two seconds it cost to line up that shot.

This time, there was no fire sprite to save her. No synth to fuel her. Only training that Randall had hammered into her over the years. She sent a silent prayer of thanks to him.

One shot, straight down into the tunnel that Hunt had made, to blast apart the last of the crystal around the core and release all that firstlight.

She knew what lining up the shot would cost her. Knew that in the second it took to aim, Rigelus would launch his power at her, and there would be no wall of Hunt's lightning to keep it at bay.

Bryce savored the whipping, wild wind around her as she teleported—one last time, propelling herself through the world.

She lifted the rifle to her shoulder, clicking off the safety, and then she was there in the core room, debris and crystal everywhere, her rifle already aimed at the hole in the center.

But Rigelus was not alone. The three other remaining Asteri now stood with him, the four of them a solid wall between Bryce and the firstlight core. At least another one was dead, if the slowing of the world a few minutes ago was any indication. But four remained.

Bryce's finger stalled on the trigger. To waste the bullet on them—

"Don't you want to know what you risk, before you act so recklessly?" Rigelus said smugly. He didn't wait for her to answer. "You destroy the firstlight core, and you destroy Midgard itself."

96

Bryce didn't lower the Godslayer Rifle. She kept it aimed at the Asteri's feet. At the hole just behind them. To get close enough, she'd have to teleport right to them, and fire straight into the hole.

"That core is tied to Midgard's very soul," Rigelus said. "You destroy it, and this entire planet will wink out of existence."

Bryce's blood chilled. She might have called bullshit had it not been for Vesperus's claims about the Cauldron.

"You made the core a kill switch for this world," Bryce breathed.

The Asteri to Rigelus's left—Eosphoros, the Morning Star—sneered, "To prevent rodents like *you* from getting any ideas about destroying us."

"Our fate," Rigelus said to Bryce, folding his hands in front of him almost beatifically, "is tied to that of this planet. You kill our source of nourishment, and you doom every living soul on Midgard as well."

"And if I call your bluff?" Bryce demanded, buying whatever time she could to sort out all she'd heard and witnessed and endured—

"Then a darkness like none you have ever known shall devour this planet, and you will all cease to exist," said the Asteri to Rigelus's right—Hesperus, the Evening Star.

"So you'd rather die," Bryce said, "than see any of us freed from you?"

"If we are denied our food, then we shall die; there is no purpose to your existence, if not to sustain us. You are chattel."

"You're fucking delusional." Bryce kept the rifle aimed at their feet. "How about I kill all of you, and leave the core here? How about that?"

"You'd have to get close enough with those blades to do so, girl," Eosphoros sneered, death in her eyes as she glanced to the Starsword at Bryce's back, to Truth-Teller sheathed at her side. "We shall not make Polaris's mistake."

They were right—Bryce knew that if she set down the gun, if she drew the blades . . . Well, they'd kill her so fast she probably wouldn't be able to draw the weapons in time.

"Think very carefully, Bryce Quinlan," Rigelus said, stepping forward with his hands raised. "One bullet from you into the core, and this world and all its innocents will be sucked into a void with no end."

The same Void that Apollion had claimed allowed him to devour the Asteri? Polaris's body had been sucked into nothing—

"You seemed so outraged in your little video," Rigelus purred, "at the deaths of those innocents in Asphodel Meadows. But what are a few hundred children compared to the millions you damn by firing that bullet?"

A void with no end . . .

"Kill her, brother," hissed the fourth Asteri, Austrus, glowing with power. "Kill her, and let us return to battle the princes before they find us down here—"

"What will it be, Bryce Quinlan?" Rigelus asked, extending a hand. "You have my word that if you do not fire that bullet, you and yours shall go free. And remain so."

The other Asteri whirled on him, outraged.

"I can teach you things you've never even dreamed of," Rigelus promised. "The language inked on your back—it is *our* language. From our home world. I can teach you how to wield it. *Any* world might be open to you, Bryce Quinlan. Name the world, and it shall be yours."

"I only want this world to be free of you," Bryce said through her teeth. "Forever."

One of the Asteri began, "How dare you speak to—" but Rigelus interrupted, attention only on Bryce, "That, too, might be possible. A Midgard of your imagining." He smiled, so earnestly she almost believed him. "Yours will be a life of comfort. I shall set you up as a *true* queen—not only of the Fae, but of all Valbara. No more Governors. No more angelic hierarchies, if that is what you and Athalar wish. If you desire the dead to be freed, then we shall find a way around death, too. They were always simply dessert to us."

"Dessert," Bryce said, hands shaking with anger. She gripped the rifle tighter.

"The secondlight shall be the dead's to keep," Rigelus went on.

But Bryce said, a familiar white haze of pure rage creeping over her vision, "They're not *dessert*. They're people. People the inhabitants of this planet knew and loved."

"A poor choice of words," Rigelus acknowledged, "and I apologize. But what you wish, you shall have. And if you desire to—"

"Enough of this catering to vermin," Eosphoros snapped. "She dies."

"I don't think so," Bryce said, and teleported directly to the Asteri. Right to the hole in the floor that Hunt had made. "I think it's your turn for that."

She fired the Godslayer Rifle into the firstlight core.

The Asteri screamed, and time dripped by as the bullet fired from the rifle, slow enough that Bryce could see the writing on its side: *Memento Mori*.

Powered by the souls of the dead, of Connor and the Pack of Devils and so many more . . . the dead sacrificing for the sake of the living. The dead, yielding eternity so Midgard might be free.

The bullet spiraled downward, into the light, toward that final crystal barrier.

Rigelus lunged for her, his hands incandescent with uncut power. Once he touched her, she'd be dead—

And maybe this was what Danika had planned all along, in putting the Horn in her, wanting her to claim that other piece of Theia's star from Avallen. Maybe this was what Urd had planned for her, had whispered she might do ever since she had accessed her power, or what Hel had imagined she and Hunt might one day do.

She wished she'd had a bit more time with Hunt. With her parents and friends. A bit more time to savor the sun, and the sky, and the sea. To listen to music, all the music she could ever hear. To dance—just one more step or spin—

Rigelus was still reaching for her arm with his bright hands; the bullet was still spiraling. And as that bullet of secondlight smashed through that final layer of crystal, as it tunneled down and down—

Bryce wished she'd had more time.

But she didn't. And if this was the time that she had been given . . . she'd make it count.

I believe it all happened for a reason. I believe it wasn't for nothing.

From far away, the words she'd spoken at the Gate the previous spring echoed.

All that had happened had been for this. Not for her, but for Midgard. For the safety and future of all worlds.

And as the bullet erupted in the firstlight core, as Rigelus's hand wrapped around her wrist and pure acid burned her skin and bones where he touched her—

Like the battery she was, she grabbed his power. Sucked it into herself.

Light met light and yet—Rigelus's starlight wasn't light at all.

It was power, yes. But it was *firstlight*. It was the power of Midgard. Of the people.

It flowed into her, so much power that it nearly knocked the breath out of her lungs. Time slowed further, and still she seized more of Rigelus's power.

His power indicator on the wall plummeted.

Rigelus reeled back, releasing her, either in pain or rage or fear, she didn't know—

His light was not his own. His light had been stolen from the people of Midgard. He was a living gate, storing that power, and just as she'd taken it from the Gates this spring, just as it had fueled her Ascent, fueled her own power to new levels . . . now it became hers.

Without the firstlight, without the people of Midgard and every other planet they'd bled dry . . . without the power of the people, these Asteri fuckers were *nothing*.

And with that knowledge, that undeniable truth, Bryce sent all that power through the Horn in her back.

Right as the core ruptured.

Midgard's kill switch flipped on. Mere feet away, the world began to cave in, sucking itself inward, obliterating everything—

Bryce willed it, and the Horn obeyed.

A portal opened—right in front of the core and the dark dot that was emerging from it, vacuuming in all life. Bryce sent the core, that lifeless, growing dot, through her portal.

The Asteri screamed again, and didn't stop. Like they knew she'd conjured her own kill switch.

A thought, and Bryce widened her portal enough that it sucked in the Asteri, their screams vanishing as they went. Rigelus and his bright hands were now a dim glow, still reaching for Midgard, clinging to it as he was pulled in.

Bryce had a heartbeat to take in what—where—she'd opened a portal to: a black, airless place, dotted with small, distant stars. A heartbeat, and then she was yanked in, too.

Straight to deep space.

97

The Asteri's crystal palace was collapsing.

Near the city walls, a crack and boom hollowed out Ruhn's ears, rocking through him. He looked back over a shoulder to see the palace's towers begin to sway and topple.

"Bryce," he gasped out.

Tharion, now awake and walking gingerly, halted, the twins—who'd been helping him along—pausing with him.

The entire world halted as a shudder went through it. As light ruptured from below the palace. A great force, like a whirlpool sucking them in, in, in, began pulling at their edges.

"Run," Tharion breathed, sensing it, too.

Nodding, Ruhn grabbed both boys by the hand. They raced the last few blocks to the city gates, Tharion struggling to keep up.

Even as Ruhn felt that tug toward the collapsing palace, and knew there would be no escaping.

Bryce had left him.

She had left him, and teleported down to those monsters alone. Hunt hadn't made it far, Holstrom on his heels, before that *boom* had rocked the palace, and the skies had opened up above somehow, and the palace was collapsing down, down, down—

It was a choice between letting Holstrom die or keep trying to make it to Bryce.

And because he knew his mate would never forgive him if he abandoned Ithan, Hunt grabbed the wolf and launched into the air, dodging falling blocks of crystal and stone and metal.

He had no idea where they landed, only that it was on the rim of a giant crater that had not been there before. It reminded him of the news footage he'd seen of what remained of Asphodel Meadows—he could only wonder if Bryce had done so intentionally.

But as Hunt shook the blood and dust from his eyes, he saw what lay at the crater's heart: a gaping void. Stars beyond it.

The force of the void yanked him inward, tugged him toward it—

"*Go,*" he ordered Holstrom. "Get as many people as you can out of the way."

Because on the other side of the portal that Bryce had somehow opened into the stars, there was a wall of impenetrable darkness. Hunt could just make out the glowing figures being sucked toward it.

Bryce had opened a black hole in the middle of Midgard.

Had she done it with the blades? Or had the joining of the Starsword and Truth-Teller merely given her the idea of how she might capture all the Asteri at once, rather than picking them off individually?

It didn't matter.

Nothing mattered, because there was a fucking black hole on the other side of that portal, and the force of it was so strong that *this* side of the portal was being sucked toward it, too—

But that didn't matter, either.

Because there, among those glowing lights of the Asteri . . . that was Bryce's starlight.

And she was headed to that black hole as well.

Bryce knew she should be dead. There was no air here, no warmth.

Maybe it was the Horn in her flesh, the Made essence of her, that kept her alive—just enough.

It had been a gamble. But she'd seen what the Starsword and Truth-Teller had done to Polaris. They had created a void that had sucked the Asteri in—the only sort of prison that might destroy a being of light. The only force in the universe that *ate* light, so strong no light could ever escape it. A portal to nowhere.

To a black hole.

Wasn't that the unholy power that Apollion possessed? The power of the Void. The antithesis of light.

The only thing that could kill a planet in one bite. Destroy the Asteri, and Midgard with them.

The Asteri knew it as well—they'd always known it, and employed it for their kill switch, to be activated upon destruction of the firstlight core.

So she'd met their black hole with one of her own. A bigger one. A black hole—a void—to *eat* other black holes.

Because Bryce couldn't let that happen to Midgard. She'd opened her portal to her black hole only wide enough for those who were right next to the core to be sucked in with it.

And now she was here, careening through space with the Asteri.

Light poured from the glowing beings around her, their screams silenced from lack of air. Behind her, the only light snuck in through a sliver she'd left behind . . . a sliver she still needed to close. One small window to Midgard. She couldn't bring herself to do it. Not yet.

She let herself look at that sliver of light, of blue sky. The last trace of home.

I believe it all happened for a reason. I believe it wasn't for nothing.

Ahead of the Asteri was the glowing mass that was the firstlight core, the black, growing hole in the heart of it . . .

The light stretched and bent as it was pulled into the yawning maw of the larger black hole. And then was gone.

Not one trace of it remained. No more kill switch, no more firstlight. Midgard was free of them.

That sliver of light thinned further. It was now too far for her to reach. She had no way of getting back to the portal. No way of propelling herself there. There was just this, the slow drift toward the event horizon of the black hole. The inevitable, crushing end.

Ahead of her, the first two Asteri, Hesperus and Eosphoros, were nearing that line of no return. They were clawing at nothing, trying to find any sort of purchase in the emptiness of space to haul them away from the yawning mouth of the black hole—

But their glowing fingers found nothing at all as they slid over that line and vanished.

Time slowed for a heartbeat—only one, time dragging, dragging—and then resumed. Their deaths had been fast. A swift swallow.

I believe it all happened for a reason. I believe it wasn't for nothing.

Rigelus and Austrus were next, but the two were clinging to each other.

No, she saw all at once: it was Austrus who was clinging, frantic as a drowning person, and Rigelus was trying to pry himself free, blasting his fellow Asteri with remnants of power that Austrus absorbed—

Perhaps if she hadn't drained Rigelus to the dregs, he might have succeeded. The Bright Hand seemed to realize it, too. Decided on a different route to free himself, because he got his feet up between them and *kicked.*

Austrus went tumbling back—straight for the event horizon. His screams made no sound.

Time slowed and shuddered as the black hole devoured him, too.

And then there was only Rigelus, still glowing—but weakly. That kick he'd given Austrus had propelled him toward Bryce. There was nothing she could do to escape him, no way to paddle out of his range—

Rigelus's expression revealed undiluted hate as he collided with her. As they spun out through space, with no meaning to *up* or *down*, and whatever protection the Horn gave her seemed to buckle in the Asteri's presence.

The Horn would bow to its maker, its master.

She needed air. She needed *air*—

Bryce shoved at him, freeing a bit of space between their bodies. Not severing contact, but enough that the Horn's protection snapped back into place, and she could breathe.

Rigelus was speaking, shouting in her face, but no words reached her. There was no sound in space. But loathing twisted his face, and she knew he beheld the same in hers as she sucked in a breath. Her last, she knew. She'd make it count, too.

Bryce grabbed his scrawny torso and wrapped her arms, then her legs around it.

Rigelus had a one-way ticket for that black hole—she'd make sure of it.

Even if she went with him.

98

His Umbra Mortis helmet discarded in the rubble beside him, Hunt stared at the giant, dark *thing* that had appeared in the center of the city and was slowly devouring everything around it.

Bryce was in that hole. A dark wind whipped at Hunt's hair, and he knew without looking who had arrived at his side.

"I told her to choose to live," Aidas murmured sadly, gazing toward the starry black expanse.

"She wouldn't be Bryce if she had chosen herself," Hunt said hoarsely. He wouldn't love her this much if she wasn't the sort of person who would have jumped in. "We have to help her," he growled, wings braced against the tug of the black hole trying to pull all of Midgard in with it.

"There's nothing that can be done," Aidas said, his voice full of sorrow.

"I have to try." Hunt's knees bent, his wings spread, preparing himself for that leap into space. To Bryce. And that eternal wall of black beyond where his mate glowed.

"You go in there, and you will die," Aidas said. "There is no air to propel you, nothing for your wings to grasp onto to carry you forward to her. You will drift, and she will still wind up with Rigelus in the Void, and you will follow her in, helpless, a few minutes later."

"But she left the portal open," Hunt said. "To Midgard."

Aidas turned those weary eyes to him. "I believe it shall shut when she and the Horn in her back are obliterated."

"She left it open to *come home*," Hunt snarled. He studied the Mask in his hands. She'd left it with him . . . why? He'd have no ability to get it back to the Fae in their home world. Hel, he couldn't even wield the damn thing. He wasn't Made; he couldn't command it.

"She is likely already dead from lack of oxygen," Aidas said softly. "I'm sorry."

"I don't accept that for one minute," Hunt raged. "I *refuse* to accept that—"

"Then go die with her," Aidas said, not unkindly. "If that's your wish, then do so now. She and Rigelus already approach the Void's edge."

Hunt studied the Mask again.

Bryce did nothing without a reason. She had left him with the Mask, knowing she was headed to her death. She'd left it with her mate . . . her mate, who had a little bit of her Made essence in him thanks to their lovemaking last night.

Which might make him capable of wielding it. For just long enough.

She had given everything for Midgard. For him.

That day last spring, when all hope had been lost, she had made the Drop alone. To save him, and to save the city—and she had done it from pure love. She had done it without expecting to come back.

Just as she must have jumped through this portal suspecting she'd never return.

Demons were spilling into the streets, and the Asterian Guard was still fighting, unaware that their remaining masters were headed toward obliteration. The mech-suits of the Fallen and their enemies clashed.

Bryce had gone into death itself for him that day in the spring.

Hunt could do no less for her.

"Athalar," Aidas said as he gazed at the hole in the world. "It is done. Come—we must finish this. Even with the Asteri gone, there are other battles to fight before the day is won."

The words might have sunk in then—*the Asteri gone*—but the ground shook behind him.

Hunt turned. A mech-suit stood there, towering over him. No pilot—this was one of the Fallen. The glowing green eyes shifted between him and the hole in the universe, the small bit of light drifting, drifting toward that infinite darkness.

The mech-suit held out a hand, and Hunt knew.

He knew which of the Fallen controlled this suit, whose soul had come to offer a hand. To help him do the impossible.

"Shahar," he said, tears falling.

The mech-suit, the Archangel's soul within it, inclined its head. Aidas took a step back, as if surprised.

In the streets, the other suits halted. Fell to their knees, bowing. Hunt could feel them—the souls of the Fallen. Swarming around him, around the suit.

But Shahar simply knelt before Hunt and opened the pilot's door.

His wings might not work in space, but the propulsion from the suit's weapons would.

Hunt didn't hesitate. He climbed in, wings furled tight in the small interior, and yanked the metal door shut.

"Thank you," he said to the Archangel, to the Fallen he now felt pressing around him.

He'd once been forced to take mech-suits apart on the battlefield to help Shahar's sister destroy humans. Now this one would help him save a life. The life that mattered to him more than any other.

Hunt didn't look at Aidas, at the collapsed palace sending debris skittering toward the portal, the black hole so enormous its pull threatened to drag them all in. Hunt just stared directly at the void as he began running, suit thundering around him, straight for that portal.

And leapt in after his mate.

It was too far.

Not for the suit, whose blasts of power sent Hunt careening

toward Bryce and Rigelus, but for the oxygen systems. They screamed at him on the screens, flashing red. Air became thin; his lungs ached—

Hunt did the only thing he could think to do. He slid the Mask onto his face.

To escape death, he'd don its trappings. The Umbra Mortis in truth.

The Mask ripped apart his soul.

Life and death—that was all that space, the universe, really was. But that chasm yawning wide, so close to Bryce and Rigelus . . . that was death incarnate.

They were struggling. He could see that now. Light flaring between them, rippling into nothing, both trying to get away from the other, to blast away—

There was only one brimstone missile left in the suit. Hunt took aim toward his mate and Rigelus. They were moving too swiftly, too closely. To shoot one would be to shoot the other.

He could have sworn a light, ghostly hand guided his to the release button.

"She'll get thrown in, too," Hunt whispered to Shahar.

That ghostly hand pressed—lightly, as if it was all she could manage—on his hand. On the button.

As if to say, *Fire.*

And the gods had never done him any favors, Urd had certainly never helped him, yet . . .

Maybe they had.

Maybe that day he'd first met Bryce, the gods had sent him there. Not to be some instrument of Hel, but because Urd knew that there would be a female who would be kind and selfless and brave, who would give everything for her city, for her planet. And that she would need someone to give everything back to *her.*

Bryce had given him a life, and a beautiful one. He didn't need all the photo evidence that had streamed in front of his face when he'd been in the Comitium's holding cell to realize it. She had brought joy, and laughter, and love, had pried him free of that cold, dark existence and pulled him into the light. Her light.

He wouldn't let it be extinguished.

So Hunt pushed the missile-launch button. One push, and it blasted from the shoulder panel on the mech-suit.

And as it left the suit, spiraling through space, golden with all that angelic wrath . . .

He felt Shahar leave with it.

Could have sworn he saw great, shining wings wrap around that missile as it spiraled through space, straight for Bryce and Rigelus.

The Fallen's cause, ended at last with this final blow.

Bryce and Rigelus halted their struggle at the glowing missile's approach.

And Hunt knew it was Shahar, it was every one of the Fallen, it was all who'd stood against the Asteri, who guided that missile for a direct hit into Rigelus's face.

It didn't explode. It launched him away from Bryce, the Bright Hand now tumbling for the event horizon, the missile with him—

And Bryce was free. Drifting.

But still too close to the edge.

Using the suit's precious cache of firepower for momentum, Hunt propelled himself forward, racing through space for his mate, his wife, his love—

The missile and Rigelus crossed the event horizon.

Time slowed.

It stretched and rippled as a flare of light plumed, either Rigelus or the erupting missile, Shahar and the Fallen's cause vanishing with it into darkness.

And then Bryce was before him, her hair floating like she was underwater. Face crusted—frozen. Unconscious.

The Mask said a different word, but he ignored it.

Ignored it and reached and reached, time still so fucking slow—

The metal hands of the suit wrapped around her waist just as time resumed. He deployed the remaining small artillery and blasted toward home. Toward the portal, now beginning to slide shut.

It could only mean one thing. The Mask had been trying to tell him, but he refused to believe it. He wouldn't believe it for one second.

But the portal was closing, getting smaller and smaller, and—

A glowing, black figure filled it. Then another.

Aidas and Apollion.

Their power grabbed the edges of the portal and held it a little wider. Held it open a moment longer.

And with what little strength he had left, Hunt threw a desperate, raging, blazing-hot rope of lightning toward Apollion. The only being on Midgard who could handle his power.

Apollion caught it, in that humanoid form once more, and pulled.

Aidas flared with black light, pushing back against the sealing portal, against Urd's wishes. Hunt was close enough to see the princes' strained faces, Apollion's teeth flashing as he dragged Hunt by his lightning, inch by inch, closer and closer. Aidas was sweating, panting as he fought to keep the portal open—

And then Ruhn was there. Starlight flaring. Pushing back against the impossible. Lidia was beside him, crackling with fire.

Tharion. Holstrom. Flynn and Dec. A fire sprite, her small body bright with flame. Isaiah and Naomi.

So many hands, so many powers, from almost every House.

The friends they'd made were what mattered in the end. Not the enemies.

Through love, all is possible.

It was love that was holding the portal open. That held it open until the very end, until Hunt and Bryce were through, crashing into the dirt of Midgard, the blue sky filling his sight and all that beautiful air filling his lungs—

The portal shut, sealing the black hole and all of space behind it.

The Asteri were gone.

Hunt was out of the mech-suit in a heartbeat, shattering the metal panel, swinging down to where Bryce lay on the ground. She wasn't moving. Wasn't breathing.

And he finally let the Mask say the word he'd been ignoring since he'd grabbed her in the depths of space.

Dead.

99

It was too long," Declan was saying as Hunt worked on Bryce's heart, his lightning slamming into her, over and over. "She was without oxygen for too long, even for Vanir. There's nothing my healing magic can do if she's already—"

Hunt blasted his lightning into her chest again.

Bryce arced off the ground, but her heart didn't start beating.

Their friends were gathered around them, shadows to his grief, this unfathomable pain.

Get up, he willed the Mask, willed her. *Get the fuck up.*

But it did not respond. Like one final *fuck you,* the Mask tumbled off his face. As if her Made essence had faded from him with her death.

"Bryce," he ordered, voice cracking. This wasn't happening, this couldn't be happening to him, not when they'd been so close—

"Blessed Luna, so bright in the sky," Flynn whispered, "spare your daughter—"

"No prayers," Hunt growled. "No *fucking* prayers."

She couldn't be dead. She had fought so hard and done so much . . .

Hunt crashed his lightning into her heart again.

It had worked before. That day of the demon attack in the spring—he'd brought her back to life.

But her heart did not answer this time.

Rigelus had used his gods-damned lightning to resurrect the Harpy—why the fuck didn't it work now? What had Rigelus known about Hunt's own power that Hunt didn't?

"Do something," Hunt snarled up at Apollion and Aidas. "You've got a black hole in your fucking mouth—you've got all the power in the galaxy," he spat at the Prince of the Pit. *"Save her."*

"I cannot," Apollion said, and Hunt had never hated anything more than he hated the grief in the prince's eyes. The tears on Aidas's face. "We do not have such gifts."

"Then find Thanatos," Ruhn ordered. "He goes around calling himself the *Prince of Souls* or whatever bullshit. Find him and—"

"He cannot save her, either," Aidas said softly. "None of us can."

Hunt looked down at his mate, so still and cold and lifeless.

The scream that came out of him shook the very world.

There was nothing but that scream, and the emptiness where she had been, where the life they were supposed to have had together should have been. And when his breath ran out, he was just . . . done. There was nothing left, and what the fuck was the point of it all if—

A gentle hand touched his shoulder. "I might be able to try something," said a female voice.

Hunt looked up to find Hypaxia Enador somehow standing beside him, the Bone Crown of the House of Flame and Shadow atop her shining black curls.

His sister was gone. Ruhn looked at Bryce's face and knew she was dead. Beyond dead.

He had no sound in his mind. Lidia stood beside him, her hand in his, her sons behind them. The boys had been the ones who'd convinced him to come back—had refused to go another step until they helped in some way.

But none of it had made a difference. Even Athalar's lightning hadn't revived Bryce.

And then Hypaxia had stepped forward, wearing that crown of bones. Somehow, she was now the Head of the House of Flame and Shadow. Offering to help.

"She'll never forgive me if you raise her into some shadow of herself," Hunt said, voice strained with tears, with his screams.

"I'm not proposing to raise her," Hypaxia assured him.

Hunt dragged his hands through his hair. "She doesn't have a soul—I mean, she does, but she sold it to the Under-King, so if that's what you need, then you're shit out of luck—"

"The Under-King is gone," Hypaxia said. Ruhn's knees wobbled. "Any bargains he made with the living or the dead are now null and void. Bryce's soul is hers to do with as she wills."

"Please—help her," Ruhn blurted, desperate. "Help her if you can."

Hypaxia met his eyes, then looked to Lidia beside him, their hands linked. She smiled.

Athalar whispered, "Anything. Whatever you need, I'll give anything."

The witch looked down at Bryce, and said to Athalar, "Not a sacrifice. A trade."

She beckoned behind her, summoning Jesiba Roga to her side.

Hunt stared at the sorceress, but Roga was only gazing at Bryce.

"Oh, Quinlan," Roga said, and there were tears gathering on her lashes.

"Priestess," Apollion hissed, and Roga lifted eyes brimming with disdain and disgust to the Prince of the Pit.

"Still wondering if I'm going to do anything with those books?" Roga snapped at Apollion. She pointed to Bryce, dead on the ground. "Don't you think if they had some power, I'd be using it *right now* to save that girl?"

Apollion glowered at her. "You're a born liar, priestess—"

"We don't have much time," Hypaxia interrupted, and even the Prince of the Pit halted at the command in her voice. "We need to act before too much damage is done to her body."

"Please," Ruhn rasped, "just explain. I know you said we didn't need to, but if we can offer something—"

"It is for me to offer," Jesiba said, and looked down again at Bryce. Tears covered the sorceress's cheeks. *Priestess,* Apollion had called her.

"To offer what?" Lidia asked.

"My life," Roga said. "My long, wicked life." She raised her eyes to Apollion again.

"That is not possible," Apollion said.

"You cursed me," Jesiba said, and as puzzled as Hunt was, he couldn't bring himself to interrupt. "You cursed me to immortality. Now I'm making it a gift: the gift of a Vanir's long life. I give it freely to Bryce Quinlan, if she wants it."

Apollion snapped, "That curse is for the *living*."

"Then it is a good thing I have a way with the dead," Hypaxia declared.

Perhaps for the first time in his existence, Apollion looked surprised. Aidas asked, "Is . . . is such a thing possible?"

Hunt said, "I offer my life, then."

"What would be the point?" Jesiba said, laughing harshly. "Save her, only to be dead yourself?"

"You . . . you'll die?" Ruhn blurted.

Jesiba smiled softly. "After fifteen thousand years, I've had my fill of Midgard."

"We must do it now," Hypaxia said. "I can feel her thinning."

Hunt didn't like that word one bit, so he said to Jesiba, "Thank you. I never knew that Quinlan . . . that she meant anything to you."

Jesiba's brows rose, and a bit of the prickly sorceress he knew returned. "Of course she does. Do you know how hard it is to find a competent assistant?"

Hunt was beyond laughter, though. "Thank you," he said again. "I . . . I hope you find peace."

Jesiba's face bloomed in a smile, and it was perhaps the first true one he'd ever seen from her. "I've already found it, Athalar. Thanks to you both." With a nod to him and Bryce, she walked up to Hypaxia and offered her hand. "Lead the House of Flame and Shadow back to the light," she said to the witch, who bowed her head.

None of them dared speak as Hypaxia began to chant.

This place was the opposite of where she'd gone during the Drop. Rather than an endless chasm, it was just . . . light. Soft, golden light. Gentle and easy on the gaze.

It was warm and restful, and she had nowhere else she really wanted to be except . . .

Except . . .

Bryce looked behind her. More light glowed in that direction.

"Looking for the exit?" said a dry female voice. "It's that way."

Bryce turned, and Jesiba was there.

The golden light rippled and faded, and they stood upon a green hill in a lush, gentle land. The land she'd glimpsed that day after the attack in the spring—when she had believed Connor and the Pack of Devils had been safe and protected in the Bone Quarter.

It was real.

"Quinlan."

She turned to Jesiba. "Are we dead?"

"Yes."

"Did the others—"

"Alive, though the Asteri are not." A wry nod. "Thanks to you."

Bryce smiled, and felt it beam through her. "Good. Good." She breathed in a lungful of the sweet, fresh air, noted the tang of salt, a hint of sea nearby—

"Quinlan," Jesiba said again. "You have to go back."

Bryce angled her head. "What do you mean?"

"To life," Jesiba said, irritable as always. "Why else do you think I'm here? I traded my life for yours."

Bryce blinked. "What? Why?"

"Holstrom can fill you in on the particulars of my existence. But let's just say . . ." Jesiba walked up to her and took her hand.

"That Archesian amulet isn't merely for protection against my books or against demons. It's a link to Midgard itself."

Bryce glanced down at her chest, the slender gold chain and delicate knot of circles dangling from it. "I don't understand."

"The amulets first belonged to the librarian-priestesses of Parthos. Each was imbued with Midgard's innate magic—the very oldest. The sort every world has, for those who know where to look."

"So?"

"So I think Midgard knows what you did, in whatever way a planet can be sentient. How you freed Avallen, not because you wanted to claim the land for yourself, but because you believed it was right."

At Bryce's surprised expression, Jesiba said, "Come, Quinlan. I know how ridiculously soft-hearted you can be." The words were dry, but her face was soft.

"What does that have to do with"—Bryce gestured around them—"all this?"

"As thanks for what you did for Midgard . . . we are being allowed this trade, as it were."

Bryce blinked, still not getting it. "A trade?"

Jesiba plowed ahead, ignoring her question. "The Parthos books are yours now. Protect them, cherish them. Share them with the world."

Bryce stammered, "*How* can you possibly, and *why* would you possibly—"

"A hundred thousand humans marched at Parthos to save the books—to save their centuries of knowledge from the Asteri. They all knew they wouldn't walk away. I had to run, that day. To protect the books, I ran from my friends and my family, who fought to buy me time." Her eyes gleamed. "You went into that portal today knowing you wouldn't walk away, either. I can offer now what I couldn't then, all those years ago. My family and friends are long gone, but I know they'd want to offer this to you, too. As our own thanks for freeing our world."

Bryce reeled. Jesiba had been at Parthos *when it fell*?

"The books are yours," Jesiba said again. "And so is the gallery's collection. The paperwork's done."

"But how did you know I'd wind up—"

"You've got one of the worst self-sacrificing streaks I've ever encountered," Jesiba said. "I had a feeling an intervention might be needed here today." She peered up at the blue sky, and smiled to herself. "Go home, Bryce. This will all be here when you're ready."

"My soul—"

"Free. The Under-King is dead. Again, Holstrom will fill you in."

Bryce's eyes stung. "I don't . . . I don't understand. I was happy to give my life—well, not *happy*, but willing—"

"I know," Jesiba said, and squeezed her hand. "That's why I'm here." She gestured behind Bryce, where a crystal doorway, reminiscent of Crescent City's Gates, now glowed. "The angel is waiting for you, Quinlan."

The angel. *Hunt.*

The thing she'd left behind. The thing that she'd been looking for, the reason she'd hesitated . . .

"This will all be here when you're ready," Jesiba repeated, then motioned to the green hills beyond. "We'll all be here when you're ready."

Far out, on a distant hill, stood seven figures.

Bryce knew them by shape, knew them by their heights and the glow around them. She picked out Connor standing tall at the back. And standing at their front, a hand upraised . . .

Bryce began crying, and it was pure joy and love that burst from her as she lifted a hand in greeting toward Danika.

Danika, here—with everyone. Safe and loved.

She heard the words on the wind, carried from her friend's soul to hers.

Light it up, Bryce.

And Bryce was laughing, laughing and sobbing as she yelled back across the lush plain and hills, *"Light it up, Danika!"*

Wolfish laughter flowed to her. And then there was a spark of light by Danika's shoulder, and Bryce knew that fire . . .

She blew a kiss to Lehabah. Through her tears, she turned back to Jesiba. "How? The secondlight—"

"It took their power. But what is eternal, what is made of love . . . that can never be destroyed."

Bryce stared at her in wonder.

Jesiba laughed. "And that's about as sentimental as I'll ever get, even here." She gave Bryce a nudge toward the crystal archway. "Live your life, Quinlan. And live it well."

Bryce nodded, and hugged Jesiba, conveying all that was in her heart.

Jesiba hugged her back—first awkwardly, then wholeheartedly. And as Bryce hugged her, she looked one more time toward the hill where Danika and Lehabah and Connor and the Pack of Devils had waved.

But they were already gone. Off to enjoy the wonders and peace of this place. It filled her heart with joy to know it.

So Bryce turned from Jesiba. From what awaited them, all of them, and walked back toward the archway.

Toward life.

Toward Hunt.

100

Bryce opened her eyes.

There were . . . a lot of people standing over her. Most of them were crying.

"This," she groaned, "is like some fucked-up version of attending your own Sailing."

Everyone was gaping at her. And Hunt—he was real, he was right there, and the shock on his face was so genuine that Bryce just laughed.

The Asteri were gone. And with them, their firstlight, secondlight, their prison of an afterlife, and those she'd loved and lost . . . they were safe, too.

All of Danika's work, fulfilled.

Bryce looked from Hunt to Ithan, also hovering over her, and gave the wolf a long, assessing look. "Who died and made you Prime?"

Ithan gaped at her, but Hypaxia—crowned with bones, for fuck's sake—smirked and said, "Sabine."

And Bryce laughed again.

"What the fuck, Quinlan?" Hunt muttered, and she looked back at her mate, whose face was so wan, his eyes so full of wonder—

She had the sense of others being there. Of Ruhn and Lidia and Flynn and Dec and Tharion and the Princes of Hel, but they all faded away before Hunt.

Bryce lifted a hand to his cheek, wiping away a tear with her thumb. "Look at my big, tough Alphahole," she said quietly, but tears thickened her voice, too.

"How can you joke at a time like this?" Hunt said, and Bryce surged forward and kissed him.

It was light and love and *life*.

She had a dim awareness of a stirring in the air around them and Ruhn saying, "Does someone, uh, want to put Jesiba's ashes in a . . . cup or something?"

But Bryce just kissed Hunt, and his arms slid around her, holding her tight to him.

Like he'd never let go.

Hunt allowed Bryce out of his sight only for a few minutes. So he could do this last, final task.

Wings of every color and the husks of the mech-suits still lay where they'd collapsed hours earlier, instantly crashing to the ground the moment the Fallen souls had vacated them.

He didn't have any particular suit in mind, but he walked among the field of them—stepping over the bodies of fallen demons and Asterian angels alike, feathers scattered everywhere, and finally halted before a hulking suit, its eyes now darkened.

"Thanks," he said quietly to the Fallen, even if their souls were now gone. Off to the place Bryce claimed they'd all go, in the end. "For having my back this one last time."

The battlefield beyond the city walls was eerily silent save for the calls of carrion-feeders, but the city behind him was a symphony of sirens and wails and screams. Of news helicopters circling, trying to find some way to convey what had happened.

Naomi had gone off to meet them, to attempt to establish some semblance of order.

"We did it," Hunt said, throat thick. "At last, we did it. The hierarchies are still here, I guess, but I promise you . . ." He swallowed hard, surveying all the cold, empty metal littering the field around him. "It's going to change from here on out."

Wings flapped overhead, and then Isaiah was there, wounds already healed beneath the blood crusted on his dark skin. His brow remained wonderfully clear of the halo.

Isaiah surveyed the mech-suits, the empty eyes, and bowed his head in silent thanks.

"Wherever they've gone," Isaiah said after a moment, "I hope it's the paradise they deserve."

"It is," Hunt said, and knew it in his heart to be true. He eyed the angel. "What's up?"

Isaiah smiled slightly. "I heard you came out here and thought you might want company. You know, someone to brood with."

Hunt chuckled. "Thanks. I always appreciate a partner-in-brooding."

Isaiah's smile broadened. But his eyes gleamed as he said, "So, after all this time, all this suffering . . . we finally saw the Fallen's cause fulfilled."

"I was just telling them that," Hunt said, gesturing to the empty husks of metal.

Isaiah clapped Hunt on the shoulder. "Thank you—for fighting for us until the end. Your mom would be proud, I think. Really damn proud, Hunt."

Hunt didn't have words, so he nodded, swallowing against the tightness in his throat. "Where do we go from here, though? I don't know shit about building governments. Do you?"

"No," Isaiah said. "But I think we're about to get a crash course."

"That's not reassuring." Hunt turned back toward the city. It was a shock to his system, as great as a zap of his lightning, to see the familiar skyline without the spires of the crystal palace.

The Asteri were *gone*.

He needed to get back to Bryce. To hold her, smell her, kiss her. No other reason than that. Than the fact that he'd come so, so close to losing her.

"Hunt," Isaiah said. The white-winged angel's eyes were solemn. "You could rule the angels, you know."

Hunt blinked slowly.

Isaiah went on, "We'll dismantle the Archangels and their schools and the hierarchies, and it'll take years, but in the meantime, we'll need a leader. Someone to guide us, rally us. Give us courage to turn from the old ways and toward something new. Something fair." He folded his wings. "That should be you."

Twice now, angels had bowed to him. Twice now, they'd given him that acknowledgment and permission. And yeah, with the Helfire in his veins, he could lead. Could blast any holdout Archangel or faction into submission.

But . . .

His phone buzzed, and he pulled it from his pocket to glance down.

Bryce Gives Me Magical Orgasms, Literally had messaged him.

Where are you?? I'm having separation anxiety! Get back here!!!

Another buzz, and she added, *After you do whatever you need to, I mean. Like, I'm supportive of you taking space for yourself and doing what has to be done.*

Another buzz.

But also get back here right now.

Hunt choked on his laugh. He had everything he needed. Everything he'd ever want.

Don't get your panties in a twist, Quinlan, he answered. *I'll be back soon.*

Then he added, *Actually, do me a favor and take your panties off altogether.*

He didn't wait for her response as he slid his phone into his back pocket and grinned at Isaiah.

His friend's eyebrows were high, no doubt surprised that he'd answered texts instead of replying to such a serious suggestion.

But Hunt had his answer. He'd had it for some time now.

He clapped Isaiah on the shoulder and said, "The angels already have a leader to steer them through this, Isaiah."

"Celestina—"

"Not Celestina." He squeezed his friend's shoulder once, then stepped back, wings flapping, readying to carry him to his wife, his mate, his best friend. To the future that awaited them. "You."

"Me?" Isaiah said, choking. "Athalar—"

Hunt lifted a few feet off the ground, hovering a beat as the autumn breeze ruffled his wings, his hair, singing of the newness of the world to come. "Lead the angels, Isaiah. I'm here if you need me."

"*Hunt.*"

But Hunt shot into the skies, headed for Bryce and whatever tomorrow might bring.

Bryce's soul was hers. It had always been hers, she supposed, but it had been . . . on loan.

Now that it was fully hers again, there was a whole new world to explore without the Asteri lurking about. A whole new afterlife, when she and Hunt were ready.

But not for a long, long time. Not while they still had so much to sort out.

There was one task she had to do immediately, though. How Isaiah managed to commandeer a helicopter to fly to Nena so quickly, Bryce had no idea. But maybe it had something to do with Celestina's pull, even from Ephraim's keep. Or maybe it was more about Celestina wanting to impress Hypaxia, who was now apparently the Head of the House of Flame and Shadow. And who didn't seem opposed to the idea of speaking to Celestina again, if the looks they'd been sneaking each other's way were any indication.

The Ocean Queen and her fleet had brought the witch over here—Hypaxia had intercepted the monarch on her way to beat the shit out of the Asteri for kidnapping Lidia's two sons. The Ocean Queen might be a piece of work, but she stood by her own. And when two children had been kidnapped from her care, she'd shown up prepared to wash the entire city away in their defense.

She and her commanders remained in the Eternal City, the threat of the tsunami she held leashed around the perimeter keeping any Asteri loyalists at bay. At least the ruler seemed too busy with the new world to deal with her petty bullshit with Tharion. For now.

It *was* a new world. In almost every sense.

Declan was already working with a team on the math of how long Midgard could run on what remained of the firstlight before it went dark, without new firstlight being fed into the power grid. Before they had to pull out the candles and watch their mobile phones slowly die. Not that they'd have any service once the grids failed.

They'd all be back to Avallen-style living. Too bad Morven wasn't around to enjoy it.

But they'd have to figure it out soon. Whether they wanted to restore the firstlight power system or try to find an alternate method. Whether they'd require people to hand over their power, or perhaps tax the uber-powerful. Require Archangels, who had power in spades, to donate some of their power to the grid. The powerful, serving the weak.

Or some shit like that. Honestly, Bryce planned to leave it to smarter minds than hers to sort out. Though she had little hope that she wouldn't have to step in to kick some ass before all was said and done. For right now . . . There was a capital city in chaos. A world turned upside down. Yet she set her sights northward.

Bryce found Nesta in the same room the female had been in before. With Ember and Randall and a handsome, vaguely familiar winged male beside them, who smelled like Nesta's mate. Sitting around a table and talking over tea and chocolate cake.

Chocolate cake, for fuck's sake.

Nesta was instantly on her feet, a long dagger in her hand. The male beside her also reached for a concealed weapon, swift as a thought.

But Bryce only gazed at her parents. Happy and at home with the Fae.

Her mom stared back at her like she'd seen a ghost. The teacup she was holding began rattling against its saucer.

Hunt spared Ember from guessing at what had passed by saying, "The Asteri are gone. Midgard is free."

A tear fell from Ember's eye. Bryce didn't think twice before stepping into that world and wrapping her arms around her mother. Holding her tight.

Ember clasped Bryce's face in her hands. "I am so proud to be your mother."

Bryce beamed, her own eyes stinging with tears, and Randall leaned in to press a kiss to her head. "You did good, kid."

Bryce threw her arms around her dad and hugged him, too. Hugged the human warrior who had served in the Asteri's armies, shredded apart his soul for them, until her mom had put him back together.

Nesta and her mate tensed, and Bryce knew Hunt had stepped into their world.

He peered around the room. Glanced at the city sparkling far below, a ribbon of river winding through it. They had to be high up on a mountain for this kind of view.

Nesta's mate said, "You have one minute before Rhys gets here and explodes."

"Oh, Rhys will be fine, Cassian," Ember said—in the Fae's language.

At Bryce's shocked face, Randall said in the same language, "It got too hard to mime everything. They gave us that bean-thing they offered you."

But Bryce shook her head. "Rhysand will be *fine*? The guy who brings darkness incarnate—"

"He and Randall bonded about being overprotective dads," Ember said. "So now Rhys knows *exactly* the sort of shit you like to pull, which apparently you pulled here, too . . ."

Bryce glanced to Nesta, who was watching warily. So Bryce reached into her jacket and pulled out the Mask. "Here. As promised."

Everyone fell silent.

And then Bryce drew Truth-Teller, and Cassian looked like he'd jump between her and Nesta. Hunt set his feet into a fighting stance in response, but Bryce just said, "Alphaholes," and laid the dagger on the table between their tea set and treats.

"You brought them back." Nesta's voice was quiet.

"Did you think I wouldn't?"

"I don't know what I thought," Nesta said, but smiled slightly.

"Poor Nesta's been in the doghouse since you took their weapons and dumped us here," Ember explained. "I tried telling Rhysand and Azriel how there's no stopping you when you've got your mind set on something, and I think Feyre—Rhysand's mate—believed me, but . . ." Ember glanced at Nesta and winced. "I apologize *again* for my daughter's behavior."

"I made the choice to give her the Mask," Nesta reminded Ember. To Bryce, she added wryly, "Your mother somehow doesn't believe that I did so willingly."

Bryce rolled her eyes at her mother. "Great. Thanks for that." She gestured to the portal shimmering behind them. "Shall we?"

Ember smiled softly. "They're truly gone, then."

"Gone, and never to be heard from again," Bryce said, her heart lifting with the words.

Ember's eyes gleamed with tears, but she turned, taking Nesta's hands and clenching them tightly in her own. "Despite the fact that my daughter lied and schemed and basically betrayed us . . . ," she started.

"Tell us how you really feel, Mom," Bryce muttered, earning an amused sidelong glance from Nesta.

But Ember continued, looking only at Nesta, "I am glad of one thing: that I was able to meet you."

Nesta's lips pressed into a thin line, and she glanced down at their joined hands.

Bryce cut in, if only to spare Nesta from her mom's increasingly weepy-looking expression, "Next time I take on intergalactic evil, I'll try to accommodate your bonding schedule."

Ember finally looked over at Bryce, glaring. "You and I are going to have *words* when we get home, Bryce Adelaide Quinlan. Leaving Cooper behind like that—"

"I know," Bryce said. She had a *lot* to answer for on that front. And apologizing to do.

"Your mother loves you," Nesta said quietly, reading the exasperation on Bryce's face. "Don't for one second take that for granted."

Bryce could only incline her head to Nesta. "I'm lucky," she admitted. "I've always been lucky to have her as a mom."

Ember really looked like she might cry now, especially as she turned back to Nesta and said, "This time with you was a gift, Nesta. It truly was."

With that, she pulled Nesta to her in a tight embrace, and Bryce could have sworn something like pain and longing crossed Nesta's expression. Like she hadn't experienced a mom-hug for a long, long time.

So Bryce gave the female some privacy to enjoy every second of that motherly embrace and turned to where Randall and Cassian stood behind them. The males had clasped arms warmly. "Thanks, friend," Randall was saying to the warrior. "For everything."

Cassian grinned, and, well, Bryce could see why Nesta might be into a male who looked like that. "Maybe we'll meet again one day, under less . . . strange circumstances."

"I hope so," Randall said, and as he passed by where Ember and Nesta were still hugging, he clapped the latter on the shoulder with fatherly affection.

Bryce's heart swelled to the point of pain as Randall approached Hunt and hugged him, too. Hunt returned the embrace, thumping her father on the back before they separated to pass through the portal together.

Ember at last pulled away from Nesta. But she gently put a hand to the female's cheek and whispered, "You'll find your way," before walking toward the portal.

Bryce could have sworn there were tears in Nesta's eyes as her mother stepped back into Midgard.

But those tears were gone when Nesta met Bryce's stare. And Cassian, like any good mate, sensed when he wasn't wanted, and walked over to the fireplace to pretend to read some sort of old-looking manuscript. Bryce knew that, *also* like any good mate, if she made one wrong move, he'd rip her to shreds. Which was precisely why Hunt had come back into the room, and was watching Nesta carefully.

"Alphaholes," Nesta echoed, eyes gleaming with amusement.

Bryce chuckled and drew the Starsword. Again, Cassian tensed, but Bryce just offered the blade to Nesta. The female took it, blinking.

"You said you had an eight-pointed star tattooed on you," Bryce explained. "And you found the chamber with the eight-pointed star in the Prison, too."

Nesta lifted her head. "So?"

"So I want you to take the Starsword." Bryce held the blade between them. "Gwydion—whatever you call it here. The age of the Starborn is over on Midgard. It ends with me."

"I don't understand."

But Bryce began backing toward the portal, taking Hunt's hand, and smiled again at the female, at her mate, at their world, as the Northern Rift began to close. "I think that eight-pointed star was tattooed on you for a reason. Take that sword and go figure out why."

101

The *Depth Charger* had anchored offshore, since the nearest port to the Eternal City was too shallow to accommodate the city-ship. Standing beside Ruhn, Lidia stared at her sons as they waited on the concrete pier while the transport pod surfaced, water sloshing off its glass dome top.

Revealing Renki and Davit, both waving wildly at the two boys standing beside Lidia.

At her sons, who were smiling at their dads, Brann enthusiastically waving back, Ace giving a smaller—but no less earnest—wave as well.

Ruhn placed a gentle hand on Lidia's back, and she leaned into the reassuring, loving touch. Her mate. Yes, she knew it without a doubt.

The glass top of the pod opened, and then Renki and Davit leapt gracefully onto the pier, Brann and Ace running for them—

It was pure love and joy, the embraces shared between the boys and their fathers. Renki had tears of relief running down his face, and Davit was holding both boys to him as if he'd never let them go again.

But Davit did let go. He crossed to Lidia in two strides and wrapped his arms around her, too. "Thank you," the male said, voice choked with tears. "Thank you." Renki was there the moment Davit pulled back, hugging her as tightly.

Lidia found herself smiling, even as her heart was again aching, and leaned away to survey her sons.

They were both considering her, Brann frowning deeply, Ace more unreadable. It was the former who said, "So this is goodbye?"

Lidia glanced to Renki and Davit, who both nodded. They'd spoken on the phone yesterday to coordinate this reunion—and what lay ahead. "Until things settle down a bit up here," Lidia said. "Above the surface, I mean."

Because even in the day since the Asteri had been vanquished, shit was already hitting the fan. The drainage of the firstlight grid was going to be a huge problem. But the Ocean Queen had fueled all her city-ships and their various pods without firstlight. With her own power. Maybe the ruler had some insight into how they might adapt their tech to move beyond consuming firstlight.

The Ocean Queen, of course, hadn't been happy when Lidia had sent a messenger to the *Depth Charger*. Lidia had kept her note short and efficient:

I trust that my services are no longer required and henceforth resign from your employ.

With gratitude for your compassion,
Lidia Cervos

The Ocean Queen had dispatched her reply—again on a briny piece of kelp—an hour later.

I have bigger issues to consider than your loyalty, Lidia Cervos. I accept your resignation, but do not fool yourself into thinking that this is the last we shall cross paths. For now, you may live your life Above.

It was the best Lidia could hope for.

Now, Lidia glanced between her sons and added, "But I'd like to see you both again. If that's okay with you."

Brann nodded, and she had no words in her head as he walked up to her and threw his arms around her.

Her son's scent, his warmth and nearness, threatened to bring her to her knees. But she managed to stay standing, knowing

Ruhn was beside her, would always be there, supporting her, as Brann pulled back, grinning.

"You're a badass," Brann said, and added, "Mom."

Even as her heart glowed with joy at the word, Lidia dared glance over his shoulder to find that Renki and Davit were grinning as broadly as Brann. Happy for her—for all of them. Her boys had a beautiful family, and perhaps, if everyone was all right with it, it was one she could find a place in. Find joy in.

Brann leaned in, pressing a kiss to Lidia's cheek that she knew she'd cherish for the rest of her existence. Then he walked over to Ruhn, and Lidia could only blink as Brann threw his arms around Ruhn, too, hugging him tight. "Thanks," Brann said. "For what you were gonna do. To save us—and our mom."

Ruhn clapped Brann on the back, and Lidia's chest filled with so much brightness she could barely contain it all. "No worries," Ruhn said. "All in a day's work for us Aux grunts."

Brann grinned, then walked back to his parents, hugging Renki again.

Lidia glanced to Ace, who was watching her warily. Knowing he wouldn't rush into her arms as Brann had, Lidia walked up to him. Slowly. Giving him time to decide what he wanted to do.

Ace held his ground, but his eyes weren't cold as he said, "Thanks for coming for us." His mouth quirked to the side. "Take care of yourself."

"I've got Ruhn watching my back," Lidia said, glancing to Ruhn. "I'll be fine."

"He *shot* you," Ace said, frowning at Ruhn.

"I shouldn't have told you that," Ruhn muttered.

Lidia smirked, but faced Ace again. "He'll pay for it, don't worry."

Ace didn't look so sure, staring Ruhn down for a moment. But when he began walking toward his dads, he stumbled, as if . . .

Lidia glared at Ruhn, who whistled innocently at the sky. Fine—let him keep his mind-speaking secrets.

Ruhn slid a hand around her waist as the boys and their parents boarded the pod. Davit slid into the pilot's seat, flicking on switches, and Brann claimed the seat beside him. Renki and Ace took the back seats, and as the pod whirred to life, they all looked at her.

Lidia offered them a small, hopeful smile. Her fingers found Ruhn's, and she gripped his hand tightly. Ruhn didn't let go.

Her sons were alive, and free, and in her life again, and it was more than she'd ever hoped for.

So the future, whatever it held . . . she'd cherish every moment of it.

Bryce was thoroughly sick of Nena's endless chill when she opened the Northern Rift again. Not to the home world of the Fae, but to Hel.

Only blackness awaited the army marching through. The beasts and flying things and the princes, who went one by one, Thanatos giving her a look that said she might have destroyed the Asteri but he was still mad about his dog, until only Apollion and Aidas stood before her in the ice and snow.

They did not seem to require coats or hats or gloves. They didn't even shiver.

Apollion said to Hunt, "Hel has no hold on you, and you have no obligation to us."

"Uh, thank you?" Hunt said. "Likewise."

Apollion threw him a half smile, then glanced to Bryce. "You did better than expected."

Bryce snapped her fingers, the sound muffled by her gloves. "*That* is what I want on my new business cards. *Bryce Quinlan: Better than Expected.*"

Apollion just smirked and walked toward the dark.

"Hey," Bryce called after the Prince of the Pit.

Apollion paused, raising a brow at her.

Bryce threw him a grin and said, "Thanks for not giving up on Midgard."

She could have sworn a kernel of compassion warmed Apollion's face before he glanced to Aidas and said, "I shall be happy to lay the matter to rest. And to see my brother at peace."

With that, he strode through the Rift.

Bryce's teeth were chattering now, but she faced Aidas. "Will we see you again?"

Aidas smiled wickedly. "Do you wish to?"

"No," Bryce said, and meant it. "Grateful as we are . . . I think we have different definitions for the word *pet*."

Aidas smiled fully this time. "Then I shall give you my gratitude, Bryce Quinlan. And bid you farewell."

"I'll be forever grateful," Bryce said to the Prince of the Chasm, "for your kindness that day at the Oracle."

His smile turned gentler. "Theia would be proud of you."

"And of you," Bryce said, the only gift she could offer to a Prince of Hel. She refrained from saying that Theia's pride meant shit to her, though. "I think you might get to hear it from her lips one day."

Aidas angled his head. Bryce had told all of them about what Jesiba had claimed. What she'd seen in that land of glowing light. "You think a Prince of Hel shall be allowed in?"

Bryce walked up to him and kissed his cheek. Icy skin met her lips. "I think a good male, regardless of where he is from, will always be allowed in."

Aidas's eyes glowed bright blue—with gratitude or longing or love, she didn't know. But the prince only nodded to her, then to Hunt, and walked through the Northern Rift into the dark.

Apollion was waiting just inside, and he took up a place beside his brother. Bryce's hand slid into Hunt's, and she lifted her other hand in farewell.

To her surprise, both princes returned the gesture.

With a ripple of thought and power, she closed the Rift. Locked it securely, leaving no cracks to slip through. Though the Asteri were gone, all their crystal Gates throughout Midgard remained intact. But for now, at least *this* particular Gate was shut completely. At long last.

"Looks like your demon-hunting days might be over," she said to Hunt.

Her mate grinned down at her, and kissed her gently, and even the frigid winds of Nena seemed to warm around them. "Guess I should file for unemployment."

Tharion Ketos stood on the outskirts of the Meat Market, looking for his wife.

Thanks to the water sprites in her employ, the Viper Queen had apparently been able to put out the blazing main building before the fire had spread, leaving the bulk of the Meat Market's interconnected warehouses intact.

Indeed, it seemed as if it was business as usual—albeit already adjusted to a new world. From the back of a truck, shady-looking grunts unloaded cannisters glowing with firstlight. Already stocking up on a product that would soon be in high demand.

Tharion didn't really know why he'd come here, when Sendes had informed him that the Ocean Queen had forgiven his disobedience. In fact, she'd made him a perfectly good offer to be a commander in her forces and work aboard the *Depth Charger*, but he'd found himself saying he had something to do first.

And then made his way back here.

The world was in upheaval. The Asteri were gone, but there was an Imperial Senate to contend with, and Archangels, and the various House Heads, and . . . maybe he should have stayed on that ship.

He didn't know why he had expected peace and comfort. Why he'd thought everyone would be happy and just . . . chill. But there were plenty of greedy fucks out there in the world, who were happy to use the shake-up to grab for power.

And he knew that the fuck who ruled the Meat Market was probably one of them. He'd have to contend with her at some point, probably someday soon.

But right now he needed to find his wife. Just to make sure she was okay. Then he could be on his way. Go to the *Depth Charger*. Or do something else, he didn't know. He figured Ogenas would guide him at some point. Maybe help him figure out his mess of a life.

Tharion slipped on the hood of his sweatshirt, checking that the gun concealed at his side was secure and ready, and walked into the warren of the Meat Market. To whatever Urd had in store for him.

He only made it one block before a female voice said from the shadows, "You have to be ten kinds of dumb to go back in there."

He halted, peering into the alley from which the voice had spoken. Two crimson eyes smoldered in the darkness.

Tharion inclined his head. "Hello, Ariadne."

102

Bryce stood in the foyer of the Autumn King's villa, surveying the field of flashing cameras, the haughty Fae nobility, and the confused-looking guards glancing between her and the crowd.

For the occasion, she'd chosen a pink dress that she knew drove Hunt to distraction. It had been either that or leggings and a T-shirt, and given that she wanted to avoid anything taking away from what she was actually doing, she'd opted for formal.

Of course, settling on the pink dress had been an ordeal in itself. There was now a giant heap of clothing in her bedroom for her to put away when she got home, which was incentive enough to draw this out for as long as possible.

But she took one look at Sathia and Flynn's sneering parents, the Lord and Lady Hawthorne having recently returned from Avallen, and decided to Hel with waiting. To Hel with all the other Fae nobility who had gathered at her invitation this morning.

She'd set foot in the city late last night, had gone right to the ruins of Asphodel Meadows, and called for this meeting the next day.

She would have done it last night, but Hunt had told her to take the time to sort out what she wanted to say. To let Marc get the paperwork ready.

The leopard shifter and Declan now stood beside the desk that had been hauled into the foyer, Ruhn and Flynn with them.

She glanced to Hunt, and he nodded subtly. It was time.

So Bryce stepped up to the desk and said to the cameras, to the Fae aristocrats, "I'll make this short and sweet, for all the busy nobles here who have to get back to champagne lunches and spa treatments."

Silence, and a frantic clicking of cameras. The videographers pressed in closer, angling their mics to pick up her every breath. One of the camera guys—a draki male—was smirking.

But Bryce kept her gaze on the cameras, on the world listening. "This is my first and only decree as the Fae Queen of Valbara and Avallen: the royal houses are ended."

She ignored the gasps and protests, and tapped the paperwork on the desk. "I've had the documents drawn up. Allow me to be perfectly clear: I am not abdicating either throne. I am no longer queen, but with this document, *no one* shall ever wear the crown again. The Fae monarchy is abolished. Forever."

From the corner of her eye, she could see Hunt grinning broadly. She wished her mom was here, but they'd decided that Ember Quinlan's presence might cause too much speculation that her human mother had pushed her to do this.

"I am donating all the Autumn King's residences in this city," Bryce said, gesturing to the elegant space around them, "to house those displaced by the attack on Asphodel Meadows. This villa in particular will be used to house children orphaned by the massacre."

One of the Fae nobles choked.

"As for the royal properties elsewhere—in Valbara and on Avallen—they will be sold to anyone who can stomach their tacky-ass decor, and the profits will go toward rebuilding Asphodel Meadows."

Bryce picked up the golden fountain pen she'd swiped from the Autumn King's study after chucking all his prisms into the trash. She planned to dismantle the orrery and sell it for scrap metal. She knew enough about how light traveled and formed—how it could break apart and come back together. She never wanted to learn another thing about light again, even her own.

"The Asteri are gone," Bryce said to the listening world, "and the Fae kingdoms with them. In their place, we will build a government built on equality and fairness. This document grants me the right to represent the Fae in the building of such a government. And nothing more."

"Traitor," hissed a Fae noble who Bryce could have sworn had sneered at her once in a restaurant, years ago.

Bryce hummed to herself, flipping the Autumn King's beloved pen between her fingers. "You guys shouldn't have granted your royals such absolute power in your quest to keep everyone else down in the dirt." She leaned over the documents. "Maybe then you could have stopped me from doing this."

The golden pen touched paper, ink blooming on the parchment.

"But you're in the mud with the rest of us now," Bryce said to the Fae as she signed her name. "Better get used to the smell."

Thus, with the stroke of the Autumn King's golden pen, the royal bloodlines of the Fae were wiped from existence.

Ruhn flicked on the lights in the apartment—for however long the place would even have power. "Bryce is going to throw a fit, but I swear it was the only one available furnished on short notice," he said to Lidia as they stepped inside the home literally a floor below Bryce's.

Lidia smiled, though, surveying the apartment that was the mirror image of Bryce's layout save for the furniture. She approached the white, gleaming kitchen. "It's lovely—really. I'll get the money wired to your account."

"Nah," Ruhn said. "Consider it a thank-you present. For bailing me out of the dungeons."

Lidia turned from the kitchen, brows high. "I think we're even by now. After . . . everything." After that shit with Pollux, which he knew would haunt his dreams for a long fucking time.

But there would be joy to light the dark memories. When he'd gone with her to return the boys to their parents, Ruhn had been content to watch the happy reunion, especially as Lidia was hugged with equal welcome and love by the boys' parents. As the boys had, in their own ways, made it clear that Lidia would be welcome in their lives.

Brann, he had no doubt, would be the easier one. But Ace . . .

Ruhn smiled to himself at the memory of how Ace had looked over at Ruhn before leaving, his dark eyes knowing. Sharp. As if to say, *Take care of my mom.*

Ruhn had answered into the kid's mind, *She can take care of herself, but I will.*

Ace's eyes had widened in shock, and he'd stumbled a step, but—with an assessing, impressed glance at Ruhn—had continued to the transport pod.

Ruhn and Lidia had spent *one* night in his shithole house, aching to fuck each other within an inch of their lives but all too conscious of his friends a thin wall away, before he'd called up a realtor and asked about finding an apartment. Immediately. With a few specific requests.

"The bedroom over there's got two beds in it," he said, pointing across the great room. "For your boys."

Her eyes were lined with silver as she faced the guest bedroom.

That had been Ruhn's main demand to the realtor: find an apartment with a guest room that had two beds. "They can visit whenever they—and you—want."

Her smile was so soft and hopeful that his heart ached. But she walked to the couch in front of the TV and sat down, as if testing it out. Testing out this house, this life.

"I think their dads will want to keep them close for a while after what happened," Lidia said, "but yes . . . I would love for them to be here sometimes."

Ruhn sank beside her on the couch. "They're going to raise Hel when they're older."

"I'm fine with that, so long as it's not literally." Lidia sighed. "I've had enough of demons for a while, however friendly."

Ruhn chuckled. "Me too."

For a few minutes, they sat in companionable silence, the apartment—*their* apartment—settling in around them.

"I can't believe we're alive," Lidia said at last.

"I can't believe the Asteri are gone."

The past few days had been such a whirlwind that he hadn't really processed all that had happened. Or the current state of the world.

Lidia said carefully, "Your sister and Athalar's intentions are good, but it's going to take a lot more than one meeting with a bunch of world leaders to sort out an entirely new system of government. Or dismantle slavery."

"I know. Bryce knows."

"Are you . . . What do you plan to do?"

It was a loaded question, but Ruhn answered, "I'll help her. I'll head up the Aux with Holstrom, I guess. Since the Fae throne's gone as of this morning." It had been a wonder to behold—Bryce standing in front of the crowd of cameras and nobles, ending the monarchies with a stroke of a pen. Their father's favorite pen, no less.

Ruhn had never been so proud to be Bryce's brother.

He smiled slightly. "The Oracle was right in a lot of ways, I guess." Lidia lifted a brow. "It wasn't just that the crown would go to Bryce, but that she'd end it. The Danaan royal line is finished."

Lidia clicked her tongue. "You're not dead or childless, after all."

"Not yet," Ruhn said, laughing again. All that time spent dreading the prophecy, worrying over his fate . . .

Lidia looked at him, in that way that no one else on Midgard did—like she saw *him*. "Are you prepared to not be a prince anymore, though? To be . . . normal?"

"I think so," he said, nudging her knee with his own. "Are you?"

"I have no idea. I don't even know what normal is," Lidia admitted.

Ruhn took her hand, linking their fingers. "How about we figure it out together, then?"

"How to be normal?"

"How to live a normal life. The normal, adult apartment's a good start. For both of us." No more veritable frat house living.

But wariness flooded her eyes. "My life is complicated."

"Whoever said normal isn't complicated?" he countered. "All I know is that whatever tomorrow or next year or the next millennium has in store for this world, I want to face it at your side."

Her expression softened. She leaned closer, brushing a strand of his hair back with her free hand.

They weren't the Hind and a Crown Prince of the Fae. Weren't Day and Night. Right then, there, they were simply Lidia and Ruhn. He wouldn't have it any other way.

But Ruhn got to his feet and walked to the kitchen, opening the fridge. The other request he'd made of the realtor: stock the fridge with one thing and one thing only.

Maybe the veritable frat house wasn't entirely gone. He walked back to the couch and handed Lidia a beer.

"As promised, Day," he said, twisting off the cap on his bottle. "One beer."

She looked at the bottle, pure delight shining on her face. She twisted the cap off her own beverage, but got to her feet and clinked her bottle against his before drinking. "To a normal life, Ruhn."

Ruhn leaned in to kiss her, and Lidia met him halfway. And the love and joy in him glowed brighter than starlight as he said against her mouth, "To a normal life, Lidia."

It would take the wolves of the Den a few days to come back from where they'd been lying low. But they *were* coming back.

Ithan didn't know if it was Amelie's order or if Perry had asked them, but everyone was returning. Perhaps just to see how shitty he'd be at leading them as Prime.

Or to assess the dynamic without the Fendyrs.

Or to get their stuff before the firstlight power grid failed and chaos reigned.

Ithan stood in the command center of the Aux headquarters,

Flynn and Dec across from him, the former eyeing Perry with an interest Ithan didn't entirely appreciate.

Perry was blushing, and Ithan didn't appreciate that, either.

But Ruhn and Lidia walked in before Ithan could say anything stupid, and the former Fae Prince said, "So, first things first: I think it sucks that we save the world and still have to be back at work two days later."

Perry laughed, and . . . okay, maybe Ithan liked the sound.

But Lidia said, grave and yet serene, "I'm expecting a report tonight regarding the status of the firstlight power grid and how we might stop it from failing. Lunathion's engineers have been meeting with the Ocean Queen to learn how she powers her ships without it and will present those findings to us. But in the meantime, we need to start assessing allies inside the city and out of it. Celestina's still dealing with Ephraim, trying to garner his support, but the other Archangels are going to start jockeying for power. If we don't want to fall back into the old ways, we need a solid plan."

"Shouldn't Athalar be here for this?" Flynn said.

"He's on his way," Ruhn said. "With Bryce. But they told us to start without them."

Dec and Flynn made kissing noises at each other, and Ithan laughed, Perry joining him.

Maybe it wouldn't be so bad. Not the being Prime part, that part he didn't particularly like, but this new future. It'd probably be batshit crazy for a while, and they'd have no shortage of enemies, but . . .

They'd also have each other. A pack. Of all Houses.

Which was why they were here. No more splintered Aux, divided among Houses and species. They'd lead by example. Starting today.

So Ithan said to Lidia and Ruhn, to Flynn and Dec and Perry, "Whatever these assholes want to throw at us, we'll throw right back at them."

"Spoken like a true sunball captain," Dec teased.

Ithan said, "Yeah." He let the word settle, and for a moment he felt it—that urge to set foot on the field, to grip that ball in his hands.

A glimmer, and it was gone, but . . . after years of nothing, he felt it. Wanted it. So Ithan grinned and added, "I am."

"That was Hypaxia on the phone," Bryce said in the sunny, open atrium of the elegant town house that would soon be the new Griffin Antiquities.

Hunt, unpacking a statue of Thurr from a crate, asked over a winged shoulder, "What'd she say?"

"That if she can find a way to stabilize the antidote, we could have it rolling out to everyone by the Spring Equinox. That is, if we still have power by then. She wants more of your lightning, by the way. She's already out of this batch of antidotes."

Bryce and Hunt had both gotten doses. The surge of magic that had resulted had been intense enough that apparently a whole new island had risen in Avallen—as if the island was now bound to her very soul. As if she and Midgard were, as Jesiba had claimed, bound together, Archesian amulet or no.

And thanks to Hunt, there had been a day straight of thunderstorms. Of course, he was fined by the city for illegal and improper weather manipulation, but *He blew his magical load* didn't really seem to hold sway when Bryce tried to explain it to the authorities.

The new power in their veins, as if returned from what the Asteri had taken, required some getting used to. And new training. Bryce could teleport in one jump between the city and her parents' house now. Which was . . . good and bad.

Good, because she could see Cooper whenever she wanted, and steal him away to the city for a hint of *real* fun. Bad, because her parents now expected her and Hunt for weekly dinners. Bryce had negotiated it down to monthly, but she knew Ember would be making a full-court press for at *least* once every two weeks.

But all of it depended on what they did next—if the firstlight power grid could hold. If it'd collapse. If they'd all have to start over again, squatting over fires in the darkness. But she—they—would proceed as usual. Let the geniuses and scientists find a way to save them this time.

"Well," Hunt said, "if Hypaxia needs someone to go beat the shit out of the Redners, I'm game. They're creeps." The former witch-queen had reluctantly partnered with Redner Industries, hoping to mass-produce the antidote.

"Scary Asshole, Part Two?"

"Happily." He turned from the crate to where Bryce was shelving books on the towering built-in unit behind her desk.

The books. The Parthos collection. No longer in darkness and hiding, but here, in the daylight, for anyone to come see. She couldn't bear to keep them locked away.

Thankfully, she'd found three new employees to help her manage the unwieldy collection. Sasa, Rithi, and Malana currently perched on a takeout container, watching an episode of *Veiled Love* on Hunt's phone where he'd propped it up against his water bottle.

They'd never replace Lehabah, but it filled something in her heart to see them. To hear Syrinx, snoring beneath her new desk, in the little nest of blankets he'd made down there. Like something had finally slid into place. Like she was exactly where she was meant to be.

"So," Hunt said, going back to unloading all the crates Hypaxia had sent over from the House of Flame and Shadow. Apparently, Jesiba had been anticipating this transfer of ownership—she'd made Ithan pack most of the artifacts up.

Bryce thought Jesiba would appreciate the Godslayer Rifle now mounted behind Bryce's desk. As much a warning to anyone who might try to steal the books as in honor of the priestess who'd guarded them for so long. That is, if the fire sprites didn't roast any would-be thief.

She didn't know where Irithys had gone, and she still wished to talk to the queen, to tell her about Lehabah, but from what Sasa had said, it sounded as if the Sprite Queen was now traveling the world, intent on freeing every last one of her people. Especially those who might be held by owners averse to the new worldwide ban on slavery.

"So . . . what?" Bryce asked Hunt, sliding a tome onto the shelf.

"So . . . are you gonna talk about the whole no-more-Fae-monarchy thing?"

"What's there to talk about?" Bryce said. "I sent out my decree. It's over. No longer my problem."

"Others might not see it that way."

"That's why, Athalar . . . ," she began, shelving another book that tried to wriggle out of her hands. She smacked it back over and shoved it onto the shelf. "That's why we're going to establish a Fae democracy. A senate, and all that crap. So the Fae can go complain to *them* about their problems."

"A senate and all that crap, huh?" Hunt said. "Sounds real official."

She turned toward him. "And what about you? How come you get to walk away from the 33rd and the angel stuff, but somehow I can't bail on the Fae drama?"

"I didn't make magic islands come flying out of the ocean and resurrect a whole territory."

"Well, Avallen's different," she sniffed.

"You just don't want to lose your new vacation home," he teased, crossing the room toward her. She let him crowd her against the bookshelf, loving his size and strength and the wall of power that was pure Hunt.

"Maybe I don't," she said, not backing down an inch. "But until the Fae can show me that they'll share Avallen with everyone, it's mine." She'd debated sending the Parthos books there, to the Avallen Archives, but she wanted them close. Wanted them accessible to everyone, not locked away on a remote island. "Or, at least, it's my responsibility," she amended.

"Yeah, well, Baxian's dying to get off the island and back into civilization, so maybe look into hiring a caretaker." Fury and June had already returned to Crescent City. There was only so much medieval living her friends could take, apparently. But Baxian had stuck it out.

She winced. The angel had been keeping the Fae in line since she and Hunt had left Avallen in his hands, taking good care of any and all refugees who made it there. Danika would have been proud. Bryce had made sure to tell the Helhound that—and about seeing his mate in the afterworld. He'd been silent enough during that call that she knew he was crying, but all he had said to Bryce was "Thank you."

"Okay, okay," Bryce said to Hunt. "Set up a democracy, find a new babysitter for Avallen, play Scary Asshole with you . . . Anything else for me to do? In addition to starting my new business?" She gestured to the soon-to-be-open gallery.

"How about hiring a sexy assistant?"

She didn't miss the heat in his eyes. The spark.

She bit her lip. "Sexy assistant, huh? You cool with going from the Umbra Mortis to fetching my coffee?"

"If it comes with the perk of kinky office sex, I'm cool with anything," Hunt growled, nipping at her ear.

"Oh, the position *definitely* comes with kinky office sex," she purred.

She felt the hardness of him push into her hip before he said, low and wicked, "Sprites—go find somewhere else to be for a while."

They grumbled, but zoomed out to the stairs, all blushing a bright pink. Syrinx dashed after them, yelping.

Bryce didn't care where they went. Not as Hunt pressed his cock against her center, and she writhed. "Get on the desk," he said, voice like gravel.

Her blood thrummed through her. "We're already late for our meeting with Ruhn and the others at the Aux."

"They can deal." His voice was pure, unrelenting sex. Her knees wobbled.

But Bryce had only taken one step toward the desk when her phone rang. Baxian.

"Call back later," Hunt said, coming to stand behind her. Sliding his hands up her thighs, bunching her skirt as he went. Yes—*fuck* yes.

Hunt's phone rang. Baxian again.

"Maybe we should . . . answer," Bryce said, though she almost didn't, considering that Hunt had a fistful of her skirt in one hand and her bare ass palmed in his other—

Hunt groaned and reached for his phone, answering with a snapped *"What."*

With her Fae ears, Bryce could hear perfectly clearly as Baxian asked, "Where's your mate?"

It was the low note of panic and urgency that had Hunt putting him on speakerphone and saying, "We're both here."

Baxian let out a shuddering breath, and Bryce's arousal vanished, cold dread filling her gut. If something had happened already, an attack on Avallen—

"I . . ." Baxian choked on the word. "There are about two dozen of them."

Bryce swapped a confused glance with Hunt and asked, "Them?"

Baxian let out a laugh that verged on hysteria. "I swear, it's like they sprang out of the earth, like they were hibernating or hiding there, I don't fucking know—"

"Baxian," Bryce said, heart thundering. *"What is it?"*

"Flying horses. Horses with *wings*."

Bryce blinked slowly. "Horses . . . with wings."

"Yes," Baxian said, his voice rising. "They're flying around and trampling everything and eating all the crops and I think you might need to come here because they seem to be the sort of thing that might belong to a Super Magical Fancy Starborn Princess . . ."

Bryce looked at Hunt, pure wonder flooding her.

"There are flying horses in Avallen," Hunt said, eyes as wide as her own, pure joy sparking there.

"In Silene's account," Bryce breathed, "she talked about her mother having flying horses. How some came here . . . and there were depictions of them in the Cave of Princes and Morven's castle. I thought they'd all been killed, but maybe . . ." Bryce shook her head. "Is it possible?" Had Helena somehow secretly kept them alive, suspended, waiting until it was safe again?

She didn't care. Not right now. "There are flying horses in Avallen," Bryce repeated to Hunt. "There are *pegasuses* in Avallen."

"Please come help me," Baxian said miserably.

"We'll be there by dawn," Bryce said, and hung up for Hunt. She met her mate's blazingly bright eyes. No more shadows, no more halo, no more pain. Never again. "Rain check on the desk sex?"

"For Jelly Jubilee in the flesh?" Hunt grinned. "Anything."

Bryce threw her arms around his neck, kissing him thoroughly, then dashed for the door.

There was an angel in her office, and a pegasus herd on Avallen. And the Asteri were gone and the dead were free . . . and though she knew there was work to do to heal Midgard, the world was out there. *Life* was out there.

So Bryce and Hunt ran out to live it.

Together.

ACKNOWLEDGMENTS

Even after so many books, I still wake up every day thankful for the incredible people that I have the honor of knowing and working with, and, with that in mind, my love and deepest gratitude go out to:

The magnificent global team at Bloomsbury: Noa Wheeler (whose editorial genius is unparalleled!), Nigel Newton, Kathleen Farrar, Adrienne Vaughan, Ian Hudson, Rebecca McNally, Valentina Rice, Erica Barmash, Angela Craft, Nicola Hill, Amanda Shipp, Marie Coolman, Lauren Ollerhead, Rebecca McGlynn, Grace McNamee, Eleanor Willis, Katie Ager, Ben McCluskey, Holly Minter, Sam Payne, Donna Mark, David Mann, John Candell, Donna Gauthier, Laura Phillips, Jaclyn Sassa, Britt Hopkins, Claire Henry, Michael Young, Nicholas Church, Brigid Nelson, Sarah McLean, Sarah Knight, Joe Roche, Fabia Ma, Sally Wilks, Inês Figueira, Jack Birch, Fliss Stevens, Claire Barker, Cristina Cappelluto, Genevieve Nelsson, Adam Kirkman, Jennifer Gonzalez, Laura Pennock, Elizabeth Tzetzo, Valerie Esposito, and Meenakshi Singh.

To Kaitlin Severini for copyediting, and Andrea Modica and Hannah Bowe for proofreading. To Elizabeth Evans, for her stellar audio adaptations, and to Carlos Quevedo, for his stunning cover art.

To the badass and brilliant team at Writers House: Robin Rue

ACKNOWLEDGMENTS

(marvelous agent and wonderful friend), Beth Miller, Cecilia de la Campa, Maja Nikolic, Kate Boggs, Maria Aughavin, Albert Araneo, Sydnee Harlan, Alessandra Birch, Sofia Bolido, Angelamarie Malkoun, Melissa Vasquez, Rosie Acacia, Lisa Castiglione, and Angela Kafka.

To the amazing team at Frankfurt Kurnit Klein & Selz: Maura Wogan, Victoria Cook, Kimberly Maynard, Louise Decoppet, Mark Merriman, Michael Ling, Michael Williams, Gregory Boyd, Edward Rosenthal, Molly Rothschild, Amanda Barkin, and Nicole Bergstrom. To Jill Gillett for her wisdom and guidance.

To my sister, Jenn, who inspires me every day, and to my dear friends who always make me smile: Julie, Megan, Katie, Steph, and Lynette. To Laura and Louisse, whose emails never fail to brighten my day.

To Ana, who takes such amazing care of my babies, allowing me to write these books.

To Josh, Taran, Sloane, and Annie: you are the greatest gifts in my life, and I love you more than words can say.

And to the readers who make all of this even possible: thank you for *everything*.